The Critics Hail Mari███████████ Darkove██ ⟨ W9-CBE-951

"A rich and highly colored tale of politics and magic, courage and pressure . . .
Topflight adventure in every way!"
—Lester Del Rey for *Analog*
(for THE HERITAGE OF HASTUR)

"May well be [Bradley's] masterpiece."
—*New York Newsday*
(for THE HERITAGE OF HASTUR)

"Literate and exciting."
—*New York Times Book Review*
(for CITY OF SORCERY)

"Suspenseful, powerfully written, and deeply moving."
—*Library Journal* (for STORMQUEEN)

"A warm, shrewd portrait of women from different backgrounds working together under adverse conditions."
—*Publishers Weekly* (for CITY OF SORCERY)

"I don't think any series novels have succeeded for me the way Marion Zimmer Bradley's DARKOVER novels did."
—*Locus* (general)

"Delightful . . . a fascinating world and a great read."
—*Locus* (for EXILE'S SONG)

"Darkover is the essence, the quintessence, my most personal and best-loved work."
—Marion Zimmer Bradley

A Reader's Guide to the Novels of Darkover

THE FOUNDING

A "lost ship" of Terran origin, in the pre-empire colonizing days, lands on a planet with a dim red star, later to be called Darkover.
DARKOVER LANDFALL

THE AGES OF CHAOS

One thousand years after the original landfall settlement, society has returned to the feudal level. The Darkovans, their Terran technology renounced or forgotten, have turned instead to freewheeling, out-of-control matrix technology, psi powers and terrible psi weapons. The populace lives under the domination of the Towers and a tyrannical breeding program to staff the Towers with unnaturally powerful, inbred gifts of *laran*.
STORMQUEEN!
HAWKMISTRESS!

THE HUNDRED KINGDOMS

An age of war and strife retaining many of the decimating and disastrous effects of the Ages of Chaos. The lands which are later to become the Seven Domains are divided by continuous border conflicts into a multitude of small, belligerent kingdoms, named for convenience "The Hundred Kingdoms." The close of this era is heralded by the adoption of the Compact, instituted by Varzil the Good. A landmark and turning point in the history of Darkover, the Compact bans all distance weapons, making it a matter of honor that one who seeks to kill must himself face equal risk of death.
TWO TO CONQUER
THE HEIRS OF HAMMERFELL
THE FALL OF NESKAYA

THE RENUNCIATES

During the Ages of Chaos and the time of the Hundred Kingdoms, there were two orders of women who set themselves apart from the patriarchal nature of Darkovan feudal society: the priestesses of Avarra, and the warriors of the Sisterhood of the Sword. Eventually these two independent groups merged to form the powerful and legally chartered Order of Renunciates or Free Amazons, a guild of women bound only by oath as a sisterhood of mutual responsibility. Their primary allegiance is to each other rather than to family, clan, caste or any man save a temporary employer. Alone among Darkovan women, they are exempt from the usual legal restrictions and protections. Their reason for existence is to provide the women of Darkover an alternative to their socially restrictive lives.

THE SHATTERED CHAIN
THENDARA HOUSE
CITY OF SORCERY

AGAINST THE TERRANS
—THE FIRST AGE (Recontact)

After the Hastur Wars, the Hundred Kingdoms are consolidated into the Seven Domains, and ruled by a hereditary aristocracy of seven families, called the Comyn, allegedly descended from the legendary Hastur, Lord of Light. It is during this era that the Terran Empire, really a form of confederacy, rediscovers Darkover, which they know as the fourth planet of the Cottman star system. The fact that Darkover is a lost colony of the Empire is not easily or readily acknowledged by Darkovans and their Comyn overlords.

REDISCOVERY (*with Mercedes Lackey*)
THE SPELL SWORD
THE FORBIDDEN TOWER
STAR OF DANGER
THE WINDS OF DARKOVER

AGAINST THE TERRANS
—THE SECOND AGE (After the Comyn)

With the initial shock of recontact beginning to wear off, and the Terran spaceport a permanent establishment on the outskirts of the city of Thendara, the younger and less traditional elements of Darkovan society begin the first real exchange of knowledge with the Terrans—learning Terran science and technology and teaching Darkovan matrix technology in turn. Eventually Regis Hastur, the young Comyn lord most active in these exchanges, becomes Regent in a provisional government allied to the Terrans. Darkover is once again reunited with its founding Empire.

THE BLOODY SUN
HERITAGE OF HASTUR
THE PLANET SAVERS
SHARRA'S EXILE
WORLD WRECKERS
EXILE'S SONG
THE SHADOW MATRIX
TRAITOR'S SUN

THE DARKOVER ANTHOLOGIES

These volumes of stories edited by Marion Zimmer Bradley strive to "fill in the blanks" of Darkovan history, and elaborate on the eras, tales and characters which have captured readers' imaginations.

THE KEEPER'S PRICE
SWORD OF CHAOS
FREE AMAZONS OF DARKOVER
THE OTHER SIDE OF THE MIRROR
RED SUN OF DARKOVER
FOUR MOONS OF DARKOVER
DOMAINS OF DARKOVER
RENUNCIATES OF DARKOVER
LERONI OF DARKOVER
TOWERS OF DARKOVER
MARION ZIMMER BRADLEY'S DARKOVER
SNOWS OF DARKOVER

THE AGES OF CHAOS

STORMQUEEN!

HAWKMISTRESS!

Marion Zimmer Bradley

DAW BOOKS, INC.
DONALD A. WOLLHEIM, FOUNDER
375 Hudson Street, New York, NY 10014

ELIZABETH R. WOLLHEIM
SHEILA E. GILBERT
PUBLISHERS
www.dawbooks.com

First Paperback Printing, May 2002
1 2 3 4 5 6 7 8 9

DAW TRADEMARK REGISTERED
U.S. PAT. OFF. AND FOREIGN COUNTRIES
—MARCA REGISTRADA
HECHO EN U.S.A.

PRINTED IN THE U.S.A.

ACKNOWLEDGMENTS

The soldier's drinking song in Part III of HAWK-MISTRESS! was suggested by the Ballad of Arilinn Tower, a "filk song" written by Bettina Helms and copyright © 1979.

STORMQUEEN!

A NOTE FROM THE AUTHOR

Ever since the third or fourth of the Darkover novels, my surprisingly faithful readers have been writing in to me, asking, in essence, "Why don't you write a novel about the Ages of Chaos?"

For a long time I demurred, hesitating to do this; to me that essence of the Darkover novels seemed to be just this—the clash of cultures between Darkovan and Terran. If I had acceded to their request to write about a time "before the coming of the Terrans," it seemed to me, the very essence of the Darkover novels would have been removed, and what remained would be very much like any of a thousand other science-fantasy novels dealing with alien worlds where people have alien powers and alien concerns.

It was my readers who finally persuaded me to attempt this. If every reader who actually writes to an author represents only a hundred who do not (and I am told the figure is higher than this) there must be, by now, several *thousand* readers out there who are interested and curious about the time known as the Ages of Chaos; the time before the Comyn had firmly established an alliance of their seven Great Houses to rule over the Domains; and also the height of the Towers, and of that curious technology known then as "starstone" and later becoming the science of matrix mechanics.

Readers of *The Forbidden Tower* will want to know that *Stormqueen* deals with a time before Varzil, Keeper of Neskaya, known as "the Good," perfected the techniques allowing women to serve as Keepers in the Towers of the Comyn.

In *The Shattered Chain*, Lady Rohana says;

> "There was a time in the history of the Comyn when we did selective breeding to fix these gifts in our racial heritage; it was a time of great tyranny, and not a time we are very proud to remember."

This is a story of the men and women who lived under that tyranny, and how it affected their lives, and the lives of those who came after them on Darkover.

—MARION ZIMMER BRADLEY

Chapter 1

The storm was wrong somehow.

That was the only way Donal could think of it . . . *wrong somehow*. It was high summer in the mountains called the Hellers, and there should have been no storms except for the never-ending snow flurries on the far heights above the timberline, and the rare savage thunderstorms that swooped down across the valleys, bouncing from peak to peak and leaving flattened trees and sometimes fire in the path of their lightning.

Yet, though the sky was blue and cloudless, thunder crackled low in the distance, and the very air seemed filled with the tension of a storm. Donal crouched on the heights of the battlement, stroking with one finger the hawk cradled in the curve of his arm, crooning half-absently to the restless bird. It was the storm in the air, the electric tension, he knew, which was frightening the hawk. He should never have taken it from the mews today—it would serve him right if the old hawkmaster beat him, and a year ago he would probably have done so without much thought. But now things were different. Donal was only ten, but there had been many changes in his short life. And this was one of the most drastic, that within the change of a few moons hawkmaster and tutors and grooms now called him—not that-brat-Donal, with cuffs and pinches and even blows, merited and unmerited, but, with new and fawning respect—young-master-Donal.

Certainly life was easier for Donal now, but the very change made him uneasy; for it had not come about from

anything he had done. It had something to do with the fact
that his mother, Aliciane of Rockraven, now shared the
bed of Dom Mikhail, Lord of Aldaran, and was soon to
bear him a child.

Only once, a long time ago (two midsummer festivals
had come and gone), had Aliciane spoken of these things
to her son.

"Listen carefully to me, Donal, for I shall say this once
only and never again. Life is not easy for a woman unprotected." Donal's father had died in one of the small wars,
which raged among the vassals of the mountain lords, before Donal could remember him; their lives had been spent
as unregarded poor relations in the home of one kinsman
after another, Donal wearing castoffs of this cousin and
that, riding always the worst horse in the stables, hanging
around unseen when cousins and kinsmen learned the skills
of arms, trying to pick up what he could by listening.

"I could put you to fosterage; your father had kinsmen
in these hills, and you could grow up to take service with
one of them. Only for me there would be nothing but to be
drudge or sewing-woman, or at best minstrel in a stranger's
household, and I am too young to find that endurable. So
I have taken service as singing-woman to Lady Deonara;
she is frail, and aging, and has borne no living children.
Lord Aldaran is said to have an eye for beauty in women.
And I am beautiful, Donal."

Donal had hugged Aliciane fiercely; indeed she was
beautiful, a slight girlish woman, with flame-bright hair and
gray eyes, who looked too young to be the mother of a
boy eight years old.

"What I am about to do, I do it at least partly for you,
Donal. My kin have cast me off for it; do not condemn me
if I am ill-spoken by those who do not understand."

Indeed it seemed, at first, that Aliciane had done this
more for her son's good than her own: Lady Deonara was
kind but had the irritability of all chronic invalids, and Aliciane had been quenched and quiet, enduring Deonara's
sharpness and the shrewish envy of the other women with
good will and cheerfulness. But Donal for the first time in
his life had whole clothing made to his measure, horse and
hawk of his own, shared the tutor and the arms-master of
Lord Aldaran's fosterlings and pages. That summer Lady

Deonara had borne the last of a series of stillborn sons;
and Mikhail, Lord of Aldaran, had taken Aliciane of Rockraven as *barragana* and sworn to her that her child, male
or female, should be legitimated, and be heir to his line,
unless he might someday father a legitimate son. She was
Lord Aldaran's acknowledged favorite—even Deonara
loved her and had chosen her for her lord's bed—and
Donal shared her eminence. Once, even, Lord Mikhail,
gray and terrifying, had called Donal to him, saying he had
good reports from tutor and arms-master, and had drawn
him into a kindly embrace. "I would indeed you were mine
by blood, foster-son. If your mother bears me such a son I
will be well content, my boy."

Donal had stammered. "I thank you, kinsman," without
the courage, yet, to call the old man "foster-father." Young
as he was, he knew that if his mother should bear Lord
Aldaran his only living child, son or daughter, then he
would be half-brother to Aldaran's heir. Already the
change in his status had been extreme and marked.

But the impending storm . . . it seemed to Donal an evil
omen for the coming birth. He shivered; this had been a
summer of strange storms, lightning bolts from nowhere,
ever-present rumblings and crashes. Without knowing why,
Donal associated these storms with *anger*—the anger of his
grand-sire, Aliciane's father, when Lord Rockraven had
heard of his daughter's choice. Donal, cowering forgotten
in a corner, had heard Lord Rockraven calling her *bitch,*
and *whore,* and names Donal had understood even less.
The old man's voice had been nearly drowned, that day,
by thunder outside, and there had been a crackle of angry
lightnings in his mother's voice, too, as she had shouted
back, "What am I to do, then, Father? Bide here at home,
mending my own shifts, feeding myself and my son upon
your shabby honor? Shall I see Donal grow up to be a
mercenary soldier, a hired sword, or dig in your garden for
his porridge? You scorn Lady Aldaran's offer—"

"It is not *Lady* Aldaran I scorn," her father snorted,
"but it is not she whom you will serve and you know it as
well as I!"

"And have you found a better offer for me? Am I to
marry a blacksmith or charcoal-burner? Better *barragana*
to Aldaran than wife to a tinker or ragpicker!"

Donal had known he could expect nothing from his
grand-sire. Rockraven had never been a rich or powerful
estate; and it was impoverished because Rockraven had
four sons to provide for, and three daughters, of whom
Aliciane was the youngest. Aliciane had once said, bitterly,
that if a man has no sons, that is tragedy; but if he has too
many, then worse for him, for he must see them struggle
for his estate.

Last of his children, Aliciane had been married to a
younger son without a title, and he had died within a year
of their marriage, leaving Aliciane and the newborn Donal
to be reared in strangers' houses.

Now, crouching on the battlements of Castle Aldaran
and watching the clear sky so inexplicably filled with lightning, Donal extended his consciousness outward, outward—
he could almost *see* the lines of electricity and the curious
shimmer of the magnetic fields of the storm in the air. At
times he had been able to call the lightning; once he had
amused himself when a storm raged by diverting the great
bolts where he would. He could not always do it, and he
could not do it too often or he would grow sick and weak;
once when he had felt through his skin (he did not know
how) that the next bolt was about to strike the tree where
he had sheltered, he had somehow *reached out* with something inside him, as if some invisible limb had grasped the
chain of exploding force and flung it *elsewhere*. The lightning bolt had exploded, with a sizzle, into a nearby bush,
crisping it into blackened leaves and charring a circle of
grass, and Donal had sunk to the ground, his head swimming, his eyes blurred. His head had been splitting in three
parts with the pain, and he could not see properly for days,
but Aliciane had hugged and praised him.

"My brother Caryl could do that, but he died young,"
she told him. "There was a time when the *leroni* at Hali
tried to breed storm-control into our *laran,* but it was too
dangerous. I can *see* the thunder-forces, a little; I cannot
manipulate them. Take care, Donal; use that gift only to
save a life. I would not have my son blasted by the lightnings he seeks to control." Aliciane had hugged him again,
with unusual warmth.

Laran. Talk of it had filled his childhood, the gifts of
extrasensory powers which were so much a preoccupation

with the mountain lords—yes, and far away in the lowlands, too. If he had had any truly extraordinary gift, telepathy, the ability to force his will upon hawk or hound or sentry-bird, he would have been recorded in the breeding charts of the *leroni,* the sorceresses who kept records of parentage among those who carried the blood of Hastur and Cassilda, legendary forebears of the Gifted Families. But he had none. Merely storm-watch, a little; he sensed when thunder-storms or even forest fire struck, and someday, when he was a bit older, he would take his place on the fire-watch, and it would help him, to know, as he already knew a little, where the fire would move next. But this was a minor gift, not worth breeding for. Even at Hali they had abandoned it, four generations before, and Donal knew, not knowing precisely how he knew, that this was one reason why the family of Rockraven had not prospered.

But this storm was far beyond his power to guess. Some-how, without clouds or rain, it seemed to center here, over the castle. *Mother,* he thought, *it has to do with my mother,* and wished that he dared run to seek her, to assure himself that all was well with her, through the terrifying, growing awareness of the storm. But a boy of ten could not run like a babe to sit in his mother's lap. And Aliciane was heavy now and ungainly, in the last days of waiting for Lord Aldaran's child to be born; Donal could not run to her with his own fears and troubles.

He soberly picked up the hawk again, and carried it down the stairs; in air so heavy with lightning, this strange and unprecedented storm, he could not loose it to fly. The sky was blue (it looked like a good day for flying hawks) but Donal could *feel* the heavy and oppressive magnetic currents in the air, the heavy crackle of electricity.

Is it my mother's fear that fills the air with lightning, as sometimes my grandsire's anger did? Suddenly Donal was overwhelmed with his own fear. He knew, as everyone knew, that women sometimes died in childbirth; he had tried hard not to think about that, but now, overwhelmed with terror for his mother, he could feel the crackle of his own fear in the lightning. Never had he felt so young, so helpless. Fiercely he wished he were back in the shabby poverty of Rockraven, or ragged and unregarded as a poor cousin in some kinman's stronghold. Shivering, he took the

hawk back to the mews, accepting the hawkmaster's reproof with such meekness that the old man thought the
boy must be sick!

Far away in the women's apartments, Aliciane heard the
continuing roll of thunder; more dimly than Donal, she
sensed the strangeness of the storm. And she was afraid.

The Rockravens had been dropped from the intensive
breeding program for *laran* gifts; like most of her generation, Aliciane thought that breeding program outrageous, a
tyranny no free mountain people would endure in these
days, to breed mankind like cattle for desired character-
istics.

Yet all her life she had been reared in loose talk of lethal
genes and recessives, of bloodlines carrying desired *laran.*
How could any woman bear a child without fear? Yet here
she was, awaiting the birth of a child who might well be
heir to Aldaran, knowing that his reason for choosing her
had been neither her beauty—although she knew, without
vanity, that it had been her beauty which first caught his
eye—nor the superb voice which had made her Lady Deonara's favorite ballad-singer, but the knowledge that she
had born a strong and living son, gifted with *laran*; that she
was of proven fertility and could survive childbirth.

*Rather, I survived it once. What does that prove, but that
I was lucky?*

As if responding to her fear, the unborn child kicked
sharply, and Aliciane drew her hand over the strings of her
rryl, the small harp she held in her lap, pressing the sidebars with her other hand and sensing the soothing effect of
the vibrations. As she began to play, she sensed the stir
among the women who had been sent to attend her, for
Lady Deonara genuinely loved her singing-woman, and had
sent her own most skillful nurses and midwives and maids
to attend her in these last days. Then Mikhail, Lord Aldaran, came into her room, a big man, in the prime of life,
his hair prematurely grayed; and indeed he was far older
than Aliciane, who had turned twenty-four but last spring.
His tread was heavy in the quiet room, sounding more like
a mailed stride on a battlefield than a soft-shod indoor step.

"Do you play for your own pleasure, Aliciane? I had
thought a musician drew most of her pleasure from ap-

plause, yet I find you playing for yourself and your women," he said, smiling, and hitched a light chair around to sit in it at her side. "How is it with you, my treasure?"

"I am well but weary," she said, also smiling. "This is a restless child, and I play partly because the music seems to have a calming effect. Perhaps because the music calms *me,* and so the child is calm, too."

"It may well be so," he said, and when she put the harp from her, said, "No, sing, Aliciane, if you are not too tired."

"As you will, my lord." She pressed the strings of the harp into chords, and sang, softly, a love song of the far hills:

> "Where are you now?
>   Where does my love wander?
>   Not on the hills, not upon the shore,
>   not far on the sea,
>   Love, where are you now?
>
> "Dark the night, and I am weary,
>   Love, when can I cease this seeking?
>   Darkness all around, above, beyond me,
>   Where lingers he, my love?"

Mikhail leaned toward the woman, drew his heavy hand gently across her brilliant hair. "Such a weary song," he said softly, "and so sad; is love truly such a thing of sadness to you, my Aliciane?"

"No, indeed not," Aliciane said, assuming a gaiety she did not feel. Fears and self-questioning were for pampered wives, not for a *barragana* whose position depended on keeping her lord amused and cheery with her charm and beauty, her skills as an entertainer. "But the loveliest love songs are of sorrow in love, my lord. Would it please you more if I choose songs of laughter or valor?"

"Whatever you sing pleases me, my treasure," Mikhail said kindly. "If you are weary or sorrowful you need not pretend to gaiety with me, *carya.*" He saw the flicker of distrust in her eyes, and thought, *I am too sensitive for my own good; it must be pleasant never to be too aware of the minds of others. Does Aliciane truly love me, or does she*

*only value her position as my acknowledged favorite? Even
if she loves me, is it for myself, or only that I am rich and
powerful and can make her secure?* He gestured to the
women, and they withdrew to the far end of the long room,
leaving him alone with his mistress; present, to satisfy the
decencies of the day that dictated a childbearing woman
should never be unattended, but out of earshot.

"I do not trust all these women," he said.

"Lord, Deonara is truly fond of me. I think. She would
not put anyone among my women with ill will to me or my
child," Aliciane said.

"Deonara? No, perhaps not," Mikhail said, remembering
that Deonara had been Lady of Aldaran for twice ten years
and shared his hunger for a child to be heir to his estate.
She could no longer promise him even the hope of one;
she had welcomed the knowledge that he had taken Aliciane, who was one of her own favorites, to his bed and
his heart. "But I have enemies who are not of this household, and it is all too easy to plant a spy with *laran,* who
can relay all the doings of my household to someone who
wishes me ill. I have kinsmen who would do much to prevent the birth of a living heir to my line. I marvel not that
you look pale, my treasure; it is hard to credit wickedness
that would harm a little child, yet I have never been sure
that Deonara was not victim to someone who killed the
children unborn in her womb. It is not hard to do; even a
little skill with matrix or *laran* can break a child's fragile
link to life."

"Anyone who wished you ill, Mikhail, would know you
have promised me that my child will be legitimated, and
would turn her evil will to me," Aliciane soothed. "Yet I
have borne this child without illness. You fear needlessly,
my dear love."

"Gods grant you are right! Yet I have enemies who
would stop at nothing. Before your child is born, I will call
a *leronis* to probe them; I will have no woman present at
your confinement who cannot swear under truthspell that
she wishes you well. An evil wish can snap a newborn
child's fight for life."

"Surely that strength of *laran* is rare, my dearest lord."

"Not as rare as I could wish it," Mikhail, Lord Aldaran,
said. "Yet of late I have strange thoughts. I find these gifts

a weapon to cut my own hand; I who have used sorcery to hurl fire and chaos upon my enemy, I feel it now that they have strength to hurl them upon me, too. When I was young I felt *laran* as a gift of the gods; they had appointed me to rule this land, and dowered me with *laran* to make my rule stronger. But as I grow old I find it a curse, not a gift."

"You are not so old, my lord, and surely no one now would challenge your rule!"

"No one dares do so openly, Aliciane. But I am alone among those who hover waiting for me to die childless. I have meaty bones to pick . . . all gods grant your child is a son, *carya*."

Aliciane was trembling. "And if it is not . . . oh, my dear lord. . . ."

"Why, then, treasure, you must bear me another," he said gently, "but even if you do not, I shall have a daughter whose dower will be my estate, and who will bring me the strong alliances I need; even a woman-child will make my position that much stronger. And *your* son shall be foster brother and paxman, shield in trouble and strong arm. I truly love your son, Aliciane."

"I know." How could she have been trapped this way . . . finding that she loved the man whom, at first, she had simply thought to ensnare with the wiles of her voice and her beauty? Mikhail was kind and honorable, he had courted her when he might have taken her as lawful prey, he had assured her, unasked, that even if she failed to give him a living son, Donal's future was secure. She felt safe with him, she had come to love him, and now she feared *for* him, too.

Caught in my own trap!

She said, almost laughing, "I need no such reassurance, my lord. I have never doubted you."

He smiled, accepting that, the courtesy of a telepath. "But women are fearful at such times, and it is sure now that Deonara will bear me no child, even if I would ask it of her after so many tragedies. Do you know what it is like, Aliciane, to see children you have longed for, desired, loved even before they were born, to see them die without drawing breath? I did not love Deonara when we were wed; I had never seen her face, for we were given to one another for family alliances; but we have endured much together, and although it may seem strange to you, child, love can come from shared sorrow as well as shared joy." His face was somber. "I love you well, *carya mea,* but it was neither for your beauty nor even for the splendor of your voice that I sought you out. Did you know Deonara was not my first wife?"

"No, my lord."

"I was wed first when I was a young man; Clariza Leynier bore me two sons and a daughter, all healthy and strong. . . . Hard as it is to lose children at birth, it is harder yet to lose sons and daughter grown almost to manhood and womanhood. And yet I lost them—one after another, as they grew to adolescence. I lost them all three, with the descent of *laran;* they died in crisis and convulsions, all of them, of that scourge of our people. I myself was ready to die of despair."

"My brother Caryl died so," Aliciane whispered.

"I know; yet he was the only one of your line, and your father had many sons and daughters. You yourself told me that your *laran* did not descend at adolescence, playing havoc with mind and body, but that you grew slowly into it from babyhood, as with many of the Rockraven folk. And I can see that this is dominant in your line, for Donal is barely ten years old, and though I do not think his *laran* is full developed yet, still he has much of it, and he at least is not like to die on the threshold. I knew that for your children, at least, I need not fear. Deonara, too, came from a bloodline with early onset of *laran,* but none of the children she bore me lived long enough for us to know whether they had *laran* or no."

Aliciane's face twisted in dismay and he laid his arm tenderly about her shoulders, "What is it, my dear one?"

"All my life I have felt revulsion for this—to breed men like cattle!"

"Man is the only animal that thinks not to improve his race," Mikhail said fiercely. "We control weather, build castles and highways with the strength of our *laran,* explore greater and greater gifts of the mind—should we not seek to better ourselves as well as our world and our surroundings?" Then his face softened. "But I understand that a woman as young as you thinks not in terms of generations,

centuries; while one is yet young, you think only of self
and children, but at my age it is natural to think in terms
of all those who will come after us when we and our children are many centauries gone. But such things are not for
you unless you wish to think of them; think of your child,
love, and how soon we will hold her in our arms."

Aliciane shrank, whispering, "You know, then, that it is
a daughter I am to bear you—you are not angry?"

"I told you I would not be angry; if I am distressed it is
only that you did not trust me enough to tell me this when
first you knew," Mikhail said, but the words were so gentle
they were hardly a reproof. "Come, Aliciane, forget your
fears; if you give me no son, at least you have given me a
sturdy foster-son, and your daughter will be a powerful
strength in bringing me a son-in-law. And our daughter will
have *laran*."

Aliciane smiled and returned his kiss; but she was still
taut with apprehension as she heard the distant crackle of
the unprecedented summer thunder, which seemed to come
and go in tune with the waves of her fear. *Can it be that
Donal is afraid of what this child will mean to him?* she
wondered, and wished passionately that she had the precog-
nitive gift, the *laran* of the Aldaran clan, so that she might
know that all would be well.

Chapter 2

"Here is the traitor!"

Aliciane trembled at the anger in Lord Aldaran's voice as he strode wrathfully into her chamber, thrusting a woman ahead of him with his two hands. Behind him the *leronis,* his household sorceress, bearing the matrix or blue starstone which somehow amplified the powers of her *laran,* tiptoed; a fragile pale-haired woman, her pallid features drawn with terror of the storm she had unleashed.

"Mayra," Aliciane said in dismay, "I thought you my friend, and friend to Lady Deonara. What has befallen that you are my enemy and my child's?"

Mayra—she was one of Deonara's robing-women, a sturdy middle-aged dame—stood frightened but defiant between Lord Aldaran's hard hands. "No, I know nothing of what that sorceress-bitch has said of me; is she jealous of my place here, having no useful work but to meddle with the minds of her betters?"

"It will not serve you to put ill names on me," said the *leronis* Margali. "I asked all these women but one question, and that under the truthspell, so that I would hear in my mind if they lied. Is your loyalty to Mikhail, Lord Aldaran, or to the *vai domna,* his lady Deonara? And if they said me *no,* or said *yes* with a doubt or a denial in their thoughts, I asked only, again under truthspell, if their loyalty were to husband or father or home-lord. From this one alone I got no honest answer, but only the knowledge that she was concealing all. And so I told Lord Aldaran that if there was a traitor among his women it could be only she."

Mikhail let the woman go and turned her around to face him, not ungently. He said. "It is true that you have been long in my service, Mayra; Deonara treats you with the kindness of a foster-sister. Is it me you wish evil, or my lady?"

"My lady has been kind to me; I am angered to see her set aside for another," said Mayra, her voice shaking. The *leronis* behind her said, in passionless tone, "No, Lord Aldaran, there she speaks no truth, either; she holds no love for you nor for your lady."

"She lies!" Mayra's voice rose to a half-shriek. "She lies—I wish you no ill save what you have brought on yourself, Lord, by taking the bitch of Rockraven to your bed. It is she who has put a spell on your manhood, that bitch-viper!"

"Silence!" Lord Aldaran quivered as if he would strike the woman, but the word was enough; everyone within range was smitten dumb, and Aliciane trembled. Only once before had she heard Mikhail use what was called, in the language of *laran,* the command-voice. There were not many who could summon enough control over their *laran* to use it; it was not an inborn gift, but one that required both talent and skilled training. And when, in that voice, Mikhail, Lord Aldaran, commanded *silence,* none within earshot could form an audible word.

The silence in the room was so extreme that Aliciane could hear the smallest of sounds: some small insect clicking in the woodwork of the paneling, the frightened breathing of the women, the far-off crackle of thunder. *It seems,* she thought, *that all through this summer we have had thunder, more than I can remember in any year before. . . . What nonsense to have in my thoughts now, when I stand before a woman who might have meant my death, had she attended my childbed. . . .*

Mikhail glanced at her, where she stood trembling and propping herself upright by the arm of a chair. Then he said to the *leronis,* "Attend the lady Aliciane, help her to sit, or to lie down on her bed if she feels better so . . ." and Aliciane felt Margali's strong hands supporting her, easing her into the chair. She shook with anger, hating the physical weakness she could not control.

This child saps my strength as never Donal did. . . . Why

am I so weakened? Is it that woman's evil will, wicked spells . . . ? Margali laid her hands on Aliciane's forehead and she felt soothing calm radiating out from them. She tried to relax under them, to breathe evenly, to calm the frantic restlessness she could sense in the movements of her child within her body. *Poor little one . . . she is afraid, too, and no wonder. . . .*

"You—" Lord Aldaran's voice commanded, "Mayra, tell me why you bear me ill will, or would seek to harm the lady Aliciane of her child!"

"Tell *you*?"

"You will, you know," Mikhail of Aldaran said. "You will tell us more than you ever believed you would say, whether you do so of your free will and painlessly, or whether it is dragged from you shrieking! I have no love for torturing womenfolk, Mayra, but I will not harbor a scorpion-ant within my chamber, either! Save us this struggle." But Mayra faced him, silent and defiant, and Mikhail shrugged faintly, a tautness Aliciane knew—and would not have dared defy—settling down over his face. He said, "On your own head, Mayra. Margali, bring your starstone—no. Better still, send for *kirizani*."

Aliciane trembled, though Mikhail was showing mercy in his own way. *Kirizani* was one of half a dozen drugs distilled from the plant resins of kireseth flowers, whose pollen brought madness when the Ghost-wind blew in the hills; *kirizani* was that part of the resin which lowered the barriers against telepathic contact, laying the mind bare to anyone who would probe within it. It was better than torture, and yet . . . She quailed, looking at the raging purpose on Mikhail's face, at the smiling defiance of the woman Mayra. They all stood silent while the *kirizani* was brought, a pale liquid in a vial of transparent crystal.

Mikhail uncapped it and said quietly. "Will you take it without protest, Mayra, or shall the women hold you and pour it down your throat like a horse being dosed?"

Mayra's face flushed; she spit at him. "You think you can make me speak with your sorcery and drugs, Lord Mikhail? Ha—I defy you! You need no evil will of mine— enough lurks already in your house and in the womb of your bitch-mistress there! A day will come when you pray you had died childless—and there will be no other! You

will take no other to your bed, no more than you have
done while the bitch of Rockraven grew heavy with her
witch daughter! My work is done, *vai dom*!" She flung the
respectful term at him like a taunt. "I need no more time!
From this day you will father neither daughter nor son—
your loins will be empty as a winter-killed tree! And you
will cry out and pray—"

"Silence that evil banshee!" Mikhail said, and Margali,
starting upright from the fainting Aliciane, raised her jeweled matrix, but the woman spit again, laughed hysterically,
gasped, and crumpled to the floor. In the stunned silence
Margali went to her, laid a perfunctory hand to her breast.

"Lord Aldaran, she is dead! She must have been spelled
to die on questioning."

The man stared in dismay at the lifeless body of the
woman, unanswered questions unspoken on his lips. He
said, "Now we shall never know what she has done, or
how, or who was the enemy who sent her here to us. I
would take my oath Deonara knows nothing of it." But the
words held a question, and Margali laid her hand on the blue
jewel and said quietly, "On my life, Lord Aldaran, the Lady
Deonara has no ill will to Lady Aliciane's child; this she
has told me often, that she is glad for you and for Aliciane,
and I know when I am hearing truth."

Mikhail nodded, but Aliciane saw the lines around his
mouth deepen. If Deonara, jealous of Lord Aldaran'a
favor, had wished Aliciane some harm, that at least would
have been understandable. But who, she wondered, knowing little of the feuds and power struggles of Aldaran, could
wish evil to a man so good as Mikhail? Who could hate
him so much as to plant a spy among his wife's waiting-
women, to do evil to the child of a *barragana,* to cast,
perhaps, *laran*-powered curses on his manhood?

"Take her away," Aldaran said at last, his voice not entirely steady. "Hang her body from the castle heights for
kyorebni to pick; she has earned no faithful servant's burial
rites." He waited, impassive, while tall guardsmen came
and bore away Mayra's dead body, to be stripped and
hanged for the great birds of prey to peck asunder. Aliciane
heard thunder crackling in the distance, then nearer and
nearer, and Aldaran came toward her, his voice now softened to tenderness.

"Have no more fear, my treasure; she is gone and her evil will with her. We will live to laugh at her curses, my darling." He sank into a chair nearby, taking her hand in gentle fingers, but she sensed, through the touch, that he, too, was distressed and even frightened. And she was not strong enough to reassure him; she felt as if she were fainting again. Mayra's curses rang in her ears, like the reverberating echoes in the canyons around Rockraven when as a child she had shouted into them for the amusement of hearing her own voice come back to her multiplied a thousandfold from all quarters of the wind.

You will father neither daughter nor son. . . . Your loins will be empty as a winter-killed tree. . . . A day will come when you pray you had died childless. . . . The reverberating remembered sound swelled, overwhelmed her; she lay back in the chair, near to losing consciousness.

"Aliciane, Aliciane—" She felt his strong arms around her, raising her, carrying her to her bed. He laid her down on the pillows, sat beside her, gently stroking her face.

"You must not be frightened of shadows, Aliciane."

She said, trembling, the first thing that came into her head. "She cursed your manhood, my lord."

"I feel not much endangered," he said with a smile.

"Yet—I myself have seen and wondered . . . you have taken no other to your bed in these days when I am so heavy, as would have been your custom."

A faint shadow passed over his face, and at this moment their minds were so close that Aliciane regretted her words; she should not have touched on his own fear. But he said, firmly putting away fear in cheerfulness, "Why, as for that, Aliciane, I am not so young a man that I cannot live womanless for a few moons. Deonara is not sorry to be free of me, I think; my embraces have never meant more to her than duty, and dying children. And in these days, it seems except for you, women are not so beautiful as they were when I was young. It has been no hardship to me, to forbear asking what is no pleasure to you to give; but when our child is born and you are well again, you shall see if that fool woman's words have any evil effect on my manhood. You may yet give me a son, Aliciane, or, if not, at least we shall spend many joyous hours together."

She said, shaking, "May the Lord of Light grant it, in-

deed." He bent and kissed her tenderly, but the touch of
his lips again brought them close, with shared fear and,
abruptly, shared pain, tearing at her.

He straightened as if shocked, calling to her women. "Attend my lady!"

She clung to his hands. "Mikhail, I am frightened," she
whispered, and picked up his thought, *Indeed this is no
good omen, that she should go into labor with the sound of
that witch's curses still in her ears.* . . . She felt, too, the
strong discipline with which he curbed and controlled even
the thought, that fear might not spiral, heightened by each
mind through which it passed. He said, with gentle command, "You must try to think of our child only, Aliciane,
and lend her strength; think of our child only—and of my
love."

It was nearing sunset. Clouds massed on the heights beyond Castle Aldaran, tall stormclouds piling higher and
higher, but where Donal soared the sky was blue and cloudless. His slight body lay stretched along a wooden frame-
work of light woods, between wide wings of thinnest leather
built out on a narrow frame. Borne up by the currents of
air, he soared, dipping a hand to either side to balance on
the strong gusts to left or to right. The air bore him aloft,
and the small matrix-jewel fastened along the crosspiece.
He had made the levitation glider himself, with only a little
help from the stable-men. Several of the boys in the household had such toys, as soon as their training in the use of
the starstones was such as to maintain their levitation skills
without undue danger. But most of the lads in the household were at their lessons; Donal had slipped away to the
castle heights and soared away alone, even though he knew
that the penalty would be to forbid him the use of the
glider, perhaps for days. He could feel the stresses, the fear,
everywhere in the castle.

A traitor executed, dying before touched, a death-spell
on her. She had cursed Lord Aldaran's manhood. . . .

Gossip had run around Castle Aldaran like wildfire,
fueled by the few women who had actually been in Aliciane's chamber and seen anything; they had seen too much
to keep silent, too little to give a true account.

She had flung curses at the little *barragana* and Aliciane

of Rockraven had fallen down in labor. She had cursed Lord Aldaran's manhood—and it was true that he had taken no other to his bed, he who had always before taken a new woman with every change of the moons in the sky. A new, ominous question in the gossiping made Donal shiver: Was it the Lady of Rockraven who had spelled his manhood so he would desire no other, that she might keep her place in his arms and in his heart?

One of the men, a coarse man-at-arms, had laughed, a deep, suggestive laugh, and said, "That one needs no spells; if Lady Aliciane cast her pretty eyes on me, I would gladly pawn my manhood," but the arms-master said firmly, "Be still, Radan. Such talk is unseemly among young lads, and look, you—see who stands among them? Go to your work; do not stand here and gossip and tell dirty tales." When the man had gone, the arms-master said kindly, "Such talk is unseemly, but it is only jesting, Donal; he is distressed because he has no woman of his own, and would speak so of any fair woman. He means no disrespect to your mother, Donal. Indeed, there will be great rejoicing at Aldaran if Aliciane of Rockraven gives him an heir. You must not be angry at unthinking speech; if you listen to every dog that barks, you will have no leisure to learn wisdom. Go to your lessons, Donal, and do not waste time resenting what ignorant men say of their betters."

Donal had gone, but not to his lessons; he had taken his glider to the castle heights and soared out on the air currents, and now rode them, distressing thoughts left behind, memory in abeyance, wholly caught up in the intoxication of soaring, bird-fashion, now swooping to the north, now turning back west to where the great crimson sun hung low on the peaks.

A hawk must fell like this, hovering. . . . Under his sensitive fingertips, the wood-and-leather wing tilted downward faintly, and he focused on the current, letting it bear him down the draft. His mind sunk into the hyperawareness of the jewel, seeing the sky not as blue emptiness but as a great net of fields and currents which were his to ride, now floating down, down until it seemed he would strike on a great crag and be dashed asunder, then at the last minute letting a sharp updraft snatch him away, hovering down the wind. . . . He floated, mindless, soaring, wrapped in ecstasy.

The green moon, Idriel, hung low, a gibbous semi-shape
in the reddening sky; the silver crescent of Mormallor was
the palest of shadows; and violent Liriel, the largest of the
moons, near to full, was just beginning to float up slowly
from the eastern horizon. A low crackle of thunder from
the massy clouds hanging behind the castle roused memory
and apprehension in Donal. He might not be chastised for
slipping away from lessons at a time like this, but if he
remained out after sunset he would certainly be punished.
Strong winds sprang up at sunset, and about a year ago,
one of the pageboys at the castle had smashed his glider
and broken an elbow on one of the rocks below. He had
been lucky, they knew, not to kill himself. Donal cast a
wary eye back at the walls of the castle, seeking for an
updraft that would carry him to the heights—otherwise he
must drift down to the slopes below the castle and carry
his glider, which was light but hugely awkward, all the way
up again. Feeling the faintest of air pressures, magnified
through the awareness of the matrix, he caught an updraft
which, if he rode it carefully, would carry him above and
behind the castle, and he could float down to the roofs.

Riding up it, he could see, with a shiver, the swollen
naked figure of the woman who hung there, her face already torn by the *kyorebni* who hovered and swooped
there. Already she was unrecognizable, and Donal shuddered. Mayra had been kind to him in her own way. Had
she truly cursed his mother? He shuddered with his first
real awareness of death.

*People die. They really die and are pecked to bits by birds
of prey. My mother could die in childbirth, too. . . .* His
body twitched in sudden terror and he felt the fragile wings
of the glider, released from control of his mind and body,
flutter and slip downward, falling. . . . Swiftly he mastered
it, brought it up, levitating his body until he caught a current again. But now he could feel the faint tension and
shock in the air, the building static.

Thunder crackled above him; a bolt of lightning flashed
to the heights of Castle Aldaran, leaving a smell of ozone
and a faint burned smell in Donal's nostrils. Behind the
deafening roar, Donal saw without hearing the flare and
play of lightning in the massed clouds above the castle. In
sudden fright, he thought, *I must get down, out of here; it*

is not safe to fly in an oncoming storm. . . . He had been told again and again to scan the sky for lightning in the clouds before letting his glider take off.

A sudden violent downdraft caught him, sent the fragile wood-and-leather apparatus plummeting down; Donal, really frightened, clung hard to the handholds, with sense enough not to try to fight it too soon. It felt as if it would smash him down on the rocks, but he forced himself to lie limp along the struts, his mind searching ahead for the crosscurrent. At just the right moment he tensed his body, focusing into the matrix awareness, felt levitation and the crosscurrent carry him up again.

Now. Quickly, and carefully. I must get up to the level of the castle, catch the first current that glides down. There is no time to waste. . . . But now the air felt heavy and thick and Donal could not read it for currents. In growing dread, he sent his awareness out in all directions, but he sensed only the strong magnetic charges of the growing storm.

This storm is wrong, too! It's like the one the other day. It's not a real storm at all, it's something else. Mother! Oh, my mother! It seemed to the frightened child, clinging to the struts of the glider, that he could hear Aliciane crying out in terror, "Oh, Donal, what will become of my boy," and he felt his body convulse in terror, the glider slipping from his control, falling . . . falling. . . . If it had been less light, less broad-winged, it would have smashed onto the rocks, but the air currents, even though Donal could not read them, bore him along. After a few moments his fall stopped, and he began to drift sideways again. Now, using *laran*—the levitational strength given body and mind by the matrix jewel—and his trained awareness searching for the traces of currents through the magnetic storm, Donal began to fight for his life. He forced away the voice he could almost hear, his mother's voice crying out in terror and pain. He forced away the fear which let him see his own body lying broken into bits on the crags below. He forced himself to submerge wholly into his own heightened *laran,* making the wood-and-leather wing extensions of his own outstretched arms, feeling the currents that blew and battered at them as if they buffeted his own hands, his own legs.

Now . . . ride it upward . . . just so far . . . try to gain a few lengths toward the west. . . . He forced himself to go limp as another smashing bolt of lightning leaped from a cloud, feeling it burst beyond him. *No control . . . it isn't going anywhere . . . it has no awareness . . .* and the maxims of the kindly *leronis* who had taught him what little he knew: *The trained mind can always master any force of nature.* . . . Ritually, Donal reminded himself of that.

I need not fear wind or storm or lightning, the trained mind can master. . . . But Donal was only ten years old, and resentfully he wondered if Margali had ever flown a glider in a thunderstorm.

A deafening crash socked him momentarily mindless; he felt the sudden drench of rain along his chilled body, and fought to stop the trembling which sought to wrest control of the fluttering wings from his mind.

Now. Firmly. Down, and down, along this current . . . right to the ground, along the slope . . . no time to play with another updraft. Down here I will be safe from the lightning. . . .

His feet had almost touched the ground when another harsh upcurrent seized the wide wings and flung him upward again, away from the safety of the slopes. Sobbing, fighting the mechanism, he fought to force it down again, throwing himself over the edge and hanging vertically, grasping the struts over his head, letting the wide wings slow his fluttering fall. He sensed, through his skin, the lightning bolt and all his strength went out to divert it, to thrust it *elsewhere*. His hands clung frantically to the struts above his head as he heard the lightning and the deafening blast, saw with dazed eyes one of the great standing rocks on the slope split asunder with a great crashing roar. His feet touched ground; he fell hard, rolling over and over, feeling the glider's struts smash and break to splinters. Pain cannoned through his shoulder as he fell, but he had enough strength and awareness left to go limp, as he had been taught to do in arms-practice, to fall without the muscular resistance which could break bones. Alive, bruised, sobbing, he lay stunned on the rocky slope, feeling the currents of lightning darting, aimlessly, around him, thunder rolling from peak to peak.

When he had recovered his breath, he picked himself up. Both wing-struts of the glider were smashed, but it could be repaired; he was lucky that his arms were not smashed like the struts. The sight of the splintered rock turned him sick and dizzy, and his head throbbed; but he realized that with all this, he was lucky to be alive. He picked up the broken toy, letting the splintered wings hang folded, and began slowly to trudge up the slope toward the castle gates.

"She hates me," Aliciane cried in terror. "She does not want to be born!"

Through the darkness that seemed to hover around her mind she felt Mikhail catch and hold her flailing hands.

"My dearest love, that is folly," he murmured, holding the woman against him, firmly controlling his own fears. He, too, sensed the strangeness of the lightning which flashed and crackled around the high windows, and Aliciane's terror reinforced his own dread. It seemed there was another in the room, besides the frightened woman, besides the calm presence of Margali, who sat with her head bent, not looking at either of them, her face blue-lighted with the glimmer of the matrix stone. Mikhail could feel the soothing waves of calm Margali sent out, trying to surround them all with it; he tried to let his own mind and body surrender to the calm, relax to it. He began the deep rhythmic breathing he had been taught for control, and after a little he felt Aliciane, too, relax and float with it.

Where, then, whence the terror, the struggle . . .

It is she, the unborn . . . it is her fear, her reluctance . . .

Birth is an ordeal of terror; there must be someone to reassure her, someone who awaits her with love. . . . Aldaran had done this service at the birth of all his children: sensing the formless fright and rage of the unformed mind, thrust by forces it could not comprehend. Now, searching his memories (had any of Clariza's children been this strong? Deonara's babes, none of them had been able even to fight for their lives, poor little weaklings . . . he reached out, searching for the unfocused thoughts of the struggling child, torn by awareness of the mother's pain and fright. He sought to send out soothing thoughts of love, of tenderness; not in words, for the unborn had no knowledge of language, but he formed them into words for his own sake and Aliciane's, to focus their emotions, to give a feeling of warmth and welcome.

You must not be afraid, little one; it will soon be over . . . you will breathe free and we will hold you in our arms and love you . . . you are long awaited and dearly loved. . . . He sought to send out love and tenderness, to banish from his mind the frightening thought of the sons and daughter he had lost, when all his love could not follow them into the darkness their developing *laran* had cast on their minds. He tried to blot out memory of the weak and pitiful struggles of Deonara's children, who had never lived to draw breath. . . . *Did I love them enough? If I had loved Deonara more, would her children have fought harder to live?*

"Draw the curtains," he said after a moment, and one of the women in the chamber tiptoed to the window and closed out the darkening sky. But the thunder roared in the room, and the flare of the lightning could be seen even through the drawn curtains.

"See how she does, the little one," the midwife said, and Margali rose quietly, came to lay gentle hands around Aliciane's body, sinking her awareness into the woman, to monitor her breathing, the progress of the birth. A woman with *laran,* bearing a child, could not be physically examined or touched, for fear of hurting or frightening the unborn with a careless pressure or touch. The *leronis* must do this, using the perception of her own telepathic and psychokinetic powers. Aliciane felt the soothing touch, and her troubled face relaxed, but as Margali withdrew she cried out in sudden terror.

"Oh, Donal, Donal—what will become of my boy?"

Lady Deonara Ardais-Aldaran, a slight aging woman, tiptoed to Aliciane's side and took the slender fingers in hers. She said soothingly, "Do not fear for Donal, Aliciane. Avarra forbid it should be needful, but I swear to you that I will, from this day forth, be foster-mother to him, as tenderly as if he were one of my own sons."

"You have been kind to me, Deonara," Aliciane said, "and I sought to take Mikhail from you."

"Child, child—this is no time to think of this; if you can give Mikhail what I could not, then you are my sister and I will love you as Cassilda loved Camilla, I swear it." Deonara bent and kissed Aliciane's pale cheek. "Set your mind at rest, *breda;* think only of this little one who comes to our arms. I will love her too."

Held tenderly in the arms of her child's father, holding the wand of the woman who had sworn to welcome her child as her own, Aliciane knew that she should be comforted. Yet, as lightning flared on the heights and rumbled around the walls of the castle, she felt terror all though and pervading her. *Is it the child's terror or mine?* Her mind swam into darkness under the soothing of the *leronis,* under the flooding reassurances of Mikhail, pouring out love and tenderness. *Is it for me or only for the child?* It no longer seemed to matter; she could see no further. Always before, she had had some faint sense of what would come after, but now it seemed there was nothing in the world but her own fear, the child's fear, in the formless, wordless rage. It seemed to her that the rage focused with the thunder, that the birth pains tearing her were brightening and darkening as the lightning came and went . . . thunder crashing not on the heights outside but in and around her own violated body . . . terror, rage, fury expending itself within her . . . the lightning bringing fury and pain. She struggled for breath and cried out and her mind sank, almost with relief, into dark, and silence, and nothingness. . . .

"Ali! She is a little fury," the midwife said, gingerly holding the struggling child. "You must calm her, *domna,* before I cut her life from her mother's, or she will struggle and bleed overmuch—but she is strong, a hearty little woman!"

Margali bent over the shrieking infant. The face was dark red, contorted into a furious scream of rage; the eyes, squinted almost shut, were a blazing blue. The round little head was covered with thick red fuzz. Margali laid her slender hands along the naked body of the child, crooning softly to her. Under the touch the baby calmed a little and stopped fighting; and the midwife was able to sever the umbilical cord and tie it. But when the woman took the infant and wrapped her in a warmed blanket, she began to shriek again and struggle and the woman laid her down, drawing back a shocked hand.

"Ai! Evanda have mercy, she is one of *those*! Well, when she is grown, the little maiden need not fear rape, if she can stroke already with *laran*. I have never heard of this in a babe so young!"

"You frightened her," Margali said, smiling; but as she took the child, her smile slid off. Like all of Deonara'a women, she had loved the gentle Aliciane. "Poor child, to lose so loving a mother, so soon!"

Mikhail of Aldaran knelt, his face drawn with anguish, beside the body of the woman he had loved. "Aliciane! Aliciane, my beloved," he mourned. Then he raised his face, in bitterness. Deonara had taken the wrapped infant from Margali and was holding it, with the fierce hunger of thwarted motherhood, to her meager breast.

"You are not ill content, are you, Deonara—that none will vie with you to mother this child?"

"That is not worthy of you, Mikhail," Deonara said, holding Aliciane's child close. "I loved Aliciane well, my lord; would you have me cast aside her child, or can I best show my love by rearing her as tenderly as if she were my own? Take her, then, my husband, until you find another love." Try as she would, Lady Aldaran could not keep the bitterness from her voice. "She is your only living child. And if already she has *laran,* she will need much care to rear her. My poor babes never lived even this long." She put the child into Dom Mikhail's arms, and he stood looking down, with infinite tenderness and grief, at his only child.

Mayra's curse rang in his mind: *You will take no other to your bed . . . your loins will be empty as a winter-killed tree.* As if his own dismay communicated itself to the infant in his arms she began to struggle again and shriek in the blanket. Beyond the window the storm raged.

Dom Mikhail looked into the face of his daughter. Infinitely precious she seemed to the childless man; the more so if the curse should be true. She was rigid in his arms, squalling, her small face contorted as if she were trying to outshout the rage of the storm outside, her tiny pink fists clenched with rage. Yet already he could see in her face a miniature blurred copy of Aliciane's—the arched brows and high cheekbones, the eyes blazing blue, the fuzz of red hair.

"Aliciane died to give me this great gift. Shall we give her her mother's name, in memory?"

Deonara shuddered and flinched. "Would you bestow on your only daughter the name of the dead, my lord? Seek a name of better omen!"

"As you will. Give her what name pleases you, domna."

Deonara said, faltering, "I would have named our first daughter Dorilys, had she lived long enough to be named. Let her bear that name, in token that I will be a mother to her." She touched the rose-petal cheek with a finger. "How do you like that name, little woman? Look—she sleeps. She is weary with so much crying. . . ."

Beyond the windows of the birth-chamber the storm muttered into silence and died away, and there was no sound but the slow dripping of the last raindrops outside.

Chapter 3

* * * Eleven Years Later * * *

It was the dark hour before dawn. Snow fell silently over the monastery of Nevarsin, already buried under deep snow.

There was no bell, or if there was, it rang silently, unheard, in Father Master's quarters. Yet in every cell and dormitory, brothers and novices and students moved silently, as if on that single noiseless signal, out of sleep.

Allart Hastur of Elhalyn came awake sharply, something in his mind tuned and receptive to the call. In the first years he had often slept through it, but no one in the monastery might waken another; part of the training here was that the novices should hear the inaudible and see what was not there to be seen.

Nor did he feel cold, though he was covered, by rule, only with the outer cowl of his long robe; he had by now disciplined his body so that it would generate heat to warm him as he slept. With no need of light, he rose, drew the cowl over the simple inner garment he wore night and day, and thrust his feet into rude sandals woven of straw. Into his pockets he thrust the small bound prayer book, the pen case and sealed ink-horn, his own bowl and spoon; now in the pockets of the robe were all the items which a monk might own or use. Dom Allart Hastur was not yet a fully sworn brother of Saint-Valentine-of-the-Snows at Nevarsin. It would be a year before he could achieve that final detachment from the world which lay below him—a troubling world, and one which he remembered every time he fastened the leather strap of his sandals; for in the world of the Domains below him, *sandal-wearer* was the ultimate insult for a male, implying effeminate behavior, or worse. Even now, as he fastened the sandal-strap, he was forced to calm his mind from that memory by the three slow breaths, pause, three more breaths paced to a murmured prayer for the cause of the offense; but Allart was painfully aware of the irony in this.

To pray for peace for my brother, who put this insult on me, when it was he who drove me here, for my very sanity's sake? Aware that he still felt anger and resentment, he did the breathing ritual again, firmly dismissing his brother from his mind, remembering the words of the Father Master.

"You have no power over the world or the things of the world, my son; you have renounced all desire for that power. The power you have come here to attain is the power over the things within. Peace will come only when you become fully aware that your thoughts are not from outside yourself; they come from within, and thus are wholly yours, the only things in this universe over which it is legitimate to have total power. You, not your thoughts and memories, rule your mind, and it is you, no other, who bid them to come and go. The man who allows his own thoughts to torment him is like the man who clasps a scorpion-ant to his breast, bidding it bite him further."

Allart repeated the exercise, and at the end of it, the memory of his brother had vanished from his mind. *He has no place here, not even in my mind and memory.* Calm now, his breathing coming and going in a small white cloud about his mouth, he left the cell and moved silently down the long corridor.

The chapel, reached by a brief passage through the falling snow, was the oldest part of the monastery. Four hundred years ago, the first band of brothers had come here to be above the world they wished to renounce, digging their monastery from the living rock of the mountain, hollowing out the small cave in which, it was said. Saint-Valentine-of-the-Snows had lived out his life. Around the hermit's remains, a city had grown: Nevarsin, the City of Snows. Now several buildings clustered here, each one built with the labor of monkish hands, in defiance of the ease of these days; it was the brothers' boast that not a single stone had been moved with the aid of any matrix, or with anything other than the toil of hands and mind.

The chapel was dark, a single small light glowing in the shrine where the statue of the Holy Bearer of Burdens stood, above the last resting-place of the saint. Allart, mov-

ing quietly, eyes closed as the rule demanded, turned into
his assigned place on the benches; as one, the brotherhood
knelt. Allart, eyes still closed by rule, heard the shuffle of
feet, an occasional stumble of some novice who must still
rely on the outer instead of the inner sight to move his
clumsy body about the darkness of the monastery. The students, unsworn, with minimal teaching, stumbled in the
darkness, ignorant of why the monks neither allowed nor
required light. Whispering, pushing one another, they stumbled and sometimes fell, but eventually they were all in
their assigned places. Again there was no discernible sound,
but the monks rose with a single disciplined movement,
following again some invisible signal from Father Master,
and their voices rose in the morning hymn:

> "One Power created
> Heaven and Earth
> Mountains and valleys
> Darkness and light;
> Male and female
> Human and nonhuman.
> This Power cannot be seen
> Cannot be heard
> Cannot be measured
> By anything except the mind
> Which partakes of this Power;
> I name it Divine. . . ."

This was the moment of every day when Allart's inward
questions, searchings, and dismay wholly vanished. Hearing
the voices of his brothers singing, old and young, treble
with childhood or rusty with age, loosing his own voice in
the great affirmation, he lost all sense of himself as a separate, searching, questing entity. He rested, floating, in the
knowledge that he was a part of something greater than
himself, a part of the great Power which maintained the
motion of moons, stars, sun, and the unknown Universe
beyond; that here he had a true place in the harmony; that
if he vanished, he would leave an Allart-sized hole in the
Universal Mind, something never to be replaced or altered.
Hearing the singing, he was wholly at peace. The sound of
his own voice, a finely trained tenor, gave him pleasure,

but no more than the sounds of each voice in the choir, even the rusty and untuneful quavering of old Brother Fenelon next to him. Whenever he sang with his brothers, he recalled the first words he had ever read of Saint-Valentine-of-the-Snows, words which had come to him during the years of his greatest torment, and which had given him the first peace he had known since he left his childhood behind.

"Each one of us is like a single voice within a great choir, a voice like no other; each of us sings for a few years within that great choir and then that voice is forever silenced, and other voices take its place; but every voice is unique and none is more beautiful than another, or can sing another's song. I call nothing evil but the attempt to sing to another's tune or in another's voice."

And Allart, reading those words, had known that from childhood he had been attempting, at the command of his father and brothers, tutors, arms-masters and grooms, servants and superiors, to sing to a tune, and in a voice, which could never be his own. He had become a *cristoforo,* which was believed unseemly for a Hastur; a descendant of Hastur and Cassilda, a descendant of gods, one who bore *laran;* a Hastur of Elhalyn, near to the holy places at Hali where the gods once had walked. All the Hasturs, from time immemorial, had worshiped the Lord of Light. Yet Allart had become a *cristoforo,* and a time had come when he had left his brethren and renounced his inheritance and come here to be Brother Allart, his lineage half forgotten even by the brethren of Nevarsin.

Forgetful of self, and yet all-mindful of his own individual and unique place in the choir, in the monastery, in the Universe, Allart sang the long hymns; later he went, his fast still unbroken, to his assigned work of the morning, bringing breakfast to the novices and students in the outer refectory. He carried the steaming jugs of tea and hot bean-porridge to the boys, pouring the food into stoneware bowls and mugs, noticing how the cold young hands curved around the heat to try to warm themselves. Most of the boys were too young to have mastered the techniques of internal heat, and he knew that some of them wore their blankets wrapped under their cowls. He felt a detached sympathy for them, remembering his own early sufferings with the cold before his untrained mind could learn how to warm his body; but they had hot food and slept under extra blankets and the more they felt the cold, the sooner they would apply themselves to conquering it.

He kept silence (though he knew he should have reproved them) when they grumbled about the coarseness of the food; here in the quarters of the children, food rich and luxurious, by contrast to that of the monks, was served. He himself had tasted hot food only twice since entering the full monastic regimen; both times when he had done extraordinary work in the deep passes, rescuing snowbound travelers. Father Master had judged the chilling of his body had gone to a point where it endangered his health, and had ordered him to eat hot food and sleep under extra blankets for a few days. Under ordinary conditions, Allart had so mastered his body that summer and winter were indifferent to him, and his body made full use of whatever food came his way, hot or cold.

One disconsolate little fellow, a pampered son of the Lowland Domains with carefully cut hair curled around his face, was shivering so hard, wrapped in cowl and blanket, that Allart while spooning him out a second portion of porridge—for the children were allowed to eat as much as they wished, being growing boys—said gently, "You will not feel the cold so much in a little while. The food will warm you. And you are warmly clad."

"Warmly?" the child said, disbelieving. "I haven't my fur cloak, and I think I am going to die of the cold!" He was near to tears, and Allart laid a hand compassionately on his shoulder.

"You won't die, little brother. You will learn that you can be warm without clothes. Do you know that the novices here sleep with neither blanket nor cowl, naked on the stone? And no one here has died of the cold yet. No animal wears clothing, their bodies being adapted to the weather where they live."

"Animals have fur," protested the child, sulkily. "I've only got my skin!"

Allart laughed and said," And that is proof you do not need fur; for if you needed fur to keep warm, you would have been born furred, little brother. You are cold because since childhood you have been told to be cold in the snow and your mind has believed this lie; but a time will come, even before summer, when you too will run about barefoot in the snow and feel no discomfort. You do not believe me now, but remember my words, child. Now eat up your porridge, and feel it going to work in the furnace of your body, to bring heat to all your limbs." He patted the tear-stained cheek, and went on with his work.

He, too, had rebelled against the harsh discipline of the monks; but he had trusted them, and their promises had been truthful. He was at peace, his mind disciplined to control, living only one day at a time with none of the tormenting pressure of foresight, his body now a willing servant, doing what it was told without demanding more than it needed for well-being and health.

In his years here he had seen four batches of these children arrive, crying with cold, complaining about harsh food and cold beds, spoiled, demanding—and they would go away in a year, or two, or three, disciplined to survival, knowing much of their past history and competent to judge their own future. These, too, including the pampered little boy who was afraid he would die of cold without his fur cloak, would go away hardened and disciplined. Without deliberation, his mind moved into the future, trying to see what would become of the child, to reassure himself. He knew it—his sternness with the child was justified. . . .

Allart tensed, his muscles stiffening as they had not done since his first year here. Automatically, he breathed to relax them, but the sudden dread remained.

I am not here. I cannot see myself at Nevarsin in another year. . . . Is it my death I see: or am I to go forth? Holy Bearer of Burdens, strengthen me. . . .

It had been this that brought him here. He was not, as some Hasturs were, *emmasca,* neither male nor female, long-lived but mostly sterile; though there were monks in this monastery who had indeed been born so, and only here had they found ways to live with this, which in these days was an affliction. No; he had known from childhood that he was a man, and had been so trained, as was fitting to the son of a royal line, fifth from the throne of the Domains. But even as a child, he had had another trouble.

He had begun to see the future almost before he was able to talk; once, when his foster-father had come to bring him a horse, he had frightened the man by telling him that he was glad he had brought the black instead of the gray he had started out with.

"How did you know I started to bring you the gray?" the man had asked.

"I saw you giving me the gray," Allart had said, "and then I saw you giving me the black, and I saw that your pack fell and you turned back and did not come at all."

"Mercy of Aldones," the man had whispered. "It is true that I came near to losing my pack in the pass, and if I had lost it I would have had to turn back, having little food for the journey."

Only slowly had Allart begun to realize the nature of his *laran;* he saw, not the one future, the true future alone, but all possible futures, fanning out ahead of him, every move he made spawning a dozen new choices. At fifteen, when he was declared a man and went before the Council of Seven to be tattooed with the mark of his Royal House, he found his days and nights torture, for he could see a dozen roads before him at every step, and a hundred choices each spurting new choices, till he was paralyzed, never daring to move for terror of the known and the new unknown. He did not know how to shut it out, and he could not live with it. In arms-training he was paralyzed, seeing at every stroke a dozen ways a movement of his own could disable or kill another, three ways every stroke aimed at him could land or fail to land. The arms-training sessions became such a nightmare that eventually he would stand still before the arms-master, cowering like a frightened girl, unable even to lift his sword. The *leronis* of his household tried to reach his mind and show him the way out of this labyrinth, but Allart was paralyzed with the different roads he could see for her training, and with his own growing sensitivity to women, could see himself seizing her mindlessly, and in the end he hid himself in his room, letting them call him coward and idiot, refusing to move or take a single step for fear of what would happen, knowing himself a freak, a madman. . . .

When Allart had finally stirred himself to make his long, terrifying journey—at every step seeing the false step which could plunge him into the abyss, to be killed or lie broken for days on the crags below the path, seeing himself fleeing, turning back—Father Master had welcomed him and heard his story, saying, "Not a freak or a madman, Allart, but much afflicted. I cannot promise you will find your true road here, or be cured, but perhaps we can teach you to live with it."

"The *leronis* thought I could learn to control it with a matrix, but I was afraid," Allart had confessed, and it was the first time he had felt free to speak of fear; fear was the forbidden thing, cowardice a vice too unspeakable to mention for a Hastur.

Father Master nodded and said, "You did well to fear the matrix; it might have controlled you through your fear. Perhaps we can show you a way to live without fear; failing that, perhaps you can learn a way to live with your fears. First you will learn that they are *yours*."

"I have always known this. I have felt guilty enough about them—" Allart protested, but the old monk had smiled.

"No. If you truly believed they were *yours,* you would not feel guilt, or resentment, or anger. What you see is from outside yourself, and may come, or not, but is beyond your control. But your fear is yours, and yours alone, like your voice, or your fingers, or your memory, and therefore yours to control. If you feel powerless over your fear, you have not yet admitted that it is yours, to do with as you will. Can you play the *rryl*?"

Startled at this mental jump, Allart admitted that he had been taught to play the small, handheld harp after a fashion.

"When your strings would not at first make the sounds you wished, did you curse the instrument, or your unskilled hands? Yet a time came, I suppose, when your fingers were responsive to your will. Do not curse your *laran* because your mind has not yet been trained to control it." He let Allart think that over for a moment, then said, "The futures you see are from outside, generated by neither memory nor fear; but the fear arises within you, paralyzing your choice to move among those futures. It is you, Allart, who create the fear; when you learn to control your fear, then you can look unafraid at the many paths you may tread and choose which you will take. Your fear is like your unskilled hand on the harp, blurring the sound."

"But how can I help being afraid? I do not *want* to fear."

"Tell me," Father Master said mildly, "which of the gods put the fear into you, like a curse?" Allart was silent, shamed, and the monk said quietly, "You speak of *being* afraid. Yet fear is something you generate in yourself, from your mind's lack of control; and you will learn to look at it and discover for yourself when you choose to be afraid. The first thing you must do is to acknowledge that the fear is *yours,* and you can bid it come and go at will. Begin with this; whenever you feel fear that prevents choice, say to yourself: 'What has made me feel fear? Why have I chosen to feel this fear preventing my choice, instead of feeling the freedom to choose?' Fear is a way of not allowing yourself to choose freely what you will do next; a way of letting your body's reflexes, not the needs of your mind, choose for you. And as you have told me, mostly, of late, you have chosen to do nothing, so that none of the things you fear will come upon you; so your choices are not made by you but by your fear. Begin here, Allart. I cannot promise to free you of your fear, only that a time will come when you are the master, and fear will not paralyze you." Then he had smiled and said, "You came here, did you not?"

"I was more afraid to stay than to come," Allart said, shaking.

Father Master had said, encouragingly, "At least you could still select between a greater and a lesser fear. Now you must learn to control the fear and look beyond it; and then a day will come when you will know that it is yours, your servant, to command as you will."

"All the Gods grant it," Allart had said, shivering.

So his life here had begun . . . and had endured for six years now. Slowly, one by one, he had mastered his fears, his body's demands, learning to seek out among the bewildering fan-shaped futures the one least harmful. Then his future had narrowed, until he saw himself only here, living one day at a time, doing what he must . . . no more and no less.

Now, after six years, suddenly what he saw ahead was a bewildering flow of images: travel, rocks and snow, a strange castle, his home, the face of a woman. . . . Allart covered his face with his hands, again in the grip of the old paralyzing fear.

No! No! I will not! I want to stay here, to live my own

destiny, to sing to no other man's tune and in no other man's voice. . . .

For six years he had been left to his own destiny, subject only to the futures determined by his own choices. Now the outside was breaking in on him again; was someone outside the monastery making choices in which he must be involved, one way or another? All the fear he had subdued in the last six years crowded in on him again; then, slowly, breathing as he had been taught, he mastered it.

My fear is my own; I am in command of it, and I alone can choose. . . . Again he sought to see, among the thronging images, one path in which he might remain Brother Allart, at peace in his cell, working for the future of his world in his own way. . . .

But there was no such future path, and this told him something; whatever outside choice was breaking in on him, it would be something which he could not choose to deny. A long time he struggled, kneeling on the cold stone of his cell, trying to force his reluctant body and mind to accept this knowledge. But in the end, as he now knew he had power to do, he mastered his fear. When the summons came he would meet it unafraid.

By midday, Allart had faced enough of the bewildering futures which spread out, diverging endlessly, before him, to know at least a part of what he faced. He had seen his father's face—angry, cajoling, complaisant—often enough in these visions to know, at least in part, what was the first trial facing him.

When Father Master summoned him, he could face the ancient monk with calm and an impassive control.

"Your father has come to speak with you, my son. You may see him in the north guest chamber."

Allart lowered his eyes; when at last he raised them, he said, "Father, must I speak with him?" His voice was calm, but the Father Master knew him too well to take this calm at face value.

"I have no reason to refuse him, Allart."

Allart felt like flinging back an angry reply, "I have!" but he had been trained too well to cling to unreason. He said quietly, at last, "I have spent much of this day schooling myself to face this; I do not want to leave Nevarsin. I have found peace here, and useful work. Help me to find a way, Father Master."

The old man sighed. His eyes were closed—as they were most of the time, since he saw more clearly with the inner sight—but Allart knew they beheld him more clearly than ever.

"I would indeed, for your sake, son, that I could see such a way. You have found content here, and such happiness as a man bearing your curse can find. But I fear your time of content is ended. You must bear in mind, lad, that many men never have such a time of rest to learn self-knowledge and discipline; be grateful for what you have been given."

Oh. I am sick of this pious talk of acceptance of those burdens laid upon us—Allart caught back the rebellious thought, but Father Master raised his head and his eyes, colorless as some strange metal, met Allart's rebellious ones

"You see, my boy, you have not really the makings of a monk. We have given you some control over your natural inclinations, but you are by nature rebellious and eager to change what you can, and changes can be made only *down there*." His gesture took in a whole wide world outside the monastery. "You will never be content to accept your world complacently, son, and now you have the strength to fight rationally, not to lash out in blind rebellion born of your own pain. You must go, Allart, and make such changes in your world as you may."

Allart covered his face with his hands. Until this moment he had still believed—*like a child, like a credulous child!*—that the old monk held some power to help him avoid what must be. He knew that six years in the monastery had not helped him grow past this; now he felt the last of his childhood drop away, and he wanted to weep.

Father Master said with a tender smile. "Are you grieving that you cannot remain a child, in your twenty-third year, Allart? Rather, be grateful that after all these years of learning, you have been made ready to be a man."

"You sound like my father!" Allart flung at him angrily. "I had that served up to me morning and night with my porridge—that I was not yet manly enough to fill my place in the world. Do not *you* begin to speak so, Father, or I shall feel my years here were all a lie!"

"But I do not mean what your father means, when I say you are ready to meet what comes as a man," Father Master said. "I think you know already what I mean by manhood, and it is not what my lord Hastur means; or was I mistaken when I heard you comfort and encourage a crying child this morning? Don't pretend you do not know the difference, Allart." The stern voice softened. "Are you too angry to kneel for my blessing, child?"

Allart fell to his knees; he felt the touch of the old man on his mind.

"The Holy Bearer of Burdens will strengthen you for what must come. I love you well, but it would be selfish to keep you here; I think you are too much needed in that world you tried to renounce." As he rose, Father Master drew Allart into a brief embrace, kissed him, and let him go.

"You have my leave to go and clothe yourself in secular garments, if you will, before you present yourself to your father." Again, for the last time, he touched Allart's face. "My blessing on you always. We may not meet again, Allart, but you will be often in my prayers in the days to come. Send your sons to me, one day, if you will. Now go." He seated himself, letting his cowl drop over his face, and Allart knew he had been dismissed from the old man's thoughts as firmly as from his presence.

Allart did not avail himself of Father Master's permission to change his garments. He thought angrily that he was a monk, and if his father liked it not, that was his father's trouble and none of his own. Yet part of this rebellion came from the knowledge that when he turned his thoughts ahead he could not see himself again in the robes of a monk, nor here in Nevarsin. Would he never come again to the City of Snows?

As he walked toward the guest chamber, he tried to discipline his breathing to calm. Whatever his father had come to say to him, it would not be bettered by quarreling with the old man as soon as they met. He swung open the door and went into the stone-floored chamber.

Beside the fire burning there, in a carven chair, an old man sat, erect and grim, his fingers clenched on the chair-arms. His face had the arrogant stamp of the lowland Hasturs. As he heard the measured sweep of Allart's robe brushing on the stone, he said irritably, "Another of you robed spooks? Send me my son!"

"Your son is here to serve you, *vai dom*."

The old man stared at him. "Gods above, is it you, Allart? How dare you present yourself before me in this guise!"

"I present myself as I am, sir. Have you been received with comfort? Let me bring you food or wine, if you wish."

"I have already been served so," the old man said, jerking his head at the tray and decanter on the table. "I need nothing more, except to speak with you, for which purpose I undertook this wretched journey!"

"And I repeat, I am here and at your service, sir. Had you a hard journey? What prompted you to make such a journey in winter, sir?"

"You!" growled the old man. "When are you going to be ready to come back where you belong, and do your duty to clan and family?"

Allart lowered his eyes, clenching his fists till his nails cut deep in his palm and drew blood; what he saw in this room, a few minutes from now, terrified him. In at least one of the futures diverging now from his every word, Stephen Hastur, Lord Elhalyn, younger brother of Regis II, who sat on the throne of Thendara, lay here on the stone floor, his neck broken. Allart knew that the anger surging in him, the rage he had felt for his father since he could remember, could all too easily erupt in such a murderous attack. His father was speaking again, but Allart did not hear, fighting to force mind and body to composure.

I do not want to fall upon my father and kill him with my two hands! I do not, I—do—not! And I will not! Only when he could speak calmly, without resentment, he said, "I am sorry, sir, to displease you. I thought you knew that I wished to spend my life within these walls, as a monk and a healer. I would be allowed to pronounce my final vows this year at midsummer, to renounce my name and inheritance and dwell here for the rest of my life."

"I knew you had once said so, in the sickness of your adolescence," Dom Stephen Hastur said, "but I thought it would pass when you were restored to health of body and mind. How is it with you, Allart? You look well and strong. It seems that these *cristoforo* madmen have not starved you nor driven you quite mad with deprivations—not yet."

Allart said amiably, "Indeed they have not, sir. My body, as you can see, is strong and well, and my mind at peace."

"Is it so, son? Then I shall not begrudge the years you have spent here; and by whatever methods they achieved this miracle, I shall forever be grateful to them."

"Then compound your gratitude, *vai dom,* by giving me leave to remain here where I am happy and at peace, for the rest of my life."

"Impossible! Madness!"

"May I ask why, sir?"

"I had forgotten that you did not know," Lord Elhalyn said. "Your brother Lauren died, three years ago; he had your *laran,* only in worse form still, for he could not manage to distinguish between past and future; and when it came upon him in all strength, he withdrew inside himself and never spoke again, or responded to anything outside, and so died."

Allat felt grieved. Lauren had been the merest child, a stranger, when he left home; but the thought of the boy's sufferings dismayed him. How narrowly he himself had escaped that fate! "Father, I am sorry. What pity you could not have sent him here; they might have been able to reach him."

"One was enough," Dom Stephen said. "We need no weakling sons; better die young than pass on such a weakness in the blood. His Grace, my brother Regis, has but a single heir; his elder son died in battle against those invaders at Serrais, and his only remaining son, Felix, who will inherit his throne, is frail in health. I am next, and then your brother Damon-Rafael. You stand within four places of the throne, and the king is in his eightieth year. You have no son, Allart."

Allart said, with a violent surge of revulsion, "With such a curse as I bear, would you have me pass it to another? You have told me how it cost Lauren his life!"

"Yet we need that foresight," Stephen Hastur said, "And you have mastered it. The *leroni* of Hali have a plan for fixing it in our line without the instability which endangered your sanity and killed Lauren. I tried to speak of this to you before you left us, but you were in no shape to think of the needs of the clan. We have made compact with the Aillard clan for a daughter of their line, whose genes have been so modified that they will be dominant, so that your children will have the sight, and the control to use it without danger. You will marry this girl. Also she has two *nedestro* sisters, and the *leroni* of the Tower have discovered a technique which will assure that you will father only sons on all of these. If the experiment succeeds, your sons will have the foresight and the control, too." He saw the disgust in Allart's face and said, enraged, "Are you no more than a squeamish boy?"

"I am a *cristoforo*. The first precept of the Creed of Chastity is *to take no woman unwilling.*"

"Good enough for a monk, not a man! Yet none of these will be unwilling when you take her, I assure you. If you wish, the two who are not your wives need not even know your name; we have drugs now which will mean that they carry away only the memory of a pleasant interlude. And every woman wishes to bear a child of the lineage of Hastur and Cassilda."

Allart grimaced in revulsion. "I want no woman who must be delivered to me drugged and unconscious. *Unwilling* does not only mean fighting in terror of rape; it would also mean a woman whose ability to give, or refuse, free consent had been destroyed by drugs!"

"I would not suggest it," said the old man angrily, "but you have made it clear that you are not ready to do your duty by caste and clan of your own free will! At your age, Damon-Rafael had a dozen *nedestro* sons by as many willing women! But you, you sandal-wearer—"

Allart bent his head, fighting the reflex of anger which prompted him to take that frail old neck between his hands and squeeze the life out of it. "Damon-Rafael spoke his mind often enough on the subject of my manhood, Father. Must I hear it from you as well?"

"What have you done to give me a better opinion of you? Where are *your* sons?"

"I do not agree with you that manhood must be measured by sons alone, sir; but I will not argue the point with you now. I do not wish to pass on this curse in my blood. I know something of *laran*. I feel you are wrong in trying to breed for greater strength in these gifts. You can see in me—and in Lauren, even more—that the human mind was never intended to bear such weight. Do you know what I mean if I speak of *recessives* and *lethal genes*?"

"Are you going to teach me my business, youngster?"

"No, but in all respect, Father, I will have no part in it. If I were ever to have sons—"

"There is no *if* about it. You must have sons."

The old man's voice was positive, and Allart sighed. His father simply did not hear him. Oh, he heard the words with his ears. But he did not listen; the words went through and past him, because what Allart was saying did not agree with the fixed belief of Lord Elhalyn—that a son's prime duty was to breed the sons who would carry on the fabled gifts of Hastur and Cassilda, the *laran* of the Domains.

Laran, sorcery, psi power, which enabled these families to excel in the manipulation of the matrix stones, the starstones amplifying the hidden powers of the mind; to know the future, to force the minds of lesser men to their own will, to manipulate inanimate objects, to compel the minds of animal and bird—*laran* was the key to power beyond imagining, and for generations the Domains had been breeding for it.

"Father, hear me, I beg you." Allart was not angry or gumentative now, but desperately in earnest. "I tell you, nothing but evil can come of this breeding program, which makes of women only instruments to breed monsters of the mind, without humanity! I have a conscience; I cannot do it."

His father sneered, "Are you a lover of men, that you will not give sons to our caste?"

"I am not," Allart said, "but I have known no woman. If I have been cursed with this evil gift of *laran*—"

"Silence! You blaspheme our forefathers and the Lord of Light who gave us *laran*!"

Now Allart was angry again. "It is you who blaspheme, sir, if you think the gods can be bent to human purposes this way!"

"You insolent—" His father sprang up, then, with an enormous effort, controlled his rage. "My son, you are young, and warped by these monkish notions. Come back to the heritage to which you were born, and you will learn

better. What I ask of you is both right and needful if the
Hasturs are to prosper. No"—he gestured for silence when
Allart would have spoken—"on these matters you are still
ignorant, and your education must be completed. A male
virgin"—try as he might, Lord Elhalyn could not keep the
contempt from his voice—"is not competent to judge."

"Believe me," Allart said, "I am not indifferent to the
charms of women. But I do not wish to pass on the curse
of my blood. And I will not."

"That is not open to discussion," Dom Stephen said,
menace in his voice. "You will not disobey me, Allart. I
would think it disgrace if a son of mine must father his
sons drugged like some reluctant bride, but there are drugs
which will do that to you, too, if you leave us no choice."

*Holy Bearer of Burdens, help me! How shall I keep from
killing him as he stands here before me?*

Dom Stephen said more quietly, "This is no time for
argument, my son. You must give us a chance to convince
you that your scruples are unfounded. I beg of you, go now
and clothe yourself as befits a man and a Hastur, and make
ready to ride with me. You are so needed, my dear son,
and—do you not know how much I have missed you?"

The genuine love in his voice thrust pain through Allart's
heart. A thousand childhood memories crowded in on him,
blurring past and future with their tenderness. He was a
pawn to his father's pride and heritage, yes, but with all
this, Lord Elhalyn sincerely loved all his sons, had been
genuinely afraid for Allart's health and sanity—or he would
never have sent him to a *cristoforo* monastery, of all places
on the face of this world! Allart thought, *I cannot even hate
him; it would be so much easier if I could!*

"I will come, Father. Believe me, I have no wish to
anger you."

"Nor I to threaten you, lad." Dom Stephen held out his
arms. "Do you know, we have not yet greeted one another
as kinsmen? Do these *cristoforos* bid you renounce kin-
ties, son?"

Allart embraced his father, feeling with dismay the bony
fragility of the old man's body, knowing that the appearance of domineering anger masked advancing weakness and
age. "All the gods forbid I should do so while you live, my
father. Let me go and make ready to ride."

"Go, then, my son. For it displeases me more than I can say, to see you in this garb so unfitting for a man."

Allart did not answer, but bowed and went to change his clothes. He would go with his father, yes, and present the appearance of a dutiful son. With certain limits, he would be so. But now he knew what Father Master had meant. Changes were needful in his world, and he could not make them behind monastery walls.

He could see himself riding forth, could see a great hawk hovering, the face of a woman . . . a woman. He knew so little of women. And now they meant to deliver up to him not one but three, drugged and complaisant . . . *that* he would fight to the end of his will and conscience; he would be no part of this monstrous breeding program of the Domains. *Never.* The monkish garb discarded, he knelt briefly, for the last time, on the cold stones of his cell.

"Holy Bearer of Burdens, strengthen me to bear my share of the world's weight . . ." he murmured, then rose and began to clothe himself in the ordinary dress of a nobleman of the Domains, strapping a sword at his side for the first time in over six years.

"Blessed Saint-Valentine-of-the-Snows, grant I may bear it justly in the world . . ." he whispered, then sighed, and looked for the last time on his cell. He knew, with a sorrowful inner knowledge, that he would never set eyes on it again.

Chapter 4

T he *chervine,* the little Darkovan stag-pony, picked its
way fastidiously along the trail, tossing its antlers in
protest at the new fall of snow. They were free of the
mountains now, Hali no more than three days' ride away.
It had been a long journey for Allart, longer than the seven
days it had taken to ride the actual distance; he felt as if
he had traveled years, endless leagues, great chasms of
change; and he was exhausted.

It took all the discipline of his years at Nevarsin to move
securely through the bewilderment of what he now saw,
legions of possible futures branching off ahead of him at
every step, like different roads he might have taken, new
possibilities generated by every word and action. As they
traveled the dangerous mountain passes, Allart could see
every possible false step which might lead him over a precipice, to be smashed, as well as the safe step he actually
took. He had learned at Nevarsin to thread his way through
his fear, but the effort left him weak and weary.

And another possibility was always with him. Again and
again, as they traveled, he had seen his father lying dead
at his feet, in an unfamiliar room.

*I do not want to begin my life outside the monastery as a
patricide! Holy bearer of Burdens, strengthen me . . . !* He
knew he could not deny his anger; that way lay the same
paralysis as in fear, to take no step for fear it would lead
to disaster.

The anger is mine, he reminded himself with firm discipline. *I can choose what I will do with my anger, and I can*

choose not to kill. But it troubled him to see again and again, in that unfamiliar scene which grew familiar as he traveled with the vision, the corpse of his father, lying in a room of green hangings bordered with gold, at the foot of a great chair whose very carvings he could have drawn, so often had he seen it with the sight of his *laran.*

It was hard, as he looked upon the face of his living father, not to look upon him with the pity and horror he would feel for the newly and shockingly dead; and it was a strain on him to show nothing of this to Lord Elhalyn.

For his father, as they traveled, had put aside his words of contempt for Allart's monkish resolution, and ceased entirely to quarrel with him about it. He spoke only kindly to his son, mostly of his childhood at Hali before the curse had descended on Allart, of their kinfolk, the chances of the journey. He spoke of Hali, and the mining done in the Tower there, by the powers of the matrix circle, to bring copper and iron and silver ore to the surface of the ground; of hawks and *chervines*, and the experiments which his brother had made breeding, with cell-deep changes, rainbow-colored hawks, or *chervines* with fantastic jewel-colored antlers like the fabled beasts of legend.

Day by day Allart recaptured some of his childhood love for his father, from the days before his *laran* and the *cristoforo* faith had separated them, and again he felt the agony of mourning, seeing that accursed room with the green hangings and gold, the great carven chair, and his father's face, white and stark and looking very surprised to be dead.

Again and again on this road other faces had begun to come out of the dimness of the unknown into the possible future. Most of them Allart ignored as he had learned in the monastery, but two or three returned repeatedly, so that he knew they were not the faces of people he *might* meet, but people who *would* come into his life; one, which he dimly recognized, was the face of his brother Damon-Rafael, who had called him sandal-wearer and coward, who had been glad to be rid of his rivalry, that he alone might be Elhalyn's heir.

I wish that my brother and I might be friends and love one another as brothers should. Yet I see it nowhere among all the possible futures. . . .

And there was the face of a woman, returning continually

to the eyes of his mind, though he had never seen her before. A small woman, delicately made, with eyes dark-lashed in her colorless face and hair like masses of spun black glass; he saw her in his visions, a grave face of sorrow, the dark eyes turned to him in anguished pleading. *Who are you?* he wondered. *Dark girl of my visions, why do you haunt me this way?*

Strange for Allart after the years in the monastery, he had begun to see erotic visions, too, of this woman, see her laughing, amorous, her face lifted to his own for a caress, closed under the rapture of his kiss. *No!* he thought. No matter how his father should tempt him with the beauty of this woman, he would hold firm to his purpose; he would father no child to bear this curse of his blood! Yet the woman's face and presence persisted, in dreams and waking, and he knew she was one of those his father would seek as a bride for him. Allart thought it would indeed be possible that he would be unable to resist her beauty.

Already I am half in love with her, he thought, *and I do not even know her name!*

One evening, as they rode down toward a broad green valley, his father began to speak again of the future.

"Below us lies Syrtis. The folk of Syrtis have been Hastur vassals for centuries; we will break our journey there. You will be glad to sleep in a bed again, I suppose?"

Allart laughed. "It is all one, Father. During this journey I have slept softer than ever I did at Nevarsin."

"Perhaps I should have had such monkish discipline, if old bones are to make such journeys! I will be glad of a mattress, if you will not! And now we are but two days' ride from home, and we can plan for your wedding. You were handfasted at ten years old to your kinswoman Cassandra Aillard, do you not remember?"

Try as he might, Allart could remember nothing but a festival where he had had a suit of new clothes and had been made to stand for hours and listen to long speeches by the grown-ups. He told his father so, and Dom Stephen said, genial once more, "I am not surprised. Perhaps the girl was not even there; I think she was only three or four years old then. I confess I, too, had doubts about this marriage. Those Aillards have *chieri* blood, and they have an evil habit of bearing, now and then, daughters who are *emmasca*—they look like beautiful women, but they never become ripe for mating, nor do they bear children. Their *laran* is strong, though, so I risked the handfasting, and when the girl had become a woman, I had our own household *leronis* examine her in the presence of a midwife, who gave it as her opinion that the girl was a functioning female and could bear children. I have not seen her since she was a tiny girl, but I am told she has grown up to be a fine-looking maiden; and she is Aillard, and that family is a strong alliance to our clan, one we need greatly. You have nothing to say, Allart?"

Allart forced himself to speak calmly.

"You know my will on that matter, Father. I will not quarrel with you about it, but I have not changed my mind. I have no wish to marry, and I will father no sons to carry on this curse in our blood. I will say no more."

Again, shockingly, the room with the green and gold hangings, and his father's dead face, swam before his mind, so strongly that he had to blink hard to see his father riding at his side.

"Allart," his father said, and his voice was kind, "during these days when we have journeyed together, I have come to know you too well to believe that. You are my own son, after all, and when you are back in the world where you belong, you will not long keep these monkish notions. Let us not speak of it, *kihu caryu*, until the time is upon us. The gods know I have no will to quarrel with the last son they have left me."

Allart felt his throat tighten with grief.

I cannot help it. I have come to love my father. Is this how he will break my will at last, not with force but with kindness? And again he looked on his father's dead face in the room hung with gold and green, and the face of the dark maiden of his visions swam before his blurring eyes.

Syrtis Great House was an ancient stone keep, fortified with moat and drawbridge, and there were great outbuildings of wood and stone, and an elaborate courtyard, under shelter of a glasslike canopy of many colors; underfoot were colored stones, laid together with a precision no workman could have accomplished, so that Allart knew the Syrtis folk were of the new-rich, who could make full use of the ornamental and difficult matrix technology to have such beautiful things constructed. *How can he find so many of the* laran-*gifted to do his will?*

The old lord Syrtis was a plump soft man, who came into the courtyard himself to welcome his overlord, falling to his knees in fawning politeness, rising with a smile that was almost a smirk when Dom Stephen drew him into a kins-man's embrace. He embraced Allart, too, and Allart flinched from the man's kiss on his cheek.

Ugh, he is like a fawning house cat!

Dom Marius led them into his Great Hall, filled with sybaritic luxury, seated them on cushioned divans, called for wine. "This is a new form of cordial, made from our apples and pears; you must try it. . . . I have a new amuse-ment; I will talk of it when we have dined," Dom Marius of Syrtis said, leaning back into the billowy cushions. "And this is your younger son, Stephen? I had heard some rumor that he had forsaken Hali and become a monk among the *cristoforos,* or some such nonsense. I am glad it is only a vicious lie; some people will say *anything.*"

"I give you my word, kinsman, Allart is no monk," Dom Stephen said. "I gave him leave to dwell at Nevarsin to recover his health; he suffered greatly in adolescence from threshold sickness. But he is well and strong, and came home to be married."

"Oh, is it so?" Dom Marius said, regarding Allart with his wide, blinking eyes, encased in wide pillows of fat. "And is the fortunate maiden known to me, dear boy?"

"No more than to me," Allart said in grudging polite-ness. "I am told she is my kinswoman Cassandra Aillard; I saw her but once, when she was a baby girl."

"Ah, the *domna* Cassandra! I have seen her in Thendara; she was present at the Festival Ball in Comyn Castle," Dom Marius said with a leer.

Allart, thought, disgusted, *He only wants us to know he is important enough to be invited there!*

Dom Marius called servants to bring their supper. He followed the recent fad for nonhuman servants, *cralmacs,* artificially bred from the harmless trailmen of the Hellers, with matrix-modified genes by human insemination. To Al-lart the creatures seemed ugly, neither human nor trailman. The trailmen, strange and monkeylike though they were, had their own alien beauty. But the *cralmacs,* handsome though some of them undeniably were, had for Allart the loathsomeness of something unnatural.

"Yes, I have seen your promised bride; she is fair enough to make even a true monk break his vows," Dom Marius sniggered. "You will have no regrets for the monastery when you lie down with her, kinsman. Though all those Aillard girls are unlucky wives, some being sterile as *riyachiyas* and others so fragile they cannot carry a child to birth."

He is one of those who like to foretell catastrophe, too, Allart thought. "I am in no great hurry for an heir; my elder brother is alive and well and has fathered *nedestro* sons. I will take what the gods send." Eager to change the subject, he asked, "Did you breed the *cralmacs* on your own estate? Father told me as we rode of my brother's experiments in breeding ornamental *chervines* through matrix-modification; and your *cralmacs* are smaller and more graceful than those bred at Hali. They are good, I remember, only for mucking out stables and such heavy work, things it would be unsuitable to ask one's human vassals to do."

He said this with a sudden pang—*How quickly I forget!*—remembering that in Nevarsin he had been taught that no honest work was beneath the dignity of a man's own hands. But the words had diverted Dom Marius again into boasting.

"I have a *leronis* from the Ridenow, captured in battle, who is skillful with such things. She thought I was kind to her, when I assured her she would never be used against her own people—but how could I trust her in such a battle?—and she made no trouble about doing other work for me. She bred me thee *cralmacs,* more graceful and shapely indeed than any I had before. I will give you breeding stock, male and female, if you will, for a wedding gift, Dom Allart; no doubt your lady would welcome handsome servants. Also the *leronis* bred for me a new strain of *riyachiyas;* will you see them, cousin?"

Lord Elhalyn nodded, and when they finished the meal the promised *riyachiyas* were brought in. Allart looked on them with an inner spasm of revulsion: exotic toys for jaded tastes. In form they were women, fair of face, slender, with shapely breasts lifting the translucent folds of their draperies, but too narrow of hip and slender of waist and long of leg to be genuine women. There were four of them, two fair-haired, two dark; otherwise identical. They knelt at Dom Marius's feet, moving sinuously, the curve of their slender necks, as they bowed, swanlike and exquisite, and Allart, through his revulsion, felt an unaccustomed stirring of desire.

Zandru's hells, but they are beautiful, as beautiful and unnatural as demon hags!

"Would you believe, cousin, that they were borne in *cralmac* wombs? They are of my seed, and that of the *leronis*," he said, "so that a fastidious man, if they were human, might say they were my daughters, and indeed, the thought adds a little—a little something," he said, sniggering. "Two at a birth—" He pointed to the fair-haired pair and said, "Lella and Rella; the dark ones are Ria and Tia. They will not disturb you with much speech, though they can talk and sing, and I had them taught to dance and to play the *rryl* and to serve food and drink. But, of course, their major talents are for pleasure. They are matrix-spelled, of course, to draw and bind—I see you cannot take your eyes from them, nor"—Dom Marius chuckled—"can your son."

Allart started and angrily turned away from the horribly enticing faces and bodies of the inhumanly beautiful, lust-inspiring creatures.

"Oh, I am not greedy; you shall have them tonight, cousin," Dom Marius said, with a lewd chuckle. "One or two, as you will. And if you, young Allart, have spent six years of frustration in Nevarsin, you must be in need of their services. I will send you Lella; she is my own favorite. Oh, the things that *riyachiya* can do, even a sworn monk would yield to her touch." He grew grossly specific, and Allart turned away.

"I beg you, kinsman," he said, trying to conceal his loathing, "do not deprive yourself of your favorite."

"No?" DomMarius's cushiony eyes rolled back, in feigned sympathy. "Is it so? After so many years in a monastery, do you prefer the pleasures to be found among the brethren? I myself seldom desire a *ri' chiyu*, but I keep a few for hospitality, and some guests desire a change now and then. Shall I send you Loyu? He is a beautiful boy

indeed, and I have had all of them modified to be almost
without response to pain, so that you can use him any way
you choose, if you desire."

Dom Stephen said quickly, seeing that Allart was about
to explode, "Indeed, the girls will do well enough for us. I
compliment you on the skill of your *leronis* at breeding
them."

When they had been taken to the suite of rooms allotted
to them, Dom Stephen said, enraged, "You will *not* disgrace us by refusing this courtesy! I will not have it gos-
siped here that my son is less than a man!"

"He is like a great fat toad! Father, is it a reflection on
my manhood that the thought of such filth overwhelms me
with loathing? I would like to fling his foul gifts in his
sniggering face!"

"You weary me with your monkish scruples, Allart. The
leroni never did better than when they bred us the *riyachiyas;* nor will your wife-to-be thank you if you refuse to
have one in your household. Can you be so ignorant as not
to know that if you lie with a breeding woman, she may
miscarry? It is part of the price we pay for our *laran,* which
we have bred with such difficulty into our line, that our
women are fragile and given to miscarry, so that we must
spare them when they are with child. If you turn your desires on a *riyachiya* only she need not be jealous, as if you
had given your affections to a real girl who would have
some claim on your thoughts."

Allart turned his face away; in the Lowlands this kind of
speech between the generations was the height of indecency, had been from the days when group marriage was
commonplace and any man of your father's age could be
your father, any woman of an age to be your mother could
have been your mother indeed; so that the sexual taboo
was absolute between generations.

Dom Stephen said defensively, "I would never so far
forget myself, Allart, except that you have not been willing
to do your duty by our caste. But I am sure you are enough
my son that you will come to life with a woman in your
arms!" He added, crudely, "You need not be scrupulous;
the creatures are sterile."

Allart thought, sick with disgust, *I may not wait for the
room with the green and gold hangings, I may kill him here*

and now, but his father had turned away and gone into his own chamber.

He thought, enraged, as he made ready for bed, of how corrupt they had become. *We, the sacred descendants of the Lord of Light, bearing the blood of Hastur and Cassilda— or was that only a pretty fairy tale?* Were the *laran* gifts of the families descended from Hastur no more than the work of some presumptuous mortal, meddling with gene-matter and brain-cells, some sorceress with a matrix jewel modifying germ plasm as Dom Marius's *leronis* did with those *riyachiyas,* making exotic toys for corrupt men?

The gods themselves—if indeed there are any gods—must turn sick at the sight of us!

The warm, luxurious room sickened him; he wished himself back at Nevarsin, in the solemn night silence. He had turned out the light when he heard an almost noiseless foot-step and the girl Lella, in her flimsy draperies, stole softly across the floor to his side.

"I am here for your contentment, *vai dom.*"

Her voice was a husky murmur; her eyes alone betrayed that she was not human, for they were dark brown animal eyes, great, soft, strangely unreadable eyes.

Allart shook his head.

"You can go away again, Lella. I will sleep alone tonight."

Sexual images tormented him, all the things he *might* do, all the possible futures, an infinitely diverging set of probabilities hinging on this moment. Lella sat on the edge of the bed; her soft slender fingers, so delicate that they seemed almost boneless, stole into his. She murmured, pleading, "If I do not please you, *vai dom,* I will be punished. What would you have me do? I know many, many ways to give delight."

He knew his father had maneuvered this situation. The *riyachiyas* were bred and taught and spelled to be irresistible; had Dom Stephen hoped she would break down Allart's inhibitions?

"Indeed, my master will be very angry if I fail to give you pleasure. Shall I send for my sister, who is as dark as I am fair? And she is even more skilled. Or would it give you pleasure to beat me, Lord? I like to be beaten, truly I do."

"Hush, hush!" Allart felt sick. "No one would want anyone more beautiful than you." And indeed, the shapely young body, the enchanting little face, the loose scented hair falling across him, were enticing. She had a sweet, faintly musky scent; somehow before he touched her he had believed that the *riyachiyas* would smell animal, not human.

Her spell is on me, he thought. How then could he resist? With a sense of deathly weariness, as he felt her slender fingertips trace a line of awareness down his bare neck from earlobe to shoulder, he thought. *What does it matter? I had indeed resolved to live womanless, never to pass on this curse I bear. But this poor creature is sterile, I cannot father a child on her if I would. Perhaps when he knows I have done his will in this, he will be less ready to put insults on me and call me less than a man. Bearer of Burdens, strengthen me! I but make excuses for what I want to do. Why should I not? Why must I alone resist what is given by right to every man of my caste?* His mind was spinning. A thousand alternate futures spun out before him: in one he seized the girl in his hands and wrung her neck like the animal he knew her to be; in another he saw himself and the girl entwined in tenderness, and the image swelled, driving the awareness of lust into his body; in another he saw the dark maiden lying dead before him. . . . *So many futures, so much death and despair.* . . . Spasmodically, desperately, trying to blot out the multiple futures, he took the girl in his arms and drew her down on the bed. Even as his lips came down on hers, he thought of despair, futility. *What does it matter, when there is all this ruin before me . . . ?*

He heard, as if from nowhere, her small cries of pleasure, and in his wretchedness, thought, *At least she is not unwilling,* and then he did not think again at all, which was an enormous relief.

Chapter 5

When he woke, the girl was gone, and Allart lay without moving for a moment, overcome with sickness and self-contempt. *How shall I keep from killing that man, that he brought this upon me . . . ?* But as his father's dead face swam before his eyes in the familiar room with green and gold hangings, he reminded himself sternly, *The choice was mine; he provided only the opportunity.*

Nevertheless, he felt overwhelming self-contempt as he moved around the room, making ready to ride. In the night past he had learned something about himself that he would rather not have known.

In his six years in Nevarsin it had been no trouble to him to keep to the womanless precincts of the monastery, to live without thought of women; he had never been tempted, even at midsummer festival when even the monks were free to join in the revelry, to seek love or its counterfeit in the lower town. So it had never occurred to him that he would find it difficult to keep his resolve—not to marry, not to father children bearing the monstrous curse of *laran.* Yet, even through his loathing and revulsion for the thing Lella was, not even human, six years of self-imposed celibacy had been cast aside in minutes, at the touch of a *riyachiya's* obscenely soft fingertips.

Now what is to become of me? If I cannot keep my resolve for a single night. . . . In the crowding, diverging futures he saw before his every step, there was a new one, and it displeased him: that he might become some such creature as old Dom Marius, refusing marriage indeed, sat-

ing his lust with these unnaturally bred pleasure girls, or
worse.

He was grateful that their host did not appear at breakfast; he found it hard enough to face his father, and the
vision of his father's dead face came near to blotting out
the real, live presence of the old man, good-natured over
his buttered bread and porridge. Sensing his son's unspoken
anger (Allart wondered if his father had had reports from
servants, or even if he had stooped low enough to question
the girl Lella, to verify that Allart had proved his masculin-
ity), Dom Stephen kept silence until they were donning
their riding-cloaks, then said, "We will leave the riding-
animals here, son; Dom Marius has offered us an air-car
which will take us directly to Hali, and the servants can
bring the riding-animals on in a few days. You have not
ridden in an air-car since you were very small, have you?"

"I do not remember that I rode in one even then," said
Allart, interested against his will. "Surely they were not
common in such times."

"No, very uncommon, and of course they are toys for
the wealthy, demanding a skilled *laran* operator as they
do," Lord Elhalyn said. "They are useless in the mountains;
the crossdrafts and winds would dash any heavier-than-air
vehicle against the crags. But here in the Lowlands it is
safe enough, and I thought such a flight would divert you."

"I confess I am curious," Allart said, thinking that Dom
Marius of Syrtis certainly spared no pains to ingratiate himself with his overlord. First he put his favorite pleasure girls
at their disposal, and now this! "But I heard at Nevarsin
that these contrivances were not safe in the Lowlands either. While war rages between Elhalyn and Ridenow, they
are all too easily attacked."

Dom Stephen shrugged, saying, "We all have *laran;* we
can make short work of any attackers. After six years in a
monastery, no doubt your fighting skills are rusty when it
comes to sword and shield, but I have no doubt you could
strike anyone who attacked us out of the sky. I have fire-
talismans." He looked shrewdly at his son, then said, "Or
are you going to tell me that the monks have made you
such a man of peace that you will not defend your life or
the life of your kinsmen, Allart? I seem to remember that
as a boy you had no stomach for fighting."

No, for at every stroke I saw death or disaster for myself or another, and it is cruel of you to taunt me with childish weakness which was no fault of mine, but of your own accursed hereditary Blood-Gift. . . . But aloud Allart said, forcing himself to ignore the shocking dead face of his father which persisted in appearing before his eyes, blurring his father's living face, "While I live, I will defend my father and my Lord to the death, and the gods do so to me and more also if I fail or falter."

Startled, warmed by something in Allart's voice, Lord Elhalyn put out his arms and embraced his son. For the first time Allart could remember, to him or anyone, the old man said. "Forgive me, dear son, that was not worthy of me. I should not so accuse you unmerited," and Allart felt tears stinging his eyes.

Gods forgive me. He is not cruel, or if he is, it is only out of fear for me, too. . . . He truly wills to be kind. . . .

The air-car was long and sleek, made of some gleaming glassy material, with ornamental stripes of silver down the length of it, a long cockpit with four seats, open to the sky. *Cralmacs* rolled it out from its shed, onto the ornamented paving of the inner courtyard, and the operator, a slender young man with the red hair which proclaimed the minor nobility of the Kilghard Hills, approached them with a curt bow, a mere perfunctory reverence; a highly trained expert, a *laranzu* of this kind, needed to be deferential to no man, not even to the brother of the king at Thendara.

"I am Karinn, *vai dom*. I have orders to take you to Hali. Please take your seats."

He left it to the *cralmacs* to lift Dom Stephen into his seat, and to fasten the straps around him, but as Allart took a place, Karinn lingered a moment before going to his own seat. He said, "Have you ever ridden in one of these, Dom Allart?"

"Not since I can remember. Is it powered by such a matrix as you alone can handle? That would seem beyond belief!"

"Not entirely; in there"—Karinn pointed—"is a battery charged with energy to run the turbines; it would indeed demand more power than one man has at his command, to levitate and move such an apparatus, but the batteries are charged by the matrix circles, and my *laran,* at this moment, is needed only to guide and steer—and to be aware of attackers and evade them." His face was somber. "I would not defy my overlord, and it is no part of my duty to refuse to do as I am bid, but—have you *laran*?"

As Karinn spoke, the unease in Allart clarified, with a sudden sharp vision of this air-car bursting asunder, exploding, falling out of the sky like a stone. Was this only a distant probability or did it truly lie before them? He had no way of knowing.

"I have *laran* enough to be uneasy at trusting myself to this contraption. Father, we will be attacked. You know that?"

"Dom Allart," Karinn said, "this contraption, as you call it, is the safest means of transport ever devised by starstone technology. You are vulnerable to attack between here and Hali, should you go a-horse, for three days; in an air-car you will be there before midday and they must place their attackers very precisely. Furthermore, it is easier to defend yourself with *laran* than against such weapons as they may send against you with armed men. I can see a day coming on Darkover when all the Great Houses will have such weapons and devices to protect themselves against envious rivals or rebellious vassals; and then there will be no more wars, either for no sane men will risk *this* kind of death and destruction. Such *contraptions* as this, *vai dom*, may be only expensive toys for rich men now, but they will bring us such an age of peace as Darkover has never known!"

He spoke with such conviction and enthusiasm that Allart doubted his own rising vision of dreadful warfare with weapons ever more dreadful. Karinn must be right Such weapons would surely restrain sane men from making war at all, and so he who invented the most terrible weapons worked the harder for peace.

Taking his seat, Allart said, "Aldones, Lord of Light, grant you speak with true vision, Karinn. And now let us see this miracle."

I have seen many possible futures which never came to pass. I have found this morning that I love my father well, and I will cling to the belief that I will never lay hands upon him, no more than I would wring the neck of that poor harmless little riyachiya in the night past. I will not fear attack, either, but I will guard against it, while I take pleasure

in this new means of travel. He let Karin show him how to
fasten the straps that would hold him in his seat if the air
became turbulent, and the device that swiveled his seat behind a magnified pane of glass, giving him instant view of
any attackers or menace.

He listened closely as the *laranzu,* taking his own seat
and fastening himself into place, bent his head in alert concentration and the battery-powered turbine began to roar.
He had practiced enough in boyhood, in the tiny gliders
levitated by small matrixes and soaring on the air currents
around the Lake of Hali, to be aware of the elementary
principles of heavier-than-air flight, but it was incredible to
him that a matrix circle, a group of close-linked telepath
minds, could charge a battery strongly enough to power
such enormous turbines. Yet *laran* could be powerful, and
a matrix could amplify the electric currents of the brain
and body enormously, a hundredfold, a thousandfold. He
wondered how many minds with *laran* it took, operating
for how long, to charge such batteries with the tremendous
humming power of those roaring turbines. He would have
liked to ask Karinn—but would not disturb the *laranzu*'s
concentration—why such a vehicle could not be adapted to
ground transit, but quickly realized that for any ground
vehicle roads and highways were needed. Someday, perhaps, roads would be practical, but on the rough terrain
from the Kilghard Hills north, ground transit would probably always be limited to the feet of men and animals.

Quickly, with the humming power, they skimmed along
a level runway surfaced with glassy material which must
have been poured there by matrix-power, too; then they
were airborne, rising swiftly over treetop sand forests, moving into the very clouds with an exhilarating speed that
took Allart's breath away. It was as far beyond the soaring
he had done on gliders, as the gliders were above the slow
plodding of a *chervine*! Karinn motioned, and the air-car
turned its vast wings southward and flew over the forests
to the south.

They had flown for a considerable time. Allart was beginning to feel the straps constricting his body, and wished he
might loosen them for a little, when he felt within himself,
with a spurt of sudden excitement, alertness and fear.

We are seen, pursued—we will be attacked!

Look to the west, Allart—

Allart squinted his yes into the light. Small shapes appeared there, one, two, three—were they gliders? If they were, such an air-car could outrun them swiftly. And, indeed, Karinn, with swift motions of his hands, was turning the air-car to evade the pursuers. For a moment it seemed they would not be followed; one of the gliding forms— *These are not gliders! Are they hawks?*—soared up, up, above them, higher and higher. It was indeed a hawk, but Allart could feel human intelligence, human awareness, watching them with malevolent will. No natural hawk had ever had eyes which glittered so, like great jewels! *No, this is no normal bird!* Restless with unease, he watched the soaring flight of the bird as it went higher and higher, winging with long, swift flapping strokes into the sky above them. . . .

Suddenly a narrow, gleaming shape detached itself from the bird and fell down, plummeting, arrowlike, toward the car. Allart's vision, even before thought, provided him with the knowledge of what would happen if that long, deadly shape, gleaming like glass, should strike the air-car: they would explode into fragments, each fragment coated with the terrible *clingfire,* which clung to what it touched and went on burning and burning, through metal and glass and flesh and bone.

Allart grasped the matrix he wore about his neck, jerked it with shaking fingers from the protecting silks. *There is so little time.* . . . Focusing into the depths of the jewel, he altered his awareness of time so that now the glassy shape fell ever more slowly, and he could focus on it, as if taking it between invisible fingers of force. . . . Slowly, slowly, carefully. . . . he must not risk having it break while it could fall into the air-car and fragments of *clingfire* destroy flesh and car. His slowed awareness spun accelerated futures through his mind—he saw the air-car exploding in fragments, his father slumping over and blazing up with *clingfire* in his hair, Karinn going up like a torch, and the air-car falling out of control, heavier than a stone . . . but none of those things would be allowed to happen!

With infinite delicacy, his mind focused into the pulsing lights of his matrix, and his eyes closed, Allart manipulated the glassy shape away from the air-car. He sensed resistance, knew the one guiding the device was fighting him for control of it. He struggled silently, feeling as if his physical hands were trying to keep hold of a greased and wriggling live thing while *other* hands fought to wrest it away, to fling it at him.

Karinn, quickly, get us higher if you can so that it will break below us. . . .

He felt his body slump against the straps as the air-car angled sharply upward; saw, with a fragment of his mind, his father collapse in his seat, thinking with swift contrition, *He is old, frail, his heart cannot take much of this . . .* but the main part of his mind was still in those fingers of force that struggled with the now-writhing device, which seemed to squirm under the control of his mind. They were nearly free of it now—

It exploded with a wild crash that seemed to rock all space and time, and Allart felt sharp burning pain in his hands; swiftly he withdrew his consciousness from the vicinity of the exploded device, but the burning still resonated in his physical hands. Now he opened his eyes and saw that the device had indeed exploded well below them, and fragments of *clingfire* were falling in a molten shower to set ablaze the forests below. But one fragment of the glassy shell had been flung upward, over the rim of the air-car, and the thin fire was spreading along the edge of the cockpit, reaching fingers of flame toward where his father lay slumped and unconscious.

Allart fought against his first impulse—to lean over and beat out the fire with his hands. *Clingfire* could not be extinguished that way; any fragment that touched his hands would burn through his clothing and his flesh and through to the bone, as long as there was anything left to be consumed. He focused again into the matrix—there was no time to take out the fire-talisman Karinn had given him, he should have had it ready!—calling his own fire and flaring it out toward the *clingfire*. Briefly it flamed high, then with a last gutter of light, the *clingfire* died and was gone.

"Father—" he cried, "are you hurt?"

His father held out shaking hands. The outer edge and the littlest finger were seared, blackened, but there was, as far as Allart could see, no greater hurt. Dom Stephen said in a weak voice, "The gods forgive me that I called your

courage into question, Allart. You saved us all. I fear I
am too old for such a struggle. But you mastered the fire
at once."

"Is the *vai dom* wounded?" Karinn called from the controls. "Look! They have fled." Indeed, low on the horizon,
Allart could see the small retreating shapes. Did they put
real birds under spell by matrix to carry their vicious weapons? Or were they some monstrous, mutant-bred things, no
more birds than the *cralmacs* were human; or some dreadful matrix-powered mechanical device that had been
brought to deliver their deadly weapon? Allart could not
guess, and his father's plight was such that he did not feel
free to pursue their attackers even in thought.

"He is shocked and a little burned," he called anxiously
to Karinn. "How long will it be before we are there?"

"But a moment or two, Dom Allart. I can see the gleam
of the lake. There, below—"

The air-car circled, and Allart could see the shoreline
and the glimmering sands, like jewels, along the shores of
Hali. . . . *Legend says that the sands where Hastur, son of
Light, walked, were jeweled from that day.* . . . And there
the curious lighter-than-water waves that broke incessantly
along the shore. To the north were shining towers, the
Great House of Elhalyn, and at the far end of the lake,
the Tower of Hali, gleaming faintly blue. As Karinn glided
downward, Allart unfastened his retraining straps and clambered to his father's side, taking the burned hands in his
own, focusing into the matrix to look with the eyes of his
mind and assess the damage. The wound was minor indeed;
his father was only shocked, his heart racing, more frightened than hurt.

Below them, Allart could see servants in the Hastur colors
running out on the landing field as the air-car descended, but
he held his father's hands in his own, trying to blot out all
that he could foresee. *Visions, none of them true . . . the air-
car did not explode inflame . . . what I see need not come—it
is only what may come, borne of my fears.* . . .

The air-car touched the ground. Allart called, "Bring my
lord's body-servants! He is hurt; you must carry him
within!" He lifted his father in his arms, and lowered him
into the waiting arms of the servants, then followed as they
carried the frail figure within.

From somewhere a familiar voice, hateful from years ago, said, "What has come to him, Allart? Were you attacked in the air?" and he recognized the voice of his elder brother, Damon-Rafael.

Briefly he described the encounter, and Damon-Rafael said, nodding, "That is the only way to handle such weapons. They used the hawk-things, then? They have sent them upon us only once or twice before, but once they burned an orchard of trees, and nuts were scarce that year."

"In the name of all the gods, brother, who are these Ridenow? Are they of the blood of Hastur and Cassilda, that they can send such *laran* weapons upon us?"

"They are upstarts," Damon-Rafael said. "They were Dry-towns bandits in the beginning, and they moved into Serrais and forced or bullied the old families of Serrais to give them their women as wives. The Serrais had strong *laran,* some of them, and now you can see the result—they grow stronger. They talk truce, and I think we must make truce with them, for this fighting cannot go on much longer. But their terms will not compromise. They want unquestioned ownership of the Domain of Serrais, and they claim that with their *laran* they have a right to it. . . . But this is no time to speak of war and politics, brother. How does our father? He seemed not much hurt, but we must get a healer-woman to him at once, come—"

In the Great Hall, Dom Stephen had been laid on a padded bench and a healer-woman was kneeling at his side, smearing ointments on the seared fingers, bandaging them in soft cloths. Another woman held a wine cup to the old lord's lips. He stretched a hand to his sons as they hurried toward him, and Damon-Rafael knelt at his side. Looking at his brother, Allart thought it was a little like looking into a blurred mirror; seven years his senior, Damon-Rafael was a little taller, a little heavier, like himself fair-haired and gray-eyed as were all the Hasturs of Elhalyn, his face beginning to show signs of the passing years.

"The gods be praised that you are spared to us now, Father!"

"For that you must thank your brother, Damon; it was he who saved us."

"If only for that, I give him welcome home," Damon-Rafael said, turning and drawing his brother into a kinsman's embrace. "Welcome, Allart. I hope you have come back to us in health, and without the sick fancies you had as a boy."

"Are you hurt, my son?" Dom Stephen asked, looking up at Allart with concern. "I saw you were in pain."

Allart spread out his hands before him. He had not been touched physically by the fire at all, but with the touch of his mind he had handled the fire-device, and the resonances had vibrated to his physical hands. There were red seared marks all along his palms, spreading up to his wrists, but the pain, though fierce, was dreamlike, nightmarish, of the mind and not of damaged flesh. He focused his awareness on it and the pain receded as the reddish marks began slowly to fade.

Damon-Rafael said, "Let me help you, brother," and took Allart's fingers in his own hands, focusing closely on them. Under his touch the red marks paled to white. Lord Elhalyn smiled.

"I am well pleased," he said. "My younger son has come back to me strong and a warrior, and my sons stand together as brothers. This day's work has been well done, if it has shown you—"

"Father!" Allart leaped toward him as the voice broke off with shocking suddenness. The healer-woman moved swiftly to his side as the old man fought for breath, his face darkening and congesting; then he slumped again, slid to the floor, and lay without moving.

Damon-Rafael's face was drawn with horror and grief. "Oh, my father—" he whispered, and Allart, standing in shock and dread at his side, looked up for the first time around the Great Hall, seeing for the first time what he had not seen in the confusion: the green and gold hangings, the great carved chair at the far end of the room.

So it was my father's Great Hall where he lay dead, and I did not even see till it was too late. . . . My foresight was true, but I mistook its cause. . . . Even knowing the many futures does nothing to avoid them. . . .

Damon-Rafael bent his head, weeping. He said to Allart, holding out his arms, "He is dead; our father has gone into the Light," and the brothers embraced, Allart trembling with shock at the sudden and unexpected descent of the future he had foreseen.

All around them, one by one, the servants knelt, turning to the brothers; and Damon-Rafael, his face drawn with grief, his breath coming ragged, forced himself to composure as the servants spoke the formula.

"Our Lord is dead. Live long, our Lord," and kneeling, held out their hands in homage to Damon-Rafael.

Allart knelt and, as was fitting and right under the law, was the first to pledge to the new overload of Elhalyn, Damon-Rafael.

Chapter 6

Stephen, Lord Elhalyn, was laid to rest in the ancient burying ground by the shores of Hali; and all the Hastur kin of the Lowland Domains, from the Aillards on the plains of Valeron, to the Hasturs of Carcosa, had come to do him honor. King Regis, stooped and old, looking almost too frail to ride, had stood beside the grave of his half-brother, leaning heavily on the arm of his only son.

Prince Felix, heir to the throne of Thendara and the crown of the Domains, had come to embrace Allart and Damon-Rafael, calling them "dear cousins." Felix was a slight, effeminate young man with gilt hair and colorless eyes, and he had the long, narrow pale face and hands of *chieri* blood. When the funeral rites were ended there was a great ceremony. Then the old king, pleading age and ill health, was taken home by his courtiers, but Felix remained to do honor to the new Lord of Elhalyn, Damon-Rafael.

Even the Ridenow lord had sent an envoy from far Serrais, proffering an unasked truce for twice forty days.

Allart, welcoming guests in the hall, came suddenly upon a face he knew—though he had never set eyes upon her before. Dark hair, like a cloud of darkness under a blue veil; gray eyes, but so darkly lashed that for a moment the eyes themselves seemed as dark as the eyes of some animal. Allart felt a strange tightening in his chest as he looked upon the face of the dark woman whose face had haunted him for so many days.

"Kinsman," she said courteously, but he could not lower

his eyes as custom demanded before an unmarried woman
who was a stranger to him.

*I know you well. You have haunted me, dreams and wak-
ing, and already I am more than half in love with you. . . .*
Erotic images attacked him, unfitting for this company, and
he struggled with them.

"Kinsman," she said again, "why do you stare at me in
such unseemly fashion?"

Allart felt the blood rising in his face; indeed it was discourtesy, almost indecency, to stare so at a woman who
was a stranger to him, and he colored at the thought that
she might possess *laran,* might be aware of the images that
tormented him. He finally found a scrap of his voice.

"But I am no stranger to you, *damisela.* Nor is it discourtesy that a man shall look his handfasted bride directly in
the face; I am Allart Hastur, and soon to be your husband."

She raised her eyes and returned his gaze fairly. But
there was tension in her voice. "Why, is it so? Still, I can
hardly believe that you have borne my image in your mind
since you last looked on my face, when I was an infant girl
of four years. And I had heard, Dom Allart, that you had
withdrawn yourself to Nevarsin, that you were ill or mad,
that you wished to be a monk and renounce your heritage.
Was it only idle gossip, then?"

"It is true that I had such thoughts for a time. I dwelt
for six years among the brethren of Saint-Valentine-of-the-
Snows, and would gladly have remained there."

*If I love this woman, I will destroy her . . . I will father
children who will be monsters . . . she will die in bearing
them. . . . Blessed Cassilda, foremother of the Domains, let
me not see so much, now, of my destiny, since I can do so
little to avert it. . . .*

"I am neither ill nor mad, *damisela;* you need not fear
me."

"Indeed," said the young woman, meeting his eyes again.
"You do not seem demented, only very troubled. Is it the
thought of our marriage which troubles you, then, cousin?"

Allart said, with a nervous smile, "Should I not be well-
content, to see what beauty and grace the gods have given
me in a handfasted bride?"

"Oh!" She moved her head, impatient. "This is no time

for pretty speeches and flatteries, kinsman! Or are you one of those who think a woman is a silly child, to be turned away with a courtly compliment or two?"

"Believe me, I meant you no discourtesy, Lady Cassandra," he said, "but I have been taught that it is unseemly to share my own troubles and fears when they are still formless."

Again the quick, direct look from the dark-lashed eyes.

"Fears, cousin? But I am harmless and a girl! Surely a lord of the Hasturs is afraid of nothing, and surely not of his pledged bride!"

Before the sarcasm he flinched. "Would you have the truth, Lady? I have a strange form of *laran;* it is not foresight alone. I do not see only the future which *will* be, but the futures which *might* come to pass, those things which may happen with ill luck or failure; and there are time when I cannot tell which of them are generated by causes now in option, and which are born of my own fear. It was to master this that I went to Nevarsin."

He heard her sharp indrawn breath.

"Avarra's mercy, what a curse to carry! And have you mastered it, then, kinsman?"

"Somewhat, Cassandra. But when I am troubled or uncertain, it rushes in upon me again, so that I do not see only the joy which marriage to one such as you might bring me." Like a physical pain in his heart, Allart felt the bitter awareness of his love, the years ahead which might turn to brightness. . . . Fiecely he slammed the inner door, closing his mind against it. Here was no *riyachiya,* to be taken without thought, for a moment's pleasure!

He said harshly, and did not know how his own pain brought a rasp to his voice and coldness to his speech, "But I see, as well, all the griefs and catastrophe which may come; and till I can see my way through the false futures born of my own fears, I can take no joy in the thought of marriage. It is intended as no discourtesy to you, my lady and my bride."

She said, "I am glad you told me this. You know, do you not, that my kinsmen are angry because our marriage did not take place two years ago, when I was legally of age. They felt you had insulted me by remaining in Nevarsin. Now they wish to be sure you will claim me without further delay." Her dark glance glinted with humor. "Not that they care a *sekal* for my wedded bliss, but they are never done reminding me how near you stand to the throne, and how fortunate I am, and how I must captivate you with my charm so you will not escape me. They have dressed me like a fashion puppet, and dressed my hair with nets of copper and silver, and loaded me with jewels, as if you were going to buy me in the market. I half expected you to open my mouth and look at my teeth to be sure my loins and withers were strong!"

Allart could not help laughing. "On that score your kinfolk need have no fear, Lady; surely no man living could find any flaw in you."

"Oh, but there is," she said ingenuously. "They were hoping you would not notice, but I will not try to hide it from you." She spread her narrow, ringed hands before him. The slender fingers were laden with jewels, but there were six of them, and as her eyes fell on the sixth, Cassandra colored deeply and tried to draw them under her veil. "Indeed, Dom Allart, I beg you not to stare at my deformity."

"It seems to me no deformity," he said. "Do you play the *rryl*? It seems to me that you could strike chords with more ease."

"Why, so it does—"

"Then let us never again think of it as defect or deformity, Cassandra," he aid, taking the slight six-fingered hands in his own and pressing his lips to them. "In Nevarsin, I saw children with six or seven fingers where the extra fingers were boneless or without tendons, so that they could not be moved or flexed; but you have full control of them, I see. I, too, am something of a musician."

"Truly? Is it because you were a monk? Most men have no patience for such things, or little time to learn them with the arts of war."

"I would rather be musician than warrior," Allart said, pressing the narrow fingers again to his lips. "The gods grant us enough peace in our days that we may make songs instead of war." But as she smiled into his eyes, her hand still against his lips, he noted that Ysabet, Lady Aillard, was watching them, and so was his brother Damon-Rafael, and they looked so self-satisfied that he turned sick. They were manipulating him into doing their will, despite his resolve! He let her hand go as if it had burned him.

"May I conduct you to your kinswoman, *damisela*?"

As the evening progressed, the festivities decorous but not somber—the old lord had been decently laid to rest, and he had a proper heir, so there was no doubt the Domain would prosper—Damon-Rafael sought out his brother. Despite the feasting, Allart noticed he was still quite sober.

"Tomorrow we ride for Thendara, where I shall be invested Lord of the Domain. You must ride with us, brother; you must be warden and heir-designate for Elhalyn. I have no legitimate sons, only *nedestro;* they will not legitimate a *nedestro* heir until it is certain that Cassilde will give me none." He looked across the room at his wife, a cold, almost bitter look. Cassilde Aillard-Hastur was a pale, slight woman, sallow and worn.

"The Domain will be in your hands, Allart, and in a sense I am at your mercy. How runs the proverb? 'Bare is back without brother.' "

Allart wondered how, in the name of all the gods, brothers could be friends, or anything but the cruelest of rivals, with such inheritance laws as these? Allart had no ambition to displace his brother as head of the Domain, but would Damon-Rafael ever believe that? He said, "I would indeed that you had left me within the monastery, Damon."

Damon-Rafael's smile was skeptical, as if he feared that his brother's words concealed some devious plot. "Is it so? Yet I watched you speaking with the Aillard woman, and it was obvious you could hardly await the ceremony. You are like to have a legitimate son before I do; Cassilde is frail, and your bride looks strong and healthy."

Allart said with concealed violence, "I am in no hurry to wed!"

Damon-Rafael scowled. "Yet the Council will not accept a man of your years as heir unless you agree to marry at once; it is scandalous that a man in his twenties should be still unwedded and without even any natural sons." He looked sharply at Allart. "Can it be that I am luckier than I think? Are you, perhaps, an *emmasca*? Or even a lover of men?"

Allart grinned wryly. "I grieve to disappoint you. But as

for being *emmasca,* you saw me stripped and shown to the Council when I came to manhood. And if you wished for me to become a lover of men, you should have made certain that I never came among the *cristoforos.* But I will return to the monastery, if you like."

He thought, for a moment, almost in elation, that this would be the answer to his torment and perplexities. Damon-Rafael did not want him to breed sons who might be rivals to his own; and so perhaps he could escape the curse of fathering sons who would carry his own tragic *laran.* If he were to return to Nevarsin . . . he was surprised at the pain of the thought.

Never to see Cassandra again. . . .

Damon-Rafael shook his head, not without regret. "I dare not anger the Aillards. They are our strongest allies in this war; and they are vexed that Cassilde had not cemented the alliance by giving me an heir of Elhalyn and Aillard blood. If you avoid the marriage I will have another enemy, and I cannot afford the Aillards for enemies. Already they fear I have found a better match for you. But I know our father had reserved two *nedestro* half-sisters of the Aillard clan for you, with modified genes, and what will I do if you should have sons by all three of them?"

Revulsion, as when Dom Stephen had first spoken of this, surged in Allart again. "I told my father I had no wish for that."

"I would rather that any sons of Aillard blood should be mine," Damon-Rafael said, "yet I cannot take your pledged wife; I have a wife of my own, and I cannot make a lady of such an exalted clan into my *barragana.* It would be a matter for blood-feud! Although if Cassilde were to die in childbirth, as she has been likely to do any time these past ten years, and may do at any time in the future, then—" His eyes sought out Cassandra where she stood near her kinswomen, appraisingly moving up and down her body; and Allart felt a quite unexpected anger. How dare Damon-Rafael talk that way? Cassandra was *his!*

Damon-Rafael said, "Almost I am tempted to delay your marriage for a year. Should Cassilde die in bearing the child she now carries, I would be free to make Cassandra my wife. I suppose they would even be grateful, when she came to share my throne."

"You speak treason," Allart said, genuinely shocked now. "King Regis still sits on the throne, and Felix is his legitimate son and will succeed him."

Damon-Rafael's shrug was contemptuous. "The old king? He will not live a year. I stood by his side today by our father's grave; and I, too, have some of the foresight of the Hasturs of Elhalyn. He will lie there before the seasons turn again. As for Felix—well, I have heard the rumors, and no doubt you have heard them, too. He is *emmasca;* one of the elders who saw him stripped was bribed, they say, and another had faulty eyesight. Whatever the truth, he has been married seven years, and his wife looks not like a woman who has been well treated in her marriage bed; nor has there ever been so much as a rumor that she was breeding. No, Allart. Treason or no, I tell you I will be on the throne within seven years. Look with your own foresight."

Allart said very quietly, "On the throne, or dead, my brother."

Damon-Rafael looked at him with enmity and said, "Those old she-males of the Council might prefer the legitimate son of a younger brother to the *nedestro* of the elder. Will you thrust your hand within the flame of Hali and pledge to support the claim of my son, legitimate or no?"

Allart fought to find the true sight through images of a kingdom raging in flames, a throne within his grasp, storms raging across the Hellers, a keep tumbling as if blasted by earthquake—*no!* He was a man of peace; he had no will to fight with his brother for a throne, see the Domains run red with the blood of a terrible fratricidal war. He bowed his head.

"The gods ordained it, Damon-Rafael, when you were born my father's eldest son. I will swear that oath you require of me, my brother and my lord."

In Damon-Rafael's look triumph mingled with contempt. Allart knew that if their positions had been reversed, he would have had to fight to the death for his inheritance. He tensed with dislike as Damon-Rafael embraced him and said, "So, I will have your oath and your strong hand to guard my sons; then perhaps the old saying is true, and I need not feel my back bare and brotherless."

He looked with regret across the room again at Cassandra, wrapped in her value veil. "I suppose—no, I am afraid you must take your bride. All the Aillards would be offended if I made her *barragana,* and I cannot keep you both unwed for another year against the possibility that Cassilde might die and I should be free to wed again."

Cassandra—in his hands? Damon-Rafael, who thought of her only as a pawn for a political alliance, to cement the support of her kinfolk? The thought sickened him. Yet Allart recalled his own resolve: to take no wife, to father no sons to bear the curse of his *laran.* He said, "In return for my support, then, brother, spare me this marriage."

"I cannot," Damon-Rafael said regretfully, "though I would willingly take her myself. But I dare not offend the Aillards that way. Never mind, you may not long be burdened with her; she is young, and many of those Aillard women have died in bearing their first child. It is likely she will do so, too. Or she may be like Cassilde, fertile enough, but bearing only stillborn babes. If you keep her breeding and miscarrying for a few years, my sons will be safe and no one would claim you had not done your best for our clan; it will be *her* fault, not yours."

Allart said, "I would not want to treat any woman so!"

"Brother, I care not at all how you treat her, so that you wed her and bed her and the Aillards are bound to us by kin-ties. I did but suggest a way you might be rid of her without discredit to your own manhood." He shrugged, dismissing the matter. "But enough of this. We will ride for Thendara tomorrow, and when the heirship is settled, then we will ride here for your wedding again. Will you drink with me?"

"I have drunk enough," Allart lied, eager to avoid further contact with his brother. His foresight had seen truly. Not in all the worlds of probability was it written anywhere that he and Damon-Rafael would be friends, and if Damon-Rafael should come to the throne—and Allart's *laran* told him that might very well be—it might be that Allart must even guard his life, and the lives of his sons.

Holy Bearer of Burdens, strengthen me! Another reason I should father no sons to come after me—that I must fear for them, too, at my brother's hands!

Chapter 7

In amiable mood, eager to do honor to his young kinsman, His Grace Regis II had agreed to perform the ceremony of marriage; his lined old face glowed with kindliness as he spoke the ritual words and locked the copper-chased bracelets, the *catenas*, first on Allat's wrist and then on Cassandra's.

"Parted in fact," he said, unlocking the bracelets, "may you never be so in spirit or in heart." They kissed, and he said, "May you be forever one."

Allart felt Cassandra trembling as they stood, hands joined by the precious metal.

She is afraid, he thought, *and no wonder. She knows nothing of me; her kinsmen sold her to me as they might have sold a hawk or brood mare.*

In earlier days (Allart had read something of Domain history at Nevarsin), marriages like this would have been unthinkable. It had been considered a form of selfishness for women to bear children to one man alone, and the gene pool had been broadened by increasing the number of possible combinations. Briefly Allart wondered if that had been how they first bred the accursed *laran* into their race; or was it true that they were descended from the children of gods who came here to Hali and fathered sons to rule over their kindred? Or were the tales true of crosses with the nonhuman *chieri*, who gave their caste both the sexless *emmasca*, and the gift of *laran*?

Whatever had happened, these long-past and mostly forgotten days of group marriage had vanished as families

began to climb to power; inheritance, and the breeding program, had made exact knowledge of paternity important.
*Now a man is judged only by his sons, and a woman by
her abilities as a breeder of sons—and she knows it is only
for this that she has been given to me!*

But the ceremony had come to a close, and Allart felt
his wife's hands cold and shaking in his as he bent to touch
her lips, briefly, in the ritual kiss which ended it, and led
her out to dance in an explosion of congratulations, goodwill, and applause from his gathered kinsmen and peers.
Allart, hypersensitive, felt the sharp-edged overtones in the
congratulatory words, and thought that few of them meant
their goodwill. His brother Damon-Rafael probably meant
his goodwill sincerely. Allart had stood before the holy
things at Hali that morning, thrusting his hand into the
cold fire that did not burn unless the speaker knew himself
forsworn, and pledged his honor as Hastur to support his
brother's wardenship of the clan, and his sons' succession
to the throne. The other kinsmen congratulated him because he had made a politically powerful alliance with the
strong clan of the Aillards of Valeron, or because they
hoped to ally themselves with him by marriage through the
sons and daughters this marriage might engender, or simply
because they took pleasure in the sight of a wedding, and
the drinking and dancing and revelry, making a welcome
break from the official mourning for Dom Stephen.

"You are silent, my husband," Cassandra said.

Allart started, hearing a pleading note in her voice. *It is
worse for her, poor girl. I was consulted—somewhat—about
this marriage; she was not even allowed to say yea or nay.
Why do we do this to our women, since it is through them
that we keep these precious inheritances which have come to
mean so much to us!*

He said gently, "My silence was not meant for you, *damisela*. This day has given me much to think about; that is
all. But I am churlish to think so deeply in your presence."

The level eyes, so deeply lashed that they appeared dark,
met his, with a gleam of humor in their depths. "Again you
are treating me like a maiden to be flattered into silence
with a pretty compliment; and I presume to remind you,
my lord, that it is hardly seemly to call me *damisela* when
I am your wife."

"God help me, yes," he said, despairing, and she looked at him, a faint frown stitching itself across her smooth brow.

"Is it so unwilling that you have been wed? I was brought up since childhood to know I must marry as my kinsmen bade me; I thought a man more free to choose."

"I think no man is free; at least, not here in the Domains." He wondered if this was why there was so much revelry at a wedding, so much dancing and drinking—in order that the sons and daughters of Hastur and Cassilda might forget they were being bred like stud-animals and brood-mares for the sake of the accursed *laran* that brought power to their line!

But how could he forget? Allart was again in the grip of the out-of-focus time sense which was the curse of his *laran,* futures diverging from this very moment with the land flaming in war and struggle, hovering hawks like those which had flung *clingfire* at his air-car, great broad-winged gliders with men hanging from them, fires rising in the forests, strange snowcapped peaks from the ranges beyond Nevarsin which he had never seen, the face of a child surrounded with the pale blaze of lightnings. . . . *Are all these things coming into my life, truly, or are they only things which may come?*

Did he have any control over any of them at all, or would some relentless fate thrust them all upon him? As they had thrust Cassandra Aillard upon him as his wife, this woman standing before him. . . . A dozen Cassandras, not one, looking up at him—aglow with love and passion he knew he could arouse, torn with hatred and loathing (yes, he could rouse that, too), limp with exhaustion, dying with a curse, dying in his arms. . . . Allart closed his eyes in a vain effort to shut out the faces of his wife.

Cassandra said, in real alarm, "My husband! Allart! Tell me what is wrong with you, I beg!"

He knew he had frightened her, and sought to control the crowding futures, to put to practice the techniques he had learned at Nevarsin, to narrow down the dozen women she had become—might become, *would* become—into the one who stood before him now.

"It is not anything you have done, Cassandra. I have told you how I am cursed."

"Is there nothing that can help you?"

Yes, he thought savagely, *it would have helped most of all if neither of us had ever been born; if our ancestors, may they freeze forever in Zandru's darkest hell, could have refrained from breeding this curse into our line!* He did not speak it, but she picked up the thought, and her eyes widened in dismay.

But just then kinsmen and kinswomen burst in on their momentary solitude. Damon-Rafael claimed Cassandra for a dance with an arrogant, "She will be all yours soon enough, brother!" and someone else thrust a glass into his hand, demanding that he join in the revelry which, after all, was in his honor!

Trying to conceal rage and rebellion—after all, he could not blame his guests for the whole system!—he let himself be persuaded to drink, to dance with young kinswomen who evidently had so little to do with his future that their faces remained reassuringly one, not altered continually by the crisscrossing probabilities of his *laran.* He did not see Cassandra again until Damon-Rafael's wife Cassilde, and their kinswomen, were leading her from the hall for the formal bedding.

Custom demanded that the bride and husband be put to bed in the presence of their assembled peers, as proof that the marriage had been duly made. Allart had read at Nevarsin that there had been a time, soon after the establishment of marriage for inheritance and the *catenas,* when public consummation had been required, too. Fortunately Allart knew that would not be demanded of him. He wondered how anyone had ever managed it!

It was not long before they led him, in a tumult of the usual jokes, into the presence of his bride. Custom demanded, too, that a bride's bedding-gown should be more revealing than anything she had ever worn before—or would ever wear again. In order, Allart thought cynically, that all might see she had no hidden flaw that would impair her value as breeding-stock!

The gods grant they have not drugged her into complaisance. . . . He looked sharply to see if her eyes were drug-blurred, whether they had dosed her with aphrodisiacs. He supposed this was merciful for a girl given unwilling to a complete stranger; no one, he supposed, would have much heart for fighting a terrified girl into submission.

Again conflicting futures, conflicting possibilities and obligations crowded into his mind with images of lust fighting for place with other futures in which he saw her lying dead in his arms. What had Damon-Rafael told him? That all of her sisters had died with the birth of their first child. . . .

With a chorus of congratulations, the kinsmen withdrew, leaving them alone. Allart rose and threw down the bar of the lock. Returning to her side, he saw the fear in her face and the gallant effort she made to hide it.

Does she fear I shall fall on her like a wild animal? But aloud he said only, "Have they drugged you with *aphrosone* or some such potion?"

She shook her head. "I refused it. My foster-mother would have made me drink it, but I told her I did not fear you."

Allart asked, "Then why are you trembling?"

She said, with that flash of spirit he had seen in her before, "I am *cold,* my lord, in this near-naked gown they insisted I must wear!"

Allart laughed. "It seems I have the better of it, then, being robed in fur. Cover yourself, then, Lady—it would have not needed that for me to desire you—I forgot, you do not like to be complimented, or flattered!" He came up and sat on the edge of the great bed beside her. "May I pour you some wine, *domna?*"

"Thank you." She took the glass, and as she sipped he saw the color come back into her face. Gratefully she tugged the fur robe up, to her shoulders. He poured some for himself, turning the stem of the goblet in his fingers, trying to think how he must say what must be said without offending her. Again the crowding futures and possibilities threatened to overwhelm him, so that he could see himself ignoring his scruples, taking her into his arms with all the pent-up passion of his life. How she would come alive with passion and love, the years of joy they would share . . . and again, confusingly, blurring the face of the woman and the moment before him, another woman's face, tawny and laughing, surrounded by masses of copper hair. . . .

"Cassandra," he said, "did you want this marriage?"

She did not look at him. "I am *honored* by this marriage. We were handfasted when I was too young to remember. It must be different for you, you are a man and have

choice, but I had none. Whatever I did as a child, I heard
nothing but this or that will or will not be suitable when
you are wed to Allart Hastur of Elhalyn."

He said, the words wrung from him, "What joy it must
be to have such security, to see only one future instead of
a dozen, a hundred, a thousand . . . not to have to tread
your way among them like an acrobat who dances upon a
stretched rope at Festival Fair!"

"I never thought of that. I thought only that your life
was more free than mine, to choose. . . ."

"Free?" He laughed without amusement. "My fate was
as sealed as yours, Lady. Yet we may still choose among
the futures I can see, if you are willing."

She said in a low voice, "What is left for us to choose
now, my lord? We are wedded and bedded; it seems to me
that no more choice is possible. Only this; you can use me
cruelly or gently, and I can bear all with patience or disgrace my caste by fighting you away and forcing you, like
the victim of some old bawdy song, to bear the marks of
my nails and teeth. Which indeed," she said, her eyes glinting up at him in a laugh, "I would think it shameful to do."

"The gods forbid you should have cause," he said. For a
moment, so poignant were the images roused by her words,
it seemed that all other futures had really been wiped out.
She was his wife, given to him consenting, even willing, and
wholly at his mercy. He could even make her love him.

*Then why do we not yield together to our destiny, my
love . . . ?*

But he forced himself to say, "A third choice remains
still, my lady. You know the law; whatever the ceremony,
this is no marriage until we make it so, and event the *catenas* can be unlocked, if we petition."

"If I should so anger my kinsmen, and bring the wrath
of the Hasturs upon them, then the string of alliances on
which the reign of the Hasturs is built will come crashing
down. If you seek to return me to my kinsmen because I
found no favor with you, there will be no peace for me,
and no happiness." Her eyes were wide and desolate.

"I thought only— A day might come when you could be
given to one more to your liking, my girl."

She said shyly, "What makes you think I could find one
more to my liking?"

He realized with sudden dread that the worst had happened. Fearing she would be given to an insensitive brute who would think of her only as a brood-mare, finding that instead he spoke to her as to an equal, the girl was ready to adore him!

If he so much as touched her hand, he knew, his resolve would vanish; he would cover her with kisses, draw her into his arms—if only to wipe out the crowding futures he could see building up from this crucial moment, wipe them all out in a single moment by *some* positive action, whatever it might be.

His voice sounded strained, even to himself. "You know the curse I bear. I see not the true future alone, but a dozen futures, any one of which may come true, or mock my by never coming to pass. I had resolved never to marry, that I might never transmit this curse to any son of mine. This was why I had resolved to renounce my heritage and become a monk; I can see, all too clearly, what marriage with you might bring about. Gods above," he cried out, "do you think me indifferent to you?"

"Are your visions always true, Allart?" she pleaded. "Why must we deny our destiny? If these things are ordained, they will come about, whatever we do now, and if not, they cannot trouble us." She raised herself to her knees, flung her arms around him.

"I am not unwilling, Allart. I—I—love you."

For the barest instant Allart could not help tightening his arms around her. Then, fighting the shamed memory of how he had surrendered to the temptation of the *riyachiya,* he seized her shoulders in his hands and thrust her away with all his strength. He heard his own voice harsh and ice-cold, as if it belonged to someone else.

"Do you still expect me to believe they have not drugged you with aphrodisiacs, my lady?"

She went rigid, tears of anger and humiliation welling in her eyes. He wanted, as he had never wanted anything in his life, to draw her back to rest against his heart.

"Forgive me," he begged. "Try to understand. I am fighting to—to find my way out of this trap they have led us into. Don't you know what I have seen? All roads lead there, it seems—that I will do what is expected of me, that I will breed monsters, children tormented worse by *laran* than ever I was, dying as my young brother died, or worse, living to curse us that they were ever born. And do you know what I have seen for you, at the end of every road, my poor girl? Your death, Cassandra, your death in bearing my child."

She whispered, her face white, "Two of my sisters so died."

"Yet you wonder why. I am not rejecting you, Cassandra. I am trying to avoid the frightful destiny I have seen for both of us. God knows, it would be easy enough. . . . Along most of the lines of my future, I see it, the course it would be easiest to take; that I should love you, that you should love me, that we will walk hand in hand into that terrible tragedy the future holds for us. Tragedy for you, Cassandra. And for me. I—" He swallowed, trying to steady his voice. "I would not bear the guilt of your death."

She began to sob. Allart dared not touch her; he stood looking down at her, heart-wrung, wretched. "Try not to cry," he said, his voice ragged. "I cannot bear it. The temptation is always there, to do the easiest thing, and trust to luck to lead us through; or if all else fails, to say, 'It is our destiny and no man can fight against fate.' For there are other choices. You might be barren, you might survive childbirth, our child might escape the curse of our joint *laran*. There are so many possibilities, so many temptations! And I have resolved that this marriage shall be no marriage at all, until I see my way clear before me. Cassandra, I beg you, agree to this."

"It seems that I have no choice," she said, and looked up at him, desolate. "Yet there is no happiness, either, in our world, for a woman who finds no favor with her husband. Until I am pregnant, my kinswomen will give me no peace. They have *laran*, too, and if this marriage is not consummated, sooner or later they will know that, too, and the same troubles we foresaw from refusing the marriage will be on us. Either way, my husband, it seems that we are the game who may stay in the trap or walk to the cookpot; either way lies ruin."

Calmed by the seriousness with which she sought to think about and evaluate their predicament, Allart said, "I have a plan, if you will follow me in it, Cassandra. Most of our kinsmen, before they come to my age, take their turn in a

Tower, using their *laran* in a matrix circle which can give energy and power and a good life to our people. I was excused this duty because of my poor health, but the obligation should be filled. Also, the life of the court is not the best life for a young wife who—" He choked on the words. "Who might be breeding. I will petition for leave to take you to the Tower of Hali, where we will do our share of work in a matrix circle. So we will not face your kinswomen or my brother, and we can dwell apart without provoking talk. Perhaps, while we are there, we can find some way out of this dilemma"

Cassandra's voice was submissive. "Let it be as you will. But our kin will think it strange that we choose this during the first days of our marriage."

"They may think what they will," Allart said. "I think it no crime to give false coin to thieves, or to lie to one who questions beyond courtesy. If I am questioned by anyone who has a right to an answer, I shall say that I shirked this obligation during my early manhood, and I wish to satisfy it now, so that you and I may go away together with no remaining unfulfilled obligations overshadowing our lives. You, my lady, may say what you will."

Her smile glinted at him; again Allart felt the wrench of heartbreak.

"Why, I will say nothing at all, my husband. I am your wife and I go where you choose to go, needing no more explanation than that! I do not say that I love this custom, nor that if you chose to demand it of me, I should obey without strife. I doubt you would find me such a submissive wife after all, Dom Allart. But I can use the custom where it suits my purposes!"

Holy Bearer of Burdens, why could not my fate have given me a woman I would be glad to put aside, not this one it would have been so easy for me to love! Exhausted with relief, he bowed his head, took up her slender fingers and kissed them.

She saw the broken weariness in his face and said, "You are very weary, my husband. Will you not lie down now and sleep?"

Again the erotic images were torturing him, but he pushed them aside. "You do not know much of men, do you, *chiya*?"

She shook her head. "How could I? Now it seems I am not to know," she said, and looked so sad that, even through his resolve, Allart felt a distant regret.

"Lie down and sleep if you will, Cassandra."

"But will you not sleep?" she asked naïvely, and he had to laugh.

"I will sleep on the floor; I have slept in worse place, and this is luxury after the stone cells of Nevarsin," he said. "Bless you, Cassandra, for accepting my decision!"

She gave him a faint smile. "Oh, I have been taught that it is a wife's duty to obey. Though it is a different obedience than I foresaw, still, I am your wife and will do as you command. Good night, my husband."

The words were gently ironic. Stretched on the soft rugs of the chamber, Allart summoned all the discipline of his years at Nevarsin and finally managed to blot out from his mind all the images of Cassandra awakened to love; nothing remained but the moment, and his resolve. But once, before dawn, he thought he could hear the sound of a woman crying, very softly, as if muffling the sound in silks and coverlets.

The next day they departed for Hali Tower; and there they remained for half a year.

Chapter 8

Early spring again in the Hellers, Donal Delleray, called Rockraven, stood on the heights of Castle Aldaran, wondering idly if the Aldaran forefathers had chosen this high peak for their keep because it commanded much of the country around. It sloped down toward the distant plains, and behind it rose toward the distant plains, and behind it rose toward the far impassable peaks where no human thing dwelled, but only trailmen and the half-legendary *chieri* of the far Hellers, in their fastnesses surrounded by eternal snow.

"They say," he said aloud, "that in the farthest of these mountains, so far in the snows that even the most skilled mountaineer would fail before he found his way through the peaks and crevasses, there is a valley of unending summer, and there the *chieri* have withdrawn since the coming of the children of Hastur. That is why we never see them now, in these days. There the *chieri* dwell forever, immortal and beautiful, singing their strange songs and dreaming immortal dreams."

"Are the *chieri* really so beautiful?"

"I do not know, little sister; I have never seen a *chieri*," Donal said. He was twenty now, tall and whiplash thin, dark-tanned, dark-browed, a straight and somber young man who looked older than he was. "But when I was very small, my mother told me once that she had seen a *chieri* in the forests, behind a tree, and that she had the beauty of the Blessed Cassilda. They say, too, that if any mortal wins through to the valley where the *chieri* dwell, and eats of their food and drinks of their magical waters, he, too, will be gifted with immortality."

"No," Dorilys said. "Now you are telling me fairy tales. I am too old to believe such things."

"Oh, you are so old," Donal teased. "I look daily to see your back stoop over with age and your hair turn gray!"

"I am old enough to be handfasted," Dorilys said with dignity. "I am eleven years old, and Margali says I look as if I were already fifteen."

Donal gave his sister a long, considering look. It was true; at eleven Dorilys was already taller than many women, and her slender body had already some hint of a woman's shapely roundness.

"I do not know if I want to be handfasted," she said, suddenly sulky. "I do not know anything of my cousin Darren! Do you know him, Donal?"

"I know him," Donal said, and his face went bleak. "He was fostered here with may other lads, when I was a boy."

"Is he handsome? Is he kind and well-spoken? Do you like him, Donal?"

Donal opened his mouth to speak and then shut it again. Darren was the son of Lord Aldaran's younger brother, Rakhal. Mikhail, Lord Aldaran, had no sons, and this marriage would mean that their children would inherit and consolidate the two estates: this was the way great Domains were built. It would be pointless to prejudice Dorilys against her promised husband because of boyish differences.

"You must not judge by that, Dorilys; we were children when we knew one another, and we fought as boys do; but he is older now, and so am I. Yes, he is good-looking enough, I suppose, as women judge such things."

"It seems hardly fair, to me," Dorilys said. "You have been more than a son to my father. Yes, he said so himself! Why can *you* not inherit his estate, since he has no son of his own?"

Donal forced himself to laugh. "You will understand these things better when you are older, Dorilys. I am no blood kin to Lord Aldaran, though he has been a kind foster-father to me, and I can expect no more than a fosterling's part in his estate; and that only because he pledged my mother—and yours—that I should be well provided for. I look for no more inheritance than this."

"That is a foolish law," Dorilys said vehemently, and Donal, seeing the signs of angry emotion in her yes, said quickly, "Look down there, Dorilys! See, between the fold in the hills, you can see the riders and the banners. That will be Lord Rakhal and his entourage riding up toward the castle, come for your handfasting. So you must run down to your nurse and let her make you beautiful for the ceremony."

"Very well," Dorilys said, diverted, but she scowled as she started down the stairway. "If I do not like him, I will not marry him. Do you hear me. Donal?"

"I hear you," he said, "but that is a little girl speaking, *chiya*. When you are a woman you will be more sensible. Your father has chosen carefully to make a marriage which will be suitable; he would not give you in marriage unless he were sure this would be the best for you."

"Oh, I have heard that again and again, from Father, from Margali. They all say the same, that I must do as I am told and when I am older I will understand why! But if I do not like my cousin Darren I will not marry him, and you know there is no one who can make me do anything I do not want to do!" She stamped her foot, her rosy face flushed with pettish anger, and ran toward the stairway leading down into the castle. As if in echo to her words, there was a faint, faraway roll of thunder.

Donal remained looking over the railing, lost in somber thought. Dorilys had spoken with the unconscious arrogance of a princess, of the pampered only daughter of Lord Aldaran. But it was more than that, and even Donal felt a qualm of dread when Dorilys spoke so positively.

There is no one who can make me do anything I do not want to do. It was all too true. Willful since birth, no one had ever dared to cross her too seriously, because of the strange *laran* with which she had been born. No one quite knew the extent to this strange power; no one had ever dared to provoke it knowingly. Even while she was still unweaned, anyone who touched her against her will had felt the power she could fling—expressed, then, only as a painful shock—but the gossip of servants and nurses had exaggerated it and spread frightening tales. When, even as a baby, she screamed in rage, or hunger, or pain, lightnings and thunder had rolled and crashed about the heights of the castle; not only the servants, but the children fostered in the castle, had learned to fear her anger. Once, in her fifth year, when a fever had laid her low, delirious for days, raving and unconscious, not recognizing even Donal or her father, lightning bolts had crashed wildly all those nights and days, striking dangerously near the towers of the castle, random, terrifying. Donal, who could control the lightnings a little himself (though nothing like this), had wondered what phantoms and nightmares pursued her in delirium, that she struck so violently against them.

Fortunately as she grew older she longed for approval and affection, and Lady Deonara, who had loved Dorilys as her own, had been able to teach her some things. The child had Aliciane's beauty and her pretty ways, and in the last year or two, she had been less feared and better liked. But still the servants and children feared her, calling her witch and sorceress when she could not hear; not even the boldness of the children dared offend her to her face. She had never turned on Donal, nor on her father, nor on her foster-mother Margali, the *leronis* who had brought her into the world; nor, during Lady Deonara's lifetime, had she ever gone against Deonara's will.

But since Deonara's death, Donal thought (sadly, for he, too, had loved the gentle Lady Aldaran), *no one has ever gainsaid Dorilys.* Mikhail of Aldaran adored his pretty daughter, and denied her nothing, in or out of reason, so that the eleven-year-old Dorilys had the jewels and play-things of a princess. The servants would not, because they feared her anger and the power which gossip had exaggerated so enormously. The other children would not, partly because she was highest in rank among them, and partly because she was a willful little tyrant who never shrank from enforcing her domination with slaps, pinches, and blows.

It is not too bad for a little girl—a pretty, pampered little girl—to be willful beyond all reason, and for everyone to fear her, and give her everything she wants. But what will

*happen when she grows to womanhood, if she does not learn
that she cannot have all things as she will? And who, fearing
her power, will dare to teach her this?*

Troubled, Donal turned down the stairs and went inside,
for he, too, must be present at the handfasting, and at the
ceremonies before hand.

In his enormous presence-chamber, Mikhail, Lord Aldaran, awaited his guests. The Aldaran lord had aged since
the birth of his daughter; a huge, heavy man, stooped now
and graying, he had something still of the look of an ancient, molting hawk; and when he raised his head it was
not unlike the stirring of some such ancient bird on its
block—a ruffle of feathers, a hint of concealed power, in
abeyance and still there, dormant.

"Donal? Is it you? It is hard to see in this light," Lord
Aldaran said, and Donal, knowing that his foster-father did
not like to admit that his eyes were not as sharp as they
had been, came toward him.

"It is I, my lord."

"Come here, dear lad. Is Dorilys ready for the ceremony
tonight? Do you think she is content with the idea of this
marriage?"

"I think she is too young to know what it means," Donal
said. He had dressed in an ornate dyed-leather suit, high
in door boots fringed at the top and carved, his hair confined in a jeweled band; about his neck a firestone flashed
crimson. "Yet she is curious. She asked me if Darren were
handsome and well-spoken, if I liked him. I gave her small
answer to that, I fear, But I told her she must not judge a
man on a boy's quarrels."

"Nor must you, my boy," Aldaran said, but he said it
gently.

"Foster-father—I have a boon to ask of you," Donal
said.

Aldaran smiled and said, "You have long known, Donal,
any gift within reason that I can give is yours for the
asking."

"This will cost you nothing, my lord, except some
thought. When the Lord Rakhal and Lord Darren come
before you tonight to discuss the matter of Dorilys's marriage gifts, will you introduce me to the company by my

father's name, and not as Donal of Rockraven as you are used to do?"

Lord Aldaran's nearsighted eyes blinked, giving him more than ever the air of some gigantic bird of prey blinded by the light. "How is this, foster-son? Would you disown your mother, or her place here? Or yours?"

"All gods forbid," Donal said.

He came and knelt at Lord Aldaran's side. The old man laid a hand on his shoulder, and at the touch the unspoken words were clear to both of them: *But only a bastard wears his mother's name. I am orphaned, but no bastard.*

"Forgive me, Donal," the old man said at last. "I am to blame. I wished—I wished not to remember that Aliciane had ever belonged to any other man. Even when she had— had left me, I could not bear to remind myself that you were not, in sober truth, my own son." It was like a cry of pain. "I have so often wished that you were!"

"I, too," said Donal. He could remember no other father, wished for no other. Yet Darren's bullying voice seemed as fresh in his ears as it had been ten years ago:

"Donal of Rockraven; yes, I know, the *barragana's* brat. Do you even know who fathered you, or are you a son of the river? Did your mother lie in the forest during a Ghost-wind and come home with no-man's son in her belly?" Donal had flown at him, then, like a banshee, clawing and kicking, and they had been dragged apart, still howling threats at each other. Even now, it was not pleasant to think of young Darren's scornful gaze, the taunts he had made.

There was tardy apology in Lord Aldaran's voice. "If I have wronged you out of my own hunger top all you my son, believe I never meant to throw doubt on the honor of your own lineage, nor to conceal it. I think in what I mean to do tonight you will find how truly I value you, dear son."

"I need nothing but that," Donal said, and sat beside him on a low footstool.

Aldaran reached for his hand and they sat like that until a servant, bringing lights, proclaimed: "Lord Rakhal Aldaran of Scathfell, and Lord Darren."

Rakhal of Scathfell was like his brother had been ten years ago, a big hearty man in the prime of life, his face open and jovial, with that good-fellowship devious men

often assume as a way of proclaiming that they are concealing nothing, when the truth is often quite the reverse. Darren was like him, tall and broad, no more than a year or
two older than Donal, sandy-red hair swept back from a
high forehead, a straight-forward look which made Donal
think, at first glance, *Yes, he is handsome, as girls reckon
such things. Dorilys will like him. . . .* He told himself that
his faint sense of foreboding was no more than a distaste
for seeing his sister taken from his own exclusive protection
and charge and given to another.

*I cannot look that Dorilys should remain with me always.
She is heir to a great Domain; I am her half-brother, no
more, and her well-being must lie in other hands than mine.*

The lord Aldaran rose from his seat and advanced a few
steps toward his brother, taking his hands warmly.

"Greetings, Rakhal. It is too long since you have come
to me here at Aldaran. How goes all at Schathfell? And
Darren?" He embraced his kinsmen, one after the other,
leading them to sit near him. "And you know my foster-
son, half-brother to your bride, Darren. Donal Delleray,
Aliciane's son."

Darren lifted his eyebrows in recognition and said, "We
were taught arms-practice together, and other things. Somehow I had thought his name was Rockraven."

"Children are given to such misconceptions," Lord Aldaran said firmly. "You must have been very young then,
nephew, and lineage means little to young lads. Donal's
grandparents were Rafael Delleray and his wife *di catenas*
Mirella Lindir. Donal's father died young, and his widowed
mother came here as singing-woman. She bore me my only
living child. Your bride, Darren."

"Indeed?" Rakhal of Scathfell looked on Donal with a
courteous interest, which Donal suspected of being as spuri-
ous as the rest of his good humor.

Donal wondered why it should matter to him what the
Scathfell clan thought of him.

*Darren and I are to be brothers-by-marriage. It is not a
relationship I would have sought.* He, Donal, was honorably
born, honorably fostered in a Great House; that should
have been enough. Looking at Darren, he knew it would
never be enough, and wondered why. Why should Darren
Aldaran, heir to Scathfell, bother to hate and resent the

half-brother of his promised wife, the fosterling of her father?

Then, looking at Darren's falsely hearty smile, suddenly he knew the answer. He was not much of a telepath, but Darren might as well have shouted it at him.

Zandru's hells, he fears my influence over Lord Aldaran! The laws of inheritance by blood are not yet so firm, in these mountains, that he is certain of what may happen. It would not be the first time a nobleman had sought to disinherit his lawful heir for one he considered more suitable; and he knows my foster-father thinks of me as a son, not a fosterling.

To do Donal credit, the thought had never crossed his mind before. He had known his place—bound to Lord Aldaran by affection, but not by blood—accepted it. Now, the thought awakened because the men of Scathfell had provoked it, he wondered why it could *not* be so; why could the man he called "Father," to whom he had been a dutiful son, not name his heir as he chose? The Aldarans of Scathfell had *that* inheritance; why should they swell their holdings almost to the size of a kingdom by adding Aldaran itself to their estate?

But Lord Rakhal had turned away from Donal, saying heartily, "And now we are brought together over the matter of this marriage, so that when we are gone, our young people may hold our joined lands for their doubled portion. Are we to see the girl, Mikhail?"

Lord Aldaran said, "She will come to greet the guests, but I felt it more suitable to settle the business part of our meeting without her presence. She is a child, not suited to listen while gray beards settle matters of dowries and marriage gifts and inheritance. She will come to pledge herself, Darren, and to dance with you at the festivities. But I beg of you to remember that she is still very young and there can be no thought of actual marriage for four years at least, perhaps more."

Rakhal chuckled. "Fathers seldom think their daughters ripe to marry, Mikhail!"

"But in this case," Aldaran said firmly, "Dorilys is no more than eleven; the marriage *di catenas* must take place no sooner than four years from now."

"Come, come. My son is already a man; how long must he wait for a bride?"

"He must wait those years," Aldaran said firmly, "or seek one elsewhere."

Darren shrugged. "If I must wait for a little girl to grow up, then I suppose I must wait. A barbarous custom this, to pledge a grown man to a girl who has not yet put aside her dolls!"

"No doubt," Rakhal of Scathfell said, in his hearty and jovial manner, "but I have felt this marriage was important ever since Dorilys was born, and have spoken often of it to my brother in the past ten years."

Darren said, "If my uncle was so opposed before this, why has he given way now?"

Lord Aldaran's shoulders went up and down in a heavy shrug. "I suppose because I am growing old and am at last resigned to the knowledge that I should have no son; and I would rather see the estate of Aldaran pass into the hands of kinfolk, than into the hands of a stranger."

Why, at this moment, after ten years, Aldaran wondered, should he think of a curse flung by a sorceress many years dead? *From this day your loins shall be empty.* It was true that he had never thought seriously, from Aliciane's death, of taking another woman to his bed.

"Of course it could be argued," Rakhal of Scathfell said, "that *my* son is lawful heir to Aldaran, anyway. The lawgivers might well argue that Dorilys deserves no more than a marriage portion, and that a lawfully born nephew is nearer in inheritance than a *barragana*'s daughter."

"I do not grant the right of those so-called lawgivers to offer any judgement in that matter!"

Scathfell shrugged. "In any case this marriage will settle it without appeal to the law, with the two claimants to marry. The estates shall be joined; I am willing to settle Scathfell on Dorilys's eldest son, and Darren shall hold Castle Aldaran as warden for Dorilys."

Aldaran shook his head.

"No. In the marriage contract it is provided; Donal shall be his sister's warden till she is five-and-twenty."

"Unreasonable," protested Scathfell. "Have you none other way to feather your fosterling's nest? If he has no property from father or mother, can you not settle some on him by gift?"

"I have done so," Aldaran said. "When he came of age,

I gave him the small holding of High Crags. It is derelict, since those who held it last spent their time in making war on their neighbors, and not in farming; but Donal, I think, can bring it back to fruitfulness. It only remains to find him a suitable wife, and that shall be done. But he shall be warden for Dorilys."

"This looks not as if you trusted us, Uncle," protested Darren. "Think you, truly, we would deprive Dorilys of her rightful heritage?"

"Of course not," said Aldaran, "and since you have no such thoughts, how can it matter to you who is warden for her fortune? Of course, if you had indeed some such notion, you would have to protest Donal's choice. A paid hireling as warden could be bribed, but certainly not her brother."

Donal heard all this in amazement. He had not known, when his foster-father sent him to report on the estate of High Crags, that Aldaran designed it for *him;* he had reported fairly on the work it would take to put it in order, and on its fine possibilities, without believing his foster-father would give him such an estate. Nor did he have any idea that Aldaran would use this marriage-contract to make him Dorilys's guardian.

On second thought, this was reasonable. Dorilys was nothing to the Aldarans of Scathfell except an obstacle in their way to Darren's inheriting. If Lord Aldaran should die tomorrow, only he, as warden, could prevent Darren from taking Dorilys immediately in marriage despite her extreme youth, after which Darren could make use of her estate as he chose. It would not be the first time a woman had been quietly made away with, once her inheritance was safely in her husband's hands. They might wait till she had borne a child, to make it look legal; but everyone knew that young wives were prone to die in childbirth, and the younger they were, the more likely to die so. Tragic, of course, but not uncommon.

With Donal as her warden, and the wardenship extended until Dorilys was a full five-and-twenty, not just old enough to marry legally and bear children, then even if she should die, Donal would be there as her warden and guardian of any child she might bear; and her estate could not fall undisputed into Darren's hands.

He thought, *My foster-father spoke truly when he said I should know tonight how much he valued me. It may be that he trusts me because he has no one else to trust. But at least he knows that I will protect Dorilys's interests even before my own.*

Aldaran of Scathfell had not accepted this peacefully; he was still arguing the point and did not cede it until Lord Aldaran reminded his brother that three other mountain lords had all made suit for Dorilys, and that she might have been handfasted at any time to anyone her father chose, even to one of the Lowlands Hasturs or Altons.

"Indeed she was pledged once before, since Deonara's Ardais kinfolk wee eager to handfast her to one of their sons. They felt they had the best claim, since Deonara never bore me a living son. But the boy died shortly afterward."

"Died? How did he die?"

Aldaran shrugged. "An accident of some sort, I heard. I do not know the details."

Nor did Donal. Dorilys had been visiting her Ardais kin at the time, and had come home shocked by the death of her promised husband, even though she had hardly known him and had not really liked him. She had told Donal, "He was a big, rough, rude boy and he broke my doll." Donal had not questioned her. Now he wondered. Young as Donal was, he knew that if some child stood in the way of an advantageous alliance, that child might not live long.

And the same could be said of Dorilys. . . .

"On this point, my mind is made up," Lord Aldaran said, with an air of good nature, but firmly. "Donal, and Donal alone, shall be warden for his sister."

"This is an insult to your kin, Uncle," Darren protested, but the Lord of Scathfell silenced his son.

"If it must be, then it must be," he said. "We should be grateful that the maiden who is to be one of our family has a trustworthy kinsman to protect her; her interests are ours, of course. It shall be as you wish, Mikhail." But his look at Donal, eyes veiled and thoughtful, put the young man on his guard.

I must look to myself, he thought. *There is probably no danger till Dorilys is grown and the marriage consummated, since if Aldaran still lived he could name another warden.*

But if Aldaran should die, or Dorilys once wedded and taken to Scathfell, my chances would not be great to live very long.

He wished suddenly that Lord Aldaran were not dealing with kinsmen. If he had been dealing with strangers he would have had a *leronis* present, with truthspell to make lying or double-dealing impossible. But, although Aldaran might not trust his kinsmen overmuch, he could not insult them by insisting on having a sorceress, and a truthspell, to bind the bargains.

They set their hands on it, and signed the contract provided—Donal, too, was required to sign—and the matter was done. Then they were all embracing as kinsmen and going down into the room where the other guests had assembled to celebrate this occasion with feasting, dancing, and revelry.

But Donal, seeing Darren of Scathfell's eyes on him, thought again, coldly, *I must guard myself.*

This man is my enemy.

Chapter 9

When they went down into the Great Hall, Dorilys was there with her foster-mother, the *leronis* Margali, receiving their guests. For the first time, she was dressed not as a little girl but as a woman, in a long gown of blue, embroidered at neck and sleeves with gold traceries. Her shining copper hair was braided low on her neck and caught into a woman's butterfly-clasp. She looked far older than her years; she might have been fifteen or sixteen, and Donal was struck by her beauty, yet he was not wholly pleased to see this abrupt change.

His foreboding was justified when Darren, presented to Dorilys, blinked at her, obviously smitten. He bowed over her hand, saying gallantly, "Kinswoman, this is a pleasure. Your father had given me to believe I was being handfasted to a little girl, and here I find a lovely woman awaiting me. It is even as I thought—no father ever believes his daughter ripe for marriage."

Donal was stricken with sudden foreboding. Why had Margali done this? Aldaran had written it so carefully into the marriage contract that there could be no marriage until Dorilys had reached fifteen. He had emphasized strongly that she was only a little girl, and now they had given the lie to that argument by presenting Dorilys before all the assembled guests as a grown woman. As Darren, still murmuring gallant words, led Dorilys out for the first dance, Donal looked after them, troubled.

He asked Margali about this, and she shook her head.

"It was not by my will, Donal; Dorilys would have it so.

I would not cross her when her mind was so strongly set to it. You know as well as I do that it is not wise to provoke Dorilys when she *will* have something. The gown was her mother's, and although I am sorry to see my little girl so grown up, still, if she is grown to it—"

"But she is *not,*" Donal said, "and my foster-father spent a considerable time convincing Lord Scathfell that Dorilys was still a child, and far too young to marry. Margali, she *is* only a little girl, you know that as well as I!"

"Yes, I know, and a very childish one, too," Margali said, "but I could not argue with her on the eve of a festival. She would have made her displeasure felt all too greatly! You know as well as I, Donal. I can sometimes get her to do my will in important things, but if I tried to enforce my will on her in little things, she would soon stop listening to me when I sought to command her I the most serious ones. Does it matter, really, what dress she wears for her handfasting, since Lord Aldaran has written it, you say, into the marriage contract, that she shall not be bound till she is fifteen?"

"I suppose not, while my foster-father is still hale and strong enough to enforce his will," Donal said, "but the memory of this may cause trouble later, if something should happen within the next few years." Margali would not betray him—she had been kind to him from earliest childhood, she had been his mother's friend—but still it was unwise to speak so of the lord of a Domain and he lowered his voice. "Lord Scathfell would have no scruples in forcing the child into marriage for his own ambitions, and to seize Aldaran for his own; nor would Darren. If she had been shown tonight for the child she is, public opinion might put some damper, however small, on any such plan. Now those who see her tonight dressed in a woman's garments, and evidently already full-grown, will not be inclined to inquire about her real age; they will simply remember that at her handfasting she looked like a grown woman, and assume that those folk of Scathfell had right on their side, after all."

Margali looked worried now, too, but she tried to shrug it aside. "I think you are letting yourself make nightmares without cause, Donal. There is no reason to think Lord Aldaran will not live another score of years; certainly long enough to protect his daughter from being taken in marriage before she is old enough. And you know Dorilys—she is a creature of whim; tonight it may please her to play the lady in her mother's gowns and jewels, but tomorrow it will be forgotten and she will be playing at leapfrog and jackstones with the other children, so that no one living could think her anything but the little child she is in truth."

"Merciful Avarra, grant it maybe so," said Donal gravely.

"Why, I see no reason to doubt it, Donal. . . . Now you must do your duty by your foster-father's guests, too: there are many women waiting to dance with you, and Dorilys, too, will be wondering why her brother does not lead her out to dance."

Donal tried to laugh, seeing Dorilys, returning at Darren's side, entirely surrounded by a group of the young men, the minor nobility of the hills, Aldaran's Guardsmen. It might be true that Dorilys was amusing herself, playing the lady, but she was making a very successful pretense of it, laughing and flirting, all too obviously enjoying the flattery and admiration.

Father will not remonstrate with her. She looks all too much like our mother; and he is proud of his beautiful daughter. Why should I worry, or grudge Dorilys her amusements? No harm can come to her among our kinsmen, at a formal dance, and tomorrow, no doubt, it will be as Margali foresaw, Dorilys with her skirts tucked up to he knees and her hair in a long tail, tearing about like the little hoyden she is, and Darren can see the real Dorilys, the child who is young enough to enjoy dressing up in her mother's frock but still far from womanhood.

Trying to thrust aside his misgivings, Donal applied himself to his duties as host, chatting politely with a few elderly dowagers, dancing with young women who had somehow been forgotten or neglected, unobtrusively coming between Lord Aldaran and importunate hangers-on who might trouble him by making inconvenient requests too publicly to be refused. But whenever his eyes turned in Dorilys's direction, he saw her surrounded by recurrent waves of young men, and she was all too evidently enjoying her popularity.

The night was far advanced before Donal had a chance to dance, at last, with his sister; so far that she thrust out her lip, pouting like the child she was, when he came up to her.

"I thought you would not dance with me at all, brother, that you would leave me to all these strangers!"

Her breath was sweet, but he smelled the traces on it of wine, and asked with a slight frown, "Dorilys, how much have you been drinking?"

She dropped her eyes guiltily. "Margali said to me that I should drink no more than one cup of wine, but it is a sad thing if at my own handfasting I am to be treated as a little girl who should be put to bed at nightfall!"

"Indeed I think you are no more," Donal said, almost laughing at the tipsy child. "I should tell Margali to come and take you to your nurse. You will be sick, Dorilys, and then no one will think you a lady, either."

"I do not feel sick, only happy," she said, leaning her head back and smiling up at him. "Come, Donal, don't scold me. All evening I have waited to dance with my darling brother; won't you dance with me?"

"As you will, *chiya.*" He led her onto the dance floor. She was an expert dancer, but halfway through the dance she tripped over the unaccustomed long skirt of her gown and fell heavily against him. he caught her close to keep her from falling, and she threw her arms about him, laying her head on his shoulder, laughing.

"O-oh, maybe I have drunk too much, as you said—but each of my partners offered to drink with me at the end of a dance and I did not know how to refuse and be polite. I must ask Margali what is polite to say in such circum—circumstanshes." Her tongue tripped on the word and she giggled. "Is this what it feels like to be drunk, Donal, giddy and feeling as if all my joints were made of strung beads like the dolls the old women sell in the markets of Caer Donn? If it is, I think I like it."

"Where is Margali?" Donal asked, looking about the dance floor for the *leronis;* inwardly he resolved there should be some harsh words spoken to the lady. "I will take you to her at once, Dori."

"Oh, poor Margali," Dorilys said with an innocent stare. "She is not well; she said she was so blinded with headache that she could not see, and I made her go to lie down and rest." She added, with a defensive out, "I was tired of having her standing over me with that reproving scowl, as if *she* were Lady Aldaran and I only a servant! I will not be ordered about by servants!"

"Dorilys!" Donal reproved angrily. "You must not speak so. Margali is a *leronis* and a noblewoman, and Father's kinswoman; you must not speak of her that way! She is no servant! And your father saw fit to put you in her care, and it is your duty to obey her, until you are old enough to be responsible for yourself! You are a very naughty little girl! You must not give your foster-mother headaches, and speak to her rudely. Now, look—you have disgraced yourself by getting tipsy in company as if you were some low-bred wench from the stables! And Margali is not even here to take charge of you!" Inwardly he was dismayed. Donal himself, her father, and Margali were the only persons on whom Dorilys had never turned her willfulness.

If she will no longer allow herself to be ruled by Margali, what are we to do with her? She is spoiled and uncontrollable, and yet I had hoped Margali could keep her in hand till she was grown.

"I am really ashamed of you, Dorilys, and Father will be very displeased when he knows how you have served Margali, who has always been so good and kind to you!"

The child said, lifting her stubborn little chin, "I am Lady Aldaran and I can do exactly what I want to do!"

Donal shook his head in dismay. The incongruity of this struck him, that she looked so much like a grown woman—and a very lovely one, at that—and spoke and acted like the spoiled and passionate child she was. *I would that Darren could see her now; he would realize what a baby she is, beyond the gown and jewels of a lady.*

Yet, Donal thought, she was not quite a baby; the *laran* she carried, already strong as his own, had allowed her to give Margali a violent headache. *Perhaps we should think ourselves fortunate that she does not seek to bring thunder and lightning upon us, as I am sure she could do if she were really angry!* Donal thanked the gods that for all Dorilys's strange *laran*, she was not a telepath and could not read his thoughts, as he could sometimes read the thoughts of those around him.

He said, coaxingly, "But you should not stay here in

company when you are drunken, *chiya;* let me take you to your nurse, upstairs. The hour is late, and soon our guests will be going to their beds. Let me take you away, Dorilys."

"I don't want to go up to bed," Dorilys said sulkily. "I have had only this one dance with you, and Father has not yet danced with me, and Darren made me promise that he should have other dances later. Look—now he comes to claim them."

Donal urged, in a troubled whisper, "But you are in no state to dance, Dorilys; you will be falling over your own feet."

"No, I will not, truly. . . . Darren," she said, moving toward her handfasted partner, raising her eyes to his with a guile that looked adult. "Dance with me; Donal has been scolding me as an older brother thinks he has the right to do, and I am weary of listening to him."

Donal said, "I was trying to convince my sister that this party has gone on long enough for a girl so young. Perhaps she will be ore ready to hear wisdom from you, Darren, who are to be her husband." *If he is drunk,* Donal thought angrily, *I will not give her into his charge, even if I must quarrel with him in this public place.*

But Darren seemed well in command of his faculties. He said, "Indeed it is late, Dorilys; what do you think—"

Abruptly there was an outcry of shouting at the far end of the hall.

"Good God!" Darren exclaimed, turning toward the clamor. "It is Lord Storn's younger son and that young whelp from Darriel Forst. They will be at blows; they will draw steel."

"I must go," Donal said in consternation, recalling his duties as his father's master of ceremonies, official host at this occasion, but he glanced, troubled, at Dorilys. Darren said, with unusual friendliness, "I will look after Dorilys, Donal. Go and see to them,."

"I thank you," Donal said, hastily. Darren was sober, and he would have a vested interest in keeping his affianced wife from behaving too scandalously in public. He hurried toward the sound of the angry words, where the two youngest members of the rival families were engaged in a loud and angry dispute. Donal was skilled at such tactics. He came quickly up to them, and by joining in the dispute, convinced each of the quarreling men that he was on *his* side; then tactfully eased them apart. Old Lord Storn took charge of his quarrelsome son, and Donal took young Padreik Darriel into his own charge. It was some time before the young man sobered, apologized, and sought out his kinsmen to take his leave; then Donal looked around the ballroom for his sister and Darren. But he could see no sign of them, and wondered if Darren had managed to persuade his sister to leave the dance floor and go to her nurse.

If he has influence over Dorilys, perhaps we should even be grateful for that. Some of the Aldarans have the commanding voice; Father had it when he was younger. Has Darren managed to use it on Dorilys?

His eyes sought for Darren, without success, and he began to feel a vague sense of foreboding. As if to emphasize his fear, he heard a faint, distant roll of thunder. Donal could never hear thunder without thinking of Dorilys. He told himself not to be ridiculous; this was the season for storms in these mountains. Nevertheless, he was afraid. Where was Dorilys?

As soon as Donal had hurried away toward the quarreling guests, Darren laid his hand under Dorilys's arm. He said, "Your cheeks are flushed, *damisela;* is it the heat of the ballroom, with so many people, or have you danced to weariness?"

"No," Dorilys said, raising her hands to her hot face, "but Donal thinks I have drunk too much wine and came to scold me. As if I were a little girl still in his care, he wanted me to be put to bed like a child!"

"It does not seem to me that you are a child," Darren said, smiling, and she moved closer to him.

"I knew you would agree with me!"

Darren thought, *Why did they tell me she was a little girl?* He looked up and down the slender body, emphasized by the long close-fitting gown. *No child this! And still they think to put me off! Does that old goat of an uncle of mine think to play for time in the hopes of making a more advantageous marriage, or give himself time to declare the bastard of Rockraven his heir?*

"Truly, it is hot here," Dorilys said, moving still closer

to Darren, her fingers warm and sweaty on his arm, and he smiled down at her.

"Come, then. Let us go out on the balcony where it is cooler," Darren urged, drawing her toward one of the curtained doors.

Dorilys hesitated, for she had been carefully brought up by Margali and knew it was not considered proper for a young woman to leave a dancing floor except with a kinsman. But she thought, defensively, *Darren is my cousin, and also my promised husband.*

Dorilys felt the cool air from the mountains towering over Castle Aldaran, and drew a long sigh, leaning against the balcony rail.

"Oh, it was so hot in there. Thank you, Darren, I am glad to be out of that crowded place. You are kind to me," she said, so ingenuously that Darren, frowning, looked at the young woman in surprise.

How childish she was for a girl so obviously adult! He wondered, fleetingly, if the girl were feeble-minded or even an idiot. What did it matter, though? She was heir to the Domain of Aldaran, and it only remained for Darren to engage her affections, so that she would protest if her kinsmen sought for some reason to deprive him of his due by breaking off the marriage. The sooner it took place, the better; it was disgraceful, that his uncle wanted him to wait four years! The girl was obviously marriageable now, and the insistence on delay seemed to him completely unreasonable.

And if she were so childish, his task would be all the easier! He pressed the hand she laid trustingly in his and said, "No man living would hesitate an instant to do such a *kindness,* Dorilys—to maneuver for a moment alone with his promised bride! And when she is as lovely as you, even the kindness becomes more of a pleasure than a duty."

Dorilys felt herself coloring again at the compliment. She said, "Am I beautiful? Margali told me so, but she is only an old woman, and I do not think she is any judge of beauty."

"You are indeed most beautiful, Dorilys," Darren said, and in the dim light streaming in patches from the ballroom she saw his smile.

She thought, *Why, he really means it; he is not only being kind to me!* She felt the first childish stirrings of awareness of her own power, the power of beauty over men. She said, "I have been told my mother was beautiful; she died when I was born. Father says I look like her; did you ever see her, Darren?"

"Only when I was a boy," Darren said, "but it is true. Aliciane of Rockraven was counted one of the loveliest women from the Kadarin to the Wall around the World. There were those who said she had put a spell on your father, but she needed no witchcraft but her own beauty. You are indeed very like her. Have you her singing voice as well?"

"I do not know," Dorilys said. "I can sing in tune, so my music-mistress says, but she says I am too young to know whether I will have a fine voice, or only a love of music and some little skill. Are you fond of music, Darren?"

"I know little about it," he said, smiling and moving closer to her, "and it needs not a beautiful voice to make a woman lovely in my eyes. Come—I am your cousin and kinsman and your promised husband; will you kiss me, Dorilys?"

"If you want me to," she said pliantly, and turned her cheek to him for his kiss. Darren, wondering again if the girl were teasing him or simply dim-witted, took her face between his hands, turning it toward him, and kissed her on the lips, his arms going around her to draw her against him.

Dorilys, submitting to the kiss, and through the tipsy blur of her sensations, felt a faint, wary stir of caution. Margali had warned her. *Oh, Margali is always trying to spoil my fun!* She leaned against Darren, letting him draw her tight against him, enjoying the touch, opening her mouth to his repeated kisses. Dorilys was no telepath, but she had *laran,* and she picked up a diffuse blur of his emotion, the arousal within him, the dim sense, *This may not be so bad after all,* and wondered why that should surprise him. Well, after all, she supposed it must be annoying for a young man to be told he was to be married off to a cousin he did not know, and she felt fuzzily glad that Darren thought her beautiful. He went on kissing her, slowly, repeatedly, sensing that she did not protest the kisses. Dorilys was too drunk, too unaware, to realize very clearly what was happening, but when his fingers moved to unlace her bodice, moving inside to cup over her bare breasts, she felt suddenly abashed and pushed him away.

"No, Darren, it is unseemly, really, you must not," she protested, feeling her tongue thick in her mouth. For the first time she was aware that perhaps Donal was right; she should *not* have drunk so much. Darren's face was flushed, and he seemed unwilling to let her go. She took his hands firmly between her strong little fingers and pushed them away.

"No, Darren, don't!" Her hands went to cover her exposed breasts; she fumbled to relace the strings.

"No, Dorilys," he said thickly, so thickly that she wondered if he had drunk too much, too. "It's all right; it is not unseemly. We can be married as soon as you will. You will like being married to me; won't you?" He drew her close and kissed her again, hard and insistently. He murmured, "Dorilys, listen to me. If you will let me take you, now, then your father will allow the marriage rites to take place at once."

Now Dorilys was beginning to be wary; she drew her mouth away from his, moved away from him, beginning, through the blur, to wonder if she should have come out here at all, alone with him. She was still innocent enough not to be quite sure what it was he wanted of her, but she knew it was something she ought not to do, and even more, something he ought really not to ask. She said, her hands trembling as she sought to lace her bodice, "My father— Margali says I am not yet old enough to be married."

"Oh, the *leronis*. What does an old virgin know of love and marriage?" Darren said. "Come here and kiss me again, my little love. No, now, be still in my arms. Here, let me kiss you—like this—"

She could feel the intensity now in the kiss, frightening, his face the face of a stranger, swollen, dark with intent, his hands no longer caressing but strong, insistent.

"Darren, let me go," she begged him. "Really, really, you must not!" Her voice was trembling in panic. "My father will not like it. Take your hands from me! I beg you, kinsman—cousin!" She pushed at him, but she was a child, and still half drunk, and Darren was a grown man, cold sober. Her blurred *laran* picked up his intent, his determination, the touch of cruelty behind it.

"No, don't fight me," he muttered. "When it is over, your father will be all too glad to give you to me at once, and that will not displease you; will it, my little one, my beauty? Here, let me hold you."

Dorilys began to struggle, in sudden terror. "Let me go, Darren! Let me go! My father will be very angry; Donal will be angry with you. Let me go, Darren, or I will cry out for help!"

She saw the awareness of that threat in his eyes, and opened her mouth to shriek for help, but he was aware of her intent and his hand, hard and determined, clasped over her mouth, smothering the cry, while he drew her closer to him. Terror suddenly gave way to anger in Dorilys. *How dare he!* Under the flooding rage, she *reached out,* in a way she had been able to do since babyhood if one touched her against her will, *striking. . . .*

Darren's hand fell from hers, and with a smothered cry, he grated with pain, "Ah, you little demon, how dare you!" and swung back his hand, striking her so hard on the cheek that she was knocked nearly senseless. "No woman alive does this to me! You are not unwilling; you want to be teased and flattered! No more; it is too late for that!"

As she fell to the floor, he knelt beside her, tearing at his clothes. Dorilys, in wild rage and fright, *struck out* again, hearing the crash of thunder through her own shriek, seeing the brilliant white flare that struck Darren. He reeled back, his face contorted, fell heavily atop her. In terror, she pushed him aside and scrambled up, gasping, sick, exhausted. He lay insensible, not moving. Never, never had she struck so hard, never. . . . *Oh, what have I done!*

"Darren," she pleaded, kneeling beside his motionless form. "Darren, get up! I didn't' mean to hurt you, only you mustn't try to maul me like that. I don't like it. Darren! Darren! Did I really hurt you? Cousin, kinsman, speak to me!" But he was silent, and in sudden terror, heedless of her disheveled hair and torn gown, she ran toward the door of the ballroom.

Donal! It was the only thought in her mind. *Donal will know what to do! I must find Donal!*

Donal, alert to his sister's cry of panic, resounding in his mind even though it was not audible within the ballroom, had made a hasty excuse to the elderly friend of his grandfather who had come to speak with him, and hurried in search of her, led by the soundless cry.

That bastard Darren! He opened the balcony door and his sister fell into his arms, her hair half unbound, her dress open at the throat.

"Dorilys! *Chiya,* what has happened?" he said, his heart pounding, his throat sticking with dread. Gods above, would even Darren presume to lay rough hands on a girl of eleven?

"Come, *bredilla.* No one must see you like this. Come, smooth your hair, *chiya;* lace your bodice, quickly," he urged, thinking grimly that this must be kept from their father. He would quarrel with his kinsmen of Scathfell. It never crossed Donal's mind that such a quarrel might redound to his personal benefit. "Don't cry, little sister. No doubt he was drunk and did not know what he was doing. Now you see why a young woman must not drink so much she has not her wits about her, to keep young men from getting such ideas. Come, Dorilys, don't cry," he begged.

She said, her voice shaking, "It's Darren . . . I hurt him. I don't know what's wrong; he just lies there and will not speak to me. He kissed me too roughly. At first I wanted him to kiss me, but then he grew rough and I made him stop, and he hit me—and I was angry and I—I made the lightning come, but I didn't want to hurt him, really I didn't. Please, Donal, come and see what is wrong with him."

Avarra, merciful goddess! Donal, his breath coming in gasps, followed his sister onto the dark balcony, kneeling beside Darren, but already he knew what he should find. Darren, his face raised to the dark sky, lay motionless, his body already growing cold.

"He's dead, Dorilys; you've killed him," he said, drawing her into his arms in fierce protectiveness, feeling her whole body shaking like a tree in the wind. Around the heights of Castle Aldaran the thunders crashed and rolled, slowly fading into silence.

Chapter 10

"And now," said Lord Scathfell somberly, "if the gods will, we shall hear the truth of this dreadful business."

The guests had been cleared away, escorted to their rooms or to their horses. Over the heights of Castle Aldaran the great red sun was beginning to show a wet crimson face through the heavy banks of cloud. Darren's body had been carried to the chapel deep in the heart of the castle. Donal had never liked Darren, but he could not keep back pity as he saw the young man lying stark and astonished, his clothing disarrayed, his head flung back in the spasm of agony and terror which had ended his life. *He came to an undignified end,* Donal thought, and would have arranged the young man's clothing in more seemly fashion; then it occurred to him that this would remove all traces of Dorilys's only defense.

Blood-guilt on so young a child, he thought with a shudder, and stepped back from the corpse and went out to Lord Aldaran's presence-chamber.

Margarli had been roused from the heavy sleep which had fallen over her at the cessation of pain; she was there, a thick shawl thrown over her night-robe, Dorilys sobbing in her arms. The girl looked like an exhausted child now, her face blotched with long crying, her hair coming down in stray locks and tendrils, her swollen eyelids drooping sleepily over her eyes. She had almost stopped crying, but every now and then a renewed spasm of sobs would shake her thin shoulders. She was sitting in Margali's lap like the child she was, though her long legs dragged on the floor. Her elaborate gown was bedraggled and crushed.

Over the child's head Margali looked at Lord Mikhail of Aldaran and said, "Will you have truthspell, then, my lord? Very well, but let me at least call her nurse and put the child to bed. She has been awake all night, and you can see—" She moved her head, indicating the weeping, disheveled Dorilys, clinging to her.

"I am sorry, *mestra*. Dorilys must remain," Aldaran said. "We must hear what she has to say, too, I fear, and under truthspell. . . . Dorilys"—his voice was gentle—"let go of your foster-mother, my child, and go and sit there beside Donal. No one will hurt you; we only want to know what happened."

Reluctantly, Dorilys loosed her grip from Margali's neck. She was rigid, gripped with terror. Donal could not help but think of a rabbithorn before a pack of mountain beasts. She came and sat on the low bench beside him. Donal put out his hand to her and the childish fingers gripped it, painfully tight. With her free hand she wiped her smeared face on the sleeve of her gown.

Margali took her matrix from the silken bag around her throat, gazed for a moment into the blue jewel, and her low, clear voice was distinctly audible, though she was almost whispering, in the silence of the presence-chamber.

"In the light of the fire of the jewel, let the truth lighten this room where we stand."

Donal had seen the setting to truthspell many times, and it had never ceased to awe him. From the small blue jewel, a glow began, slowly suffused the face of the *leronis,* crept out into the room, creeping slowly from face to face. Donal felt the shimmer of the light on his own face, saw it glowing on the blotched face of the child at his side, saw it lightening the face of Rakhal of Scathfell and the paxman who stood motionless at his back. In the blue light Mikahil of Aldaran looked more than ever like some aged and molting bird of prey, motionless on his block, but when he raised his head the power and the menace were there, silent potential.

Margali said, "It is done, my lord. The truth alone may be spoken here while this light endures."

Donal knew that if falsehoods were knowingly spoken

under the truthspell, the light would vanish from the face of the speaker, showing instantly that he lied.

"Now," said Mikhail of Aldaran, "you must tell us what you know of this, Dorilys. How came Darren to die?"

Dorilys raised her face. She looked pitiable, her face smeared and blotched with weeping, her eyes swollen, and again she wiped her nose on the elaborate sleeves of her gown. She clung hard to Donal's hand, and he could feel her trembling. Aldaran had never before used the commanding voice on his daughter. After a moment she said, "I—I didn't know he was dead," and blinked rapidly as if she were about to cry again.

Rakhal of Scathfell said, "He is dead. My eldest son is dead. Have no doubt about that, you—"

"Silence!" with the sound of the commanding voice, even Lord Scathfell let his voice die into quiet. "Now, Dorilys, tell us what befell between Darren and you. How came the lightnings to strike him?"

Dorilys slowly gained command of her voice. "We were warm from dancing, and he said we should go out on the balcony. He bean to kiss me, and he—" Her voice shook again, uncontrollably. "He unlaced my gown and touched me, and he would not stop when I bade him." She blinked hard, but the truthlight on her face did not falter. "He said I should let him take me now so that Father could not delay the marriage. And he kissed me roughly; he hurt me." Her hands went up to cover her face, and she shook with a fresh outburst of sobs.

Aldaran's face was sent like stone. He said, "Don't be afraid, my daughter; but you must let our kinsmen see your face."

Donal took Dorilys's hands in his. He could feel the agony of her fear and shame as if it were pulsing out through her small hands.

She said, stammering, into the unflickering truthlight, "He—he hit me hard when I pushed him away, and he knocked me down on the floor, and then he got down on the floor beside me, and I was—I was scared, and I hit him with the lightnings. I didn't want to hurt him; I only wanted him to take his hands off me!"

"You! You killed him, then! You struck him with your

witch-lightnings, you fiend from hell!" Scathfell rose, advanced from his seat, his hand raised as if to strike.

"Father! Don't let him hurt me!" Dorilys cried out in shrill terror. A blue blaze of lightning struck outward, and Rakhal of Scathfell reeled back, stopped dead in his tracks, clutching at his heart. The paxman came and supported his faltering lord to his seat.

Donal said, "My lords, if she had not struck him down, I would myself have called challenge on him! To seek to ravish a girl of eleven!" His hand clutched at his sword as if the dead man stood before him.

Aldaran's voice was filled with sorrow and bewilderment as he turned to Lord Scathfell. "Well, my brother, you have seen. I regret this, more than I can say; but you have seen the truthlight on the child's face, and it seems to me there is little fault in her, either. How came your son to attempt a thing so unseemly at his own handfasting—to try to rape his intended bride?"

"It never occurred to me that he would need to rape," Scathfell said, anger beating through his words. "It was I who told him, simply, to make sure of her. Did you truly think we would agree to wait for years while you sought out a more advantageous marriage? A blind man could have seen that the girl was marriageable, and the law is clear: if a handfasted couple lie together, the marriage is legal from that moment. It was I who told my son to make sure of his bride."

"I should have known," Aldaran said bitterly. "You did not trust me, brother? But here stand the *leronis* who brought my daughter to the light. Under truthspell, Margali, how old is Dorilys?"

"It is true," the *leronis* said into the blue truthlight. "I took her from Aliciane's dead body eleven summers ago. But even if she had been of marriageable age, my lord of Scathfell, why should you connive at the seduction of your own niece?"

"Yes, we should hear that, too," Mikhail of Aldaran said. "Why, my brother? Could you not trust the dues of kin?"

"It is you who have forgotten kinship's dues," Scathfell flung at him. "Need you ask, brother? When you would have had Darren wait years while you schemed to find

some way to give all to the bastard of Rockraven, whom
you call fosterling. That bastard son you will not even
acknowledge!"

Without stopping to think, Donal rose from his seat and
stepped to the paxman's place, three steps behind Mikhail
of Aldaran. His hand hovered a few inches above his
sword-hilt. Lord Aldaran did not look around at Donal,
but the words were wrenched from him.

"Would to all the gods that your words were true! Would
that Donal had been born of my blood, lawfully or unlawful! No man could ask more in kinsman or son! But alas—
alas, with grief I say it—and in the light of truthspell, Donal
is not my son."

"Not your son? Truly?" Scathfell's voice was contorted
with fury. "Why, then, why else would an old man so forget
kinship's dues if he were not unseemly besotted with the
boy? If not your son, then it must be he is your minion!"

Donal's hand flashed to sword-hilt. Aldaran, sensing his
intent, reached out and gripped Donal's wrist in steel fingers, squeezing until Donal's hand relaxed and he let the
sword slide back into the scabbard, undrawn.

"Not beneath this roof, foster-son; he is still our guest."
Then he let Donal's wrist go, advancing on the lord of
Scathfell, and Donal thought again of a hawk swooping on
his prey. "Had any man but my brother spoken such words
I would tear the lie from his throat. Get out! Take up the
body of that foul ravisher you called son, and all your lack-
eys, and get you gone from my roof before indeed I forget
the dues of kin!"

"Your roof indeed, but not for long, my brother," Scathfell said between his teeth. "I will tear it down stone from
stone around your head, ere it goes to the bastard of
Rockraven!"

"And I will burn it over my own head, before it goes to
any son of Scathfell," Lord Aldaran retorted. "Be gone
from my house before high noon, else my servants shall
drive you forth with whips! Get you back to Scathfell, and
think lucky I do not harry you forth from that stronghold
as well, which you hold by my favor. I make allowance for
your grief, or I would have revenge in your heart's blood
for what you have said and done here today! Get you gone

to Scathfell, or where you will, but come into my presence
no more, nor call me again brother!"

"Brother no more, nor overlord," Scathfell said in a rage.
"The gods be thanked, I have other sons, and a day will
come when we hold Scathfell of our own right, and not by
your leave and favor. A day will come when we hold Aldaran as well, and yonder murdering sorceress who hides
behind the mask of a weeping girl-baby shall be held to
account with her own blood! From hence, Mikhail of Aldaran, look to yourself, and your witch-daughter, and to the
bastard of Rockraven whom you will not own your son!
The gods alone know what hold he has on you! Some filthy
spell of witchcraft! I will breathe no longer this air polluted
with the foul sorceries of this place!" Turning, his paxman
at his heels, Lord Scathfell went forth, with a slow and
measured step, from Aldaran's presence-chamber. His last
look was for Dorilys, a look so full of loathing that Donal
turned cold.

*When brethren are at odds, enemies step in to widen the
gap,* Donal thought. Now his foster-father had quarreled
with all his kin. *And I, who alone stand by him now—I am
not even his son!*

When the folk of Scathfell had departed, Margali said
firmly, "Now, my lord, by your leave, I shall take Dorilys
away to her bed."

Aldaran, starting out of a brooding apathy, said, "Yes, yes,
take the child away, but return to me here when she sleeps."

Margali took the sobbing child away, and Aldaran sat
motionless, head down, lost in thought.

Donal forbore to disturb him, but when Margali returned, he asked, "Shall I go?"

"No, no, lad, this concerns you, too," Aldaran said, sighing as he looked up at the *leronis.* "No blame to you, Margali, but what are we to do now?"

Margali said, shaking her head, "I cannot control her any
more, my lord. She is strong and willful, and soon the
stresses of puberty will be upon her. I beg you, Dom Mikhail, to place her in charge of someone stronger than I, and
better fitted to teach her control of her *laran,* or worse
things than this may follow."

Donal wondered, *What could be worse than this?*

As if picking up the unspoken question, Aldaran said, "Every other child I have fathered has died in adolescence of the threshold sickness which is the curse of our line. Must I fear that for her, too?"

Margali said, "Have you thought, my lord, of sending her to the *vai leroni* of Tramontana Tower? They would care for her, and teach her the uses of her *laran*. If anyone alive could bring her through adolescence unharmed, it is they."

Donal thought, *That is certainly the right solution.* "Yes, Father," he said eagerly. "You will remember how kind they were to me whenever I went there. They would have been glad to have me among them, if you could have spared me from your side. Even so, they always welcomed me among them as guest and friend, and they taught me much about the use of my *laran*, and would have gladly taught me more. Send Dorilys to them, Father."

Aldaran's face had brightened imperceptibly; then he frowned again. "To Tramontana? Would you shame me before my neighbors, then, Donal? Am I to show my weakness, that they can spread the word aboard to all the folk in the Hellers? Am I to be made the subject of gossip and scorn?"

"Father, I think you wrong the folk of Tramontana," Donal said, but he knew it would do no good. He had reckoned without Dom Mikhail's pride.

Margali said, "If you will not entrust her to your neighbors at Tramontana, Dom Mikhail, then I beg of you to send her to Hali or Neskaya, or to one of the Towers in the Lowlands. I am no longer young enough, or strong enough, to teach her or control her. All the gods know, I have no wish to part with her. I love her as if she were my own child, but I cannot handle her anymore. In a Tower they are schooled to do so."

Aldaran thought about that for some time. Finally he said, "I think she is too young to be sent to a Tower. But there are old ties of friendship between Aldaran and Elhalyn. For the sake of that old friendship, perhaps the lord of Elhalyn will send a *leronis* from Hali Tower to care for her. This would excite no comment. Any household with *laran* has need of some such person, to teach the young people of that household. Will you go, Donal, and ask that someone shall come to Aldaran to dwell in our household and teach her?"

Donal rose and bowed. The thought of Dorilys, safe in Tramontana Tower among his friends, had attracted him; but perhaps it had been too much to ask that his foster-father should make his weakness known to his neighbors. "I shall ride today, if you will, my lord, as soon as I can assemble an escort befitting your rank and dignity."

"No," Aldaran said, heavily. "You will ride alone, Donal, as befits a suppliant. I have heard that there is a truce between the Elhalyn and the Ridenow; you will be safe enough. But if you go alone, it will be clear that I am beseeching their help."

"As you will," Donal said. "I can ride tomorrow, then. Or even this night."

"Tomorrow will be time enough," Aldaran said. "Let the folk of Scathfell get well away to their homes. I want no word of this to get around the mountains."

Chapter 11

At the far end of the Lake of Hali, the Tower rose, a narrow, tall structure, made of pale translucent stone. Most of the more demanding work of the matrix circle was done at night. At first Allart had not understood this, thinking it superstition or meaningless custom. As time passed, however, he had begun to realize that the night hours, while most people slept, were the most free of intruding thoughts, the random vibrations of other minds. In the deserted night hours, the matrix circle workers were free to send their conjoined minds into the matrix crystals which enormously amplified the electronic and energon vibrations of the brain, transforming power into energy.

With the tremendous power of the linked minds and the giant artificial matrix lattices which the technicians could build, these mental energies could mine deep-buried metals to the surface in a pure molten flow; could charge batteries for the operation of air-cars or the great generators which lighted the castles of Elhalyn and Thendara. Such a circle had raised the glistening white towers of the castle at Thendara from the living rock of the mountain peak where it stood. From the many Towers like this one flowed all the energy and technology of Darkover, and it was the men and women of the Tower circles who created it.

Now, in the shielded matrix chamber—shielded, not only by taboo and tradition, and the isolation of Hali, but by force-fields which could strike an intruder dead or mindless—Allart Hastur sat before a low, round table, hands and mind linked with the six others of his circle. All the energies of his brain and body were concentrated into a single flow toward the Keeper of the circle. The Keeper was a slight, steel-strong young man; his name was Coryn, and he was a cousin of Allart's, about his own age. Seated before the giant artificial crystal, he seized the massed energon flows of the six who sat around the table, pouring them through the intricate inner crystal lattices, directing the stream of that energy into the rows of batteries ranged before them on the low table. Coryn did not move or speak, but as he pointed a narrow, commanding hand toward one battery after another, the linked, blank-faced members of the circle poured every atom of their focused energies into the matrix and through the body of the Keeper, sending enormous charges of energy into the batteries, one by one.

Allart was ice-cold, cramped, but he did not know it; he was unaware of his body, unaware of anything except the pouring streams, the flow of energy which rushed through him. Dimly, without thought, it reminded him of the ecstatic union of minds and voices of the morning hymns of Nevarsin, this sense of unique blending and separateness, of having found his own place in the music of the universe. . . .

Outside the circle of linked hands and minds, a white-robed woman sat, her face in her hands, nothing visible but the falling streams of her long copper-colored hair. Her mind moved ceaselessly around and around the circle, monitoring one after another of the motionless figures. She eased the tension of a muscle before it could impair concentration, soothed a sudden cramp or itch before it could intrude into the concentration of the man or woman in the circle; made certain breathing did not falter, nor any of the small automatic movements which kept the neglected bodies in good order—the rhythmic blinks of the eyes to avoid strain, the faint shift of position. If breathing faltered, she went into rapport with the breather and starting the smooth rhythm again, lending smooth pace to a faltering heart. The linked members of the circle were not conscious of their own bodies, had not been conscious of them for hours. They were aware only of their linked minds, floating in the blazing energies they poured into the batteries. Time had stopped for them in an endless instant of massive union; only the monitor was conscious of the passing hours. Now, not seeing but sensing that the hour of sunrise was still some time away, she was aware of some tension in the circle that should not be there, and sent her questing mind from one to another of the linked figures.

Coryn. The Keeper himself, trained for years in mind and body to endure just this strain . . . no, he was in no distress. He was cramped, and she checked his circulation; he was cold but was not yet aware of it. His condition had not altered since the early hours of the night. Once his body was linked and locked into one of the comfortably balanced postures he could maintain unmoving for hours, it was well with him.

Mira? No, the old woman who had been monitor before Renata herself was calm and unaware, floating peacefully in the energy nets, focused on the outflows of force, random dreaming, blissful.

Barak? The sturdy, swarthy man, the technician who had built the artificial matrix lattice to the requirements of this circle, was cramped. Automatically Renata descended into his body-awareness, eased a muscle before pain could intrude into his concentration. Nothing else was amiss with him.

Allart? How had a newcomer to the circle come to have such control? Had it been his Nevarsin training? His breathing was deep and slow, unfaltering, the flow of oxygen to his limbs and heart unceasing. He had even learned the most difficult trick of a matrix circle, the long hours unmoving, without undue pain or cramping.

Arielle? She was the youngest of the circle in years, yet at sixteen she had spent a full two years here in Hali, and had achieved the rank of mechanic. Renata checked her carefully: breathing, heart, the sinuses which sometimes gave Arielle trouble because of the dampness here in the lake country. Arielle was from the southern plains. Finding nothing amiss, Renata checked further. No, nothing wrong, not even a full bladder to cause tension. Renata thought, *I wondered if Coryn had made her pregnant, but it is not that. I checked her carefully before she entered the circle, and Arielle knows better than that. . . .*

It must be the other newcomer, then, Cassandra. . . . Carefully monitoring, she checked heart, breathing, circulation. Cassandra was cramped, but not in much pain from it, not enough to notice. Renata felt Cassandra's awareness, a random troubled flutter, and sent a quick, reassuring thought to calm her before it could disturb the others. Cassandra was new to this work, and had not yet come to take the routine intrusion of a monitor's touch on body and mind with complete acceptance. It took Renata some seconds to soothe Cassandra before she could go into the deeper internal monitoring.

Yes, it is Cassandra. It is her strain we are all sharing. . . . She should not have come into the circle at this time, with her woman's cycles about to come upon her. I thought she knew better than that. . . . But Renata never thought of blaming Cassandra, only herself. *I should have made certain of that.* Renata knew how hard it was, in the early days of learning, to confess weakness or admit to limitations.

She moved into rapport with Cassandra, trying to calm her tension, but she realized Cassandra was not yet able to work with her in that kind of total closeness. She sent a careful, warning thought to Coryn, a gentle touch akin to the softest of murmurs.

We must break soon . . . be ready when I signal to you.

The flow of energies did not pause or falter, but the barest outside flutter of Coryn's attention replied, *Not yet; there is still an entire row of batteries which must be charged,* then he sank back into the linkage of the circle without a ripple.

Now Renata was troubled. The word of the Keeper was law in the circle; yet it was the responsibility of the monitor to keep custody of the well-being of the bodies of the linked members. So far she had carefully shielded her thoughts and her concern from all of them, but from somewhere she felt, now, a faint awareness, a withdrawal of total energy from the circle, which should not have been there. *Allart is aware of Cassandra. He is too aware of her for this stage. He should not, linked into the circle like this, know she is alive, any more than another.* As yet it was only a flicker and she compensated by gently nudging Allart's awareness back to his own focus of energy. She tried to hold Cassandra steady, as if, on a steep stairway, she had lent the other woman the support of her arm. But once the intensity of concentration was broken, something in the stream of energies faltered, wavered, as a wind ruffles the face of the waters. One by one she felt the disturbance run around the circle, only a flicker, but at this high level of concentration, disrupting. Barak shifted his weight uneasily, Coryn coughed. Arielle snuffled, and Renata felt Cassandra's breathing falter, grow heavy. Now imperative, she sent out a second warning:

We must break, Coryn. It is near time . . .

This time the backlash was definitely irritable, and it reverberated through all the linked minds like an alarm bell. Allart heard the sound in his mind as he had heard the soundless bells of Nevarsin, and began slowly to recover his independent focus. Coryn's irritation was like a stinging slap; he felt it like the twitching of some internal strand as he felt Cassandra's consciousness drop away. It was like plucking forth an ingrown strand, as if some deep root planted in his being was jerked forth all bloody. One by one he felt the circle break and disintegrate, not the gentle withdrawal it had been in the earlier times, but this time falling apart painfully. He heard Mira gasping with effort, Arielle sniffle as if she were going to cry. Barak groaned, stretching a painfully cramped limb. Allart knew enough not to move too quickly at first; he moved with the slowest, most careful of motions, as if coming awake from a very deep sleep. But he was troubled and distressed. What had happened to the circle? Certainly their work had not been completed. . . .

One by one, around the table, the others were coming up from the depths of the matrix trance. Coryn looked white and shattered. He did not speak, but the intensity of his anger, directed at Renata, was painful to them all.

I told you, not yet. Now we will have this all to do again, for less than a dozen batteries. . . . Why did you break just now? Was there anyone in this circle too weak to endure for just a little more? Are we children playing jackstones, or a responsible mechanics' circle?

But Renata paid no attention, and Allart, his conscious mind flicking back into focus, saw that Cassandra had fallen sideways, her long dark hair scattered along the tabletop. He shoved back his low chair and sprang to her side, but Renata was there before him.

"No," she said, and with a flicker of dismay, Allart heard the commanding voice focused against him. *"Don't touch her!* This is my responsibility!" In his extreme sensitization Allart picked up the thought Renata had not spoken aloud: *You have done too much already; you are responsible for this. . . .*

I? Holy Bearer of Burdens, strengthen me! I, Renata?

Renata was kneeling beside Cassandra, her fingertips spread at the back of Cassandra's neck, just touching her at the nerve center there. Cassandra stirred, and Renata said soothingly, "It's all right, love; you're all right now."

Cassandra murmured, "I'm so cold, so cold."

"I know, it will pass in a few minutes."

"I'm so sorry. I didn't mean—I was sure—" Cassandra looked around, dazed, at the edge of tears. She flinched before Coryn's angry glare.

"Let her alone, Coryn. It's not her fault," Renata said, not looking up.

Coryn said, with a gesture of deep irony, *"Z'par servu, vai leronis. . . .* Have we your leave to test the batteries? While you minister to your bride?"

Cassandra was struggling against sobs. Renata said, "Don't mind Coryn; he is as tired as we all are. He didn't mean that as it sounded."

Arielle went to a side table, took up a metal tool—the matrix circles had first call on all the scarce metals of Darkover—and, wrapping her hand in insulating material, went to the batteries, touching them one after another to elicit the spark indicating they were fully charged. The other members of the circle rose cautiously, stretching cramped bodies. Renata still knelt at Cassandra's side; finally she withdrew her hands from the pulse circuits at the other woman's throat.

"Try to stand up now. Move around if you can."

Cassandra chafed her thin hands together. "I am as cold as if I had spent the night in Zandru's coldest hell. Thank you, Renata. How did you know?"

"I am a monitor. It is my duty to know such things." Renata Leynier was a slight, tawny young woman, with masses of copper-gold hair, but her mouth was too wide for beauty, her teeth somewhat crooked, her nose splotched with freckles. Her eyes, though, were wide and gray and beautiful.

"When you have had a little more training, Cassandra,

you will be able to sense them for yourself, and tell us when you are not well enough to join a circle. At such a time, as I thought you knew, your psychic energy leaves your body with your blood, and you need all your strength for yourself. Now you must go to bed and rest for a day or two. Certainly you must not work in the circle again, or do any work demanding so much effort and concentration."

Allart came toward them, troubled. "Are you ill, Cassandra?"

Renata answered for her. "Overwearied, no more, and in need of food and rest." Mira had gone to a cupboard at the far end of the room and was setting out some of the food and wine kept there so that the circle members could refresh themselves at once from the tremendous energy-drains of their work. Renata went and searched among the provisions for a long bar of compressed nuts, sticky with honey. She put it into Cassandra's hand, but the dark-haired woman shook her head.

"I do not like sweets. I will wait for a proper breakfast."

"Eat it," Renata said, in command voice. "You need the strength."

Cassandra broke off a piece of the sticky confection and put it into her mouth. She grimaced at the cloying taste, but chewed it obediently. Arielle joined them, and throwing down the tool and taking a handful of dried fruits, she put them greedily into her mouth. When she could speak plain she said, "The last full dozen of the batteries are not charged, and the last three we finished will have to be done again; they are not to full capacity."

"What a nuisance!" Coryn glared at Cassandra.

"Let her alone!" Renata insisted. "We have all been beginners!"

Coryn poured himself some wine and sipped it. "I am sorry, kinswoman," he said at last, smiling at Cassandra, his normal good nature taking over again. "Are you wearied, cousin? You must not exhaust yourself for a few batteries."

Arielle wiped her fingers, sticky with the honeyed fruit. "If there is any work more tedious from Dalereuth to the Hellers than charging batteries, I cannot imagine it."

"Better that than mining," Coryn said. "Whenever I work with metals, I come out exhausted for half a moon.

I am glad there is no more work to be done this year. Every time we go into the earth for mining, I come back to consciousness feeling as if I had lifted every spoonful of it with my own two hands!"

Allart, disciplined by the years of arduous physical and mental training at Nevarsin, was less weary than the others, but his muscles were aching with tension and inactivity. He saw Cassandra break another piece of the sticky honey-nut confection, felt her grimace as she put it into her mouth. They were still in rapport and he felt her revulsion for the oversweet stuff as if he were eating it himself.

"Don't eat that if you don't like it. Surely on the shelves there is something more to your liking," he said, and turned to rummage in them.

Cassandra shrugged. "Renata said this would restore me more quickly than anything else. I don't mind."

Allart took a piece of it himself. Barak, who had been sipping a cup of wine, finished it and came toward them.

"Are you recovered, kinswoman? The work is indeed fatiguing when you are new to it, and there are no suitable restoratives here." He laughed aloud. "Perhaps you should have a spoonful or so of kireseth honey; it is the best of all restoratives after long weariness, and you especially should—" Abruptly he coughed and turned away, pretending he had choked on the last swallow in his glass, but they all heard the words in his mind as if he had spoken them aloud. *You especially should take such restoratives, since you are so new-made a bride and have more need of them.* . . . but before the words had escaped his tongue, Barak had recalled what indeed they all knew, having been in close telepathic rapport with Allart and Cassandra: the real state of affairs between them.

The only amend he could make for the tactless jest was to turn away, pretend the words unthought as they had been unspoken. There was a brief silence in the matrix chamber and then they all began talking very loudly and all at once about something else. Coryn took up the metal tool and checked a couple of the batteries himself. Mira rubbed her cold hands and said she was ready for a hot bath and a massage.

Renata put an arm around Cassandra's waist.

"You, too, sweetheart. You are cold and cramped. Go

down now; send for some proper breakfast and have a hot
bath. I will send my own bath-woman; she is extra skilled
at massage, and can loosen those tight muscles and nerves
of yours so you can sleep. Don't feel guilty. All of us over-
worked in our first season here. No one likes to admit
weakness, and we have all done it. When you have had
some hot food and a bath and massage, then lie down and
sleep. Have her put hot bricks at your feet and cover you
well."

Cassandra demurred. "I do not like to deprive you of
her services."

"*Chiya,* I do not let myself get into such a state anymore.
Go now. Tell Lucetta I said to tend you as she does me
when I am out of the circle. Do as you are told, cousin.
This is my business, to know what you need even when
you do not know it yourself," she said. Allart thought she
sounded motherly, as if she were a generation Cassandra's
senior, instead of a girl Cassandra's own age or less.

"I will go down, too," Mira said. Coryn drew Arielle's
hand through his arm and they left together. Allart was
about to follow when Renata laid a feather-light hand on
his arm.

"Allart, if you are not too weary, I would like a word
with you."

Allart had been thinking of his luxurious room on a
lower floor, and a cool bath, but he was not really weary;
he said so, and Renata nodded.

"If this is the training of the Nevarsin brethren, perhaps
we should acquire it for our circles. You are as steady and
unwearied as Barak, and he has been part of our circles
almost as long as I have been alive. You should teach us
something of your secrets! Or do the brethren pledge you
to secrecy?"

Allart shook his head. "It is only a discipline of
breathing."

"Come. Shall we walk outdoors in the sunshine?"

Together they went down to the ground level, stepped
through the force-field which protected the Tower circle
against intrusion when they were working, and went into
the growing brilliance of the morning. Allart walked silently
beside Renata. He was not unduly tired, but he was tense
and sleepless, his nerves jangling. As always when he re-

laxed his barriers even a little, his *laran* wove conflicting futures around him, diverging but just as perceptible as the green lawns sloping away toward the lake and the cloudy shores of Hali.

Silent, they walked side by side along the shore. Liriel, the violet moon, just past full, was setting dimly over the lake. Green Idriel, the palest of crescents, hung high and pale over the faraway rim of mountains.

Allart knew—he had known when first he set eyes on Renata—that this was the other of the two women he had seen again and again, and again, in the diverging futures of his life. From that first day in the Tower he had been on guard against her, speaking no more than the barest courtesies, avoiding her as much as it was possible to avoid anyone in the close quarters of the Tower. He had come to respect her competence as a monitor, to value her quick laughter and good humor, and this morning, watching her ministering to Cassandra's collapse, he had been touched by her kindness. But until this moment they had never exchanged a single word outside the line of their duties in the circle.

Now hampered by fatigue he saw Renata's face, not as it was—gentle, impersonal, withdrawn, the look of a Tower-trained monitor at work, speaking of professional things—but as it might be in any of the diverging, fanning futures which *might* come to pass. Although he had barricaded himself against it, never allowing such thoughts freedom, he had seen her warmed by love, known the tenderness she could summon, had possessed her as if in a dream. This, overlaid upon the real state of affairs between them, confused and embarrassed him, as if he must face a woman about whom he had dreamed erotically, and conceal it from her. No. No woman had any part in his life except Cassandra, and he had firmly resolved how limited *that* part should be. He steeled himself against any lowering of these barriers and looked on Renata with the cold, impersonal gaze, almost hostile, of the Nevarsin monk.

They walked together, hearing the whispering sound of the soft cloud-waves. Allart had grown up on the shores of Hali, and had heard it all his life, but now he seemed to hear it freshly through Renata's ears.

"I never tire of this sound. It is so like, and so unlike, water. I suppose no one could swim in this lake?"

"No, you would sink. Slowly, it is true, but you would sink; it will not hold you up. But you can breathe it, you know, so it does not matter if you sink. Many times in my boyhood I have walked along the lake-bottom to watch the strange things within it."

"You can breathe it? And you will not drown?"

"No, no, it is not water at all—I do not know what it is. If you breathe it too long, you will become faint, and feel too weary even to take breaths, and there is some danger that you will become unconscious and die without remembering to breathe. But for a little while it is exhilarating. And there are strange creatures. I do not know whether to call them fish or bird, nor could I say whether they swim in the cloud or fly through it, but they are very beautiful. They used to say that to breathe the cloud of the lake conferred long life and that was why we Hasturs are long-lived. They say, too, that when Hastur, the son of the Lord of Light, fell to the shores at Hali, he gave immortality to those who dwelt there, and that we Hasturs lost that gift because of our sinful lives. But these things are all fairy tales."

"You think so being a *cristoforo*?"

"I think so being a man of reason," Allart said, smiling. "I cannot conceive of a god who would meddle with the laws of the world he created."

"Yet the Hasturs are long-lived, in truth."

"I was told at Nevarsin that all those of the blood of Hastur bear *chieri* blood; and the *chieri* are all but immortal."

Renata sighed. "I have heard, too, that they are *emmasca,* neither man nor woman, and thus free of the perils of being either. I think I envy them that."

It struck Allart that Renata gave tirelessly of her own strength; yet there was none to care if she herself was over-wearied.

"Go and rest, kinswoman. Whatever you have to say to me, it cannot be so urgent that it cannot wait till you have had the food and rest to which you were so quick to send my dear lady."

"But I would rather say it while Cassandra is sleeping. I must say it to one of you, and though I know you will think it an intrusion, you are older than Cassandra and better able to endure what I must say. Well, enough of apology and preamble. . . . You should not have come here with Cassandra new-made a bride and your marriage still unconsummated."

Allart opened his mouth to speak, but she gestured him to silence. "I warned you, remember, that you would think it an intrusion of your privacy and hers. I have been in the Tower since I was fourteen; I know the courtesies of such things. But also I am monitor here, and responsible for the well-being of everyone in the Tower. Anything which interferes—no, hear me out, Allart—anything which impairs your functioning, disrupts us all. I knew before you had been here three days that your bride was virgin still, but I did not intrude, not then. I thought perhaps you had been married for political reasons and did not like one another. But now, after half a year, it is obvious that you are madly in love. The tension between you is disrupting us all, and making Cassandra ill. She is so tense all the time that she cannot even properly monitor the state of her own nerves and body, which she should be able to do by now. I can do it for her, a little, when you are in the circle, but I cannot do it all the time and I ought not to do for her what she should learn to do for herself. Now, I am sure you had some good reason for coming here in this state, but whatever your reasons, you knew too little of how a Tower circle must function. You can endure this; you have had the Nevarsin training and you can function even when you are unhappy. Cassandra cannot. It is as simple as that."

Allart said defensively, "I did not think Cassandra was so unhappy."

Renata looked at him and shook her head. "If you do not know, it is only that you have not allowed yourself to know. The wisest thing would be to take her away until things are settled between you; then, if you wish, you can return. We are always in need of trained workers, and your training at Nevarsin is very valuable. As for Cassandra, I think she has the talent to become a monitor, even a technician if the work interests her. But not now. This is a time for the two of you to be alone, not disrupting us all with your unsolaced needs."

Allart listened, cold with dismay. His own life had been lived so long under iron discipline that it had never occurred to him that his own needs, or Cassandra's unhappiness, could interfere to a hair's weight with the circle. But of course he should have known.

"Take her away, Allart. Tonight would not be too soon."

Allart said through mounting misery, "I would give all I possess, I think, if I were free to do that. But Cassandra and I have pledged one another—"

He turned away, but the thoughts were clear in his mind, and Renata looked at him in dismay.

"Cousin, what could prompt you to a vow so rash? I do not speak only of your duty to kinsmen and clan."

"No," said Allart. "Don't speak of that, Renata, not even in friendship. I have heard all too much of that and I need no one to remind me. But you know what kind of *laran* I have and what a curse it has been to me. I would not perpetuate it in sons and grandsons. This breeding program among those families with *laran,* which prompts you to speak of duty to caste and kin, it is wrong, it is evil. I will not pass it on!" He spoke vehemently, trying to blot out the sight of Renata's face, not as it was, grave with kindly concern, but as it might be, all pity wakened, tenderness and passion.

"A curse indeed, Allart! I, too, have many fears and doubts about the breeding program. I do not think any woman in the Domains is ever free of them. Yet, Cassandra's unhappiness, and yours, is needless."

"There is more, and worse," Allart said desperately. "At the end of every road I can foresee, it seems, Cassandra lies dead in bearing my child. Even if I could compromise my conscience to father a child who might bear this curse, I could not bring that fate on her. So we have pledged to live apart."

"Cassandra is very young and a virgin," Renata said, "and may be excused for knowing no better than that, though it seems wicked to me to keep a woman in ignorance of anything which may so closely affect her life. But surely the choice you have made is too extreme, since it is apparent even to outsiders that you love each other. You can hardly be unaware that there are ways—" She turned her face away, embarrassed, as she spoke. Such things were not spoken of much even between husband and wife. Allart was embarrassed, too.

She cannot be older than Cassandra! In the name of all

*the gods, how does a young woman, gently reared, of good
family and still unmarried, come to know of such things?*

The thought was very clear in his mind, and Renata could
not help picking it up. She said dryly, "You have been a
monk, cousin, and for that reason alone I am willing to
admit that perhaps you really do not know the answer to
that question. Perhaps you still believe that it is men alone
who have such needs, and that women are immune to them.
I do not want to scandalize you, Allart, but women in the
Tower need not, and cannot, live by the foolish laws and
customs of this time, which pretend that women are no
more than toys to serve men's desires, with none of their
own, save to breed sons for their clans. I am no virgin,
Allart. Any one of us—man or woman—must learn, before
we have been long in the circle, to face our own needs and
desires, or we cannot put all our strength into the work we
do. Or, if we try, such things happen as befell this morning—or worse, much worse."

Allart looked away from her, embarrassed. His first, almost automatic thought was pure reaction to his childhood
teachings. *The men of the Domains know this, and still let
their women come here?*

Renata shrugged, answering the unspoken question.

"It is the price they pay for the work we do—that we
women shall to some extent be freed, for our term here, of
the laws which emphasize inheritance and breeding. I
think most of them choose not to inquire too closely. Also,
it is not safe for a woman working in the circles to interrupt
her term with pregnancy." She added after a moment, "If
you wish, Mira can instruct Cassandra—or I myself. Perhaps she would take it more easily from a girl her own
age."

*If anyone had told me, while I dwelt at Nevarsin, that
there was any woman alive with whom I could speak openly
of such things, and that woman neither wife nor kinswoman,
I would never have believed it. I had never thought there
could be simple honesty between man and woman, this way.*

"That would solve our worst fears, indeed, while we
dwelt in the Tower. Perhaps we can have—this much. Indeed, we spoke of this, a little." Cassandra's words echoed
in his mind as if they had been spoken only moments ago,
not half a season gone by:

"I can bear it, as things are now, Allart, but I do not know if I could hold to such a resolve. I love you, Allart. I cannot trust myself. Sooner or later I would want your child, and it is easier this way, without the possibility and the temptation. . . ."

Hearing the echo in his mind, Renata said indignantly, "Easier for *her,* perhaps—" and stopped herself. "Forgive me, I have no right. Cassandra, too, is entitled to her own needs and desires, not to what you or I think she *ought* to feel. When a girl has been taught, since she was old enough to understand the words, that a woman's reason for living is to bear children to her husband's caste and clan, it is not easy to change that, or to find some other purpose for living." She fell silent, and Allart thought her voice sounded too bitter for her youth. He wondered how old she was, and they were so close in rapport that Renata answered the unspoken question.

"I am only a month or two older than Cassandra. I am not yet free of the desire to bear a child someday, but I had fears very like yours about this breeding program. Of course it is only men who are allowed to voice such fears and qualms; women are not supposed to think of such things. I sometimes feel that women in the Domains are not supposed to think at all! But my father was indulgent with me, and I won the promise that I should not marry till I was twenty, and that I might have training in a Tower, and I have learned much. For instance, Allart, if you and Cassandra chose to have a child, and she became pregnant, then with the aid of a monitor she could probe the unborn deeply, into the very germ plasm. If it should bear the kind of *laran* you fear, or any lethal recessive which could kill Cassandra in bearing it, she need not bring it to birth."

Allart said violently, "It is evil enough that we Hasturs meddle with the stuff of life of breeding *riyachiyas* and such abominations by genetic manipulation of our seed! But to do that with my own sons and daughters? Or to destroy, willingly, a life I myself have given? The thought sickens me!"

"I am not the keeper of your conscience, or of Cassandra's," Renata said. "This is only one choice; there must be others more to your liking. Yet I think it a lesser evil. I know that someday I shall be forced to marry, and if I am pledged to bear children to my caste, I will find myself caught between two choices which seem to me almost equally cruel: to bear, perhaps, monsters of *laran* to my caste, or to destroy them unborn in my womb." Allart saw her shudder.

"It was for this I became a monitor, that I might not contribute, unknowing, to this breeding program which has brought these monstrosities into our race. Now, *knowing* what I must do has made it the less endurable; I am not a god, to determine who will live and who will die. Perhaps you and Cassandra have done right after all, to give no life you must take away again."

"And while we await these choices," Allart said bitterly, "we charge batteries so that idle folk may play with air-cars, and light their homes without dirtying their hands on resin and pitch, and mine metals to spare others the labor of bringing them from the ground, and we create weapons ever more fearful, to destroy lives over which we have no shadow of right."

Renata went very white. "No! Now, *that* I had not heard. Allart, is this your foresight, is war to break out again?"

"I saw, and spoke unthinking," Allart said, staring at her in dread. The sounds and sights of war were already around him, blurring her presence, and he thought, *Perhaps I will be killed in battle, be spared further wrestling with destiny or conscience!*

"It is your war and none of mine," she said. "My father has no quarrel with Serrais and no allegiance to Hastur; if the war breaks out anew, he will send for me, demanding again that I return home to marry. Ah, merciful Avarra, I am filled with good advice as to how you and your lady shall conduct your marriage and I have neither courage nor wisdom to face my own! Would that I had your foresight, Allart, to know which of many evil choices would bring the least of wrong."

"Would that I could tell you," he said, taking her hands for a moment. With the gesture Allart's *laran* clearly showed Renata and himself riding away northward together . . . where? For what purpose? The image faded and was gone, to be replaced by a whirl of images: The swooping flight of a great bird—or was it truly a bird? A child's face terrified, frozen in the glare of lightnings. A rain of *clingfire* falling, a great tower breaking, crumbling, smashing into rubble. Renata's face all ablaze with tenderness, her body under his own. . . . Dazed with the swirling pictures, he struggled to shut away the crowding futures.

"Perhaps *this* is the answer!" Renata said with sudden violence. "To breed monsters and let them loose on our people, make weapons ever more fearful, wipe out our accursed race and let the gods make another, a people without this dreadful, monstrous curse of *laran!*"

In the aftermath of her outburst it was so still that Allart could hear somewhere the morning sounds of wakening birds chirping, the soft wet sounds of the cloud-waves along the shores of Hali. Renata drew a long, shuddering breath. But when she spoke again she was calm, the disciplined monitor.

"But this is afar from what it was laid on me to say to you. For the sake of our work, you and Cassandra must not again work in the same matrix circle until all is well with you; till you have given and received your love and come to terms with it, or until you have decided for all time that it shall never be so, and you can be friends without indecision or desire. For the time, perhaps, you can be placed in different circles for working; after all, there are eighteen of us here, and you can work separately. But if you do not go away together, one of you must go. Even in separate circles, there is too much tension between you for you to dwell together under this roof. I think you should be the one to go. You have had, at Nevarsin, some teaching to master your *laran,* and Cassandra has not. But it is for you to say, Allart. In law, your marriage has made you Cassandra's master, and if you wish to exercise the right, the keeper of her will and conscience, too."

He ignored the irony. "If you think it would profit my lady to remain," he said, "then she shall stay and I will go." Bleakness came over him. He had found happiness at Nevarsin and been driven forth, never to return. Now he had found useful work here, the full possession of his *laran* gift, and was he to go forth from here, too?

Is there no place for me on the face of this world? Must I forever be driven, homeless, by the winds of circumstance? Then he was wryly amused at himself. He complained because his *laran* showed him too many futures, now he was dismayed because he saw none. Renata, too, was driven by choices not under her own control.

"You have worked all the night, cousin," he said, "and then you have stayed here and wrestled with my troubles and my wife's, and taken no thought for your own weariness."

Her smile glinted deep in her eyes, though it did not reach her mouth. "Oh, it has eased me to think of troubles other than my own; didn't you know that? The burdens of others are light to the shoulders. But I will go and sleep. And you?"

Allart shook his head. "I am not sleepy. I think perhaps I will go and walk in the lake for a little while, look at the strange fish or birds or whatever they may be and try to decide again what they are. Did our forefathers breed them, I wonder, with their passion for breeding strange things? Perhaps I, too, will find peace in regarding something afar from my own troubles. Bless you, kinswoman, for your kindness."

"Why? I solved nothing. I have given you more worries, that is all," she said. "But I will go and sleep, and perhaps dream an answer to all our troubles. Is there such a *laran* as that, I wonder?"

"Probably," Allart said, "but no doubt it has been given to someone who knows not how to use it for his own good; that is how these things happen in this world. Otherwise we might somehow find our way out of these worries and be like the game-pawn which manages to wriggle off the board without being captured. Go and sleep, Renata. All gods forbid you should bear the burden of our fears and worries, even in dreams."

Chapter 12

That evening, when Allart joined the members of his circle in the lower hall at Hali, he found them all talking excitedly, the six who had worked with him that morning, and all the others. Across the room he caught Renata's eyes; she was pale with dread. He asked Barak, who stood at the edge of the circle, "What is it, what's happened?"

"The war is upon us again. The Ridenow have launched an attack with bowmen and *clingfire* arrows, and Castle Hastur, in the Kilghard Hills, is under siege by air-cars and incendiaries. Evey able-bodied man of Hastur and Aillard allegiance is out to combat the fire raging in the forests, or to defend the castle. We had word from the relays at Neskaya. Arielle was in the relay nets and heard—"

"Gods above," Allart said, and Cassandra came and stood looking up at him, troubled.

"Will the lord Damon-Rafael send for you, my husband? Must you go to the war?"

"I do not know," he said. "I was long enough in the monastery that my brother may think me too little skilled in campaign and strategy, and wish another of his paxmen to command the men." He fell silent, thinking, *If one of us must go, perhaps it is better if I go to war. If I do not come back, then she will be freed, and we will be out of this hopeless impasse.* The woman was looking up at him, her eyes filled with tears, but he kept his face cold, impassive, the disciplined and impersonal glance of the monk. He said,

"Why are you not resting, my lady? Renata said you would be ill. Should you not keep your bed?"

"I heard the talk of war and I was frightened," she said, seeking for his hand, but he gently drew it away, turning to Coryn.

The Keeper said, "I would think you better employed here, Allart. You have the strength that makes our work easier, and since the war has broken out again, we are sure to be asked to make *clingfire* for weapons. And since we are to lose Renata—"

"Are we to lose Renata?"

Coryn nodded. "She is a neutral in this war; her father has already sent word on the relays that she must be sent home under a safe-conduct. He wishes her out of the combat area at once. I am always sorry to lose a good monitor," Coryn added, "but I believe, with training, Cassandra will be equally skillful. Monitoring is not difficult, but Arielle is better as a technician. Do you think, Renata, that you will have time to instruct Cassandra in the techniques of monitoring before you go?"

"I will try," Renata said, coming toward them, "and I will stay as long as I can. I do not want to leave the Tower—" and she looked up at Allart helplessly. He remembered what she had told him only that morning.

"I shall be sorry to see you go, kinswoman," he said, taking her hands gently in his own.

"I would rather stay here with you," she said. "Would that I were a man like you and free to choose."

"Ah, Renata," he said, "men are not free either, not free to refuse war and dangers. I who am a Hastur lord can be sent unwilling into battle as if I were the least of my brother's vassals."

They stood for a moment, hands clasped, unaware of Cassandra's eyes on them, nor did either of them see her leave the hall. Then Coryn came up to them.

"How we shall need you, Renata! Lord Damon-Rafael has sent to us already for a new supply of *clingfire* and I have devised a new weapon that I am eager to experiment with." He took a careless seat in the window, as merrily as if he were devising a new sport or game. "A homing device set to a trap-matrix to kill only a particular enemy, so that if we aim it—for instance—at Lord Ridenow, it will do no good for his paxmen to throw himself in front of his lord's body. Of course we would have to get his thought-pattern, resonances from some captured article of his clothing, perhaps, or better yet, jewelry he has worn next to his body. Or by probing some captured man of his. Such a weapon will harm no one else, for nothing but the particular pattern of *his* mind will detonate it; it will fly to *him,* and him *only,* and kill him."

Renata shuddered, and Allart absentmindedly stroked her hand.

"*Clingfire* is too hard to make." Arielle said. "I wish they could find some better weapon. First we must mine the red stuff from the ground, then separate it atom by atom by distilling at high heat, and that is dangerous. Last time I worked with it, one of the glass vessels exploded; fortunately I was wearing protective clothing, but even so—" She thrust out her hand, showing a wicked scar, round, cicatrized, a deep depression in the flesh. "Only a fragment, only a grain, but it burned to the bone and had to be cut away."

Coryn lifted the girl's hand to his lips and kissed it. "You bear an honorable scar of war, *preciosa*. Not many women do. I have devised vessels which will not break at whatever heat; we have all put a binding spell on them so that they cannot shatter no matter what happens. Even if they should crack or break, the binding spell will hold them so that they stay in their shape and will not fly and shatter and injure the bystanders."

"How did you do that?" Mira asked.

"It was easy," Coryn said. "You set their pattern with a matrix so they can take no other shape. They can crack, and their contents can leak out, but they cannot fly asunder. If they are smashed the pieces will sooner or later settle gently down—we cannot put gravity wholly in abeyance— but they will not fly with enough strength to cut anyone. But to work with a ninth-level matrix, as we must do when refining *clingfire,* we need a circle of nine, and a technician, or better yet, another Keeper, to hold the binding spell on the vessels. I wonder," Coryn added, gazing at Allart, "would you make a Keeper, given training?"

"I have no such ambitions, kinsman."

"Yet it would keep you away from the war," Coryn said frankly, "and if you feel guilt at that, remember you will be better employed here, and not without risk. None of us is free of scars. Look," he added, holding up his hands, showing a deep, long-healed burn. "I took a backflow once, when a technician faltered. The matrix was like a live coal. I thought it would burn to the bones of my hands like *clingfire.* As for suffering—well, if we are to be working circles of nine, night and day, for the making of weapons— well, we will suffer, and our women with us, if we must spend so much time in the circles."

Arielle colored as the men standing around began to chuckle softly; they all knew what Coryn meant: the major side effect of matrix work, for men, was a long period of impotence. Seeing Allart's stiff smile, Coryn chuckled again.

"Perhaps we should all be monks, and trained to endure *that,* with cold and hunger," he said, laughing. "Allart, tell me. I have heard that on your way from Nevarsin you were attacked by a *clingfire* device which exploded—but you managed to wrest it loose so that it exploded at a distance. Tell me about that."

Allart told what he could remember of the episode, and Coryn nodded gravely. "I had thought of such a missile, making it superfragile, to be filled either with *clingfire* or with ordinary incendiaries. I have one which will set an entire forest ablaze, so that they must withdraw fighting men to fight the fire. And I have a weapon which is like those fancy drops our artisans make, which can be struck with hammers or trodden on by beasts, and will not break, but the merest touch against the long glass tail and they shatter into a thousand fragments. This one cannot be prematurely exploded as you did with the one sent against your father, because nothing, *nothing,* will explode it except the detonating thoughts of the one who sent it. I am not sorry for the end of the truce. We must have a chance to try these weapons somewhere!"

"Would they might stay forever untried!" Allart said with a shudder.

"Ah, there speaks the monk," Barak said. "A few years will cure you of such treasonous nonsense, my lad. Those Ridenow usurpers who would crowd their way into our

Domain are many and fertile, some of the fathers with six
or seven sons, all land-hungry and quarrelsome. Of *my* father's seven sons, two died at birth and another when *laran*
came on him at adolescence. Yet it seems to me almost
worse to have many sons who survive to manhood, so that
an estate must be cut into slivers to support them all; or
they must range outward, as those Ridenow have done,
seeking lands enough for them to rule, and conquer."

Coryn smiled without even a trace of mirth. "True," he
said. "One son is needful, so needful they will do anything
to insure that one survives; but if two should live, it is too
many. I was the younger son, and my elder brother is well
pleased that I should dwell here as Keeper, powerless in
the great events of our time. *Your* brother is more loving,
Allart—at least he has given you in marriage!"

"Yes," Allart said, "but I have sworn to uphold his claim
to the throne, should anything befall King Regis—may his
reign be long!"

"Already his reign has been overlong," said a Keeper
from one of the other circles. "But I am not looking forward with any pleasure to what will come when your
brother and Prince Felix begin to struggle for the throne.
War with Ridenow is evil enough, but a war of brethren
within the Hastur Domain would be far worse."

"Prince Felix is *emmasca,* I have heard," Barak said. "I
do not think he will fight to keep his crown—eggs can't
fight stones!'

"Well, he is safe enough while the old king lives," Coryn
said. "But after that it is only a matter of time till he is
challenged and exposed. Whom, I wonder, did they bribe,
to let him be named as heir in the first place? But perhaps
you were fortunate, Allart, for your brother needed your
support badly enough to find you a wife, and a lovely and
winning lady she is indeed."

"I thought I had seen her here but a moment ago," said
the other Keeper, "but now she is gone."

Allart looked around, suddenly filled with a nameless
foreboding. A group of the younger women of the Tower
were dancing at one end of the long room; he had thought
her among them. Again he saw her lying dead in his
arms . . . but he dismissed the picture as an illusion born
of fear and his mental disquiet.

"Perhaps she has gone upstairs to her room again. Renata bade her keep her bed, for she was not well, and I was surprised she had come down at all tonight."

"But she is not in her room," Renata said, coming to them, picking up his thought, her face white. "Where can she have gone, Allart? I went to ask if she wished me to instruct her as a monitor, and she is not within the Tower at all."

"Merciful Avarra!" Suddenly the diverging futures crashed in upon him again and Allart knew where Cassandra had gone. Without a word of leavetaking he turned away from the men and hurried out, going through halls and corridors, stepping through the force-field and out of the Tower.

The sun, a great crimson ball, hung like fire on the distant hills, coating the lake with flame.

She saw me with Renata. I would not touch her hand, though she was weeping; yet I kissed Renata before her eyes. Only in friendship, as I might have comforted a sister, only because I could touch Renata without that agony of love and guilt. But Cassandra saw and did not understand. . . .

He shouted Cassandra's name, but there was no reply, only the soft splashing sound of the cloud-waters. He flung off his outer garment and began to run. At the very edge of the sand he saw two small high-heeled sandals, dyed blue, not kicked this way and that but lined up with meticulous care, as if she had knelt here, delaying. Allart kicked off his boots and ran into the lake.

The strange cloud-waters enfolded him, dim, strange, and the thick, foggy sensation surrounded him. He breathed it in, feeling the curious exhilaration it gave at first. He could see quite clearly, as if through a thin morning mist. Brilliant creatures—fish or bird?— glided past him, their shimmering orange and green colors like nothing he had ever seen, except the lights behind his eyes when he had been given a dose of *kirian,* the telepathic drug which opened the brain. . . . Allart felt his feet falling lightly on the weedy bottom of the lake as he began to run along the lake bed.

Something had passed this way, yes. The fish-birds were gathering, drifting in the cloud-currents. Allart felt his running feet slowing. The heavy gas of the cloud was beginning to oppress him now. He sent out a despairing cry: *"Cassandra!"*

The cloud of the lake would not carry sound; it was like being at the bottom of a very silent well, silence engulfing and surrounding him. Even at Nevarsin he had never known such silence. The fish-birds drifted past him, noiseless, curious, their luminescent colors stirring reflections in his brain. He was dizzy, light-headed. He forced himself to breathe, remembering that in the strange gaseous cloud of the lake, there was none of that element which triggered the breath reflex in the brain. He must breathe by effort and will; his brain would not keep his body breathing automatically.

"Cassandra!"

A faint, distant flicker, almost pettish. . . . *"Go away. . . ."* and it was gone again.

Breathe! Allart was beginning to tire; here the weeds were deeper, thicker, and he had to force his way through him. *Breathe! In and out, remember to breathe. . . .* He felt a long slimy trail of weed lock around his ankle, had to stoop and disengage it. *Breathe!* He forced himself to struggle on, even as the brilliantly colored fish-birds began to cluster around him, their colors blurring before his eyes. His *laran* rushed upon him, as always when he was troubled or fatigued, and he saw himself sinking down and down into the gas and ooze, lying there quiet and content, suffocating in happy peace because he had forgotten how to breathe. . . . *Breathe!* Allart struggled to draw in another damp breath of the gas, reminding himself that it would support life indefinitely; the only danger was forgetting to breathe it in. Had Cassandra already reached this point? Was she lying, comfortably dying—a painless ecstatic death—here at the bottom of the lake?

She wanted to die, and I am guilty. . . . Breathe! Don't think of anything now, just remember to breathe. . . .

He saw himself carrying Cassandra from the lake, still, lifeless, her long hair lying black and dripping across his arm . . . saw himself bending over her, lying in the swaying grasses in the lake bed, taking her in his arms, sinking down beside her . . . no more *laran*, no trouble, no more fear, the family curse ended forever for them both.

The fish-birds moved, agitated, around him. Before his feet, he saw a flicker of pale blue, no color ever to be seen at the bottom of the lake. Was it the long sleeve of Cassandra's gown? *Breathe*. . . . Allart bent over her. She was lying there, on her side, her eyes open and still, a faint joyous smile on her lips, but she was too far gone to see Allart. His heart clutching, he bent over her, lifted her lightly into his arms. She was unconscious, faint, her body lolling against him in the drifting weeds. *Breathe! Breathe into her mouth; it is the gas in our expelled breath which triggers breathing.* . . . Allart tightened his arms about her and laid his lips against hers, forcing his breath into her lungs. As if in reflex, she breathed, a long deep breath, and was still again.

Allart lifted her and began to carry her back along the lake bed, in the dim cloudy light reddened now by the setting sun, and terror suddenly struck him. *If it grows dark, if the sun sets, I will never find my way to the shore in the darkness. We will die here together.* Again he bent over her, forcing his expelled breath into her mouth; again he felt her breathe. But the automatic breathing-mechanism was gone in Cassandra, and he did not know how long she could survive without it, even with the oxygen of the reflex breaths he forced her to take, every two or three steps, by breathing into her mouth. And he had to hurry, before the light was gone. He struggled along in the growing darkness, holding her in his arms, but he had to stop every two or three breaths, to breathe life into her again. Her heart was beating. If she would only breathe . . . if he could only rouse her enough to remember to breathe. . . .

The last few steps were nightmare. Cassandra was a slight woman, but Allart was not a big man, either. As the cloud-fog grew shallower, he finally abandoned any attempt to carry her and dragged her along, stooping and holding her under the shoulders, every two or three steps stopping to force his breath into her lungs. At last his head broke out into air and he gasped air convulsively, hearing it sob in and out of his lungs. Then, with a final effort, he grabbed Cassandra up and held her with her head out of the cloudy gas, stumbling drunkenly toward the shore, collapsing beside her on the grass. He lay beside her, breathing into her mouth, pressing her ribs, until after several breaths she shuddered and gasped and let out a strange wailing cry, not unlike the cry of a newborn child as his lungs filled with the first breath. Then he heard her begin to breathe normally again. She was still unconscious, but after a little, in the gathering darkness, he felt her thoughts touch his. Then she whispered, still faintly, only a breath, "Allart? Is it you?"

"I am here, my beloved."

"I am so cold."

Allart caught up the garment he had flung away, wrapped it tightly around her. He held her, close-folded, murmuring hopeless endearments.

"Preciosa . . . bredhiva . . . my treasure, my cherished, why . . . how . . . I thought I had lost you forever. Why did you want to leave me?"

"Leave you? No," she whispered. "But it was so peaceful in the lake, and all I wanted was to stay there forever in the silence, and not to fear anymore, or cry anymore. I thought I could hear you calling me, but I was so weary. . . . I only lay down to rest a little, and I was so tired, I could not rise. I could not seem to breathe, and I was afraid . . . and then you came . . . but I knew you did not love me."

"Not love you? Not want you? Cassandra—" Allart found that he could not speak. He pulled her close to him, kissed her on the cold lips.

Moments later he took her up again in his arms and carried her into the Tower, through the lower hall. The other members of the matrix circles, assembled there, stared at him with shock and amazement, but there was something in Allart's eyes that kept them from speaking or approaching the couple. He felt Renata watching them, felt the curiosity and horror from them all. Briefly, without thinking about it, he saw himself as he must appear in their eyes, soaked and bedraggled, bootless, Cassandra's drenched garments soaking the cloak he had wrapped around her, her long dark hair streaming dampness and entangled weeds. Before the grim concentration in his face they drew aside as he went through the hall and up the long stairs; not to the room where she had slept, alone, since they had come here, but along a wide hallway on the lower floors of the Tower, to his own room.

He shut and locked the door behind him and knelt beside her, with shaking hands removing the soaked clothing, wrapping her warmly in his own blankets. She was still as death, pale and unmoving against the pillow, her damp hair hanging lifelessly down.

"No," she whispered. "You are to leave the Tower and you did not even tell me. I felt it would be better to die than to stay here alone, with all the others mocking me, knowing I am wed and no wife, that you did not love me or want me."

"Not love you?" Allart whispered again. "I love you as my blessed forefather loved Robardin's daughter on the shores of Hali centuries ago. Not want you, Cassandra?" He held her to him, covering her with kisses, and he felt that his kisses were breathing life into her as the breath of his lungs had given her life at the depths of the lake. He was almost beyond thought, beyond remembering the pledge they had made to one another, but a final, despairing thought crossed his mind before he drew the blankets aside.

I can never let her go, not now. Merciful Avarra, have pity on us!

Chapter 13

Allart sat at Cassandra's side, looking into her sleeping face. Physically she was not much the worse for her experience in the lake. Even now he was not certain whether it had been a genuine attempt at suicide, or only an impulse born of deep unhappiness, compounded by illness and exhaustion. But in the days since then he had hardly left her side. He had come so close to losing her!

The others in the Tower had left them much to themselves. As they had known the state of affairs between himself and Cassandra, he sensed they knew the change that had come, but it did not seem to matter.

Now, he knew, as soon as Cassandra was able to leave her bed, some decision must be made. Should he leave the Tower and take her with him, send her to a place of safety (for if they were making weapons here, the Tower would be under attack), or should he go away himself and leave her here for the *laran* training he knew she must have?

Yet again and again, his own *laran* gave him visions of riding away to the north, Renata at his side. Cassandra's absence from these visions frightened him. What was to become of her?

He saw strange banners overhead, war, the clashing of swords, the explosion of strange weapons, fire, death. *Maybe that would be best for us both. . . .*

He found it impossible to keep to the disciplined calm he had learned at Nevarsin. Cassandra was ever-present in his mind, his thoughts and emotions as hypersensitive to her as his body.

He had broken the pledge they had made to one another.

After seven years in Nevarsin, I am still weak, still driven by the senses and not by the mind. I took her without thought, as if she had been one of old Dom Marius's pleasure girls.

He heard the soft knock at the door, but even before it registered on his ears, he knew—*it has come.* He stooped and kissed the sleeping woman, with an aching sense of farewell, then went to the door, opening it in a split second after the knock, so that Arielle blinked in surprise.

"Allart," she whispered. "Your brother, the lord Elhalyn, is below in the Stranger's Hall and asks to speak with you. I will remain with your wife."

Allart went down to the Stranger's Hall, the only room in the Tower into which outsiders were permitted to come. Damon-Rafael was there, his paxman noiseless and unmoving at his back.

"You lend us grace, brother. How may I serve you?"

"I suppose you have heard of the truce's end?"

"Then you have come to summon me to arms?"

Damon-Rafael said with a contemptuous laugh, "Do you suppose I should come myself for that? Anyhow, you would serve me better here; I have little faith, after all those years of monkish seclusion, in your skill at arms or any of the manly arts. No, brother, I have another mission for you, if you will accept it."

It took all of Allart's hard-won discipline to remain silent at the taunt, remarking quietly that he was at the service of his brother and his overlord.

"You have dwelled beyond the Kadarin; have you ever traveled to the Aldaran lands, near Caer Donn?"

"Never; only to Ardais and Nevarsin."

"Still, you must know that clan grows over-powerful. They hold Castle Aldaran at Caer Donn, as well as Sain Scarp and Scathfell; and they make alliances with all the others, with Ardais and Darriel and Storn. They are of Hastur kin, but Lord Aldaran came not to my accession as lord of Elhalyn, nor has he come to midsummer festival in Thendara for many years. Now, with this war breaking forth again, he is like a great hawk in his mountain aerie, ready to swoop down on the Lowlands whenever we are torn by strife and cannot resist him. If all those who owe allegiance to Aldaran were to strike us at once, Thendara itself could not hold. I can foresee a day when all the Domains from Dalereuth to the Kilghard Hills might lie under the lordship of Aldaran."

Allart said, "I knew not you had the foresight, brother."

Damon-Rafael moved his head with a quick, impatient gesture. "Foresight? That takes not much reading! *When kinsmen quarrel, enemies step in to widen the gap.* I am trying to negotiate another truce—it profits us nothing to set the land aflame—but with our cousins of Castle Hastur under seige, it is not easy. Our carrier-birds are flying night and day with secret dispatches. Also, I have *leroni* working in relays to send messages, but of course we can entrust nothing secret to them; what is known to one is known to all with *laran.* Now we come to the service I ask of you, brother."

"I listen," Allart said.

"It is long since a Hastur sent a kinsman on diplomatic mission to Aldaran. Yet we need such a tie. The Storns hold lands to the west of Caer Donn, close to Serrais across the hills, and they might find it useful to join with the Ridenow. Then all of the alliances within the Hellers could be drawn into this war. Do you think you might persuade Lord Aldaran to hold himself and his liegemen neutral in this war? I do not think he would join it on our side, but he might be willing to stay out of it entirely. You are Nevarsin-trained; you know the language of the Hellers well. Will you go for me, Allart, and try to keep Mikhail, Lord Aldaran, from joining in this war?"

Allart studied his brother's face. This seemed all too simple a mission. Did Damon-Rafael plot some treachery, or did he simply want Allart out of the way, so that the Hasturs of Elhalyn would not have loyalties divided between the brothers?

"I am at your command, Damon-Rafael, but I know little diplomacy of that sort."

"You will carry letters from me," Damon-Rafael said, "and you will write secret dispatches and send them to me by carrier-birds. You will write open dispatches, which spies on both sides will certainly see; but you will also write secret dispatches, and send them under a matrix-lock which none but I can open or read. Surely you can arrange a lock spelled shut so that if other eyes fall upon them they will be destroyed?"

"That is simple enough," Allart staid, and now he understood. There could not be many people to whom Damon-Rafael would willingly give the unique pattern of his own body and brain to set a matrix-lock; such a lock was a common tool for assassins, like the homing device Coryn had mentioned.

So I am one of the two or three persons living to whom Damon-Rafael will entrust that power over him; because I am sworn to defend him and his sons.

"I have arranged it so you will have a cover for your mission," Damon-Rafael said. "We have captured an envoy from Aldaran, fearing he had been sent to declare for the Ridenow. But the messenger, when my household *leronis* probed his sleep, told us he was on a personal mission for Lord Aldaran. I don't know all the details, but it has nothing to do with the war. His memory has been matrix-cleansed, and when he speaks with your Keeper, which he will do soon, I suppose, he will not know that he has ever captured or that he has been probed at all. I have arranged with our cousin Coryn that you will be, ostensibly, in charge of the truce flag which will escort Aldaran's messenger northward to the Kadarin. No one will notice if you simply continue and ride with them to Aldaran. Is that satisfactory to you?"

What choice have I? But I have known for days now that I must ride northward; only I did not know it was to Aldaran. And what has Renata to do with this? But loud he said to Damon-Rafael only, "It seems you have thought of everything."

"At sunset, my paxman will ride here to give you documents qualifying you as my ambassador, and instructions for sending messages, and access to carrier-birds." He rose, saying, "If you wish, I will pay a courtesy visit to your lady. It should be thought this is a family visit without any secret purpose."

"I thank you," Allart said, "but Cassandra is not well, and has kept her bed. I shall convey her your respectful compliments."

"Do so, by all means," Damon-Rafael said, "although, I suppose, since you have chosen to dwell with her in the

Tower, there is no reason to send congratulations. I do not imagine she is already carrying your child."

Not now, perhaps never. . . . Allart felt again the surge of desolation. He said aloud only, "No, we have not as yet any such good fortune." Damon-Rafael had no way of knowing the real state of affairs between himself and Cassandra, neither the pledge they had made one another nor the circumstances in which it had been broken. He was only twisting a knife at random. There was no need to waste anger on his brother's malice, but Allart was angry.

Still, he was bound to obey Damon-Rafael as overlord of Elhalyn, and Damon-Rafael was so far right. If the Northmen from the Hellers joined this war, there would be ravage and disaster.

I should be grateful, he thought, *that the gods have sent me such an honorable way to serve in this war. If I can persuade the Aldarans to neutrality I will indeed do well for all the vassals of Hastur.*

As Damon-Rafael rose to depart, Allart said, "Truly, I thank you, brother, for entrusting me with this mission," and his words were so heartfelt that Damon-Rafael stared at him with surprise. When he embraced Allart at parting there was a touch of warmth in the gesture. The two would never be friends, but they were nearer to it at this moment than they had been for years or Allart knew it sadly—were ever likely to be again.

Later that night he was summoned again to the Stranger's Hall, this time, he supposed, to meet with Damon-Rafael's envoy, bearing safe-conducts and dispatches.

Coryn met him outside the door.

"Allart, do you speak the languages of the Hellers?"

Allart nodded, wondering if Damon-Rafael had taken Coryn into his confidence and why.

"Mikhail of Aldaran has sent us a messenger," Coryn said, "but his command of our language is uncertain. Will you come and speak to him in his own tongue?"

"Gladly," Allart said, and thought, *Not Damon-Rafael's envoy, then, but Aldaran's messenger. Damon-Rafael said he had been mind-probed. I think that unjust, but, after all, this is war.*

When he came with Coryn into the Stranger's Hall, he

recognized the messenger's face. His *laran* had shown it to him again and again, though he had never known why: a dark-haired, dark-browed, youthful face, looking at him with tentative friendliness. Allart greeted him in the formal speech of the Hellers.

"You lend us grace, *siarbainn,*" he said, giving it the special inflection which made the archaic word for stranger mean, *friend-still-unknown.* "How may I serve you?"

The strange youth rose and bowed.

"I am Donal Delleray, foster-son and paxman to Mikhail, Lord Aldaran. I bring his words, not my own, to the *vai leroni* of Hali Tower."

"I am Allart Hastur of Elhalyn; this, my kinsman and cousin, Coryn, *tenerézu* of Hali. Speak freely."

He thought, *Surely this is more than coincidence, that Aldaran should send a messenger just as my brother devises his plan. Or did he devise his plan to fit the messenger's coming? The gods strengthen me—I see plots and counterplots everywhere!*

Donal said, "First, *vai domyn,* I am to bear you Lord Aldaran's apologies for sending me in his place. He would not hesitate to come as suppliant and petitioner, but he is old, and hardly fitted to bear the long road from Aldaran. Also, I can ride more quickly than he. Indeed, I had thought to be here within eight days' ride, but I seem to have lost a day on the road."

Damon-Rafael and his damned mind-probing, Allart thought, but he said nothing, waiting for Donal to make his request.

Coryn said, "It is our pleasure to do courtesy to Lord Aldaran; what does he ask?"

"Lord Aldaran bids me say that his daughter, his only living child and heir, is cursed with *laran* such as he has never known before. The aged *leronis* who has cared for her since her birth no longer knows what to do with her. The child is of an age when my father fears lest threshold sickness destroy her. He comes, then, as suppliant, to ask of the *vai leroni* if they know of one who will come to care for her during these crucial seasons."

This was not unknown, that a Tower-trained *leronis* might go to guide and care for some young heir during the troubled years of adolescence, when threshold sickness took such toll of the sons and daughters of their caste. A *laranzu* from Arilinn Tower had first counseled Allart to seek sanctuary at Nevarsin. And, Allart thought, if Aldaran was beholden to Hali for such a service, Aldaran would be all the more ready to refrain from angering Elhalyn by coming into this war.

Allart said, "The Hasturs of Elhalyn, and those who serve them in Hali Tower, will be pleased to serve Lord Aldaran in this matter." He asked Coryn in their own language, "Who shall we send?"

"I thought you would go," Coryn said. "You are none too eager to remain and become entangled in this war."

"I shall go, indeed, at my brother's bidding and on his mission," Allart said, "but it is not seemly that a *laranzu* shall have the training of a maiden. Surely she needs a woman to guide her."

"Yet there is none to spare," said Coryn. "Now that I am to lose Renata, I shall need Mira for monitoring. And, of course, Cassandra is not even well enough trained for monitoring, far less for work of this sort, teaching a young girl to control her gift."

Allart said, "Could not Renata fulfill this mission? It seems to me that this would remove her from the combat zone, as much as returning to Neskaya."

"Yes, Renata is the obvious choice," Coryn said, "but she is not to go to Neskaya. Did you not hear? No," he answered his own question. "While Cassandra has been ill, you have stayed with her and you did not hear the word from the relays. Dom Erlend Leynier has sent word that she is not to go to Neskaya Towers but to go home to her wedding. It has twice been delayed already. I do not think she would wish to delay it again to go to some godforgotten corner of the Hellers, to teach some barefoot mountain girl how to handle her *laran*!"

Allart looked apprehensively at young Donal. Had he heard the offensive remark? But Donal, like a proper messenger, was staring straight before him, appearing neither to hear or see anything but what concerned him directly. If he *did* know enough of the Lowland tongue to understand Coryn's words, or had enough *laran* to read their thoughts, neither Coryn nor Allart would ever know.

"I do not think Renata is in such a great hurry to be married," Allart demurred.

Coryn chuckled. "I think you mean *you* are in no hurry for Renata to be married, cousin." Then, at the glare of rage in Allart's eyes, he said hastily, "I was but jesting, cousin. Tell young Delleray that we will ask the *damisela* Renata Leynier if she will undertake the journey northward."

Allart repeated the formal phrases to Donal, who bowed and replied, "Say to the *vai domna* that Mikhail, Lord Aldaran, would not have her make this tremendous service unremunerated. In gratitude, she will be dowered as if she were his younger daughter, when the time comes for her to marry."

"That is generous," Allart said, as indeed it was. The use of *laran* could not be bought or sold like ordinary service; tradition stated it should be used only in service to caste or clan and was not for hire. This was the usual compromise. The Leyniers were wealthy, but they had no such wealth as the Aldarans, and this would give Renata the dower of a princess.

After a few more courtesies, they had young Donal conducted to a chamber to await the final arrangements. Coryn said regretfully, as he and Allart went through the forcefield into the main part of the Tower, "Perhaps I should have arranged this journey for Arielle. She is a Di Asturien, but she is *nedestro* and has no dower to speak of. Even if my brother would give me leave to marry, which is not likely, he would not allow me to wed with a poor girl." He laughed bitterly. "But it matters now . . . even if she were dowered with all the jewels of Carthon, a Hastur of Carcosa could not wed with a *nedestro* of Di Asturien; and if Arielle had such a dowry, her father would surely offer her to another, and I should lose her."

"You are long unmarried," Allart said, and Coryn shrugged.

"My brother is not eager for me to have an heir. I have *laran* enough, and I have fathered half a dozen sons for their accursed breeding program, on this girl and that, but I have not bothered to see the babes, though they say they all have *laran*. It is better not to get too fond of them, since

I understand that every attempt to breed the Hastur gift to Aillard or Ardais has meant they die in threshold sickness, poor little brats. It is hard on their mothers, but I have no intention of letting myself be heart-wrung, too."

"How can you take it so casually?"

For a moment the mask of indifference broke and Coryn looked out at him in real distress.

"What else can I do, Allart? No son of Hastur has a life he can call his own, while the *leroni* of this damned stud-service they call our caste make all our marriages and even arrange the fathering of our bastards. But we are not all like you, able to tolerate living the life of a monk!" Then he was stony-faced, impassive again. "Well, it is not an unpleasant duty to my clan, after all. While I dwell here as Keeper, there are plenty of times when I am no use to any woman, which is almost as good as being a monk. . . . Arielle and I are willing to take what we can have when occasion permits. I am not like you, a romantic seeking a great love," he added defensively, and turned away. "Will you ask Renata if she will go, or shall I?"

"You ask her," Allart said. He knew already what she would say, knew they would ride northward together. He had seen it again and again; it could not be avoided.

Was it unavoidable, then, that he would love Renata, forgetting his love and his honor and his pledge to Cassandra?

I should never have left Nevarsin, he thought. *Would that I had flung myself from the highest crag before I let them force me away!*

Chapter 14

Renata hesitated at the door of the room, then, knowing that Cassandra was aware of her presence, went in without knocking. Cassandra was out of bed, although she still looked pale and exhausted. She had some needlework in her hands, and was setting small precise stitches in the petal of an embroidered flower, but as Renata's eyes fell on it Cassandra colored and put it aside.

"I am ashamed to waste time on so foolish and womanly a pastime."

Renata said, "Why? I, too, was taught never to let my hands sit idle, lest my mind find nothing to occupy itself but too much brooding on my own problems and miseries. Although my stitches were never so fine as yours. Are you feeling better now?"

Cassandra sighed. "Yes, I am well again. I suppose I can take my place among you. I suppose—" Renata, the empath, knew that Cassandra's throat closed, unable to speak the words. *I suppose they all know what I tried to do; they all despise me. . . .*

"There is not one of us feels anything for you save sympathy, sorrow that you could have been so unhappy among us, and none of us spoke or tried to ease your suffering," Renata said gently.

"Yet I hear whispers around me; I cannot read what is happening. What are you concealing from me, Renata? What are you all hiding?"

"You know that the war has broken out afresh," Renata began.

"Allart is to go to war!" It was a cry of anguish. "And he did not tell me."

"If he has hesitated to say this, *chiya*, surely it is only that he fears you might be overcome again by despair, and act rashly."

Cassandra lowered her eyes; gently as the words were spoken, they were a reproof, and well-deserved. "No, that will not happen again. Not now."

"Allart is not to go to war," Renata said. "Instead, he is being sent outside the combat area. A messenger has come from Caer Donn, and Allart is being sent to escort him, under a truce-flag. Lord Elhalyn has sent him on some mission to the mountain people there."

"Am I to go with him?" Cassandra caught her breath, a flush of such pure joy spreading over her face that Renata was reluctant to speak and banish it.

At last she said gently, "No, cousin. That is not your destiny now. You must stay here. You have great need of the training we can give, to master your *laran*, so that you will never again be overcome like that. And since I am to leave the Tower, you will be needed as a monitor here. Mira will begin at once to teach you."

"I? A monitor? Truly?"

"Yes. You have worked long enough in the circle so that your *laran* and your talents are known to us. Coryn has said that you will make a monitor of great skill. And you will be needed soon. With Allart's and my departure, there will hardly be enough trained workers here to form two circles, and not enough trained to monitor."

"So." Cassandra was silent a moment. "In any case, I have an easier lot than other women of my clan, who have nothing to do but watch their husbands ride forth to battle and perhaps death. I have useful work to do here, and Allart need have no fear that he leaves me with child." To answer Renata's questioning look, she said, "I am ashamed, Renata. Probably you do not know . . . Allart and I made one another a pledge, that our marriage would remain unconsummated. I—I tempted him to break that vow."

"Cassandra, Allart is not a child or an untried boy. He is a grown man, and fully capable of making such a decision for himself." Renata smothered an impulse to laugh. "I doubt he would be complimented by the thought that you ravished him against his will."

Cassandra colored. "Still, if I had been stronger, if I had been able to master my unhappiness—"

"Cassandra, it's done and past mending; all the smiths in Zandru's forges can't mend a broken egg. You are not the keeper of Allart's conscience. Now you can only look ahead. Perhaps it is just as well that Allart must leave you for a time. It will give you both the opportunity to decide what you wish to do in the future."

Cassandra shook her head. "How can I alone make a decision that concerns us both? It is for Allart to say what shall come afterward. He is my husband and my lord!"

Suddenly Renata was exasperated. "It is that attitude which has led women to where they are now in the Domains! In the name of the Blessed Cassilda, child, are you still thinking of yourself only in terms of a breeder of sons and a toy of lust? Wake up, girl! Do you think it is only for that Allart desires you?"

Cassandra blinked, startled. "What else am I? What else can any woman be?"

"You are not a woman!" Renata said angrily. "You are only a child! Every word you say makes it evident! Listen to me, Cassandra. First, you are a human being, a child of the gods, a daughter of your clan, bearing *laran.* Do you think you have it only that you may pass it on to your sons? You are a matrix worker; soon you will be a monitor. Do you honestly think you are no good to Allart for anything but to share his bed and to give him children? Gods above, girl, *that* he could have from a concubine, or a *riyachiya.* . . ."

Cassandra's cheeks flushed an angry red. "It is not seemly to talk about such things!"

"But only to *do* them?" Renata retorted, at white heat. "The gods created us thinking creatures; do you suppose they meant woman to be brood animals alone? If so, why do we have brains and *laran,* and tongues to speak our thoughts, instead of being given only fair faces and sex organs and bellies to bear our children and breasts to nourish them? Do you believe the gods did not know what they were doing?"

"I do not believe there are any gods at all," Cassandra retorted, and the bitterness in her voice was so great that Renata's anger vanished. She, too, had known that kind of bitterness; she was not yet free of it.

She put her arms around the other girl, and said tenderly, "Cousin, you and I have no reason to quarrel. You are young and untaught; as you learn, here, to use your *laran,* perhaps you will come to think differently about what you are, within yourself—not only as Allart's wife. Someday you may be the keeper of your own will and conscience, and not rely on Allart to make the decisions for both of you, nor lay on him the burden of your sorrows as well as his own."

"I never thought of that," said Cassandra, hiding her face against Renata's shoulder. "If I had been stronger, I would not have laid this burden upon him. I have put upon him the guilt for my own unhappiness which drove me into the lake. Yet he was only doing what he felt he must do. Will they teach me here to be strong, Renata? As strong as you?"

"Stronger, I hope, *chiya,*" Renata said, kissing the other girl on the forehead, yet her own thoughts were grim. *I am full of good advice for her, yet I cannot handle my own life. For the third time, now, I run away from marriage, into this unknown mission at Aldaran, for a girl I do not know and for whom I care nothing. I should stay here and defy my father, not run away to Aldaran to teach some unknown girl how to use the* laran *that her foolish forefathers bred into her mind and body! What is this girl to me, that I should neglect my own life to help her gain command of hers?*

Yet she knew it had all been determined by what she was—a *leronis,* born with the talent, and fortunate enough to have been given Tower training to master it. Thus in honor bound to do whatever she could to help others less fortunate master their own unasked for, undesired *laran.*

Cassandra was calm now. She said, "Allart will not go without bidding me farewell . . . ?"

"No, no, of course not, my child. Coryn has already given him leave to withdraw from the circle, so this last night you spend under one roof, you may spend together to say your farewells." She did not tell Cassandra that she herself was to accompany Allart on his ride northward; that would be for Allart to tell her, in his own time and in his own way. She only said, "In any case, as things are between you now, one of you should go. You know that when serious work begins in the circle, you must remain apart and chaste."

"I do not understand that," Cassandra said. "Coryn and Arielle—"

"—have worked together for more than a year in the circle; they know the limits of what is allowed and what is dangerous," Renata said. "A day will come when you will know it, too, but as you are now, it would be difficult to recall or keep to those limits. This is your time to learn, with no distractions, and Allart would be"—she smiled at the other girl, mischievously—"a distraction. Oh, these men, that we can neither live at peace with them—nor without them!"

Cassandra's laughter was momentary. Then her face convulsed again with weeping. "I know that all you say is true, and yet I cannot bear to have Allart leave me. Have you never been in love, Renata?"

"No, not as you mean it, *chiya.*" Renata held Cassandra close to her, torn, with the empath *laran,* anguished with the other woman's pain, as Cassandra sobbed helplessly against her breast.

"What can I do, Renata? What can I do?"

Renata shook her head, staring bleakly into space. *Will I ever know what it is to love that way? Do I want to know, or is such love as this only a trap into which women walk of their own free will, so that they have no more strength to rule their own lives? Is this how the women of the Comyn have become no more than breeders of sons and toys of lust?* But Cassandra's pain was very real to her. At last she said, hesitating, shy before the depths of the other woman's emotion, "You could make it impossible for him to leave you, if you grieve like this, cousin. He would be too fearful for you, too guilty at the thought of leaving you to such despair."

Cassandra struggled to control her sobs. Finally she said, "You are right. I must not add to Allart's guilt and grief with my own. I am not the first, nor the last wife of a Hastur who must see him ride away from her, with no knowledge of when, or ever, he will return; but his honor and the success of his mission are in my hands, then. I must not hold that lightly. Somehow"—she set her small chin stubbornly—"I will find the strength to send him away from me; if not gladly, at least I will try to make sure that he goes without fear for me to add to his own."

It was a small party that rode north from Hali the next day. Donal, as a suppliant, had ridden alone; Allart himself had only the banner-bearer to which, as heir to Elhalyn, he was entitled, and the messenger with a truce-flag; not so much as a single body-servant. Renata, too, had dispensed with lady companions, saying that in time of war such niceties need not be observed; she had brought only her nurse Lucetta, who had served her since childhood, and would have dispensed even with this attendance, save that an unmarried woman of the Domains could not travel without any female attendance.

Allart rode silently, apart from the rest, tormented by the memory of Cassandra at the moment of their parting, her lovely eyes filled with the tears she had struggled so valiantly not to shed before him. At least he had not left her pregnant; so far the gods had been merciful.

If there were any gods, and if they cared what befell mankind. . . .

Ahead he could hear Renata chatting lightheartedly with Donal. They seemed so young, both of them. Allart knew he was only three or four years older than Donal, but it seemed he had never been as young as that. *Seeing what will be, what may be, what may never be, it seems I live a lifetime in every day that passes.* He envied the boy.

They were riding through a land bearing the scars of war, blackened fields with traces of fire, roofless houses, abandoned farms. So few travelers passed them on the road that after the first day Renata did not even bother to keep her cloak modestly folded about her face.

Once an air-car flew low overhead; it circled, dipped low to scrutinize them, then turned about and flew back southward. The guardsman with the truce-flag dropped back to ride at Allart's side.

"Truce-flag or not, *vai dom,* I wish you had agreed to an escort. Those bastards of Ridenow may choose not to honor a truce-flag; and seeing your banners, it might occur to them that it would be worth much to capture the heir to Elhalyn and hold him to ransom from his Hastur kinfolk. It would not be the first time such a thing had happened."

"If they will not honor a flag of truce," Allart said reasonably, "it will avail us nothing to defeat them in this war, either, for they would not honor our victory or the terms of surrender. I think we must trust our enemies to abide by the rules of war."

"I have had small faith in the rules of war, Dom Allart, since first I saw a village burned to ashes by *clingfire*—not soldiers alone, but old men and women and little children. I would prefer to trust in the rules of war with a considerable escort at my back!"

Allart said, "I have not foreseen it with my *laran*, that we will be under attack."

The Guardsman only said dryly, "Then you are fortunate, *vai dom*. I have not the consolation of foresight or other sorcery," and fell into stubborn silence.

On the third day of the journey, they crossed a pass which led downward to the Kadarin River, which separated the Lowland Domains from the territories held by the mountain folk—Aldaran, Ardais, and the lesser lords of the Hellers. Before they rode downward, Renata turned back to look over the lands from which they had come, where most of the Domains lay spread out before them. Renata looked on the distant hills and Towers, then cried out in dismay—forest fire was raging across the Kilghard Hills away south.

"Look where it rages!" she cried. "Surely it will trespass on Alton lands." Allart and Donal, both telepaths, picked up her thought! *Will my home, too, lie in flames down there in a war which is none of ours?* Aloud she only said, her voice shaking, "Now I wish I had your foresight, Allart."

The panorama of the Domains below them blurred before Allart's eyes and he closed them in a vain attempt to shut out the diverging futures of his *laran*. If the powerful clan of the Altons was drawn into this war by an attack on their home country, no homestead or estate anywhere in the Domains would be safe. It would not matter to the Altons whether their homes were burned by fires deliberately set, or by those raging out of control after being set to attack elsewhere.

"How dare they use forest fire as a weapon," Renata

demanded furiously, "knowing it cannot be controlled, but is at the mercy of winds over which they have no power."

"No," said Allart, trying to comfort her. "Some of the *leroni*—you know that—can use their powers to raise clouds and rain to dampen the fires, or even snow to smother them."

Donal drew his mount close to Renata's. "Where lies your home, Lady?"

She pointed a slender hand. "There, between the lakes of Miridon and Mariposa. My home is beyond the hills, but you can see the lakes."

Donal's dark face was intent, as he said, "Have no fear, *damisela.* See—it will move upward along that ridge"—he pointed—"and there the winds will drive it back upon itself. It will burn out before tomorrow's sunset."

"I pray you are right," she said, "but surely you are only guessing?"

"No, my lady. Surely you can see it, if you will only calm yourself. Certainly you, who are Tower-trained, can have no difficulty in reading how the air currents *there* will move this way, and the wind will rise *there*. You are a *leronis*; you must see that."

Allart and Renata regarded Donal in wonder and amazement. Finally Renata said, "Once when I was studying the breeding program, I read something of such a *laran* as that, but it was abandoned because it could not be controlled. But that was not in the Hastur kin, nor in the Delleray. Are you perhaps akin to the folk of Storn or Rockraven?"

"Aliciane of Rockraven—she who was fourth daughter to old Lord Vardo—was my mother."

"Is it so?" Renata looked at him with open curiosity. "I believed that *laran* extinct, since it was one of those which came on a child before birth and usually killed the mother who bore such a child. Did your mother survive your birth?"

"She did," Donal said, "but she died in bearing my sister Dorilys, who is to be in your care."

Renata shook her head. "So the accursed breeding program among the Hastur kin has left its mark in the Hellers, too. Had your father any *laran*?"

"I do not know. I cannot recall that I ever looked on his face," Donal said, "but my mother was no telepath, and

Dorilys—my sister—cannot read thoughts at all. Such telepathy as I have must be the gift of my father."

"Did your *laran* come on you in infancy, or suddenly, in adolescence?"

"The ability to sense air currents, storms, has been with me as long as I can remember," Donal said. "I did not think it *laran* then, merely a sense everyone had to greater degree or less, like an ear for music. When I grew older I could control the lightning a little." He told how in childhood he had diverted a bolt of lightning which might, otherwise, have struck the tree under which he and his mother had sheltered. "But I can do it only rarely and in great need, and it makes me ill; so I try only to read these forces, not to control them."

"That is wisest," Renata confirmed. "Everything we know of the more unusual *laran* has taught us how dangerous it is to play with these forces; rain at one place is drought at another. It was a wise man who said, *'It is ill done to chain a dragon for roasting your meat.'* Yet I see you bear a starstone."

"A little, and only for toys. I can levitate and control a glider, such things as that. Such small things as our household *leronis* could teach me."

"Were you a telepath from infancy, too?"

"No; that came on me when I was past fifteen, when I had ceased to expect it."

"Did you suffer much from threshold sickness?" Allart asked.

"Not much; dizziness, disorientation for half a season or so. Mostly I was distressed because my foster-father forbade me my glider for that time!" He laughed, but they could both read his thoughts: *I never knew how deeply my foster-father loved me, till I felt how deeply he feared then to lose me when I fell ill with threshold sickness.*

"No convulsions?"

"None."

Renata nodded. "Some strains have it more severely than others. You seem to have the relatively minor one, and Lord Aldaran's kin the lethal form. Is there Hastur blood in your family?"

"*Damisela,* I have not the faintest notion," Donal said stiffly, and the others heard his resentment as if he had spoken the words aloud: *Am I a racing* chervine *or a stud animal to be judged on my pedigree?*

Renata laughed aloud. "Forgive me, Donal. Perhaps I have dwelt too long in a Tower and had not considered how offensive another might consider such a question. I have spent so many years studying these things! Although indeed, my friend, if I am to care for your sister I must indeed study her lineage and pedigree as seriously as if she were a racing animal or a fine hawk, to find out how this *laran* came into her line, and what lethals and recessives she may be carrying. Even if they are quiet now, they could cause trouble when she comes to womanhood. But forgive me, I meant no offense."

"It is I should beg your pardon, *damisela,* for being churlish when you are studying ways to help my sister."

"Let us forgive one another then, Donal, and be friends."

Allart, watching them, felt sudden bitter envy of these young people who could laugh and flirt and enjoy life even when burdened with impending disasters. Then he was suddenly ashamed of himself. Renata had no light burden; she could have placed all the responsibility on father or husband, yet she had worked since her childhood to know what she should do, how best to take responsibility, even if it meant destroying the life of an unborn child and bearing the reproach toward a barren woman in the Domains. Donal had had no careless youth either, living with the knowledge of his own strange *laran* which could destroy him and his sister.

He wondered if every human being, indeed, walked through life on a precipice as narrow as his own. Allart realized that he had been acting as if he alone bore an intolerable curse, and all others were lighthearted, carefree. He watched Renata and Donal laughing and jesting, and then he thought, and it was a new and strange thought to him, *Perhaps Nevarsin gave me too exaggerated a seriousness about life. If they can live with the burdens they bear, and still be light of heart and enjoy this journey, perhaps they are wiser than I.*

When he rode forward to join them he was smiling.

They came to Aldaran late in the afternoon of a gray and rainy day, little spits of sleet hiding in the wind and rain. Renata had wrapped her cloak over her face and protected her cheeks with a scarf, and the banner-bearer had put away his flag to protect it and rode muffled in his thick cape, looking dour. Allart found that the increasing altitude made his heart pound, so that he felt light-headed. But with every day's ride Donal had seemed to cast off care and to look merry and youthful, as if the altitude and the worsening weather were only a sign of homecoming; even in the rain he rode bareheaded, the hood of his riding-cloak cast back, disregarding the sleet on his face, which was reddened with the wind and cold.

At the foot of the long slope that led upward to the castle, he paused and waved in a signal, laughing. Renata's nurse grumbled, "Are we to ride ordinary animals up that goat-track, or do they think we are hawks that can fly?" Even Renata looked a little daunted by the last steep path.

"*This* is the Aldaran keep? It seems as inaccessible as Nevarsin itself!"

Donal laughed. "No, but in the old days, when my foster-father's forebears had to keep it by force of arms, this made it impregnable—my lady," he added, with sudden self-consciousness. During the days of the journey they had become "Allart" and "Renata" and "Donal" to one another; Donal's sudden return to formal courtesy made them realize that whatever happened, this period of forgetfulness was ended and the burden of their separate destinies lay upon them again.

"I trust the soldiers on those walls know we are not come to attack," grumbled the guardsman who had borne the truce-flag.

Donal laughed and said, "No, we should be small indeed for a war party, I think. Look—there is my foster-father on the battlement, with my sister. Evidently he knew of our arrival."

Allart saw the blank look slide down over Donal's face, the look of the telepath in contact with those out of earshot.

A moment later Donal smiled gaily and said, "The horse path is not so steep, after all. On the far side of the castle there are steps carved from the rock, two hundred and eighty-nine of them. Would you prefer to climb up that way, perhaps? Or you, *mestra*?" he added to the nurse, and she made a sound of dismay. "Come, my foster-father awaits us."

During the long ride, Allart had made use of the techniques he had learned at Nevarsin, to keep the crowding futures at a distance. Since he could do nothing whatever about them, he knew that allowing himself to dwell upon them, with morbid fears, was a form of self-indulgence he could no longer give mental lease. He must deal with whatever came, and look ahead only when he had some reasonable chance of deciding which of the possible futures could be rationally affected by some choice actually within his own power to control. But as they reached the top of the steep slope, coming in out of the sleet and winds of the height into a sheltered courtyard, with servants crowding about to take the horses, Allart knew he had lived this scene before in memory or foresight. Through the momentary disorientation he heard a shrill childish voice crying out, and it seemed to him that he saw a flare of lightnings, so that he physically shrank from the voice, in the moment before he actually *heard* it clearly. It was simple after all, no danger, no flare of strange lightning, nothing but a joyous child's voice calling out Donal's name—and a little girl, her long plaits flying, ran from the shelter of an archway and wrapped him in her arms.

"I knew it must be you, and the strangers. Is this the woman who is to be my guardian and teacher? What is her name? Do you like her? What is it like in the Lowlands? Do flowers truly bloom there all year as I have heard? Did you see any nonhumans as you traveled? Did you bring me back any gifts? Who are these people? What kind of animals are they riding?"

"Gently, gently, Dorilys," reproved a deep voice. "Our guests will think us mountain barbarians indeed, if you chatter like an ill-taught *gallimak*! Let your brother go, and greet our guests like a lady!"

Donal let his sister cling tightly to his hand as he turned to his foster-father, but he let her go as Mikhail of Aldaran took him into a close embrace.

"Dearest lad, I have missed you greatly. Now will you not present our honored guests?"

"Renata Leynier, *leronis* of Hali Tower," Donal said. Renata made a deep curtsy before Lord Aldaran.

"Lady, you lend us grace; we are deeply honored. Allow me to present my daughter and heir, Dorilys of Rock-raven."

Dorilys lowered her eyes shyly as she curtsied.

"S'dia shaya, domna," she said bashfully.

Then Lord Aldaran presented Margali to Renata. "This is the *leronis* who has cared for her since she was born."

Renata looked sharply at the old woman. Despite her pale, fragile features, her graying hair and the lines of age in her face, she still bore the indefinable stamp of power. Renata thought, *If she has been in the care of a* leronis *since she was born, and Aldaran felt still that she needed stronger care and control—what, in the name of all the gods, does he fear for this charming little girl?*

Donal was presenting Allart to his foster-father. Allart, bowing to the old man, raised his eyes to look into the hawklike face of Dom Mikhail, and knew abruptly that he had seen this face before, in dreams and foresight, knew it with mingled affection and fear. Somehow this mountain lord held the key to his destiny, but he could see only a vaulted room, white stone like a chapel, and flickering flames, and despair. Allart fought to dismiss the unwelcome, confusing images until some rational choice could be made among them.

My laran *is useless,* he thought, *save to frighten me!*

As they were being led through the castle to their rooms, Allart found himself nervously watching for the vaulted room of his vision, the place of flames and tragedy. But he did not see it, and he wondered if it was anywhere at Castle Aldaran at all. Indeed, it might be anywhere—or, he thought bitterly, nowhere.

Chapter 15

Renata woke to sense the presence of an outsider; then she saw Dorilys's pretty, childish face peeping around a curtain.

"I am sorry," Dorilys said. "Did I wake you, *domna*?"

"I think so." Renata blinked, grasping vaguely at fragments of a disappearing dream: fire, the wings of a glider, Donal's face. "No, it does not matter, child; Lucetta would have waked me soon to go down to dinner."

Dorilys came around the curtain and sat on the edge of the bed. "Was the journey very tiring, *domna*? I hope you will have recovered soon from your fatigue."

Renata had to smile at the mixture of childishness and adult courtesy. "You speak *casta* very well, child; is it spoken so much here?"

"No," Dorilys said, "but Margali was schooled in the Domains, at Thendara, and she said I should learn to speak it well so that if I went to Thendara there would be none who could call me mountain barbarian."

"Then Margali did well, for your accent is very good."

"Were you trained in a Tower, too, *vai leronis*?"

"Yes, but there is no need to be so formal as all that," Renata said, spontaneously warming to the girl. "Call me cousin or kinswoman, what you will."

"You look very young to be a *leronis*, cousin," Dorilys said, choosing the more intimate of the two words.

Renata said, "I started when I was about your age." Then she hesitated, for Dorilys seemed childish for the fourteen or fifteen she looked. If she was to educate Dorilys, as a nobleman's daughter, she must quickly put a stop to so big a girl running about the courtyards with her hair flying, racing and shouting like a little girl. She wondered if, indeed, the girl was somewhat lacking in wit. "How old are you . . . fifteen?"

Dorilys giggled and shook her head. "Everyone says I look so, and Margali wearies me night and day with telling me I am too old to do this and too big to do that, but I am only eleven years old. I shall be twelve at a summer harvest."

Abruptly Renata revised her perceptions of the girl. She was not, then, a childish and ill-educated young woman, as she looked, but a highly precocious and intelligent pre-adolescent girl. It was perhaps her misfortune that she looked older than her years, for everyone would expect Dorilys to have a degree of experience and judgment she could hardly possess at that age.

Dorilys asked, "Did you like being a *leronis*? What is a monitor?"

"You will find that out when I monitor you, as I must do before I begin to teach you about *laran*," Renata said.

"What did you do in the Tower?"

"Many things," Renata said. "Bringing metals to the surface of the ground for the smiths to work them, charging batteries for lights and air-cars, working in the relays to speak without voice to those in the other Towers, so that what was happening in one Domain could be known to all, much faster than a messenger could ride. . . ."

Dorilys listened, finally letting out a long, fascinated sigh. "And will you teach me to do those things?"

"Not all of them, perhaps, but you shall know such things as you have need to know, as the lady of a great Domain. And beyond that, such things as all women should know if they are to have control of their own lives and bodies."

"Will you teach me to read thoughts? Donal and Father and Margali can read thoughts and I cannot, and they can talk apart and I cannot hear, and it makes me angry because I know they talk about me."

"I cannot teach you that, but if you have the talent I can teach you to use it. You are too young to know whether you have it or not."

"Will I have a matrix?"

"When you can learn to use it," Renata said. She thought it strange that Margali had not already tested the child, taught her to key a matrix. Well, Margali was well on in years; perhaps she feared what her charge, headstrong and lacking in mature judgment, would do with the enormous power of a matrix. "Do you know what your *laran* is, Dorilys?"

The child lowered her eyes. "A little. You know what happened at my handfasting. . . ."

"Only that your promised husband died very suddenly."

Suddenly Dorilys began to cry. "He died—and everyone said I had killed him, but I didn't, cousin. I didn't want to kill him—I only wanted to make him take his hands off me."

Looking at the sobbing child, Renata's first, spontaneous impulse was to put her arms around Dorilys and comfort her. *Of course she hadn't meant to kill him! How cruel, to let a child so young carry blood-guilt!* But in the instant before she moved, an intuitive flash of second thought kept her motionless.

However young she was, Dorilys had *laran* which could kill. This *laran,* in the hands of a child too young to exercise rational judgment about it . . . the very thought made Renata shudder. If Dorilys was old enough to possess this terrifying *laran,* she was old enough—she would *have* to be old enough—to learn control, and its proper use.

Controlling *laran* was not easy. No one knew better than Renata, a Tower-trained monitor, how difficult it could be, the hard work and self-discipline which went even into the earliest stages of that control. How could a spoiled, pampered little girl, whose every word had been law to her companions and adoring family, find the discipline and the inner motivation to tread that difficult path? Perhaps the death she had wrought, and her guilt and fear about it, might be fortunate in the long run. Renata did not like to use fear in her teaching, but at the moment she did not know enough about Dorilys to throw away any slight advantage she might have in teaching the girl.

So she did not touch Dorilys, but let her cry, looking at her with a detached tenderness of which her calm face and manner gave not the slightest hint. At last she said, voicing the first thing she herself had been taught in the early discipline of Hali Tower, "*Laran* is a terrible gift and a terrible responsibility, and it is not easy to learn to control it. It is your own choice whether you will learn to control it, or whether it will control *you*. If you are willing to work hard, a time will come when you will be in command, when you will use your *laran* and not let it use you. That is why I have come here to teach you, so that such a thing cannot happen again."

"You are more than welcome here at Aldaran," Mikhail, Lord Aldaran said, leaning forward from his high seat and catching Allart's eyes. "It is long since I had the pleasure of entertaining one of my Lowland kin. I trust we will make you welcome. But I do not flatter myself that the heir to Elhalyn did the service which any paxman or banner-bearer could do, just for the sake of showing me honor. Not when the Elhalyn Domain is at war. You want something of me— or the Elhalyn Domain wants something, which may not be the same thing at all. Will you not tell me your true mission, kinsman?"

Allart pondered a dozen answers, watching the play of firelight on the old man's face, knowing it was the curious foresight of his *laran* which caused that face to wear a hundred aspects— benevolence, wrath, offended pride, anguish. Had his mission alone the power to raise all those reactions in Lord Aldaran, or was it something yet to pass between them?

At last, weighing each word, he said, "My lord, what you say is true, although it was a privilege to travel north with your foster-son, and I was not sorry to be at some distance from this war."

Aldaran raised an eyebrow and said, "I would have thought in time of war you would have been unwilling to leave the Domain. Are you not your brother's heir?"

"His regent and warden, sir, but I am sworn to support the claim of his *nedestro* sons."

"It seems to me you could have done better for yourself than that," Dom Mikhail said. "Should your brother die in battle, you seem better fitted to command a Domain than any flock of little boys, legitimate or bastard, and no doubt the folk of your Domain would rather have it so. There's a true saying: *when the cat's a kitten, rats make play in the kitchen!* So it goes with a Domain; in times like this, a strong hand is needful. In wartime a younger son, or one whose parentage is uncertain, can carve out for himself a position of power as he could never do at any other time."

Allart thought, *But I have no ambition to rule my Domain.* However, he knew that Lord Aldaran would never believe this. To men of his sort, ambition was the only legitimate emotion for a man born into a ruling house. *And it is this which keeps us torn with fratricidal wars. . . .* But he said nothing, if he did, Aldaran would immediately jump to the conclusion that he was an effeminate, or, worse, a coward. "My brother and overlord felt I could better serve my Domain on this mission, sir."

"Indeed? It must be more important than I had believed possible," Aldaran said, and he looked grim. "Well, tell me about it, kinsman, if it is a mission of such great moment to Aldaran that your brother must entrust it to his nearest rival!" He looked angry and guarded, and Allart knew he had not made a good impression. However, as Allart broached his mission, Aldaran slowly relaxed, leaning back in his chair, and when the young man had done he nodded slowly, letting out his breath with a long sigh.

"It is not so bad as I feared," he said. "I have foresight enough, and I could read your thoughts a little—not much; where did you learn to guard them so?—and I knew you came to speak of this war to me. I feared you had come, for the sake of the old friendship between your father and me, to urge me to join with your folk in this war. Though I loved your father well, *that* I would have been reluctant to do. I might have been willing to aid in the defense of Elhalyn, if you were hard pressed, but I would not have wished to attack the Ridenow."

"I have brought no such request, sir," Allart said, "but will you tell me why?"

"Why? Why, you ask? Well, tell me, lad," Aldaran said. "What grudge have you against the Ridenow?"

"I, myself? None, sir, save that they attacked an air-car in which I was riding with my father, and brought about his death. But all the Domains of the Lowlands have a grudge against the Ridenow because they have moved into the old Domain of Serrais and have taken their women in marriage."

"Is that such a bad thing?" Aldaran asked. "Did the women of Serrais ask your aid against these marriages, or prove to you that they had been married against their will?"

"No, but—" Allart hesitated. He knew it was not lawful for women of the Hastur kin to marry outside that kinfolk. As the thought crossed his mind, Aldaran picked it up and said, "As I thought. It is only that you want these women for your own Domain, and those close akin to you. I had heard that the male line of Serrais is extinct: it is this inbreeding which has brought that line to extinction. If the women of Serrais wed back into the Hastur kin, I know enough of their bloodlines to predict that their *laran* will not survive another hundred years. They *need* new blood in that House. The Ridenow are healthy, and fertile. Nothing better could happen to the Serrais women than for the Ridenow to marry into their kindred."

Allart knew that his face betrayed his revulsion, though he tried to hide it. "If you will forgive plain speaking, sir, I find it revolting to speak of the relationships between men and women only in terms of this accursed breeding program in the Domains."

Aldaran snorted. "Yet you think it fitting to let the Serrais women be married off to Hasturs and Elhalyns and Aillards all over again? Isn't that breeding them for their *laran,* too? They wouldn't survive three more generations, I tell you! How many fertile sons have been born to Serrais in the last forty years? Come, come, do you think the lords who rule at Thendara are so charitable that they are trying to preserve the purity of Serrais? You are young, but you can hardly be so naïve as that. The Hastur kin would let Serrais die out before they let outlanders breed into it, but these Ridenow have other ideas. And that is the only hope for Serrais—some new genes! If you are wise, you people in the Domains will welcome the Ridenow and bind them to your own daughters with marriage ties!"

Allart was shocked. "The Ridenow—marry into the Hastur kin? They have no part in the blood of Hastur and Cassilda."

"Their sons will have it," Aldaran said bluntly, "and with new blood, the old Serrais line may survive, instead of breeding itself into sterility, as the Aillards are doing at

Valeron, and as some of the Hasturs have done already. How many *emmasca* sons have been born into the Hasturs of Carcosa, or of Elhalyn, or Aillard, in the last hundred years?"

"Too many, I fear." Against his will Allart thought of the lads he had known in the monastery; *emmasca,* neither male nor wholly female, sterile, some with other defects. "But I have not studied the matter."

"Yet you presume to form an opinion on it?" Aldaran raised his eyebrows again. "I heard you had married an Aillard daughter; how many healthy sons and daughters have you? Though I need hardly ask. If you had, you would hardly be willing to swear allegiance to another man's bastards."

Stung, Allart retorted, "My wife and I have been wedded less than half a year."

"How many healthy legitimate sons has your brother? Come, come, Allart; you know as well as I that if your genes survive, they will do so in the veins of your *nedestro* children, even as mine. My wife was an Ardais, and bore me no more living children than your Aillard lady is likely to bear you."

Allart lowered his eyes, thinking with a spasm of grief and guilt, *It is no wonder the men of our line turn to riyachiyas and such perversions. We can take so little joy in our wives, between guilt at what we do to them, or fear for what will befall them!*

Aldaran saw the play of emotion on the young man's face and relented. "Well, well, there is no need to quarrel, kinsman; I meant no offense. But we have followed a breeding program, among the kin of Hastur and Cassilda, that has endangered our blood more than any upstart bandits could do—and salvation may take strange forms. It seems to me that the Ridenow will be the salvation of Serrais, if you folk at Elhalyn do not hinder them. But that is neither here nor there. Tell your brother that even if I wished to join in the war, which I do not, I could do nothing of the sort. I am myself hard-pressed; I have quarreled with my brother of Scathfell, and it troubles me that he has, as yet, sought no revenge. What is he plotting? I have meaty bones to pick, here at Aldaran, and it seems to me sometimes that the other mountain lords are like *kyorebni,*

circling, waiting. . . . I am old. I have no legitimate heir,
no living son at all, no single child of my own blood save
my young daughter."

Allart said, "But she is a fair child—and a healthy one,
it seems—and she possesses *laran*. If you have no son,
surely you can find somewhere a son-in-law to inherit
your estate!"

"I had hoped so," Aldaran said. "I think now it might
even be well to marry her to one of those Ridenow, but
that would bring down all the Elhalyn and Hastur kindred
as well. It must depend, also, on whether your kinswoman
can help her to survive the threshold at adolescence. I lost
three grown sons and a daughter so. When I sought to wed
into a line—such as my late wife, Deonara of Ardais—
whose *laran* came early upon them, the children died before birth or in infancy. Dorilys survived birth and infancy,
but with her *laran*, I fear she will not survive adolescence."

"The gods forbid she should die so! My kinswoman and
I will do all that we can. There are many ways now of
preventing death in adolescence. I myself came near it, yet
I live."

"If that is so," Aldaran said, "then am I your humble
suppliant, kinsman. What I have is yours for the asking.
But I beg you, remain and save my child from this fate!"

"I am at your service, Lord Aldaran. My brother has
bidden me remain while I can be of use to you, or as long
as needful to persuade you to remain neutral in this war."

"That I promise you," Aldaran said.

"Then you may command me, Lord Aldaran." Then Allart's bitterness broke through. "If you do not hold me too
greatly in contempt, that I am not eager to return to the
battlefield, since that seems to you the most fitting place
for the young men of my clan!"

Aldaran bent his head. "I spoke in anger. Forgive me,
kinsman. But I have no will to join this stupid war in the
Lowlands, even though I feel the Hasturs should test the
Ridenow before they admit them into their kindred. If
the Ridenow cannot survive, perhaps they do not truly deserve to come into the line of Serrais. Perhaps the gods
know what they are doing when they send wars among
men, so that old lines of blood, softened by luxury and
decadence, may die out, and new ones prevail, or come

into them; new genetic material with traits tested by their ability to survive."

Allart shook his head. "This may have been true in the older days," he said, "when war was truly a test of strength and courage, so that the weaker did not survive to breed. I cannot believe it is so *now*, my lord, when such things as *clingfire* kill the strong and the weak alike, even women and little children who have no part in the quarrels of the lords . . ."

"Clingfire!" Lord Aldaran whispered. "Is it so, then— that they have begun to use *clingfire* in the Domains? But surely they can use it but little; the raw material is hard to mine from the earth and deteriorates so rapidly once it is exposed to the air."

"It is made by matrix circles in the Towers, my lord. This is one reason I was eager to leave the area of this war. I would not be sent cleanly into battle, but would be put to make the hellish stuff." Aldaran closed his eyes as if to shut out the unbearable.

"Are they all madmen, then, below the Kadarin? I had thought sheer sanity would deter them from weapons which must ravage conquerer and conquered alike! I find it hard to believe in any man of honor loosing such terrible weapons against his kin," Aldaran said. "Remain here, Allart. All the gods forbid I should send any man back into such dishonorable warfare!" His face twisted. "Perhaps, if the gods are kind, they will exterminate one another, like the dragons if legend who consumed one another in their fire, leaving their prey to build on the scorched ground beneath them."

Chapter 16

Renata, head lowered, hurried across the courtyard at Aldaran. In her preoccupation, she ran hard into someone, murmured an apology, and would have hurried on, but felt herself caught and held.

"Wait a moment, kinswoman! I have hardly seen you since I came here," Allart said.

Renata, raising her eyes, said, "Are you making ready to return to the Lowlands, cousin?"

"No, my lord of Aldaran has invited me to remain, to teach Donal something of what I learned at Nevarsin," Allart said. Then, looking full into her face, he drew a breath of consternation. "Cousin, what troubles you? What is so dreadful?"

Confused, Renata looked at him, saying, "Why, I do not know." Then, dropping into full rapport with his thoughts, she saw herself as she looked in his eyes—drawn, pale, her face twisted with grief and tragedy.

Is this what I am, or what I shall be? In sudden fear, she clung for a moment to him, and he steadied her, gently.

"Forgive me, cousin, that I frightened you. Indeed, I am beginning to feel that much of what I see exists only in my own fear. Surely there is nothing so frightful here, is there? Or is the *damisela* Dorilys such a little monster as the servants say?"

Renata laughed, but she still looked troubled. "No, indeed; she is the dearest, sweetest child, and as yet she has shown me only her most biddable and loving face. But— Oh, Allart, it is true! I am frightened for her; she bears a truly dreadful *laran,* and I am afraid for what I must say to the lord Aldaran, her father! It cannot but make him angry!"

"I have seen her only for a few minutes," Allart said. "Donal was showing me how he controls the glider-toys, and she came down and begged to fly with us; but Donal said she must ask Margali, that he would not take the responsibility of letting her come. She was very cross, and went off in a great sulk."

"But she did not strike at him?"

"No," said Allart. "She pouted and said he did not love her, but she obeyed him. I would not want to let her fly until she could control a matrix, but Donal said he was given one when he was nine, and learned to use it without trouble. Evidently *laran* comes early on the Delleray kindred."

"Or on those of Rockraven," Renata said, but she still looked troubled. "I would not want to trust Dorilys with a matrix yet; perhaps never. But we will speak of that later. Lord Aldaran has agreed to receive me, and I must not keep him waiting."

"Indeed you must not," Allart said, and Renata went across the courtyard, frowning.

Outside the presence-chamber of the lord Aldaran, she found Dorilys. The little girl looked more controlled and civilized today, her hair neatly plaited, her dress an embroidered smock.

"I want to hear what you say to my father about me, cousin," she said, sliding her hand confidingly into Renata's.

Renata shook her head. "It is not good for little girls to listen to the councils of their elders," she said. "I must say many things which you would not understand. I give you my word that everything concerning you will be told to you when the proper time comes, but that proper time is not now, Dorilys."

"I am not a little girl," Dorilys said, thrusting her lip out.

"Then you should not behave like one, pouting and stamping your foot as if you were five years old! Certainly such behavior will not convince me that you are old enough to listen with maturity to talk about your future."

Dorilys looked more rebellious than ever. 'Who do you

think you are, to talk that way to me? I am Lady of Aldaran!"

"You are a child who will one day be Lady of Aldaran," Renata said coldly, "and I am the *leronis* whom your father saw fit to entrust with the task of teaching you proper behavior befitting that high place."

Dorilys pulled her hand free of Renata's, staring sulkily at the floor. "I will not be spoken to in that way! I will complain of you to my father, and he will send you away if you are not kind to me!"

"You do not know the meaning of the word unkindness," Renata said mildly. "When I entered the Tower of Hali as a novice to learn the art of monitor, no one was allowed to speak to me for forty days, nor to look into my eyes. This was to strengthen my reliance upon my *laran*."

"I wouldn't have put up with it," Dorilys said, and Renata smiled.

"Then they would have sent me home, knowing I did not have the strength and self-discipline to learn what I must learn. I will never be unkind to you, Dorilys, but you must master yourself before you are fit to command others."

"But it is different with me," Dorilys argued. "I am Lady of Aldaran, and already I command all the women in the castle, and most of the men, too. You are not the Lady of your Domain, are you?"

Renata shook her head. "No, but I am a Tower monitor. And even a Keeper is taught so. You have met your brother's friend, Allart. He is Regent of Elhalyn, yet at Nevarsin, for his training, he slept naked on stone for three winters, and never spoke in the presence of any monk superior to him."

"That's *horrible,*" Dorilys said, making a face.

"No. We undertake these disciplines voluntarily, because we know we need to discipline our bodies and minds to obey us, so that our *laran* will not destroy us."

"If I obey you," Dorilys asked craftily, "will you give me a matrix and teach me to use it, so that I can fly with Donal?"

"I will when I think you can be trusted with it, *chiya,*" Renata said.

"But I want it *now,*" Dorilys argued.

Renata shook her head. "No," she said. "Now go back
to your rooms, Dorilys, and I will see you when I have
finished with your father." She spoke firmly, and Dorilys
started to obey; then, after a few steps, she whirled around,
stamping her foot angrily.

"You will not use command-voice on me again!"

"I will do what I think fit," said Renata, unmoved. "Your
father has put me in charge of you. Must I tell him I find
you disobedient, and ask him to command you to obey me
in all things?"

Dorilys shrank. "No, please—don't tell Father on me,
Renata!"

"Then obey me at once," Renata repeated, using the
forbidden command-voice. "Go back and tell Margali you
have been disobedient, and ask her to punish you."

Dorilys's eyes filled with tears, but she moved away, lagging, out of the courtyard, and Renata let her breath go.

*How would I have forced her to obey if she had refused?
And a time will come when she will refuse, and I must be
prepared for that!*

One of the servants was staring, wide-eyed, having observed the little interchange. Renata picked up the woman's
thoughts without trying: *I have never seen my little lady
obey like that . . . without a word of protest!*

So it was the first time Dorilys had to obey against her
will, Renata thought. Margali, she knew, would punish Dorilys gently, only by setting her to sew long and uninteresting
seams on skirts and shifts, and forbidding her to touch her
embroidery-frames. *It will not hurt our little lady to learn
to do tasks for which she has no liking or talent.*

But the confrontation had hardened her will for what she
knew would be a difficult meeting with Lord Aldaran. She
was grateful that he had agreed to receive her in the small
study where he wrote his letters and saw the *coridom* about
the business of his estates, rather than in the formal
presence-chamber.

She found him dictating to his private secretary, but he
broke off when she came in, and sent the man away. "Well,
damisela, how are you getting along with my daughter? Do
you find her obedient and biddable? She is headstrong, but
very sweet and loving."

Renata smiled faintly. "She is not very loving at this moment, I fear," she said. "I have had to punish her, to send her to Margali to sit over her sewing for a while, and learn to think before she speaks."

Lord Aldaran sighed. "I suppose no child can be brought up without some punishment," he said. "I gave Donal's tutors leave to beat him, if they must, but I was gentler with him than my father with me, for I forbade his tutors to strike him hard enough to leave bruises; while as a boy I often was beaten so that I could not sit in comfort for days. But you will not need to beat my daughter, I hope?"

"I would prefer not to," Renata said. "I have always thought that solitary meditation over some tedious or boring task is punishment enough for most misbehavior. Still, I wish you would tell her, sometime, what you have told me, my lord. She seems to feel that her rank should excuse her from punishment or discipline."

"You would like me to tell her that my tutors had leave to beat me when I was a lad?" Lord Aldaran chuckled. "Very well, I shall do so, by way of reminding her that even I have had to learn to rule myself. But did you come only for leave to punish my daughter, Lady? I had thought that when I put her in your charge, you would take that for granted."

"And so I do," Renata said. "But I had something far more serious to discuss with you. You brought me here because you feared the strength of your daughter's *laran*, did you not? I have monitored her carefully, body and brain; she is still several moons short of puberty, I judge. Before that comes upon her, I would like to ask leave to monitor you, my lord, and Donal as well."

Lord Aldaran raised his eyebrows curiously. "May I ask why, *damisela*?"

"Margali has already told me all she can remember of Aliciane's pregnancy and confinement," Renata said, "so that I know some of what Dorilys inherited from her mother. But Donal, too, bears the heritage of Rockraven, and I would like to know what recessives Dorilys may be carrying. It is simpler to check Donal than to go into germ plasm. The same with you, my lord, since Dorilys bears not only your heritage but that of all your line. I would also like access to your genealogies, so that I can see if there are any traces in *your* line of certain kinds of *laran*."

Lord Aldaran nodded. "I can see that you should be armed with such knowledge," he said. "You may tell the keeper of the Aldaran archives that I give you freedom of all our records. Do you think, then, that she will survive threshold sickness in adolescence?"

"I will tell you that when I know more of what lies within her genes and heritage," Renata said. "I will do what I can for her, I swear it, and so will Allart. But I must know what I am facing."

"Well, I have no particular objection to being monitored," Lord Aldaran said, "although it is a technique with which I am not familiar."

"Deep monitoring of this sort was developed for the matrix circles working on the higher levels," Renata said. "When we had done using it for that, we found it had other uses."

"What must I do, then?"

"Nothing," Renata said. "Simply make your mind and body as quiet and relaxed as you can, and try to think of nothing at all. Trust me; I shall not intrude into your thoughts, but only into your body and its deeper secrets."

Aldaran shrugged. "Whenever you like," he said.

Renata reached out, beginning the slow monitoring process; first monitoring his breathing, his circulation, then going deeper and deeper into the cells of body and brain. After a long time she gently withdrew, and thanked him, but she looked troubled and abstracted.

"What is the verdict, *damisela*?"

"I would rather wait until I have seen the archives, and worked with Donal," she said, and bowed to him, leaving the room.

A few days later, Renata sent word asking if Lord Aldaran could receive her again.

When she came into his presence this time, she wasted no words.

"My lord, is Dorilys your only living child?"

"*Yes,* I told you that."

"I know she is the only child you acknowledge. But is that only a manner of speaking, or the literal truth? Have you any unacknowledged bastards, by-blows, any child at all born of your blood?"

Aldaran shook his head, troubled.

"No," he said. "Not one. I had several children by my first marriage, but they died in their adolescence, of threshold sickness; and Deonara's babes all died before they were weaned. In my youth I fathered a few sons here and there, though none survived adolescence. As far as I know, Dorilys alone, on the face of this world, bears my blood."

"I do not want to anger you, Lord Aldaran," Renata said, "but you should get you another heir at once."

He looked at her, and she saw the dismay and panic in his eyes.

"Are you warning me that she, too, will not survive adolescence?"

"No," said Renata. "There is every reason to hope she will survive it; she may even become something of a telepath. But your heritage should not rest on her alone. She might, as Aliciane did, survive the bearing of a single child. Her *laran,* as near as I can tell, is sex-linked; one of the few gifts that are. It is recessive in boys; Donal has the ability to read air currents and air pressure, to feel the winds and sense the movement of storms, and even to control the lightning a little, though not to draw it or to generate it. But this gift is dominant in females. Dorilys might survive the birth of a son. She could not survive the birth of a daughter gifted unborn with such *laran.* Donal, too, should be warned to father only sons, unless he wishes to see their mothers struck down by this *laran* in their unborn daughters."

Aldaran took this in slowly. At last he said, his face gray with torment, "Are you saying that Dorilys killed Aliciane?"

"I thought you knew that. This is one reason the Rockraven gift was abandoned by the breeding program. Some daughters, without the full strength of *laran* themselves, nevertheless had it to pass on to *their* daughters. I think Aliciane must have been one of these. And Dorilys had the full *laran.* . . . During her birth—tell me—was there a storm?"

Aldaran felt his breath catch in his throat, recalling how Aliciane had cried out, in terror, "She hates me! She doesn't want to be born!"

Dorilys killed her mother! She killed my beloved, my

Aliciane. . . . Desperately, struggling for fairness, he said, "She was a newborn child! How can you blame her?"

"Blame? Who speaks of blame? A child's emotions are uncontrolled; they have had no training in controlling them. And birth is terrifying for a child. Did you not know that, my lord?"

"Of course! I was present when all of Deonara's babes were born," he said, "but I could calm them to some extent."

"But Dorilys was stronger than most babes," Renata said, "and in her fear and pain, she struck—and Aliciane died. She does not know this; I hope she will never know. But, knowing this, you can see why it is not safe to rely on her, alone, to pass your blood to future generations. Indeed, it would be safer for her never to marry, though I shall teach her, when she comes to womanhood, how to conceive sons only."

"Would Aliciane had had such teaching," said Lord Aldaran, with great bitterness. "I did not know this technique was known in the Domains."

"It is not very commonly taught," Renata said, "although those who breed *riyachiyas* know it, to breed nothing but females. It has not been taught lest the lords of great estates, hungry for sons, should upset the balance nature has given us, so that there would be too few women born. Yet, in such a case as this, I think, where such a frightful *laran* can strike the unborn, I think it justified. I will teach Dorilys, and Donal, too, if he wishes."

The old man bowed his head. "What am I to do? She is my only child!"

"Lord Aldaran," Renata said quietly, "I would like your permission, if I think it needful, to burn out her *laran* in adolescence to destroy her psi centers within the brain. It might save her life—or her reason."

He stared at her in horror. "Would you destroy her mind?"

"No. But she would be free of *laran,*" Renata said.

"Monstrous! I refuse absolutely!"

"My lord," Renata said, and her face was drawn, "I swear to you. If Dorilys were the child of my own womb, I would ask you the same. Do you know she has killed three times?"

"Three? *Three*? Aliciane; Darren, my brother's son—but that was justified, he attempted to ravish her!"

Renata nodded. She said, "She was handfasted once before, and the child died, did he not?"

"I thought that was an accident."

"Why, so it was," said Renata. "Dorilys was not six years old. She knew only that he had broken her doll. She had blocked it from her mind. When I forced her to remember it, she cried so pitifully, I think it would have melted the heart of Zandru's self! So far she strikes only in panic. She would not, I think, even have killed the kinsman who tried to rape her, but she had no control. She could not stun, only kill. And she may kill again. I do not know if anyone living can teach her enough control over this kind of *laran.* I would not burden her with guilt, if she strikes again in a moment of fear or panic."

Renata hesitated. Finally she said, "It is well known: power corrupts. Even now, I think, she knows no one dares to defy her. She is headstrong and arrogant. She may like the knowledge that everyone fears her. A girl on the threshold of adolescence has many troubles; at such times girls dislike their faces, their bodies, the color of their hair. They think others dislike them, because they have so many anxieties they cannot yet focus. If Dorilys comforts herself for these anxieties with the knowledge of her power—well, I know *I* would be frightened of her under these conditions!"

Aldaran stared at the floor of the room, black and white and inlaid with a mosaic of birds. "I cannot consent to having her *laran* destroyed, Renata. She is my only child."

"Then, my lord," Renata said bluntly, "you should marry again and get you another heir before it is too late; and at your age you should lose no time."

"Do you think I have not tried that?" Aldaran said bitterly. Then, hesitating, he told Renata of the curse.

"My lord, surely a man of your intelligence knows that the power of such a curse is upon your mind, not your manhood."

"So I told myself for many years. Yet I felt no desire for any woman, for many years after Aliciane died. After Deonara died, and I knew I had only a single *nedestro* girl-child surviving, I took others to my bed; yet none of them quickened. Of late I have begun to believe the curse had struck me before the sorceress voiced it, for while Aliciane was heavy with my child I took no other. For me that was unknown, that I should live half a year with no woman for my bed." He shook his head, apologetically. "Forgive me, *damisela.* Such talk is unseemly to a woman of your years."

"Speaking of such things I am not a woman but a *leronis,* my lord. Don't trouble yourself about that. Have you never been monitored to test this, my lord?"

"I did not know such a thing was possible."

"I will test it, if you will," Renata said matter-of-factly. "Or if you would rather—Margali is your kinswoman, and nearer to your years—if it would trouble you less. . . ."

The man stared at the floor. "I would feel less shamed before a stranger, I think," he said in a low voice.

"As you will." Renata quieted herself and sank deep into the monitoring of body and brain; cell deep.

After a time she said regretfully, "You are cursed, indeed, my lord. Your seed bears no spark of life."

"Is such a thing possible? Did the woman merely know my shame, or did she cause this—this—" His voice died, between rage and dismay.

Renata said quietly, "I have no way of knowing, my lord. I suppose it is possible that some enemy could have done this to you. Although no one trusted with a matrix in the Towers would be capable of such a thing. We are sworn with many oaths against such abuse of our powers."

"Can it be reversed? What the powers of sorcery have done, can they not undo?"

"I fear not, sir. Perhaps if it had been known at once, something— but after so many years, I fear it is an impossible task."

Aldaran bowed his head. "Then I must pray to all the gods that you can somehow bring Dorilys undamaged through adolescence. She alone bears the heritage of Aldaran."

Renata pitied the old man; he had had to face some painful and humiliating truths today. She said gently, "My lord, you have a brother, and your brother has sons. Even if Dorilys should not survive this—although, indeed, I pray Avarra may guard her from all harm—the Aldaran heritage will not be wholly lost. I beg you, sir, be reconciled to your brother."

Aldaran's eyes blazed with sudden, terrible exploding rage.

"Have a care, my girl! I am grateful for all you have done, and all you will do, for my child, but there are some things even you cannot say to me! I have sworn that I will tear down this castle stone by stone ere it falls to any son of Scathfell! Dorilys will reign here after me, or none!"

Cruel, arrogant old man! Renata found herself thinking. *It would serve you right if that came, indeed, to pass! His pride is stronger than his love for Dorilys, or he would spare her this terrible destiny!*

She bowed. "Then there is no more to be said, my lord. I will do what I can for Dorilys. Yet I beg you to remember, sir, that the world will go as it will, and not as you or I would have it go."

"Kinswoman, I beg you, be not angry. I beg you not to let your anger at this sharp-tongued old man make you any less a friend to my little girl."

"Nothing could do that," Renata said, softening against her will to the old man's charm. "I love Dorilys, and I will guard her as much as I may, even against herself."

When she had left Aldaran, she walked for a long time on the battlements, troubled. She faced a very serious ethical problem. Dorilys probably could not survive childbirth. Could she reconcile it to her own strict code, to let the girl come unknowing to womanhood with that shocking curse? Should she warn Dorilys of what lay ahead for her?

She thought, angry again, that Lord Aldaran would expose Dorilys to such a death rather than accept the knowledge that his brother of Scathfell might inherit his domain.

Cassilda, blessed mother of the Hastur kin, she thought. *All gods be praised that I am not lord of a Domain!*

Chapter 17

Summer in the Hellers was beautiful; the snows receded to the highest peaks, and even at dawn there was little rain or snow.

"A beautiful season, but dangerous, cousin Allart," Donal said, standing at the height of the castle. "We have fewer fires than the Lowland Domains, for our snows remain longer, but our fires rage longer because of the resin-trees, and in the heat of these days they give off the volatile oils which ignite so quickly when the summer lightning storms rage. And when the resin-trees ignite—" He shrugged, spreading his hands, and Allart understood; he, too, had seen the volatile trees catch fire and go up like torches, throwing off showers of sparks which fell in liquid rain, spreading flame through the whole forest.

"It is a miracle that there are any resin-trees left, if this happens year after year!"

"True; I think if they grew less swiftly, these hills would be bare and the Hellers a wasteland from the Kadarin to the Wall around the World. But they grow swiftly, and in a year the slopes are re-covered."

Allart said, fastening the straps of the flying-harness around his waist, "I have not flown in one of these since I was a boy. I hope I have not lost the knack!"

"You never lose it," Donal said. "When I was fifteen and ill with threshold sickness, I could not fly for almost a year. I was dizzy and disoriented and when I was well again I thought I had forgotten how to fly. But my body remembered, as soon as I was airborne."

Allart drew the last buckle tight. "Have we far to fly?"

"Riding, it would be more than most animals could do in two days; it lies by paths mostly straight up and down. But as the *kyorebni* fly, it is little more than an hour's flight."

"Would it not be simpler to take an air-car?" Then Allart remembered he had seen none in the Hellers.

Donal said, "The folk of Darriel experimented with such things. But there are too many crosscurrents and cross-drafts among the peaks here; even with a glider you must pick your day carefully for flying, and be wary of storms and changes in the wind. Once I had to sit on a crag for hours, waiting for a summer storm to subside." He chuckled with the memory. "I came home as bedraggled and sad as a rabbithorn who has had to yield his hole to a tree-badger! But today, I think, we will have no such trouble. Allart, you are Tower-trained, do you know the folk at Tramontana?"

"Ian-Mikhail of Storn is Keeper there," Allart said, "and I spoke with all of them in the relays, from time to time, during my half-year at Hali. But I have never been to Tramontana in the flesh."

"They have always welcomed me there; indeed, I think they are always glad of visitors. They sit like hawks in their aerie, seeing no one from midsummer festival to midwinter night. It will be a pleasure for them to welcome you, cousin."

"And for me," Allart said. Tramontana was the most distant and farthest northward of the Towers, in almost total isolation from the others, though its workers passed messages through the relay-nets and exchanged information about the work they had done in developing new uses for matrix science. It had been the workers at Tramontana, he remembered, who devised the chemicals for fire-fighting, where they could be found in the deep caves under the Hellers, refining them, devising new ways to use them, all with the matrix arts.

"Is it not true that they have worked with matrixes to the twenty-fifth level?"

"I think so, cousin. There are thirty of them there, after all. It may be the farthest of the Towers, but it is not the smallest."

"Their work with chemicals is brilliant," Allart said, "although I think I would be afraid to do some of the things they have done. Yet their technicians say that once the lattices are mastered, a twenty-sixth-level matrix is no more dangerous than a fourth-level. I do not know if I would wish to trust myself to the concentration of twenty-five other people."

Donal smiled ruefully. "I wish I knew more of these things. I know only what Margali has taught me, and what little they have had leisure to tell me, when I visit there, and I have seldom been given leave to stay more than a single day."

"Indeed, I think you would have made a mechanic, or perhaps even a technician," Allart said, thinking of how swiftly the lad had responded to his teaching, "but you have another destiny."

"True; I would not abandon my father, nor my sister, and they need me here," Donal said. "So there are many things I shall never do with a matrix, for they need the safety of a Tower. But I am glad to have learned what I could, and for nothing am I more glad than this," he added, touching the leather-and-wood struts of the glider. "Are we ready to go, cousin?"

He stepped to the edge of the parapet, fluttered the long extended leather flaps of the glider wings to catch the air current, then stepped off into the air, soaring upward. Allart, his senses extended, could just feel the edge of the current; he stepped to the parapet edge, feeling an inner cramping at the height, the glimpse of the fearful gulf below him. Yet if a boy like Donal could fly without fear over that height. . . . He focused on the matrix, stepped free, and felt the sudden dizziness of the long drop and swoop outward, the tug of the current that bore him upward. His body swiftly balanced itself, lying along the inner struts, leaning this way and that as he mastered the balance of the toy. He saw Donal's glider, soaring hawklike above him, and caught an updraft carrying him along until they flew side by side.

For the first minutes Allart was so preoccupied with the mastery of the glider that he did not look down at all, his entire consciousness caught up into the delicate balances, the pressure of the air and the energy currents he could dimly sense, all around him. Somehow it made him think of his days at Nevarsin, when he had first mastered his *laran* and had learned to see human beings as swirls, energy-nets of force like streaming currents, without the awareness of flesh and blood, of his *solid* body. Now he sensed that the insubstantial air was filled with the same streaming currents of force. *If I have taught Donal much, he has given me no less in return, teaching me this mastery of air currents and the streams of force which permeate the air as they do the land and the waters. . . .* Allart had never before been aware of these currents in the air; now he could almost *see* them, could pick and choose among them, riding them up, up to a height where the winds dashed against the frail glider, racing along on the tremendous airstream, then picking a convenient current to dip down again to a safer height. He began, as he lay along the struts now, leaving a fragment of his consciousness to control the glider, to look down at the mountain panorama laid out below him.

Below them a quiet mountainous countryside stretched out, slope after slope of hills covered with dark forest, now and then the thickness giving way to slanted rows of trees, marching mechanically up and down a hillside—nut-farms, or plantations of edible fungus in the forest. Hillsides had been cleared for grasses where herds grazed, dotted with small huts where the herd-keepers lived, and now and again, beside the course of a racing mountain stream, a waterwheel set up for the making of cheeses, or the fibers which, matrix-enhanced, could be extracted from the bulk of the milk after whey and curds had been pressed out. He smelled the odd reek of a felting-mill, and another of a mill where the scraps left after timbering were pressed into paper. On a rocky slope, he saw the entrance to a network of caves where the forge-folk lived and saw the glow of their fires, where flying sparks could not endanger forests or populated areas.

As they flew on, the hills became higher and more deserted. He felt Donal's touch on his thoughts—the boy was developing into a skilled telepath who could attract his attention without troubling it— and Allart followed him down a long draft between two hills, to where the white glareless stone of Tramontana Tower gleamed in the noon-light. He saw a sentry on the heights raise his hand in

greeting, and followed as Donal swooped down, folding the
wings of his glider as he landed on his feet, sinking grace-
fully to his knees and rising in a single controlled movement, whipping off the glider wings in a long trail behind
him; but Allart, less skilled at this game, found himself
knocked off his feet, in a disorderly tangle of struts and
ropes. Donal, laughing, came to help him disentangle
himself.

"Never mind, cousin. I have landed that way many times
myself," he said, though Allart wondered how many years
it had been since he had done so. "Come, Arzi will take
your glider and keep it safe against our return," he added,
gesturing to the bent old man who stood beside him.

"Master Donal," said the old man, in a dialect so thick
that even Allart, who knew most of the Hellers dialects,
found it hard to follow. "A joy, as ever, to welcome ye
back among us. Y' lend us grace, *dom'yn*," he added, including Allart in his rude bow.

Donal said, "This is my old friend Arzi, who has served
the Tower since before I was born, and welcomed me here
three or four times a year since I was ten years old. Arzi—
my cousin, Dom Allart Hastur of Elhalyn."

"Vai dom." Arzi's bow was almost comical in its depth
and deference. "Lord Hastur lends us grace. Ah, it's a
happy day—the *vai leronyn* will be glad indeed to welcome
ye, Lord Hastur."

"Not Lord Hastur," Allart said gently, "only Lord Allart,
my good man, but I thank you for your welcome."

"Ah, it's been many, many years since a Hastur came
among us," Arzi said. "Be pleased t' follow me, *vai
domyn*."

"Look what the winds have brought us," called a merry
voice, and a young girl, tall, slender, with hair as pale as
snow on the distant peak, came running toward Donal,
holding out her hands to him in welcome. "Donal, how
glad we all are to see you again! But you have brought a
guest to us!"

"I am glad to return, Rosaura," Donal said, embracing
the girl as if they were long-lost kin. The girl stretched out
her hands to welcome Allart, with the swift touch of telepaths to whom this was more natural than the touch of

fingertips. Allart, of course, had known who she was even
before Donal spoke the name, but as they brushed against
one another her face lighted again with a quick smile.

"Oh, but you are Allart, who was at Hali for half a year.
I had heard you were in the Hellers, of course, but I had
no notion fortune would bring you here to us, kinsman.
Have you come to work with Tramontana Tower?"

Donal was watching with amazement at this meeting.
"But you have not been here before, cousin," he said to
Allart.

"That is true," Rosaura said. "Until this hour, none of
us have looked upon our kinsman's face, but we have
touched him in the relays. This is a glad day for Tramontana, kinsman! Come and meet the rest of us." Rosaura
took them inside, and quickly they were surrounded by
more than a dozen young men and women—some of the
others were at work in the relays, others asleep after a
night of work—all of whom welcomed Donal almost as one
of themselves.

Allart's emotions were mixed. He had managed not to
think too much about what he had left behind at Hali
Tower, and now he was meeting, face to face, minds he
had touched in the relays there, putting faces and voices
and personalities to people he had known only in the elu-
sive, bodiless touch of mind to mind.

"Are you coming to Tramontana to stay, cousin? We can
use a good technician."

Regretfully, Allart shook his head. "I am committed elsewhere, though nothing would please me more, I think. But
I have been long at Aldaran, without much new from the
outside world. How goes the war?"

"Much as before," said Ian-Mikhail of Storn, a slight,
dark young man with curling hair. "There was a rumor that
Alaric Ridenow, him they call the Red Fox, had been slain,
but it was false. King Regis lies gravely ill, and Prince Felix
has summoned the Council. If he should die, may his reign
be long, there will be need for another truce while Felix is
crowned, should he ever be crowned. And among your own
kinsmen, Allart, word came through the relays that a son
was born to your brother's lady in the first tenday of the
rose month. The boy does well, though the lady Cassilde

has not recovered her strength and could not suckle him herself. There is some fear that she will not recover. But the boy has been proclaimed your brother's heir."

"The gods be thanked, and Evanda the merciful smile on the child." Allart spoke the formula with real relief.

Now Damon-Rafael had a legitimate son; there was no question whether the Council would choose a legitimate brother over a *nedestro* son.

Yet, among the crowding futures, Allart saw himself crowned at Thendara. Angrily he tried to slam the door on his *laran* and the unwelcome possibilities. *Have I some taint of my brother's kind of ambition, after all?*

"And," said Rosaura, "I spoke with your lady but three days ago, in the relays."

Allart's heart seemed to clutch painfully and knock against his ribs. Cassandra! How long had it been since he had called her image to mind? "How does my lady?"

"She seems well and content," Rosaura said. "You knew, did you not, that she has now been appointed full monitor for Coryn's circle at Hali?"

"No, I had not heard."

"She is a powerful telepath in the relay-nets. I wonder you could bring yourself to leave her behind. You have not been long married, have you?"

"Not yet a year," Allart said. *No, not long, a painfully short time to leave a beloved wife. . . .* He had forgotten that he was among trained telepaths, a Tower circle; for a moment he had dropped his barriers, saw the pain in his thoughts reflected all around him.

He said, "The fortunes of war, I suppose. The world will go as it will and not as you or I would have it." He felt sententious, prim, as he mouthed the cliché, but they displayed the bland unrevealing non-contact, the mental turning-away which is the courtesy among telepaths when truths too revealing have been shown. He recovered his composure while Donal spoke of their errand.

"My father sent me for the first of the fire-chemicals to be taken to the station at the heart of the resin-tree forest; the others can be sent more slowly, with pack-animals. We are building a new fire station on the peak. The talk became general, of fire-fighting, of the season and the early storms.

One of the *leronyn* took Donal to make up a packet of the chemicals which could be carried back on the gliders, and Rosaura drew Allart aside.

"I regret the necessities which parted you so soon from your bride, kinsman; but if you like, and if Cassandra is in the relays, you can speak with her."

Faced with the possibility, Allart felt his heart clenched. He had resigned himself, told himself that if he never saw Cassandra again, at least they avoided the grimmest of the futures he had seen. Yet he knew he could not forbear this chance to speak with her.

The matrix chamber was like any other, the vaulted roof and blue window-lights below it admitting soft radiance, the monitor screen, the great relay lattice. A young woman in the soft loose robe of a matrix worker knelt before it, her face blank and calm with the distant look of a matrix technician with the mind attuned elsewhere, thoughts caught up in the relay-nets that linked all the telepaths in all the Towers of Darkover.

Allart took his place beside the girl in the relays, the inner part of his thoughts still troubled.

What shall I say to her? How can I meet her again, even this way?

But the old discipline held, the ritual breaths to calm his mind, his body locking itself in one of the effortless postures which could be maintained indefinitely without too much fatigue.

He cast himself into the vast spinning darkness, like the swoop of the glider over the great gulf. Thoughts whirled and spun past him like distant conversation in a crowded room, meaningless because he was unaware of their origin or context. Slowly, as he became more aware of the structure of the relay-net tonight, he felt a more definite touch, Rosaura's voice.

Hali. . . .

We are here, what would you have?

If the lady Cassandra Aillard-Hastur is among you, her husband is with us at Tramontana and begs a word with her. . . .

Allart, is it you? As recognizable as her bright hair, her gay girlish smile, he touched Arielle. *I think Cassandra is sleeping, but for this she will be glad to be wakened. Bear my greetings to my cousin Renata; I think of her often with love and blessings. I will waken Cassandra for you.*

Arielle was gone. Allart was back in the floating silence, messages slipping past him without impinging on any part of his mind which could remember or register them. Then, without warning, she was *there,* beside him, around him, a presence almost physical. . . . *Cassandra!*

Allart, my beloved. . . .

The texture of tears, of amazement, disbelief, reunion; an instant, timeless (three seconds? three hours?), of absolute, ecstatic joining, like an embrace. It was like nothing except the moment when he had first possessed her and in that moment felt the barriers drop, felt her mind yield and blend into his, a joining more complete, a mutual surrender more total than the union of their bodies. Wordless, but complete; he was lost in it, felt her lose herself in it.

It could not be sustained for long at such a level; he felt it drop away, recede into ordinary thought, ordinary contact.

Allart, how came you to Tramontana?

With the foster-son of Aldaran, to collect the first of the fire-fighting chemicals for the high fire season; it is upon us in the Hellers. He flashed to her a picture of the long, ecstatic flight here, the swoop of the glider, the wind racing past head and body.

We have had fires here, too. The Hali Tower was attacked with air-cars and incendiaries. He saw ravening flames on the shore, explosions, an air-car struck down and burning like a meteor as it fell, exploded by the linked minds of eleven at Hali, the dying shrieks of the flyer who had brought it in, drugged and suicidal. . . .

But you are safe, my beloved?

I am safe, although we are all weary, working day and night. . . . Many things have happened to me, my husband. I shall have much to tell you. When will you return to me?

That must be as the gods will, Cassandra, but I shall not delay any longer than I must. . . . As he formed the word-thoughts he knew they were true. The part of wisdom might be never to see her again. But even now he could foresee a day when he would hold her in his arms again, and he knew abruptly that even if death were the penalty, he would not turn away . . . nor would she.

Allart, are we to fear the entrance of the Aldarans into

this war? Since you left us for the Hellers, we have all feared that more than anything else.

No, Aldaran is much beset by strife with his kin; he bears neither loyalty nor grudge to either side. I am here to teach laran *to Lord Aldaran's foster-son while Renata cares for his daughter. . . .*

Is she very beautiful? In her thoughts, wordless yet unmistakable, he sensed rancor, jealousy. Was it for Renata or the unknown daughter? He heard her unspoken answer: *both. . . .*

Very beautiful, yes. . . . Allart kept his thoughts light, amused. *She is eleven years old . . . and no woman on the face of this world, not the Blessed Cassilda within her shrine, is half so beautiful as you, my beloved. . . .* Then another moment of the wholly blissful, ecstatic merging, joining, as if they were clasped together, with everything that they were, bodies, minds, souls. . . . He must break it. Cassandra could not long sustain this, not if she was working as a monitor. Slowly, reluctantly, he let the contact drop away, disappear, fade into nothingness, but his whole mind and body were still full of her as if he could feel the print of her kiss on his mouth.

Dazed, weary, Allart let himself come back to awareness of the matrix chamber, cold and blue, around him, of his own cramped and shivering body. Slowly, after a long time, he moved, rose, quietly tiptoed out of the matrix chamber, leaving the workers in the relay-nets undisturbed. As he made his way down the long twisting stairs, he did not know whether or not he was grateful for the chance to speak with her.

It has forged anew a bond which it would have been better to break. In that long joining he had picked up many things which he had not, with his conscious mind, really understood, but he sensed that Cassandra, too, had tried in her own way to break that bond. He was not resentful. They were still bound, more strongly than ever, with the bonds of desire and frustration.

And love? *And love?*

What is love, anyway? Allart was not sure whether the thought was his own, or one he had somehow picked up from the confused mind of his young wife.

Rosaura met him at the bottom of the stairs. If she noted

his dazed face, the traces of tears around his eyes, she said nothing; there were certain courtesies among Tower telepaths, where no strong emotion could ever be concealed. She only said, quietly matter-of-fact, "After a contact across so much space, you will be drained and weary. Come, cousin, and refresh yourself."

Donal joined them at the meal, and half a dozen of the workers in the Tower who were not at their duties or resting. They were all a little manic with the relaxation of strain, the rare treat of company in their isolated place. Allart's sorrow and revived longing for Cassandra were swept away on a tide of jesting and laughter. The food was strange to Allart, though good; a sweet white mountain wine he had never tasted, mushrooms and fungus cooked in a dozen different ways, a soft white boiled tuber or root of some kind mashed into little cakes and fried in fragrant oil, but there was no meat. Rosaura told him that they had resolved to experiment here with a diet of no animal flesh and see if it sensitized their awarenesses. This seemed strange and a little silly to Allart, but he had lived for years with such a diet at Nevarsin.

"Before you go, we have a message for your foster-father, Donal," Ian-Mikhail said. "Scathfell has sent embassies to Sain Scarp, to Storn, to Ardais and Scaravel, and to the Castamirs. I do not know what it is all about, but as overlord to Scathfell he should be told. Scathfell would not trust it to the relays, so I fear it is some secret conspiracy, and we had heard rumors of a breach between your father and Lord Scathfell. Lord Aldaran should be warned."

Donal looked troubled. "I thank you on my foster-father's behalf. Of course we knew some such things must be happening, but our household *leronis* is old, and has been much occupied with the care of my sister, so we had heard nothing by way of the overworld."

"Is your sister well?" Rosaura asked. "We should have liked to have her here with us at Tramontana for her testing."

"Renata Leynier has come from Hali to care for her during adolescence," Donal said, and Rosaura smiled.

"Renata from Hali; I know her well in the relays. Your sister will be well with her, Donal."

Then it was time to make ready and go. One of the

monitors brought them neatly made-up packets of the chemicals which, mixed with water or other fluids, would expand enormously into a white foam that would cover an incredible expanse of fire. More would be sent as soon as land convoy could be arranged. Donal went up to the high walk behind the tower and stood there scanning the skies. When he descended, he looked grave.

"There may be storms before sunset," he said. "We should lose no time, cousin."

This time Allart felt no hesitation about stepping off, drifting on a rising current of air, using the power of his matrix to carry him up and up, soaring. Yet he could not wholly give himself to the enjoyment of the experience.

The contact with Cassandra, blissful as it had been, had left him drained and troubled. He tried to put aside all these thoughts, flying demanded concentration on his matrix; preoccupation with outside thoughts was a luxury he could not afford. Yet again and again he saw faces cast before him by his *laran*: a big hearty man who oddly resembled Dom Mikhail of Aldaran; Cassandra weeping alone in her room at Hali, then rising and composing herself to work in the relays; Renata facing Dorilys with angry challenge. . . . He brought himself back by force of will to the heights, the soaring rush of air past the glider, the air currents tingling painfully in his outstretched fingertips as if each finger were the pinion of a soaring hawk, himself neither man nor bird, swooping on the air. He knew that in this moment he shared Donal's inner fantasy.

"There are storms ahead," said Donal. "I am sorry to take you so far from our way when you are not used to flying, but we must go around them. It is not safe to fly so near a storm. Follow me, cousin." He caught a handy air current and let himself drift, matrix-aided, away from the straight line to Aldaran.

Allart could see the storm ahead of them, sensing rather than seeing the charges of electricity leaping from cloud to cloud. They circled in a long, slow spiral almost to the ground, and Allart sensed Donal's exasperation.

Are we going to have to land somewhere and wait out the storm? I would risk it, but Allart is unaccustomed to flying. . . .

I will risk what you risk, kinsman Donal.

Follow me, then. It is like dodging a rain of arrows, but I have done it more than once. . . . He dipped his wings, soared upward on a fast current, then darted swiftly between two clouds. *Quickly! A charge of lightning has just struck and there is a little time until another can build up!*

Allart felt the curious harsh tingle, and again they ran the gauntlet of darting lightning. He would have hung back, but he trusted Donal's *laran* to guide them through, Donal knowing where and precisely *when* the lightning would strike. Yet Allart felt cold chills strike him. They flew through a sudden small rain squall and he clung, drenched and icy, to the struts of the glider, his wet clothes freezing against his skin. He followed Donal on the long sickening swoop of downdraft, snatched up at the last minute to ride a current up and up till they hung circling above the heights of Castle Aldaran.

Donal instructed, a voice in his mind: *We cannot go down at once; there is too much charge on our gliders and clothing. When we put foot to ground it would knock us senseless. We must circle a while; soar, spread your hands to drain off the charge. . . .*

Allart, following instructions, drifting in lazy, dreamy circles, knew that Donal was in the hawk-persona again, projecting himself into the mind and thoughts of a great bird. Circling above the castle; Allart had leisure to look down at Aldaran. In these months past it had become a second home to him, but now he beheld, with a sense of foreboding, a long caravan of riders winding up to the gates. Turning, Allart sent out a wordless cry of warning to Donal, as the caravan leader drew and brandished a sword, the sound of his yelling *almost* audible to Allart where he hung high above the battlements, above the steep tumbling waterfall.

"But there is no one there, kinsman," Donal said, troubled. "What ails you? What did you see? Truly, there is no one there."

Dazed, Allart blinked, a sudden giddiness making his wings flutter, and he tilted, automatically, to balance on the air. The road to Aldaran lay bare and deserted in the thickening twilight—neither riders, nor armed men, nor banners. His *laran* had shown him, only his *laran,* the foresight of what might, or might never, come to pass. It was gone.

Donal fluttered, swooped sidewise. His agitated alarm prompted Allart to follow him quickly. "We must get down, even if we are knocked senseless," he, shouted, then sent a swift, agitated thought to Allart: *There is another storm coming.*

But I see no clouds.

This storm needs no clouds, Donal thought in dismay. *This is the anger of my sister, generating lightning. The clouds will come. She would not strike us, knowing, but still we must get down as quickly as we can.*

He let himself drop on a swift current, shifting his weight on the glider so that he hung, vertically, using his weight and twisting his body like an acrobat to send the glider downward. Allart, more cautious and less experienced, followed a more conservative downward spiral, but he felt, still, the jolt of painful electricity as his feet touched the ground behind the castle. Donal, unbuckling his harness and shoving the glider in a jumble of ropes at the servant who came hurrying to take it, murmured, "What can it be? What has happened to upset or frighten Dorilys?" With a word of apology to Allart, he hurried away.

Chapter 18

Renata, too, heard the muttering of the summer thunder, without thinking too much about it, as she moved through the castle halls on her way to Dorilys's apartments for their daily late-afternoon lesson.

Because Dorilys was younger than the novice workers in any Tower—and also because Dorilys had not, as they did, sought out this training of her own free will, pledging herself to endure uncomplaining all the discomforts and difficulties of the work—Renata had tried to make the teaching easy and pleasant, to devise games and amusements which would develop the girl's use of *laran* without tedious exercises to tire or bore her. Dorilys was still too young to be tested formally for telepathy which rarely developed much in advance of puberty, but other forms of *laran* were earlier to arise, and Renata judged that Dorilys had a considerable amount of clairvoyance and, probably, some telekinetic power in addition to her formidable gift of generating or controlling lightnings. So she had taught her with simple games: hiding sweets and toys and letting her find them with her *laran,* blindfolding her and having her find her way among intricate obstacle courses of furniture or unfamiliar parts of the castle; having her pick her own possessions, blindfolded, out of a jumble of similar ones, by the "feel" of her own magnetism attached to them. She was a quick pupil, and enjoyed the lessons so much that on two or three occasions Margali had actually controlled her rebellious young charge by threatening to deprive her of them, as she did with her music lessons, unless she satisfactorily finished the other tasks of which she was not so fond.

As far as Renata could tell, Dorilys was wholly without the two gifts which would have made her a trainable Tower worker: telepathy, defined as the ability to read or pick up deliberate thought; and empathy, or the ability to feel another's emotions or physical sensations in her own mind and body. But either might develop at adolescence—they often did—and if, at that time, she had some control of her own energy currents and flows, there would be less danger of the dreaded threshold sickness.

If it could only develop earlier—or later! It was the scourge of all the families with *laran* that these troubling facilities should develop at the same time the child was going through the physical and emotional upheavals of puberty. So many of those who bore these gifts found that the sudden onset of psi powers, developing sexuality, and the hormonal and temperamental liability of these times were an overload on body and brain. They developed enormous upheavals; sometimes crisis, convulsions, and even death followed. Renata herself had lost a brother to threshold sickness; no *laran* family survived unscathed.

Dorilys carried Aldaran blood on his father's side, not the relatively stable Delleray, which was akin to the Hastur. What Renata knew of the Aldaran and Rockraven lines did not make her entirely hopeful, but the more Dorilys knew of the energy currents in her body, the nerve flows and energon runs, the more likely she would be to survive these upheavals without undue difficulty.

Now, as she approached Dorilys's rooms, she sensed overtones of annoyance, weary patience (Renata herself considered the old *leronis* virtually a saint for putting up with this difficult and spoiled little girl), and the arrogance of Dorilys when she was crossed. Dorilys had seldom shown this pettish side to Renata, for she admired the young *leronis* and wanted her goodwill and liking. But she had never been disciplined firmly, and found it difficult to obey when her emotions went otherwise. It did not make it easier that, since Darren of Scathfell had been struck down, Margali was afraid of her charge, and could not conceal it.

I am afraid of her, too, Renata thought, *but she does not*

know it, and if I ever let her know, I will never again be
able to teach her anything!

Outside the door, she heard Dorilys's voice, just a petulant grumble. She heightened her sensitivity to hear Margali's firm answer.

"No, child. Your stitching is a disgrace. There will be no
music lesson, nor any lesson with the lady Renata, until
you have taken out all those clumsy stitches and done them
properly." She added, in a coaxing tone, "You are not so
clumsy as that; you are simply not trying. You can sew very
neatly when you choose, but today you have decided you
do not want to sew, and so you are deliberately making a
mess of what you do. Now take out all of those stitches—
no, use the proper ripping tool, child! Don't try to take
them out with your fingers, or you will tear the cloth! Dorilys, what is the matter with you today?"

Dorilys said, "I don't like sewing. When I am Lady of
Aldaran I will have a dozen sewing-woman, and there is
no reason I should learn. The lady Renata will not deprive
me of my lesson because *you* say so!"

The rude and spiteful tone of her words decided Renata.
The sewing was not important, but the self-discipline of
working carefully and conscientiously at a task for which
she had neither talent nor taste was a valuable teaching.
Renata, a trained empath and monitor, felt as she opened
the door the deep searing pain across Margali's forehead,
the lines of weariness in the older woman's face. Dorilys
was up to her old trick of giving Margali headaches when
the older woman would not give her everything she wanted.
Dorilys was sitting over the hated sewing, looking sweet
and compliant, but Renata could see, as Margali could not,
the triumphant smirk on her face as Renata came through
the door. She flung the sewing to the floor, and rose, hurrying to Renata.

"Is it time for my lesson, cousin?"

Renata said coldly, "Pick up your sewing and put it away
properly in its drawer—or better yet sit down and finish it
as you should."

"I don't have to learn to sew," Dorilys said, pouting.
"My father wants me to learn those things which *you* can
teach me!"

"What I can teach you best," Renata said firmly, "is to

do what you have to do, when you have to do it, as well as you can do it, whether you want to do it or not. I do not care whether you can sew neatly or whether your stitches stagger like a *chervine* drunken on windfall apples"—Dorilys gave a small, triumphant giggle—"but you will not use your lessons with me to get the better of your foster-mother, or to evade what she wants you to do." She glanced at Margali, who was white with pain, and decided the time had come for a showdown.

"Is she giving you headaches again?"

Margali said faintly. "She knows no better."

"Then she shall learn better," Renata said, her voice icy. "Whatever it is that you are doing, Dorilys, you will release your foster-mother at once, and you will kneel and beg her pardon, and then *perhaps* I shall continue to teach you."

"Beg *her* pardon?" Dorilys said incredulously. "I won't!"

Something in the tilt of the small chin, though Dorilys was said to resemble her dead mother, suddenly made Renata think of Lord Aldaran himself. *She has her father's pride,* she thought, *but she has not yet learned to mask it in courtesy and expedient compromise and charm. She is still young and we can see this willfulness in all its naked ugliness. Already she does not care who she hurts, as long as she gets her own way. And to her, Margali is not much better than a servant. Nor am I; she obeys me because it pleases her.*

She said, "I am waiting, Dorilys. Beg Margali's pardon at once, and never do so again!"

"I will, if she will promise not to order me around anymore," Dorilys said sullenly.

Renata set her lips. So it was really a showdown, then. *If I back down, if I allow her to set her own terms, she will never obey me again. And this teaching may save her life. I do not want power over her, but if I am to teach her, she must learn obedience; to rely on my judgment until she can trust her own and control it.*

"I did not ask you on what terms you would beg her pardon," Renata said. "I simply told you to do it. I am waiting."

"Renata," Margali began.

But Renata said quietly. "No, Margali. Keep out of this.

You know as well as I what the first thing is she must learn." To Dorilys she said, her voice a whiplash, using the trained command-voice, "Kneel down at once and beg pardon of your foster-mother!"

Dorilys dropped automatically to her knees; then, springing up, she cried out shrilly, "I have told you never to use command-voice on me! I will not allow it, and neither will my father! *He* would not see me humiliated by begging *her* pardon!"

Dorilys. Renata thought, *should have been thoroughly spanked before she was old enough, or strong enough, to get such exaggerated ideas of her own importance. But everyone has been afraid of her, and would not cross her. I do not blame them. I am afraid of her, too.*

She knew she faced an angry child whose anger had killed. *Yet I still have the upper hand. She is a child and she knows she is in the wrong, and I am a trained Tower technician and monitor. I must teach her, now, that I am stronger than she is. Because a day will come, when she is full-grown, when no one will be strong enough to control her; and before that time has come, she must be capable of controlling herself.*

Her voice was a whiplash. "Dorilys, your father gave me charge of you in all things. He told me that if you disobeyed, I had his leave to beat you. You are a big girl, and I would not like to humiliate you *that* way, but I tell you— unless you obey me at once, and beg pardon of your foster-mother, I shall do exactly that, as if you were a baby too small to listen to the voice of reason. Do as I tell you, and at once!"

"I will not," cried Dorilys, "and you cannot make me!" As if to echo her words, there was a harsh mutter of thunder outside the windows. Dorilys was too angry to hear it, but she sensed it, and flinched.

Renata thought, *Good. She is still a little afraid of her own power. She does not want to kill again. . . .*

Then Renata felt across her own forehead the searing pain, like a tightening band . . . was she picking this up from Margali, with her own empath power? No; a quick look at the angry child showed her that Dorilys was taut, frowning, tense, concentrated with gritted anger. Dorilys was doing to her what she had done to Margali.

The little devil! Renata thought, torn between anger and unwilling admiration of the child's power and spirit. *If only all that strength and defiance can be turned to some useful purpose, what a woman she will make!* Focusing on her matrix—which she had never done before in Dorilys's presence, except to monitor her—Renata began to fight back, reflecting the energy at Dorilys. Slowly her own pain diminished and she saw the girl's face go white with strain. She kept her voice calm with an effort.

"See? You cannot serve me so, Dorilys. I am stronger than you. I do not want to hurt you, and you know it. Now obey me, and we will have our lesson."

She felt Dorilys strike out, angrily. Summoning all her own strength, she caught and held the child as if she had wrapped her physically in her arms, restraining body and mind, voice and *laran*. Dorilys tried to cry out, "Let me go," and discovered, in terror, that her voice would not obey, that she could not make a single move. . . . Renata, sensitive, empath, felt Dorilys's terror as if it were in her own body, and ached with pity for her.

But she must know that I am strong enough to protect her from her own impulses, that she cannot strike me down without thinking, as she did with Darren. She must know that she is safe with me, that I will not let her hurt herself, or anyone else.

Now Dorilys was really afraid. For a moment, watching her bulging eyes, the frantic small trapped movements of her muscles, Renata felt such pity that she could not endure it. *I do not want to hurt her, or to break her spirit, only to teach her . . . to protect her from her own terrible power! Someday she will know it, but now she is so frightened, poor little love. . . .*

She saw the small muscles in Dorilys's throat moving, struggling to speak, and released the hold on the child's voice; saw the tears starting from Dorilys's eyes.

"Let me go, let me go!"

Margali turned entreating eyes on her; she, too, was suffering, seeing her beloved nursling so helpless.

The old *leronis* whispered, "Release her, Lady Renata. She will be good; won't you, my baby?"

Renata said, very gently, "You see, Dorilys, I am still stronger than you. I will not allow you to hurt anyone, not even yourself. I know you do not really want to hurt or kill anyone for a moment's anger because you cannot have your own way in all things."

Dorilys began to sob, still held rigidly motionless in the grip of Renata's *laran*.

"Let me go, cousin, I beg you. I will be good. I will, I promise. I am sorry."

"It is not to me you must apologize, child, but to your foster-mother," Renata reminded her gently, releasing her hold on the little girl.

Dorilys dropped to her knees and managed to sob out, "I am sorry, Margali. I did not mean to hurt you; I was only angry," before she collapsed into incoherent crying.

Margali's thin fingers, gnarled now with age, gently stroked Dorilys's soft cheek. "I know that, dear heart. You would never hurt anyone; it is only that you do not think."

Dorilys turned to Renata and whispered, her eyes wide with horror, "I could have—could have done to you what I did to Darren—and I love you, cousin, I love you." She flung her arms around Renata, and Renata, still shaking, wrapped her arms around the thin, shaking child.

"Don't cry anymore, sweetheart. I won't let you hurt anyone. I promise," she said, holding her tight. "I won't ever let you hurt anyone." She took her kerchief, dried Dorilys's eyes. "Now put away your sewing properly, and we will have our lesson."

She knows, now, what she is capable of doing, and she is beginning to be wise enough to be afraid of it. If I can only manage to control her until she is wise enough to control herself!

Outside the window the storm had died to a distant rumble, and then to nothing, silence.

But, hours later, Renata faced Allart, shaking with long-suppressed tension and fear.

"I was stronger than she—but not enough," she whispered. "I was so frightened, kinsman!"

He said soberly, "Tell me about it. What are we to do with her?"

They were sitting in the drawing room of the small and luxurious suite of rooms which Lord Aldaran had ordered placed at Renata's disposal.

"Allart, I hated to frighten her that way! There should be a better way to teach her than fear!"

"I do not see what choice you had," Allart said soberly. "She must learn to fear her own impulses. There is more than one kind of fear." This discussion intensified many of his own old anxieties, roused by contact with Cassandra, by the long flight with Donal, the surroundings of the Tower at Tramontana. "My own battle was fought with fear, the kind of fear that paralyzed me and kept me from action. I find little that is good in that kind of fear. Until I mastered it, I could do nothing. But it seems to me that she knows too little of caution, and fear may have to serve her until she learns rational caution."

Renata repeated what she had thought during the battle of wills. "If there were only some way to harness all that strength, what a woman she could be!"

"Well," said Allart, "that is, after all, why you are here. Don't be discouraged, Renata. She is very young and you have time."

"But not enough time," Renata said. "I fear puberty will come on her before the winter's end, and I do not know if that is enough time to teach her what she must learn, before that dreadful stress is placed on her."

"You can do no more than your best," Allart said, wondering if the images in his mind—a child's face circled by lightning, Renata's weeping in the vaulted room, her body swollen in pregnancy—were true images or fear alone. How could he distinguish between what would happen, what must happen, what might never happen?

Time is my enemy. . . . For everyone else it runs one way only, but for me it straggles and bends upon itself and wanders into a land where never is as real as now. . . .

But he banished self-pity and preoccupation again, looking into Renata's troubled eyes. She seemed so young to him, no more than a girl herself, and burdened with such dreadful responsibility! Searching for something to lighten her dread, he told her, "I spoke through the relays to Hali; I bear greetings and love for you from Arielle."

"Dear Arielle," Renata said. "I miss her, too. What news from Hali, cousin?"

"My brother has a son, born to his wife and therefore legitimate," Allart said. "And our king lies gravely ill and

Prince Felix has summoned the Council. I know little more than that. Hali was attacked by incendiaries."

Renata shivered. "Was anyone hurt?"

"No, I think not. Cassandra would surely have told me if there had been any serious injuries. But they are all overwearied, working night and day," Allart said. Then he came out with what had been on his mind since he had spoken with his wife in the relays. "It weighs on me that I am here in safety when she must face such dangers! I should care for her and protect her, and I cannot."

"You face your own dangers," Renata said gravely. "Do not grudge her the strength to face her own. So she is full monitor now? I knew she had the talent, if she could endure the training."

"Still, she is a woman, and I am better fitted to endure danger and hardship."

"What troubles you, kinsman? Do you fear that if she is no longer dependent on you, she will not turn to you with love?"

Is it only that? Am I truly as selfish as that, that I want her weak and childlike, so that she will turn to me for strength and protection? He had picked up many things from Cassandra's mind in their long, intense rapport that she had not consciously told him, and which he was only now beginning to bring into awareness. The timid childlike girl, swayed by impulse, wholly dependent on his love and care, had become a strong Tower-trained monitor, a woman, a skilled *leronis*. She still loved him, deeply, passionately—their communion had left him no doubt of that—but he was no longer the only thing in her world. Love had taken its place among many forces now motivating her, and was not the only one she would act upon.

It was painful for him to realize this; more painful to realize how unhappy the thought made him.

Would I truly have wanted to keep her like that, timid, virginal, frightened, belonging to me alone, seeing the world only through my eyes, knowing only what I wanted her to know, being only what I desired in a wife? Custom, the traditions of his caste and his pride of family, cried out, *Yes, yes!* But the larger world he had begun to see prompted him to be ashamed of that.

Allart smiled ruefully, thinking this was not the first time

Renata had interceded for his wife's own good. Now there were other roads for Cassandra besides the solitary one he had seen at the end of their love, that she must inevitably die in bearing his child. How could he resent anything which removed that continuing terror from his mind?

"I am sorry, Renata! You came to me for comfort, and as usual, you have ended by comforting and reassuring *me*! Indeed, I wish I knew more of Dorilys's *laran,* so I could advise you, but I agree with you that it will be a catastrophe if we cannot teach her in time. I saw Donal's in action today, and it is most impressive—more even than when he read which way the fire would move. Now that the fire season is starting," Allart suggested tentatively, "perhaps you could take her to the fire station, high on the peaks, and let Donal try to teach her a little of how to use this. He knows more of it than either you or I."

"I think perhaps I must do that," Renata agreed. "Donal, too, has survived the threshold, and it may give her confidence that she can do the same. I am glad that she does not read my thoughts; I do not want her to be terrified of what may come upon her with her womanhood, but she must be prepared to face that, too. . . . She wants more than anything else to learn to fly, as the boys in the castle do before they are anywhere near her age. Margali says it is unseemly for a girl, but since her *laran* has to do with the elements, she should learn to face them close at hand." Renata laughed and admitted, "I, too, would like to learn. Are you going to go all stiff and monkish on me and say it is unsuitable for a woman as for a young girl?"

Allart laughed, signaling with the gesture of a fencer who acknowledges a hit. "Are my years in Nevarsin still so plainly visible, cousin?"

"Dorilys will be so happy when I tell her," Renata said, laughing, and Allart realized again, suddenly, how very young she was. She had the self-imposed dignity and sober manners of the monitor, she had assumed formal manners and self-discipline to teach Dorilys, but she was really only a young girl herself who should be as lighthearted and carefree as Dorilys.

"Then, Donal shall teach you both to fly," he said. "I will speak with him, while you teach her to master a matrix and the art of levitating with it."

Renata said, "I think she is old enough to learn to use a matrix. Now she will learn quickly, and not waste her energies upon testing me."

"It will make it easier to go to the fire station," Allart told her, "since the ride is difficult, and many of the men who work there, watching for fires, find it simpler to fly to the peaks." He glanced self-consciously at the night beyond the windows. "Cousin, I must go; it is very late."

He rose, their hands touching with the fingertip-touch of telepaths, somehow more intimate than a handclasp. They were lightly in rapport, still, and as he looked down into her lifted face, he saw it aglow, warmed with passion. He was aware of her all over again as he had taught himself not to be; the close contact with Cassandra, barriers down, had broken the facade of monklike austerity, of indifference to women, which he kept so firmly in place. She blurred into a dozen women in that momentary touch, his *laran* showing him the possible and the likely, the known and the impossible; and almost without volition, before he was fully aware of what he was doing, he had drawn her into his arms, was crushing her to him, breathless.

"Renata, Renata—"

She met his eyes, with a troubled smile. They were in such close contact that it was impossible to conceal his sudden awareness and hunger for her, and her immediate and unashamed response to it.

"Cousin," she said gently. "What is it that you want? If I have roused you without meaning it, I am sorry. I would not knowingly have done so, simply to show my power over you. Or is it only that you are very much alone and longing for anyone who can give you comfort, and sympathy?"

He drew away from her, dazed, but struck by her calm, her complete lack of shame or confusion. He wished that he himself were as calm.

"I am sorry, Renata. Forgive me."

"For what?" she asked, her smile glinting deep in her eyes. "Is it an offense to find me desirable? If so, I hope I shall be offended that way many times." Her small hand closed on his. "It is not so serious a thing as that, cousin. I only wanted to know how seriously you intended it; that is all."

Allart muttered miserably, "I don't know." Confusion,

loyalty to Cassandra, the memory of shame and disgust because he had been unable to resist the temptation of the *riyachiya* his father had pushed into his arms, overwhelmed him. Was it *this* which had led him to embrace Renata? The knowledge that she actually shared this upsurge of need and emotion confused him all over again.

A woman he could love without fear, one who was not wholly dependent on him. . . . Then came a shaming thought: *Or am I doing this because Cassandra is no longer wholly mine?*

She said, laughing up at him, "Why do you refuse for yourself a freedom you have given to her?"

He almost stammered, "I do not want to—to use you for my own need, as if you were no more than a *riyachiya.*"

"Ah, no, Allart," she said in asmall voice, clinging to him. "I, too, am alone and in need of comfort, kinsman. Only I have learned that it is nothing shameful to say so and acknowledge it, and you have not, that is all. . . ."

What Allart saw in her face shocked him with its openness. He held her close to him, realizing suddenly that for all her strength, for all her invulnerable skill and wisdom, she was a girl, and frightened, and like himself facing troubles far beyond her ability to solve.

What have the men and women of the Domains done to one another, so that everything between us must be shrouded in fear or guilt for what has been or what may be. It is so rare that there can be simple kindliness or friendship between us, like this.

Holding Renata close in his arms, bending to kiss her very tenderly, he said almost in a whisper, "Let us comfort one another, then, cousin," and led her into the inner room.

Chapter 19

Dorilys was wildly excited, chattering like a child half her age, but a little abashed when Margali dressed her in clothing borrowed from one of the young pages. Margali, too, was skeptical.

"Was this necessary, Lady Renata? She is hoyden enough already, without tearing about in boys' clothes!" She looked with frowning disapproval at Renata, who had borrowed a pair of breeches from the hall-steward's fifteen-year-old son.

Renata said, "She must learn to work with her *laran*, and to do that, she must confront the elements where they are, not where we might like them to be. She has worked very hard to master the matrix, so that I promised she might fly with Donal when she had done so."

"But is it really needful for her to wear those unseemly breeches? It seems not modest to me."

Renata laughed. "For flying? How modest would it be, do you think, if her gown should fill with the wind like a great sail and fly up about her ears? Those unseemly breeches seem to me the most modest garment she could possibly wear for flying!"

"I had not thought of that," the old *leronis* confessed, laughing. "I, too, longed to fly when I was a young girl. I wish I were coming with you!"

"Come along, then," Renata invited. "Surely you have skill enough to learn to control the levitators!"

Margali shook her head. "No, my bones are too old. There is a time to learn such things, and when that time is past, it is too late. It's too late for me. But go, Renata. Enjoy it—and you, too, darling," she added, kissing Dorilys's cheek. "Is your tunic fastened? Have you a warm scarf? It is sure to be cold on the heights."

Despite her brave words, Renata felt uneasy. Not since she was five years old had she showed the shape of her limbs in any public place. When they joined Allart and Donal in the courtyard, they, too, seemed abashed and did not look at her.

Renata thought, *I hoped Allart had more sense! I have shared his bed, and yet he looks everywhere but at me, as if it came as a great surprise to him that I had legs like everyone else! How ridiculous is custom!*

But Dorilys was quite without self-consciousness, strutting in her breeches, demanding to be noticed and admired.

"See, Donal! Now I will be able to fly as well as any boy!"

"And has Renata taught you to practice with the matrix, raising and lowering other objects before you tried it with yourself?"

"Yes, and I am good at it. Didn't you say I was good at it, Renata?"

Renata smiled. "Yes, I think she has a talent for it, which a little practice will sharpen into skill."

While Donal showed his sister the mechanism of the glider-toys, Allart came to help Renata with her straps. They stood side by side, watching Dorilys and her brother. The night they had spent together had cemented and strengthened their friendship; it had not really changed its nature. Renata smiled up at Allart, acknowledging his help, realizing with pleasure that she thought of him as she always did, as a friend, not a lover.

I do not know what love is. I do not think I really want to know. . . .

She was fond of Allart. She had liked giving him pleasure. But both had been content to leave it there, a single shared impulse of loneliness, and not to build it into anything it was not. Their needs were basically too different for that.

Donal was now showing Dorilys how to read the air currents carefully, how she could use the focus of her matrix to amplify them and make them more perceptible to her senses. Renata listened carefully; if lads in the Hellers mastered these tricks before they were ten years old, surely a trained matrix worker could do it, too!

Donal made them all practice a while on the flat windswept area behind the castle, running with the winds and letting themselves rise on the currents, soaring high and circling, swooping down. Finally he declared himself satisfied and pointed to the peak far above them, where the fire station commanded a view of the whole valley beyond Caer Donn.

"Do you think you can fly so far, little sister?"

"Oh, yes!" Dorilys was flushed and breathless, little tendrils of fine copper hair escaping from the long braid at her back, her cheeks whipped to crimson with the wind. "I love it. I would like to fly forever!"

"Come, then. But stay close to me. Don't be afraid; you can't fall, not as long as you keep your awareness of the air currents. Now, lift your wings, like this—"

He watched her step off and soar upward on a long rising current, rising and rising over a long gulf of sky. Renata followed, feeling the draft take her and toss her high, seeing Allart rising behind her. Dorilys caught a downdraft and was circling, hovering like a hawk, but Donal gestured her onward.

Higher and higher they flew, rising through a damp white cloud, emerging above it; now hovering and turning, soaring down until they came to rest on the peak. The fire watch station was an ancient structure of cobblestone and timbers; the ranger, a middle-aged man, long and lean, with pale gray eyes and the weathered look of one who spends much of his time peering into unfathomable distances, came to greet them, in surprise and pleasure.

"Master Donal! Has Dom Mikhail sent you with a message for me?"

"No, Kyril; it is only that we wished my sister to see how the fire station is managed. This is Lord Allart Hastur, and the lady Renata Leynier, *leronis* of Hali."

"You are welcome," the man said, courteously, but without undue servility; as a skilled professional, he owed deference to no one. "Have you ever been up to the peak before, little lady?"

"No. Father thought it too far for me to ride; also, he said you were too busy here during the fire season for guests."

"Well, he was right," Kyril said, "but I will be glad to show you what I can as I have leisure. Come inside, my dear."

Inside the station were relief maps of the entire valley, a replica in miniature of the tremendous full-circle panorama seen from the windows of the building on every side. He pointed out to her the cloud-cover over parts of the valley, the areas marked on his map which had been burned over in recent seasons, the sensitive areas of resin-trees which had to be watched closely for any stray spark.

"What is that light flashing, Master Kyril?"

"Ah, you have sharp eyes, little one. It is a signal to me, which I must answer." He took a mirrored-glass device with a small mechanical cover which could be opened and closed swiftly, and stepping to the opened window, began to flash a patterned signal into the valley. After a moment the flashing in the valley resumed. Dorilys started to ask a question, but he motioned her to be quiet, then bent over his map, marked it with chalk, and turned back to her.

"Now I can explain to you. That man signaled to me that he was building a cookfire there, while the herdman take their count of his cattle. It is a precaution so that I will not think a forest fire has begun and call men together to fight it. Also, if the smoke remains more than a reasonable time for a herdman's cookfire, I will know it is out of control and can dispatch someone to help with it before it spreads too far. You see"—he gestured in a circle all around the fire-tower—"I must know at every moment where every wisp of smoke is, in all this country, and what causes it."

"You have the chemicals from Tramontana?" Donal asked.

"The first lot reached me just in time to stop a serious outbreak in the creek-bed there," he said, indicating it on the map. "Yesterday a consignment was brought here, and others stored at the foot of the peak. It is a dry year, and there is some danger, but we have had only one bad burn, over by Dead Man's Peak."

"Why is it called Dead Man's Peak?" Dorilys asked.

"Why, I do not know, little lady; it was so called in my father's time and my grandfather's. Perhaps at some time, someone found a dead man there."

"But why would anyone go there to die?" Dorilys asked, looking up at the far crags. "To me it looks more like a hawk's nest."

"There were hawks there once," Kyril said, "for I climbed to take some when I was a young man. But that was long, long ago." He looked at the distant sea of smoke and flame; to the others it was blurred by distance. "There have been no hawks there for years. . . ."

Renata interrupted the conversation, saying, "Dorilys, can you tell where the fire on that slope will move next?"

Dorilys blinked, her face going blank, staring into the distance. After a moment she gestured, and for a moment Allart, astonished, realized she was speaking so rapidly it was gibberish.

"What, child?" Renata asked, and Dorilys came back to herself.

She said, "It is so hard to say it in words, when I can *see* the fire where it was and where it is and where it is moving, from its start to its finish."

Merciful Avarra, Allart thought. *She sees it in three dimensions of time—past and present and future. Is it any wonder we find it hard to communicate with her!* The second thought that hit him, hard, was that this might somehow have some bearing on his own curious gift . . . or curse!

Dorilys was trying to focus down, to search, struggling, for words to communicate what she saw.

"I can see where it started, there, but the winds drove it down the watercourse, and it turned—look—into the . . . I can't say it! Into those net things at the edge of the windstream. Donal," she appealed, "*you* see it, don't you?"

He came and joined her at the window. "Not quite what you see, sister. I think perhaps no one sees it quite as you do; but can you see where it will move next?"

"It has moved—I mean, it will move *there,* where they will have the men all ganged together to fight it," she said. "But it will come there only because *they* come. It can feel—No, that isn't right! There aren't any words." Her face twisted and she looked as if she were almost crying.

"My head hurts," she said plaintively. "Can I have a drink of water?"

"There is a pump behind the door," the man Kyril said. "The water is good; it comes from a spring behind the station. Be sure to hang up the cup when you have drunk, little lady." As she went in quest of her drink, Renata and Donal exchanged long looks of amazement.

Renata thought, *I have learned more about her* laran *now in a few minutes than I have learned in half a season. I should have thought to come here before.*

Kyril said in a low voice, "You know, of course, that there are not any men fighting the fire now; they controlled it and left it to burn out along the lower crags. Yet she saw them. I have seen nothing like this since the sorceress Alarie came here once with a fire-talisman to gain command of a great fire, when I was a young man. Is the child a sorceress, then?"

Renata, disliking the ancient word smacking so much of superstition, said, "No; but she has *laran,* which we are trying to train properly, to see these things. She took to the gliders like a young bird to the air."

"Yes," Donal said. "It took me far longer to master them. Perhaps she sees the currents more clearly than I can. For all we know, they are solid to her, something she can almost touch. I think Dorilys could learn to use a fire-talisman; the forge-folk have them, to bring metals from the ground to their forges."

Renata had heard of this. The forge-folk had certain especially adapted matrixes, which they used for mining and for that purpose only; a technique both more crude and more developed than the highly technical mining methods of the Towers. She had the Tower technician's distrust of matrix methods developed in this catch-as-catch-can, pragmatic way, without theory.

Kyril looked into the valley, saying, "The cookfire is out," and erased the chalk mark on his map. "One less trouble, then. That valley is all as dry as tinder. May I offer you some refreshment, sir? My lady?"

"We have brought food with us," Allart said. "Rather, we would be honored if you would share our meal." He began to unwrap the packages of dried fruit, hard-baked bread, and dried meat that they had brought.

"I thank you," Kyril said. "I have wine here, if I may offer you a cupful, and some fresh fruit for the little lady."

They sat near the window so that Kyril could continue his watch. Dorilys asked, "Are you alone here all the time?"

"Why, no, lady. I have an apprentice who helps me, but he has gone down the valley today to see his mother, so for the day I am alone. I had not thought I would be entertaining guests." He drew out his clasp-knife from his heavy boot and began to peel her an apple, spiraling the peel into delicately cut designs. She watched with fascination, while Renata and Allart watched the clouds moving slowly across the valley far below them, casting strange shadows. Donal came and stood behind them.

Renata asked him, in a low voice, "Can you, too, sense where the storms will move?"

"A little, now, when I can see them spread out this way before me. I think perhaps that when I am watching a storm I move a little outside of time, so that I see the *whole* storm, from start to finish, as Dorilys saw the whole fire a little while ago." He glanced back at Dorilys, who was eating her apple, chattering with the ranger. "But somehow at the same time I see the lightnings in sequence, one after another, so that I know where each one will strike and which first, because I can see the pattern of where they move *through* time. That is why, sometimes, I can control them—but only a little. I cannot *make* them strike anywhere, as my sister does," he added, lowering his voice so that it would not carry to the little girl. "I can only, now and again, divert them so that they will *not* strike where they have already begun to move."

Allart listened, frowning, thinking of the sensitive divisions of time which this gift took. Donal, picking up his thoughts, said, "I think this must be a little like your gift, Allart. You move outside time, too; do you not?"

Allart said, troubled, "Yes, but not always into *real* time. Sometimes, I think, a kind of probability time, which will never happen, depending on the decisions of many, many other people, all crisscrossing. So that I see only a little part of the pattern of what will be or what *may* be. I don't think a human mind could ever learn to sort it all out."

Donal wanted to ask some questions about whether Al-

lart had ever tested his gift under *kirian,* one of the telepathic drugs in use in the Towers, for it was well known
that *kirian* somehow blurred the borders between mind and
mind so that telepathy was easier, time not quite so rigid.
But Renata was following her own line of question, her
mind again on her charge.

"You all saw how the fire troubled her," she said. "I
wonder if that has something to do with the way she uses
her gift—or strikes. Because in anger or confusion, she no
longer sees a pattern of time clearly; for her there is nothing but that one moment, of rage, or anger, or fear. . . .
She cannot see it as only one of a progression of moments.
You spoke of a fever she had as a child, when storms raged
around the castle for days, and you wondered what dreams
or delirium prompted them. Possibly there was some damage to the brain. Fevers often impair *laran.*" She considered
for a long moment, watching the slow inexorable drifting
of the storm clouds below them, which now masked a siz-
able part of the valley floor.

Dorilys came up behind them, winding her arms around
Renata like an affectionate kitten trying to climb into a lap.

"Is it me you are talking about? Look down there, Renata. See the lightning inside the cloud?"

Renata nodded, knowing the storm was just beginning to
build up enough electrical potential to show lightnings; she
herself had not seen lightning yet.

"But there are lightnings in the air even when there are
no clouds and no rain," Dorilys said. "Can't you see them,
Renata? When I use them, I don't really *bring* them, I just
use them." She looked sheepish, guilty, as she added,
"When I gave Margali a headache, and tried to do it with
you, I was using those lightnings I couldn't *see.*"

Merciful gods, Renata thought, *this child is trying to tell
me, without knowing the words, that what she does is to tap
the electrical potential field of the planet itself!* Donal and
Allart, picking up the thought, turned startled eyes on her,
but Renata did not see them, suddenly shuddering.

"Are you cold, cousin?" the child asked solicitously. "It
is so warm. . . ."

*All the gods at once be thanked that at least she cannot
read minds as well. . . .*

Kyril had come over to the window, looking with concentrated attention at the curdled mass of gray that was the storm center and the lightnings just beginning to be visible within it. "You asked about my work, little lady. This is a part of it, to watch where the storm center moves, and see if it strikes anywhere. Many fires are set by lightning, though sometimes no smoke can be seen for a long time after." He added, with an apologetic glance at the noblemen and Renata, "I think perhaps that some unknown forefather endowed me with a little foresight, because sometimes when I see a great strike I know that it will later blaze up. And so I watch it with a little more care, for some hours."

Renata said, "I would like to inquire into your ancestors, and find how even this diluted trace of *laran* came into your blood."

"Oh, I know *that*," Kyril said, again almost apologetic. "My mother was a *nedestro* of the old lord of Rockraven's brother—not he who rules there now, but the one before him."

So how can I say there is any laran *gift which is all evil, without potential use for good?* Renata thought. Kyril had turned his own small inherited gift to a useful, skilled, and harmless profession.

But Donal was following his own thoughts.

"Is it so, then, Kyril? Why, then, we are kinsmen."

"True, Master Donal, though I never sought to bring myself to their notice. Saving your presence, they are a proud people, and my mother was too humble for them. And I have no need of anything they could give."

Dorilys slid her hand confidingly through Kyril's. "Why, then, we are related, too, kinsman," she said, and he smiled and patted her cheek.

"You are like your mother, little one; she had your eyes. If the gods will, you will have inherited her sweet voice, as you have her pretty ways."

Renata thought, *How she charms everyone, when she is not being proud or sullen! Aliciane must have had that sweetness.*

"Come here, Dorilys," she said. "Look at the storm; can you see where it will move?"

"Yes, of course," Dorilys narrowed her eyes and

squinted her face in a comical way, and Allart glanced at Renata for permission to question her pupil.

"Is its course fixed, then, not to be changed at all?"

Dorilys said, "It's *awfully* hard to explain, kinsman. It could go this way or that, if the wind changed, but I can only see one or two ways the wind could change. . . ."

"But the path is fixed?"

"Unless I tried to move it," she said.

"*Could* you move it?"

"It's not so much that *I* could move it," Dorilys frowned in fierce concentration as she fumbled for words she had never been taught and did not know existed. "But I can see all the ways it *could* move. Well, let me show you," she said.

Allart, sliding lightly into rapport with her mind, began to sense and see the thick gray high-piled storm clouds as she saw them, everywhere at once. Yet he could trace where the storm was now, where it had been, and at least four ways it *might* be.

"But what will be cannot be altered; can it, little cousin? It follows its own laws; does it not? You have nothing to do with it."

She said, "There are places I could move it and places I could *not*, because the conditions are not right for it to go there. It's like a stream of water," she said, fumbling. "If I put rocks in it, it would go around the rocks, but it could go either way. But I couldn't make it jump out of the stream-bed, or run back uphill; do you understand, cousin? I can't explain," she said plaintively. "It makes my head ache. Let me *show* you. See?" She pointed to the enormous anvil-shaped storm mass below. His sensitivity keyed into hers, he suddenly saw with his own gift, the probable track of the storm with others less probable *through* and *over* the most likely path; it faded into the nothingness of total unlikeliness and then impossibility at the far outer edges of his perception. Then Dorilys's strange gift was *his own* gift, expanded, altered, strangely different, but basically the same: to see all the *possible* futures, the places where the storm *might* strike, the places where it might *not* because of its own nature. . . .

And she could choose between them like himself, to a

very limited degree because of the forces outside herself which moved them. . . .

As I saw my brother on the throne, or dead, within seven years. There was no third choice, that he could choose to remain content as Lord Elhalyn, because of what he is. . . .

He felt almost overwhelmed by this sudden insight into the nature of time, and probability, and of his own *laran*. But Renata was more practical.

"Can you actually control it, then, Dorilys? Or just tell where it will go?" Allart followed her thought. Was this simply precognition, foreknowledge, or was it like the power of levitation, moving an inanimate object?

"I can move it anywhere it *could* go," she said. "It could go there or there"—she pointed—"but not *there* because the wind couldn't change that fast, or that hard. See?" Turning back to Kyril, she asked, "Is it likely to start a fire now?"

"I hope not," the man said soberly, "but if the storm should move down toward High Crags there, where the resin-trees grow so thickly, we could have a bad fire."

"Then we will not let it strike there," Dorilys said, laughing. "It won't hurt anything if the lightning strikes down there, near Dead Man's Peak, where it is already all burned over; will it?" As she spoke a great blue-white bolt of lightning ripped from cloud to earth, striking Dead Man's Peak with a searing blaze, leaving a glare of sparks on all their eyes. After a second or two they heard the great crash of the thunder rolling over them.

Dorilys laughed in delight. "It is better than the fire-toys the forge-folk set off for us at midwinter!" she cried, and again the great flare of lightning arched across the sky, and again, while she laughed excitedly, pleased with the new ability to do what she would with the gift she had borne, not knowing it, all her life. Again and again the great blue-white, green-white bolts ripped and flamed down on Dead Man's Peak, and Dorilys shrieked with hysterical laughter.

Kyril stared at her, his eyes wide with awe and dread. "Sorceress," he whispered. "Storm queen. . . ."

Then the lightnings died, the thunders rumbled and rolled into silence, and Dorilys swayed and leaned against Renata, her eyes dark circled, smudged with fatigue. Again she was a child exhausted, white and worn. Kyril lifted her tenderly and carried her down a short flight of stairs. Renata followed him. He laid her on his own bed.

"Let the little one sleep," he said.

As Renata bent over the child to pull off her shoes, Dorilys smiled up at her wearily and was at once asleep.

Donal looked at her, questioning, as she came back to them.

"She is already asleep," Renata said. "She could not fly like this; she has exhausted herself."

"If you wish," Kyril said diffidently, "you and the little lady can have my bed, *vai domna,* and tomorrow, when the sun comes out, I can flash a signal for them to bring riding animals for you to return home that way."

"Well, we shall see," Renata said. "Perhaps when she has slept a while, she will have recovered enough to fly back to Aldaran." She moved behind him to the window, watching as his brow ridged in a worried frown.

"Look. The lightning has struck there, in that dry canyon," he pointed. Renata, with all her extended perception, could not see the slightest wisp of smoke, but she did not doubt that *he* saw it. "There is no sun for me to flash a signal. By the time it comes out again the fire will have taken hold there, but if I could reach anyone—"

Allart thought, *We should have telepaths stationed on these watchtowers, so that they could reach others stationed below at such times. If someone were standing by in the nearest village, armed with a matrix, Kyril or another could signal to have the fire put out.*

But Donal was thinking of the requirements of the moment. He said, "You have the fire-fighting chemicals I brought from Tramontana. I will fly there in my glider and spread the chemicals where the lightning struck. That will damp the fire before it really starts."

The old ranger looked at him, troubled. "Lord Aldaran would be ill pleased if I let his foster-son run such a danger!"

"It is no longer a question of *letting* me, old friend. I am a grown man, and my foster-father's steward, and responsible for the well-being of all these people. They shall not be ravaged by fire if I can prevent it." Donal turned, breaking into a run, down the stairs and through the room where Dorilys still lay in her stunned sleep. Kyril and Renata hurried after him. He was already buckling himself into his flying-harness.

"Give me the chemicals, Kyril."

Reluctantly the ranger handed over the sealed water-cylinder, the packet of chemicals. When mixed together, they would expand into a foam that could cover and smother an extraordinary expanse of flames.

As he moved toward the open space, before he could break into the run of takeoff, she stopped him.

"Donal, let me go, too!" Would they really let him fly alone into such danger?

"No," he said gently. "You are too new to flying, Renata. And there is some danger."

She said aloud, and knew her voice was shaking, "I am not a court lady, to be sheltered against all dangers. I am a trained Tower worker, and I am used to sharing all the dangers I see!"

He reached out, took her shoulders gently between his hands. "I know," he said softly, "but you have not the experience of flying; I should be hindered by having to stop and make certain you knew precisely what to do, and there is need for haste. Let me go, cousin." His hands on her shoulders tightened and he pulled her into a quick, impulsive embrace.

"There is not as much danger as you think, not for me. Wait for me, *carya*." He kissed her, swiftly.

She stood, still feeling the touch of his lips, watching him run toward the edge of the cliff, wings tilted to catch the wind. Donal soared off, and she stood shading her eyes against the glare, watching the glider shrink to hawk-size, sparrow-size, a pinpoint dipping behind the clouds. When it was gone she blinked hard, turned, and made her way inside the fire station.

Allart was standing at the windows, watching intently. He said as she joined him, "Since Dorilys showed me what she sees, I am somehow a little more able to control my foresight. It is a matter of shifting the perceptions for all times and seeing which is most real. . . ."

"I am so glad, cousin," she said, and meant it, knowing how painfully Allart had struggled with this curse of *laran*. But in spite of her very real concern for Allart, who was her kinsman, her lover, her friend, she discovered that she had no time to think of Allart now. All of her emotional tension was stretched outward, focused on that small distant fleck which was Donal's glider, hovering high above the valley, dipping slowly, slowly down, skirting the edge of the storm-pattern. And suddenly, all her emotion, all the empathic *laran* of a Tower-trained monitor, surged into awareness, identity, and she *was* Donal. She was . . .

. . . flying high above the valley, sensing the taut energy-net currents strung across the sky as if they were banners flying from the heights of the castle, snapped in the wind, trailing forces. He spread his fingertips to drain off the tingle of the electricity, hovering, soaring, all his attention focused on the spot on the forest floor that Kyril had pointed out to him.

A thin wisp of smoke, curling, half concealed by leaves and the long gray-green needles of evergreens, lying fallen and crisped by forst and sun on the ground. . . . It could smolder there unseen for days before blazing into a fire that could ravage all of the valley. . . . It had been well that he came. This was all too near the estate of High Crags which his foster-father had given him.

I am a poor man. I have nothing to offer Renata even if such a lady would be my wife . . . nothing but this poor estate, here in fire-country and ravaged again and again by fire. I had thought I could marry, establish a household. Yet now it seems to me all too little to offer my dear lady. Why do I think she would have me?

(Standing frozen, intent at the wide windows, Renata shivered, not really *there* at all. Allart, turning to speak, saw it and let her be.)

Again, Renata's awareness merged with his, Donal dropped down and down, hanging from the struts of the glider. He circled the small trailing wisp of smoke, studying it, unaware of how the storm above him moved and drifted and rumbled. The glider was dropping swiftly now, the wide wings slowing his fall just enough so that he could land on his feet, fall forward, braking his fall with his outstretched hands. He did not bother to unfasten the glider harness as he pulled the sealed water-cylinder from its place under the strut. After tearing it open with his teeth he tucked it under his arm while he ripped open the small packet of chemicals;

then he dropped the chemicals into the water, held the
pliable cylinder over and wisp of smoke, and watched as
the green foam bubbled and surged out, foaming up and
up endlessly, aiming and spilling around the forest floor,
soaking quickly into the ground. The smoke was gone; only
the last remnants of the oozing foam remained. Like all
fire-fighters, Donal was astonished anew at how quickly a
fire, once controlled at its source, could subside as if it had
never been.

*The most fickle of the elements, easiest to call, most diffi-
cult to control. . . .* The words came from nowhere in his
mind and were as swiftly gone again. He folded the limp
bag which had once been the water-cylinder, its imperme-
able material still smelling faintly of chemical slime, and
tucked it under one of the ropes of the glider harness.

This was so simple; why did Renata fear for me? Looking
into the sky, he knew. The clouds had gathered again
around him, and it was certainly no weather for flying.
There was no rain here, the air still heavy and sullen, oppressive and thick; but above him on the slopes of Dead
Man's Peak, the storm raged, heavy rain and black clouds
laced intermittently by flares of lightning arching from
cloud to the waiting ground. He was not really afraid, for
he had been flying since he was a small boy. Frowning, he
stood for a moment studying sky and air currents, the pattern of the storm, the winds, trying to calculate his best
chances of return to the fire station with the least danger
or difficulty.

*At least the storm on Dead Man's Peak has drowned the
last vestiges of the fire. . . .* Scanning the sky, Donal whipped
off the glider harness and tucked the contraption, wings
folded, under his arm. Walking very far with the wings
trailing offered too much drag, and there was also the danger of catching and snagging them on something. He
climbed a small, steep hillside from where he knew he
could catch a wind, strapped himself into the glider harness
again, and tried to take off. But the winds were swirling,
capricious. Twice he made a short run, tried to catch
enough wind in his wings to take off, but each time the
wind shifted around and spilled him, once with a painful
tumble to the ground.

Picking himself up, bruised, Donal swore. Was Dorilys

playing again with winds and air currents, shifting wind and magnetic fields without knowing he was down there? No, surely, Renata and Allart would keep her from trying any such tricks. But if she were still sleeping, still enormously nerved up from the excitement of the day, her first flight, the effort of controlling her gift? Did her dreaming mind shift winds and air at will, then?

Without enthusiasm he contemplated the distant peak where the fire station stood. Was he going to have to climb up there on foot? He could hardly do that before dark. The road was good enough, for supplies had to be brought up to the fire station every tenday; he had heard this road had been matrix-surfaced, in the time of Dom Mikhail's grandfather. But, still, he did not want to climb it. The best that could be said for it was that it was less trouble than scrambling up a rocky hillside. Yet if he could not catch a wind steady enough to lift him, with the aid of his matrix crystal, he must trudge up that road, carrying the glider under his arm!

He looked again at the sky, heightening his sensitivity to wind and air. The only wind steady enough to bear him up was blowing steadily toward the storm over Dead Man's Peak. Yet if he could ride up on this wind, catching a cross-current somewhere that would carry him back toward the fire station . . . there was some risk to it, yes. If the wind was too brisk, he would be carried along into the storm raging there.

Yet if he took the time to climb all that way, it would be dark and dangerous. He must risk the wind blowing toward the peak. He took a little extra time to make certain his straps were snug and secure, inspected the struts and their fastenings, and finally discarded the plastic fabric of the water-container. It could be reclaimed some other time, and even a little extra weight might make the difference in what was going to be a fairly tricky flying maneuver. Then he ran toward the edge of the hill, focusing on his matrix, letting the wind and the force of levitation bear him upward; felt, with relief, the wind catch in the broad edge-planes of his glider and carry him up and outward, along on the rising current of the solid draft.

He rose, soaring high, racing along on the wind with such force that every strut and rope of the glider shuddered and he could hear a high singing note above the roar of wind past his ears. He felt a curious, cold, exhilarating fear, his senses strained to their limit, taken up with the delight of soaring on the wind. *If I fall I could be smashed—but I will not fall!* Like a hawk in its native element he circled, looking down at the valley below, the ragged rents in the clouds over the fire station, the thickly piled storm clouds, sullen with lightning, over Dead Man's Peak. Circling again, he caught a cross-draft which would take him in the general direction of the fire station; he tilted his wings into it, a bird in his element, every sense given into the ecstasy of the flight. He was not aware of Renata's mind linked with his, but he found himself thinking, *I wish Renata could see this as I see it.* Somehow in his mind he linked the ecstasy of that soaring long glide, the rush of wind past the struts, with the moment, all too brief, when he had held her and felt her mouth on his own. . . .

Lightning crackled ominously, the metal clips at the end of the struts gleamed, suddenly, with bluish light, and Donal, tingling with undischarged electricity, realized that the storm had begun to move, swiftly on the wind, down the valley toward the fire station. He could not even descend; carrying this much electrical charge, he could not touch ground or he would be killed. He must circle until the charge was drained away. Through the sudden thunder, he realized that he was very much afraid. The storm was moving the wrong way. It should have drifted out past Dead Man's Peak and now it was turning back. Suddenly he remembered the day of Dorilys's birth, the day of his mother's death. The storm had been wrong then, too! Dorilys, asleep, dreaming dreams of terror and power, reaching out to tap the forces of the storm. But why would she focus them on him, even in sleep?

Does she know that she is no longer the only female creature in my thoughts and in my heart? He fought to keep his place in the air, despite the stubborn downdraft that sought to carry him downward to the open space behind the fire station. He knew he must circle once more. Again the crackle of thunder in the air deafened him, and gusts and spurts of cold rain chilled him. Once again he felt the lightning moving around him, and with every last atom of his *laran* he reached out, *twisted* something, thrust it *elsewhere. . . .*

It was gone. Thunder crackled through his body and he fell like a stone, with his last strength catching a current which could bring him in at the very edge of the open space behind the fire station. Or would he miss it, go tumbling down the side of the mountain to wind up, smashed, far below? Half-unconscious, he saw someone running below him, running toward where he would land. He fell heavily, staggering. His feet touched ground, and Renata caught him in her arms and held him, drenched and senseless against her for a moment before his weight overwhelmed her and they fell, together.

Wrung, exhausted, Renata held the unconscious Donal against her breast. His face was cold with rain and for a terrified moment she did not know if he were alive, then she felt the warmth of his breath against her, and her own world started to move again.

Now do I know what it is to love. To see nothing ahead except the one . . . to know, now, kneeling here as he lies stricken in my arms, that if he had been killed, in a very real sense I would have died here, too. . . . Her fingers fumbled on the straps, loosening the miraculously undamaged glider. But his eyes opened; he pulled her down to him and their lips met, in a sudden, profound quiet. They neither saw nor heeded Allart and Kyril watching them. Once and for all, now and forever, they knew they belonged to one another. Whatever happened afterward would simply be confirmation of what they already knew.

Chapter 20

As long as she lived, Renata knew, nothing in mind or memory would ever match the splendor of this season—high summer in the Hellers, and Donal at her side. Together they flew along the long valleys in their gliders, soaring from peak to peak, hiding beneath the crags from the summer storms, or lay side by side in the hidden canyons, hour after hour, watching clouds move across the sky, and turning from the sky to the green earth and to one another.

Day by day Dorilys came nearer to mastery of her strange gift, and Renata began to be more optimistic. Perhaps all would be well. Probably Dorilys should never risk bearing a child, certainly never a girl child, but she might survive puberty undamaged. In the flood of her own love, Renata felt she could not endure to rob Dorilys of that promise, that hope.

And I mocked Cassandra! Merciful Avarra, how young I was, how ignorant!

On one of the long, brilliant summer afternoons, they lay hidden in a green valley, looking up at the heights where Dorilys, with a few of the lads from the castle, was soaring like a bird, wheeling on the updrafts.

Donal said, "I am skilled enough with a glider, but I never could ride the winds as she does. I would not have dared. None of the boys is half so skilled or so fearless."

"None of them has her gift," Renata said, looking up into the dizzying violet depths of the sky, and blinking with sudden tears. Sometimes it seemed to her, in this first and last summer of their love, that Dorilys had become her own child, the girl child she knew she would never dare to bear to her lover; but Dorilys was theirs, theirs to teach and train, theirs to love.

Donal leaned over suddenly and kissed her, and then touched her eyelashes with a light finger. "Tears, beloved?"

Renata shook her head. "I have been looking too long into the sky, watching her."

"How strange this is," Donal said, taking her hands in his and kissing the slender fingers. "I had never thought—" His voice trailed off, but they were so deeply in rapport that Renata could follow his unspoken thoughts.

I never thought love would come to me like this. I knew that someday, soon or late, my foster-father would find me a wife, but to love like this . . . it does not seem real. I must somehow find courage to tell him, sometime. . . . Donal tried hard to imagine himself going against custom and civilized behavior, walking into his foster-father's study and saying to him, "Sir, I have not waited for you to find me a bride. There is a woman I wish to marry. . . ." He wondered if Dom Mikhail would be very angry with him; or, worse, if he would blame Renata.

But if he knew that there would never again be any happiness in life for me, except with Renata. . . . He wondered if Dom Mikhail could possibly ever have known what it was to love. *His* marriages had been properly arranged by his family; what could he possibly know of the emotion that swept them both up this way? He felt the wind blow cold on him and shivered, feeling a distant premonitory breath of thunder.

"No," Renata said. "She knows the storm currents too well; she is not in any danger. Look! All the lads are following her now—" She pointed upward at the line of children, tipping and circling on the wings of the wind, arrowing back like a flight of wild birds toward the distant high crags of Aldaran. "Come, dear love. The sun will set soon, and the winds grow so strong at sunset; we must go back and join them."

His hands trembled as he helped her to fasten the straps of her glider.

She whispered, "Of all the things you have shared with me, Donal, perhaps this is the most wonderful. I do not know if any other woman in the Hellers has ever been able to fly like this." Donal saw, in the gathering sunset crimsons, the flicker of a tear on her lashes; but without a rebuff, she evaded his thoughts, tipping the wings of her glider and running away down the long valley, catching a swift draft and soaring up, up, and away from him, to hang on a long drift of air until he flew at her side.

That evening in the hall, when Dorilys had made her good nights and been sent away, Aldaran gestured to Allart and Renata to remain. The musicians were playing and some of the house-folk were dancing to the sound of the harps, but Dom Mikhail frowned as he spread out a letter.

"Look here. I sent an embassy to Storn to open negotiations for a marriage with Dorilys. Last year they were willing to speak of nothing else, but this year I receive only a reply that since Dorilys is so young, perhaps we should speak of it again when she is of an age to be married. I wonder—"

Donal said bluntly, "Dorilys has been handfasted twice, and both her affianced husbands met a violent death soon after. Dorilys is clever, and beautiful, and her dower is Castle Aldaran; but it would be surprising if it were not remarked that those who seek to wed her do not live long."

Allart said, "If I were you, Lord Aldaran, I would wait to think further of marriage until Dorilys has passed puberty and is free of the danger of threshold sickness."

Aldaran said, his breath caching in his throat, "Allart, have you foreseen . . . will she die of threshold sickness like the children of my first marriage?"

Allart said, "I have seen nothing of the kind." He had tried, very hard, not to look ahead. It seemed now that he saw nothing except disasters, many of which could not be tied down to time or place. Again and again he had seen Castle Aldaran under siege, arrows flying, armed men striking, lightnings aflare and striking down on the keep. Allart had tried to do as he did at Nevarsin—to barricade it all away from his mind, to see *nothing;* for most of what he saw were lies and meaningless fear.

"Foresight is useless here, my lord. If I should see a hundred different possibilities, still, only one of them can come to pass. So it is meaningless to see ahead and fear the other ninety-and-nine. But if it were inevitable that Dorilys should die in threshold sickness at puberty, I do not think I would be able to *avoid* seeing it; and I have not."

Dom Mikhail leaned his head in his hands, and said, "Would that I had some trace of your gift, Allart! For it seems to me that this is clear sign that the folk of Storn have been in communication with my brother of Scathfell; and they will not anger him because he still hopes to win Aldaran somehow, if I die without son or son-in-law to hold it for me. And *that*," he said, pausing and moving his head with that quick hawklike movement, "will never be, while the four moons ride in the heaven and snow falls in midwinter!"

His eyes fell on Donal, and softened, and all of them could follow what he was thinking, that it was high time Donal, at least, was wed. Donal tensed knowing this was not the time to speak and cross him, but Dom Mikhail said only, "Go, children, join the dancers in the hall, if you will. I must think what to say to my kinsman of Storn," and Donal breathed again.

But later that night, Donal said, "We must not delay much longer, beloved. Or a day will come when he will summon me and say, 'Donal, here is your bride,' and I will be put to the trouble of explaining to him why I cannot marry whatever spiritless daughter of one of his vassals he has found for me. Renata, shall I journey to the Kilghard Hills and make suit, then, in my own name for your hand? Would Dom Erlend, do you think, give his daughter to a poor man, lord of no more than the small holding at High Crags? You are daughter to a powerful Domain; your kinsmen will say I was quick to go wooing a rich dower."

Renata laughed. "I have but a small dower of my own; I have three older sisters. And my father is so displeased that I have come here without his consent that he may even refuse me that! Such dower as I have is from Dom Mikhail, for my care of Dorilys, and he will hardly be sorry to keep it in his own family!"

"Still, he has been kinder to me than any father of my own blood could have been, and he deserves better of me than this double-dealing. Nor do I want your kinsmen to think I have seduced you while you dwelt under my foster-father's roof, perhaps for the sake of that very dower."

"Oh, that wretched dower! I know you do not care for that, Donal."

"If it is necessary, my love, I will give up all claim on it and take you in your bare shift," he said seriously.

Renata laughed and pulled his head down to her. "You would take me better without it," she teased, loving the way he still blushed like a boy half his age.

She had never believed she could be so wholly lost to everything except her love. She thought, *For all my years in the Tower, for all the lovers I have taken, I might as well have been a child Dorilys's age! Once I knew what love could be, all the rest meant nothing, nothing at all, less than nothing. . . .*

"Still, Renata," Donal said, resuming the conversation at last, "my foster-father should know."

"He is a telepath. I am sure he knows. But I think he has not yet decided what he means to do about it," Renata said, "and it would be quite unkind of us to force it upon his attention!"

Donal had to be content with that, but he wondered. How could Dom Mikhail ever have thought that Donal would go against custom this way, and turn his thoughts, unpermitted, upon a marriageable woman without the consent of her kin? He felt strange, alienated from the pattern he knew his life should have taken.

Looking at the troubled face of her lover, Renata sighed. In her solitary struggles with conscience in the Tower, she had realized that inevitably she must break away from the traditional patterns allotted to a woman of her clan. Donal had never, till now, faced the necessity for change.

"I shall send to my father, then, when it is too late for him to reply before midwinter, telling him that we are to be married at midwinter-night—if you still want me."

"If I still want you? Beloved, how can you ask?" Donal reproached, and the rest of their conversation was not held in words.

Summer drew on. The leaves began to turn, Dorilys celebrated her birthday, and the first of the harvest was gathered in. On a day when all of Aldaran's people had gone out to see the great wagons filled with sacks of nuts and jugs of the oil pressed from them borne into one of the outlying barns, Allart found himself standing next to Renata in an outlying part of the courtyard.

"Are you to remain for the winter, kinsman? I shall not leave Dorilys till she is safely past puberty; but you?"

"Donal has asked me to stay, and Dom Mikhail as well. I shall remain until I am summoned by my brother." Beyond the words Renata sensed weariness and resignation. Allart was painfully longing for Cassandra; in one of his secret dispatches he had asked leave to return, which Damon-Rafael had refused.

Renata smiled, an ironic smile. "Now that your brother has a legitimate son, he is in no hurry for you to rejoin your wife, and perhaps father sons who might contest that claim to the Domain."

Allart sighed, a sound too weary, Renata thought, for a man as young as Allart. "Cassandra will bear me no children," he said. "I will not bring that danger upon her. And I have sworn in the fires of Hali to support the claim of my brother's sons, legitimate or *nedestro,* to the Domain."

Renata felt the tears which had been so near the surface for days now welling up and brimming over in her eyes. To keep them back, she made her voice hard and ironic. "To the Domain—yes, you have sworn. But to the crown, Allart?"

"I want no crown," Allart said.

"Oh, I believe you," Renata's voice was waspish. "But will that brother of yours ever believe that?"

"I do not know." Allart sighed. Did Damon-Rafael truly believe that Allart could not resist the temptation to wrest the Domain—or the crown—from his hands? Or did he simply wish to place the powerful lord Aldaran under an obligation to Elhalyn? Damon-Rafael would need allies, if he chose to struggle with Prince Felix for the throne at Thendara.

That struggle would not come for a while. Old King Regis still clung to life, and the Council would not disturb his deathbed. But when the king lay in an unmarked grave at Hali beside his forefathers, as the custom was, then— *then* the Council would not be slow to demand that Prince Felix display his fitness to inherit his father's throne.

"An *emmasca* might make a good king," Renata said, following his thoughts effortlessly, "but he can found no dynasty. Felix will not inherit. And I read the last dispatch, too. Cassilde never recovered after the birth of her son, and died a few tendays after. So your brother has a legitimate son, but is seeking again for a wife. Now, no doubt, he repents he was so quick to marry you to Cassandra."

Allart's mouth curled in distaste, remembering what Damon-Rafael had said on that subject. "If Cassilde should die, as she has been likely to do any time these past few years, I would be free to take Cassandra myself." How could even his brother have spoken that way of the woman who had borne him a dozen children, only to see them die?

Allart said, "Perhaps it is better this way," but he sounded so dreary that Renata could not keep back the tears. He tipped his face gently up to his. "What is it, cousin? You are ever eager to comfort my troubles, yet you speak never of your own. What ails you, kinswoman?" His arms went out to encircle her, but it was the affectionate touch of a brother, a friend, not a lover, and Renata knew it. She sobbed, and Allart held her gently.

"Tell me, *chiya*," he said, as tenderly as if she were Dorilys's age, and Renata struggled to hold back her tears.

"I haven't told Donal. I wanted to have his child. If it were so with me, my father could not force me to come home to Edelweiss and marry whatever man he had chosen for me. . . . And so I conceived, but after a day or so, monitoring, I discovered that the child was female; and so I—" She swallowed, and Allart could feel her pain like a great agony within himself. "I could not let it live. I—I don't regret it; who could, with that curse on the line of Rockraven? And yet—I look at Dorilys and I cannot help but think, I have had to destroy what could have been like *that*, beautiful and—and—" Her voice broke and she sobbed helplessly for a moment against Allart.

And I thought I could force a choice like this upon Cassandra. . . . There was nothing Allart could say. He held Renata, letting her cry softly against him.

She quieted at last, murmuring, "I know I did right. It had to be. But I—I couldn't tell Donal, either."

What in the name of all the gods, are we doing to our women? What have we wrought in our blood and genes, to bring this on them? Holy Bearer of Burdens, it is your blessing, not your curse, that I am parted from Cassandra. . . .

Even as he spoke he seemed to see Cassandra's face, racked with fear, fear like Renata's. Trying to put it aside, he tightened his arms around Renata and said gently, "Still you know you have done right, and that knowledge will strengthen you, I hope." Then, slowly, searching for words, he told her of the moment of foresight, when he had seen her far advanced in pregnancy, terrified, despairing. "I have not seen that of late in my visions," he reassured her. "Probably that possibility existed only during the short time you were actually pregnant, and afterward—afterward, that future simply ceased to be; since you had taken the action which could prevent it. Don't be regretful."

Still, he was unsure: he had not seen *anything* of late. He had tried hard to blot out *any* use of his foresight and its dreadful thronging possible futures. Was it true that now, with the female child Renata had conceived already destroyed, there was no cause for fear? But he had reassured her. She looked calmer, and he would not disturb her again.

"I *know* I did right," Renata said. "Yet of late Dorilys has grown so sweet, so biddable and gentle. Now that she has some command of her *laran*, the storms seem to rage no longer."

Yes, thought Allart. *It has been long since my sleep or my waking was disturbed by those dreadful visions of a vaulted room, of a child's face framed in awful lightnings. . . .* Had all these tragedies, too, moved out of the realm of the possible, as Dorilys mastered her terrible gift?

"Yet, in a way, that makes it worse," Renata said, "to know there might have been another such child, and now she will never live . . . Well, I suppose I must simply think of Dorilys as the daughter I shall never dare to have. . . . Allart, she has invited her father and Donal to hear her play and sing this afternoon; will you come, too? She has begun to develop a truly fine singing voice; will you come and hear it?"

"With pleasure," Allart said sincerely.

Donal was there already, and Lord Aldaran, and several of the women of the household, including Dorilys's music-mistress, a young noblewoman of the house of Darriel. Darkly beautiful, with dark hair and dark-lashed eyes, she reminded Allart briefly of Cassandra, though they were not really much alike. Still, as Lady Elisa sat with her head bent over the *rryl,* tuning the strings, he noted that she, too, had six fingers on her hands. He remembered what he had said to Cassandra at their wedding, "May we live in a time when we can make songs, not war!" How brief that hope had been! They lived in a land torn with war among mountains and Domains alike, Cassandra in a Tower beset by air-cars and incendiaries, Allart in a land aflame with forest fire and raging lightnings, striking like arrows. Startled, he looked around the quiet room, out at the quiet skies and hills beyond. No sound of war, no breath. His damned foresight again, no more, in the calm room where Lady Elisa touched the sidebars of the harp, and said, "Sing, Dorilys."

The child's voice, sweet and mournful, began an old song of the far hills:

"Where are you now?
Where does my love wander?"

Allart thought such a song of hopeless love and longing ill placed on the lips of a young maiden, but he was entranced by the loveliness of the voice. Dorilys had grown considerably that autumn; she was taller, and her breasts, though small, were already well formed under her childish smock, the young body nicely rounded. She was still long-legged, awkward—she would be a tall woman. Already she was taller than Renata.

Dom Mikhail said as she finished her song, "Indeed, my darling, it seems you have inherited your mother's superb voice. Will you sing me something less mournful?"

"Gladly." Dorilys took the *rryl* from Lady Elisa. She adjusted the tuning slightly, then began to strum it casually and sing a comical ballad from the hills. Allart had heard it often at Nevarsin, though not in the monastery; a rowdy song about a monk who carried, in his pockets, as a good monk should, all the possessions he was allowed to own.

"In the pockets, the pockets,
Fro' Domenick's pockets.
Those wonderful pockets he wore round his waist,
The pockets he stuffed every morning in haste;

Whatever he owned at the start of the day,
He stuffed in his pockets and went on his way."

The audience was chuckling before long at the ever-increasing and ridiculous catalog of the possessions borne in the legendary monk's pockets.

"Whatever he owned at the start of the day,
He stuffed in his pockets and went on his way.
A bowl and a spoon and a book for his prayers,
A blanket to shield him against the cold airs,
A pencase to write down his prayers and his letters,
A warm cozy kneepad to kneel to his betters,
A nutcracker handled in copper and gold . . ."

Dorilys herself was struggling to keep her face straight as her audience began to chuckle, or giggle, or in the case of her father, throw back his head and guffaw with laughter at the absurdity of some of the contents of:

"The pockets, the pockets, Fro' Domenick's pockets . . ."

She had reached the verse which detailed:

"A saddle and bridle, some spurs and a rein
In case he was given a riding *chervine,*
A good-handled basin, a razor of—"

Dorilys broke off, uncertainly, as the door opened, and Lord Aldaran turned in anger on his paxman, who had entered with such lack of ceremony.

"Varlet, how dare you break into the room of your young mistress this way!"

"I beg the young lady's pardon, but the matter is extremely urgent. Lord Scathfell—"

"Come, come," Aldaran said irritably. "Even if he were at our gates with a hundred armed warriors, my man, it would not excuse such a lack of courtesy!"

"He has sent you a message. His messenger speaks of a demand, my lord."

After a moment Mikhail of Aldaran rose. He bowed to

Lady Elisa and to his daughter with as much courtesy as if
Dorily's little schoolroom had been a presence-chamber.

"Ladies, forgive me. I would not willingly have interrupted your music. But I fear I must ask permission to
withdraw, daughter."

For a moment Dorilys gaped; he asked *her* permission
to come and go? It was clearly the first time he had extended this grown-up formal politeness; but then the beautiful manners in which Margali and Renata had schooled
her came to her aid. She dropped him so deep a curtsy that
she nearly sank to her knees.

"You are welcome to come and go at your own occasions, sir, but I beg you to return when you are free."

He bent over her hand. "I shall indeed, my daughter.
Ladies, my apologies." he added, extending the bow to
Margali and Renata, then he said curtly, "Donal, attend
me," and Donal rose and hurried after him.

When they had gone, Dorilys tried to resume her song,
but the heart had gone out of the occasion and after a little
it broke up. Allart went down into the courtyard where the
riding animals were stabled, and the escort of the diplomatic mission from Scathfell was tethered. Among them he
could see other badges of different mountain clans, that
armed men came and went in the courts, but they shifted
like water and were not there when he looked again. He
knew that his *laran* painted hallucinations for him of things
that might never be. He tried to thread his way through
them, to see into time, but he was not calm enough, and
what he sensed—he was not consciously reading the minds
of those who had brought Scathfell's demand, but they, too,
were broadcasting their emotions all over the landscape—
was not conducive to calm.

War? Here? He felt a pang of grief for the long beautiful
summer, so irrevocably shattered. *How could I sit at peace
when my people are at war and my brother prepares to strive
for a crown? What have I done to deserve this peace, when
even my beloved wife faces danger and terror?* He went to
his room and tried to calm himself with the Nevarsin
breathing disciplines, but he could not concentrate with the
visions of war, storms, and riots crowding eyes and brain,
and he was grateful when, after a considerable time, he was
summoned to Aldaran's presence-chamber.

He had expected to confront the embassy from Scathfell, as he had seen them so often in his vision, but no one was there except Aldaran himself, staring gloomily at the floor in front of his high seat, and Donal, pacing nervously back and forth.

As Allart came in Donal gave him a quick look of gratitude and entreaty mingled.

"Come in, cousin," Dom Mikhail said. "Now indeed do we need the advice of kinsmen. Will you sit?"

Allart would have preferred to stand, or to pace like Donal, but he took the seat Dom Mikhail indicated. The old man sat with his chin in his hands, brooding. At last he said, "Do you sit, too, Donal! You drive me mad pacing there like a berserker possessed by a raging wolf," and waited for his foster-son to seat himself beside Allart. "Rakhal of Scathfell—for I will not yield him the name of brother—has sent me an envoy with demands so outrageous that I can no longer bear them in calm. He sees fit to demand that I shall choose without delay, preferably before midwinter, one of his younger sons—I suppose I should be honored that he leaves it up to me to choose which of his damned whelps I will have—to be formally adopted as my heir, since I have no legitimate son, nor, he says, am I likely to have one at my age." He picked up a piece of paper lying on the seat where he cast it, and crumpled it again in his fist. "He says I should invite all men to witness what I have done in declaring a son of Scathfell my heir, and then—will you listen to the insolence of the man!—he says, *then you may live out your few remaining years in such peace as your other deeds allow.*" He clenched the offending letter in his fist as if it were his brother's neck.

"Tell me, cousin. What am I to do with that man?"

Allart stared, appalled. *In the name of all the gods,* he thought, *what does he mean by asking me? Does he think seriously that I am capable of advising him on such a matter?*

Aldaran added, more gently, and also more urgently, "Allart, you were schooled at Nevarsin; you know all our history, and all the law. Tell me, cousin. Is there no way at all that I can keep my brother of Scathfell from grasping my estate even before my bones are cold in my grave?"

"My lord, I do not see how they can compel you to adopt your brother's son. But I do not know how you can keep Lord Scathfell's sons from inheriting after you; the law is not clear about female children." *And if it were,* he thought almost in despair, *is Dorilys truly fit to rule?* "When a female heir is given leave to inherit, it is usually because all concerned feel that her husband will make a suitable overlord. No one will deny you the right to leave Aldaran to Dorilys's husband."

"And yet," Aldaran said, with painstaking fingers smoothing out the crumpled letter, "look—the seals of Storn, and Sain Scarp, and even of Lord Darriel, hung about this letter, as if to lend their strength to this—this ultimatum he has sent. No wonder Lord Storn made me no reply when I sought his son for Dorilys. Each of them is afraid to ally himself with me lest he alienate all the others. Now, indeed, do I wish the Ridenow were not entangled in this war against your kin, or I should offer Dorilys there." He was silent a moment, brooding. "I have sworn I will burn Aldaran over my own head ere it goes to my brother. Help me find a way, Allart."

The first thought that flashed into Allart's mind—and later, he was grateful that he had had sense enough to barricade it so that Aldaran could not read it—was this: *My brother Damon-Rafael has but lately lost his wife.* But the very thought filled his mind with erupting visions of dread and disaster. The effort to control them kept him silent in consternation, while he remembered Damon-Rafael's prediction that had sent him here: "I fear a day when all our world from Dalereuth to the Hellers will bow before the might of Aldaran."

Noting his silence, Dom Mikhail said, "It is a thousand pities *you* are wed, cousin. I would offer my daughter to *you.* . . . But you know my will. Tell me, Allart. Is there no way at all in which I can declare Donal my heir? It is he who has always been the true son of my heart."

"Father," Donal entreated, "don't quarrel with your kinsmen about me. Why set the land aflame in a useless war? When you have gone to join your forefathers—may that day be far from you, dear foster-father—what will it matter to you, then, who holds Aldaran?"

"It matters," said the old man, his face set like a mask

in stone. "Allart, in all your knowledge of the law, is there no single loophole through which I might bring Donal into this inheritance?"

Allart set his mind to consider this. He said at last, "None, I think, that you could use, but these laws about blood inheritance are not yet so strong as all that. As recently as seven or eight generations ago, you and your brothers and all your wives would have dwelt together, and the eldest among you, or your chosen leader, would have chosen for heir the son who looked most likely and capable, not the eldest son of the eldest brother, but the *best*. It is custom, not law, that has foisted this rule of primogeniture and known fathering on the mountains. Yet if you simply proclaim that you have chosen Donal by the old law and not the new, then there will be war, my lord. Every eldest son in the mountains will know his position threatened, and his younger brother or his remote kinsmen more his enemy than now."

"It would be simpler," said Aldaran with great bitterness, "if Donal were a waif or an orphan, and not the son of my beloved Aliciane. Then could I wed him to Dorilys, and see my daughter protected and my estate in the hands of the one who knows it best and is best fitted to care for it."

Allart said, "That could still be done, my lord. It would be a legal fiction—as when the lady Bruna Leynier, sister of the heir who had been killed in battle, took her brother's widow and his unborn child under her protection in free-mate marriage, so that no other marriage could be forced upon the widow and the child's rights set aside. They say that she commanded the guards, too, in her brother's place."

Aldaran laughed. "I thought that only a jesting tale."

"No," said Allart. "It happened, indeed. The women dwelt together for twenty years, until the unborn child was grown to manhood and could claim his rights. Folly, perhaps, but the laws could not forbid it. Such a marriage has a legal status at least—a half-brother and half-sister can marry if they will. Renata has told me it is best for Dorilys to bear no children, and Donal could father a *nedestro* heir to succeed him."

He was thinking of Renata, but Mikhail of Aldaran raised his head with a quick, decisive movement. "Legal fiction be damned," he said. "That is our answer, then, Donal. Allart is mistaken in what Renata said. I remember it well! She said Dorilys should not bear a *daughter,* but it would be safe for her to bear a son. And she has Aldaran blood, which would mean that Donal's son would be an Aldaran heir, and thus entitled to inherit after them. Every breeder of animals knows this is the best way to fix a desired trait in the line, to breed back with the same genetic materials. So that Dorilys will bear to her half-brother the son Aliciane should have given *me*—Renata will know how to make sure of that—and the fire-control and lightning-control talents redoubled. We must be careful for a few generations not to allow any daughters to be born, but so much the better, so that the line will flourish."

Donal stared at his foster-father, appalled. "You cannot possibly be serious, sir!"

"Why not?"

"But Dorilys is my sister—and only a little girl."

"Half-sister," Aldaran said, "and not such a little girl as all that. Margali tells me she will come to womanhood sometime this winter, so there is not even long to wait before we can tell them a true Aldaran heir is to inherit."

Donal stared at his father, stricken, and Allart could tell he was thinking of Renata, but Mikhail of Aldaran was too intent on his own will to have the slightest scrap of *laran* left over for reading his foster-son's thoughts. But as Donal opened his mouth to speak, Allart saw, all too clearly, the old man's face darkening and twisting, stricken, the roaring of the brain. Allart clamped the boy's wrist in his hand, forcing the picture of Aldaran's attack on Donal, hard, his thoughts strong as the command-voice: *In the name of all the gods, Donal, don't quarrel with him now! It would be the death of him!* Donal fell back into his seat, the words unspoken. The picture of Lord Aldaran stricken down at the words vanished into the limbo of those things which now would not come to pass, and Allart saw it thin out and vanish, relieved and yet troubled.

I am not a monitor, but if he stands so near to death, we must tell Renata. He should be monitored. . . .

"Come, come," Aldaran said gently. "Your scruples are foolish, my son. You have known for many years that Dorilys must marry as soon as she is grown, and if she must be wed before she is full-grown, will it not be easier for her to marry someone she knows and loves well? Would you not use her more gently than some stranger? It is the only way I can think of, that you should marry Dorilys and father a son upon her—as things are now," he added, frowning a little.

Allart, startled and shocked, realized it was probably just as well for Dorilys that Lord Aldaran was very old and considered himself past fathering an heir.

"As for this thing," Aldaran said, crushing Scathfell's letter again and flinging it to the floor, "I think I shall use it to wipe myself, and send it *so* to my brother, to show him what I think of his ultimatum! At the same time I shall invite him to witness your wedding."

"No," whispered Donal. "Father, I beg you—"

"Not a word, my son; my mind is made up." Aldaran rose and embraced Donal. "Since first Aliciane brought you into this house, you have been my beloved son; and this will make it legitimate. Will you deny me that, dear lad?"

Donal stood helpless, unable to speak his protest. How could he cast his foster-father's love and concern back at him at that moment?

"Call my scribe," said Lord Aldaran. "I shall take pleasure in dictating a letter to Lord Scathfell, inviting him to the wedding of my daughter and heir with my chosen son."

Donal made a final plea. "You know, my father, that this is a declaration of war? They will come against us in force."

Aldaran gestured at the window. Outside the gray skies were blurring with the fall of daytime snow, the first of the year. "They will not come now," he said. "Winter is upon us. They will not come till spring thaw. And then—" He threw back his head and laughed, and Allart felt chills down his spine, thinking of the raucous scream of a bird of prey. "Let them come. Let them come when they will. We will be ready for them!"

Chapter 21

"**B**ut truly there is no woman in the world whom I wish to marry," Donal said, "except for you, my beloved." Until Renata had come into his life, he had never believed that he would have any choice in the matter—nor did he particularly want it, provided his bride-to-be was neither sickly nor a shrew, and he had trusted his foster-father to make sure of that. He had wasted very little thought on the matter.

Renata saw all these thoughts—and the almost unconscious resentment in Donal, that he had had to face this enormous change in his life pattern—and reached out to take his hand. "Indeed I am to blame, my love. I should have done as you wished, and married you at once."

"No one speaks of blame, *carya mea,* but what are we to do now? My foster-father is old, and today I truly feared he would be stricken down as I spoke, had not Allart prevented me. All the gods forgive me, Renata, I could not help thinking—if he should die, then would I be free of this thing he asks." Donal covered his face with his hands, and Renata, watching him, knew that his present upheaval was her doing. It was she who had inspired him to set himself against his foster-father's wishes.

At last she said, keeping her voice calm with considerable effort, "Donal, my beloved, you must do what you feel is right. The gods forbid I should try to persuade you against your conscience. If you think it wrong to go against your foster-father's will, then you must obey him."

He raised his face, struggling with the effort not to break

down. "In the name of the merciful gods, Renata, how could I possibly want to obey him? Do you think I *want* to marry my sister?"

"Not even with Aldaran as the dower?" she asked. "You cannot tell me that you have no desire to inherit the Domain."

"If I could do it justly! But not like this, Renata, not like this! I would defy him, but I cannot speak that word if it would strike him dead, as Allart fears! And the worst of it is—if you desert me now, if I should lose you—"

Quickly she reached out and took his hands in hers. "No, no, my love. I will not desert you, I promise it! That was not what I meant! I meant only that if you are forced into this marriage, it can be the legal fiction he wishes it to be, or wished it to be at first."

Donal swallowed hard. "How can I ask that? A noblewoman of your rank cannot become a *barragana*. This would mean I can never offer you what you should have in honor, the *catenas* and honorable recognition as my wife. My own mother was a *barragana*. I know what life would be for our children. Daily they taunted me, called me brat and bastard and things that made less pleasant hearing. How could I bring that upon any child of mine? Merciful Evanda, there were times I hated my own mother, that she had exposed me to such things!"

"I would rather be *barragana* to you than wear the *catenas* for another, Donal."

He knew she spoke truth, but confused resentment made him lash out, "Truly? What you mean, I suppose, is that you would rather be *barragana* to Aldaran than wife to the poor farmer of High Crags!"

She looked at him in dismay. *Already it has made us quarrel!*

"You do not understand me, Donal. I would rather be *yours,* as wife, freemate, or *barragana,* than marry some man my father chose for me without my knowledge or consent, were that man Prince Felix on his throne at Thendara. My father will be angry when he hears that I dwell openly in your house as *barragana,* but it will mean he cannot dispose of me to some other man, for there are those who would not have me upon such conditions, and I am beyond the reach of his anger—or his ambition!"

Donal felt guilty, knowing *he* could not so have defied his foster-father; and now, having defied *her* kin, Renata had nowhere else to go. He knew he should be equally brave, refuse Lord Aldaran's command, and insist upon marrying Renata at once, even if his foster-father were to disinherit him and drive him forth.

Yet, he thought, miserably, *I cannot quarrel with him. It is not only for my own sake, but I would not leave him at the mercy of the folk of Scathfell, and the other mountain lords who hover to pick his bones the moment they see him helpless!* His foster-father had no one else. How could he leave him alone? Yet it seemed that honor demanded he do just that.

He covered his face with his hands.

"I feel torn in pieces, Renata! Loyalty to you—and loyalty to my father. Is this, I wonder, why marriages are arranged by kinfolk, so that such terrible conflicts of loyalty cannot arise?"

As if Donal's tormented self-questioning could reverberate throughout Castle Aldaran, Allart, too, was troubled, restlessly pacing in his allotted chamber.

He thought, *I should have let Donal speak. If the shock of knowing he could not always have his own way should have killed Dom Mikhail, then we can well spare such tyrants, seeking always to impose their own will on others, despite their conscience. . . .* All the rage and resentment Allart had felt against his own father, he was ready to pour out on Lord Aldaran.

For this damned breeding program he will wreck Donal's life, and Dorilys's—before she is even out of childhood— and Renata's! Does he care about anything except a legitimate heir of Aldaran blood?

But then, belatedly, Allart began to be fair. He thought, *No, it is not all Dom Mikhail's fault. Donal is to blame, too, that he did not go at once to Dom Mikhail when first he fell in love with Renata, and ask for her in marriage. And I am to blame, that I listened to his request for some legal loophole. It was I who put it into his head that Donal and Dorilys could be married even as a legal fiction! And it was my damned foresight that made me prevent Donal from speaking out! Again I was swayed by a happening that might never have come to pass!*

My laran *has brought this upon us all. Now somehow I must manage to master it, to thread my way and see through time, to discover what will happen among the many futures I see.*

He had blocked it for so long. For many moons now, he had spent much of his emotional energy trying to see *nothing,* to live in the moment as others did, not letting himself be swayed by the shifting, seductive possibilities in the many futures. The thought of opening his mind to it all was terror, a fear that was almost physical. Yet that was what he must do.

Locking his door against intrusion, he went about his preparations with as much calm as he could summon. Finally he stretched out on the stone floor, closing his eyes and breathing quietly in the Nevarsin-trained manner, to calm himself. Then, struggling against panic—he *couldn't* do this, he had spent seven years in Nevarsin learning how *not* to do this—he lowered the self-imposed barriers and reached out with his *laran.* . . .

For an instant—timeless, eternal, probably not much more than half a second, but seeming like a million years inside his screaming senses—all of time rushed in on him, past and present, all of the deeds of his forefathers that had resulted in this moment. He saw a woman walking by the lake of Hali, a woman of surpassing beauty with the colorless gray eyes and moonlight hair of a *chieri;* he glimpsed memories of forests and peaks; he saw other stars and other suns, a world with a yellow sun with only a single pale moon in the sky; he looked out on a black night of space; he died in snow, in space, in fire, a thousand deaths crammed into a single moment; he fought and died screaming on a battlefield; he saw himself die curled into fetal position and withdrawing into himself beyond thought as he had almost done in his fourteenth year; he lived a hundred thousand lives in that one shrieking moment, and knew his body convulsing into spasms of terror, dying. . . . He heard himself cry out in agony and knew he was insane, that he would never come back. . . . He fought for a moment to slam the gates he had opened, knew it was too late. . . .

And then he was Allart again, and knew he had only this single life, *now;* the others were irrevocably past or had yet to be. But in this single life (and how narrow it looked, after those centuries upon centuries of split-second awareness that he *was,* he *had been,* he *would be*) still spread out before him, infinitely reduplicating itself, with every move he made hundreds of new possibilities were created and others were wiped out forever. He could see now how every move he had made since his childhood had either opened up opportunities or closed off other paths for all time. He could have taken the path of pride in strength and weaponry, set himself to best Damon-Rafael at swordplay and combat, become his father's most needed son. . . . He could have somehow arranged it so that Damon-Rafael died in childhood, become his father's heir. . . . He could have remained forever in the safe and sheltered walls of Nevarsin, disinherited. . . . He could have plunged into the world of the senses that he had discovered, an infinite temptation, in the arms of a *riyachiya.* . . . He could have choked out the life of his father, in his humiliated pride. . . . Slowly, through the crowding pasts, he could see the inevitability of the choices that had led him to this moment, to this crossroads. . . .

Now he was *here,* at this crucial moment in time, where his past choices, willing or unwilling, had led him. Now his future choices must be made in full knowledge of what they might bring. In that overloaded moment of total awareness, he accepted responsibility for what had been, and for what would be, and began to look carefully ahead.

Dorilys's words flashed through his mind: "It's like a stream of water. If I put rocks in it, it would go around the rocks, but it could go either way. But I couldn't make it jump out of the stream-bed, or run back uphill. . . ."

Slowly he began to see, with that curious extended perception, what lay ahead; the most likely thing straight before him, it seemed, fanning out to the wildest possibilities at the far edges of his awareness. He saw immediately before him the possibilities that Donal would accept; would defy; would take Renata and be gone from Aldaran; would take Dorilys and father *nedestro* children upon Renata. He saw that Dom Erlend Leynier might join forces with Scathfell against Aldaran in retaliation for the insult to his daughter. (He should warn Renata of that—but would she care?) Again and again, he saw the often repeated vision of Scathfell's armed men upon Aldaran in the spring, so that once again Aldaran must be kept by force of arms. . . . He saw remoter possibilities: that Lord Aldaran would indeed be struck down by a massive stroke, would die or lie helpless for months and years, while Donal struggled with his unwilling regency for his sister . . . that Lord Aldaran would recover and drive Scathfell away with his superior armed might . . . that Lord Aldaran would somehow be reconciled to his brother. . . . He saw Dorilys dying in threshold sickness when womanhood came upon her . . . dying while delivering the child Donal swore he would never father upon her . . . surviving to give Donal a son, who would inherit only the Aldaran *laran* and die of threshold sickness in his teens. . . .

Painfully, painstakingly, Allart forced himself to thread his way through all the possibilities. *I am not a god! How can I tell which of these things would be best for all? I can only say what would be least painful for Donal or for Renata, whom I love. . . .*

Now, against his will, he began to see his own future. He would return to Cassandra . . . he would not return but would dwell forever in Nevarsin or, like Saint-Valentine-of-the-Snows, alone in a solitary cave in the Hellers till death . . . he would be reunited ecstatically with Cassandra . . . he would die at the hands of Damon-Rafael, who feared treachery . . . Cassandra would dwell forever in the Tower . . . she would die in bearing his child . . . she would fall into the hands of Damon-Rafael, who had never ceased to regret that he had given her to Allart instead of making her his own *barragana*. . . . This jolted Allart completely out of the reverie of crowding futures and probabilities, to look more closely at *that* one.

Damon-Rafael, his own wife dead, and his single legitimate son dead before weaning. . . . Allart had not known that; it was pure foresight, *laran*. But was it true or only a fear born of his consciousness of Cassandra and Damon-Rafael's unscrupulous ambition? Abruptly something his father had said when speaking of his handfasting to Cassandra surged back into his mind.

"You will be married to a woman of the Aillard clan,

with genes specially modified to control this *laran*. . . ."
Allart had heard his father, but he had not been listening.
He had heard only the voice of his own fear. But Damon-
Rafael *had* known. It would not be the first time that a
Domain chief, powerful and ambitious, had taken the wife
of his younger brother . . . *or his brother's widow. If I
return to claim Cassandra for my wife, Damon-Rafael will
kill me.* With a craven pang, Allart wondered how he could
avoid this fate, the fate it now seemed he saw everywhere.

*I shall return to the monastery, take vows there, never to
return to Elhalyn. Then Damon-Rafael will take Cassandra
for his wife, and seize the throne of Thendara from the faltering hands of the young* emmasca *who sits there now. Cassandra will mourn for me, but when she is queen at
Thendara she will forget. . . .*

And Damon-Rafael, his ambition satisfied, will be content.
Then horror flared upon Allart, seeing what kind of king
his brother would be. Tyranny—the Ridenow would be
wiped out wholly so that the women of Serrais could be
bred into the line of Elhalyn, the Hasturs of Hali and Valeron would be assimilated into the single line of Elhalyn, so
many alliances entered into that the Domains themselves
would become only vassals to the Hastur of Elhalyn, reigning from Thendara. Damon-Rafael's greedy hands would
reach out to bring all of the known world from Dalereuth
to the Hellers under the domain of Elhalyn. All this would
happen in the name of bringing peace . . . peace under the
despotism of Damon-Rafael and the sons of Hastur!

*Inbreeding, sterility, weakness, decadence, the inflow of
barbarians from the Dry-towns and hill country . . . sack,
looting, ravage, death. . . .*

*I do not want a crown. Yet no man living could rule this
land worse than my brother. . . .*

By main force Allart shut off the flow of images. Somehow, he must prevent this from occurring. Now for the
first time he let himself think seriously of Cassandra. How
casually he had almost stepped aside, leaving her to become
Damon-Rafael's prey—for, queen or no, no woman would
ever be more than this to his brother, a toy of lust and a
pawn of ambition. Damon-Rafael had brought an almost
certain death upon Cassilde, not caring as long as she bore

him a legitimate son. He would not hesitate to use Cassandra the same way.

Then something in Allart that he had crushed and subdued and trampled suddenly reared up and said, *No! He shall not have her!*

If she had wanted Damon-Rafael, if she had even been ambitious for the crown, then, with agony never to be weighed or measured, Allart might have stepped aside. But he knew her too well for that. It was his responsibility— and his *right,* his unchallenged right—to protect and reclaim her for himself.

Even now, my brother might be reaching out his hand to take her. . . .

Allart could see ahead into all possible futures, but he could not see what was actually happening now at a distance—not without the aid of his matrix. Slowly, stretching his cramped muscles, he stood up and looked around the chamber. The night had passed, and the snow; crimson dawn was breaking over the Hellers outside his window, showing snowclad peaks flashing red sunlight. With the weather-wisdom of the mountains, which he had learned at Nevarsin, he knew the storm was gone, for a time at least.

With the starstone in his hand, Allart resolutely focused on his thought, enormously amplified by the matrix, over the long spaces that lay between. *What befalls at Elhalyn? What is happening in Thendara?*

Slowly, pinpointed as if he were seeing it with his physical eyes through the small end of a lens, tiny and sharp-edged and brilliant, a picture formed before his eyes.

Along the shores of Hali, where the unending waves that were not water splashed and receded forever, a procession wound its way, with the banners and flags of mourning. Old King Regis was being carried to the burial ground at the shores of Hali, there to lie, as custom demanded, in an unmarked grave among the former kings and rulers of the Domains. In that procession, face after face flashed before Allart's eyes, but only two made any impression on him: One, the narrow, pale sexless face of Prince Felix, sad and fearful. It would not be long, Allart knew, looking at the rapacious faces of the nobles in his train, before Prince Felix was stripped naked and forced to yield his crown to

one who could pass on blood and genes, the precious *laran.*
The other was the face of Damon-Rafael of Elhalyn, next
heir to the crown of Thendara. As if already tasting his
victory, Damon-Rafael rode with a fierce smile on his face.
Before Allart's eyes the picture blurred, not into what was
now, but what would be, and he saw Damon-Rafael
crowned in Thendara, Cassandra, robed and jeweled as a
queen, at his side, and the powerful lords of Valeron, cemented in close alliance through kinfolk, standing behind
the new king Damon-Rafael. . . .

War, decadence, ruin, chaos. . . . Allart suddenly knew
he stood at the crux of a line of events which could alter
forever the whole future of Darkover.

*I wish my brother no harm. But I cannot let him plunge
all of our world into ruin. There is no journey that does not
begin with a single step. I cannot prevent Damon-Rafael
from becoming king. But he will not cement the Aillard alliance by making my wife his queen.*

Allart put the matrix aside, sent for his servants and had
food brought, eating and drinking without tasting, to
strengthen him against what he knew must come. That
done, he went in search of Lord Aldaran. He found Dom
Mikhail in high good humor.

"I have sent the message to my brother of Scathfell, inviting him to the wedding of my daughter and my beloved
foster-son," he said. "It is a stroke of genius. There is no
other man into whose hands I would so willingly give my
little daughter for her safety and protection lifelong. I shall
tell her today what we intend, and I think she, too, will be
grateful, that she need not be given into a stranger's
hands. . . . You are responsible for this splendid solution,
my friend. I wish I could somehow repay you with some
equal kindness! How I would like to be a fly upon the
wall when my brother of Scathfell reads the letter I have
sent him!"

Allart said, "As a matter of fact, Dom Mikhail, I have
come to ask you a great favor."

"It would be a pleasure to grant you whatever you ask,
cousin."

"I wish to send for my wife, who dwells in Hali Tower.
Will you receive her as a guest?"

"Willingly," Dom Mikhail said. "I will send my own

guard as escort, if you wish it, but the journey is precarious at this time of year; ten days' ride from the Lowlands with the winter storms coming on. Perhaps you could eliminate the time it would take my men to travel to the lake of Hali and fetch her, if you sent to Tramontana Tower with a message through the relays that she should set forth at once. I could send men to meet her on the way and escort her. I suppose she could find her own escort from Elhalyn."

Allart looked troubled. He said, "I do not want to trust her to my brother, and I am reluctant that her going should be known."

Dom Mikhail looked at him sharply. "Is it like that? I suggest, then, that you go at once with Donal to Tramontana, and try to persuade them to bring her here at once, through the Tower relays. It is not often done in these days—the expenditure of energy is out of all reason—unless the need is desperate. But if it is as important as that—"

Allart said, "I did not know that could still be done!"

"Oh, yes, the equipment is still there in the Tower, matrix-powered. Perhaps, with your help, they could be persuaded. I would suggest that you ride to Tramontana, however, rather than flying; the weather is not good enough at this season for that. . . . Still, speak with Donal. He knows all that there is to know about flying in the Hellers at any season." He rose, courteously dismissing the younger man.

"It will be a pleasure to welcome your wife as my guest, cousin. She will be an honored guest at my daughter's wedding."

"Yes, of course we can fly there," Donal said, glancing at the sky. "We will have at least a day free of snow, but of course we cannot return the same day. If there must be work done within the relays, you would be too exhausted, and so would your lady. I suggest that we leave for Tramontana as soon as we can, and that I give orders for mounts to be sent after us, including one for your wife, gentle and suited to a lady's riding."

They set forth later that morning. Allart did not speak of Donal's approaching marriage, fearing it might be a sore point with him, but Donal brought it up himself. "It cannot be before midwinter night," he said. "Renata has moni-

tored Dorilys and she says she will not mature before that.
And she has had such ill fortune with handfastings that
even Father hesitates to subject her to another such
ceremony."

"Has she been told?"

"Yes, Father told her," Donal said, hesitating, "and I
spoke with her, a little, after. . . . She is only a child. She
has only the haziest idea of what marriage means."

Allart was not so certain, but after all it was Donal's
affair, and Renata's, not his. Donal turned to catch the
wind, tilted his glider wings with the control, and soared
upward on a long drift of air.

Once airborne, as always, the troubles of the world
slipped away from Allart's thoughts; he gave himself up to
it without thought, riding the achingly cold air in a kind of
ecstasy, matrix-borne, hawk-free. He was almost regretful
when he came in sight of Tramontana Tower, but not quite.
There lay his path to Cassandra.

As he turned the glider over to Arzi he pondered that.
Perhaps, rather than bringing her here to a cowardly safety,
he should return to Hali and face his brother. No, he knew
with that cold new inner knowledge; if he should venture
anywhere within Damon-Rafael's grasp his life would not
be worth the smallest coin.

Inside himself he mourned. *How have we come to this,
my brother and I?* Yet he put his grief aside, steadying
himself to face the *tenerézu* of the Tower with his request.

Ian-Mikhail frowned, and Allart thought he would refuse
out of hand. "The power is there," he said, "or can be
summoned. Yet I am very reluctant to entangle Tramontana in the affairs of the Lowlands. Are you very sure there
is danger to your wife, Allart?"

Allart found in his mind only the certain knowledge that
Damon-Rafael would not hesitate to seize her, as he had
seized Donal. Donal, close by, reading his thoughts, flushed
with anger.

"*That* I had never known until this moment. It is well
for Lord Elhalyn that my foster-father did not know!"

Ian-Mikhail sighed. "Here we are at peace; we make no
weapons and take part in no wars. But you are one of us,
Allart. We must safeguard your lady from harm. I cannot
imagine it. I, too, was schooled at Nevarsin, and I would

rather lie with a corpse or a *cralmac* than an unwilling woman. But I have heard that your brother is a ruthless man, and ambitious beyond measure. Go, Allart. Communicate with Cassandra through the relays. I will summon the circle for tonight."

Allart went to the matrix chamber, calming himself for the work, casting himself into the spinning darkness of the relays, riding the web of electrical energies as earlier that day he had ridden the air drafts of the winter sky. Then, without warning, he felt the intimate touch on his mind. He had not hoped for such luck; Cassandra herself was in the relays.

Allart? Is it you, love?

Surprise and wonder, an amazement that was near to tears. . . . *You are at Tramontana? You know we are all in mourning here for the old king?*

Allart had seen, though no one had thought to tell him formally here.

Allart, a moment before you begin whatever business brought you to Tramontana. I am—I do not want to trouble you, but I am afraid of your brother. He paid me a courtesy call, saying marriage-kin should know one another; and when I spoke my sympathy at Cassilde's death and the death of his young son, he spoke of a time gone by when brothers and sisters held all their wives in common, and he looked at me so strangely. I asked what he meant and he said a time would come when I would understand, but I could not read his thoughts. . . .

Until this moment Allart had hoped it was fantasy born of his fear. Now he knew his foresight had been true.

It was for this I came here, beloved. You must leave Hali and come to me in the mountains.

Ride there at this season? In the Hellers?

He could feel her fear. Nevarsin-trained, Allart had no fear of the killing weather of the Hellers, but he knew her fright was genuine. *No. Even now the circle is gathering, to bring you here through the screens. You do not fear that, do you, love?*

No. . . . But the faraway denial did not sound quite sure.

It will not be long. But go and ask the others to come.

Ian-Mikhail came into the matrix chamber, now wearing the crimson robe of Keeper. Behind him Allart could see the girl Rosaura whom he had met here before, and half a dozen of the others. The white-robed monitor was working with the dampers, adjusting them to compensate for the presence of an outsider, setting up the force-lock which made it impossible for any outsider to intrude, body or mind, into the space or time where they were working. Then Allart felt the familiar body-mind touch and knew he was being monitored for his presence in the circle. He felt grateful to them, not knowing how to express it, that they were willing to tolerate the presence of someone outside their closed and intimate circle. Yet he was not wholly an outsider; he had touched them more than once when he worked in the relay-nets. He was *known* to them, and he felt obscurely comforted.

I have lost my brother. Damon-Rafael is my enemy. Yet will I nevermore be wholly brotherless, having worked in the relays which touch mind to mind all over this world. I have sisters and brothers in Hali and Tramontana, and at Arilinn and Dalereuth and all of the Towers. . . .

Damon-Rafael and I were never brothers in that sense.

Ian-Mikhail of Storn was gathering the circle now, motioning each of them to his or her place. Allart counted nine in the circle, and he came and sat in the ring of joined bodies, not touching anywhere but close enough to feel one another as electrical fields. He saw the inner swirlings within forcefields that were the others in the circle; saw the field begin to build around Ian-Mikhail as the Keeper seized the tremendous energies of the linked matrices and began to twist and direct them into a cone of power on the screen before them. Having worked only with Coryn as Keeper, whose mental touch was light and almost imperceptible, by contrast Allart felt that Ian-Mikhail caught him, wrenched at him, almost brutally, placing him within the circle, but there was nothing of malice in the strength. It was simply the distinct way he worked; everyone used his or her psi powers in a particular way.

Once in the circle, locked into the ring of minds, individual thought faded, gave way to a humming awareness of joined, concentrated *purpose.* Allart could sense the force building inside the screen, a vast enormous singing silence. Dimly in the distance he touched other familiar minds: Coryn, like a brief handclasp; Arielle a riffle of air, wavering, perceptible; Cassandra. . . . They were *there,* they were *here*—then he went blind and deaf with the searing overload, the sting of ozone in his nostrils, the enormous flaring, searing energies, like lightning crashing on the heights.

Abruptly the pattern broke, and they were separate individuals again, and Cassandra, dazed and white, was kneeling on the stones before the circle.

She reeled, about to fall, but Rosaura reached out and steadied her; then Allart was there, lifting her in his arms. She looked up at him in exhaustion and terror.

Ian-Mikhail said with a faint laugh, "You are as wearied as by the ten days' ride, kinswoman. There has been a certain amount of energy expended, however it was done. Come with us, then. We must eat and rebuild our forces. Tell us all the news from Hali, if you will."

Allart was faint with the terrible hunger of the energy-drain. For once, he found himself eating the heavily sweetened reserve foods in the matrix chamber without nausea or distaste. He was not enough of a technician to understand the process which had teleported Cassandra through space across the ten days' ride between the Towers, but she was here, her hand clasped tight in his, and that was enough for him.

The white-robed monitor came and insisted on monitoring them both. They didn't protest.

As they ate, Cassandra told the news from Hali. The death and burial of the old king; the Council summoned to test Prince Felix—not yet crowned, probably never to be crowned; the upheaval in Thendara among the people who supported the gentle young prince. There had been a renewed truce with the Ridenow which Hali Tower had been forced to use for the stockpiling of *clingfire.* Cassandra showed Allart one of the characteristic burns on her hand.

Allart listened with amazement and wonder. His wife. Yet he felt he had never seen this woman before. When last he had seen her she had been childlike, submissive, still sick with the recoil of her suicidal despair. Now, after a scant half year, she seemed years older; her very voice and gestures stronger, more definite. This was no timid girl but a woman, poised, confident, sure of herself, talking casually and competently with the other monitors about the professional requirements of their exacting work.

What have I to give to a woman like this? Allart wondered. *She clung to me, then, because I was stronger and she needed my strength. But now that she does not need me, will she love me?*

"Come, cousin," Rosaura said. "I must find you some clothes; you cannot travel in what you wear now."

Cassandra laughed, looking down at the loose, warm white monitor's robe which was her only garment.

"Thank you, kinswoman. I came away in haste without leisure to pack my belongings!"

"I will find you travel clothing, and a change or so of underlinen," Rosaura said. "We are much of a size. And when you reach Castle Aldaran, I am sure they can find you suitable garments."

"Am I going with you to Aldaran, Allart?"

Ian-Mikhail said, "Unless you would rather stay here with us . . . we are always in need of competent monitors and technicians."

There was something of the old childlike Cassandra in the way she clasped his hand.

"I thank you, kinsman. But I will go with my husband."

The night was far advanced, snow beating furiously around the heights of the Tower. Rosaura showed them to a room made ready on the lower floor.

Allart wondered again, when they were alone. *What have I to give a woman like this? A woman, and no longer in need of my strength!* But as he turned to her, he felt the barriers going down, one after another, so that their minds merged before he even touched her. He knew nothing was gone between them that could make a difference.

In gray dawnlight they were roused by a sudden knocking at the door. It was not really very loud, but somehow had a frantic sound, a commotion that made Allart sit up and stare wildly around him for some cause, some reason behind the violent disturbance. Cassandra sat up and looked at him in the dim light, frightened.

"What is it? Oh, what is it?"

"Damon-Rafael," Allart said, before realizing that this was madness. Damon-Rafael was ten days away in the Lowlands and there was no way he could intrude here. Yet, as he opened the door, the sight of Rosaura's pale, frightened face was a shock. Had he *really* expected to see his brother, armed for combat or kill, ready to break into the room where he slept, reunited with his wife?

"I am sorry to disturb you," Rosaura said, "but Coryn of Hali is in the relays and he says he must speak with you at once, Allart."

"At this hour?" Allart said, wondering who had suddenly gone mad, for the dawn was just beginning to merge into pink at the edge of the sky. Nevertheless he dressed in haste, and hurried up the long stairs to the matrix chamber because he felt too confused to trust himself to the rising-shaft.

A young technician Allart did not know was in the relays. "You are Allart Hastur of Elhalyn? Coryn of Hali has insisted we waken you."

Allart took his place inside the relay circle, and reaching out, felt Coryn's light touch on his mind.

Kinsman? At such an hour? What can be happening at Hali?

I do not like it any better than you do. But a few hours past, Damon-Rafael, Lord Elhalyn, came raging to the doors of Hali, demanding that we turn your wife over to him, as hostage against your treachery. I knew not that there was madness in our kindred, Allart!

Not madness, but a touch of laran, *and a very little of my own foresight,* Allart sent back an answer. *Did you tell him you had sent her here?*

I had no choice, Coryn replied. *Now he has demanded that we attack Tramontana Tower with our powers, unless they agree quickly to send her back, and preferably you, too. . . .*

Allart whistled in dismay. Hali was bound, by law and custom, to use its powers for the Elhalyn overlord. They could strafe Tramontana with psychic lightnings, till the workers in the Tower were dead or mindless. Had he brought ruin on the friends here who had brought Cassandra to him? How could he have entangled them in his own family troubles? Well, it was too late now to regret.

Coryn said, *We refused, of course, and he gave us a day and a night to reconsider our answer. By the time he comes again we must be able to tell him, in a way that will satisfy his own* leronis *that neither of you is in Tramontana and that such strafing would be useless.*

Be very sure, we shall be gone from Tramontana before daylight, Allart assured him, and allowed the contact to break.

Chapter 22

They set forth at the break of day, afoot, Tramontana kept no mounts and, in any case, their escort, with travel gear, had set forth yesterday at the same hour as Donal and Allart in their gliders. There was only one road, and sometime today they would meet the party from Aldaran on it.

The important thing was to be gone from Tramontana so that Hali could justly refuse to strafe the other Tower. *We cannot bring disaster upon our brothers and sisters of Tramontana, not when they have made themselves vulnerable for our sake.*

Cassandra looked up at him as they walked down the steep path side by side, and it seemed to Allart that the look she gave him was one of awful vulnerability. Once again, in life and death, he was responsible for this woman. He did not speak, but moved close to her.

"All the gods be thanked for the fine weather," Donal said. "We are but ill equipped to ravel more than a day in these hills. But the party from Aldaran has tents and shelter, blankets and food; once we meet them, we could, if need struck us, camp for a few days should a storm come up." His trained eyes scanned the sky. "But it seems to me unlikely that there will be such a storm. If we meet with them on the road a little after midday, as we most probably will, we can reach Aldaran sometime tomorrow in the afternoon."

As he spoke a small thrill of dread struck inward at Allart. For a moment it seemed that he walked through whirling snow, a raging wind, and Cassandra was gone from his side. . . . No! It was gone. No doubt Donal's words had roused fear of one of those remotely possible futures which would probably never come to pass As the sun rose above its mantle of crimson cloud on the distant peaks, he put back the cowl of his traveling-cloak—borrowed from Ian-Mikhail, for he had not been able to wear heavy garments in the glider, and all of his cold-weather gear was with the escort party from Aldaran; they had, of course, expected to wait in comfort at Tramontana until the escort came for them. Donal was similarly burdened with a borrowed cloak—for, although the weather seemed incredibly fine for the season, no one ventured forth in winter in the Hellers without clothing against a sudden storm, no matter how unlikely. Cassandra was dressed in clothing somewhat too short for her, borrowed from Rosaura. The colors, designed for the tawny-russet Rosaura, made her delicate dark beauty look quenched and colorless, and the short skirt displayed her ankles a little more than was strictly seemly, but she made a joke of it.

"All the better for walking on these steep paths!" She bundled up Rosaura's bright green travel-cloak and wadded it carelessly under her arm. "It is all too warm for this; I would as soon not be burdened with carrying it," she said, laughing.

"You do not know our mountains, Lady," Donal said soberly. "If even a little wind springs up, you will be glad of it."

But as the sun climbed the sky, Allart's confidence grew. After more than an hour of walking, Tramontana was lost to sight behind a shoulder of the mountain, and Allart felt relieved. Now indeed they were gone from Tramontana, and when Damon-Rafael came to Hali and demanded that they should be yielded up to him, Tramontana could honestly say they were out of reach.

Would he vent his wrath upon the Hali circle, anyway? Most probably he would not. He needed their goodwill for the war he was waging against the Ridenow, needed them to make the weapons which gave him tactical and military advantage—and Coryn was an inspired deviser of weapons. *All too inspired,* Allart thought. *If the Domain were in my hands I should make peace at once with the Ridenow, and*

*truce lasting enough that we could settle our differences in
a meaningful way. Aldaran is right; we have no cause to
war with the Ridenow at Serrais. We should welcome them
among us, and be grateful if the* laran *of Serrais is kept alive
in the women they have wed.*

After several hours of walking, as the sun heightened to
noon, Donal and Allart, too, had taken off their heavy
cloaks and even their outer tunics. The people at Tramontana had given them ample food for a meal or two by the
way—"In case," they said, "your escort should be somewhat delayed by the road; riding-animals can go lame or
rockfalls obstruct the roads for a little"—and they sat on
rocks beside the road, eating hard flat cakes of journey-
bread and dried fruit and cheese.

"Merciful Avarra," Cassandra said, gathering up the
remnants, "it seems they have given us enough for a tenday! Surely there is no sense to carrying all this!"

Allart shrugged, stuffing the packets in one of the pockets of his outer tunic. Something in the gesture made him
think of mornings at Nevarsin, stowing the few things he
was allowed to possess in the pockets of his robe.

Donal, taking the remaining packages of food, seemed
to share a part of the joke. "I feel like Fro' Domenick,
with his pockets bulging," he said, and whistled a snatch of
Dorilys's song.

Little more than a year ago, Allart thought, *I was resigned
to living the rest of my life within the walls of a monastery.*
He looked at Cassandra, who had tucked up her skirts almost to her knees and climbed a little stone wall to come
at a stream that trickled down, clear and cool, from the
heights. She bent to cup the water in her hands for a drink.
*I thought I could spend all my life as a monk, that no
woman could ever mean anything to me, yet it would rend
me asunder now to be parted from her.* He climbed across
the wall, and bent beside her to drink, and as their hands
touched, he wished suddenly that Donal was not with them;
then he almost laughed at himself. Surely there had been
times in the summer past when Renata and Donal had
suffered *his* presence as unwillingly as he now tolerated
Donal's company.

They sat for a while beside the road, resting, feeling the
warmth of the sun on their heads, and Cassandra told him

about her training as a monitor, and of the work as a mechanic. He touched the bone-deep *clingfire* scar on her hand with a twinge of horror, glad suddenly that she was out of the reach of war. In return he told her a little of Dorilys's strange gift, touching lightly on the horror of the deaths following her handfastings, and talking of how they had flown among the storms.

"You shall try it, too, kinswoman," Donal said, "when the spring comes."

"I wish I might, but I do not know if I would care to wear breeches, even for that."

"Renata does," Donal said.

Cassandra laughed gaily. "She has always had more daring than I!"

Donal said, suddenly subdued, "Allart is my dear cousin and friend and I have no secrets from his wife. Renata and I were to be married at midwinter. But now my father has other wishes." Slowly, he told her of Aldaran's plan, that he and Dorilys should marry, so he might legally inherit Aldaran. She looked at him in kindly sympathy.

"I was fortunate. My kinfolk gave me to Allart when I had never seen him, but I found him such a one as I could love," she said. "Yet I know it is not always so, nor even very often, and I know what it is to be parted from a loved one."

"I will *not* be parted from Renata," Donal said, low and fierce. "This mockery of marriage with Dorilys will be no more than a fiction, to endure no longer than my father lives. Then, if Dorilys will have it so, we will find her a husband and go forth, Renata and I. Or if she has no will to marry, I will remain as warden in her time. If it is her wish to adopt one of my *nedestro* sons as her heir, well and good; and if not, well and good also. I will not defy my father, but I will not obey him, either. Not in this; not if he wishes me to take my half-sister to bed and father a son upon her!"

"I should think that should be as Dorilys wills it, kinsman. The lady of Aldaran, if she is lawfully wed to another, cannot create scandal by taking guardsmen or mercenaries to her bed . . . and she may not have any wish to live loveless and childless."

Donal looked away from her. "She may do as she wills,

but if she has sons they will not be of my fathering. Allart has told me enough of what the breeding program and its inbreeding has already done among our people. My mother reaped that bitter fruit, and I will sow no more of it."

Before the fierceness of that, Cassandra recoiled. Allart, sensing her unease, picked up her cloak and said, "I suppose we should go on. The escort can travel faster than we can, but still, even an hour's walking to meet them will lessen the time we must spend on the road tomorrow."

The path was less steep now, but the sunshine was patched with shadows as long feathery traces of gray cloud moved across the sky. Donal shivered and looked nervously toward the heights, darkening with thick gray masses, but he said nothing, only fastening the neck of his cloak.

Allart, picking up his apprehension, thought, *It would be well if we met with the escort as soon as might be.*

A little more walking, then, and the sky was hidden entirely with cloud, and Allart felt a snowflake strike his face. They were drifting slowly down, spiraling as they fell. Cassandra caught the snowflakes in her hand, marveling, childlike, at their size. But Allart had lived at Nevarsin and he knew something of the storms in the Hellers.

So Damon-Rafael may have had his way after all. By driving us forth in winter from the safety of Tramontana Tower, when storms are rather more likely than not, he may have rid himself without effort of a dangerous rival. . . . And if I die in this storm, then there is no one to stand against my brother's will to power. Allart's *laran* began to overpower him again, bringing him obsessive pictures of ruin and terror, wars raging, lands ravaged and burned, a true age of chaos all over Darkover from Dalereuth to the Hellers.

Scathfell, too, might fall upon Aldaran, and with Donal gone, there will be no one to stand against him. Between them, Scathfell and my brother will tear all this land asunder!

"Allart," Cassandra said, picking up from his mind some of the images of ruin and chaos, "what is wrong?"

And I have Cassandra to protect, not only against my brother, but against all the rage of the elements!

"Will it be a blizzard?" she asked, suddenly frightened, and he looked at the thickening snowfall.

"I am not sure," he said, watching Donal thrust up a wetted finger into the wind and turn it slowly around, trying to sense where the wind came from. "But there is some danger, though not immediate. We may meet the escort on the way before it gets any worse. They have food and clothing and gear for shelter, and then there will be nothing to fear."

But even as he spoke, he met Donal's eyes and knew that it was worse than he thought. The storm was coming *from* the direction of Aldaran; therefore it had probably already forced the escort to stop and make camp on the way. They would not be able to see the road ahead and the animals would not be able to find their footing in the heavy snow. There was no blame to the escort party; they would have believed Allart and Donal and Allart's lady safe and among friends in Tramontana Tower.

How could they be expected to guess at Damon-Rafael's malice?

Cassandra looked terrified. *If she is reading my mind, no wonder,* Allart thought, and applied himself to the task of calming her fears. He had too much respect for her to offer her a pacifying lie, but things were not as bad as she feared, either.

"One of the first things I learned at Nevarsin, was the art of finding shelter in unlikely places, and how to come through these sudden storms without disaster. Donal," he said, "is there any man among the escort with a scrap of *laran,* so that you and I could reach him and tell the escort of our plight?"

Donal stopped to consider. At last he said regretfully, "I fear not, cousin. Although it would not hurt to try; some few men can receive thoughts, though they could not send them and do not think of it as *laran.*"

"Try, then, to reach them," Allart instructed. "For they have every reason to believe us safe at Tramontana. They should know that this is not so. Meanwhile—" He cast his eyes around, searching for shelter, trying to think ahead along the road to see if there was an old building of any kind, a lean-to, a deserted barn, even some inhabited dwelling where they might be given shelter.

But as far as his clairvoyance could see, there was none The country they traveled might have been virgin to all human feet for all time, for any traces of mankind's passing here. He had seen no print of habitation since the small stone wall near where they had eaten their midday meal.

It had been years since he had had to use his mountain-survival training; not since his third year at Nevarsin, when he had been sent forth barehanded in his monk's cowl into the teeth of the harshest season, to bring back proof of his fitness for the next level of training. The old brother who had taught him had said, "After some deserted human dwelling, next best is a thicket of trees close-set; after that, a rock-ledge facing away from the wind and with some vegetation." Allart wrinkled his forehead, trying to remember, searching out ahead of him, letting his *laran* have full play as he sought to spy ahead in time what lay along each of the directions they might take from here.

Is there time to return to Tramontana? Mentally retracing his steps, he saw along that line of probability only their three dead bodies, huddled and frozen at the side of the road.

For once in his life he was grateful for his *laran,* which allowed him to see clearly ahead on every choice they might make; because on the choices they made now, their very lives would certainly depend. He saw along the road directly ahead that the path narrowed; where blinded by the ever-thickening snow, they might miss their footing, go plunging into a chasm hundreds of feet deep, their bodies never found. They must go no farther along this road. Following his clear warning, Cassandra and Donal stopped and awaited his guidance. They were now only blurred cloaked shapes in the thickening snow, and a high wind had begun to scream down from the heights.

A little way ahead of them, a pathway led up to a clustered formation of rocks, close gathered to give almost as much shelter as a building. Allart started to direct them up to it, then hesitated, searching with his *laran* along that line of probability. He flinched, in panic; the cluster of rocks was the nest of banshee-birds, the evil flightless carnivores who lived above the timberline and were drawn by an unfailing tropism to anything with the body-heat of life. They must not go *that* way!

They could not remain here; the wind was strong enough to fling them off the ledge, and the snow thick around

them. Already Cassandra was shivering, the borrowed
travel-cloak never intended for a serious storm. Allart and
Donal, more used to mountain weather, were not cold, but
Allart was beginning to be frightened. They could not go
back to Tramontana. They could not climb up where the
banshees nested. They could not go ahead on the road to
the narrowing path over the abyss. And they could not stay
here. Was there no alternative to their death then? Was it
ordained by fate that they should die in this blizzard?

*Holy Bearer of Burdens, strengthen me. Help me to see a
way,* Allart prayed. He had almost forgotten how to pray
since leaving the monastery, and fear for himself would not
have done it, but Cassandra, shivering in his arms, spurred
him to explore every avenue.

They could not return to Tramontana, but a little way
back along the path was the stone wall. It was long abandoned and falling down, but it would provide better shelter
than the open path; and behind it—he saw now with both
memory and *laran*—a thick set clump of evergreens.

"We must go back to where we ate our midday meal,"
he said, pitching his voice carefully above the shriek of
the wind.

Slowly, holding on to one another, for the snow was wet
and slippery underfoot, they retraced their steps. It was
slow, hard going. Donal, who had spent all his life in these
mountains, was surefooted as a mountain cat, but Allart
had been years away from the crags around Nevarsin, and
Cassandra was wholly unaccustomed to these roads. Once
she slipped and fell full length in the snow, her thin borrowed dress soaked to the knees, her hands torn on the
rocks under their coat of snow, and she lay there chilled
and sobbing with pain. Allart lifted her to her feet, his face
set with determination. But she had twisted knee and ankle
in the fall, and Donal and Allart had almost to carry her
the last few hundred steps to the rock wall, to lift her over
it and help her into the thick enclosure of the clumped
trees. As they were down into it, Allart's *laran* screamed
at him that this was the place of his death. He saw their
three bodies, entangled, clutching one another for warmth,
frozen and stark. He had to force himself down into the
enclosure made by the trees.

Gnarled and old, twisted by the violence of mountain

storms for half a century or more, the trees wove close, and inside their circle the wind was less, though they could hear it screaming outside, and there was a patch of ground unmarred by the heavy snow. Allart laid Cassandra down on the ground, folding her cloak so it kept the worst of the cold from her, and began to examine her injured leg.

"There is nothing broken," she said shakily, after a moment, and he remembered that she was a trained Tower monitor, skilled at penetrating the bodies of herself and others for whatever was wrong inside. "The ankle is painful but nothing is harmed; only a tendon pulled a little . . . but the kneecap has been twisted out of its place."

As Allart turned his attention to the knee he saw the kneecap wrenched to the side of the leg, the place rapidly swelling and darkening.

She said, drawing a terrified breath, "Donal, you must hold my shoulders, and you Allart, you must grasp my knee and ankle like this—" She gestured. "No! Lower down, with that hand—and pull hard. Don't worry about hurting me. If it is not returned to its place at once I could be lamed for life."

Allart steeled himself to follow her instructions. She was braced and tense, but despite her courage, a shriek was forced between her teeth as he gripped the dislocation and twisted it, hard, back into its place, feeling the grating as the kneecap slid back into its socket. She fell back in Donal's arms and for a moment it seemed she had fainted, but she had closed her eyes and was again monitoring to see what had happened.

"Not quite. You must turn my foot to one side—I cannot move it myself—so it will fall back into place. Yes," she said, between clenched teeth, as Allart obeyed her. "That will do. Now tear my under-petticoat and bandage it tightly," she said. Tears came to her eyes again, not only of pain, but of embarrassment as Allart lifted her to remove her under-garment, although Donal modestly turned away.

When the hurt knee had been tightly bandaged in trips of cloth, and Cassandra, white and shivering, had been wrapped in her cloak, and was resting on the ground, Allart soberly took stock of their chances here. Outside, the storm had not nearly reached its height, and night, as he imagined, was not far away, though already it was dark, a thick, heavy twilight that had nothing to do with the actual hour. They had with them only the remnants of their picnic lunch, enough for a couple of sparse meals. These storms sometimes lasted for two or three days, or more. Under ordinary conditions, any of them could have gone without a few meals, but not if the cold should become really severe.

They could probably manage for two or three days. But if the storm should last much longer than that, or if the roads should become impassable, their chances were not good. Alone, Allart would have wrapped himself tightly in his cloak, found the most sheltered spot possible, and let himself sink into the tranced sleep he had learned at Nevarsin, slowing his heartbeat, lowering his body temperature, all the requirements of his body—food, sleep, warmth—in abeyance. But he was responsible for his wife, and for young Donal, and they had not had his training. He was the oldest and the most skilled.

"Your cloak is the thinnest, Cassandra, and the least useful to us for warmth. Spread it on the ground like this, here, so it will keep the cold of the earth from rising," he directed. "Now, our two cloaks over the three of us. Cassandra is the least accustomed to the cold of the mountains, so we will put her between us." When they were all three huddled together, back to front, he could feel Cassandra's shivering subside somewhat.

"Now," he said gently, "the best thing to do is to sleep if we can; above all, not to waste energy in talking."

Outside the shelter where they lay, the wind howled, snow coming down endlessly in streaks white against the black night. Inside, only random flurries blew through the tightly laced branches. Allart let himself drift into a light trance, holding Cassandra close in his arms so that he would know if she stirred or had any need of him. At last he knew that Donal, at least, slept; but Cassandra, though she lay quiet in his arms, did not sleep. He was aware of the sharp pain in her injured leg, keeping her concentration at bay. At last she turned in his arms to face him, and he clasped her tight.

She whispered, "Allart, are we going to die here?"

Reassurance would have been easy—and false. No matter what, there must be truth between them, as there had been from the first moment they met. He fumbled in the dark for her slender fingers and said, "I don't know *preciosa*. I hope not."

His *laran* showed him only darkness ahead. Through the touch of her hands he could feel the pain stabbing at her. She tried carefully to shift her weight without disturbing Donal, who was curled close against her body. Allart half rose, kneeling and lifted her, changing her position. "Is that easier?"

"A little." But there was not much he could do in their cramped shelter. This had been the worst of all mischances; even if there were a break in the weather, they could not now seek better shelter, for Cassandra would probably not be able to walk for several days. Tended, put at once into a hot bath, given massage and treatment by a matrix-trained *leronis* to halt the swelling and bleeding within the joint, it might not have been very serious; but long exposure to cold and immobilization did not promise well for swift healing Even if conditions had been right, Allart had but small training in those skills. Rough and ready first aid he could give, indeed, but nothing more complicated.

"I should have left you safe at Hali," he groaned, and she touched his face in the darkness.

"There was no safety for me there, my husband. Not with your brother at my door."

"Still, if I have led you to your death—"

"It might equally have been my death to stay there," she said, and amazingly, even in this extremity, he caught a flicker of laughter in her voice. "Had Damon-Rafael sought to take me unwilling, he would have found no submissive woman in his bed. I have a knife and I know how— and where—to use it." He heard her voice tighten. "I doubt he would have let me live to spread the tale of that humiliation."

"I do not think he would have had to use force," Allart said bleakly. "More like, you would have been drugged into submission, without will to resist."

"Ah, no," she said, and her voice thrilled with an emotion he could not read. "In that case, my husband, I would have known where to turn the knife ere they brought me to *that*."

Allart felt such a thickening in his throat that he could not force an answer. What had he done to deserve this

woman? Had he ever believed her timid, childlike, fearful?
He caught her tightly against him, but aloud he only said,
"Try to sleep, my love. Rest your weight against me, if it
is easier. Are you too cold now?"

"No, not really, not close to you this way," she said, and
was still, breathing long, calm breaths in and out.

But have I given her freedom or only a choice of deaths?

The night crawled by, an eternity. When day broke it
was only a little lessening of the darkness, and for the three
in the hollow, cramped and restless, it was torment. Allart
cautioned Donal, crawling outside for a call of nature, not
to go more than a step or two from the thicket, and when
he staggered back inside, battered and already snow covered, he said that outside the wind was so heavy he could
hardly stand. Allart had to carry Cassandra in his arms; she
could not set her foot to the ground. Later he meted out
most of the food from the day before. The snow showed
no sign of abating; as far as Allart could tell, the world
outside their tree-cluster ended an arm's length away in a
white blur of snowy nothingness.

He let his *laran* range out cautiously ahead. Almost in
every instance he saw their lives end *here,* yet there had to
be other possibilities. If it were his ordained fate to die
here, and if bringing Cassandra from the Hali would lead
inevitably to his death and hers in the snow, then why had
his *laran* shown him no trace of it, ever, in any line of
probability that he had foreseen to this time?

"Donal," he said, and the younger man stirred.

"Cousin . . ."

"You have more of the weather gift than I. Can you read
this storm and discover how far it extends, and how long
it will take to move past us?"

"I will try," Donal sank inward in consciousness, and
Allart, lightly in rapport, saw again the curious extended
sense of pressures and forces, like nets of energy upon the
surface of the ground, and in the thin envelope of air above
it. Finally, returning to surface consciousness, Donal said
soberly, "Too far, I fear. And it is moving sluggishly.
Would that I had my sister's gift, to control the storms and
move them here and there at my will!"

Suddenly Allart knew that was the answer, as he began

to see ahead again. His *laran* was real foresight, yes; he could dislocate time and stand outside it, but it was limited by his own interpretation of what he saw. For that reason it would always be unreliable as a sole guide to his actions. He must never be content with an obvious future; there was always the probability, however small, that interaction with someone whose actions he could not foresee would alter that future beyond recognition. He could rule his *laran*, but as with his matrix jewel, he must never let it rule him instead. Yesterday he had used it to find safety here and avoid the most obvious deaths lying in wait; it had worked to avert imminent death until he could explore some other probability.

"If we could somehow make contact with Dorilys—"

"She is not a telepath," Donal said, sounding doubtful. "Never have I been able to reach her with my thoughts." Then he lifted his eyes and said, "Renata . . . Renata is a telepath. If one of you two could manage to reach Renata—"

Yes, for Renata was the key to control of Dorilys's power.

Allart said, "*You* try to reach her, Donal."

"But—I am not so strong a telepath."

"Nevertheless. Those who have shared love, as you two, can often make such a link when no other can. Tell Renata of our plight, and perhaps Dorilys can read the storm, or help it to pass more quickly beyond us!"

"I will do what I can," Donal said. Drawing himself upright, the cloaks still hunched around him, he drew out his matrix and began to focus himself within it. Allart and Cassandra, clinging together beneath the remaining cloak, could almost see the luminous lines of force spreading out, so that Donal seemed no more than a solid network of swirling energies, fields of force. . . . Then, abruptly, the contact flared and Allart and Cassandra, both telepaths, could not close away that amplified rapport.

Renata!

Donal! The joy and blaze of that contact spilled over to Cassandra and Allart, as if she touched them, too, embraced them.

I was fearful, with this storm! Are you safe? Have you remained at Tramontana, then? I feared when it broke that

*the escort would be forced to turn back; did they meet with
you, then?*

No, my beloved. quickly, in rapid mental images, Donal
sketched their plight. He interrupted Renata's horrified reaction. *No, love, don't waste time and strength that way.
Here is what you must do.*

Of course, Dorilys can help us, and the swift touch,
awareness. *I will find her at once, show her what to do.*

The contact was gone. The lines of force faded out and
Donal shivered under the doubled cloaks.

Allart handed him the last of the food, and said, when
he protested, "Your energy is drained with the matrix; you
need the strength."

"Still, your lady—" Donal protested, but Cassandra
shook her head. In the gray snowlight she looked pale,
drawn, deathly.

"I am not hungry, Donal. You need it far more than I.
I am cold, so cold. . . ."

Quickly Allart knew what she meant and what faced her
now. He said, "What is it with the leg, then?"

"I will monitor and be sure," she said, a flicker of a smile
touching her face, a wry smile indeed. "I have not wanted
to know the worst, since there seems nothing I could do to
mend it, however bad it may be." But he saw her look go
abstracted, focused inward. Finally, reluctant, she said, "It
is not good. The cold, the forced inactivity—and in the
lower part of that leg the circulation is already impaired,
so that it is more susceptible to chilling."

There was nothing Allart could say but, "Help may soon
reach us, my love. Meanwhile—" He took off his outer
tunic, began to wrap it around the injured knee to protect
it, and wrapped her in his under-cloak, remaining in his
undertunic and breeches. At their shocked protest, he said
with a smile, "Ah, you forget; I was a monk at Nevarsin
for six years, and I slept naked in worse weather than this."
Indeed, the old lessons took over; as the cold struck his
now unprotected flesh, he began automatically the old
breathing, flooding his body with inner warmth. He said,
"Truly, I am not cold. Feel and see. . . ."

Cassandra reached out her hand, wondering. "It is true!
You are warm as a furnace."

"Yes," he said, taking her chilly fingers in his and laying them under his arm. "Here, let me warm your hands."

Donal said, in astonishment, "I would that you could teach me that trick, cousin."

Feeling enormously genial with the sudden flooding warmth, Allart replied, "It needs little teaching. We teach it to the novices in their first season with us, so that before a few tendays have passed, they are romping half naked in the snow. Children who are crying with the cold in their first few days soon begin to run about in the courtyards without even remembering to put on their cowls."

"Is it a secret of your *cristoforo* religion?" Donal asked suspiciously.

Allart shook his head. "No, only a trick of the mind; it needs not even a matrix. The first thing we tell them is that cold is born of *fear;* that if they needed protection against cold, they would have been born with fur or feathers; that the forces of nature protect even the fruits with snow-pods if they need them; but man, being born naked, needs no protection against he weather. Once they come to believe that, that mankind wears clothes because he wishes to, for modesty or for decoration, but not to shelter against the weather, then the worst is over and soon they can adjust their bodies to cold or heat as they wish." He laughed, knowing the euphoria of the extra oxygen he was taking into his body was beginning to act upon him, to be converted into warmth. "I am less cold than I was last night under our shared cloaks and body warmth."

Cassandra tried to imitate his breathing, but she was in severe pain, and this inhibited her concentration, while Donal was wholly untrained.

Outside, the storm raged even more fiercely, and Allart lay down between the two, trying to share with them his warmth. He was desperately anxious about Cassandra; if she suffered much more pain and chilling, her knee might not heal for a long time, perhaps never wholly restore itself. He tried to conceal his anxiety from her, but the same closeness which had enabled Donal to reach Renata—without a Tower screen, through an open matrix-link alone—meant he and Cassandra were similarly linked and, especially at this close range, could not conceal a fear so strong from one another.

She reached for his hand and murmured, "Don't be frightened. The pain is not so bad now; truly it is not."

Well, when they reached Aldaran, Margali and Renata could tend her; for now there was nothing to be done. In the dimness he held the slight six-fingered hand in his, felt the knotted scar of the *clingfire* burn. She had endured war and fear and pain before this; he had not brought her out of peaceful life into danger. If he had simply substituted one danger for another, still, he knew, it was the danger which she had freely chosen for another less to her liking, and that was all any human being could ask in such days. Comforted a little, he dropped off, for a time, to sleep, held in her arms.

When he woke it was to hear a cry from Cassandra.

"Look! The storm has cleared!" He looked up, dazed, at the sky. It had stopped snowing entirely, and clouds were tearing across the sky at a wild pace.

"Dorilys," Donal said. "No storm ever moved across these hills at such a pace." He drew a long, shaking breath. "Her power—the power we have all feared so much—has saved all our lives."

Allart, sending his *laran* out across the country around, realized that the escort had been weathered in on the other side of the ledge he had hesitated to face in the storm. Now, as soon as they could bring their riding-animals across it—a matter of a few hours, certainly—help would be with them, food and shelter and care.

It had not been Dorilys's *laran* alone that had saved them, he thought soberly. The *laran* he had considered a curse had now proved its worth—and its limitations.

I cannot ignore it. But I must never wholly rely on it, either. I need not hide from it in terror, as I did all those years in Nevarsin. But I cannot let it wholly rule my actions.

Maybe I am beginning to know its limitations, Allart thought. It suddenly occurred to him that he had thought of Donal as very young, childishly young. Yet he himself, he realized, was no more than two years Donal's senior. With a completely new humility, free for once in his life of self-pity, he thought, *I am still very young myself. And I may not be given enough time to learn wisdom. But if I live, I may find that some of my problems were only because I was too young, and too foolish to know I was only too young.*

Cassandra was lying on his cloak, gray with pain and exhausted. He turned to her, and was touched that she tried to smile and appear brave. Now he could reassure her honestly, without hiding his own fear. Help was on the way and would reach them soon; there was only a little more time to wait.

Chapter 23

Donal Delleray, called Rockhaven, and Dorilys, heir to Aldaran, were formally married by the *catenas* on midwinter night.

It was not a festive occasion. The weather prevented, as often in the Hellers, inviting any but the nearest of Aldaran's neighbors; and of those invited, many chose not to come, in which Aldaran saw, rightly or not, a sign that they had chosen to align with his brother of Scathfell. So that the marriage was held in the presence of the immediate household alone, and even among these there was murmuring.

This kind of marriage, half-brother to half-sister, had once been commonplace in the early days of the breeding program, especially among the great nobles of the Domains—and imitated, like all such customs, by their inferiors. But it had fallen now into disuse and was regarded as mildly scandalous.

"They do not like it," said Allart to Cassandra as they went into the great hall where the festive supper, and the ceremony, and afterward the dance for the household, were all to be held. She was leaning heavily on his arm; she still walked with a dragging limp, memento of their ordeal in the snow, despite the best care Margali and Renata could give. It might heal with time, but it was still difficult for her to walk without help.

"They do not like it," he repeated. "Had anyone other than Dom Mikhail given orders for such a thing, they would have defied him, I think."

"What is it they do not like? That Donal shall inherit Aldaran when he is not of the blood of Hastur and Cassilda?"

"No," said Allart. "As far as I can tell from talking to Aldaran's vassals and household knights, that pleases them rather than otherwise; none of them has any love for Scathfell, nor any wish to see him rule here. If Dom Mikhail had given it out, true or not, that Donal was his *nedestro* son and would inherit, they would have stood by him to the death. Even if they knew it was false, they would have treated it as a legal fiction. What they do not like is this marriage of brother and sister."

"But this is a legal fiction, too," Cassandra protested.

Allart said, "I am not so sure of that. And neither are they. I still feel guilty that it was my own careless words which put this mad idea into Dom Mikhail's mind. And those who support Dom Mikhail in this—well, they do it as if they were humoring a madman. I am not so sure they are wrong," he added after a moment. "All madmen do not rave and froth at the mouth and chase butterflies in midwinter snow. Pride and obsession like Dom Mikhail's come near to madness, even if they are couched in reason and logic."

Since the bride was a little girl, the guests could not even hope to lighten the occasion with the jokes and rough horseplay which usually marked a wedding, culminating in the rowdy business of putting the bride and groom to bed together. Dorilys was not even full-grown, far less of legal age to be married. No one had wanted to rouse in Dorilys any bitter memories of her last handfasting, and so there had been no question of presenting her as a grown woman. In her childish dress, her copper hair hanging in long curls about her shoulders, she looked like a child of the household who had been allowed to stay up for the festivities, rather than like the appointed bride. As for the bridegroom, though he made an attempt to give decent lip service to the occasion, he looked grim and joyless, and before they went into the hall, the guests observed that he went toward a group of the bride's waiting-women and called Renata Leynier apart, talking with her vehemently for some minutes. A few of the house-folk, and most of the servants, knew the true state of affairs between Donal and

Renata, and shook their heads at this indiscretion in a man about to be wed. Others, looking at the little bride, surrounded by her nurses and governesses, compared her mentally with Renata and did not censure him.

"Whatever he says, whatever mummery he may make with the *catenas,* this is no more than a handfasting, and not a legal wedding. In law, even a *catenas* marriage is not legal till it is consummated," Donal argued. Renata, about to tell him that this point was still being argued before the Council and the lawgivers of the land, knew that he needed reassurance, not reason.

"It will make no difference to me! Swear it will make no difference to you, Renata, or I will defy my foster-father here and now, before all his vassals!"

If you were going to defy him, Renata thought in despair, *you should have done so from the beginning, certainly before things went this far! It is too late for public defiance without destroying both of you!* Aloud she said only, "Nothing could make any difference to me, Donal; you know that too well to need any oaths, and this is neither the time nor the place. I must go back to the women, Donal." But she touched his hand lightly, with a smile that was almost pity.

We were so happy this summer! How could we come to this? I am not blameless; I should have married him at once. To do him justice, he wished for that. Renata's thoughts were in turmoil as she walked, with Dorilys's women, into the hall.

Dom Mikhail was standing by the fireplace, lighted with the midwinter-fires kindled that day with sunfire, token of the return of light from the darkest day, greeting each of his guests in turn. Dorilys made her father a formal curtsy, and he bowed to her, kissed her on either cheek, and set her at his right side, at the high table. Then, one by one, he greeted the women.

"Lady Elisa, I would like to express my gratitude for your work in cultivating the lovely voice my daughter has inherited from her mother," he said, bowing. "Kinswoman Margali, again at this season I am grateful to you that you have taken a mother's place with my orphaned child. *Damisela*"— he bowed over Renata's hand—"how can I express my pleasure in what you have done for Dorilys? It is the greatest pleasure to welcome you to my—to my festal board," he said, stumbling. Renata, a telepath and keyed to the highest level of sensitivity at this moment, knew with a moment of anguish that he had started to say, "to my family," and then had remembered the real state of affairs between herself and Donal, and forborne to speak those words.

I always thought he knew, Renata thought, blind with pain. *Yet it means more to him, to carry out this plan of his!* Now she even regretted the scruples that had prevented her from again becoming pregnant by Donal at once.

If I had come to midwinter night visibly pregnant with Donal's child, would he have had the insolence to give Donal in marriage to another before my very eyes? When he insists that I have been the salvation of Dorilys? Could I have forced his hand that way? She walked to her seat, blinded by tears, in a welter of regrets and anxieties.

Although Aldaran's cooks and stewards had done their best, and the feast spread before them was notable, it was a joyless occasion. Dorilys seemed nervous, twisting her long curls, at once restless and sleepy. At the close of the meal Dom Mikhail signaled for attention, and called Donal and Dorilys to him. Cassandra and Allart, seated side by side at the far end of the high table, watched in tension, Allart braced for some untoward explosion, either from Donal, guarded and miserable behind a taut facade of civility, or from one of the sullen stewards and household knights at high table or lower hall. But no one interrupted. Watching Dom Mikhail's face, Allart thought no one would have dared to cross him now.

"This is indeed a joyous occasion for Aldaran," said Dom Mikhail.

Allart, briefly meeting Donal's eyes, shared a thought with him, quickly barricaded again. *Like Zandru's hell it is!*

"On this day of revelry it is my pleasure to place the guardianship of my house and my only heir, still a minor, Dorilys of Aldaran, into the hands of my beloved foster-son Donal of Rockraven."

Donal flinched at the name which proclaimed him bastard, and his lips moved in inaudible protest.

"Donal Delleray," Dom Mikhail corrected himself, reluctantly.

Allart thought, *Even now he does not wish to face the fact that Donal is not his son.*

Aldaran placed the twin bracelets of finely chased copper—engraved and filigreed, and lined on the side nearest the skin with gold plating so that the precious metal would not irritate the skin— on Donal's right wrist and Dorilys's left. Allart, looking down at the bracelet on his own wrist, held out his hand to Cassandra. All around the hall married couples were doing the same, as Aldaran spoke the ritual words.

"As the left hand to the right, may you be forever at one; in caste and clan, in home and heritage, at fireside and in council, sharing all things at home and abroad, in love and in loyalty, now and for all time to come," he said, locking bracelets together. Smiling for a moment despite his disquiet, Allart fitted the link of his own bracelet into that of his wife and they clasped hands tightly. He picked up Cassandra's thought, *If only it were Donal and Renata . . .* and felt again a surge of anger at this travesty.

Aldaran unlocked the bracelets, separated them. "Separated in fact, may you be joined in heart as in law," he said. "In token I bid you exchange a kiss."

All through the hall, married couples leaned toward one another to proclaim again their bond, even those, Allart knew, who were not on good terms with one another at ordinary times. He kissed Cassandra tenderly, but he turned his eyes away as Donal bent forward, just touching Dorilys's lips with his own.

Aldaran said, "May you be forever one."

Allart caught Renata's eye, and thought, *Desolate. Donal should not have done this to her. . . .* He still felt a strong sense of closeness to her, of responsibility, and he wished he knew what he could do. *It is not even as if Donal himself were happy about this. They are both wretched.* He damned Dom Mikhail for his obsession, and guilt lay heavy on him. *This was my doing. I put it into his head.* He wished heartily that he had never come to Aldaran at all.

Later there was dancing in the hall, Dorilys leading the dance with a group of her women. Renata had helped her to devise this dance and danced with her in the first measures, hands interlaced with the child's as they went through the ornate measures.

Allart watched her and thought, *They are not rivals; they*

are both victims. He saw Donal watching them both, and abruptly turned away, returning to the sidelines where Cassandra, still too lame for dancing, sat among a group of the old woman.

The night wore on, Aldaran's vassals and guests dutifully trying to put some jollity into the occasion. A juggler performed magic tricks for the household, bringing coins and small animals from the unlikeliest places, scarves and rings out of nowhere; in the end he brought a live songbird from Dorilys's ear and presented it to her, then retired, bowing. There were minstrels to sing old ballads, and in the great hall, more dancing. But it was not like a wedding, nor like an ordinary midwinter feast. Every now and then someone would start to make the kind of rowdy joke suitable for a wedding, then remember the real state of affairs and nervously break off in mid-sentence. Dorilys sat beside her father in the high seat, Donal at her side for a long time someone had found a cage for her songbird and she was trying to coax it to sing, but the hour was late and the bird drooping on its perch. Dorilys seemed to droop, too. Finally Donal, desperate at the silent tension and the joyless gathering, said, "Will you dance with me, Dorilys?"

"No," said Aldaran. "It is not seemly that bride and groom dance together at a wedding."

Donal turned on his foster-father a look of fury and despair. "In the name of all the gods, this pretense—" he began, then sighed heavily and dropped it. Not at a feast, not before all their assembled house-folk and vassals. He said with heavy irony, "God forbid we should do anything out of custom, such as might cause scandal among our kin," and turned, beckoning Allart from his wife's side. "Cousin, take my sister out to dance, if you will."

As Allart led out Dorilys to the floor, Donal looked once at Renata, in despair, but before his father's eyes he bowed to Margali. "Foster-mother, will you honor me with a dance, I beg?" and moved away with the old lady on his arm.

Afterward he danced dutifully with other of Dorilys's women, Lady Elisa and even her aged, waddling nurse. Allart, watching, wondered if this was intended to lead up to a situation where it would seem obvious for Donal to dance with Renata; but as Donal returned old Kathya to the women, they came face to face with Dorilys, who had been dancing with the *coridom* of the estate.

Dorilys looked up at Donal sweetly, then beckoned to Renata and in a clear, audible voice, filled with a false and sugary sweetness, said loudly, "You must dance with Donal, Renata. If you dance with a bridegroom at midwinter, you, too, will be married within the year, they say. Shall I ask my father to find you a husband, cousin Renata?" Her smile was innocent and spiteful, and Donal clenched his teeth as he took Renata's hand and led her onto the dancing floor.

"She should be spanked!"

Renata was almost in tears. "I thought—I thought she understood. I had hoped she was fond of me, even that she had come to love me! how could she—"

Donal could only say, "She is overwrought. The hour is late for her, and this is a trying occasion She cannot help but remember, I suppose, what happened at her handfasting to Darren of Scathfell. . . ." As if to underline his anger it seemed, though he could not be sure whether he really heard it or remembered it, that he heard a curious premonitory rumble of thunder.

Renata thought, *Dorilys has been on her good behavior of late. She cooperated with me on moving the storm which menaced Allart and Cassandra and Donal, and is now proud of her talent, proud that it saved lives. But she is only a child, spoiled and arrogant.*

Allart, across the room and seated at Cassandra's side, heard the thunder, too, and for a moment it seemed like the voice of his *laran,* warning him of storms to break over Aldaran. . . . For a moment it seemed that he stood in the courtyard of Aldaran keep, hearing thunders strike and break over the castle; he saw Renata's face pale and distraught with the lightnings . . . he heard the cries of armed men and actually started, wondering if the castle were truly under assault, until he recalled that it was midwinter night.

Cassandra clasped his hand. "What did you see?" she whispered.

"A storm," he said, "and shadows, shadows over Aldaran." His voice died to a whisper, as if he heard the thunders again, though this time it was only in his mind.

When Donal returned to the high seat of his foster-father

he said firmly, "Sir, the hour is late. Since this will not end like a traditional wedding, with a bedding as well, I have given orders for the guesting-cup to be brought and the minstrels dismissed."

Aldaran's face turned dark with sudden flaring anger.

"You take all too much on yourself, Donal! I have given no orders to that effect!"

Donal was startled, mystified at the sudden rage. Dom Mikhail had left all such things in his hands for the last three midwinter feasts. He said reasonably, "I did as you have always bidden me to do, sir. I acted upon my own best judgment." He hoped that by quoting his foster-father's own words he could calm him.

Instead, Dom Mikhail leaned forward with clenched hands and demanded, "Are you so eager to rule all in my place, then, Donal? That you cannot wait for my word—"

Donal thought, bewildered, *Is he mad? Is his mind going?*

Dom Mikhail opened his mouth to say more, but the servants had already entered bearing the jeweled cup containing a rich mixture of wine and spices, which would go around, shared from hand to hand. It was offered to Dom Mikhail, who held it motionless between his two hands for so long that Donal trembled. Courtesy finally conquered. Dom Mikhail set the cup to his lips, bowed to Donal, and handed him the cup. In his turn Donal barely tasted the mixture, but steadied it for Dorilys to taste, and passed it on to Allart and Cassandra.

The abortive scene had put a damper on what little remained of festivity. One by one, as they sipped from the cup, the guests bowed to Lord Aldaran and withdrew. Dorilys suddenly began to cry, noisy childish crying which suddenly escalated into screaming, bawling hysteria.

Dom Mikhail said helplessly, "Why, Dorilys, child," but she shrieked louder than ever when he touched her.

Margali came to enfold the child in her arms. "She is exhausted, and no wonder. Come, come, my little love, my baby. Let me take you away to your bed. Come, my darling, my bird, don't cry anymore," she crooned.

Dorilys, surrounded by Margali and Elisa and old Kathya, was half carried from the hall. The few remaining guests, embarrassed, slipped away to their beds.

Donal, crimson and raging, picked up a glass of wine and emptied it at a single swallow, then refilled it with angry determination. Allart went toward him to speak, then sighed and withdrew. There was nothing he could do for Donal now, and if Donal chose to get himself drunk, it was only a fitting end to this enormous fiasco of a festival. Allart joined Cassandra at the door, and went silently, at her side, down the hallway toward their own rooms.

"I do not blame the child," Cassandra said, painfully dragging herself upward on the stairs, holding to the railing. "It cannot be easy to be displayed as a bride before all these folk, and everyone staring and talking scandal about this wedding, and then to be put to bed in the nursery as if nothing had happened. Some wedding for the child! And some wedding night!"

Allart said gently, taking her by the elbow to steady her lagging step, "As I remember, my beloved, you spent your wedding night alone."

"Yes," she said, turning her eyes on him and smiling, "but my bridegroom was not abed with someone he loved better, either. Do you think Dorilys does not know Donal shares Renata's bed? She is jealous."

Allart scoffed. "Even if she does know—at her age, would it mean anything to her? She may be jealous because Donal cares more for Renata than he does for her, but he is only her big brother; surely it does not mean to her what it would have meant to you!"

"I am not so sure," Cassandra said. "She is not so young as most people think. In years—yes, I grant you, she is a child. But no one with her gift, no one with two deaths behind her, no one with the training she has had from Renata, is really a child, whatever the years may indicate. Merciful gods," she whispered, "what a tangle this is! I cannot imagine what will come of it!"

Allart, who could, was wishing that he could not.

Very late that night, Renata, in her solitary room, was wakened by a sound at her door. Instantly knowing who was there, she opened it to see Donal, disheveled, swaying on his feet, very drunk.

"On this night—is it wise, Donal?" she asked, but she

knew he was beyond caring for that. She could feel the despair like physical pain in him.

"If you turn me away now," he raged, "I shall throw myself from the heights of this castle before the dawn!"

Her arms went out to hold him against her, compassionately; to draw him inside, to shut the door after him.

"They may marry me to Dorilys," he said, with drunken earnestness, "but she will never be my wife. No woman living shall be my wife but you!"

Merciful Avarra, what will become of us? she thought. Renata was a monitor; there could have been no worse time for him to come to her like this, and yet she knew, sharing with him all the rage and despair of the humiliating night past, that she could deny him nothing, nothing that could ease even a little the pain of what had happened. She knew, too, with a despairing foresight, that she would come from this night bearing his son.

Chapter 24

Late in the winter, Allart met Cassandra on the stairway which led into the south wing of Castle Aldaran, where the women spent much of their time at this season in the conservatory rooms which caught the winter sun.

"It is a bright day," he said. "Why not come and walk with me in the courtyard? I see so little of you these days!" Then, laughing, he checked himself. "But no, you cannot— this afternoon is your festival in the women's quarters for Dorilys; is it not?"

Everyone at Castle Aldaran knew that in the last tenday Dorilys had first shown the signs of maturity—an official occasion for rejoicing. During the last three days she had been distributing her toys and playthings, her dolls and her favorite childish garments, among the children in the castle. The afternoon would be the private quasi-religious celebration among the women which marked leaving the company of the children and entering the society of the women.

"I know her father has sent her a special gift of some sort," Allart said.

Cassandra nodded. "And I am embroidering her some bands for a new shift," she said.

"What goes on at these women's affairs, anyhow?" Allart asked.

Cassandra laughed gaily. "Ah, you must not ask me that, my husband," she aid, and then, with mock seriousness, "There are some things it is not good for men to know."

Allart chuckled. "Now there is a byword I have not

heard since I left the company of the *cristoforos*. And I suppose we will not have your company at dinner either!"

"No. Tonight the women will dine together for her festival," Cassandra said.

He stooped to kiss her hand. "Well, then, bear Dorilys my congratulations," he said, and went out, while Cassandra, holding carefully to the railing—her lame knee had bettered somewhat, but was still troublesome on the stairs—went up toward the conservatory.

During the winter the women spent much of their time here, for these rooms alone caught the winter sun. They were bright with plants blooming in the light of the solar reflectors, and in the last tenday, in preparation for this celebration, branches of fruit-blossom had been brought inside and forced in the sunlight to adorn the gathering. Margali, as household *leronis* and also as Dorilys's foster-mother, was in charge of the ceremonies. Most of the women of the castle were present, the wives of the stewards and household knights and other functionaries, Dorilys's own waiting-women, a few of her favorites among the servant-women, and her own nurses, governesses, and teachers.

First she was taken to the chapel, and a lock of her hair was cut and laid upon the altar of Evanda, with fruit and flowers. After this Margali and Renata bathed her—Cassandra, as the highest in rank of the lady guests, had been invited to assist at this ritual—and dressed her from the skin out in new clothes, doing up her hair in a woman's coiffure. Margali, looking at her nursling, remembered how different she looked from when, less than a year ago, she had been masquerading in woman's garments at her handfasting.

Part of the purpose of this party, in earlier days, had been to make, for the new member of the woman's community, such things as she would need in her adult life; a remnant of a harsher time in the mountains. It was still, by tradition, a party at which all women brought their sewing, and everyone took at least a few stitches in items intended for the guest of honor. As they sewed, the harp went from hand to hand, each of the women being expected to sing a song, or tell a story, to amuse the others. Elisa had had the tall harp brought from the schoolroom and sang mountain ballads. A variety of dainties had been provided for refreshments, including some of Dorilys's favorite sweets, but Renata noticed that she only nibbled at them listlessly.

"What is the matter, *chiya*?"

Dorilys passed her hand over her eyes. "I am tired and my eyes hurt a little. I don't feel like eating."

"Come now, it is too late for that," one of them teased. "Two or three days ago was your time for headaches and vapors of that sort, if you must! You should be perfectly well again by now!" She examined the length of linen in Dorilys's lap.

"What are you making, Dori?"

Dorilys said with dignity, "I am embroidering a holiday shirt for my husband," and moved her wrist to display the *catenas* bracelet on it. Renata, watching her, suddenly did not know whether to laugh or cry. Such a traditional bridelike occupation, and the child had been given into a marriage which would never be more than a mockery! Well, she was still very young, and it would not hurt her to embroider a shirt for the big brother she loved and who was, in his eyes of the law, her husband.

Elisa finished her ballad, and turned to Cassandra.

"It is your turn. Will you favor us with a song, Lady Hastur?" she asked deferentially.

Cassandra hesitated, feeling shy, then realized that if she refused it might be taken as an indication that she considered her self above this gathering.

"With pleasure," she said, "but I cannot play on the tall harp, Elisa. If someone will lend me a *rryl*—"

When the smaller instrument was fetched and tuned, she sang for them, in a sweet husky voice, two or three of the songs of the Valeron plains, far away. These were new to the mountain women, and they asked for more, but Cassandra shook her head.

"Another time, perhaps. It is Dorilys's turn to sing for us, and I am sure she is eager to try out her new lute," she said. The lute, an elaborate gilded and painted one, adorned with ribbons, was Lord Aldaran's gift to his daughter on this occasion, replacing the old one of her mother's on which she had learned to play. "And I am sure she would welcome a rest from sewing!"

Dorilys looked up languidly from the mass of linen on her knees. "I don't feel like singing," she said. "Will you excuse me, kinswoman?" She drew her hand across her eyes, then began to rub them. "My head aches. Do I have to do any more sewing?"

"Not unless you wish, love, but we are all sewing here," Margali said. In her mind was a gently amused picture, which Cassandra and Renata could both read clearly, that Dorilys was all too ready to develop headaches when it came to doing the hated sewing.

"How dare you say that about me," Dorilys cried out, flinging the shirt in a wadded muddle to the floor. "I am really sick, I am not pretending! I don't even want to sing, and I *always* want to sing—" And suddenly she began to cry.

Margali looked at her in dismay and consternation. *But I didn't open my mouth! Gods above, is the child a telepath, too?*

Renata said gently, "Come here, Dorilys, and sit by me. Your foster-mother did not speak; you read her thoughts, that is all. There is no need to be troubled."

But Margali was not accustomed to barricading her thoughts from Dorilys. She had come to believe that her charge had no trace of telepathic power, and she could not prevent the swift thought that flashed through her mind.

Merciful Avarral This, too? Lord Aldaran's older children so died when they were come to adolescence, and now it is beginning with her, too!

Dismayed, Renata reached out to try to barricade the thoughts, but it was too late; Dorilys had read them already. Her sobbing died and she stared at Renata in frozen terror.

Cousin! Am I going to die?

Renata said firmly, aloud, "No, of course not. Why do you think we have been training and teaching you, if not to strengthen you for this? I had not expected it quite so soon, that is all. Now don't try to read anymore; you haven't the strength. We will teach you to shut it out and control it."

But Dorilys was not hearing her. She was staring at them in a nightmare of panic and dread, their thoughts mirrored back at them in the first frightening moment of overload.

She stared around her like some small trapped animal, her mouth open, her eyes so wide with terror that the whites showed all around the shrunken pupils.

Margali got up and went to her foster-child, trying to take her into a comforting embrace. Dorilys stood rigid, unmoving, unaware of the touch, unable to perceive anything but the massive onslaught of internal sensation. When Margali would have lifted her into her arms, she struck out unknowing, striking Margali with a painful shock that crumpled the old woman against the wall. Elisa hurried to her aid, lifting Margali, and the woman sat there staring in shock and consternation.

To turn on me this way . . . on me?

Renata said, "She doesn't know what she is doing, Margali; she doesn't know anything. I can hold her," she added, reaching out to hold the girl motionless as she had done when Dorilys first defied her, "but this is serious; she must have some *kirian.*"

Margali went for the drug, and Elisa, at a word from Renata, asked the guests to leave. Too many minds nearby would confuse Dorilys more frighteningly. She should be in the presence of only a few she trusted. When Margali returned with the *kirian,* only Renata, Cassandra, and Margali herself remained.

Renata went to Dorilys, trying to make contact with the terrified girl, isolated behind her panicked barricade of fear. After a time Dorilys began to breathe more easily, her eyes unlocked from their rigid, rolled-up unseeing position. When Margali held the vial of *kirian* to her lips swallowed it without protest. They laid her on a couch and tucked a blanket around her, but when Renata knelt at her side to monitor her, she cried out again in panic and sudden terror.

"No, no, don't touch me, don't!" Thunder suddenly crashed around the heights of the castle, a rattling roar.

"*Chiya.* I won't hurt you, really. I only want to see—"

"Don't touch me, Renata!" Dorilys shrieked. "You want me to die, and then *you* can have Donal!"

Shocked, Renata recoiled. Such a thought had never crossed her mind, but had Dorilys probed to a level of which even Renata herself was unaware? Fiercely dismissing the guilt, she held out her arms to the girl.

"No, darling, no. Look—you can read my thoughts if you

will and see what nonsense that is. I want nothing more
than to have you well again."

But, Dorilys's teeth were chattering, and they knew she
was in no state to listen to reason. Cassandra came and
took her place; she could not kneel because of her lame
knee, but she sat on the edge of the couch beside Dorilys.

"Renata would never hurt you, *chiya,* but we do not want
you to upset yourself either. I am a monitor, too. I will
monitor you. You are not afraid of me, are you?" She
added to Renata, "When she is calmer, she will know the
truth."

Renata moved away, still so horrified by Dorilys's sudden
attack that she was almost incapable of rational thought.
*Has she lost her senses? Does threshold sickness presage
madness also?* She had been prepared for Dorilys to show
ordinary sisterly jealousy because Donal was no longer specially hers; she had not been prepared for the intense emotion of this.

*Damn that mad old man, if he has encouraged her to
believe this will be anything but a legal fiction!* Although
Renata had hoped very soon to reveal to Donal that she
was bearing his son— for now she was certain, and she had
monitored the unborn, germ-deep, to be certain it bore no
lethals—she realized that it must be kept secret for a while
longer. If Dorilys were sick and unstable, this would only
hurt her more.

Cassandra went through the monitoring process; then, as
the *kirian* began to take effect, lowering Dorilys's terrified
defenses against the new sense which had frightened her
so, Dorilys quieted, her breathing growing more steady.

"It's stopped," she said at last, and her face was calm,
her heart no longer racing with panic. Only the memory of
fear remained. "Will it—will it start again?"

"Probably," Cassandra said, but stilled Dorilys's look of
swift panic with, "It will grow less troubling as you grow
used to it. Each time it will be easier, and when you are
fully mature, you will be able to use it as you do your sight,
to look selectively as you wish, near and far, and to shut
out everything you do not want."

"I'm afraid," Dorilys whispered. "Don't leave me alone."

"No, my lamb," Margali said. "I will sleep in your room
as long as you need me."

Renata said, "I know Margali has been like a mother to you, and you want her near you, but truly, Dorilys, I am more skilled in this and I could help you more if you needed it for the next few nights."

Dorilys held out her arms, and Renata came into them. The girl hid her face against Renata's shoulder. "I'm sorry, Renata. I didn't mean it. Forgive me, cousin . . . you know I love you. Please, stay with me."

"Of course, darling," Renata said, holding her in a reassuring hug. "I know, I know. I have had threshold sickness, too. You were scared, and all kinds of wild ideas were flooding into your mind at once. It is hard to control when it comes on you so suddenly like that. From now on we must work a little every day with your matrix, to help you control it; because when it comes on you again you must be prepared."

I wish that we had her in a Tower. She would be safer there, and so would all of us, she thought. She felt Cassandra echo the wish as the thunder rolled again and crackled in the air outside the castle.

In the great hall Allart heard the thunder, and so did Donal. Donal never heard thunder, no matter how or where, without thinking of Dorilys; and Dom Mikhail evidently followed his thoughts.

"Now that your bride is become a woman, you can go about the business of fathering an heir. If we know there is to be a son with Aldaran blood, then we will indeed be ready to defy Scathfell when he comes on us—and spring is not far," Aldaran said with a fierce smile. But Donal's face was taut with rejection, and Dom Mikhail looked at him and scowled.

"Zandru's hells, lad! I do not expect that a child so young should attract you too much as a lover! But when you have done your duty to your clan, you can have as many other women as you will. No one will gainsay that! The important thing now is to give the Domain a legitimate, *catenas* heir, fathered in lawful marriage!"

Donal made a gesture of rejection. *Are all old people always so cynical?* At the same moment he felt his foster-father's thoughts crossing and reinforcing his, with a kind of rueful affection.

Are all young people always so foolishly idealistic? Mikhail of Aldaran reached out to clasp his foster-son's hand.

"My dear boy, think of it this way. this time next year there will be an heir to Aldaran, and you will be his regent lawfully," he said.

As he spoke Allart almost gasped aloud, for his *laran* clearly showed it. In this great hall where they now sat, he could see it as clearly as if it were at this moment present to his eyes: Dom Mikhail, looking older, stooped and aged, held up a blanketed child—newborn, only a small red oval of baby face between the folds of the fleecy shawl—proclaiming Aldaran's heir. The cries of acclamation were so loud that for a moment Allart could not believe the others could not hear them. . . . The images were gone, had yet to be. But he was deeply shaken.

Would Donal, then, actually father a child on his little sister? Would this be the heir to Aldaran? His foresight seemed so clear and unequivocal! Donal picked it up from his mind and sat staring at him, helplessly, but some hint of it spilled over to the old man and he grinned in fierce triumph, seeing in Allart's mind the heir with whom he was obsessed.

At that moment Margali and Cassandra entered the hall, and Aldaran looked at them with a benevolent smile.

"I had not thought your merrymaking would end so quickly, ladies. When the hall-steward's daughter came of age, there was dancing and singing in the women's rooms until midnight was past—" He broke off abruptly. "Margali, kinswoman, what is wrong?"

But he read the truth quickly in her face.

"Threshold sickness! Merciful Avarra!"

Suddenly, from ambition and paranoia, he was only a concerned father again. His voice shook when he said, "I had hoped she would be spared this. Aliciane's *laran* came on her early, and she had no crisis at puberty, but there is a curse on my seed . . . my older sons and daughter so died." He bowed his head. "I have not thought of them in years."

Allart saw them in his mind, reinforced by the memories of the old *leronis:* a dark, laughing boy; a smaller, more solid boy with a mop of riotous curls and a triangular scar on his chin; a delicate, dreamy dark girl who somehow, in the lift of her small head, had something of a look of Dorilys, too. . . . Allart felt in himself the anguish of the father who had seen them sicken and die, one after another, all their promise and beauty wiped out. He saw in the older man's mind a terrible picture, never to be effaced or forgotten: the girl lying arched, convulsed, her long hair matted, her lips bitten through so that her face was smeared with blood, the dreamy eyes those of an agonized maddened animal. . . .

"You must not despair, cousin," Margali said. "Renata has trained her well, to endure this. Often the first attack of threshold sickness is the most severe so that if she survives that, the worst is over."

"It is often so," Dom Mikhail said, his voice brooding inward on horror. "It was so with Rafaella, one day laughing and dancing and playing her harp; and the next day, the very next, a screaming, tormented thing going into convulsion after convulsion in my arms. She never opened her eyes again to know me. When at last she ceased to struggle, I did not know whether to be more grieved, or more glad that she had come to the end of her agony. . . . But Dorilys has survived."

"Yes," Cassandra said compassionately, "and she did not even go into crisis, Dom Mikhail. There is no reason to think she will die."

Donal's voice was fierce, angry. "Now do you see, Father, what was on my mind? Before we speak of getting her with child, can we at least be sure she will live to womanhood?"

Aldaran flinched, as with a crushing blow. In the dying thunder past the windows, there was suddenly a crash and a rumble, and rain smote them, sluicing down and rattling, pounding, like the tramp of Scathfell's armies on the march toward them.

For now the spring thaw was upon the Hellers, and the war was upon them.

Chapter 25

For the first moon of spring it rained incessantly, and Allart, welcoming the rain because he knew it would keep Scathfell's armies from the road, still fretted with indecision. Damon-Rafael had sent a message expressing kindly concern, which to Allart's perception read false in every line of it, and ended by ordering his brother home at the earliest moment when the roads were open and he was able to travel.

If I return home now, Damon-Rafael will kill me. It is as simple as that. . . . Treason. I am forsworn. I gave my oath that I would support his rule, and now I know I will not. My life is forfeit to him, for I have broken my oath, in thought if not in deed . . . yet. So indecision made him linger at Aldaran, glad of the spring rains which kept him there.

Damon-Rafael is not sure, not yet. But if the roads are open and still I do not come—then I am a traitor, my life forfeit. And he wondered what Damon-Rafael would do when there was no longer any room for doubt.

Meanwhile, Dorilys had had a few repeated attacks of threshold sickness, but they had not been very severe, and at no time had Renata considered her life to be in danger. Renata had stayed with her tirelessly—though on one occasion she said to Cassandra, with the wry lift of a smile, "I do not know if she truly wishes to keep me at her side— or whether she feels that when I am with her, at least I am not with Donal." Both women knew there was another thing, unspoken.

Soon or late, she must know that I am bearing Donal's child. I do not want to hurt her or cause her any more grief.

Donal, whenever he saw Dorilys—which was seldom, for he was organizing the defenses of Aldaran against the attack which they knew would come with the spring—was kindly and attentive, the loving elder brother he had always been. But whenever Dorilys spoke the words "my husband," he never answered with anything except an indulgent laugh, as if this were indeed a childish game they were playing, and he humoring her in it.

During these days when Dorilys was subject to recurring attacks of disorientation and upheaval—her telepathic sense not yet under control, plunging her into a nightmare of terror and overload— she and Cassandra had become very close. Their shared love of music cemented this bond. Dorilys was already a talented player on the lute; Cassandra taught her to play a *rryl* as well, and she learned from the older woman some of the songs of Cassandra's faraway homeland at Valeron.

"I cannot see how you can endure to live in the Lowlands," Dorilys said. "I could not live without the mountain peaks surrounding me. It must be so dismal there, and so dull."

Cassandra smiled. "No, sweetheart, it is very beautiful. Sometimes here I feel the mountains are closing around me so that I can hardly breathe, as if the peaks were the bars of a cage."

"Really? How strange! Cassandra, I cannot play that chord as you do at the end of the ballad."

Cassandra took the *rryl* from her hand and demonstrated. "But you cannot finger it as I do. You will have to ask Elisa to show you the fingering," Cassandra said, and spread out her hand before Dorilys. The girl stared, wide-eyed.

"Oh, you have six fingers on your hand! No wonder I cannot play it as you do! I have heard that is a sign of *chieri* blood, but you are not *emmasca* as the *chieri* are; are you, cousin?"

"No," Cassandra said, smiling.

"I have heard—Father told me that the king in the Lowlands is *emmasca*, so they will take the throne from him this summer. How terrible for him, poor king. Have you ever seen him? What is he like?"

"He was only the young prince when I saw him last," said Cassandra. "He is quiet, and sad faced, and I think he would have made a good king, if they had been willing to let him reign."

Dorilys bent over the instrument, experimentally fingering the chord she could not play again and again. Finally she gave up the attempt. "I wish I had six fingers," she said. "There is no way I can play it properly! I wonder if my children will inherit my musical talents, or only my *laran*."

"Surely you are too young to be thinking yet about children," Cassandra said, smiling.

"In a few more moons, I will be capable of bearing. You know there is a great need for a son of Aldaran blood." She spoke so seriously that Cassandra felt a great wrench of pity.

This they do to all the women of our caste! Dorilys has hardly put away her dolls, and already she can think of nothing but her duty to her clan! After a long silence, hesitating, she said, "Perhaps—Dorilys, perhaps you should not have children, with this curse of *laran* you bear."

"As a son of our house must risk death in war, so a daughter of a great house must risk everything to give children to her caste." She repeated it simply and positively, and Cassandra sighed.

"I know, *chiya*. Since I was a child younger than you, I, too, heard that day in and day out, as a religion it was impious to doubt, and I believed it as you do now. But I feel you should be old enough to decide."

"I *am* old enough to decide," said Dorilys. "You do not have that kind of problem, cousin. *Your* husband is not heir to a Domain."

"You did not know?" Cassandra said. "Allart's elder brother will be king, if the *emmasca* of Hali is dethroned. This brother has no legitimate sons."

Dorilys stared at her. She said, "You could be queen," and her face held awe. Evidently she had had no idea of Allart's caste; he was only her brother's friend. "Then Dom Allart, too, stands desperately in need of an heir, and you are not yet bearing him one." Her eyes held a hint of reproach.

Hesitant, Cassandra explained the choice they had made.

"Now, perhaps, with what I know, it might be safe, but we will wait till we are sure. Till we are very sure. . . ."

"Renata said I should bear no daughters," Dorilys said, "or I might die as my mother died in giving me birth. But I am not sure I trust Renata anymore. *She* loves Donal, and she does not want me bearing his children."

"If that is true," Cassandra said very gently, "then it is only that she fears for you, *chiya.*"

"Well, in any case, I should have a son first," Dorilys said, "and then I will decide. Perhaps, when I give him a son, Donal will forget Renata, because I will be the mother of his heir." Her young arrogance was so great that Cassandra felt troubled, and again assailed by doubts.

Could she cement her bond with Allart best by giving him the son he must have, if they were not to deny him the throne like Prince Felix? They had not spoken of this seriously for some time.

I would give anything, to be so sure of myself as Dorilys But she changed the subject firmly, taking the *rryl* on her lap again, and placing Dorilys's fingers on the strings.

"Look, I think perhaps if you hold it this way, you can play that chord, even with only five fingers," she said.

Again and again, as the days passed, Allart wakened to the awareness of Aldaran under siege, then knew that the reality was not yet with them, that it was only his foresight which spread the inevitable visibly before him. That it was inevitable he knew perfectly well.

"At this season," Donal said one morning, "the spring storms would have subsided in the Lowlands, but I do not know how the weather goes at Scathfell or Sain Scarp, or whether their armies can move. I shall go up to the watchtower, which commands all the country around, and see if there is any suspicious movement on the roads."

"Take Dorilys with you to the watchtower," Allart advised. "She can read the weather even better than you."

Donal hesitated and said, "I am reluctant, always, to meet with Dorilys now. Especially now that she can read my thoughts a little, as well. I am not happy that she has become a telepath."

"Still, if Dorilys feels she can be of use to you somehow,

that you are not altogether avoiding her . . ." Allart
suggested.

Donal sighed. "You are right, cousin. Besides, I cannot
avoid her entirely." He dispatched a servant to his sister's
rooms, thinking, *Would it be altogether bad, then, to give
Dorilys what my father wishes of me? Perhaps, if she has
what she wants of me, she will not grudge me Renata, and
we need not struggle so hard to keep it from her. . . .*

Dorilys looked like the springtime itself, in a tunic embroidered with spring leaves, her shining hair braided low
on her neck and caught with a woman's butterfly-clasp. Allart could see the dissonance in Donal's mind between his
memories of the child, and the tall, graceful young woman
she had become. He bowed over her hand, courteously.

"Now I see that I must call you *my lady,* Dorilys," he
said lightly, trying to make it a joke. "It seems that my little
girl is gone forever. I have need of your talents, *carya,*" he
added, and explained what he wanted of her.

At the very topmost spire of Castle Aldaran, the watchtower shot up for the height of another floor or two, an
astonishing feat of engineering, and one which Allart could
not figure out. It would have had to be done by matrix,
working with a large circle. This great height commanded
all of the country around to a great distance. While they
climbed to the Tower, the window-slits showed them it was
wrapped in fog, and cloud, but by the time they emerged
into the high chamber, the clouds were already thinning
and moving away. Donal looked at Dorilys in delighted
surprise, and she smiled, almost a smug smile.

"To dispel fogs of that sort—even as a baby I think I
could do *that,* she said. "And now it is nothing. It takes
only the lightest thought, without effort, and if you wish to
see clearly—I remember when I was little you brought me
up here, Donal, and let me look through Father's collection
of big spyglasses."

Allart could see the roads below them aswarm with
movement. He blinked, knowing they were not there, not
yet; then shook his head, trying to clarify present from future. It was true! Armies moved on the road, though not
yet at the gates of Aldaran.

"We need not fear," Donal said, trying to reassure Dorilys. "Aldaran has never been captured by force of arms. We could hold this citadel forever, had we food enough; but they will be at our gates within a tenday. I will put on a glider-harness and go out to spy where they go, and bring back news of how many men move against us."

"No," Allart said. "If you will let me presume to advise you, cousin, you will not go yourself. Now that you are to command, your place is here where any one of your vassals who needs to consult with you can find you at once. You must not risk yourself on a task which any one of your lads could do for you."

Donal made a gesture of repugnance. "It goes against me—to order any man into a danger I will not face myself," he said, but Allart shook his head.

"You will face your own dangers," he said, "but there are dangers for the leaders and dangers for the followers, and they are not interchangeable. From now on, cousin, your flying must be a recreation for times of peace."

Dorilys touched Donal's arm, very lightly. She said, "Now that I am a woman—can I still fly, Donal?"

Donal said, "I do not see why you should not, when there is peace again, but you must ask our father about that, *chiya,* and Margali."

"But I am your wife," she aid, "and it is for *you* to give me commands."

Caught between exasperation and tenderness, Donal sighed. He said, "Then, *chiya,* I command you to seek Margali's advice in this, and Renata's. I cannot advise you." Her face had clouded ominously at the mention of Renata, and Donal thought, *Someday I must tell her, very clearly, how it stands with me and Renata.* He said aloud, an arm gently about her shoulders, "*Chiya,* when I was fourteen and my *laran* was coming on me, as it is upon you now, I was forbidden to fly for more than half a year, since I was never sure when an attack of disorientation and giddiness would come upon me. For that reason, it would please me better if you did not seek to fly until you are sure you can master it."

"I will do exactly as you say, my husband," she said, looking up at him with a look of such adoration that he quailed.

When she had gone away, Donal looked at Allart in despair. "She seems not like a child! I cannot think of her as a child," he said, "and that is my only defense now, to say she is a child and too young."

Allart was painfully reminded of his own emotional conflict over the *riyachiyas,* with this difference—that they were sterile and not altogether human and whatever he did with them could affect only his own self-esteem and not the *riyachiyas* themselves. But Donal had been placed in the position of playing a god with the life of a real woman. How could he advise Donal? He had consummated his own marriage, against his own better judgment, and for much the same reasons—because the girl wished for it.

He said soberly, "Perhaps it would be better not to think of Dorilys as a child, cousin. No girl given the training she has had can be altogether a child. Perhaps you must begin to think of her as a woman. Try to come to agreement with her in that way, as a woman old enough to make her own decisions; at least when the threshold sickness has left her free of impulse and sudden brainstorms."

"I am sure you are right." Almost gratefully, Donal recalled himself to duty. "But come—my father must be told that there is movement on the roads, and someone must be sent to spy out where they are!"

Aldaran greeted the news with a fierce smile.

"So it has come!" he said, and Allart thought again of the old hawk, mantling, spreading his wings, eager for a last flight.

As armed men crossed the Kadarin and moved northward into the Hellers, Allart, seeing them with his *laran,* knew with a sinking heart that some of these men moved northward against *him;* for among the armed men there were some with the fir-tree badge of the Hasturs of Elhalyn, with the crown that distinguished it from the Hasturs of Carcosa and Castle Hastur.

Day after day, he and Donal returned to the watchtower, awaiting the first sign of the armies' imminent approach at the castle.

But is this real, or does my laran *show me what might never come to pass?*

"It is real, for I see it, too," Donal said, reading his thoughts. "My father must be told of this."

"He wished to keep from entanglement in Lowland wars," Allart said. "Now, by sheltering me and my wife, he has made an enemy, and Damon-Rafael has made common cause with Scathfell against him." As they turned to go down into the castle, he thought, *Now, truly, I am brotherless. . . .*

Donal laid a hand on his arm. "I, too, cousin," he said.

On an impulse, neither moving first, but simultaneously, they drew their daggers. Allart smiled, laid the hilt of his to the blade of Donal's; then slid Donal's into his own sheath. It was a very old pledge; it meant that neither would ever draw steel against the other in any cause whatever. Donal sheathed Allart's dagger. They embraced briefly, then, arms linked, went down to Dom Mikhail.

Allart, comforted by the gesture, felt a moment's hesitation.

Perhaps I was wrong. I must be careful what alliances I make, do nothing it would embarrass me to retract should I one day sit on the throne. . . . He broke off the thought impatiently.

Already, he thought with a flare of self-hatred, *I am thinking in terms of what is expedient, like a politician—like my brother!*

As they came into the courtyard and began to cross it, one of the servants suddenly pointed upward.

"There—there! What is that?"

"It is only a bird," someone said, but the man cried out, "No, that is no bird!"

Shading his eyes, Allart looking up into the sun, seeing *something* there, wheeling, slowly spiraling down, a slow and ominous descent. Fear and agony clutched at him. *This is some work of Damon-Rafael's, an arrow launched by Damon-Rafael at my heart,* he thought, almost paralyzed. In a spasm of dread he realized, *Damon-Rafael has the pattern of my matrix, of my soul. He could aim one of Coryn's fearful weapons at me, without fear it will kill any other.*

In that moment he felt Cassandra's thoughts entangled in his own; then there was a blaze of lightning in the clear sky, a cry of pain and triumph, and the broken thing that was *not* a bird fell, like a stone, arrested in midair, splattering fire from which the servants edged back in terror. A woman's dress had been caught in the terrible stuff. One of the stablemen grabbed her and shoved her bodily into one of the washing-tubs that stood at the end of the court. She screamed with pain and outrage, but the fire sizzled and went out. Allart looked at the fire and the broken bird still squirming with dreadful pseudo-life as he came near.

"Bring water, and douse it wholly," he ordered.

When the contents of two or three laundry-tubs had been flung on it and the fire was wholly out, he looked at the faintly squirming thing with terrible repugnance. The woman who had been pushed into the first laundry-tub had hauled herself out, dripping.

"You were fortunate," Donal said before she could protest. "A drop of *clingfire* splattered on you, my good woman. It would have burned up your dress and burned through your flesh to your bones and gone on burning until the burned flesh was cut away."

Allart stamped on the broken thing of metal coils and wheels and pseudo-flesh, again and again, until it lay in shattered fragments which were still, faintly, moving. "Take this," he directed one of the stablemen. "Pick it up on your shovels. Do not touch it with your bare hands, and bury it deep in the earth."

One of the guardsmen came and looked, shaking his head.

"Gods above! Is *that* what we must face in this war? What devilry sent *that* against us?"

"The lord Elhalyn, who would be king over this land," said Donal, his face like stone. "If it were not for my sister's command of the lightning, my friend and my brother would now lie here burning!" He turned, sensing Dorilys running down the inner stairs, Cassandra following more slowly, with all the haste her lamed leg would allow. Dorilys ran to Donal and caught him close in her arms.

"I felt it! I felt it hovering over us. I have struck it down," she cried. "It did not strike at you or Allart! I saved you, I saved you both!"

Indeed you did," Donal said, holding the girl in his arms. "We are grateful to you, my child, we are grateful! Truly you are what Kyril called you that day at the fire station— queen of storms!"

The girl clung to him, her face lighted with such joy that

Allart felt sudden fear. It seemed to him that lightnings played all over Castle Aldaran, thought he sky was wholly clear again, and that the air was heavy with fire.

Was *this* what lay ahead in this war? Cassandra came to him, holding him, and he felt her fear like his own, and remembered that she had known the pain of a *clingfire* burn.

"Don't cry, my love. Dorilys saved me," he said. "She struck down Damon-Rafael's evil contrivance before it reached me. I suppose he would not believe I could escape this one, so it is not likely he will send another such thing against me."

But even as he comforted her, he was still afraid. This war would not be ordinary mountain warfare, but something quite new and terrible.

Chapter 26

If there had ever been room for doubt in Allart's mind about the coming war, there was none now. On every road leading to the peak of Aldaran, armies were gathering. Donal, massing the defenses, had stationed armed men ringing the lower slopes, so that for the first time in Donal's memory Castle Aldaran was actually the armed fortress it had been built to be.

A messenger had come into the castle under truce-flag. Allart stood in Aldaran's presence-chamber, looking at Mikhail of Aldaran on his high seat, calm, impassive, menacing. Dorilys sat beside him, with Donal standing at her side. Even Allart knew that Dorilys's presence was no more than the excuse for Donal's.

"My lord," the messenger said, and bowed, "hear the words of Rakhal of Scathfell, demanding certain observances and concessions from Mikhail of Aldaran."

Aldaran's voice was surprisingly mild. "I am not accustomed to receive demands. My brother of Scathfell may legitimately require of me whatever is customary from overlord to vassal. Say therefore to Lord Scathfell that I am dismayed that he should demand of me anything which he has only to request on the proper terms."

"It shall be so spoken," said the messenger. Allart, knowing that the messenger was a Voice, or trained speaker who would be able to relay up to two or three hours of such speech and counter-speech without the slightest variation in phrasing or emphasis, was certain the message would be relayed to Scathfell in Aldaran's very intonation.

"With that reservation, my lord Aldaran; hear the words of Rakhal of Scathfell to his brother of Aldaran." The stance and the very vocal timbre of the messenger altered slightly, and although he was a small man, and his voice light in texture, the illusion was eerie; it was as if Scathfell himself stood in the hall. Donal could almost hear the good-humored bullying voice of Lord Rakhal of Scathfell as the messenger spoke.

"Since you, brother, have made of late certain unlawful and scandalous dispositions regarding the heritage of Aldaran, therefore I, Rakhal of Scathfell, warden and lawful heir to the Domain of Aldaran, and pledged to support and uphold the Domain should your illness, infirmity, or old age make you unfit to do so, declare you senile, infirm, and unfit to make any further decisions regarding the Domain. Therefore I, Rakhal of Scathfell, am prepared to assume wardenship of the Domain in your name. Therefore I demand"—Lord Aldaran's fists clenched at his side at that repeated word, *demand*—"that you deliver up to me at once possession of Castle Aldaran, and the person of your *nedestro* daughter Dorilys of Rockraven, in order that I may suitably bestow her in marriage for the ultimate good of the realm. As for the traitor Donal of Rockraven, called Delleray, who has unlawfully influenced your sick mind to do malice and scandal to this realm, I, warden of Aldaran, am disposed to offer amnesty, provided that he leaves Castle Aldaran before sunrise and goes where he will, never to return or to step within the borders of the realm of Aldaran, or his life shall be forfeit and he shall be slain like an animal by any man's hand."

Donal stiffened, but his mouth took on a hard, determined line.

He wants Aldaran, Allart thought. Perhaps at first he was willing to step aside for Aldaran's kinsmen. But now it was obvious that Donal had become accustomed to thinking of himself as his foster-father's lawful successor and heir.

The Voice went on, and his voice altered faintly, his very posture changing somewhat. Although Allart had seen the technique before, it was now as if a quite different man stood before him, even the lines of his face changing. But what they had in common was arrogance.

"Furthermore, I, Damon-Rafael of Elhalyn, rightful king

of the Domains, demand of Mikhail of Aldaran that he shall at once deliver to me the person of the traitor Allart Hastur of Elhalyn and his wife Cassandra Aillard, that they may be duly charged with plotting against the crown; and that you, Mikhail of Aldaran, present yourself before me to discuss what tribute shall be paid from Aldaran to Thendara that you may continue during my realm to enjoy your Domain in peace."

Still again the messenger's voice and bearing altered, and again it was as if Rakhal of Scathfell stood before them.

"And should you, my brother of Aldaran, refuse any of these demands, I shall feel empowered to enforce them upon your stronghold and yourself by force of arms if I must."

The messenger bowed a fourth time and remained silent.

"An insolent message," Aldaran said at last, "and if justice were done, he who spoke it should be hanged from the highest battlement of this castle, since in serving my brother you are also pledged to serve his overlord, and I am he. Why, then should I not treat you as a traitor, fellow?"

The messenger paled, but his face betrayed no twitch of personal reaction, as he said, "The words are not mine, Lord, but those of your brother of Scathfell and His Highness Elhalyn. If the words offend you, sir, I beg of you to punish their originators, not the messenger who repeats them upon command."

"Why, you are right," Aldaran said mildly. "Why beat the puppy when the old dog annoys me with barking? Bear *this* message, then, to my brother of Scathfell. Say to him that I, Mikhail of Aldaran, am in full enjoyment of my wits, and that I am his overlord by oath and custom. Say to him that if justice were done, I should dispossess him of Scathfell, which he holds by my favor, and proclaim him outlaw in this realm as he has presumed to do with the chosen husband of my daughter. Say further to my brother that as for my daughter Dorilys, she is already wedded by the *catenas,* and he need not trouble himself to find a husband for her elsewhere. As for the lord Damon-Rafael of Elhalyn, say to him that I neither know nor care who reigns within the Lowlands across the Kadarin, since within this realm I acknowledge no reign save my own, but that if he who would be king in Thendara should invite me as his equal to witness his crowning, we will then discuss the exchange of diplomatic courtesies. As for my kinsman and guest Allart Hastur, he is welcome at my household and he may make to Lord Elhalyn such answer as he chooses, or none at all."

Allart wet his lips, too late realizing that even this gesture would be faithfully reproduced by the messenger standing before him, and wished he had not betrayed that small weakness. At last he said, "Say to my brother Damon-Rafael that I came here to Aldaran as his obedient subject and that I have faithfully performed all that he asked of me. My mission completed, I claim the right to domicile myself where I choose without consulting him." *A poor answer,* he thought, and cast about for the best way to continue. "Say further that the climate of Hali did not agree with my wife's health and that I removed her from Hali Tower for her health and safety." *Let Damon-Rafael chew on that!*

"Say at last," he added, "that, far from plotting against the crown, I am a faithful subject of Felix, son of the late king, Regis. If Felix, lawful king of Thendara, bids me at any time to come and defend his crown against any who would conspire to seize it, I am at his command. Meanwhile I remain here at Aldaran lest the lawful king Felix accuse me of conspiring to seize his rightful throne."

Now, he thought, *it is done and irrevocable. I could have sent a message of submission to my brother, and pleaded that as Aldaran's guest I could raise no hand against him. Instead, I have declared myself his foe.*

Allart resisted the temptation to look ahead and see, with his *laran,* what might befall when Damon-Rafael and Lord Scathfell received that message. He might foresee a hundred things, but only one could come to pass, and there was no sense in troubling his mind with the other ninety and nine.

There was silence in the presence-chamber while the trained Voice digested the message. Then he said, "My lords, those who dispatched me foresaw some answer such as this and bade me say thus:

"To Donal of Rockraven, called Delleray, that he is declared outlaw in this realm and that any man who slays him shall do so from this day forth without penalty. To Allart

Hastur, traitor, we offer nothing save the mercy of his brother should he come and make submission to him before sundown of this day. And to Mikhail of Aldaran, that he shall surrender Castle Aldaran, and all those within it, to the last woman and child, forthwith, or we shall come and take it."

There was another of those long silences. At last Aldaran said, "I do not plan to visit my Domain in the near future. If my brother of Scathfell has nothing better to do with his seed-time and harvest than sit like a dog outside my gates, he may stay there as long as it pleases him. However, should he injure man or woman, child or animal lawfully under my protection, or should he step beyond the line of my armed men so much as the width of my smallest finger, then I shall hold that as reason to annihilate him and his armies, and declare his holding of Scathfell forfeit. As for him, if I take him here I shall certainly hang him."

Silence. When it was obvious that he had no more to say, the messenger bowed.

"My lord, the message shall be delivered faithfully as spoken," he said. Then, the truce-flag before him, he withdrew from the room. Even before he had reached the door, Allart knew that there was no mistaking what the future would be.

It was war.

But then, he had never been in any doubt of that.

It was not long in coming. Within an hour of the departure of the Voice, a flight of fire-arrows winged up from below. Most of them fell harmlessly on stone, but a few landed on wooden roofs or on bales of fodder stacked within the courtyard for the animals, and the laundry-tubs of water were again put into play for extinguishing them before the fire could spread.

After the fires had been put out, silence again. This time it was an ominous silence, the difference, Donal thought, between warfare impending and warfare begun. Donal ordered all the remaining fodder doused down heavily with water from the inside wells. But the fire-arrows had only been the formal answer to the challenge, ". . . should he step beyond the line of my armed men so much as the width of my smallest finger. . . ."

Inside the courtyard, all were ready to repel a siege. Armed men were stationed at the head of every small path leading upward, in case anyone should break through the outer ring of men around the entire mountain. Food and fodder had been stockpiled long since, and there were several wells within the enclosure of the castle, living springs in the rock of the mountain. There was nothing to do but wait. . . .

The waiting continued for three days. Guards stationed in the watchtower, and those in the line around the lower peaks, reported no activity in the camp below. Then, one morning, Donal heard cries of consternation in the courtyard and hurried out to see what had happened.

The guardsmen were cooking their breakfast around fires kindled within hearthstones laid at the far end, but the cooks, and those who were carrying water to the animals, stared in fear at the water flowing from the pipes: thick, red, and sluggish, with the color, the consistency, and even the smell of freshly spilled blood. Allart, coming to see, looked at the frightened faces of the guardsmen and soldiers, and knew that this was serious. The success in outlasting a siege depended almost entirely on the water supply. If Scathfell had somehow managed to contaminate the springs which watered the castle, they could not hold out more than a day or two. Before sunset some of the animals would begin to die; then the children. There was nothing but surrender before them.

He looked at the stuff flowing from the pipes. "Is it only this spring? Or is the other one, which runs into the castle, contaminated also?" he asked.

One of the men spoke up. "I went into the kitchens, Dom Allart, and it's just like this."

Dom Mikhail, hastily summoned, bent over the stuff, let it run into his hand, grimacing at the thick texture and the smell: then experimentally lifted his hand to his mouth to taste. After a moment he shrugged, spit it out.

"How did they get at the wells, I wonder? The answer to that is that they *could* not; and therefore they *did* not." He touched the matrix about his neck. He took another mouthful and when he sit it out the water ran clear from his lips.

"Illusion," he said. "A remarkably realistic and disgusting illusion, but illusion nevertheless. The water is clean and wholesome; they have only set a spell on it so that it looks, and tastes, and worst of all smells like blood."

Allart bent to sip the stuff, feeling the surge of nausea because to all appearance he was drinking a stream of fresh blood . . . but it was water to the texture and feel, despite the sickening smell and taste.

"Is this to be witch-war, then?" the guard demanded, shaking his head in consternation. "Nobody can drink *that* stuff."

"I tell you, it's water, and perfectly good water," Aldaran said impatiently. "They've just made it *look* like blood."

"Aye, Lord, and smell and taste," said the cook. "I tell *you*—none will drink of it."

"You'll drink of it or go dry," Donal said impatiently. "It's all in your mind, man; your throat will feel it as water, whatever the look of it."

"But the beasts will not drink of it, either," said one of the men, and indeed they could hear the noises of restless animals from inside the barns and stables, some of them kicking and rearing.

Allart thought, *Yes, this is serious. All beasts fear the blood-smell. Furthermore, the men here are afraid, so we must show them quickly that they need not fear such things.*

Aldaran said, sighing, "Well, well, I had hoped we could simply ignore it, let them think their spell had no effect." But while they might at last coax or persuade the men to ignore the look and taste of the water, the effort of this would sap their morale. And the animals could not be persuaded by reason to ignore it. To them, smell and taste *were* the reality of the water, and they might easily die of thirst within reach of all the water they could drink, rather than violate their instincts by drinking what their senses told them was freshly spilled blood.

"Allart, I have no right to ask you to aid in the defense of my stronghold."

"My brother has seized the crown and makes common cause with *yours*, kinsman. My life is forfeit if I am taken here."

"Then see if we can find what in Zandru's seven hells they are doing down there!"

"There is at least one *laranzu* bearing a matrix," Allart

said, "and perhaps more. But this is a simple spell. I will see what I can do."

"I need Donal here for the defense of the outwalls," Aldaran said.

Allart nodded. "So be it." He turned to one of the servants, who stood staring at the water that still flowed, like fresh blood, in a crimson stream from the pipe, and said, "Go to my lady, the lady Renata, and Margali, and ask that they join me in the watchtower as soon as they may."

He added, turning to Dom Mikhail, "By your leave, kinsman, it is isolated enough that we can work in peace."

"Give what orders you will, kinsman," Aldaran said.

Within the watchtower, when the women joined him, he said, "You know?"

Renata made a wry face, saying, "I know. My maid came shrieking in when she went to draw my bath, screaming that blood flowed from the taps. I suspected even then that it was illusion, but I could not convince my servingwomen of that!"

"I, too," Margali said. "Though I knew it illusion, I felt I would rather go dirty than bathe in the stuff, or thirsty than drink of it. Dorilys was terrified. Poor child, she has had another attack of threshold sickness. I had hoped she was past it, but with all this emotional upheaval—"

"Well, first we must see how it is done," Allart said. "Cassandra, you are a monitor, but you, Renata, have had the most training. Do you wish to work central to what we are doing?"

"No, Allart. I—I dare not," she said reluctantly.

Immediately Cassandra picked up her meaning. She put her arm around her kinswoman. "I had not known . . . you are pregnant, Renata!" Cassandra said, in astonishment and dismay. After all Renata had said to them . . . but it was done, and nothing to argue now. "Very well. You can monitor outside the circle, if you wish, though I do not think it is needed for this. . . . Margali?"

A blue light began to glimmer from the three matrixes as they focused upon them; after a moment Cassandra nodded. It had been, indeed, the simplest of spells.

"There is no need for anything," she said, "except to reinforce nature. That water shall be what it is, and nothing more."

Joined, they sank into the surrounding energy patterns, repeating the simplest of the awarenesses, the old elemental pattern: *Earth and air and water and fire, soil and rock and wind and sky and rain and snow and lightning. . . .* As the rhythm of nature moved within them and over them, Allart felt even Renata drop into the simple spell . . . for this, in tune with nature instead of wrenching it to their patterns, could do nothing but good even to her unborn child. It repeated simply that he must be what nature had made him. As they searched out the fabric of the vibration that had set the illusion on the springs below the castle, they knew that every spring and every tap and pipe now flowed clear spring water from the rock. Remaining for a moment in the smooth resting rhythm of nature, they felt Dorilys, too, and Donal and Lord Aldaran—everyone within the castle who bore a matrix and could use *laran*—reinforced and strengthened by it. Even those who had not this awareness sensed the smooth rhythm, to the lowliest beasts in the courtyards and stables. The sun, too, seemed for a moment to shine with a more brilliant crimson light.

All of nature is one, and all that one is harmony. . . . To Cassandra, the musician, it was like a great chord, massive and peaceful, lingering and dying away into silence, but still heard, somewhere. . . .

Dorilys came softly into the watchtower room. After a moment the rapport fell quietly apart, without any tactile break, and Margali smiled and stretched her hand to her foster-daughter.

"You look well again, sweetheart."

"Yes," Dorilys said, smiling. "I was lying on my bed, and suddenly I felt—oh, I don't know how to tell you—*good,* and I knew you were working here, and I wanted to come and be with you all." She leaned against her foster-mother, with a sweet and confiding smile. "Oh, Kathya said I must tell you that the water flows clean again in bath and pipes, and you can break fast when you will."

The healing-spell was made, Allart knew. It would be that much harder for Scathfell's hordes to use the powers of sorcery or matrix science against them, when these did any violence to nature. The best thing was that they had done this without even harming the *laranzu* who had set the spell; for his attempted evil he had been returned good.

Holy Bearer of Burdens, grant it stops at this, Allart thought. But despite the flow of happiness and well-being in every nerve, he knew it could not stop here. Having barred their attack by illusion, the forces commanded by Scathfell and Damon-Rafael must turn, at least for now, to more conventional warfare.

He said as much to Dom Mikhail, later that day, but Lord Aldaran looked pessimistic.

"Castle Aldaran can stand through any ordinary siege, and my brother of Scathfell knows it. He will not be content with that."

"Yet I foresee," Allart said, hesitating, "that if we use ordinary warfare only, it will go hard with both sides. It is not even sure that we shall win. But if they manage to lure us into a battle by matrix technology, then nothing can come but catastrophe. Lord Aldaran, I have pledged that I will do what I can to aid you. Yet I beg you, Dom Mikhail. Try to keep this warfare to ordinary methods, even if the victory comes harder in this way. You have said yourself that this castle can withstand any ordinary siege. I beg you not to let them force us into doing their kind of battle."

Lord Aldaran noted that Allart's face was pale, and that he was trembling. Part of him understood and took in fully all that Allart was saying; the part of him that had been repelled when Allart spoke of *clingfire* used in the Lowlands. Yet a part of him, the skilled old soldier, veteran of many forays and campaigns in the mountains, looked at Allart and saw only the man of peace, afraid of the desolation of war. His sympathy was not unmixed with contempt, the contempt of the natural warrior for the man of peace, the soldier for the monk. He said, "I wish it might be kept, indeed, to lawful weapons of war. Yet already your brother has sent evil birds and *clingfire* against us. I fear he will not be content to throw catapults against us and storm our walls with scaling ladders and armed men. I will pledge you this; that if he does not use his dreadful weapons against us, I will not be the first to use *laran* against him. But I have no Tower circle at my command to stockpile ever more frightful weapons against my enemies. If Damon-Rafael has brought Tower-created weapons to place at the command of my brother of Scathfell, I cannot hold him off forever with men armed only with arrows and dart-guns and swords."

That was only reasonable, Allart thought in despair. Would he allow Cassandra to fall into the hands of Damon-Rafael, simply because he was reluctant to use *clingfire?* Would he see Donal hanged from the castle wall, Dorilys carried off to a stranger's bed? Yet he *knew,* beyond all shadow of a doubt, that if *laran* were used, beyond this simple spell which reaffirmed that nature was one and nothing out of harmony with it could long exist, then . . .

Allart's ears were full of cries of future lamentation . . . Dom Mikhail stood before him bowed with weeping, aged beyond recognition in a single night, crying out, "I am accursed! Would that I had died with neither daughter nor son." Renata's face swam before him, convulsed, anguished, dying. The terrible flare of lightning stunned his senses, and Dorilys's face showed livid in the storm's glare. . . . He could not endure the possible futures; neither could he shut them out. The weight of them cut off speech, cut off everything but dread. . . .

Shaking his head despairingly at Lord Aldaran, he went away.

But for a time indeed, it seemed that the attackers had been frustrated and must fall back on ordinary weapons. All that day, and all through the night, catapults thudded against the castle walls, some varied with flights of fire-arrows. Donal kept men with tubs of water continually on the alert, and even some of the women were pressed into service watching for fires and hauling tubs of water where they could be used at once to extinguish fires in the wooden outbuildings. Just before dawn, while most of the castle's guard were busy scurrying here and there putting out a dozen small fires, an alarm was suddenly sounded calling every able-bodied man to the walls to repel a party on scaling ladders. Most of them were cut down and thrown from the heights, but a few managed to break inside, and Donal, with half a dozen picked men, had to face them in the first hand-to-hand battle of the inner courtyard. Allart, fighting at Donal's side, took a slight slash in one arm, and Donal sent him to have it tended.

*   *   *

Allart found Cassandra and Renata working alongside the healer-women.

"All the gods be thanked it is no worse," said Cassandra, very pale.

"Is Donal hurt?" Renata demanded.

"Nothing to worry about," Allart said, grimacing as the healer-woman began to stitch his arm. "He cut down the man who gave me *this*. Dom Mikhail did never better for himself or Aldaran than when he had Donal trained in warfare. Young as he is, he has everything under complete control."

"It is quiet," Cassandra said, with a sudden deep shudder. "What devilry are those folk down there contemplating now?"

"Quiet, you say?" Allart looked at her in astonishment; then realized that it was indeed quiet, a deep ominous quiet both inside and out. The screaming sound of the shells and missiles breaking against the castle wall had ended. The sounds he heard so clearly were all inside his own head, were the possibles and might-never-be's of his *laran*. For the moment it was quiet indeed, but the sounds he could *almost* hear told him this was only a lull.

"My beloved, I wish that you were safe at Hali, or in Tramontana."

She said, "I would rather be with you."

The healer-woman finished bandaging his arm and strapped it in a sling. She handed him some reddish sticky fluid in a small cup. "Drink this; it will keep your wound from fevering," she said. "Rest your arm if you can; there are others who can bear a sword into the fight." She drew back in dismay as the cup fell from Allart's suddenly lax hand, the red fluid running like blood on the stone floor.

"In Avarra's name, my lord!"

But even as she stooped to mop up the mess the outcry Allart had already heard through his *laran* broke out in the courtyard; unceremoniously Allart rose and ran down the inner stairs, hearing the commotion. There was a crowd in the inner court, edging back from a burst container which lay on the stone, oozing a strange-looking yellow slime. As the slime spread, the very stone of the courtyard smoked and burned and fell away into great gaping holes, eaten away like cold butter.

"Zandru's hells!" burst out one of the guardsmen. "What is *that*? More wizard hellcraft?"

"I know not," Dom Mikhail said, sobered. "I have never seen anything like it before."

One of the courageous soldiers came forward, to try to heave some fragments of the container aside. He fell back, howling in agony, his hand seared and blackened with the stuff.

"Do *you* know what this is, Allart?" Donal asked.

Allart pressed his lips tight. "No sorcery, but a weapon devised by the Towers—an acid that will melt stone."

"Is there nothing we can do about it?" Lord Aldaran asked. "If they throw many of those against our outwalls, they will melt the very castle about our ears! Donal, send men to check the boundaries."

Donal pointed to a guardsman. "You, and you, and you, take your paxmen and go. Take straw shields; it will not harm the straw—See where it has splashed on the fodder—but if it touches metal you will be stifled by the acid fumes."

Allart said, "If it is acid, take the ash-water you use for mopping in the dairy and stables, and perhaps it will stop the acid from eating through the stone." Although the strong alkali did indeed neutralize the acid and keep it from spreading, several of the men were splashed by the strong lye. Where the courtyard had been eaten by the acid, even where treated afterward with the lye-water, holes were eaten in boots and whole areas had to be fenced off so that the men would not be injured by trespassing on them. There had been a few direct hits on the stone of the outwalls, and the stone was eaten away and crumbling; worse, the supply of lye-water was soon exhausted. They tried to use substitutes, such as soap and animal urine, but they were not strong enough.

"This is dreadful," Dom Mikhail said. "They will have our walls down at this rate. Surely this is Lord Elhalyn's doing, kinsman. My brother of Scathfell has no such weapons at his command! What can we do, kinsman? Have you any suggestions?"

"Two," Allart said, hesitating. "We can put a binding-spell on the stone, so that it cannot be eaten away by any unnatural substance, but only by those things intended to destroy stone. It would not stand against earthquake or time or flood, but I think it may stand against these unnatural weapons."

So once again the Tower-trained personnel took their place in the matrix chamber. Dorilys joined them, pleading to take a hand.

"I can monitor," she begged, "and Renata would be free to join you in the circle."

"No," Renata said quickly, thanking all the gods that Dorilys's telepathy was still untrained and erratic. "I think, if you will, you can take a place in the circle, and I will monitor from outside."

As monitor for the circle Dorilys would know at once why Renata could not join it now.

It goes against me to deceive her this way. But a time will soon come when she is strong and well, and then Donal and I will tell her, Renata thought.

Fortunately, Dorilys was sufficiently excited at being allowed to take a place inside the circle, her first formal use of a matrix except to levitate her own glider, that she did not question Renata. Cassandra held out her hand and the girl took her place beside Cassandra. Again, the circle was formed, and once again they sent out the spell that was only a strengthening of nature's own forces.

The rock is one with the planet on which it is formed, and man has so shaped it as it was determined. Nothing shall change it or alter. The rock is one . . . one . . . one. . . .

The binding-spell was set. Allart, individual consciousness lost behind the joined consciousness of his circle, was aware of the shaped rocks of the castle, of their hard integrity; of the fact that the impact of explosive shells and the chemical slime was harmlessly bouncing away, repelled, the yellow slime rolling down the outside, leaving long, evil-looking streaks, but not crumbling stone or melting it.

The rock is one . . . one . . . one. . . .

From outside the circle, a careful thought reached them.

Allart?

Is it you, brédu?

It is Donal. I have stationed men on the outwalls to pick off their cannoneers with arrows, but they are out of range. Can you make a darkness about them so that they cannot see where to shoot?

Allart hesitated. It was one thing to affirm the integrity of nature's creation by forcing water to remain, untampered, as water, and stone to remain impervious to things nature had never intended to destroy stone. But to tamper with nature by creating darkness during the hours of light . . .

Dorilys's thoughts wove into the circle. *It would be in tune with the forces of nature if a thick fog should come up. It often happens at this season, so that no man on the hillside can see beyond the reach of his own arms!*

Allart, searching a little way ahead with his *laran*, saw indeed that there was a strong probability of thick fog arising. Focusing on the joined matrixes again, the workers concentrated upon the moisture in the air, the nearing clouds, to wrap the whole of the mountainside in a thick curtain, rising from the river below, until all of Castle Aldaran and the nearby peaks lay shrouded in darkening fog.

"They will not lift this night," said Dorilys with satisfaction.

Allart dissolved the circle, admonishing his group to go and rest. They might be needed again soon. The sound of shelling had stopped, and Donal's men below had a chance to clean up the residue of acids and lye. Renata, running the body-mind monitor's touch over Dorilys, was struck with something new in her.

Was it only the healing-spell earlier? She seemed calmer, more womanly; no longer even a little like a child. Renata, recalling how she herself had grown swiftly into adulthood in her first season in the Tower, knew that Dorilys had made some such enormous leap into womanhood, and inwardly gave thanks to all her gods.

If she has stabilized, if we need no longer fear her childish explosions, if she is beginning to have judgment and skill to match her power—perhaps then, soon, soon, it will be over and Donal and I will be free. . . .

With a surge of the old love for Dorilys, she drew the girl close and kissed her. "I am proud of you, *carya mea*," she said. "You have acquitted yourself as would a woman

in the circle. Now go and rest, and eat well, so that you
will not lose your strength when we need you again."

Dorilys was glowing.

"So I am doing my part, like Donal, in the defense of
my home," she exclaimed, and Renata shared her innocent pride.

So much strength, she thought, *and so much potential.
Will she win through after all?*

The thick fog continued to shroud the castle hour upon
hour, enclosing in mystery what the attacking armies were
doing down below. Perhaps, Allart thought, they were simply waiting—waiting, as were those in the besieged castle,
for the fog to lift so that they cold resume the attack. For
Allart's part, he was wholly content to wait.

This breathing spell, after the hectic opening days of the
siege, was appreciated by them all. At nightfall, since even
the watch on the castle walls could do little, Allart went to
dine alone with Cassandra in their rooms. By common consent they avoided speaking of the war; there was nothing
they could do about it. Cassandra called for her *rryl,* and
sang to him.

"I said upon the day of our wedding," she said, looking
up from the instrument, "that I hoped we might live in
peace and make songs, not war. Alas for that hope! But
even in the shadow of war, my dearest, there can still be
songs for us."

He took the thin fingers in his hands and kissed them.

"So far, at least, the gods have been good to us," he said.

"It is so still, Allart! They might have all gone away in
the night, it is so quiet below!"

"I would that I knew what Damon-Rafael was doing,"
Allart said, roused to new unquiet. "I do not think he will
be content to sit there at the bottom of the hill, without
throwing some new weapon into the gap."

"It would be easy for you to find out," she hazarded, but
Allart shook his head.

"I will not use *laran* in this war unless I am forced to do
so. Only to defend us from certain catastrophe. Damon-
Rafael shall not make of me the excuse to bring his frightful kind of war to this country."

About midnight the sky suddenly began to clear, the fog first thinning, then blowing away in little wisps and ragged shreds. Overhead three of the four moons floated, brilliant and serene. Violet Liriel was near the zenith, full and brilliant. Blue Kyrrdis and green Idriel hung near the western edge of the mountains. Cassandra was sleeping, had been sleeping for hours, but Allart, seized by strange unease, slid quietly from bed and into his clothes. Hurrying down the hallway, he saw Dorilys in her long white chamber-robe, her hair hanging loose down her back. She was barefoot, her snub-nosed face a pale oval in the dimness.

"Dorilys? What is Margali thinking of to let you wander like this in your night-garb at this hour?"

"I could not sleep, Dom Allart, and I was uneasy," the girl said. "I am going down to join Donal near the outwall. I suddenly woke and felt that he was in danger."

"If he is truly in danger, *chiya,* the last place he would want you is beside him."

"He is my husband," the child said adamantly, raising her face to Allart. "My place is at his side, sir."

Paralyzed by the strength of her obsession, Allart could do nothing. After all, this was the only thing she could share with Donal. Since Allart himself had been reunited with Cassandra, he had been highly sensitized to loneliness. It struck him at that moment that Dorilys was almost wholly alone. She had left the society of children irrevocably. Yet among the adults she was still treated as a child. He did not protest, but began to move toward the outer stairs, hearing her behind him. After a moment he felt her small dry hand, a child's hand and warm like a little animal's paw, slide into his. He clasped it, and they hurried together across the courtyard to Donal's post at the outwalls.

Outside, the night had grown bright and cloudless, with only a single low bank of cloud hanging at the horizon. The moons floated high and clear, in a sky so brilliantly lighted that no single star was visible anywhere in the sky. Donal was standing, arms folded, atop the outwall, but as Allart hurried toward him, someone spoke in a low, reproachful voice.

"Master Donal, I beg you to come off the wall. You are all too good a target standing there," and Donal slid down off the wall.

Not too soon; an arrow came whistling out of the darkness, harmlessly flying past where Donal had just been standing. Dorilys ran and caught him around the waist.

"You must not stand there like that, Donal. Promise me you will never do so again!"

He laughed noiselessly, bending to kiss her, a light brotherly peck, on the forehead. "Oh, I am in no danger. I wanted to see if anyone was still down there and awake, after all, or if they had all gone away; as in that quiet and fog it seemed they might well have done."

It had been Allart's own thought—that they were too quiet, that some devilry was afoot. He asked Donal, "Did the fog lift of itself?"

"I am not sure. They have more than one *laranzu* down there, and it lifted, indeed, all too quickly," Donal said, wrinkling up his forehead. "But at this season the fog does blow away sometimes, exactly like that. I cannot tell."

Suddenly, to Allart, the air was filled with cries and exploding fire. "Donal! Call the watch!" he cried. Almost before the words escaped his lips, an air-car flashed by overhead, and several small shapes fell slowly toward the ground, almost lazily, like snowflakes, falling open as they moved and pouring liquid streaks of fire toward the castle roofs and the court.

"*Clingfire!*" Donal leaped for an alarm bell, but already several of the wooden roofs were blazing up and fire was lighting the whole courtyard. Men poured into the court, only to be stopped, screaming, by the streams of unquenchable fire. One or two went up like human torches, shrieking all the time, until the howls died away and they lay, their corpses still smoking and flaming, lifeless on the stone. Donal leaped to push Dorilys under an overhanging stone cave, but drops of the liquid fire rolled off and caught her chamber-robe, which blazed up wildly. She screamed in terror and pain, as Donal dragged her toward a tub of water and literally flung her into it. Her dress sizzled and went out, but a drop of the stuff had fallen on her skin and was burning, burning inward. She kept shrieking, a wild, almost inhuman sound, maddened with the pain.

"Keep back! Keep in the lee of the building!" Donal yelled. "There are more of them overhead!"

Dorilys was screaming and struggling between his hands, maddened with agony. Overhead, thunder suddenly crackled and flared, lightnings seared and struck here, there. . . . Abruptly one of the air-cars overhead went up in a great burst of fire and fell, a flaming ruin, into the valley. Another great bolt struck a second air-car in midair, exploding it into showers of fire. Rain sliced down hard, drenching Allart to the skin Donal had fallen back from Dorilys in terror. Screaming, maddened, the child was shaking her fist at the sky, striking with great sizzling bolts here, there, everywhere. A final air-car split with a huge explosion and fell apart over the attacking camp below, sending forth shrieks and howls of pain as the *clingfire* fell back on its launchers. Then silence, except for the heavy, continuing rumble of the rain, and Dorilys's stabbing screams of pain as the *clingfire* continued to eat inward on her wrist, penetrating to the bone.

"Let me take her," Renata said, running up barefoot in her nightgown. The girl sobbed and cried out and tried vainly to push her away. "No, darling, no. Don't struggle! This must be done or it will burn your arm away. Hold her, Donal."

Dorilys screamed again with pain as Renata scraped away the last remnants of the *clingfire* from the burned flesh, then collapsed against Donal. All around the courtyard men were gathering, silent, awed. Renata tore Dorilys's charred chamber-robe to bandage her arm. Donal held her against him, soothingly, rocking her.

"You saved us all," he whispered. "Had you not struck at them, so much *clingfire* could have burned Aldaran over all our heads!"

Indeed, Allart thought. Damon-Rafael and Scathfell had thought to take Aldaran unawares, unprepared for this kind of attack. Had the contents of three air-cars all carrying *clingfire* struck them, all of Castle Aldaran would have been burned to the ground. Had they exhausted their arsenal, then, hoping to win at one stroke? Had Dorilys decisively defeated them, then, in this one stroke? He looked at the child, weeping now in Renata's arms with the pain of her burns.

She had saved them all, as she had saved him, before, from Damon-Rafael's evil bird-weapon.

But he did not think this would be the end.

Chapter 27

There were still fires to be put out, where the *clingfire* had set buildings alight. Five men were dead, and a sixth died as Renata knelt to look at him. Four more had *clingfire* burns deep enough that even Allart knew they would not live out the day, and a dozen more had minor burns which must be treated and every scrap of the terrible stuff scraped away, disregarding screams and pleas for mercy. Cassandra came and took Dorilys away to be put to bed, her bandages soaked in oil. But when all had been done, Donal and Allart stood on the outwall, looking down at the camp of the besiegers where fires still raged and flared.

The rain had subsided as soon as Dorilys was calm, and in any case it would take long, heavy soaking rain to put out *clingfire* blazes. Now Donal had no fear of arrows out of darkness. He said, stepping down from the wall, "Scathfell and his folks will have more than enough to do this night in their own camp. I will leave a small watch, but no more. Unless I am gravely mistaken, they will have no leisure to mount another attack for a day or so!"

He set a few picked men as guards, and went to see how Dorilys fared. He found her abed, restless, her eyes bright and feverish, her arm freshly bandaged. She reached with her free arm for his hand and pulled him down at her side.

"So, you have come to see me. Renata was not being cruel to me, Donal. I know it now; she was scraping away the fire so that it would not burn my arm to the bone. It nearly did, you know," she said. "Cassandra showed me.

She has a scar almost exactly like mine will be, and from *clingfire,* too."

"So you, too, will bear an honorable scar of warfare from the defense of our home," Donal said. "You saved us all."

"I know." Her eyes flickered, and he could see the pain in them. Far away he could hear a distant rumble of thunder. He sat beside her, holding the small hand that stuck out below the heavy bandage.

"Donal," she said, "now that I am a woman, when shall I be really your wife?"

Donal turned his eyes away, grateful that Dorilys was still a very erratic telepath. "This is no time to speak of that, *chiya,* when we are all fighting for survival. And you are still very young."

"I am not so young as all that," she insisted. "I am old enough to work in a matrix circle as I did with Allart and the others, and old enough to fight against those who are attacking us."

"But, my child—"

"Don't call me that! I am not a child!" she said with a small, imperious flare of anger; then laid her head against his arm, with a sigh that was not, indeed, childlike. "Now that we are entangled in this war, Donal, there should be an heir to Aldaran. My father is old, old, and this war ages him day by day. And today—" Suddenly her voice began to shake uncontrollably. "I don't think I had ever thought of this before, but suddenly I knew you could die—or I could die, Donal, young as I am. If I should die before you, never having borne you a child, you could be driven forth from Aldaran, since you are not blood-kin. Or if—if you should die, and I had never had your child, I could be flung into some stranger's bed for the dower of Aldaran. Donal, I am afraid of *that.*"

Donal held her small hand in his. All this was true, he thought. Dorilys might be the only way he could hold this castle which had been his only home from childhood. It was not even as if she were unwilling. He, too, after the long days of battle and siege, was all too aware of the vulnerability of his own body. He had seen men blaze up like living flames, seen them die fast and slow, but die nonetheless. And Dorilys was his, legally given in marriage with the consent of her father. She was young, but she was moving quickly, quickly, into womanhood. . . . His hand tightened on hers.

"We shall see, Dorilys," he said, drawing her close for a minute. "When Cassandra tells me that you are old enough to bear a child without danger, then, if you still wish for it, Dorilys, it shall be as you desire."

He bent down and would have kissed her on the forehead, but she clung to him with surprising strength, pulling him down so that their lips met, with passion that was not at all childlike. When at last she released him Donal was dizzy. He straightened up and left the room quickly, but not before Dorilys, with her erratic telepathic sense, still unreliable, had picked up his thought, *No, Dorilys is a child no more.*

Quiet. Quiet. All was silent in Castle Aldaran . . . all was silent in the camp of the besiegers below. All day the dreadful silence hung over the land. Allart, high in the watchtower, setting again a binding-spell on the castle walls, wondered what new devilry this quiet presaged. So sensitized had he become by this prolonged warfare by matrix that he could almost *feel* them plotting—or was it an illusion?—and his *laran* continued to present pictures of the castle falling in ruins, the very world trembling. Toward midday, all over the castle, all at once, men began shrieking and crying out, with nothing visible the matter with them. Allart, in the tower room with Renata, Cassandra, and the old sorceress Margali—Dorilys had kept her bed, for her arm still throbbed with pain, and Margali had given her a strong sleeping draft—had his first warning when Margali raised her hands to her head and began to weep aloud.

"Oh, my baby, my little one, my poor lamb," she cried. "I must go to her!" She ran out of the room, and almost at the same moment Renata caught her hands against her breast, as if struck by an arrow there, and cried out, "Ah! He is dead!" While Allart stared at her in amazement, at the slammed door still quivering behind Margali, he heard Cassandra screaming. All at once it seemed to him that she was gone, that the world grew dark, that somewhere behind a locked door she fought a deathly battle with his brother, that he must go to her and protect her. He had actually

risen and taken a step to the door on a mad dash to rescue
Cassandra from the ravisher, when he saw her across the
room, kneeling, swaying in anguish and tearing at herself,
keening as if she knelt above a corpse.

A tiny shred of rationality struggled for what felt like
hours inside Allart. *Cassandra is in no need of rescue, if
yonder she sits wailing as if the one she loved best lay dead
before her.* . . . Yet within his mind it still seemed that he
heard screams of terror and anguish, that she was calling
to him, crying out.

*Allart! Allart! Why do you not come to me? Allart, come
come quickly* . . . and a long, terrified shriek of desperate
anguish.

Renata had risen, and was making her way on faltering
feet to the door. Allart caught her around the waist.

"No," he said. "No, kinswoman, you must not go. This
is bewitchment. We must fight it; we must set the
binding-spell."

She fought and struggled in his arms like a mad thing,
kicking, scratching at his face with her nails as if he were
not Allart at all but some enemy bent on murder or rape,
her eyes rolled inward in some wholly interior terror, and
Allart knew she neither saw nor heard him.

"No, no, let me go! It's the baby! They're murdering our
baby! Can't you see where they have him there, ready to
fling him from the wall? Ah, merciful Avarra . . . let me
go, you murdering devils! Take me first!"

Icy chills chased themselves up and down Allart's spine
as he realized that Renata, too, fought against some wholly
internal fear, that she saw Donal, or the child who was not
yet even born, in deadly danger. . . .

Even while he held her he struggled against the conviction that, somewhere, Cassandra was screaming his name,
weeping, pleading, begging him to come to her. . . . Allart
knew that if he did not quickly still this he would succumb
also and run wildly down the stairs seeking her in every
room of the castle, even though his mind told him she knelt
there across the room, wholly caught up into some such
internal ritual of terror as held Renata.

He snatched out his matrix, focused into it.

Truth, truth, let me see truth . . . *earth and air and water
and fire* . . . *let Nature prevail free of illusion* . . . *earth and*

air and water and fire. . . . He had no strength for anything but this, the most basic of spells, the first of prayers. He strove to drive out the nonexistent, dying sound of Cassandra's screams for mercy in his ears, the terrible guilt that he lingered here while she struggled somewhere with a ravisher. . . .

Quiet spread through his mind, the silence of the healing-spell, the silence of the chapel at Nevarsin. He entered into the silence and, for a timeless moment, was healed. Now he saw only what was there in the room, the two women in the grip of terrifying illusion. He focused first on Renata, willing her to quiet with the pulse of the healing-spell. Slowly, slowly, he felt it enter her mind, calm her, so that she stopped struggling, stared around her with a great amazement.

"But none of it was true," she said in a whisper. "Donal—Donal is not dead. Our child—our child is not even born. Yet I *saw* Allart, I saw where they held them and I could not reach them."

"A spell of terror," Allart said. "I think everyone saw what he or she most feared. Come quickly—help me to break it!"

Shaken, but strong again, Renata took her matrix, and at once they focused on Cassandra. After a moment her smothered cries of terror stopped, and she looked at them, dazed with dread, then blinked, realizing what had happened. Now with three minds and three matrixes focused, they sent the healing-spell beating out through all the castle, and from cellar to attic and everywhere in the crowded courtyard, servants and soldiers and guardsmen and stableboys came out of the dazed trance wherein each had heard the cries of whoever he loved best and fought blindly to rescue that one from the hands of a nameless enemy.

At last all the castle lay under the rhythm of the healing-spell, but now Allart was shaking in dread. Not, this time, the dread of nameless persecution, but something all too real and frightful.

If they have begun to fight us this way, how can we hold them at bay? Here within the castle Allart had only the two women, old Margali, the still older Dom Mikhail, and Donal, if he could dare to take him from the defense of the castle against attackers who were all too tangible. In fact, Allart feared that this was just the tactic they would use—to distract the fighting men while they attacked, under cover of the great fear they could project. He hurried in search of Dom Mikhail, for a council of war.

"You know what we have had to fight," he said. The old lord nodded, his face grim, his eyes hawk-bright, menacing.

"I thought I stood and watched my best-loved die again," he said. "In my ears was the curse of a sorceress I hanged from these walls thirteen years gone by, jeering at me that a day would come when I would cry out to the gods in grief that I had not died childless." Then he seemed to start awake and shake himself like a mantling hawk on the block. "Well, she is dead and her malice with her."

He pondered for a time.

"We must attack," he said. "They can wear us down quickly, if we must be alert night and day for that kind of attack, and we cannot be ever on the defense. Somehow we must send them howling. We have only one weapon strong enough to rout them."

"I did not know that we had any such weapon," Allart said. "Of what do you speak, my lord?"

Dom Mikhail said, "I speak of Dorilys. She commands the lightning. She must strike them with storm, and utterly destroy their camp."

Allart looked at him in consternation.

"My lord Aldaran, you must be mad!"

"Kinsman," Aldaran said, his eyes flaring displeasure, "I think you forget yourself!"

"If I have angered you, sir, I beg your pardon. Let my love for your foster-son—yes, and for your daughter, too—be my excuse. Dorilys is only a child, and the lady Renata—yes—and my wife also have done their utmost to teach her to master and control her gift, never to use it unworthily. If you ask her now to direct it in rage and destruction on the armies below us, can you not see, my lord, you wipe out all we have done? As a young child, twice, she killed, striking with a child's uncontrolled anger. Can you not see, if you use her this way—" Allart stopped, trembling with apprehension.

Dom Mikhail said, "We must use such weapons as we have to hand, Allart." He raised his head and said, "You did not complain when she struck down the evil bird your brother sent against you! Nor did you hesitate to ask her to use her gift to move the storm which had you trapped in the snow! And she struck down the air-cars which would have spread enough *clingfire* here to burn Castle Aldaran into a smoking ruin!"

"All this is true," Allart said, shaking with earnestness, "but in all this she was defending herself or others against the violence of another. Can you not see the difference between defense and attack, sir?"

"No," Aldaran said, "for it seems to me that in this case attack is the only defense, or we may be struck down at any moment by some weapon even more frightful than those they have loosed on us already."

Sighing, Allart made his last plea.

"Lord Aldaran, she has not yet even recovered from her threshold sickness. I saw, when we were at the fire station, how over use of her *laran* left her sick and weak, and then she was not yet come to the threshold of maturity this way. I am really afraid of what may happen if you put further strain on her powers just now. Will you wait, at least, until we truly have no other choice? A few days, even a few hours—"

The father's face contracted with fear, and Allart knew that for the moment, at least, he had won his victory.

"Cassandra and I will go again to the watchtower and keep vigil so they will not take us unaware again. No matter how many *leroni* they have down there, they must have exhausted themselves with that spell of terror. I think they must rest before they try anything more like *that,* or worse."

Allart's prediction proved true, for all during that day and night, only a few flights of arrows flew against the walls of the castle. But at dawn the next morning, Allart, who had snatched a few hours of sleep, leaving Cassandra on watch in the tower room, was wakened by ominous rumbling far away. Confused, trying to flood away sleep

by splashing cold water on his face, he tried to identify
the sound. Cannon? Thunder? Was Dorilys angered or
frightened again? Had Aldaran broken his pledge not to
use her except in extremity? Or was it something else?

He hurried up the stairs to the watchtower, but as he
went, the stairs seemed to sway under his feet and he
had to clutch at the handrail, his *laran* suddenly envi-
sioning the cracks spreading in the tower walls, the tower
splitting and crumbling, falling.

He burst into the tower room, his face white, and Cassandra, seated before the matrix, looked up at him in
sudden terror, picking up his dread.

"Come down," he said quickly. "Come out of here, at
once, my wife." As she hurried down the stairs he saw
again the great cracks widening in the staircase, the
rumbling. . . . They fled down the stairs, hand in hand,
Cassandra stumbling on her lame knee, and at last Allart
turned back, caught her up in his arms and carried her
down the last few steps, not stopping even to breathe,
hurrying along the hall. Out of breath, he set her on her
feet and stood clinging to a doorframe in the corridor,
her arms around him. Then the floor beneath their feet
swayed and rumbled, there was a great sound like the
splitting asunder of the world, and the floor of the tower
they had just left heaved and buckled upward. The stairs
broke away from the wall, stones fell outward, crumbling,
and then the whole tower split and fell, crashing in heavy
thunder down upon the roofs of the keep, stones cascading into the courtyards, falling into the valley below,
touching off rockfalls and landslides. . . . Cassandra buried her face in Allart's chest and clung to him, shaking
with dread. Allart felt his knees buckling and they slid
together to the floor, as it swayed and shook under them.
Finally the noise died away, leaving only silence and
strange, ominous grumbles and crunching sounds from
the ground under them.

Slowly they clambered to their feet. Cassandra had injured her lame knee freshly in their fall; she had to cling
to Allart to stand. They stared up at the great gap and
thick foggy dawn where once a tall tower had risen, by a
near-miracle of matrix engineering, three flights of stairs

toward the sun. Now there was nothing but a great pile of stone and rubble and plaster fallen inward, and a huge gap through which the morning rain was drizzling in.

"What, in the name of all the gods was *that*?" Cassandra finally inquired, stunned. "An earthquake?"

"Worse, I fear," Allart said. "I do not know what kind of *leroni* they have down there, or what they are using against us, but I am afraid it is something worse than even Coryn would invent."

Cassandra scoffed, "No matrix known could do *that*!"

"No single matrix, no," Allart said, "and no technician. But if they have one of the great matrix screens, they could explode this planet to its core, if they dared." His mind clamored, *Would even Damon-Rafael risk laying waste this land he seeks to rule?* But his mind provided him with a grim answer.

Damon-Rafael would not be at all averse to showing his power over a part of the world for which he had no immediate need and which he considered expendable. And after this, no one would dare to challenge him.

Scathfell might be malicious and eager to rule in his brother's shoes, but Damon-Rafael was the culprit this time. Scathfell wished to rule in Castle Aldaran, not to destroy it.

Now they became aware, through the gap in the castle walls, of cries and commotion below, and Allart recalled himself to duty.

"I must go and see if anyone has been hurt by falling stones, and how it fares with Donal, my sworn brother," he said, and hurried away. But even as he went he felt the castle trembling again beneath him, and wondered what new devilry was afoot. Well, Cassandra could warn the women without his help. He hurried down into the courtyard, where he found chaos unbelievable. One of the outbuildings had been buried entirely beneath the falling stones of the tower, and a dozen men and four times as many animals were dead in the ruins; others had been crushed by falling debris.

Dom Mikhail was there, leaning heavily on Donal's arm. He was still in his furred bed-gown, his face gray and fallen in; Allart thought he looked twenty years older in a single night. He clung to his foster-son as he moved carefully among the ruin in his courtyard. As he saw Allart his thin mouth stretched in a travesty of a smile.

"Cousin, the gods be thanked, I feared that you and your lady had fallen with the tower and been killed. Is the lady Cassandra safe? What, in the name of all Zandru's demons, have they done to us now? It will take us half a year to clear away this chaos! Half the dairy animals have been killed; the children will go wanting milk this winter. . . ."

"I am not certain," Allart said soberly, "but I must have every man or woman in this stronghold who is able to use a matrix, and organize our defenses against it. We are but ill prepared, I fear, for this kind of warfare."

"Are you sure of that, my brother?" Donal asked. "Surely earthquakes have been known in the mountains before this!"

"It was no earthquake! I am as sure of that as if Damon-Rafael stood before me laughing at what he had done!"

Dom Mikhail knelt beside the body of a fallen man, only crushed legs protruding from a block of fallen stone larger than a man. "Poor fellow," he said. "At least his death must have been swift. I fear that those buried in the stables had a death more fearful. Donal, leave the guardsmen to bury the dead; Allart has more need of you now. I will send everyone with *laran* to you, so that you can see what has been sent us."

"We cannot meet in the tower now," Allart said grimly. "We must have a room somewhat isolated from the grief and fright of those who are clearing away the ruin, Lord Aldaran."

"Take the women's conservatory; perhaps the peace of the flowering plants there will create an atmosphere you can use."

As Donal and Allart entered the castle once again, Allart could feel, through the soles of his feet, a renewed faint tremor. Again he wondered what happened. He felt a spasm of dread, remembering how near Cassandra had come to being trapped in the falling tower.

Donal said, "I wish that our friends in Tramontana were here. They would know how to deal with this!"

"I am glad that they are not," Allart replied. "I would not have the Towers drawn into the wars in this land!"

The sun was just coming through the clouds as they entered the conservatory, and the calm brilliance of the sun light, the solar collectors spreading light, the faint, pleasant damp smell of herbs and flowering leaves, felt strangely at odds with the dread and fear Allart could feel from the men and women who were joining him there. Not only Cassandra, Renata, Margali, and Dorilys, but two or three of the women he had not seen before, and half a dozen of the men. Each one bore a matrix, though Allart sensed that more than half of these had only minimal talent and could do little more than open a matrix-lock or operate some such toy as the gliders. After a time Dom Mikhail, too, came in.

Allart glanced at Cassandra. She had been in a Tower longer than he, she was, perhaps, better trained, and he was willing to allow her to conduct this search, but she shook her head.

"You are Nevarsin-taught; you are less subject to fear and confusion than I."

Allart was not so sure, but he accepted her decision and looked around the circle of men and women.

"I have no time to test you one by one and assess the level of your training; I must trust you," he said. "Renata, you were four years a monitor. You must set a guard around us, for we expose ourselves to those who are trying to destroy this castle and all those in it, and we are vulnerable. I must find what they are using against us, and if there is any defense against it. You must lend us your strength, and our lives are in all of your hands."

He looked around the room, at the men and women who shared with him a spark of this gift of the great families. Did they all have some trace of the far-off kin to the gods; were they all somehow descended via the breeding program from the blood of Hastur and Cassilda? Or did all men, in truth, have some trace, more or less, of these powers? Always before he had depended on his equals, his kinsmen; now he was in the hands of commoners, and it sobered him, and humbled him, too. He was afraid to trust them, but he had no choice.

He linked his mind first with Cassandra, then with

Donal; then, one by one, with the others in the circle, picking up traces of their emotion as he did so . . . fear, anger at what was being sent against them, disquiet at this unusual operation, strangeness. . . . He felt Dorilys drop into the linkage, sensing her fury at the attackers who had dared to do this to her home. . . . One by one, he picked up every man and woman in the circle, and sank into the joined consciousness, moved outward and outward, searching sifting. . . .

It seemed a very long time before he felt the link fall apart and Allart raised his head, looking sobered.

"It is no natural matrix they are using against us," he said, "but one constructed artificially within the Towers by a technician. With it, they are seeking to alter the natural vibration of the very rock of the mountain beneath us." As he spoke, he put out a hand and he could feel through the walls the very faint trembling of the walls which reflected the deeper trembling within the foundations and the veined metal and layers of old rock beneath.

Dom Mikhail had not shaved; beneath the untidy stubble of grayish beard his face was deathly pale. "They will bring down the castle about our heads! Is there no defense, Allart?"

"I do not know," Allart said. "All of us together could hardly stand against a matrix that size." Was there indeed any hope, or should Aldaran capitulate and surrender before his entire castle collapsed in ruin around him? "We could try to put a binding-spell upon the rock of the mountain," he said, hesitating. "I do not know if it would hold. Even with all of us, I am not sure it would hold. But it seems our only hope."

Dorilys sprang to her feet. She had come to the conservatory, with her matrix, not bothering to dress; she sat in her long-sleeved childish nightgown, her hair unbraided and falling about her shoulders like a cascade of new copper. "But I have a better idea," she cried. "*I* can break their concentration; can I not, Father? Donal, come with me."

Allart watched, in consternation, as she hurried from the room. In a whisper, from the men and women, commoners, around the room, he heard again the name they had given her.

"Stormqueen. Our little lady, our little sorceress, she can

raise a storm and give those folk down there something else to think about, indeed!"

Allart appealed to Dom Mikhail.

"My lord—"

Slowly, the old lord of Aldaran shook his head. "I see no other choice, cousin. It is that, or surrender at once."

Allart lowered his eyes, knowing that Dom Mikhail spoke no more than truth.

Already, as he followed toward the high battlement where Dorilys stood with Donal, he could see the clouds thickening and gathering. Then he shrank from the open window as Dorilys raised her arms, crying out wordlessly. Power seemed to burst from her, so that she was no longer only a young woman in a nightgown, her hair falling about her shoulders; above their heads the storm burst like one of the explosive shells, with a great thunderbolt and a flare of lightning that seemed to split the sky asunder. Torrential rains poured down, wiping out eyesight below, but through the welter of noise, the crash upon crash of thunder and the glare that hurt his eyes and split the heavens apart, Allart sensed what was happening below.

Floodwaters washing down on the camp at the foot of the mountain. Thunder, deafening and stampeding their riding-animals, spreading panic in human and nonhuman alike. Lightning ripping through the tent where the matrix workers sat over their great unnatural stone, searing them blind and deafened, some of them burned out or dead. Rain, pouring soaking rain, pounding and drumming, beating their camp into the ground, driving around every rock or tree where they might take shelter, reducing everything that had life in that camp to naked, soaked animal humiliation. Lightning again kindling fires to roar through their tents, searing, raging, beating everything to the ground.

Never had Allart known such a storm. Cassandra clung to him, as it raged on and on over their heads, burying her head and sobbing in fear. Allart held himself tensed against the noise and devastation, as if it raged through his whole body. But Dom Mikhail's face held a fierce exultation as he stood there, hour after hour, watching the storm wreak desolation and ruin in the camp of Scathfell and Damon-Rafael below them.

At last, at long last, it began to subside. Small rollings

and rumblings of thunder remained, dying away in shudders of sound on the distant hills, and the rain began to grow weaker. As the sky cleared to whitish shreds of cloud, Allart looked down into the valley. The valley lay stunned, quiet, a few fires still roaring out of control in the camp, side by side with flooding streams which had left their beds and raged over the countryside. There seemed no sign of life below.

Dorilys swayed, her face very white, and fell against Donal in a faint. He picked her up tenderly and carried her inside.

She has saved us, Allart thought, *at least for now. But at what cost?*

Chapter 28

It was high noon before there was any sign of life from the camp of Lord Scathfell below. There were still more rumbles and noise of ominous thunder high above them, crashing around the peaks, and Allart wondered if Dorilys, in her exhausted sleep, still dreamed of the dreadful battle, if these thunders reflected her nightmares.

Renata said that Dorilys taps the magnetic potential of the planet, he reflected. *I can well believe it! But with all that power flowing through her poor little body and brain, can she survive it undamaged?*

He wondered if Aldaran, in the long run, would not have done better to surrender. What kind of father love would expose a beloved child to that?

But near midday the thunders died away, and Cassandra, who had been summoned to monitor Dorilys and care for her, reported that she had wakened and eaten and fallen into normal sleep. Still, Allart felt a dreadful unease, and it seemed to him that unending lightnings still played around the castle. Donal, too, looked deeply troubled, and although he had gone to supervise the men who were burying the dead and clearing rubble from the fallen tower, he kept returning, stealing up to the door of her room and standing there to listen to her breathing. Renata came to look at him, in dread and pleading, but he avoided her eyes.

The woman wondered, in dread, *Has he been seduced at the thought of all this power? What has happened to Donal?* And she, too, was afraid for Dorilys, wondering what the use of that blasting force had done to the girl she loved.

An hour or two past noon, a messenger appeared on the road leading up to the castle, still washed-out and runneled with water flooding from the heights, partially blocked with stones that had fallen when the tower collapsed. The message was relayed to Donal, who took it to Dom Mikhail at once.

"Father, your brother of Scathfell has sent a messenger asking if he may come to negotiate terms with you."

Aldaran's eyes glinted, fierce and bright, but he said calmly, "Tell my brother of Scathfell I will hear what he has to say."

After a time, the leader of the opposing army came up the path, afoot, followed by his paxman and two guards. As he crossed the line of siege he said to the single man stationed there, "Wait till I return." Donal, who had come to escort him into Aldaran's presence, received the most contemptuous glare, but Scathfell looked beaten nevertheless, and they all knew he had come to surrender. There was too little left of his army, and nothing of Damon-Rafael's weaponry. He had come, Donal knew, to try to save what little he could out of defeat.

Lord Aldaran had made ready to receive his brother in his presence-chamber, and he entered the room with Dorilys on his arm. Donal thought of the last time they had all been together in this room. Scathfell looked older, grimmer, aged by the crushing weight of defeat. He glared at Donal, and at Dorilys in her blue gown, and looked with grim appraisal at Allart when he was named. Even though Allart had been styled traitor and rebel, Scathfell still looked on him with the habitual respect, amounting to awe, of a younger son and minor noble before a Hastur lord.

"Well, my brother," Aldaran said at last. "Much has passed between us since last you came into this hall. I had never thought to see you here again. Tell me—why have you asked for my presence? Have you come to surrender yourself and beg my pardon for your rebellion against my lawful demands?"

Scathfell swallowed heavily before he could speak. At last he said with great bitterness, "What other choice have I now? Your witch-daughter there has routed my armies and killed my men as she struck down my son and heir.

No man living can stand against such sorcery. I have come to ask for compromise."

"Why should I compromise with you, Rakhal? Why should I not strip you of your lands and honors, which you hold at my pleasure, and send you forth naked and yelping like a beaten hound, or hang you from my battlements to show all men how I shall deal henceforth with all rebels and traitors?"

"I do not stand alone," Rakhal of Scathfell said. "I have an ally who is, perhaps, even more powerful than you and your witch-brat together. I am bidden to say that if I do not return before sunset, Damon-Rafael will gather his forces and shake apart this mountain beneath you, and Aldaran will fall over your head. You had a taste of that power this morning at sunrise, I think. Men and armies can be scattered and beaten, but if you wish this land to be rent in a dozen parts by sorcery, it will be your doing and not mine. However, he has no desire to destroy you now that you know his power. He asks only that he shall be allowed to speak with his brother, both unarmed, in the space between our armies, before sunset."

"Allart Hastur is my guest," Aldaran said. "Should I deliver him over to his brother's sure treachery?"

"Treachery? Between brethren and Hasturs both?" asked Scathfell, and his face showed honest outrage. "He would make peace with his brother as I, Mikhail, would make peace with mine." Clumsily, unaccustomed, he bowed to one knee.

"You have beaten me, Mikhail," he said. "I will withdraw my armies. And, believe me, it was none of my doing that broke your tower. Truly, I spoke against it, but the lord Damon-Rafael wished to display his power before the northlands."

"I believe you." Aldaran looked at his brother with a great sadness. "Go home, Rakhal," he said. "Go in peace. I ask only that you take oath to honor the husband of my daughter as next heir after me, and never to raise hand or sword against him, openly or by stealth. If you will take this oath in the light of truthspell, you may enjoy Scathfell forevermore, without harassment from me or mine."

Scathfell raised his head, rage and contempt vying on his face.

Donal, watching him, thought, *My father should not have pressed this now! Did he think I could not hold Aldaran after him?* Yet it seemed that Scathfell would capitulate.

"Call your *leronis* and set the truthspell," he said, his face set and unsmiling. "Never did I think I would come to this at your hands, my brother, or that you would exact such humiliation from me." He stood restless, as Margali was summoned, shifting from foot to foot. As the *leronis* came, he made as if to go to his knees before Donal and Dorilys. Then suddenly he cried, "No!" and bounded to his feet.

"Take oath never to contest the bastard of Rockraven, and that hell-brat of yours? Zandru take me first! Rather will I strike and rid the earth of their sorcery," he cried, and suddenly there was a dagger in his hand. Donal cried out and flung himself in front of his sister, but there was a shrill shriek from Dorilys, an exploding blue flare of lightning in the room, searing the air white, and Scathfell fell, convulsing briefly into an agonized arch, then lay still, half his face blackened and burned away.

There was silence in the room, the silence of shock and sheer horror. Dorilys cried out, "He would have killed Donal! He would have killed us both! You saw the dagger," and she covered her face with her hands. Donal, struggling to control his nausea, unfastened the cloak around his throat and cast it mercifully over the blackened body of Scathfell.

Mikhail of Aldaran said hoarsely, "It is no dishonor to kill a man forsworn, who seeks to do murder on the very ground of surrender. There is no shame to you, daughter." But he left his high seat and came down into the room, kneeling by his brother's body, pulling back the cloak from his face.

"Oh, my brother, my brother," he mourned, and his eyes were blazing and tearless. "How did we come to this?" He bent, kissing the blackened brow; then gently drew the cloak over Scathfell's face again.

"Bear him down to his men," he said to Scathfell's pax-man. "You are witness that there was no treachery save his own. I will take no revenge; his son may hold Scathfell after him. Though it would be only fair if I gifted Donal

with Scathfell for amends, and gave them only the farm at
High Crags in its stead."

The paxman, knowing that what Aldaran said was true,
bowed silently.

"It shall be as you say, Lord. His eldest son Loran is
turned seventeen and shall assume rule over Scathfell. But
what am I to say to the lord Hastur?" He amended quickly,
"To His Highness, Damon-Rafael, king over this land?"

Allart suddenly left his place. He said, "My brother's
quarrel is with me, Lord Aldaran. I will go down and meet
him, unarmed, as he has asked."

Cassandra cried out, "Allart, no! He means treachery!"

"Still, I must face him," Allart said. It was his doing
which had entangled the house of Aldaran in this Lowland
war, when they had enough trouble of their own. Now,
unless Allart went to him, Damon-Rafael would destroy
Aldaran around their heads. "He said that he wished to
compromise with his brother as Lord Scathfell wished to
come to terms with *you;* and I think, at that moment, Scathfell spoke only truth. I do not think he moved against
Donal by foresight but upon impulse, and he has paid for
it. It may be that my brother wishes only to persuade me
that he is indeed rightfully king over this land, and ask my
support. It is true that before I knew what I did, I pledged
to support him in this. He is right to call me traitor, perhaps. I must go down and speak with him."

Cassandra came and clutched at him, holding him
motionless.

"I will not let you go! I will not! He will kill you, and
you know it!"

"He will not kill me, my wife," said Allart, putting her away
with more force than he had ever before used against her. "But
I know what I must do, and I forbid you to hinder me."

"You forbid me?" She stood away from him, angry now.
"Do what you feel you must, my husband," she said, her
teeth set, "but say to Damon-Rafael that if he harms you,
I shall raise every man, every woman, and every matrix in
the Hellers against him!"

Yet as he went slowly down the mountainside, Cassandra's face seemed to go with him, and his *laran* spread
pictures of disaster before him.

Damon-Rafael will almost certainly try to kill me. Yet I must kill him first, as I would kill a maddened beast, raging and ready to bite. If he becomes king over this land, then there will be ruin and disaster such as the Domains have never known.

I never wanted to rule. I never wanted power; I have no ambitions of that kind. I would have been content to dwell within the walls of Nevarsin, or within the Tower at Hali or Tramontana. Yet now that my laran *has shown me what must come to pass if Damon-Rafael comes to the throne, I must somehow stop that from happening. Even if I must kill him!*

The hand he had thrust into the fires of Hali throbbed, as if reminding him of the oath he had sworn and was now breaking.

I am forsworn. But I am a Hastur, descendant of the Hastur who was said to be son to a god; and I am responsible for the well-being of this land and its people. I will not loose Damon-Rafael upon them!

It was not long to the camp, but it seemed the distance to the world's end, and his *laran* spread dissolving pictures before him, of things which might be, which would be, which could be if he did not take care, which would never be. In all too many of these futures he lay lifeless among the stones fallen from the tower, with Damon-Rafael's knife in his throat, and Damon-Rafael went on to level the walls of Aldaran, to possess northlands and Domains, to reign in tyranny and power for many years, riding rough-shod over all the remaining freedoms of men, razing their defenses with weapons ever more powerful, and at last invading even their very minds with his *leroni*, making them all obedient slaves to his will, their own wishes and enterprises burned away.

His heart cried out, as Mikhail of Aldaran had cried out a little while ago, *Ah, my brother, my brother, how did we come to this?*

Damon-Rafael was not an evil man. But he had pride, and a will to power, and he felt honestly that he knew what was best for all men.

He is not unlike Dom Mikhail. . . . But Allart shuddered away from that thought. He was lost again in terrifying vision, blotting out the present, of this land under the rule of the tyrant Damon-Rafael.

Yet my brother is not evil. Does he even know this?

At last he came to a stop, and he saw that he stood on a leveled place in the road, with fallen debris of the tower all around him. At the far end of the leveled space, his brother Damon-Rafael was standing and watching him.

Allart bowed, without speaking.

His *laran* was screaming, *this is the place, then, of my death.* But Damon-Rafael was alone, and he seemed unarmed. Allart spread his hands to display that he was unweaponed, too, and the brothers advanced, step by step, toward one another.

Damon-Rafael said, "You have a loyal and a loving wife, Allart. It will grieve me to take her from you. Yet you were reluctant to wed her, and even more reluctant to bed her, so I suppose it will not trouble you much to give her up to me. The world and the kingdom are full of women, and I shall make sure you are wed to one you will like just as well. But Cassandra I must have; I need the support of the Aillards. And I have discovered that her genes were modified before puberty, so that she can bear me a son with the Hastur gift controlled by the Aillard."

Allart cleared his throat and said, "Cassandra is my wife, Damon-Rafael. If you loved her, or if she were ambitious to be queen, I would step aside for you both. But I love her, and she loves me, and you care nothing for her, save as a pawn of political power. Therefore I will not yield her up to you. I will die first."

Damon-Rafael shook his head. "I cannot afford to take her over your dead body. I would greatly prefer not to come to the throne over a brother's death."

Allart smiled fiercely. He said, "Then I can inconvenience you somewhat in coming to the throne, if only by my death!"

"I do not understand this," Damon-Rafael said. "You asked me to spare you this marriage to the Aillard woman, and now you speak romantically of love. You swore to support me for the throne, and now you refuse your support and strive to hinder me! What has happened, Allart? Is that what love for a woman can do to a man? If so, I am glad I have never known such love!"

"When I pledged my support to you," Allart said, "I did not know what would befall if you were to be king. Now I have pledged myself to support Prince Felix."

"An *emmasca* cannot be king," Damon-Rafael said. "that is one of our oldest laws."

"If you were fit to be king," Allart retorted, "you would not be on the road with an army, trying to extend your reign to the northlands! You would wait until the council offered you the throne, and seek their advice."

"How could I better serve my kingdom, than by extending its might and power across the Hellers as well?" Damon-Rafael said. "Come, Allart, there is no reason we should quarrel. . . . Cassandra has a *nedestro* sister, as like to Cassandra as twin to twin. You shall have her for your wife, and be my chief councillor. I shall need someone with your foresight and strength. *Bare is back without brother . . .* that is what they say, and believe me, it is true. Let us amend our differences, embrace and be friends."

Then it is hopeless, Allart thought. Even as Damon-Rafael held out his arms for the offered embrace, Allart was aware of the dagger concealed by stealth in his brother's hand.

So he would not even face me openly, but would embrace me and stab me to the heart even while I went to his arms, he mourned. *Oh, my brother. . . .* As he moved into Damon-Rafael's embrace, he reached out with his *laran,* trained and honed to skill in the Tower and at Nevarsin, and held Damon-Rafael motionless, the dagger revealed now in his hand.

Damon-Rafael struggled, held motionless, but Allart shook his head sadly.

"So you seek to embrace and stab at once, brother? Is this the kind of statecraft you think will make you king? No. Damon-Rafael," he said sorrowfully, and reaching out into Damon-Rafael's mind, made contact. "See what kind of king you would make, my brother who has renounced the tie of brotherhood."

He felt his *laran* flooding the future through Damon-Rafael's mind: conquest, blood and rapine, the relentless rise to power, laying waste the Domains to wilderness and a stunned conquest they called peace by default . . . men's minds burned into blind obedience, the land shattered and torn with war waged with greater and greater weapons, all men bowing down before a king who had become not the just ruler and protector of his people, but their tyrant, despot, hated as no man had ever been hated within the realm. . . .

"No, no," Damon-Rafael whispered, struggling with the dagger in his hand. "Show me no more. I would not be like that."

"No, my brother? You have the Hastur *laran* which sees all choices; see for yourself what manner of king you would be," Allart said, releasing his hold on his brother's mind but holding him motionless. "Face no man's judgment but your own. Look within."

He watched Damon-Rafael, saw the look of dread and horror spreading over his face, slow dawning of awareness, conviction. Then, with a maddened effort, Damon-Rafael freed himself from Allart's hold and raised the dagger. Allart stood his ground, knowing that within a moment he might lie at his brother's feet—or had Damon-Rafael seen himself clearly enough to take warning?

"I will not be such a king," Damon-Rafael whispered, just loud enough for Allart to hear. "I tell you I will *not,*" and with one swift movement he raised the dagger and plunged it deep into his own breast.

He crumpled to the ground, whispered, "Even your foresight cannot see all ends, little brother," and coughed out a stream of bright red blood. Allart felt his brother's dying mind fade into silence.

Chapter 29

The armies in the valley below had departed, but thunder still rolled and crunched around the heights, and stray bolts of lightning ripped across the mountains. As she went into the lower hall of Castle Aldaran, Cassandra gave Allart a quick, frightened look.

"It has not stopped thundering—not once, not for a moment—since she struck Scathfell down. And you know she will not let Renata near her."

Donal sat with Dorilys's head in his lap; the girl looked ill and feverish. She held Donal's hand tightly clasped in hers and would not release it. The blue eyes were closed, but she opened them, painfully, as Cassandra came to her side.

"The thunder hurts my head so," she whispered. "I can't make it stop. Can't you help me turn off the lightning, Cassandra?"

Cassandra bent over her. "I will try. But I think it is only that you are overwearied, *chiya.*" She took the lax fingers in hers, fell back with a cry of pain, and Dorilys burst into violent crying.

"I didn't mean to do that, I didn't! it keeps happening and I cannot stop it! I hurt Margali; I did it to Kathya while she was dressing me. Oh, Cassandra, make it stop, make it stop! Can't anybody make the thundering go away?"

Dom Mikhail came and bent over her. His face was drawn and troubled. "Hush, hush, my precious, no one is blaming you!" He turned a look of agony on Cassandra.

"Can you help her? Donal, you have that kind of *laran*, too; can you do nothing for her?"

"I wish indeed that there was something I could do," Donal said, cradling the girl in his arms. She relaxed against him, and Cassandra, steadying herself, braced and took the girl's hand in her own again. This time nothing happened, but she felt frightened, even while she tried to relax herself into the calm detachment of a monitor. She looked once at Renata, over Dorilys's head, and Renata picked up her thought: *I wish she would let you do this; you have so much more experience than I.*

"I will give you something to make you sleep," she said at last. "Perhaps all you need is rest, *chiya.*"

When Renata brought the sleeping draft, Donal held the vial to her lips Dorilys swallowed it obediently, but her voice was plaintive when she said, "I am so afraid to sleep now. My dreams are so dreadful, and I hear the tower falling, and the thunder is inside me. The storms are all inside my head now. . . ."

Donal stood up, Dorilys in his arms. "Let me carry you to your bed, sister," he said, but she clung to him.

"No, no! Oh, please, please, I'm afraid to be alone. I'm so afraid. Please stay with me, Donal! Don't leave me!"

"I will stay with you until you are asleep," Donal promised, sighing, and signaled to Cassandra to come with them.

She followed as he carried Dorilys along the hall and up the long staircase. At the end of the hallway the roofing had been roughly repaired, but a great pile of stone and fallen plaster and debris still blocked the hall. Cassandra thought, *It is no great wonder she hears it in her nightmares!*

Donal carried Dorilys into her room, laying her on the bed and summoning her women to loosen her clothing, remove her shoes. But even when she was tucked under her quilts she would not release his hand. She murmured something Cassandra did not hear. Donal stroked her forehead gently, with his free hand.

"This is no time to speak of that, *chiya.* You are ill. When you are well and strong again, and wholly free of threshold sickness—then, yes, if you wish it. I have promised you." He bent to kiss her lightly on the forehead, but she pulled at his head with both hands so that their lips met, and the kiss she gave him was not a child's kiss or a sister's. Donal drew away, looking troubled and embarrassed.

"Sleep, child, sleep. You are wearied; you must be strong and well tonight for the victory feast in the Great Hall."

She lay back on her pillow, smiling.

"Yes," she said drowsily. "For the first time I shall sit in the high seat as Lady of Aldaran . . . and you beside me . . . my husband. . . ."

The drowsiness of the strong sleeping medicine was already taking her. She let her eyes fall shut, but she did not loosen her grip on Donal's hand, and even when she slept it was some time before her fingers relaxed enough so that he could draw his hand free. Cassandra, watching, was embarrassed at having witnessed this, even though she knew perfectly well that this was one reason Donal had wanted her there.

She is not herself. We should not blame her for what happens when she is under such stress, poor child. But inside herself Cassandra knew that Dorilys was perfectly well aware what she was doing, and why.

She is too old for her years. . . .

When they returned to the hall, Renata raised questioning eyes to them, and Donal said, "Yes, she sleeps. But in the name of all the gods, cousin, what did you give her to work so quickly?"

Renata told him, and he stared at her in consternation.

"*That?* To a child?"

Dom Mikhail said, "That would be a dose overlarge for a grown man dying of the black rot! Was that not dangerous?"

"I dared give her nothing less," Renata said. "Listen." She held up a hand for silence and overhead they could hear the crackle and crumble of thunder in the cloudless sky. "Even now she dreams."

"Blessed Cassilda, have mercy!" Dom Mikhail said. "What ails her?"

Renata said soberly, "Her *laran* is out of control. You should never have allowed her to use it in the war, my lord. Her control was broken down when she loosed it against the armies. I first saw it in the fire station, when she played with the storms, and became overexcited and dizzy. You remember, Donal! But she had not then come

to her full strength or womanhood. Now—all the control I
taught her has faded from her mind. I do not know what
we can do for her." She turned, made a deep reverence
to Aldaran.

"My lord, I asked you this once before, and you refused.
Now, I think, there is no choice. I implore you. Let me
burn out her psi centers. Perhaps now, while she sleeps, it
could still be done."

Aldaran looked at Renata in horror.

"When her *laran* has saved us all? What would that do
to her?"

"I think—I *hope,*" Renata said, "that it would do no
more than take away the lightnings that torment her so.
She would be without *laran,* but she wishes for that now.
You heard her beg Cassandra to take away the thundering.
She would perhaps be no more, and on less, than an ordinary woman of her caste, ungifted with *laran,* yes, but having her beauty, still, and her talents, and her superb voice.
She could still—" She hesitated, choked over the words,
and went on, looking straight at Donal, "She could still
give an heir of Aldaran blood to your clan, gifted with the
laran in her genes. She should never bear a daughter, but
she could give Aldaran a son, if need be."

Donal had told her of the promise he had made to Dorilys, during the siege of Castle Aldaran.

"It is no more than fair," Renata had said then. *If Dorilys must be bound all her life by the* catenas *in a marriage
forced on her before she is old enough to know anything of
marriage or of love, where she will have the name and dignity of a wife but never a husband's love, it is only fair that
she should have something of her very own, something to
love and cherish. I do not grudge her a child for Aldaran.
It would be better if she would choose some other than
Donal for the fathering, but as her life must be ordered, it
is not likely she will come to know any man well enough
for such a purpose. And it is Lord Aldaran's will that Donal's son should reign here when he is gone. I do not begrudge Dorilys a child of Donal's. It is I who am his wife,
and we all know it, or will know it, in time to come.*

Now Renata looked at Lord Aldaran, pleading, and Allart remembered the moment when he had seen with his
laran, in this very hall, the vassals of Aldaran acclaiming a

child whom he held up before them, proclaiming the new
heir of Aldaran blood. Why, Allart wondered, should his
foresight show him only this one moment? It seemed that
all else was blurred into nightmare and thundercloud. But
they saw it in Allart's mind, all the telepaths there assembled, and Aldaran said "I told you so!" with that fierce,
hawklike glance.

Donal lowered his head and would not meet Renata's
eyes.

"It seems terrible to do that to her, when she has saved
us all. Are you sure it would do no worse to her than this—
to destroy the psi centers and leave the rest undamaged?"
Lord Aldaran said.

Renata said reluctantly, "My lord, no *leronis* living could
make such a pledge. I love Dorilys as if she were my own,
and I would give her the uttermost of my skill and strength.
But I do not know how much of her brain has been invaded
by the *laran*, or damaged by these storms. You know that
electrical discharges *within* the brain reflect themselves as
convulsive seizures in the body. Dorilys's *laran* somehow
translates the electrical discharges *in* the brain to thunder
and lightnings in the electrical field of the planet. Now that
is out of control. She said the thunders were *inside* her
now. I do not know how much damage has been done. It
might be that I would have to destroy some part of her
memory, or of her intelligence."

Donal was white with dread. "No!" he said, and it was
a prayer. "Would she be an idiot, then?"

Renata would not look at him. She said, very low, "I
cannot swear that the possibility is beyond belief. I would
do my best for her. But it could indeed be so."

"No! All gods help us—no, kinswoman!" Aldaran said,
the old hawk roused. "If there is the slightest chance—no,
I cannot risk it. Even if all should go for the best, cousin,
a woman who is heir to Aldaran cannot live as a commoner, without *laran*. She would be better dead!"

Renata bowed, a submissive gesture. "Let us hope it does
not come to that, my lord."

Lord Aldaran looked around at them all. "I shall see you
tonight at the victory feast within this hall," he said. "I
must go and give orders that all is done as I command."
He went from the hall, his head erect and arrogant.

Renata, watching him go, thought, *It is his moment of triumph. He has Aldaran now, unchallenged, despite the ruin of the war. Dorilys is a part of that triumph. He wants her at his side, a threat, a weapon for the future.* Suddenly she shuddered, hearing the thunders, soft and dying overhead.

Dorilys slept, her terror and rage diminished by the drug. But she would wake. And what then?

The thunders were still silent late that evening, as the sun set. Allart and Cassandra stood on the balcony above their suite, looking down into the valley.

"I can hardly believe the war is over," Cassandra said.

Allart nodded. "And most likely the war with the Ridenow as well; it was my father and Damon-Rafael who wished to conquer them and drive them back to the Drytowns. I do not think anyone else cares if they remain at Serrais; certainly the women of Serrais, who wedded them and welcomed them there, do not."

"What is going to happen in Thendara now, Allart?"

"How should I know?" Her husband's smile was bleak. "We have had proofs enough of the inadequacy of my foresight. Most likely Prince Felix will reign until the council declares his heir. And you know, and I know, whom they are likely to choose."

She said, with a little shiver, "I do not want to be queen."

"Nor I to be king, beloved. But we both knew, when we became entangled in the great events of our time, that there would be no help for it." He sighed. "My first act, if it is so, will be to choose Felix Hastur as my principal Councilor. He was born to the throne, and reared to the knowledge of ruling; also, he is *emmasca* and long-lived, as with those of *chieri* blood, and he may live through two or three reigns. Since he can raise up no son to supplant me, he will be the most useful and disinterested of advisers. Between the two of us, he and I may together make something like a king."

He put his arm around Cassandra, drew her close. Damon-Rafael had reminded him; with Cassandra's modified genes, the blend of Hastur and Aillard might, after all, be viable in a child of theirs. Cassandra, following his thoughts, said aloud, "With what I have learned in the Tower I can make certain I will conceive no child who will kill me in the bearing, or carry lethal genes which will destroy him at puberty. There will be some risk, always. . . ." She raised her eyes to his and smiled. "But after what we have survived together, I think we can risk that much."

"There will be time for that," he said, "but if there should be no such good fortune, Damon-Rafael has half a dozen *nedestro* sons. One of them, at least, should have the stuff to make a king. I think I have had lesson enough in the pride that drives a man to seek a crown for his own sons." He could see, shadowy and blurred in the future, the face of a lad who would follow him to the throne, and that it was a child of Hastur blood. But whether it was a son of his own, or the son of his brother, he did not know, or care.

He was weary, and more grieved than he wanted to let himself know, at his brother's death. He thought, *Even though I had resolved to kill him if I must, even though it was I who held up the mirror of his own heart and thus forced him to turn the knife on himself, I am grieved.* He knew he would never be wholly free of grief and guilt for the decision which had been, whether anyone else ever knew it or not, the first conscious act of his reign. And he knew he would never cease to mourn—not for the power-hungry potential tyrant he had driven to suicide, but for the big brother he loved, who had wept with him at their father's grave.

But *that* Damon-Rafael had died long ago, long ago—if he had ever lived outside Allart's own imagination!

Faint thunder rumbled in the sky, and Cassandra started, then, looking at the rain falling, a dark streak, across the valley on the peaks, she said, "I think it is only a summer storm. Yet I can never hear lightning now—" She broke off. "Allart! Do you think Renata was right? Should you have persuaded Dom Mikhail to let Renata destroy her *laran* as she slept?"

"I do not know," Allart said, troubled. "After what has befallen, I am not eager to trust my own foresight now. But I, too, found my *laran* a curse, when I was a boy on the threshold of manhood. Had any offered me such a release then, I think I would have taken it with gladness. And yet—and yet—" He reached out for her, drew her to him, remembering those agonized days when he had cowered, paralyzed, under the *laran* which had become such a dreadful curse. It had stabilized when he came to manhood; he knew now that he would never have been more than half alive without it. "When she comes to maturity, Dorilys, too, may find stability and strength, and be the stronger for these trials."

As I have been. And you, my beloved.

"I should go to her," Cassandra said uneasily, and Allart laughed.

"Ah, that is like you, love—you who are to be queen, to rush off to the bedside of a sick maiden, and one who is not even to be one of your subjects!"

Cassandra raised her small head proudly.

"I was monitor, and healer, before ever I thought of being a queen. And I hope I shall never refuse my skill to anyone who stands in need of it!"

Allart raised her fingertips to his lips and kissed them.

"The gods grant, beloved, that I shall be as good a king as that!"

Within the castle, Renata heard the thunder, and thought of Dorilys as she readied herself for the victory feast.

"If you have any influence with her at all, Donal," she said, "you will try to persuade her that I mean her well. Then, perhaps, I can work with her, to rebuild the control I had begun to teach her. It would be easier to retrace what she and I had done than to begin again with a stranger."

"I will do that," Donal said. "I do not fear for her; never once has she turned on me, nor on her father, and if she has control enough for that, I have no doubt she can learn control in other things. She is weary now, and frightened, and in the grip of threshold sickness. But when she is well again, she will recapture her control. I am sure of it."

"God grant you are right," she said, smiling, trying to hide her fears.

Abruptly, he said, "At the victory feast, beloved—I want to tell my father, and Dorilys, how it stands with us."

Renata shook her head vehemently. "I do not think it is the right time, Donal. I do not think she can bear it yet."

"Yet," Donal said, frowning, "I am reluctant to lie to her. I wish it had been you, rather than Cassandra, who saw how she clung to me, when I carried her to her bed. I want her to know that I will always cherish her and protect her, but I do not want her to misunderstand, either, or to have a false impression of how things are to be between us. At this feast-when she sits at my side as my wife—" He stopped, troubled, thinking of the kiss Dorilys had given him, which was not a sister's kiss at all.

Renata sighed. At least a part of Dorilys's trouble was threshold sickness, the emotional and physical upheaval which often disturbed a developing telepath in adolescence. Aldaran had lost three nearly grown children that way. Renata, a monitor, and Tower-trained, knew that part of the danger in threshold sickness was the enormous upsurge, at the same time, of telepathic forces, mingled with the stresses of developing, yet not controlled, sexuality. Dorilys had come young to that, too. Like a plant in a forcing-house, the use of her *laran* powers had created all the other upheavals and upsurges, too. Was it any wonder, filled with all this new power and awareness, that she turned to the older boy who had been her special champion, her idol since she was a baby, her protector—and now, by this cruel farce she was too young to understand, her husband as well?

"It is true that she survived her first attack of threshold sickness, and the first attack is often the worst. Perhaps, if she wakes well and coherent—but at this victory feast, Donal? When first she sits at your side, acknowledged your wife? Would you spoil her pleasure in *that,* then?"

"What better time?" Donal asked, smiling. "But even before Dorilys, I want you to tell my father how it is to be with us. He should know that you bear my *nedestro* child. It is not the heir he wants for Aldaran. But he should know that this child will be shield-arm and paxman to Aldaran house as I have been since my mother brought me here as a child. Truly, my dear love, we cannot keep it secret much longer. Pregnancy, like blood-feud, grows never less with secrecy. I would not have it thought that I am cowardly, or ashamed of what I have done. Once known and acknowledged, beloved, your status is protected. Even Dorilys, by civilized custom, knows it is a wife's duty to see to the well-being of any child her husband may father. At this point in her life, I think, any duty properly belonging to a wife will please Dorilys. She was so pleased when Father said she should sit as heir at the victory feast, beside her consort."

"Perhaps you are right," Renata said, remembering Dorilys, who hated sewing, proudly embroidering a holiday shirt for Donal—a traditional bride's task. Donal was right; his marriage to Dorilys was a legal fiction, but custom should be observed, and it was his duty to tell Dorilys that another woman bore his child.

Donal remembered that he had been present—a boy just turned ten years old—when Dom Mikhail had informed Lady Deonara that Aliciane of Rockraven was pregnant with his child. Deonara had risen, embraced Aliciane before all the house-folk, and led her from the women's table to the high seat, formally sharing a drink of wine from the same cup, in token that she would accept the coming child. Renata laughed uneasily at the thought of this ritual with Dorilys.

"Yet you have loved her tenderly," Donal urged, "and I think she will remember that. Also there is this to consider. Dorilys is impulsive and given to fierce tempers, but she is also very conscious of her dignity before the house-folk, as Lady of Aldaran. Once she has been forced to be polite to you at a formal occasion, like this, she will remember how kind you have been to her. Nothing would please me more than to see you reconciled. She will know that I love her. I honor her, I will always care for her. I will even, if it is really her will, give her a child. But she will know what she can expect from me, and what she cannot."

Renata sighed and took his hands.

"As you will, then, beloved," she said. "I can refuse you nothing."

There was a time, not a year past, when I was proud to say to Cassandra Aillard that I did not know what it was to love a man, to suspend my own better judgment to do his will. Do all women come to this, soon or late? And I dared to judge her for that!

Later that evening, when Donal met her at the door of the feasting hall, and himself conducted her to her seat at the women's table, Renata thought that she might as well have shouted it aloud before all the assembled house-folk of Castle Aldaran. She did not care. If all had gone rightly, she and Donal would have been married at midwinter night, and worn the *catenas*. Aldaran had forced another marriage on Donal, but she was neither the first woman nor the last to cling to a lover forced into an expedient marriage with someone else.

She watched Donal as he took his seat at the high table. He had looked handsome to her even in the old rubbed-leather riding-breeches and faded jerkin he had worn during the siege, but now he had put on his finest garments. Firestones hung gleaming at his throat and a jeweled sword at his side. His hair was curled and there were rings on his fingers; he looked handsome and princely. Old Dom Mikhail, in his long furred robe of dark green, with wide sleeves and a jeweled belt, looked proud, but benevolent, too. Dorilys's chair was empty, and Renata wondered if she were still in her drugged sleep. No doubt sleep would do her more good than feasting. Beside Donal and Lord Aldaran at the high table were only Allart and Cassandra, as honored guests of highest rank, and the *leronis* Margali, who was a noblewoman and Dorilys's foster-mother. Under ordinary conditions, Renata sat there herself, as Dorilys's companion and teacher, and so did the *coridom* or estate steward, the chief of the hall-stewards, the castellan, and three or four other functionaries of Castle Aldaran. But at such a solemn feast, only the immediate family and any guests of rank equal to Aldaran's own, or higher, were seated beside the lord Aldaran. The nobles and functionaries were seated either at the women's table where Renata sat, with Lady Elisa and the other women of the estate, or at the men's table with the household knights and important men of the castle.

The lower hall was crowded with those of lower rank, soldiers, guardsmen, servants, everyone down to the stablemen and dairy-women.

"Why are you looking like that at Dorilys's empty chair?" Cassandra asked.

"I thought for a moment that she was there," Allart murmured, disquieted. He had seen for a moment a strange flare of lightning, and thought, *I am weary. I still start at shadows. Perhaps it is only the aftermath of the siege!*

Dom Mikhail leaned toward Margali, asking what had

delayed Dorilys. After a moment he nodded, rose from his chair, and addressed the folk assembled in the Great Hall.

"Let us give thanks to the gods that the armies which surrounded us are vanquished and gone to their own place. What they have destroyed will be rebuilded; what they have broken shall be mended." He raised his cup. "First let us drink to honor those who have given their lives in this warfare."

Allart rose with the others, drinking silently from his cup in honor to the dead.

"Now I shall speak of the living," Lord Aldaran said. "I hereby state that any child of any man who died in the siege of this castle shall be fostered in my house, or the household of one of my vassals, according to his father's rightful station, commoner or noble."

There was an outcry of thanks for the lord Aldaran's generosity; then he spoke again.

"Furthermore, if their widows wish to marry again, my stewards shall see to finding them suitable husbands, and if not, they shall be helped to respectable livelihoods."

When the outcry had died down this time, he said, "Now let us eat and drink, but drink first in honor of him who best defended the castle—my foster-son Donal of Rockraven and husband of my daughter, Dorilys, Lady of Aldaran."

Under the cover of the cries of acclamation, Cassandra said, "Would that Dorilys were here, to know herself so honored."

"I do not know," Allart said slowly. "I think perhaps she has already too much pride in her own power and station."

Dom Mikhail glanced to where Allart sat with Cassandra. "I would that you might remain to help me set my Domain in order, cousin. Yet I have no doubt that before very long they will summon you to Thendara. With your brother dead, you are heir to the Domain of Elhalyn." He looked at Allart, suddenly cautious. Dom Mikhail had become aware that he was no longer dealing with a kinsman, a friend, a fellow noble, but with a future ruler with whom he must one day soon have careful, tactical diplomatic dealings. A Hastur lord, one who might before midsummer day sit on the throne of Thendara.

It seemed to Allart that every word Dom Mikhail spoke was fenced about with sudden caution.

"I hope we will always be friends, cousin."

Allart said, heartfelt, "I hope, indeed, that there will always be friendship between Thendara and Elhalyn." But he wondered, *Can I never again know any real friendships, any simple personal relationships?* The thought depressed him.

Dom Mikhail said, "It will take us half a year to clear away the rubble of the fallen tower; perhaps twice that to rebuild, if we do it by ordinary means. What do you think, Donal—shall we send for a matrix crew, perhaps from Tramontana, perhaps from the Lowlands, to come and clear away this rubble?"

Donal nodded. "We must think of the folk who have had to be away from their homes because of the armies; already the spring planting is delayed, and if it must wait much longer, we will have hunger in these hills at harvest."

Dom Mikhail said, "Yes, and they can design the tower anew, and raise it again by matrix. It would be costly and long, but it would give pride to Castle Aldaran, and when your children and Dorilys's rule here someday, you will wish for a point of vantage to command the country around. Though, indeed, I think it will be long, very long, before anyone sends armed might against the stronghold of Aldaran!"

"May that day be far," Donal said. "I hope you will sit in this high seat for many years to come, my father." He rose and bowed. "By your leave, sir," he said, and left his seat, going to the women's table where Renata sat.

"Come with me, love, and speak with my father. Then, when Dorilys comes later to join us, he will know the truth, and there will be honesty among us all."

Renata smiled and took his offered hand. Part of her felt naked and exposed by the way in which he had sought her out, but she realized that this was a part of the price she paid for her love. She could have chosen to go away, to return to her family, when Donal was married to another. A conventional woman would have done so. She had chosen to remain here as Donal's *barragana,* and she was not ashamed of it. Why should she hesitate to cross the little space between the women's table and the high seat, to sit at Donal's side?

Allart watched with apprehension, wondering what would happen when Renata and Dorilys came face to face. No . . . Dorilys was not here; she had not come into the hall. Yet his *laran* showed him weird out-of-focus pictures of Dorilys's face, of Renata, distraught. He started to rise from his seat, then realized in despair that there was nothing he could do, nothing to focus on, nothing had happened *yet;* but the noise and confusion in the hall, pictured by his *laran,* paralyzed him. He stared around, bewildered by the pandemonium of his *laran,* and the actual present Great Hall, with only the cheerful noises of many people loudly eating and drinking at a holiday feast.

Renata said, "I love Dorilys well. I would not for worlds step on the hem of her garment. I still feel we should not tell her this until we are sure that she is free of threshold sickness."

"But if she finds it out of herself, she will be very angry, and rightly so," Donal argued, leading Renata toward the high seat. "We should tell my father, even if there is no need to tell Dorilys at once."

"What is it that you will say to my father and not to me, my husband?"

The light, childish voice dropped into the silence, shattering it like breaking glass. Dorilys, in her holiday gown of blue, her hair coiled low on her neck, and somehow looking more childish than ever in her woman's garments, came walking across the floor, dazed, almost as if she were sleepwalking. Allart and Margali rose, and Dom Mikhail held out his hand to Dorilys, saying, "My dear child, I am glad you are well enough to join us," but she paid no attention, her eyes fixed on Donal and Renata, hand in hand before her.

She cried out suddenly, "How dare you speak like that about me, Renata!"

Renata could not conceal a start of surprise and guilt. But she looked at Dorilys and smiled.

"Dear child," she said, "I have said nothing about you except what shows my love and concern, as always. If there is anything we have not told you, it has been only to save

you distress while you were overwearied and ill with threshold sickness." But her heart sank as he saw the look in
Dorilys's eyes, dark, strained, clutching sanity about her
with painful concentration, and she realized that Dorilys,
as she had done on the day of her festival, was reading
thoughts again; not clearly like a skilled telepath, but errati-
cally, with crazy, patchy incompleteness. Then Dorilys cried
out in rage and sudden comprehension, turning on Donal.

"You!" she cried, in a frenzy. "You have given to *her*
what you denied to *me!* Now you think—you scheme that
she will bear the new heir to Aldaran!"

"Dorilys, no," Renata protested, but Dorilys, beside herself, would not hear.

"Do you think I cannot see it? Do you think I do not
know that my father has always schemed that *your* child
should be heir? He would let you father a child on some
outsider to supersede *mine.*"

Donal reached for her hands, but she wrenched them
away.

"You promised, Donal," she cried shrilly. "You promised, and tried to soothe me with lies, as if I were a child
to be petted and told fairy tales, and while you lied to me,
all that time you planned that *she* should bear your first
son. But she shall not, I swear it! I will strike her first!"

Lightning flared in the hall, a crash of thunder, loud and
almost deafening. In the shocked silence as it died away,
Cassandra rose, taking a frantic step toward Dorilys.

"Dorilys, dear child, come to me."

"Don't touch me, Cassandra!" Dorilys shrieked. "You
have lied to me, too. You are *her* friend, not mine! You
schemed with her, knowing what she planned behind my
back. I am alone here; there is none to love me."

"Dorilys, there is none here does *not* love you," Donal
said.

But Dom Mikhail had risen, somber and angry. He raised
a hand and said, using command-voice, *"Dorilys! I say,
be still!"*

The girl stood motionless, shocked into silence.

"This is an outrage!" Lord Aldaran said, towering over the
child. "How dare you create such an unseemly uproar at a
festival? How dare you speak so to our kinswoman? Come
and sit here in your proper place by me, and be silent!"

Dorilys took a step toward the high table, and Renata thought, her heart churning with relief, *After all, even with her power, she is a child; she is accustomed to obey her elders. She is still young enough to obey her father without question.*

Dorilys took another step under the command-voice; then she broke free.

"No!" she cried out, whirling, stamping her foot in the willful fury Renata had seen so often in her first days at the castle. "I will not! I will not be humiliated this way! And you, Renata, you who have dared to step on my garment this way, in pride of what you have had from my husband when I have had only empty words and promises and a child's kiss on the forehead, you shall not flaunt your belly at me. You shall not!" She whirled, her face ablaze with the lightning flare.

And Allart saw what once he had foreseen in this hall, a child's face all ablaze with lightning. . . .

Renata took a panicked step backward, tripping over a piece of furniture. Donal cried out, "Dorilys, no! No! Not at her!" and flung himself between Renata and Dorilys, shielding Renata with his body. "If you are angry, speak your anger to me alone—" Then he broke off, with an inarticulate sound, and staggered and his body twitched, caught in the lightning flare. He jerked violently, convulsed, fell, his body crisped and blackened like a blasted tree, twitched again, already lifeless, and lay without moving on the stone pavement.

It had all happened so swiftly that there were many in the lower hall who had heard nothing except cries and accusations. Margali still sat with her mouth open, staring stupidly at her charge, not believing what she saw. Cassandra still stood with her arms extended toward Dorilys, but Allart caught her and held her motionless.

Dom Mikhail took one step toward Dorilys, and staggered. He stopped, swaying, holding himself upright with both hands on the edge of the table. His face was congested and dark with blood, and he could hardly speak. His voice held a terrible bitterness.

"It is the curse," he said. "A sorceress foretold this day, that I should cry out to the gods above and below, would to all of the gods that I had died childless." Moving slowly,

an old, broken-winged hawk, he came slowly to where
Donal lay, fell to his knees beside him.

"Oh, my son," he whispered. "My son, my son . . ." and
raised his face, set and rigid as if carved in stone, to Dorilys.

"Strike me down, too, girl. Why do you wait?"

Dorilys had not moved; she stood as if turned to stone,
as if the lightning which had struck Donal down had struck
her, too, turning her motionless. Her face was a terrible,
tragic mask, her eyes blank and unmoving. Her mouth was
open, as if in a soundless scream, but she did not move.

Allart breaking the frozen stasis, began to move to Dom
Mikhail's side, but a wild flare of lightning suddenly blazed
in the hall, and Dorilys disappeared in its flare. Allart fell
back dazed by the shock. Another and another lightning
bolt crackled in the room, and they could see Dorilys now,
her eyes mad and blazing. Another lightning bolt and another seared at random around the room, and in the lower
hall a man leaped up, twitched, and fell dead. One by one,
everyone edged back, step by step, from where Dorilys
stood, surrounded by the crazed flare of lightning, deafened
by thunder; back, and back from where she stood like a
statue of some terrible goddess etched in lightning. Her
face was not a child's face. It was not even human anymore.

Only Renata dared the lightning. Perhaps, Allart thought
in some horrified corner of his mind where he could still
think, perhaps Renata simply had no more to lose. She
took a step toward Dorilys; another. Another. Dorilys
moved for the first time since she had struck Donal down,
a menacing gesture, but Renata did not pause or flinch,
advancing step by step toward the core of those terrible
lightnings where Dorilys blazed like some figure of legendary hells.

Dom Mikhail said brokenly, "No, Lady Renata. No, no—
stand back from her. Not you, too, Renata—not you, too."

Allart heard in his mind a clamor, a confusing babble, a
wild interplay of confused possibilities there—gone, retreating, surging up again—as Renata moved, slowly and
steadily, toward Dorilys, where she stood over Donal's
dead body. He saw Renata fall blasted, saw her strike Dorilys with her own *laran* and hold her motionless, as she had
done when Dorilys was a willful child; he heard her cursing
Dorilys, pleading with her, defying her, all at once in the

wild surge of futures from this moment that would be, might be, would never be. . . .

Renata spread her arms wide. Her voice was anguished but steady, clearly audible.

"Dorilys," she said in a whisper. "Dorilys, my little girl, my darling—"

She rose from where she had fallen and took a step and another, and Dorilys came into her arms, was folded close to her breast. The lightnings died. Suddenly Dorilys was only a little girl again, clasped in Renata's arms, sobbing tempestuously.

Renata held her, soothing her, stroking her, murmuring soft love words, tears raining down her own face. Dorilys looked around her, dazed.

"I feel so sick, Renata," she whispered. "What has happened? I thought this was a festival. Is Donal very angry with me?" Then she shrieked, a long, terrible cry of horror and realization, and crumpled, a limp, lifeless-looking unconscious heap in Renata's arms.

Overhead the thunder muttered and died and was still.

Chapter 30

"It is too late," Renata repeated. "I do not know if it will ever be safe to let her wake again."

Overhead the thunder rattled at random, striking sudden searing bolts around the towers of Aldaran, and Allart wondered, with a shudder, what dreams disturbed Dorilys's sleep. Dreadful ones, no doubt.

In the stunned moment following Dorilys's realization of what she had done, Renata had managed to get her to swallow a dose of the same strong drug she had given her before. Almost as soon as she had swallowed it, the moment of sanity had faded from her eyes and the terrible core of lightning had begun to build up around her again. But the drug had taken over with merciful quickness before more than a few random bolts had struck, and she had sunk into her present unquiet stupor, the storms raging overhead but not striking near.

"We cannot give her that drug again," Renata repeated. "even if I could get her to take it again—and I am not sure of that—it would almost certainly kill her."

Aldaran said, with terrible bitterness, "Better that, than that she should destroy us all as she destroyed my boy." His voice broke and the terrible glazed brightness of his eyes was worse than weeping. "Is there no hope, Renata? None?"

"I am afraid that even when I asked you, before," Renata said, "it was too late. Too much of her mind, too much of the brain itself has been destroyed and invaded by the lightnings. It is too late for Dorilys, my lord. I fear you must accept that; our only concern now is to make sure she does not destroy too much outside herself, in her own death."

The father shuddered. Finally he said, "How can we make sure of that?"

"I do not know, my lord. Probably no one with this lethal gift has ever survived so near maturity, and so we have only the faintest notion of its potential. I must consult with those in Tramontana Tower, or perhaps at Hali, to be certain what we can do, and how we can best make her harmless during"—Renata swallowed, struggling to control herself—"during what little time remains to her. She can tap the whole electrical potential of the planet, my lord. I beg you not to underestimate the damage she can still do, if we frighten her."

"I am cursed," said Aldaran, softly and bitterly. "I was cursed the day she was born, and I did not know it. You tried to warn me, and I did not hear. It is I who deserve death, and it took only my children, my innocent children."

"Let me go and consult my colleagues in the towers, Lord Aldaran."

"And spread far and wide the news of the shame of Aldaran? No, Lady Renata. It was I who brought this awful curse to our world; without malice, and in love, but still it was I. Now I shall destroy it."

He drew his dagger, raised it above Dorilys, and brought it suddenly striking down. But from the prostrate form there came a blue flash and Aldaran fell back, knocked half across the room, the breath gone from his body. When Allart picked him up he struggled for breath and for a moment Allart feared he was dying.

Renata shook her head sadly.

"Had you forgotten, my lord? She is a telepath, too. Even in her sleep, she can sense your intent. Although I do not think she would want to live if she knew, there is something in that brain that will protect itself. I do not think we can kill her. I must go to Hali or to Tramontana, my lord."

Lord Aldaran bowed is head.

"As you will, kinswoman. Will you make ready to ride?"

"There is no time for that—and no need. I will go through the overworld."

Drawing out her matrix, Renata composed herself for the journey. With one part of herself she was grateful for this disturbance, this desperate need; it deferred the moment when she must face the unendurable fact of Donal's death. Unasked, Cassandra came to keep watch beside Renata's body while she made the journey through the intangible realms of the mind.

It was like stepping out of a garment suddenly grown unimaginably too large. For an instant, in the grayness of the shadow-world overlaying the solid and tangible world, Renata could see her body, looking as lifeless as Dorilys's, wearing the elaborate gown she had put on for the victory feast which had turned to defeat, and Cassandra motionless beside her. Then, moving with the swiftness of thought, she stood on the high peak of Tramontana Tower, wondering why she had been drawn here . . . then, in the crimson garment of a Keeper, she saw Ian-Mikhail of Tramontana.

He said gently, "So Donal is dead, suddenly and by violence? I was his friend, and his teacher. I must seek him out in the Realms Beyond, Renata. If he died suddenly, and by violence, he may not know he is dead; his mind may be trapped near to his body and he may be helplessly trying to reenter it again. I was uneasy about him; yet I did not know what had befallen him until I saw you, cousin."

In the intangible spaces of the overworld, where a physical touch could register only as an idea, he gently touched her hand.

"We share your grief, Renata. We all loved him; he should have been one of us in Tramontana. I must go to him." She saw the small premonitory stirring of the gray spaces which presaged Ian-Mikhail's withdrawing of his thoughts and presence from her, and caught at his presence with a despairing thought that disturbed the overworld like a cry.

"What of Dorilys, kinsman? What shall we do for her?"

"Alas. I do not know, Renata. Her father would not entrust her to us, and we do not know her. It is a pity; we might have found a way to help her control her *laran*. But the records of the breeding programs are at Hali and Arilinn. Perhaps they have had some experience, or some advice. Delay me no more, sister; I must go to Donal

Renata watched his image in the overworld recede, grow

distant. He was going to seek out Donal, dead so suddenly by violence, make certain he did not linger, trapped, near his useless body. Dully Renata envied him. She knew that contact between the dead and the living was perilous for both, and thus forbidden. The dead must not be encouraged to remain too near the grief of the bereaved; the living must not be drawn into realms where, as yet, they had no business. Ian-Mikhail, trained from adolescence to the detachment of a Keeper's vows, could safely perform this office for his friend without being drawn into overmuch concern. Even so, Renata knew, had Donal been a member of his immediate family, Ian-Mikhail would have ceded this task to another, less personally concerned.

Weary, uncertain, remembering only Donal and her loss, Renata turned her thoughts toward Hali. She struggled for calm, knowing that too much emotion would force her off this plane altogether, but it threatened to overcome her. She knew that if she did not banish the tormenting memories she would break altogether, retreat into the dreamstuff of the overworld, and never return.

But the grayness of the overworld seemed unending, and while she could see the dimness of the Tower of Hali in the distance, it seemed that although she tried to move toward the Tower, her limbs would not obey her, nor her unruly thoughts. She moved forever in gray uninhabited mental wastelands. . . .

Then, very far away, in the distance, it seemed that she saw a familiar figure, young, laughing, very far away, too far to reach. . . . Donal! Donal, so very far from her! In this realm where thoughts were pliable, something survived. . . . She began to hurry after the retreating figure, sending out a cry of joy.

Donal! Donal, I am here! Wait for me, beloved. . . .

But he was very far away. He did not turn or look at her. She thought, with a last moment of rationality, *No; it is forbidden. He has gone into a realm still denied, still inaccessible. This could draw me after him . . . too far. . . .*

I will not go too far. But I must see him again. I must see him only this once, say the good-byes of which we were so cruelly cheated . . . only this once, and then nevermore. . . .

She hurried after the retreating figure, her thoughts seeming to bear her along swiftly through the grayness of

the overworld. When she looked around all the familiar
landmarks, the last sight of Hali Tower, had vanished, and
she was wholly alone in grayness, with nothing but he small,
retreating figure of Donal just at the horizon, drawing her
on. . . .

*No. This is madness! It is forbidden. I must return before
it is too late.* She had known this from her first years in the
Tower, that there could not be, *must* not be, any intrusion
by the living into whatever realms belonged to the dead,
and she knew why. But caution was almost gone in her
now. In the despair of grief, she thought, *I must see him
once more, only once, must kiss him, must say good-bye. . . .
I must or I cannot live! Surely it cannot be forbidden, only
to say good-bye. I am a trained matrix worker. I know what
I am doing, and it will give me the strength to go on living
without him. . . .*

A final touch of intruding sanity made her wonder if it
were truly Donal there on the horizon, leading her away.
Or was it an illusion, born of grief and longing, unwilling-
ness to accept the irrevocability of death? Here in the
realms of thought, her mind could build an illusion of
Donal and follow it till she joined him in those realms.

I do not care! I do not care! It seemed that she was
running, running after the retreating form, then more
slowly, more despairing, her pace slackening. Unable to
move, she sent out a final despairing cry:

Donal! Wait—

Suddenly the grayness lightened, thinned, a shadowy
form barred her way, and a voice spoke her name; a familiar, gentle voice.

"Renata. Kinswoman, cousin—Renata, no."

She saw Dorilys standing before her, not the terrifying
inhuman lightning flare, not the queen of storms, but the
old Dorilys, the little Dorilys of that summer of her love.
In this fluid world where all things were as the mind pictured them, Dorilys was the little girl she had been, her
hair in a long plait, one of her old childish dresses barely
reaching her ankles.

"No, Renata, love, it is not Donal. It is an illusion born
of your longing, an illusion you would follow forever. Go
back, dear. They need you, *there*—"

Suddenly Renata saw the hall in Castle Aldaran, where her lifeless body lay, watched by Cassandra.

Renata stopped, looking at Dorilys before her.

She had killed. Killed Donal . . .

"Not I, but my gift," Dorilys said, and the childish face was tragic. "I will kill no more, Renata. In my pride and willfulness I would not listen, and now it is too late. You must go back and tell them; I must never wake again."

Renata bowed her head, knowing the child spoke truth.

"They need you, Renata. Go back. Donal is not here," Dorilys said. "I, too, could have followed him forever over that horizon. Only, perhaps, now, when there is no pride or desire to blind me, I can see clearly. All my life, I never saw more of Donal than *that*, an illusion, to my own willful belief that he would be what I wanted him to be. I—" Renata saw her face flicker and move and she saw the child Dorilys might have been, the woman she was becoming, would now never be. "I knew he was given to you; I was too selfish to accept it. Now I have not even what he would have given me, willingly. I wanted what he could give only to you."

She gestured. "Go back, Renata. It is too late for me."

"But what will become of you, child?"

"You must use your matrix," Dorilys said, "to isolate me behind a force-field like the ones at Hali . . . you told me of them, shielding things too dangerous to use. You cannot even kill me, Renata. The gift in my brain works independent now of the real *me*—I do not understand it, either— but *it* will strike to protect my body if I am attacked. Even though I no longer desire to live. Renata, cousin, promise me you will not let me destroy any more of those I love!"

It could be done, Renata thought. *Dorilys could not be killed. But she could be isolated, her life-forces suspended, behind a force-field.*

"Let me sleep so, safe, until it is safe for me to wake," Dorilys said, and Renata trembled. This would isolate Dorilys in the overworld, alone, behind the force-field which would barricade even her mind.

"Darling, what of you, then?"

Her smile was childish and wise.

"Why, with such a long time—although time, I know,

does not exist *out here*—I shall perhaps learn wisdom, at
last, if I continue to live. And if I do not"—a curious,
distant smile—"there are others who have gone before me.
I do not believe wisdom is ever wasted. Go back, Renata.
Do not let me destroy anyone else. Donal is gone beyond
my reach, or your's. But you must go back, and you must
live, because of his child. He deserves some chance at life."

With those words Renata found herself lying in the chair
in the Great Hall at Castle Aldaran, with the storms breaking above the castle heights. . . .

"It can be done," Allart said at last quietly. "Among the
three of us, it can be done. Her life-forces can be lowered
to where she is no danger. Perhaps she will die; perhaps,
only, they will be in abeyance and someday she may wake
in safety, in control. But more likely she will sink and sink,
and finally, perhaps many years or centuries from now, she
will die. In either case she is free, and we are safe. . . ."

So it was done, and she lay as Allart had foreseen with
his *laran,* motionless on the bier in the great vaulted room
which was the chapel of Castle Aldaran.

"We shall bear her to Hali," Allart said, "and there lay
her within the chapel, forever."

Lord Aldaran took Renata's hand. "I have no heir; I am
alone and old. It will not be long. Kinswoman," he added,
looking into her eyes, "will you wed me by the *catenas?* I
have nothing to offer you save this: that if I acknowledge
your child my son and heir, there is none alive who can
gainsay me."

Renata bowed her head. "For the sake of Donal's son.
Let it be as you will, kinsman," and Aldaran held out his
arms and folded her in them. He kissed her, tenderly and
without passion, on the forehead; and with that the flood-
gates broke, and for the first time since Donal had been
stricken down before her, Renata began to weep, crying
and crying as if she would never cease.

Allart knew at last that this death would not strike down
Renata also. She would live, and someday she would even
recover. A day would come when Aldaran would proclaim
Donal's son heir to Aldaran in this very room, as Allart's
laran had foreseen. . . .

They rode forth the next morning at daybreak, Dorilys's
body sealed in her force-field within its casket, to bear her

to Hali, there to lie forever. Allart and Cassandra rode beside her. Above them, on the highest balcony of Aldaran, Renata and old Dom Mikhail watched them go, silent, motionless, bowed with mourning.

Allart thought, as they rode down the pathway, that he could never cease to mourn—for Donal, struck low in the midst of victory; for Dorilys, in her beauty and willfulness and pride; for the proud old man who stood above them, broken; and for Renata at his side, broken by grief.

I, too, am broken. I will be a king, and I do not want to reign. Yet I alone can save this realm from disaster, and I have no choice. He rode, head bowed, hardly seeing Cassandra at his side, until at last she reached to him and closed her slender six-fingered hand over his as they rode.

"A time will come, my dear love," she said, "when at last we may make songs, not war. My *laran* is not as yours. But I foresee it."

Allart thought, *I am not alone . . . and for her sake I must not grieve.* He raised his head, setting his face firmly against the future, and threw up a hand in final farewell to Castle Aldaran, which he would never see again, and in parting from Renata, from whom, he knew, he parted only for a little while.

As he rode down the path from Aldaran, following the cortege that bore the stormqueen to her last resting place, he prepared himself to meet on the road the men who were, even now, riding toward him to offer him the unwanted crown. Overhead the sky was gray and still, and it seemed that no thunder had ever troubled those quiet places.

HAWKMISTRESS!

Book One:

FALCONSWARD, in the Kilghard Hills

Chapter 1

Romilly was so weary that she could hardly stand on her feet.

It was dark in the mews, with no light but a carefully shielded lantern hanging from one rafter; but the eyes of the hawk were as bright, as untamed and filled with rage as ever. No, Romilly reminded herself; not rage alone, but terror.

She is afraid. She does not hate me; she is only afraid.

She could feel it all inside herself, that terror which pounded behind the rage, until she hardly knew which was herself—weary, her eyes burning, ready to fall into the dirty straw in an exhausted heap—and what was flooding into her mind from the brain of the hawk; hatred, fear, a wild frenzy of hunger for blood and for freedom.

Even as Romilly pulled the small sharp knife from her belt, and carefully cut a piece from the carcass placed conveniently near, she was shaking with the effort not to strike out, to pull away in a frenzy from the strap that held her— *no, not her, held the hawk*—to the falcon-block; *merciless leathers, cutting her feet*—

The hawk bated, wings flapping and thrashing, and Romilly jerked, with a convulsive reflex action, and the strip of raw meat fell into the straw. Romilly felt the struggle inside herself, the fury and frenzy of terror, as if the leather lines holding the big bird to the block were tying her too, cutting into her feet in agony . . . she tried to bend, to search for the meat calmly, but the emotions of the hawk, flooding into her mind, were too much for her. She flung her hands over her eyes and moaned aloud, letting it all become part of her, the crashing frenzy of wings, beating, beating . . . once, the first time this had happened to her, more than a year ago, she had run out of the mews in panic, running and running until she stumbled and skidded and fell, a hand's-breadth from the edges of the crags that tumbled down from Castle Falconsward to the very rocks of the Kadarin far below.

She must not let it go so deep into her mind, she must remember that she was human, was Romilly MacAran . . . she forced her breathing back to calm, remembering the words of the young *leronis* who had talked with her, briefly and in secret, before returning to Tramontana Tower.

You have a rare gift, child—one of the rarest of the gifts called laran. *I do not know why your father is so bitter, why he will not let you and your sister and brothers be tested and trained to the use of these gifts—surely he must know that an untrained telepath is a menace to herself and to everyone around her; he himself has the gift in full measure!*

Romilly knew; and she suspected the *leronis* knew, too, but out of loyalty to her father she would not speak of it outside the family, and the *leronis* was a stranger, after all; The MacAran had given her hospitality, as with any guest, but had coldly refused the purpose of the woman's visit, to test the children of Falconsward for *laran* gifts.

"You are my guest, *Domna* Marelie, but I have lost one son to the accursed Towers which blight our land and lure the sons of honest men—aye, and their daughters too—from home and family loyalties! You may shelter beneath this roof while the storm lasts, and have all that belongs to a guest in honor; but keep your prying hands from the minds of my children!"

Lost one son to the accursed Towers, Romilly thought, remembering her brother Ruyven who had fled to Neskaya Tower, across the Kadarin, four years ago. *And like to lose another, for even I can see that Darren is more fit for the Tower or the monastery of Nevarsin, than for the Heirship to Falconsward.* Darren would have been still in Nevarsin, as custom demanded of a nobleman's son in the hill country, and had wished to remain; but, obedient to their father's will, returned to his duties as the Heir.

How could Ruyven desert his brother that way? Darren cannot be Heir to Falconsward without his brother at his side. There was less than a year between the brothers, and they had always clung together as if they were twin-born; but they had gone together to Nevarsin, and only Darren had returned; Ruyven, he told her father, had gone to the Tower. Ruyven had sent a message, which only their father had read; but then he had flung it into the midden and from that moment he had never spoken Ruyven's name, and forbidden any other to speak it.

"I have but two sons," he said, his face like stone. "And one is in the monastery and the other at his mother's knee."

The *leronis* Marelie had frowned as she remembered, and said to Romilly, "I did my best, child, but he would not hear of it; so you must do the best you can to master your gift, or it will master you. And I can help you but little in what time I have; and I am sure that if he knew I had spoken to you like this, he would not shelter me this night. But I dare not leave you without some protection when your *laran* wakens. You are alone with it, and it will not be easy to master it alone, but it is not impossible, for I know of a few who have done it, your brother among them."

"You know my brother!" Romilly whispered.

"I know him, child—who, think you, sent me here to speak with you? You must not think he deserted you without cause," Marelie added gently, as Romilly's lips tightened, "He loves you well; he loves your father, too. But a cagebird cannot be a falcon, and a falcon cannot be a *kyorebni*. To return hither, to live his life without full use of his *laran*—that would be death for him, Romilly; can you understand? It would be like being made deaf and blind, without the company of his own kind."

"But what can this *laran* be, that he would forsake us all for it?" Romilly had cried, and Marelie had only looked sad.

"You will know that when your own *laran* wakens, my child."

And Romilly had cried out, "I hate *laran*! And I hate the Towers! They stole Ruyven from us!" and she had turned away, refusing to speak again to Marelie; and the *leronis* had sighed and said, "I cannot fault you for loyalty to your father, my child," and gone away to the room assigned to her, and departed the next morning, without further speech with Romilly.

That had been two years ago, and Romilly had tried to

put it from her mind; but in this last year she had begun to realize that she had the Gift of the MacArans in fullest measure—that strangeness in her mind which could enter into the mind of hawk, or hound, or horse, or any animal, and had begun to wish that she could have spoken with the *leronis* about it. . . .

But that was not even to be thought about. *I may have* laran, she told herself again and again, *but never would I abandon home and family for something of that sort!*

So she had struggled to master it alone; and now she forced herself to be calm, to breathe quietly, and felt the calming effect of the breathing composing her mind as well and even soothing, a little, the raging fury of the hawk; the chained bird was motionless, and the waiting girl knew that she was Romilly again, not a chained thing struggling in a frenzy to be free of the biting jesses. . . .

Slowly she picked that one bit of information out of the madness of fear and frenzy. *The jesses are too tight. They hurt her.* She bent, trying to send out soothing waves of calm all around her, into the mind of the hawk—*but she is too mad with hunger and terror to understand, or she would be quiet and know I mean her no harm.* She bent and tugged at the slitted straps which were wound about the hawk's legs. At the very back of her mind, carefully blanked out behind the soothing thoughts she was trying to send out to the hawk, Romilly's own fear struggled against what she was doing—once she had seen a young hawker lose an eye by getting too close to a frightened bird's beak-but she commanded the fear to be quiet and not interfere with what she had to do—if the hawk was in pain, the frenzy and fear would be worse, too.

She fumbled one-handed in the semidarkness, and blessed the persevering practice which had taught her all the falconer's knots, blindfolded and one-handed; old Davin had emphasized that, again and again, *most of the time you will be in a dark mews, and one hand will be busy about your hawk.* And so, hour after hour, she had tightened and loosened, tied and untied these same knots on twig after twig before ever she was let near the thin legs of any bird. The leather was damp with the sweat of her fingers, but she managed to loosen it slightly—not too much or the bird would be out of the jesses and would fly free, perhaps breaking her wings inside the walls of the mews, but loose enough so that it was no longer cutting into the leathery skin of the upper leg. Then she bent again and fumbled in the straw for the strip of meat, brushing the dirt from it. She knew it did not matter too much—birds, she knew, had to swallow dirt and stones to grind up their food inside their crops—but the dirty bits of straw clinging to the meat revolted her and she picked them fastidiously free and, once again, held out her gloved hand to the hawk on the block. Would the bird ever feed from her hand? Well, she must simply stay here until hunger overcame fear and the bird took the meat, or they would lose this hawk, too. And Romilly had resolved this would not happen.

She was glad, now, that she had let the other bird go. At first she had it in her mind, when she had found old Davin tossing and moaning with the summer fever, that she could save both of the hawks he had taken three days before. He had told her to let them both go, or they would starve, for they would not yet take food from any human hand. When he had captured them, he had promised Romilly that she should have the training of one of them while he was busied with the other. But then the fever had come to Falconsward, and when he had taken the sickness, he had told her to release them both—there would be other seasons, other hawks.

But they were valuable birds, the finest *verrin* hawks he had taken for many seasons. Loosing the larger of the two, Romilly had known Davin was right. A hawk like this was all but priceless—King Carolin in Carcosa had no finer birds, Davin had said, and he should know; Romilly's grandfather had been hawkmaster to the exiled King Carolin before the rebellion which had sent Carolin into the Hellers and probably to death, and the usurper Rakhal had sent most of Carolin's men to their own estates, surrounding himself with men he could trust.

It had been his own loss; Romilly's grandfather was known from the Kadarin to the Sea of Dalereuth as the finest man with hawks in the Kilghard Hills, and he had taught all his arts to Mikhail, now The MacAran, and to his commoner cousin Davin Hawkmaster. *Verrin* hawks, taken full-grown in the wild, were more stubborn than hatchlings reared to handling; a bird caught wild might let itself starve before it would take food from the hand, and better it should fly free to hatch others of the same fine breed, than die of fear and hunger in the mews, untamed.

So Romilly, with regret, had taken the larger of the birds from the mews, and slipped the jesses from the leathery skin of the leg; and, behind the stables, had climbed to a high rock and let her fly free. Her eyes had blurred with tears as she watched the falcon climb out of sight, and deep within her, something had flown with the hawk, in the wild ecstasy of rising, spiraling, free, *free* . . . for an instant Romilly had seen the dizzying panorama of Castle Falconsward lying below, deep ravines filled to the brim with forest, and far away a white shape, glimmering, that she knew to be Hali Tower on the shores of the Lake . . . *was her brother there, even now?* . . . and then she was alone again, shivering with the cold on the high rock, and her eyes were dazzled from staring into the light, and the hawk was gone.

She had returned to the mews, and her hand was already outstretched to take the other one and free it as well, but then the hawk's eyes had met her own for a moment, and there had been an instant when she knew, a strong and dizzying knowledge within her, *I can tame this one, I need not let her go, I can master her.*

The fever which had come to the castle and struck down Davin was almost her friend. On any ordinary day, Romilly would have had duties and lessons; but the governess he shared with her younger sister Mallina had a touch of the fever, too, and was shivering beside the fire in the school-room, having given Romilly permission to go to the stables and ride, or take her lesson-book or her needlework to the conservatory high in the castle, and study there among the leaves and flowers—the light still hurt *Domna* Calinda's eyes. Old Gwennis, who had been Romilly's nurse when she and her sister were little children, was busy with Mallina, who had a touch of fever, though she was not danger-ously ill. And the Lady Luciella, their stepmother, would not stir from the side of nine-year-old Rael, for he had the fever in its most dangerous form, the debilitating sweats and inability to swallow.

So Romilly had promised herself a delicious day of free-dom in stables and hawk-house—was *Domna* Calinda really enough of a fool to think she would spend a day free of lessons over her stupid lesson-book or needlework? But she had found Davin, too, sick of the fever, and he had welcomed her coming—his apprentice was not yet skilled enough to go near the untrained birds, though he was good enough to feed the others and clean the mews—and so he had ordered Romilly to release them both. And she had started to obey—

But this hawk was *hers*! Never mind that it sat on its block, angry and sullen, red eyes veiled with rage and terror, bating wildly at the slightest movement near her, the wings exploding in the wild frenzy of flapping and thrashing; it was hers, and soon or late, it would know of the bond between them.

But she had known it would be neither quick nor easy. She had reared eyasses—young birds hatched in the mews or captured still helpless, accustomed before they were feathered to feed from a hand or glove. But this hawk had learned to fly, to hunt and feed itself in the wild; they were better hunters than hawks reared in captivity, but harder to tame; two out of five such birds, more or less, would let themselves die of hunger before they would feed. The thought that this could happen to *her* hawk was a dread Romilly refused to face. Somehow, she would, she *must* bridge the gulf between them.

The falcon bated again, thrashing furious wings, and Romilly struggled to maintain the sense of *herself,* not merging into the terror and fury of the angry bird, at the same time trying to send out waves of calm. *I will not hurt you, lovely one. See, here is food.* But it ignored the signal, flapping angrily, and Romilly struggled hard not to shrink back in terror, not to be overcome with the flooding, surging waves of rage and terror she could feel radiating from the chained bird.

Surely, this time, the beating wings had flapped into quiet sooner than before? The falcon was tiring. Was it growing weaker, would it fight its way down into death and exhaustion before it was ready to surrender and feed from the gauntlet? Romilly had lost track of time, but as the hawk quieted and her brain cleared, so that she knew again that she was Romilly and not the frenzied bird, her breathing quieted again and she let the gauntlet slip for a moment from her hand. Her wrist and shoulder felt as if they were

going to drop off, but she as not sure whether it was because the gauntlet was too heavy for her, (she had spent
hours holding it at arm's length, enduring the pain of
cramped muscles and tension, to accustom herself to its
weight) or whether it had something to do with the
frenzied beating of her wings . . . no. No, she must remember which
was herself, which the hawk. She leaned back against the
rough wall behind her, half-closing her eyes. She was almost asleep on her feet. But she must not sleep, nor move.

You don't leave a hawk at this stage, Davin had told her.
Not for a moment. She remembered asking, when she was
small, not even to eat? And he had snorted, "If it comes
to that, you can go without food and water longer than a
hawk can; if you can't out-wait a hawk you're taming, you
have no business around one."

But he had been speaking of himself. It had not occurred
to him, then, that a girl could tame a hawk or wish to. He
had indulged her wish to learn all the arts of the falconer—
after all, the birds might one day be hers, even though
she had two older brothers; it would not be the first time
Falconsward had passed down through the female line, to
the strong husband of the woman heir. Nor was it unknown
for a woman to ride out, with a docile and well-trained
bird; even Romilly's stepmother had been known to ride
forth, a delicately trained bird, no larger than a pigeon,
adorning her wrist like a rare jewel. Although Luciella
would never have touched one of the *verrin* hawks, and the
thought that her stepdaughter would wish to do so had
never entered her mind.

But why not? Romilly asked herself in a rage. *I was born
with the MacAran Gift; the laran which would give me mastery over hawk or horse or hound. Not* laran, *I will never
admit that I have that evil curse of the Hastur-kinfolk; but
the ancient Gift of the MacArans . . . I have a right to that,
it is not* laran, *not really. . . . I may be a woman, but I am
as much a MacAran as my brothers!*

Again she stepped toward the hawk, the meat extended
on the gauntlet, but the hawk thrust up its head and the
beady eyes stared coldly at Romilly; it moved away, with
a little hop, as far away as the dimensions of the block
allowed. She could sense that the jesses were no longer
giving it pain. She murmured small sounds of reassurance,

and her own hunger came surging up inside her. She should have brought some food in her pocket for herself, she had seen Davin, often enough, thrust cold meats and bread into his pouch so that he could munch on something while he waited out the long stay with a hawk. If only she could sneak away for a moment to the kitchen or pantry—and to the privy, too; her bladder ached with tension. Her father or brothers could have stepped away, turned aside for a moment, undone breeches and relieved themselves against the wall, but Romilly, though she contemplated it for a moment, would have had too many strings and fastenings to undo, even though she was wearing a pair of Ruyven's old breeches. But she sighed, staying where she was.

If you can't wait out a hawk, Davin had said, *you have no business around one.* That was the only real disadvantage she could think of for a girl, around the stables, and this was the first time it had been any real disadvantage for her.

You're hungry too, she said silently to the hawk, *come on, here's food, just because I'm hungry doesn't mean you can't eat, you stubborn thing, you!* But the hawk made no move to touch the food. It moved a little, and for a moment Romilly feared it would explode into another of those wild bursts of bating. But it stayed still, and after a moment she relaxed into the motionless quiet of her vigil.

When my brothers were my age, it was taken for granted— a MacAran son should train his own hound, his own horse, his own hawk. Even Rael, he is only nine, but already Father insists he shall teach his dogs manners. When she had been younger—before Ruyven had left them, before Darren was sent to Nevarsin—her father had been proud to let Romilly work with horses and hounds.

He used to say; Romilly's a MacAran, she has the Gift; there's no horse she can't ride, no dog she can't make friends with, the very bitches come and whelp in her lap. He was proud of me. He used to tell Ruyven and Darren that I would be a better MacAran than either of them, tell them to watch my way with a horse.

But now—now it makes him angry.

Since Ruyven had gone, Romilly had been sternly turned over to her stepmother, expected to stay indoors, to "behave like a lady." She was now almost fifteen; her younger sister Mallina had already begun dressing her hair with a woman's butterfly-clasp, Mallina was content to sit and learn embroidery stitches, to ride decorously in a lady's saddle, to play with little stupid lap-dogs instead of the sensible herding-dogs and working-dogs around the pastures and stables. Mallina had grown into a fool, and the dreadful thing was that their father preferred her as a fool and wished audibly that Romilly would emulate her.

Never. I'd rather be dead than stay inside the house all the time and stitch like a lady. Mallina used to ride well, and now she's like Luciella, soft and flabby, she startles away when a horse moves its head near her, she couldn't ride for half an hour at a good gallop without falling off gasping like a fish in a tree, and now, like Luciella, she simpers and twitters, and the worst thing is, Father likes them that way!

There was a little stir at the far end of the hawk-house, and one of the eyasses there screamed, the wild screaming sound of an untrained fledgling that scents food. The sound sent Romilly's hawk into a wild explosion of bating, and Romilly, one with the mad flapping of wings, the fierce hunger gripping like claws in her belly, knew that the hawk-master's boy had come into the hawk-house to feed the other birds. He went from one to another, slowly, muttering to them, and Romilly knew it was near sunset; she had been there since mid-morning. He finished his work and raised his head to see her.

"Mistress Romilly! What are you doing here, *damisela*?"

At his voice the hawk bated again, and Romilly felt again the dreadful ache, as if her hands and arms would drop off into the straw. She struggled to keep herself free of frenzy, fear, anger, blood-lust—*blood bursting forth, exploding into her mouth under tearing beak and talons* . . . and forced herself to the low tone that would not further terrify the frenzied bird.

"I am manning this hawk. Go away, Ker, your work is finished and you will frighten her."

"But I heard Davin say the hawk's to be released, and The MacAran's in a rage about it," Ker mumbled. "He didna' want to lose the *verrin* birds, and he's threatened Davin wi' being turned off, old man that he is, if he loses them—"

"Well, Father's not going to lose this one, unless you

frighten her out of her senses," Romilly said crisply, "Go
away, Ker, before she bates again—" for she could feel the
trembling build in the bird's body and mind, she felt if
that flapping frenzy exploded again she would collapse with
exhaustion, scream herself in fury and frustration. It made
her voice sharp. "Go away!"

Her own agitation communicated itself to the bird; it
burst into the frenzied flapping of wings again, surges of
hatred and terror coming and going, threatening to drown
all her own awareness and identity. She fought it, silently,
trying to cling to calm, to send out calm to the terrified
bird. *There, there, lovely one, no one shall harm you, see,
here is food . . .* and when she knew who or where she was
again, the boy had gone.

He had left the door open, and there was a draught of
cold air from the evening mists; and soon the night's rain
or snow would start to fall—damn the wretch! She stole
for a few seconds on tiptoe away from the block to draw
the door closed—it would avail her nothing to tame this
hawk if all the birds died with the cold! Once away from
the bird's side, she began to wonder what she was doing
here and why. How was it that she thought that she, a
young woman, could accomplish something at which even
the skilled Davin failed two out of five times? She should
have told the boy that the bird was at the end of exhaustion, have him come and take over . . . she had seen what
he could do with a wild, raging, exhausted stallion from the
wild herds of the ravines and outer hills. An hour, maybe
two, with her father at one end of a lunge line and the
stallion at the other, and he would come to the bridle,
lower his big head and rub it against The MacAran's
chest . . . surely he could still save this bird, too. She was
weary and cold and exhausted, she longed for the old days
when she could climb into her father's lap and tell him all
her troubles. . . .

Then the voice struck through to her, angry and cold—
but there was tenderness in it too; the voice of Mikhail,
lord of Falconsward, The MacAran.

"Romilly!" he said, shocked but compassionate, "Daughter, what do you think you are doing? This is no task for
a maiden, manning a *verrin* hawk! I gave orders to that
wretch Davin and he lies slack in bed while one hawk is

mishandled by a child, and the other, I doubt not, starved on its block. . . ."

Romilly could hardly speak through the tears threatening to surge up inside her and break her control.

"The other hawk flies free to hatch more of her kind," she said, "I released her myself at dawn. And this one has not been mishandled, Father—"

At the words and movement the hawk bated again, more fiercely than before, and Romilly gasped, struggling to keep her sense of self against the fury of thrashing wings, the hunger, the blood-lust, the frenzy to break free, fly free, dash itself to death against the dark enclosing beams . . . but it subsided, and Romilly, crooning to the bird, sensed another mind touching hers, sending out waves of calm . . . *so that's how Father does it,* she thought with a corner of her mind, brushed a dripping lock of hair out of her eyes and stepped toward the hawk again.

Here is food, come and eat . . . nausea rushed through her stomach at the smell and sight of the dead meat on the gauntlet. *Yes, hawks feed on fresh-caught food, they must be tamed by starvation into feeding on carrion. . . .*

Abruptly the touching of minds, girl, man, hawk, broke, and Mikhail of MacAran said harshly, "Romilly, what am I to do with you, girl? You have no business here in the hawk-house; it is no work for a lady." His voice softened. "No doubt Davin put you up to this; and I'll deal with him. Leave the meat and go, Romilly. Sometimes a hawk will feed from an empty block when she's hungry enough, and if she does we can keep her; if not, Davin can release her tomorrow, or that boy of his can do something for once to earn his porridge! It's too late tonight for her to fly. She won't die, and if she does, it won't be the first hawk we've lost. Go in, Romilly, get a bath and go to your bed. Leave the hawks to the hawkmaster and his boy—that's why they're here, love, my little girl doesn't need to do this. Go in the house, Romi, child."

She swallowed hard, feeling tears break through

"Father, please," she begged, "I'm sure I can tame her. Let me stay, I beg of you."

"Zandru's hells," the MacAran swore, "If but one of your brothers had your strength and skill, girl! But I'll not have it said that my daughters must work in mews and stable! Get you inside, Romilly, and not another word from you!"

His face was angry and implacable; the hawk bated again, at his anger, and Romilly felt it surging through her too, an explosion of fury, frustration, anger, terror. She dropped the gauntlet and ran, sobbing with rage, and behind her, her father strode out of the mews and locked it behind him.

Romilly went to her room, where she emptied her aching bladder, ate a little bread and honey and drank a cup of milk from the tray one of the serving-women brought her; but her mind was still with the chained, suffering, starving hawk in the mews.

It would not eat, and soon it would die. It had begun, just a little, to trust Romilly . . . surely, the last two or three times it had bated, before her father had disturbed them, it had quieted sooner, feeling her soothing touch. But now it would surely die.

Romilly began to draw off her shoes. The MacAran was not to be disobeyed, certainly not by his daughter. Even Ruyven, six feet tall and almost a man, had never dared open disobedience until the final break. Romilly, Darren, Mallina—all of them obeyed his word and seldom dared even a look of defiance; only the youngest, spoilt little Rael, would sometimes tease and wheedle and coax in the face of his father's edicts.

In the next room, past the glass doors separating their chambers, Mallina already slept in her cot, her pale-red hair and lacy nightgown pale against the pillow. Lady Calinda had long gone to her bed, and old Gwennis drowsed in a chair beside the sleeping Mallina; and although Romilly was not glad of her sister's illness, she was glad that the old nurse was busy about her sister; if she had seen Romilly in her current state—ruefully, Romilly surveyed her filthy and sweat-soaked clothes—there would have been an argument, a lecture, trouble.

She was exhausted, and thought longingly of clean clothes, a bath, her own soft bed. She had surely done all she could to save the hawk. Perhaps she should abandon the effort. It might feed from the block; but once it had done that, though it would not die, it could never be tamed enough to feed from the hawker's hand or gauntlet, and

must be released. Well, let it go then. And if, in its state
of exhaustion and terror, it would not feed from the block,
and died . . . well, hawks had died before this at
Falconsward.

*But never one with whom I had gone so deeply into
rapport. . . .*

And once again, if she were still standing, exhausted and
tense, in the hawk-house, she felt that furious frenzy building up again . . . even safely tied to the block, the hawk in
her terrified threshing could break her wings . . . never to
fly again, to sit dumb and broken on a perch, or to die . . .
*like me inside a house, wearing women's clothes and
stitching at foolish embroideries. . . .*

And then she knew she would not let it happen that way.

Her father, she thought with detachment, would be very
angry. This time he might even give her the beating he had
threatened last time she disobeyed him. He had never, yet,
laid a hand on her; her governess had spanked her a time
or two when she was very small, but mostly she had been
punished with confinement, with being forbidden to ride,
with harsh words or loss of some promised treat or outing.

This time he will surely beat me, she thought, and the
unfairness surged within her; *I will be beaten because I cannot resign myself to let the poor thing die or thrash itself to
death in terror. . . .*

*Well, I shall be beaten then. No one ever died of a beating,
I suppose.* Romilly knew already that she was going to defy
her father. She shrank from the thought of his rage, even
more than from the imagined blows, but she knew she
would never be able to face herself again if she sat quietly
in her chamber and let the hawk die.

She should have released them both yesterday at dawn,
as Davin said. Perhaps she deserved a beating for that disobedience; but having begun, it would be too cruel to stop
now. At least, Romilly thought, she could understand why
she was being beaten; the hawk would not understand the
reasons for the long ordeal till it was finished. Her father
himself had always told her that a good animal handler
never began anything with hawk or hound or horse, that
he could not finish; it was not fair to a dumb creature who
knew nothing of reason.

If, he had told them once, *you break faith with a human*

being for some reason which seems good to you, you can at least explain to him or her. But if you break faith with a dumb creature, you have hurt that creature in a way which is unforgivable, because you can never make it understand. Never in her life had Romilly heard her father speak of faith in any religion, or speak of any God except in a curse; but that time, even as he spoke, she had sensed the depths of his belief and knew that he spoke from the very depths of his being. She was disobeying him, yes; but in a deeper sense she was doing what he had taught her to think right; and so, even if he should beat her for it, he would one day know that what she had done was both right and necessary.

Romilly took another swallow of water—she could face hunger, if she must, but thirst was the real torture; Davin usually kept a water pail within reach when he was working a hawk, and Romilly had forgotten to set a pail and dipper within reach. Then she slipped quietly out of the room. With luck, the hawk would "break" before dawn—would feed from the gauntlet, and sleep. This interruption might lose the hawk, she knew—if it did not soon feed, it would die—but at least she would know that she, who had confined it there, had not been the one to break faith and abandon it to death.

She had already left the chamber when she turned and went back for her flint-and-steel lighter; doubtless, her father or the hawkmaster's boy would have extinguished the lantern and she would have to relight it. Gwennis, in the room beyond the glass doors, stirred and yawned, and Romilly froze, but the nurse only bent to feel Mallina's forehead to see if her fever had broken, sighed, and settled back in her chair without a glance in Romilly's direction.

On noiseless feet, she crept down the stairs.

Even the dogs were sleeping. Two of the great grey-brown hounds called Rousers were asleep right across the doorway; they were not fierce dogs, and would not bite or attack even an intruder unless he offered to hurt them, but they were noisy creatures, and in their friendly, noisy barking, their function was to rouse the household against intruder or friend. But Romilly had known both dogs since they were whelped, had given them their first solid tidbits when they left off sucking their dam; she shoved them slightly away from the door, and the dogs, feeling a familiar and beloved hand, only snuffled a little in their sleep and let her pass.

The light in the hawk-house had indeed been extinguished. As she stepped across the doorsill she thought of an old ballad her own mother had sung in her childhood, of how, at night, the birds talked among themselves when no human creature was near. She found she was walking tip-toe, half expecting to overhear what they might be saying. But the birds in the mews where the tame ones were kept were only hunched forms on the blocks, fast asleep, and she felt from them only a confused silence.

I wonder if they are telepathic among themselves, she wondered, *if they are aware of one another's fear or pain?* Even the *leronis* had not been able to tell her this. Now, she supposed, most of the birds, at least, were head-blind, without telepathic awareness or *laran,* or they would all be awake and restless now; for Romilly could still feel, beating up at her in waves of dread and fury, of hunger and rage, the emotions of the great *verrin* hawk.

She lighted the lamp, with hands that shook. Father had never believed, then, that it would feed from the block; he certainly knew that no hawk would feed in darkness. How could he have done that? Even if he was angry with her, Romilly, he need not have deprived her hawk of its last chance at life.

Now it was all to do again. She saw the dead meat lying on the block; unpecked, untouched. The hawk had not fed. The meat was beginning to smell rancid, and Romilly had to overcome her own revulsion as she handled the dead thing—*ugh, if I were a hawk I wouldn't touch this carrion either.*

The hawk bated again in its frenzy and Romilly stepped closer, crooning, murmuring calm. And after a few seconds the thrashing wings quieted. Could it be that the hawk remembered her? Perhaps the interruption had not wholly wrecked her chances. She slid her hand into the gauntlet, cut a fresh strip of meat from the carcass and held it out to the bird, but again it seemed that the disgust of the dead smell was more sickening and overpowering than it had been.

Was she feeling, then, what the hawk felt? For a moment, in a dizzy wave of sickness, Romilly met the great yellow-green eyes of the bird, and it seemed to her that she was badly balanced on some narrow space without any proper place to stand, unfamiliar leather chafing her ankles, and that some strange and hateful *presence* was there, trying to force her to swallow some revolting filthy mess, absolutely unfit to eat . . . for a split second Romilly was again a child too young to speak, tied into her high chair and her nurse was spooning some horrid nasty stuff down her throat and she could only struggle and scream. . . .

Shaken and sick, she stepped back, letting the dead carcass fall to the floor. Was *that* how the hawk regarded her? She should have let the hawk fly, she could never live with such hatred . . . *do all the animals we master hate us like that? Why, then, a trainer of horses and hounds is more evil than a molester of children . . . and he who takes a hawk from the sky, to chain it on a block, he is no better than a rapist, a violator of women. . . .* But the bating, struggling hawk was off her perch this time, and Romilly moved forward, patiently adjusting the block so that the hawk could find a secure place to stand, until it found its feet and balanced securely again.

Then she stood silent, trying not to trouble the hawk even with breath, while the battle went on inside her mind. Part of her fought with the chained hawk, terror and rage contending for place, but Romilly, in her own struggle for interior calm, filled her mind with the memory of the last time she had hunted with her own favorite falcon . . . soaring upward with it, striking, and something inside her remembered clearly that sudden feeling, which in herself would have been pride and pleasure, as the hawk fed from her glove . . . and she knew it would have been stronger still if she herself had trained the hawk; that pleasure in accomplishment, that sense of sudden union with the bird, would have been deeper still.

And she had shared the delight, inarticulate, impossible to frame in words, but a joy deep and swelling, when her favorite bitch brought her puppies to her; the animal's pleasure at the caress was something like the love she felt for her own father, her joy and pride at his rare praise. And even though she had felt the real pain and fear when a young horse struggled against bridle and saddle, she had shared in the communion and trust between horse and rider, and known it for real love, too; so that she loved to ride breakneck, knowing she could come to no harm while the horse carried her, and she let the horse go at her own pace and pleasure, sharing the delight in the running. . . .

No, she thought, it is not a violation to teach or train an animal, no more than when nurse taught me to eat porridge, even though I thought it nasty at first and wanted nothing but milk; because if she had fed me upon milk and babies' pap after my teeth were grown, I would have been sickly and weak, and needed solid food to grow strong. I had to learn even to eat what was good for me, and to wear clothes even though, no doubt, I would sooner, then, have been wrapped in my blankets like a swaddled baby! And later I had to learn to cut my meat with knife and fork instead of gnawing at it with fingers and teeth as an animal would do. And now I am glad to know all these things.

When the hawk bated again, Romilly did not withdraw from the fear and terror, but let herself share it, whispering half aloud, "Trust me, lovely one, you will fly free again and we will hunt together, you and I, as friends, not as master and slave, I promise you. . . ."

She filled her mind with images of soaring free above the trees in sunlight, trying to open her mind to the memory of the last time she had hunted; seeing the bird come spiraling down with its prey, of tearing apart the freshly killed meat, so she could give the bird its share of the kill . . . and again, with an urgency that made her feel sick, she felt the maddening hunger, the hawk's mind-picture of striking, fresh blood flowing into her mouth . . . her own human revulsion, the hawk's hunger, so mingled in her that she hardly knew which was which. Sensing that hunger, she held out the strip of rabbithorn meat, but now the smell revolted her as much as the hawk; she felt that she would vomit.

But you must eat and grow strong, *preciosa,* she sent out the thought again and again, feeling the hawk's hunger, her weakening struggles. *Preciosa; that is your name, that is what I will call you, and I want you to eat and grow strong, Preciosa, so we can hunt together, but first you must trust me and eat . . . I want you to eat because I love you and I want to share this with you, but first you must learn to eat from my hand . . . eat, Preciosa, my lovely one, my darling, my beauty, won't you eat this? I don't want you to die. . . .*

Hours, she felt, must have crawled by while she stood there, tensed into the endless struggle with the weakening hawk. Every time the frenzied bating was weaker, the surges of hunger so intense that Romilly's own body cramped with pain. The hawk's eyes were as bright as ever, as filled with terror, and from those eyes it all flooded into Romilly, too, in growing despair.

The hawk was weakening, surely; if she did not feed soon, after all this struggle, she would die; she had taken no food since she was captured four days ago. Would she die, still fighting?

Maybe her father had been right, maybe no woman had the strength for this. . . .

And then she remembered the moment when she had looked out from the hawk's eyes and she, Romilly Mac-Aran, had not even been a memory, and she had been something other than human. Fear and despair flooded her; she saw herself ripping off the gauntlet, beaten to take up her needlework, letting walls close round her forever. A prisoner, more a prisoner than the chained hawk, who, at least, would now and then have a chance to fly, and to feel again the soaring ecstasy of flight and freedom. . . .

No. Rather than live like that, prisoner, she too would let herself die. . . .

No; there must be a way, if only I can find it.

She would not surrender, never admit that the hawk had beaten her. She was Romilly MacAran, born with the Mac-Aran Gift, and she was stronger than any hawk. She would not let the hawk die . . . no, it was not "the hawk" any more, it was Preciosa, whom she loved, and she would fight for her life even if she must stand here till they dropped together and died. One more time she reached out, moving fearlessly into the bird-mind, this time aware fully of herself as a shadowy and now familiar torture in Preciosa's mind, and the sickening, rank smell of the meat on the gauntlet . . . for a moment she thought Preciosa would go into another frenzy of bating, but this time the bird bent its head toward the meat on the glove.

Romilly held her breath. *Yes, yes, eat and grow stronger . . .* and then Romilly was overcome by sickness,

feeling that she would vomit where she stood from the
sickening rotten smell of the meat.

*Now she wants to eat, she would trust me, but she cannot
eat this now; perhaps if she had taken it before she was so
weak, but not now . . . she is no carrion feeder. . . .*

Romilly was overcome by despair. She had brought the
freshest food she could find in the kitchens, but now it was
not fresh enough; the hawk was beginning to trust her,
might perhaps have taken food from her gauntlet, if she
had brought something she could actually have managed to
swallow without sickness . . . a rat scurried in the straw,
and she discovered that she was looking out from the bird's
eyes with real hunger at the little animal. . . .

Dawn was near. In the garden outside she heard the
chirp of a sleepy wraithbird, and from the cotes the half-
wakened chirp of the caged pigeons who were sometimes
roasted for special guests or for the sick. Even before the
thought was clear in her mind she was moving, and at the
back of her thoughts she heard herself say, *the fowl-keeper
will be very angry with me, I am not allowed to touch the
pigeons without leave,* but the hunger flooding through her
mind, the bird-mind, would not be denied. Romilly flung
away the piece of dead rabbithorn meat, flinging it on the
midden; it would rot there, or some scavenger would find
it, or one of the dogs who was less fastidious in feeding.
There was a fluttering, flapping stir as she thrust her hand
into the pigeon-cote and brought out one, flapping its wings
and squawking; its fear filled her with something that was
half pain and half excitement, adrenalin running through
her body and cramping her legs and buttocks with familiar
dread; but Romilly had been farm-bred and was not squeamish; fowl were for the pot in return for safe cotes and
lifelong grain. She held the struggling bird for an instant
for brief regret between her hands, then fought one-handed
to hold it while she got the gauntlet on again. She thrust
into the hawk-mind, without words, a swift sharp awareness
of hunger and fresh food . . . then, with one decisive movement, wrung the pigeon's neck and thrust the still-warm
corpse toward Preciosa.

For an instant, one more time, it seemed that the bird
was about to explode into a last frenzy of bating, and Romilly felt the sickness of failure . . . but this time the hawk

bent her head and with a thrust so swift that Romilly could not follow it with her eyes, stabbed with the strong beak, so hard that Romilly staggered under the killing thrust. Blood spurted; the hawk pecked one more time and began to eat.

Romilly sobbed aloud through the flooding ecstasy of strength filling her as she felt the bird tear, swallow, tear again at the fresh meat. "Oh, you beauty," she whispered, "You beauty, you precious, you wonder!"

When the hawk had fed . . . she could feel the dulling of hunger, and even her own thirst receded . . . she set it on the block again, and slipped a hood over Preciosa's head. Now it would sleep, and wake remembering where its food came from. She must leave orders that food for this hawk must be very fresh; she would have birds or mice killed freshly for it until Preciosa could hunt for herself. It would not be long. It was an intelligent bird, or it would not have struggled so long; Romilly, still lightly in link with the bird, knew that now Preciosa would recognize her as the source of food, and that one day they would hunt together.

Her arm felt as if it would fall off; she slipped off the heavy gauntlet, and wiped her forehead with a sweaty arm. She could clearly see light outside the hawk-house; she had stood there all night. And as she took conscious note of the light—soon the household would be stirring—she saw her father and Davin standing in the doorway.

"Mistress Romilly! Have you been here all night?" Davin asked, shocked and concerned.

But her father's temples were swollen with rage.

"You wretched girl, I ordered you back to the house! Do you think I am going to let you defy me like this? Come out of there and leave the hawk—"

"The hawk has fed," said Romilly, "I saved her for you. Doesn't that mean anything?" And then all her fury flooded through her again, and like a bating hawk, she exploded. "Beat me if you want to—if it's more important to you that I should act like a lady and let a harmless bird die! If that is being a lady, I hope I shall never be one! I have the *laran*—" in her anger she used the word without thinking, "and I don't think the gods make mistakes; it must mean that I am meant to use it! It isn't my fault that I have the MacAran Gift when my brother doesn't, but it was given to me so that now I didn't have to stand by and let Preciosa die. . . ." and she stopped, swallowing back sobs that threatened to choke her voice entirely.

"She's right, sir," said old Davin slowly. "She's not the first lady of MacAran to have the Gift, and, be the gods willing, she won't be the last."

The MacAran glared; but he stepped forward, took up a feather, and gently stroked the breast of the drowsing hawk. "A beautiful bird," he said, at last. "What did you call her? Preciosa? A good name, too. You have done well, daughter." It was wrenched out of him, unwilling; then he scowled, and it was like the flood of fury flooding through the hawk.

"Get you gone from here, inside the house, and have a bath and fresh clothes—I will not have you filthy as a stable wench! Go and call your maid, and don't let me see you beyond the house door again!" And as she slipped past him she could feel that blow he started to give her, then held back—he could not bring himself to strike anything, and she *had* saved the life of the hawk. But out of his rage of frustration he shouted after her at the top of his lungs, "You haven't heard the last of this, damn you, Romilly!"

Chapter 2

Romilly stared out the window, her head in her hands. The great red sun was angling downward from noon; two of the small moons stood, pale dayshine reflections, in the sky, and the distant line of the Kilghard Hills lured her mind out there in the sky, with the clouds and the birds flying. A page of finished sums, put side, lay before her on the wooden desk, and a still-damp page of neatly copied maxims from the *cristoforo* Book of Burdens; but she did not see them, nor did she hear the voice of her governess; Calinda was fussing at Mallina for her badly blotted pages.

This afternoon, when I have done flying Preciosa to the lure, I will have Windracer saddled, and carry Preciosa before me on my saddle, hooded, to accustom her to the horse's smell and motion. I cannot trust her yet to fly free, but it will not be long. . . .

Across the room her brother Rael scuffled his feet noisily, and Calinda rebuked him with a silent shake of her head. Rael, Romilly thought, was dreadfully spoiled now—he had been so dangerously ill, and this was his first day back in the schoolroom. Silence fell over the children, except for the noisy scratching of Mallina's pen, and the almost-noiseless click of Calinda's knotting-pins; she was making a woolly undervest for Rael, and when it was finished, Romilly thought, not without malice, then she would only face the problem of getting Rael to wear it!

Her eyes glazed in a drowse of perfect boredom, Romilly stared out the window, until the quiet was interrupted by a noisy wail from Mallina.

"Curse this pen! It sheds blots like nuts in autumn! Now I have blotted another sheet!"

"Hush, Mallina," said the governess severely. "Romilly, read to your sister the last of the maxims I set you to copy from the Book of Burdens."

Sighing, recalled against her will to the schoolroom, Romilly read sullenly aloud. "A poor worker blames only the tool in his hand."

"It is not the fault of the pen if you cannot write without blots," Calinda reproved, and came to guide the pen in her pupil's hand. "See, hold your hand so—"

"My fingers ache," Mallina grumbled, "Why must I learn to write anyway, spoiling my eyes and making my hands hurt? None of the daughters of High Crags can write, or read either, and they are none the worse for it; they are already betrothed, and it is no loss to them!"

"You should think yourself lucky," said the governess sternly, "Your father does not wish his daughters to grow up in ignorance, able only to sew and spin and embroider, without enough learning even to write 'Apple and nut conserve' on your jars at harvest time! When I was a girl, I had to fight for even so much learning as that! Your father is a man of sense, who knows that his daughters will need learning as much as do his sons! So you will sit there until you have filled another sheet without a single blot. Romilly, let me see your work. Yes, that is very neat. While I check your sums, will you hear your brother read from his book?"

Romilly rose with alacrity, to join Rael at his seat; anything was better than sitting motionless at her desk! Calinda bent to guide Mallina's hand on her pen, and Rael leaned against Romilly's shoulder; she gave the child a surreptitious hug, then dutifully pointed her finger at the first hand-lettered line of the primer. It was very old; she had been taught to read from this same book, and so, she thought, had Ruyven and Darren before her—the book had been made, and sewn, by her own grandmother when her gather had first learned to read; and written in the front were the crudely sprawled letters that said *Mikhail Mac-Aran, his own book.* The ink was beginning to fade a little, but it was still perfectly legible.

"The horse is in the stable," Rael spelled out slowly,

"The fowl is in the nest. The bird is in the air. The tree is in the wood. The boat is on the water. The nut is on the tree. The boy is in the—" he scowled at the word and guessed. "Barn?"

Romilly chuckled softly. "I am sure he wishes he were, as you do," she whispered, "but that's not right, Rael. Look, what is that first letter? Spell it out—"

"The boy is in the kitchen," he read glumly. "The bread is in the—pan?"

"Rael, you're guessing again," she said. "Look at the letters. You know better than that."

"The bread is in the oven."

"That's right. Try the next page, now."

"The cook bakes the bread. The farmer—" he hesitated, moving his lips, scowling at the page. "Gathers?"

"That's right, go on."

"The farmer gathers the nuts. The soldier rides the horse. The groom puts the saddle on the horse. Romy, when can I read something that makes sense?"

Romilly chuckled again. "When you know your letters a bit better," she said. "Let me see your copybook. Yes, your letters are written there, but look, they sprawl all over the line like ducks waddling, when they should march along neatly like soldiers—see where Calinda ruled the line for you?" She put the primer aside. "But I will tell Calinda you know your lesson, shall I?"

"Then perhaps we can go out to the stables," whispered Rael. "Romy, did father beat you for taming the hawk? I heard Mother say he should."

I doubt that not at all, Romilly thought, but the Lady Luciella was Rael's mother and she would not speak evil of her to the child. And Luciella had never been really unkind to her. She said "No, I was not beaten; father said I did well—he would have lost the hawk otherwise, and *verrin* hawks are costly and rare. And this one was near to starving on its block—"

"How did you do it? Can I tame a hawk some day? I would be afraid, they are so fierce—"

But he had raised his voice, and Calinda looked up and frowned at them. "Rael, Romilly, are you minding the lesson?"

"No, *mestra,*" said Romilly politely, "he has finished, he read two pages in the primer with only one mistake. May we go now?"

"You know you are not supposed to whisper and chatter when you are working," said the governess, but she looked tired, too. "Rael, bring me your sheet of letters. Oh, this is disgraceful," she said, frowning, "Why, they are all over the page! A big boy like you should write better than this! Sit down, now, and take your pen!"

"I don't want to," Rael sulked, "My head hurts."

"If your head hurts, I shall tell your mother you are not well enough to ride after your lesson," said Calinda, hiding the smile that sprang to her lips, and Rael glumly sat down, curled his fist around the pen and began to print another series of tipsy letters along the line, his tongue just protruding between his teeth, scowling over the page.

"Mallina, go and wash the ink from your fingers. Romilly, bring your embroidery-work, and you may as well bring Mallina's too," said the governess, bending over Rael's desk. Romilly, frowning, went to the cupboard and pulled out her workbasket and her sister's. She was quick enough with her pen, but, she thought angrily, *put a needle in my hand and I might as well have a hoof instead of fingers!*

"I will show you one more time how to do the knot-stitch neatly," said Calinda, taking the grubby, wrinkled linen in her own hands, trying to smooth it, while Romilly pricked her finger threading the needle and yelped like a puppy. "This is a disgrace, Romilly; why, Rael could do better if he tried, I do believe!"

"Then why not let Rael do it?" Romilly scowled.

"For shame, a big girl, almost fifteen, old enough to be married," Calinda said, glancing over Rael's shoulder. "Why, what have you written here?"

Startled by the tone in the woman's voice, Romilly looked over her small brother's shoulder. In uneven printing, he had lettered *I wish my brother Ruyven come home.*

"Well, I do," said Rael, blinking his eyes hard and digging his fists into them.

"Tear it up, quickly," said Calinda, taking the paper and suiting the action to the word. "If your father saw it—you know he has ordered that your brother's name is not to be mentioned in this house!"

"I didn't mention it, I only printed it," said Rael angrily, "and he's *my* brother and I'll talk about him if I want to! Ruyven Ruyven, Ruyven—so *there*!"

"Hush, hush, Rael," said Calinda, "We all—" she broke off, thinking better of what she had begun to say, but Romilly heard it with her new senses, as clearly as if Calinda had said, *We all miss Ruyven.* More gently, Calinda said, "Put your book away, and run along to your riding-lesson, Rael."

Rael slammed his primer into his desk and raced for the door. Romilly watched her brother enviously, scowling at the wrinkled stitchery in her hand. After a minute Calinda sighed and said, "It is hard for a child to understand. Your brother Darren will be home at Midsummer, and I am glad—Rael needs his brother, I think. Here, Romilly, watch my fingers—wrap the thread *so,* three times around the needle, and pull it through—see, you can do it neatly enough when you try."

"A knot-stitch is easy," said Mallina complacently, looking up from her smooth panel of bleached linen, where a brilliant flower bloomed under her needle.

"Aren't you ashamed, Romilly? Why, Mallina has already embroidered a dozen cushion-covers for her marriage-chest, and now she is working on her wedding sheets—"

"Well," said Romilly, driven to the wall, "What do I need of embroidered cushion-covers? A cushion is to sit on, not to show fancy stitching. And I hope, if I have a husband, he will be looking at me, and not the embroidered flowers on our wedding sheets!"

Mallina giggled and blushed, and Calinda said, "Oh, hush, Romilly, what a thing to say!" But she was smiling. "When you have your own house, you will be proud to have beautiful things to adorn it."

I doubt that very much, Romilly thought, but she picked up the stitchery-piece with resignation and thrust the needle through it. Mallina bent over the quilt she was making, delicately appliqued with white starflowers on blue, and began to set tiny stitches into the flame.

Yes, it was pretty, Romilly thought, but why did it matter so much? A plain one would keep her just as warm at night, and so would a saddle-blanket! She would not have minded, if she could have made something sensible, like a riding-cloak, or a hood for a hawk, but this stupid flower-pattern, designed to show off the fancy stitching she hated! Grimly she bent over her work, needle clutched awkwardly in her fist, as the governess looked over the paper of sums she had done that morning.

"You have gone past my teaching in this, Romilly," the governess said at last, "I will speak to *Dom* Mikhail, and sk if the steward can give you lessons in keeping account-books and ciphering. It would be a pity to waste an intelligence as keen as yours."

"Lessons from the steward?" said a voice from the door-way. "Nonsense, *mestra*; Romilly is too old to have lessons from a man, it would be scandalous. And what need has a lady, to keep account-books?" Romilly raised her head from the tangle of threads, to see her stepmother Luciella coming into the room.

"If I could keep my own accounts, foster-mother," Romilly said, "I need never be afraid I would be cheated by a dishonest steward."

Luciella smiled kindly. She was a small plump woman, her hair carefully curled, as meticulously dressed as if she were about to entertain the Queen at a garden-party. She said, "I think we can find you a husband good enough that he will see to all that for you, foster-daughter." She bent to kiss Mallina on the cheek, patted Romilly's head. "Has Rael gone already to his riding-lesson? I hope the sun will not be too strong for him, he is still not entirely recovered." She frowned at the tangled threads and drunken line of colored stitching. "Oh, dear, dear, this will never do! Give me the needle, child, you hold it as if it were a currycomb! Look, hold it like this. See? Now the knot is neat—isn't that easier, when you hold it so?"

Grudgingly, Romilly nodded. *Domna* Luciella had never been anything but kind to her; it was only that she could not imagine why Romilly was not exactly like Mallina, only more so, being older.

"Let me see you make another one, as I showed you," Luciella said. "See, that is much better, my dear. I knew you could do it, you are clever enough with your fingers— your handwriting is much neater than Mallina's, only you will not try. Calinda, I came to ask you to give the children a holiday—Rael has already run off to the stables? Well enough—I only need the girls, I want them to come and be fitted for their new riding-habits; they mus be ready when the guests come at Midsummer."

Predictably, Mallina squealed.

"Am I to have a new riding-habit, foster-mother? What color is it? Is it made of velvet like a lady's?"

"No, my dear, yours is made of gabardine, for hard wear and more growing," said Luciella, and Mallina grumbled "I am tired of wearing dresses all clumsy in the seams so they can be let out when I grow half a dozen times, and all faded so everyone can see where they have been let out and the hem let down—"

"You must just hurry and finish growing, then," said Luciella kindly, "There is no sense making a dress to your measure when you will have outgrown it in six months wear, and you have not even a younger sister to pass it on to. You are lucky you re to have a new habit at all, you know," she added smiling, "You should wear Romilly's old ones, but we all know that Romilly gives her riding-clothes such hard wear that after half a year there is nothing at all left of them—they are hardly fit to pass on to the dairy-woman."

"Well, I *ride* a horse," Romilly said, "I don't sit on its back and simper at the stableboy!"

"Bitch," said Mallina, giving her a surreptitious kick on the ankle, "You would, fast enough, if he'd look at you, but nobody ever will—you're like a broom-handle dressed up in a gown!"

"And you're a fat pig," retorted Romilly, "You couldn't wear my cast-off gowns anyway, because you're so fat from all the honey-cakes you gobble whenever you can sneak into the kitchen!"

"Girls! Girls!" Luciella entreated, "Must you always squabble like this? I came to ask a holiday for you—do you want to sit all day in the schoolroom and hem dish-towels instead?"

"No, indeed, foster-mother, forgive me," said Romilly quickly, and Mallina said sullenly, "Am I supposed to let her insult me?"

"No, nor should you insult her in turn," said Luciella, sighing. "Come, come, the sewing-women are waiting for you."

"Do you need me, *vai domna*?" Calinda asked.

"No, go and rest, *mestra*—I am sure you need it, after a morning with my brood. Send the groom first to look for Rael, he must have his new jacket fitted today, but I can wait till he has finished his riding-lesson."

Romilly had been apprehensive, as she followed her stepmother into the room where the sewing-women worked, light and airy with broad windows and green growing plants in the sunny light; not flowers, for Luciella was a practical woman, but growing pots of kitchen herbs and medicinals which smelled sweet in the sun through the glass. Luciella's taste ran heavily to ruffles and flounces, and, from some battles when she was a young girl, Romilly feared that if Luciella had ordered her riding-clothes they would be some disgustingly frilly style. But when she saw the dark-green velvet, cut deftly to accentuate her slenderness, but plainly, with no trim but a single white band at her throat, the whole dress of a green which caught the color of her green eyes and made her coppery hair shine, she flushed with pleasure.

"It is beautiful, foster-mother," she said, standing as still as she could while the sewing-women fitted it with pins to her body, "It is almost too fine for me!"

"Well, you will need a good one, for hawking and hunting when the people from High Crags come for the Midsummer feasting and parties," said Luciella, "It is well to show off what a fine horse-woman you are, though I think you need a horse better suited to a lady than old Windracer. I have spoken to Mikhail about a good horse for you—was there not one you trained yourself?"

Romilly's delighted gasp made her stepmother smile. She had been allowed to help her father in training three of the fine blacks from the Lanart estates, and they were all among the finest horses to grace the stables at Falconsward. If her father agreed that she might have one of *those* horses—she thought with delight and pleasure of racing over the hills on one of the spirited blacks, with Preciosa on her arm, and gave Luciella a spontaneous hug that startled the older woman. "Oh, thank you, thank you, step-mother!"

"It is a pleasure to see you looking so much like a lady," Luciella said, smiling at the pretty picture Romilly made in the green habit. "Take it off now, my dear, so it can be stitched. No, Dara," she added to the sewing-woman who was fitting Mallina's habit over her full young breasts, "Not so tight in the tunic there, it is unseemly for so young a girl."

Mallina sulked, "Why must all my dresses be cut like a child's tunic? I have already more of a woman's figure than Romilly!"

"You certainly have," Romilly said, "If you grow much more in the tits, you can hire out for a wet-nurse." She looked critically at Mallina's swelling body, and the younger girl snarled, "A woman's habit is wasted on you, you could wear a pair of Darren's old britches! You'd rather run around looking like a stableboy, in a man's old leathers, like one of the Sisterhood of the Sword—"

"Come, come," said Luciella peacefully, "Don't make fun of your sister's figure, Romilly, she is growing faster than you, that is all. And you be quiet too, Mallina; Romilly is grown, now, and your father has given strict orders that she is not to ride astride in boots and breeches any more, but is to have a proper lady's habit and a lady's saddle for Midsummer, when the people from High Crags will be coming here for hawking and hunting, and perhaps Aldaran of Scathfell with his sons and daughters, and some of the people from Storn Heights."

Mallina squealed with pleasure—the twin daughters of Scathfell were her closest friends, and during the winter, heavy snowfalls had separated Falconsward from Scathfell or from High Crags. Romilly felt no such pleasure—Jessamy and Jeralda were about her own age, but they were like Mallina, plump and soft, an insult to any horse that carried them, much more concerned with the fit of their riding-habits and the ornaments of saddle and reins than in the well-being of the horses they rode, or their own riding-skill. The oldest son at High Crags was about Ruyven's age and had been his dearest friend; he treated Romilly and even Darren as silly children. And the folk from Storn were all grown, and most of them married some with children.

Well, perhaps she would have a chance to ride with her father, and with Darren who would be home from Nevarsin, and to fly Preciosa; it would not be too bad, even if, while there were guests, she must wear a lady's riding-habit and use a lady's saddle instead of the boots and breeches more suitable for hunting; the guests would only be here for a few days and then she could go back to her sensible boy's clothes for riding; she was willing to dress up properly to meet her parents' guests. She had learned, as a matter of course, to manage proper riding-skirts and a lady's saddle when there were guests, and to please her stepmother.

She was humming when she returned to her room to change her dress for riding; perhaps she would take Rael with her when she went to exercise Preciosa to the lure, the long line whirled around her head with scraps of meat and feathers to train and exercise a hawk. But when she searched behind her door for the old boots and breeches she always wore for riding—they were an ancient pair of Ruyven's—they could not be found.

She clapped her hands to summon the maid who waited on the children, but it was old Gwennis who came.

"What is this, Nurse? Where are my riding-breeches?"

"Your father has given strict orders," Gwennis said, "Lady Luciella made me throw them out—they're hardly fit for the hawkmaster's boy now, those old things. Your new habit's being made, and you can wear your old one till it's ready, my pet." She pointed to the riding-skirt and tunic laid out on Romilly's bed. "Here, my lamb, I'll help you lace it up."

"You threw them out?" Romilly exploded, "How dared you?"

"Oh, come, don't talk like that, my little love, we all have to do what Lady Luciella says, don't we? That habit still fits you fine, even if it's a little tight at the waist—see, I let it out for you yesterday, when Lady Luciella told me."

"I can't ride Windracer in this!" Romilly wadded up the offending skirts and flung them across the room. "He's not used to a lady's saddle, and I hate it, and there aren't gusts or anything like that! Get me some riding breeches," she stormed, but Gwennis shook her head sternly.

"I can't do that, lovey, your father's given orders, you're not to ride in breeches any more, and it's about time, you'll be fifteen ten days before Midsummer, and we must think now about getting you married, and what man will want to marry a hoyden who races around in breeches like some camp-follower, or one of those scandalous women of the Sisterhood, with sword and ears pierced? Really, Romy, you should be ashamed. A big girl like you, running off to the hawk-house and staying out all night like that—it's time you were tamed down into a lady! Now put on your riding-skirts, if you want to ride, and let's not have any more of this nonsense."

Romilly stared in horror at her nurse. So this was to be her father's punishment. Worse, far worse than a beating, and she knew that from her father's orders there would be no appeal.

I wish he had beaten me. At least he would have been dealing with me, directly, with Romilly, with a person. But to turn me over to Luciella, to let her make me into her image of a lady. . . .

"It's an insult to a decent horse," Romilly stormed, "I won't do it!"

She aimed a savage kick at the offending habit on the floor.

"Well, then, lovey, you can just stay inside the house like a lady, you don't need to ride," said Gwennis complacently, "You spend too much time in the stables as it is, it's time you stayed more in the house, and left the hawks and horses to your brothers as you should."

Appalled, Romilly swallowed down a lump in her throat, looking from the habit on the floor to her beaming nurse. "I expected this of Luciella," she said, "she hates me, doesn't she? It's the sort of spiteful thing Mallina might do, just because she can't ride a decent horse. But I didn't think you'd join with them against me, Nurse!"

"Come, you mustn't talk like that," Gwennis said, clucking ruefully, "How can you say that about your kind step-mother? I tell you, not many stepmothers with grown daughters are as good to them as Lady Luciella is to you and Mallina, dressing them up in beautiful things when you're both prettier than she is, knowing Darren's to be Lord here and her own son only a younger son, not much better than a *nedestro*! Why, your own mother would have had you out of breeches three years ago, she'd never have let you run around all these years like a hoyden! How can you say that she hates you?"

Romilly looked at the floor, her eyes stinging. It was true; no one could have been kinder to her than Luciella. It would have been easier if Luciella had ever showed her the slightest unkindness. *I could fight against her, if she was cruel to me. What can I do now?*

And Preciosa would be waiting for her; did Gwennis really think she would leave her own hawk to the hawkmaster's boy, or even to Davin himself? Her hands shook with fury as she pulled on the detested habit, threadbare blue gabardine and in spite of Gwennis's alternations, still too tight in the waist, so that the lacings gaped wide over her under-tunic. Better to ride in skirts than not to ride at all, she supposed, but if they thought they had beaten her this easily, they could think again!

Will she even know me in this stupid girl's oufit?

Fuming, she strode toward the stables and hawk-house, tripping once or twice over the annoying skirts, slowing her step perforce to a proper ladylike pace. So Luciella would bribe her with a pretty habit, to soften the blow? Just like a woman, that silly devious trick, not even telling her outright that she must put aside her riding-breeches!

Inside the hawk-house, she went directly to the block, slipping on her old gauntlet and taking Preciosa up on her arm. With her free hand she stroked the hawk's breast with the feather kept for that purpose—the touch of a hand on the hawk's fathers would take the coating from the feathers and damage them. Preciosa sensed her agitation and moved uneasily on her wrist, and Romilly made an effort to calm herself, taking down the hanging lure of feathers and signalling to the boy Ker.

"Have you fresh meat for Preciosa?"

"Yes, *damisela,* I had a pigeon just killed for the table and I kept all the innards for her, they haven't been out of the bird more than ten minutes," Ker said, and she sniffed suspiciously at the fresh meat, then threaded it on to the lure. Preciosa smelled the fresh food and jerked uneasily and fluttered; Romilly spoke soothingly to her, and walked on, kicking the skirt out of her way. She went into the stableyard and loosed the jesses, whirling the lure high over her head; Preciosa flung herself upward, the recoil thrusting

Romilly's hand down, and wheeled high into the sky over the stableyard, stooping down swiftly on the lure, striking almost before it hit the ground. Romilly let her feed in peace for a moment before calling her with the little falconer's whistle, which the bird must learn to associate with her food, and slipping the hood over her head again. She handed the lure to Ker and said, "You whirl it; I want to watch her fly."

Obediently the hawkmaster's boy took the lure and began to whirl it over his head; again Romilly loosed the hawk, watched her fly high, and descend to Romilly's whistle to the flying bait. Twice more the maneuver was repeated, then Romilly let the hawk finish her meal in peace, before hooding her and setting her back on the block. She stroked her again and again tenderly with the feather, crooning nonsense words of love to her, feeling the sense of closeness and satisfaction from the fed hawk. She was learning. Soon she would fly free and catch her own prey, and return to the wrist. . . .

"Go and saddle Windrace," she said, glumly adding, "I suppose you must use my sidesaddle."

The groom would not look at her.

"I am sorry, *damisela*—The MacAran gave strict orders. Very angry, he was."

So this, then, was her punishment. More subtle than a beating, and not her father's way—the delicate stitches set by Luciella's hand could be clearly seen in this. She could almost hear in her imagination the words her stepmother must have used; see, a big girl like Romilly, and you let her run about the stables, why are you surprised at anything she might do? But leave her to me, and I will make a lady of her. . . .

Romilly was about to fling at the groom, angrily, to forget it, a sidesaddle was an insult to any self-respecting horse . . . but on her arm Preciosa bated in agitation, and she knew the bird was picking up her own rage—she struggled for calm and said quietly, "Very well, put a lady's saddle on her, then." Anger or no, sidesaddle or no, Preciosa must be habituated to the motion of the horse; and a ride on a lady's saddle was better than no ride at all.

But she thought about it, long and hard, as she rode that day. Appeal to her father would be useless: evidently he had turned responsibility over to Luciella, the new riding-habit had been only a signal showing which way the wind now blew. No doubt, a day would come when she would be forbidden to ride at all—no, for Luciella had told her of his plans to give her a good horse. But she would ride as a lady, decorously because no horse could do anything better than a ladylike trot with a lady's sidesaddle; ride cumbered in skirts, unable even to school her hawk properly; there was no proper room for a hawk as there was a man's saddle where she could carry the block before her. And soon, no doubt, she would be forbidden the stables and hawk-house except for such ladylike rides as this. And what could she do about it? She was not yet of age—she would be fifteen at Midsummer, and had no resource except to do as her father and guardians bade her. It seemed that the walls were closing about her.

Why, then, had she been given this *laran*, since it seemed that only a man had the freedom to use it? Romilly could have wept. Why had she not, then, been born a man? She knew the answer that would be given her, if she asked Luciella what she would do with her Gift; it is, the woman would say, so that your sons will have it.

And was she nothing but a vehicle for giving some unknown husband sons? She had often thought she would like to have children—she remembered Rael as a baby, little and cunning and as soft and lovable as an unweaned puppy. But to give up everything, to stay in the house and grow soft and flabby like Luciella, her own life at an end, living only through her children? It was too high a price to pay, even for babies as adorable as that. Furiously, Romilly blinked back tears, knowing that the emotion would come through to hawk and horse, and disciplined herself to quiet.

She must wait. Perhaps, when her father's first anger had cooled, he could be made to see reason. And then she remembered; before Midsummer, Darren would be home, and perhaps he, as her father's sole remaining heir, could intercede for her with her father. She stroked the hawk with its feather to quiet her, and rode back toward Falconsward with a glimmer of hope in her heart.

Chapter 3

Ten days before Midsummer, on Romilly's fifteenth birthday, her brother Darren came home.

It was Rael who saw the riders first, as the family sat at breakfast on the terrace; the weather was so fine that Luciella had given orders for breakfast to be served on that outdoor balcony overlooking the valley of the Kadarin. Rael had taken his second piece of bread and honey to the railing, despite Luciella's gentle reprimand that he should sit down nicely and finish his food, and was hanging over the edge, throwing crumbs of bread at the broad leaves of the ivy that crawled up the sides of the castle toward the high balcony.

"Look, Mother," he called, "there are riders, coming up the path—are they coming here, do you think? Father, do you see?"

The MacAran frowned at the child, raising his cup to his lips. "Hush, Rael, I am talking to your mother—" but Romilly abruptly knew who the riders were.

"It is Darren," she cried, and flew to the railing. "I know his horse—I am going down to meet him!"

"Romilly! Sit down and finish your food," Luciella scolded, but Romilly was already out the door, her braids flapping against her shoulderblades, and flying down the long stairway. Behind her she heard the clattering of Rael's boots, and laughed at the thought of Luciella's disquiet— the peaceful meal had been disrupted for good, this time. She licked her fingers, which were sticky with honey, and went out into the courtyard, Rael behind her; the boy was hanging on the big gates, calling to the yard-men to come and open them.

"It is my brother Darren—he is coming!"

Good-naturedly, the men came and began to tug on the doors, even before the sound of the horses' hooves reached them; Rael was a favorite, spoiled by everyone. He clung to the gates, laughing, as the men shoved them under him, and waved his arm excitedly at the riders.

"It is Darren, and there is someone with him, Romilly, come and see, come and meet him!"

But Romilly hung back a little, suddenly shy, conscious of her hastily-braided, crooked hair, her smeared fingers and mouth, the bread and honey still in her hand; she flung it quickly to the yard-dog and rubbed her kerchief over the sticky smears of her mouth. Why did she feel like this? It was only Darren and some friend he had made at the monastery. Darren slid from his horse and Rael was clambering all over him, hugging him, talking so fast he could hardly be understood. Darren laughed, set Rael down and came to take Romilly into his arms.

"You have grown, sister, you are almost a woman."

"It's her birthday, Darren, what did you bring her?" Rael demanded, and Darren chuckled. He was tall and thin, his red hair clustered in thick curls over his eyes, his face had the indoor pallor of a winter spent among the snows of Nevarsin.

"I had forgotten your birthday, sister—will you forgive me? I will have a gift for you at Midsummer," he said.

"It is gift enough that you have come today, Darren," she said, and pain struck through her; she loved Darren, but Ruyven was the brother to whom she had always been closest, while Mallina and Darren had always shared everything. And Ruyven would not come home, would never come home. Hatred for the Towers who had taken her brother from her surged within her, and she swallowed hard, flicking away angry tears.

"Father and Luciella are at breakfast," she said, "Come up to the terrace, Darren; tell the *coridom* to have your saddlebags taken to your room." She caught his hand and would have drawn him along, but he turned back to the stranger who had given his horse to the groom.

"First I want you to know my friend," he said, and pulled

the young man forward. "Alderic of Castamir; my oldest sister Romilly."

Alderic was even taller than Darren, his hair glinting with faint copper through gold; hi eyes were steel-grey, set deep beneath a high forehead. He was shabbily dressed, an odd contrast to the richness of Darren's garments—Darren, as the eldest son of Falconsward, was richly clad in rust-colored velveteen trimmed with dark fur, but the cloak the Castamir youngster wore was threadbare, as if he had had it from his father or even his grandfather, and the mean edging of rabbithorn wool was coming away in places.

So he has made a friend of a youth poorer than himself, no doubt brought him here because his friend had not the means to journey to his home for the holidays. Darren is always kind. She put kind welcome, too, and a trace of condescension, into her voice, as she said, "You are welcome, *dom* Alderic. Come up and join my parents at breakfast, will you not? Garin—" she beckoned to the steward, "Take my brother's bags to his room, and put dom Alderic's things in the red chamber for the moment unless the Lady Luciella gives other orders, it will be good to have him close to my brother's quarters."

"Yes, come along." Darren linked arms with Romilly, drew Alderic with them up the stairs. "I cannot walk if you hang on me like that, Rael—go ahead of us, do!"

"He has been missing you," Romilly said, "And—" she had started to speak of their other brother, but this was to bring family matters out before a stranger; she and Darren would have time enough for confidences. They reached the terrace, and Darren was enfolded in Mallina's arms, and Romilly was left to present Alderic of Castamir to her father.

The MacAran said with grave courtesy, "You are welcome to our home, lad. A friend of my son has a friend's welcome here. Are you akin to Valdrin Castamir of Highgarth? He and I were in the guard of King Rafael before the king was most foully murdered."

"Only distantly, sir," said Alderic. "Knew you not that Lord Valdrin was dead, and his castle burnt about his ears with *clingfire* because he sheltered Carolin in his road to exile?"

The MacAran swallowed visibly. "Valdrin dead? We

were playfellows and *bredin*," he said, "but Valdrin was
always a fool, as any man is a fool who meddles in the
affairs of the great folk of the land."

Alderic said stiffly, "I honor the memory of the Lord
Valdrin for his loyalty to our rightful king in exile, sir."

"Honor," the MacAran said bitterly, "Honor is of no use
to the dead, and to all of his folk whom he entangled in
the quarrel of the great ones; great honor to his wife and
little children, I doubt it not, to die with the flesh burnt
from their very bones? As if it mattered to me, or to any
reasonable man, which great donkey kept the throne warm
with his royal backsides while better men went about
their business?"

Romilly could see that Alderic was ready with a sharp
answer, but he bowed and said nothing; he would not offend his host. Mallina was introduced to Alderic and sim-
pered up at him, while Romilly watched in disdain—
anything in breeches, she thought, and Mallina willingly
practices her silly womanish wiles on him, even this shabby
political refugee Darren picked up at Nevarsin and brought
home, no doubt to give the boy a few good meals—he
looked him as a rake, and no doubt, as Nevarsin, they feed
them on porridge of acorns and cold water!

Mallina was still chattering to the young men.

"And the folk from Storn Heights are coming, and the
sons and daughters of Aldaran of Scathfell, and all during
the Midsummer-festival there will be parties and hawkings
and hunts, and a great Midsummer-dance—" and she
slanted her long-lashed eyes at Alderic and said, "Are you
fond of dancing, *dom* Alderic?"

"I have done but little dancing since I was a child," said
Alderic, "I have danced only the clodhopper-dances of the
monks and novices when they dance together at midwinter—but I shall expect you to teach them to me, *damisela*."
He bowed to her and to Romilly, but Mallina said, "Oh,
Romilly will not dance with men— she is more at home in
the stables, and would rather show you her hawks and
hounds!"

"Mallina, go to your lessons," said Luciella, in a voice
that clearly said, *I'll deal with you later, young lady.* "You
must forgive her, *dom* Alderic, she is only a spiteful child."

Mallina burst into tears and ran out of the room, but Alderic smiled at Romilly and said, "I too feel more at ease in the company of hawks and horses than that of women. I believe one of the horses we brought from Nevarsin is yours?"

"It belonged to—" Darren caught his father's scowl and amended, "a relative of ours; he left it in Nevarsin to be returned to us." But Romilly intercepted the glance that passed between Darren and Alderic and knew that her brother had confided the whole story to his friend. How far, she wondered, had that scandal spread, that the son of The MacAran had quarreled with his family and fled to a Tower?

"Romilly," said her father, "should you not be in the schoolroom with Mistress Calinda?"

"You promised me a holiday on my birthday," Romilly reminded her stepmother, and Luciella said with an ill grace, "Well, as I have promised—I suppose you want to spend the time with your brother. Go, then, if you wish."

She smiled at her brother and said, "I would like to show you my new *verrin* hawk—"

"Romilly trained it herself," Rael burst out, while her father frowned. "When Davin was sick. She waited up all night until it would feed, and the hawkmaster said that father could not have done better himself—"

"Aye," The MacAran said roughly, "your sister has done what you would not do, boy—you should take lessons from her in skill and courage! Would that she had been the boy, and you the maiden, so that you might put skirts about your knees and spend the day in scribbling and embroidering within the house—"

Darren flushed to the roots of his hair. He said, "Do not mock me before my friend, Father. I will do as well as I am able, I pledge to you. But I am as the Gods made me, and no other. A rabbithorn cannot be a war-horse and will only become a laughing-stock if he should try."

"Is that what they have taught you among the damned monks?"

"They taught me that what I am, I am," said Darren, and Romilly saw the glint of tears in his eyes, "and yet, Father, I am here at your will, to do my poor best for you."

Romilly could hear, as plain as if the forbidden name had been spoken, *it is not my fault that I am not Ruyven, nor was it my doing that he went from here.*

The MacAran set his massive jaw, and Romilly knew that he, too, heard the forbidden words. He said, scowling, "Take your brother to the hawk-house, Romy, and show him your hawk; perhaps it will shame him into striving to equal what a girl can do."

Darren opened his mouth to speak, but Romilly nudged him in the ribs, as if to say, *Let us go while we can, before he says worse.* Darren said, muffled, "Come along, Alderic, unless hawks weary you," and Alderic, saying something courteous and noncommittal, bowed to The MacAran and to Lady Luciella and went with them down the stairs.

For the last few days Preciosa had been placed on her block among the already-trained hawks; moving quietly, Romilly slid gauntlet on wrist and took up the bird, then returned to the two young men.

"This is Preciosa," she said, pride swelling her voice, and asked Darren, "Would you like to hold her for a moment while I fetch the lures and lines? She must learn to tolerate another's hand and voice—"

But as she moved toward him, he flinched away, in a startled movement, and Romilly, sensing how the fear in him reverberated in the bird-mind, turned her attention to soothing Preciosa, stroking her with a feather. She said, not reproving, but so intent on what she was doing that she did not stop to think how her words would sound to another, "Never move so quickly around a hawk—you should know that! You will frighten her—one would think you were afraid of her!"

"It is only—I am not used to be so close to anything so large and so fierce," Darren said, biting his lip.

"Fierce? Preciosa? Why, she is gentle as a puppy dog," Romilly said, disbelieving. She beckoned to the hawk-master's boy. "Fetch the lures, Ker—" and when he brought them, she examined the bait, frowning and wrinkling up her nose.

"Is this what you have for the other hawks? Do you think they are carrion feeders? Why, a dog would turn away from this in disgust! I have orders that Preciosa was to have fresh-killed meat, mice if nothing better was available from the kitchens, but nothing as old and rank as this."

"It's what Davin had set aside for the birds, Mistress Romilly."

Romilly opened her mouth to give him the tongue-lashing he deserved, but even before a sound was out, the hawk on her wrist bated furiously, and she knew her own anger as reaching Preciosa's mind. She drew a long breath and said quietly, "I will have a word with Davin. I would ask no decent hawk to feed on this garbage. For now, go and fetch me something fresh-killed for my bird; if not a pigeon, take one of the dogs and find mice or a rat, and at once."

Darren had drawn back from the frenzied flapping of wings, but as Ker scuttled away to obey orders, he said, "I see that working with the hawk has at least given you some command of that temper and tongue, Romy—it has been good for you!"

"I wish Father would agree to that," Romilly said, still stroking Preciosa with the feather, trying to calm her. "But birds are like babies, they pick up the emotions of those who tend them, I really do not think it is more than that. Have you forgotten when Rael was a babe, that nurse Luciella had for him—no, I cannot bring her name to mind just now—Marja, Moyra, something of that sort—Luciella had to send her away because the woman's older son drowned, and she wept when she saw Rael, and it gave him colic, so that was when Gwennis came to us—"

"No, it is more than that," said Alderic, as they moved out of the darkness of the hawk-house into the tiled court-yard, "There is a well-known *laran,* and it appeared first, I am told, among the Delleray and MacAran folk; empathy with hawk and horse and sentry-bird . . . it was for *that* they trained it, in warfare in the days of King Felix. Among the Delleray folk, it was tied to some lethal genes and so died away, but MacArans have had the Gift for generations."

Darren said with an uneasy smile, "I beg you, my friend, speak not of *laran* so freely when my father is by to hear."

"Why, is he one who would speak of sweetnut-blossom because snowflakes are too cold for him?" Alderic asked with a grin. "All my life I have heard of the horses trained by The MacAran as the finest in the world, and *Dom* Mikhail is one of the more notable of MacAran lords. Surely he knows well the Gifts and *laran* of his house and his lady's."

"Still, he will not hear the word spoken," said Darren, "Not since Ruyven fled to the Tower, and I blame him not, though some would say I am the gainer by what Ruyven has done . . . Romilly, now while Father is not by, I will say this to you and you may tell Mallina secretly; I think Rael is too young to keep it to himself, but use your own judgment. At the monastery, I had a letter from Ruyven; he is well, and loves the work he does, and is happy. He sends his love and a kiss to all of you, and bids me speak of him again to Father when I judge the time is right."

"Which will be when apples and blackfruit grow on the ice cliffs of Nevarsin," said Romilly, "You were there, you know what he feels—"

Darren shook his head. "Ah, no, sister, I am not so much a telepath as you, though I knew that he was angry—"

Romilly turned on him, blinking in disbelief. "Can you not hear a thing unless it is spoken aloud?" she demanded, "Are you head blind like the witless donkey you ride?"

Slow color, the red of shame, suffused Darren's face as he lowered his eyes. "Even so, sister," he said, and Romilly shut her eyes as if to avoid looking on some gross deformity. She had never known or guessed this, she had always taken it for granted that all her siblings shared the Gift she had come to take for granted even before she knew what it was.

She turned with relief to Davin, who was coming through the courtyard. "Was it you, old friend, gave orders to feed the hawks on the offal of the kitchens, and not even fresh at that?" She pointed at the pan of offending refuse; Davin picked it up, sniffed disdainfully at it, and put it aside.

"That lazybones of a lad brought *this*? He'll make no hawker! I sent him for fresher food from the kitchens, but Lady Luciella says there are to be no more fresh birds killed for hawk-bait; I doubt not Ker was too lazy to catch mice, but I'll find something fresher to exercise your hawk, Mistress Romilly."

Alderic asked, "May I touch her?" And took the feather from Romilly's hand, stroking the hawk's sleek feathers.

"She is indeed beautiful; *verrin* hawks are not easy to keep, though I have tried it. Not with success, unless they were yard-hatched. And this was a haggard? Who trained her?"

"I did, and am still working with her; she has not yet flown free," Romilly said, and smiled shyly at his look of amazement.

"You trained her? A girl? But why not, you are a Mac-Aran. In the tower where I dwelt for a time, some of the woman tamed and flew *verrin* hawks taken in the wild, and we are apt to say there, to one who has notable success with a hawk, *Why, you have the hand of a MacAran with a bird. . . ."

"Are there MacArans in the Towers, then, that they should say so?" Romilly asked, "I knew not that there were any MacArans within their walls, until my brother went thither—"

Alderic said, "The saying was known in my father's time and in his father's—the Gift of a MacAran." The word he used was not the ordinary word in the Kilghard Hills, *laran,* but the old casta word *donas.* "But your father is not pleased, then, to have a son in the Tower? Most hill-folk would be proud."

Darren's smile was bitter. "I have no gift for working with animals—and small gift for anything else, save learning; but while Ruyven was my father's heir it did not matter; I was destined for the monastery, and if was happy with the Brotherhood. Now he will even try to hammer this bent nail into the place laid out for my brother—"

"Have you not a third brother?" Alderic asked, "Is the little lad who greeted you *nedestro,* or feebleminded, that your father cannot give a son to St.-Valentine-of-the-Snows and rear Rafael, Rael, whatever you called him, to the lordship of Falconsward? Or, seeing what Mistress Romilly can do—" his smile was generous, and Romilly blushed. But Darren said bitterly, "You do not know my father—" and broke off while Romilly was still pondering this; did it seem reasonable to Alderic, then, that she might even take Ruyven's place at Falconsward?

"I've brought fresh-killed meat for your hawk, Mistress Romilly," Davin said, coming into the stableyard, "One of the cooks had just killed a fowl for roasting at dinner; she let me have the innards for your bird, and I gave orders for the freshest offal of every day to be put aside for you in the morning; that garbage Ker brought was from the day before, because one of the cooks put it aside for the dogs, and he was too busy eyeing the wenches in the kitchen to ask for the fresh meat. He'll never make a hawker, that one! I swear, I'd turn him off for a *sekal,* and start teaching little Master Rael the handling!"

Romilly chuckled. "Luciella would have much to say about that," she told him, "but put Ker to feeding the pigs or tending the kennels, and surely there must be someone on the estate who has some hawk-sense!"

Darren grinned mirthlessly. He said, "Try Nelda's boy Garris; he was festival-got, and rumor speaks wide about who had his fathering. If he's good with the beasts, it will bring him under my father's eye, which Nelda was too proud to do. Once I suggested he should be put to share lessons with Rael, and our great Lady and Mistress Luciella had fits—one would think I'd suggested bringing the pig-boy in to dine at the high table."

"You should know that Luciella hears only what she wants to hear," said Romilly. "Perhaps she thought that bastardy is like fleas, catching. . . ." She fumbled for the lures and lines, cumbered with Preciosa's weight on her wrist. "Damnation, Darren, can't you hold her for me a moment? If not, for charity's sake, at least thread the meat on the lure—she smells it and will go wild in a moment!"

"I will take her, if you will trust me with your hawk," said Alderic, and held out his arm. "So, will you come to me, pretty one?" Carefully, he lifted the nervous hawk from Romilly's wrist to his own. "What is it you call her, Preciosa? And so she is, are you not, precious one?"

Romilly watched jealously as the hooded hawk settled down comfortably on Alderic's wrist; but Preciosa seemed content and she turned to tying the line around the meat, so that Preciosa could not snap it away too swiftly, and must bring it down to the ground to eat, as a good hunting-hawk must learn to do; badly tamed hawks tended to snatch food from a lure in midair, which taught them little about hunting practice. They must be taught to bring the prey down to their master, and to wait until the meat was given to them from the hand.

"Give me the line and lure," said Darren. "If I can do nothing else, I can at least throw out the lure—"

Romilly handed it to him with relief. "Thank you—you are taller than I, you can whirl it higher," she said, and took Preciosa again on her wrist. One handed, she slipped the hood from the hawk's head, raising her arm to let it fly. Trailing its lines, the hawk rose higher, higher—coming to the end of the line, Romilly saw it turn its head, see the fling, whistling lure—swiftly, dropping with suddenly folded wings, it descended on the lure, seizing it with beak and talons, and dropped swiftly to Romilly's feet. Romilly gave the sharp whistle which the hawk was being taught to associate with food, and scooped Preciosa up on her glove, tearing the food from the lure.

Preciosa was bending so swiftly to the food that she hopped sidewise on Romilly's arm, her claws contracting painfully in the girl's thinly-clad forearm above the gauntlet. Blood burst out, staining her dress; Romilly set her mouth and did not cry out, but as the crimson spread across the blue fabric, Darren cried out sharply.

"Oh, sister—!"

Preciosa, startled by the cry, lost her balance and fell, bated awkwardly, her wings beating into Darren's face; Romilly reached for her, but Darren cried out in panic and flung up his hands to ward away the beak and talons which were dangerously close to his face. At his scream, Preciosa tottered again and flew upward, checking with a shrill scream of rage at the end of her lines.

Her jaws set, Romilly hissed in a whisper "Damn you, Darren, she could have broken a flight-feather! Don't you know better than to move that fast around a hawk? Get back before you frighten her worse than that!"

Darren stammered "You—you—you're bleeding—"

"So what?" Romilly demanded harshly, shoved him back with a rough hand, an whistled softly, coaxingly to Preciosa. "I might better bring Rael into the hawk-house, you lackwit! Get out of here!"

"And this is what I have for a son and heir," said The MacAran bitterly. He was standing in the door of the hawk-house, watching the three young people unseen. His voice, even in his anger, was low—he knew better than to raise

his voice near a frightened bird. He stood silent, staring
with his brows knitted in a scowl, as Romilly coaxed the
hawk down to her wrist and untangled the lines. "Are you
not ashamed, Darren, to stand by while a little girl bests
you at what should come by instinct to any son of mine?
But that I knew your mother so well, I would swear you
had been fathered by some chance-come beggar of the
roads. . . . Bearer of Burdens, why have you weighted my
life with a son so unfit for his place?" He grabbed Darren's
arm and jerked him inside the hawk-house; Romilly heard
Darren cry out and her teeth met in her lip as if the blow
had landed on her own shoulders.

"Get out there, now, and try to behave like a man for
once! Take this hawk—no, not like that, damnation take
you, you have hands like great hams for all your writing
and scribbling! Take the hawk out there and exercise her
on a lure, and if I see you ducking away from it like that,
I swear I'll have you beaten and sent to bed with bread
and water as if you were Rael's age!"

Alderic's face was dead white and his jaw set, but he
bent his eyes on the backs of his hands and did not speak.
Romilly, fighting for calm—there was no sense in upsetting
Preciosa again—threaded meat on the lure again. Without
words, Alderic reached for the line and began to swing it
high, and Romilly watched Preciosa wing off, both of them
trying to ignore Darren, his face red and swollen, clumsily
trying to unhood a strange hawk at the far end of the stableyard. It was all they could do for Darren now.

She thought; *at least, he is trying. Perhaps that is braver
than what I did, defying Father; I had the Gift, I was only
doing what is natural for me, and Darren, obeying, is going
against everything which is natural to him. . . .* and her
throat swelled as if she would cry, but she fought the tears
back. It would not help Darren. Nothing would help him
except trying to conquer his own nervousness. And, somewhere inside her, she could not help feeling a tiny sting of
contempt . . . *how could he bungle anything which was so
easy and simple?*

Chapter 4

Romilly did not see the first of the guests arrive for the Midsummer-feast; the day had dawned clear and brilliant, the red sun rising over just a hint of cloud at the horizon. For three days there had been neither snow nor rain, and everywhere in the courtyard flowers were bursting into bloom. She sat up in her bed, drawing a breath of excitement; today she was to fly Preciosa free for the very first time.

This was the final excruciating test for hawk and trainer. All too often, when first freed, the hawk would rise into the sky, wing away into the violet clouds—and never return. She faced that knowledge; she could not bear to lose Preciosa now, and it was all the more likely with a haggard who had hunted and fed for herself in the wild.

But Preciosa would return, Romilly was confident of that. She flung off her nightgown and dressed for the hunt; her stepmother had hd her new green-velvet habit laid enticingly ready, but she put on an old tunic and shirt, and a pair of Darren's old breeches. If her father was angry, then he must be angry as he would; she would not spoil Preciosa's first hunt by worrying about whether or not she spotted her new velvet clothing.

As she slipped out into the corridor she stumbled over a basket set in her door; the traditional Midsummer-gift from the men of the family to mothers, sisters, daughters. Her father was always generous; she set the basket inside, rummaged through it for a handy apple and a few of the sweets that always appeared there too, and thrust them into her pockets—just what she wanted for hunting, and after a moment she pocketed a few more for Darren and Alderic. There was a second basket there too; Darren's? And a tiny one clumsily pasted of paper strips, which she had seen Rael trying to hide in the schoolroom; she smiled indulgently, for it was filled with a handful of nuts which she knew he had saved from his own desserts. What a darling he was, her little brother! For a moment she was tempted to ask him, too, on this special ride, but after a minute of reflection she sighed and decided not to risk her stepmother's anger. She would arrange some special treat for him later.

She went silently down the hallway and joined Darren and Alderic, who were waiting at the doorway, having let the dogs outside—it was, after all, well after daylight. The three young people went toward the stable.

Darren said, "I told Father we were going hawking at dawn. He gave you leave to fly his racer if you would, Alderic."

"He is generous," said Alderic, and went quietly toward the hawk.

"Which one will you take, Darren?" asked Romilly, slipping Preciosa on to her wrist. Darren, raising his eyes to her with a smile, said, "I think you know, sister, that I take no pleasure in hawks. If father had bidden me to exercise one of his birds, I would obey him; but in honor of the holiday, perhaps, he forbore to lay any such command on me."

His tone was so bitter that Alderic looked up and said, "I think he means to be kind, *bredu.*"

"Aye. No doubt." But Darren did not raise his head as they went across to the stable, where the horses were ready.

Romilly set Preciosa on the perch as she saddled her own horse. She would not command any man to disobey her father against his conscience; but she would not ride sidesaddle on this holiday ride, either. If her father chose to punish her, she would accept whatever he chose to do.

It was sheer ecstasy to be on a horse again in proper riding clothes, feeling the cool morning wind against her face, and Preciosa before her on the saddle, hooded but alert. She could feel a trickle of awareness from the bird which was blended of emotions Romilly herself could not identify . . . not quite fear as she had come to know it, not quite excitement, but to her great relief it was wholly un-mixed with the terrifying rage she had felt when she began training the hawk. The clouds melted away as they rode into the hills, and under their horses' hooves there was only the tiniest crackling of frost.

"Where shall we go, Darren? You know these hills," Alderic asked, and Darren laughed at them.

"Ask Romilly, not me, my—" he broke off sharply and Romilly, raising her eyes suddenly from her bird, inter-cepted the sharp, almost warning look Alderic gave the younger man. Darren said quickly, "My sister knows more of the hills and of the hawks than I do, Lord 'Deric."

"This way, I think," she said, "To the far horse-pasture; we can fly the birds there and none will disturb us. And there are always small birds and small animals in the coverts."

As they topped the rise they looked down on the pasture, a wide stretch of hillside grassland, dotted here and there with clumps of berry-briars, small bushes and underbrush. A few horses were cropping the bunchy grass, green with summer, and the fields and bushes were coated with clus-ters of blue and yellow wildflowers. Insects buzzed in the grass; the horses raised their heads in alert inquiry, but seeing nothing to disturb them, went on nibbling grass. One small filly flung up her head and came trotting, on spindly legs, toward them; Romilly laughed, slid from her horse and went to nuzzle the baby horse; she came not much higher than Romilly's shoulder.

"This is Angel," she said to the young men, "She was born last winter, and I used to feed her with apple scraps— no, Angel, that's *my* breakfast," she added, slapping the soft muzzle away from the pocket where the horse was trying to rummage. But she relented and pulled her knife, cutting a small slice of apple for the filly.

"No more, now, it will give you a bellyache," she said, and the little animal, evidently taking her word for it, trot-ted off on her long spindly legs.

"Let us go on, or old Windy will be on us," she said laughing, "He is out to pasture in this field. He is too old a gelding for the mares to take any notice of him, and his teeth are almost too old to chew grass; Father would have

him put down this spring, but, he said he should have one
last summer and before winter comes, he will send him
quietly to his rest; he should not have to endure another
winter of cold with his old joints."

"I will grieve when that is my task," said Darren, "we
all learned to ride on him, he was like an old rocking-chair
to sit on." He looked with a distant sadness at the aged,
half-blind pony chomping at soft grass in a corner of the
field. "I think Father spared him because he was Ruyven's
first horse. . . ."

"He had a good life, and will make a good end," said
Alderic, "Unlike men, horses are not allowed to live till
they are senile and half mad . . . if they gave men such
mercy as that, I should not—there would not now be a
usurper king on the throne in Hali and—and the king
would not now be wandering in his exile."

"I do not understand," said Romilly. Darren frowned,
but Alderic said, "You are not old enough to remember
when King Felix died? He was more than a hundred and
fifty, an *emmasca,* very old and without sons; and he had
long outlived sense and wit, so he sought to put the eldest
son of his youngest brother on the throne, rather than his
next brother's elder son, who was rightfully Heir. And so
the Lord Rakhal, who flattered and cozened an old and
senile king and got the Regents all in his hand with bribes
and lies, an aged lecher from whom no woman is safe, nor,
'tis said, the young son of any courtier who would like to
curry favor, sits on the throne of the Hasturs at Hali. And
Carolin and his sons wander across the Kadarin, at the
mercy of any bandit or robber who would like the bounty
set on their heads by our most gracious Lord Rakhal . . .
for I will never give him the name of king."

"Do you know the—the exiled king?"

Darren said, "The young prince was at Nevarsin among
the monks for a time; but he fled when word came that
Lord Rakhal sought him there."

"And you support the young prince and the—the king
in exile?" Romilly asked.

"Aye. That I do. And if some kindly courtier had relieved the ancient Felix of his life before 'twas a burden to
him, Carolin would now rule in Hali as a just king, rather
than turning the holy city of the Hasturs into a—a cesspool

of filth and indecencies, where no man dares come for justice without a bribe in hand, and upstart lordlings and outlanders wrangle and divide our land among them!"

Romilly did not answer; she knew nothing of courts and kings, and had never been even so far as the foothill city of Neskaya, far less into the lowlands, or near to the Lake of Hali. She reached for Preciosa's hood, and then hesitated, showing Alderic the courtesy due a guest.

"Will you fly first, sir?"

He smiled and shook his head. "I think we are all as eager as you to see how Preciosa has come through her training."

With shaking hands, Romilly slipped the hood from Preciosa's head, watching the hawk mantling her feathers. Now. Now was the test, not only of her mastery of the hawk, but of the hawk's acceptance of her training, the hawk's tie to her. She felt she could not bear to see this hawk she had loved, over whom she had spent so many anxious and painful hours, fly from her and never return. It flashed through her mind, *is this how Father feels now that Ruyven has gone?* Yet she must try the hawk in free flight. Otherwise, she was no more than a tame cagebird, sitting dull on a block, not a wild hawk at all. But she felt tears blurring her sight as she raised her fist and felt the hawk balance a moment, then, with a single long wing-stroke, fly free.

She rose on a long, slanting arch into the sunlight, and Romilly, her mind full of anxious thoughts—will she fly well, has this long period of inactivity dulled her flight?—watched her rise. And something in her rose with the hawk, feeling the wordless joy of the morning sun on her wings, the light dazzling her eyes as she winged upward, rose, hovered, soared—wheeled and winged strongly away.

Romilly let out a long breath. She as gone, she would not return—

"You have lost her, I fear," said Alderic at last. "I am sorry, *damisela.*"

Loss and pain, and a sharing of ecstasy, battled in Romilly. Free flight, something of her soaring with the hawk . . . and then fading away in the distance. She shook her head. If she had lost the hawk, then she had never really possessed her. She thought, *I would rather lose her than tie her to me against her will. . . .*

Why cannot Father see that? She knew the thought was Darren's, because of the bitterness. Then he was not head-blind? Or was his telepathy erratic, as hers had once been, coming only rarely and when she was deeply moved . . . her own had strengthened when she had begun working with the animals, but Darren had none of that gift. . . .

So Preciosa was free, and it was all an illusion. She might as well sit quietly in the house and mind her stitchery for all it would profit her to hang about the hawk-house, trying like a man to work with the birds. . . .

And then it seemed that her heart would stop. For through the infinite pain of loss, a thread of awareness stole, high flight, the world laid out beneath her like one of the maps in her schoolbooks, only colored and curiously sharp, with a sight stronger than her own, and little flickers of life coming from there, small birds in flight, small animals in the grass. . . .

Preciosa! The hawk was still in rapport, the hawk had not flown wild! Darren said something; she did not hear. She heard Alderic saying, "Don't waste your voice, *bredu*, she cannot hear you. She is with the hawk. . . ."

Romilly sat, with automatic habit, in the saddle, upright, silent, but the real part of her soared over the high pasture, keen with hunger, in the ecstasy of the flight. Supernaturally keen, her sight and senses, aware of the life of small birds, so that she felt she was smacking her ips and almost giggled and broke out of the rapport with the absurdity of it, sudden burning hunger and a desire almost sexual in its ferocity . . . down. Down on long soaring wings, the beak striking, blood bursting into her mouth, the sudden fierce-ness of bursting life and death. . . .

Down. Wavering down. She had just enough of her self-hood left to hold out her fist rock-steady, under the sudden jarring stop of a heavy hawk laden with her kill. She felt tears streaming down her face, but there was no time for emotion; her knife was in her free hand as she cut the head away, thrust her portion, headless rabbit, into her wallet with the freer hand; all her own awareness was feeding with the greedy hawk on her portion. Alderic had loosed his own hawk, but she did not know; she as weeping outright with love and relief as she slipped the hood on Preciosa's head.

Preciosa had come back. She had returned of her free will, out of freedom into bondage and the hood. She choked back her tears as she stroked the hawk with the feather, and knew her hands were shaking.

What have I done to deserve this? How can I possibly be worthy of it? That a wild thing should give up her freedom for me . . . what can I possibly do to make me worthy enough for that gift?

Later they ate the apples and sweets that Romilly had brought, before riding back, through the growing light, to Falconsward. As the young people came through the court-yard the saw strange horses being unsaddled there, one with the banners of Aldaran of Scathfell, and knew that the highest-born of the guests had arrived.

Alderic asked, anxiously, "Is old lord Gareth still Lord of Scathfell?"

"He is not, my lord; Gareth of Scathfell is not more than forty-nine," said Romilly. Alderic looked relieved, and Romilly intercepted a questioning look between Darren and Alderic. Alderic said shortly, "He might well know me by sight."

"Do you not trust to the laws of—" Darren began, frowned in Romilly's direction, and broke off, and Romilly, bending her head over her hawk, thought; *what kind of fool do they think me? I would need be deaf, blind, dumb and head-blind as well, not to know he is allied in partisan-ship to Carolin in exile, perhaps the young prince himself. And I know as well as he why my father must get no word of it.*

"True; Old Gareth died three winters gone, sir," Darren said, "and was half-blind at that. Will all of the folk of Scathfell be here, Romilly?"

Romilly, relieved that the tension had passed, began to recite the grown sons and daughters of the middle-aged lord of Scathfell; his Heir, yet another Gareth ("But they call him Garris, in lowland fashion," she added), "*Dom* Garris is not wed, he has buried three wives; I think he is only in his thirtieth year, but looks older, and is lame with a wasting disease of one leg."

"And you dislike him," said Alderic, and she grinned, her impish smile. "Why, how could you possibly know that, Lord Alderic? But it is true; he is always fumbling the maidens in corners, he was not above pawing at Mallina last year, when she had not even put up her hair. . . ."

"Lecherous old goat!" Darren said, "Did Father know?"

"None of us wanted a quarrel with neighbors; Luciella only told Mallina and me to keep away from him if we could do so without being uncivil. Then there is *Dom* Edric, who is blind, and his wife Ruanna, who keeps the estate books as well as any man. And there are the young twins, Cathal and Cinhil, they are not so young either—they are Ruyven's age; twenty-two. And Cathal's wife, who was one of my childhood friends—Darissa Storn. Cinhil is not wed, and Father once spoke of betrothing us, but nothing came of it, which gladdened my heart—I would not want to live at Scathfell, it is like a bandit's hold! Though I would not mind being close to Darissa, and Cinhil is a nice enough boy."

"It seems to me you are over young to be wedded," said Alderic, and Darren laughed. "Women marry young in these hills, and Romilly is fifteen. And, I doubt not, she thinks it long till she is in a home of her own, and out from Luciella's guidance—what's the ancient saying, *where two women rule a hearthfire, the thatch may burn with the sparks flying* . . . yet I think Father could do better for Romilly than a younger son, a fourth son at that. Better lady in a cottage than serving-woman in a castle, and when *Dom* Garris weds again—or if old Scathfell should take a wife— Cinhil's wife would be lowest of all, not much better than waiting-women to all the rest. Darissa was pretty and bright when she was wedded, and now she looks ten years older than Cathal, and all out of shape with bearing children."

"I am in no haste to marry," Romilly said, "And there are men enough, I suppose, in these hills; Manfred Storn is Heir to Storn Heights, and he is about Darren's age, so it's likely, when I am old enough to marry, Father will speak to old Lord Storn. The folk of High Crags will be coming too, and they have a couple of unmarried sons and daughters, it's likely that they will marry Rael into that kindred, or me." She shrugged. "What does it matter, after all? Men are all alike."

Alderic chuckled. "By those words I know how young you are, Mistress Romilly—I hope your father does not seek to have you married till you are old enough to distinguish between one man or another, or you may awaken some day and discover you are married to the very last man on earth you would have sought for husband. Shall we go in the house? The sun is high, and your stepmother said something of a festival breakfast—and I smelled the cooks making spicebread as we passed the kitchens!''

Romilly only hoped, now, that she could get up to her room unobserved, to change her clothing and bathe before the festal meal. But, coming around a corridor, she almost bumped into a tall, pale, fattish man with fair hair, coming from the big bathing-room with hot pools, fed by volcanic springs. He was wrapped in a loose robe and his hair as damp and mussed; he had evidently gone to soak away the fatigue of riding. Romilly curtseyed politely as she had been taught, then remembered that she was wearing breeches— curse it! If she had gone on about her business he might simply have taken her for an out-of-place servant boy on some errand. Instead his pale flabby face tightened in a dimply creased smile.

"Mistress Romilly," he said, his eyes sliding up and down her long legs, "An unexpected pleasure. Why, what a pair of legs you have, girl! And you have—grown," he added, the pallid china-blue eyes resting on the straining laces of the old tunic pulled over her full breasts, "It will be a pleasure to dance with you tonight, now I have had the delights of seeing what so many women so carefully conceal from their admirers. . . .''

Romilly flushed, feeling heat in her face, ducked her head and escaped. Through the scalding heat flooding to her ears, she thought, wretchedly, *Now do I know what Luciella meant, that I was too big to run about in breeches— I might as well be naked, the way he looked at me.* All her life she had run about in her brother's clothes, as free of self-consciousness or shame as if she were another lad; now, under the man's lustful eyes, she felt as if her body had actually been rudely handled; her breasts prickled and there was a curious crawling sensation lower down in her belly.

She took refuge in her room, her heart pounding, and went swiftly to the washstand, splashing her hot face with cold water to cool it.

"Luciella was right. Oh, why didn't she tell me?" she wondered wretchedly, then realized that there was no way to speak of it, and if she had been told, without this experience, she would only have laughed it away. Her hands were still shaking as she undid the laces of the boy's tunic, dropped the breeches to the floor, and for the first time in her life, looked clearly in the mirror and saw her body as a woman's. She was still slender, her breasts scarcely rounded, the hips scarcely more flared than a boy's, and the long legs were really boyish. *But,* she thought, *if ever I wear boy's clothes again, I shall be sure they fit me loosely enough that I truly look like a male.*

Through the glass connecting doors to Mallina's room she saw her sister exploring her Midsummer-baskets; like Romilly herself, she had three, which made Romilly turn back to her father's generous basket, with more fruits and sweets than flowers—The MacAran had quite a realistic view of little girl's appetites, which were just as greedy as those of young boys—and the smaller basket she thought was from Darren. Now, examining it closely, she realized that it was filled with garden and hothouse flowers, exquisitely arranged, and with one or two exotic fruits which he must have gotten in Nevarsin, since they did not grow near Falconsward. Then she saw the card, and read in surprise;

> I have neither sister or mother to receive
> Midsummer-Gifts; accept these with my
>   homage, *Alderic, student.*

Mallina burst into her room.

"Romy, aren't you dressed yet? We mustn't be late for Festival breakfast! Are you going to wear your holiday gown? Calinda is with Mother, will you button the back of my dress for me? What beautiful flowers, Romy! Mine are all garden flowers, though there is a beautiful bunch of ice-grapes, as sweet as honey—you know, they leave them on the trees in Nevarsin till they freeze, like redfruit, and then they lose their sourness and grow sweet . . . Romy, who do you think he is? He looks so romantic—do you think *Dom* Alderic is trying to court one of us? I would be happy indeed to be betrothed to him, he is so handsome and gallant, like the hero of some fairy-tale—"

"What a silly chatterbox you are, Mally," said Romilly, but she smiled, "I think he is a thoughtful guest, no more; no doubt he has sent to Mother a basket as fine as this."

"*Domna* Luciella will not appreciate it," Mallina said,

"Still she thinks Festival Night is a heathen observance not worthy of a good *cristoforo;* she scolded Calinda because she had Rael making Festival baskets, but Father said everyone deserved a holiday and one excuse was a good as another for giving the farm workers a day of leisure and some well-deserved bonus gifts, and he should let Rael enjoy the Festival while he was still a child—he would be as good a *cristoforo* as he need, if he as a good boy and minded the Book of Burdens."

Romilly smiled. "Father has said much the tame every Festival since I can remember," she said, "And I doubt not he likes spicebread and sweetbaked saffron cakes and fruits as well as anyone else. He quoted from the Book of Burdens that the beast should not be grudged his grain, nor the worker his wage, nor his holiday, and father may be a harsh man, but he is always just to his workmen." She did up the last button on the gown and spun her sister around. "How fine you are, Mally! But it is fortunate you do not wear this dress on a work day—it needs a maid to do it up for you! That is why I had my festival gown made with laces, so I could do it up for myself." She finished fastening the embroidered cuffs of her under-tunic, slipped the long loose surplice, rust-red and embroidered with butterflies, over her head, and turned for Mallina to pin up her braid at her neck with the butterfly-clasp that modestly hid the neck of her frock.

Mallina turned to choose a flower for her hair from the baskets. "Does this rose-plant suit me? It is pink like my dress . . . oh, Romy, look!" she said, with a scandalized half-breath, "Saw you not, he has put golden-flower, *dorilys,* into your basket!"

"And so what, silly?" asked Romy, choosing the blue *kireseth* blossom for her knotted braid, but Mallina caught her hand.

"No, indeed, you must not, Romilly—what, don't you know the flower-language? The gift of golden-flower is—well, the flower is an aphrodisiac, you know as well as I do what it means, when a man offers a maiden *dorilys.* . . ."

Romilly blushed, again feeling the lustful eyes on her. She swallowed hard—Alderic, was he too looking at her with this kind of greed? Then common sense came back. She said crisply, "Nonsense; he is a stranger to these hills, that is all. But if that kind of talk is commonplace among silly girls, I will not wear the flower—shame to them, for it is the prettiest of all the flowers, but do you choose me a flower, then, for my braids."

The sisters went down in their finery to the family feast, bearing with them, as custom dictated, the fruits from their festival baskets to be shared with father and brothers. The family was gathered in the great dining-hall rather than the small room used for family meals, and *Domna* Luciella was there, welcoming her guests. Rael was there in his best suit, and Calina in a new gown too, dark and decent as suited her station, but well-made and new, not a shabby or out-worn family castoff; Luciella was a kind woman, Romilly thought, even to poor relations. Darren wore his best clothing too, and Alderic, though his best was sombre as befitted a student at Nevarsin, and bore no trace of family colors or badges. She wondered who he was, and kept to herself the thought that had come to her, that he might well be one of the king's men, exiled, or even the young prince . . . no, she would say nothing; but she wished that Darren had trusted her with his secret.

The middle-aged Gareth of Scathfell, as the man of highest rank in the assembly, had been given the high seat usually assigned to The MacAran at his own table; her father had taken a lower place. The young couples and single men and women were at a separate table; Romilly saw Darissa seated beside Cathal and would have joined her friend, but her stepmother gestured to an empty seat left beside *Dom* Garris; Romilly blushed, but would not incite a confrontation here; she took her seat, biting her lip and hoping that in the very presence of her parents he would say nothing to her.

"Now, clothed as befits your beauty, you are even more lovely, *damisela*," he said, and that was all; the words were perfectly polite, but she looked at his pale slab of face with dislike and did not answer. But after all, he had done nothing, the words had been polite enough, what could she say, there was no way she could complain of him.

There were delicacies of every kind, for this was break-fast and mid-day meal in one; the feasting went on for some time, and before the dishes were cleared, the musicians had come in and begun to play. The curtains had been drawn back to their furthest to let in the midsummer sun, and the doors flung open; the furniture in the lower hall had been moved away to clear it for dancing. As Darren led his sister out for the first dance, as custom demanded, she heard them discussing, at the high table, the men that had been sent out to seek the exiled Carolin.

"It's nothing to me," The MacAran said, "I care not who sits on the throne; but I'll not have my men bribed to be thief-takers, either. There was a time when MacArans ruled this as a kingdom; but then, we had little to do but keep it by force of arms, and I've no wish to make my lands an armed camp, and the Hasturs are welcome to rule as they will; but I curse their brotherslaying wars!"

"I had heard word that Carolin and his older son had crossed the Kadarin," Lord Scathfell said, "No doubt to seek refuge with my cousin of Aldaran—there is old hatred between the Hastur-kin and the Aldarans."

Her father drew up his mouth in a one-sided grin. "None so keen at the hunting of wolves as the dog with wolf blood," he said, "Were not the Aldarans, long ago, come from that same Hastur-blood?"

"So they say," Lord Scathfell said with a grim nod, "I put no stock in all those tales of the children of Gods . . . though, the Gods know, there is *laran* in the Aldaran line, even among my own sons and daughters, as among yours; have you not one son in a Tower, *Dom* Mikhail?"

Her father's brow clouded. "Not by my will or wish, nor by my leave," he spat out, "I give no name of son to him who dwells among the *Hali'imyn!*" On his lips the harmless word was an obscenity; he calmed himself with an effort and added, "But this is no talk for a festal board. Will it please you to dance, my Lord?"

"I will leave that for younger folk," said Lord Scathfell, "But lead your lady out to dance if you will," he added, and The MacAran turned dutifully to Lady Luciella and led her on to the dance floor.

After the first ceremonious dance, the younger folk gathered for a ring-dance, all the young men in the outer ring, all the girls and women in the inner one; the dancing grew riotous after a bit, and Romilly saw Darissa drop out of the dancers, her hand pressed to her side; she went to fetch her friend a drink, and sat beside her, chatting. Darissa wore the loose ungirdled gown of a pregnant woman, but even so she loosed the clasps on her tunic, and fanned herself—she was red and panting.

"I shall dance no more till this one is born," she said, pressing her long fingers against her swollen body, "He holds his own dance, I think, and will dance from now till harvest-time, mostly when I am trying to sleep!" Cathal came and bent solicitously over his wife, but she gestured him back to the dancing. "Go and dance with the men, my husband, I will sit here for a little and talk with my old playmate—what have you been doing with yourself, Romilly? Are you not betrothed yet? You are fifteen now, are you not?"

Romilly nodded. She was shocked at her friend, who had been so pretty and graceful but three years ago; now she had grown heavy-footed, her small breasts swollen and thick beneath the laces of her gown, her waist clumsy. In three years, Darissa had had two children and now she was bearing another already! As if reading her thoughts, Darissa said with a bitter twist of her lips, "Oh, I know well, I am not so pretty as I was when I was a maiden—enjoy your last year of dancing, Romilly, 'tis likely that next year you too will be on the sidelines, swelling with your first; my husband's father spoke of wedding you to Cinhil, or perhaps Mallina; he thinks her more docile and lady-like."

Romilly said in shock, "But need you have another so soon? I should think two in three years was enough—"

Darissa shrugged and smiled. "Oh, well, it is the way of things—this one I think I will feed at my own breast and not put out to nurse, and perhaps I will not get with child again this year. I love my little ones, but I think three is enough for a time—"

"It would be more than enough for me for a lifetime," said Romilly vigorously, and Darissa laughed. "So say we all when we are young girls. Lord Scathfell is pleased with me because I have already given them two sons, and I hope this one is a daughter; I would like a little girl—later I will take you to see my babies; they are pretty children, little Gareth has red hair; maybe he will have *laran,* a magician for the Towers—"

"Would you want him to—?" Romilly murmured, and Darissa laughed. "Oh, yes, Tramontana Tower would be ready to take him, the Aldarans are Hastur-kin from away back before the Hundred Kingdoms, and they have old ties with Tramontana." She lowered her voice. "Have you truly no news of Ruyven? Did your father really disown him?"

Romilly nodded, and Darissa's eyes widened; she and Ruyven had played together as children, too.

"I remember, one year at Midsummer, he sent me a Festival-basket," she said, "and I wore the sprig of golden-flower he sent me; but at the end of that Festival, Father betrothed me to Cathal, and we have been happy enough, and now there are our children—but I think kindly of Ruyven, and I would gladly have been your sister, Romilly. Do you think The MacAran will give you to Cinhil if he should ask? Then should we be sisters indeed—"

"I do not dislike Cinhil," Romilly said, but inwardly she shrank away; three years from now, then, would she be like Darissa, grown fat and short of breath, her skin blotched and her body misshapen from breeding? "The one good thing about such a marriage would be, it would bring me close to you," she said truthfully, "but I see no haste to marry; and Luciella says, fifteen is too young to settle down; she would as soon not have us betrothed till we are seventeen or more. One does not breed a good bitch in her first heat."

"Oh, Romilly," Darissa said, blushing, and they giggled together like children.

"Well, enjoy the dancing while you can, for your dancing days will be over soon," Darissa said. "Look, there is Darren's friend from the monastery—he looks like a monk in his dark suit; is he one of the brethren, then?"

Romilly shook her head. "I know not who he is, only that he is a friend of Darren's and of the Castamir clan," she said, and kept her suspicions to herself. Darissa said, "Castamir is a Hastur clan! I wonder he will come here freely—they held by the old king, I heard. Does your father hold to Carolin, or support the new king?"

"I do not think Father knows or cares, one king or another," said Romilly, but before she could say more, Alderic stood beside them.

"Mistress Romilly? It is a set dance—will you partner me?"

"Do you mind being left alone, Darissa?"

"No, there is Cathal; I will ask him to fetch me a glass of wine," Darissa said, and Romilly let Alderic draw her into the forming set, six couples—although one of them was Rael and Jessamy Storn who was eleven, and half a head taller than her partner. They faced one another, and Darren and Jeralda Storn, at the head of the line, led off, taking hands, circling each couple in the complex figures of the dance. When it came Alderic's turn she reached confidently for his hands; they were square, hard and warm, not the soft hands of a scholar at all, but calloused and strong like a swordsman's. An unlikely monk, indeed, she thought, and put her mind to the intricacies of the dance, which at the end of the figure put her opposite Darren, and then opposite her brother Rael. When the set brought her briefly into partnership, crossing hands and circling with Cinhil, he squeezed her hand and smiled, but she cast her eyes down and did not return the smile. So Lord Scathfell thought to marry her to Cinhil this year, so she could be fat and swollen with baby after baby like Darissa? Not likely! Some day, she supposed, she would have to be married, but not to this raw boy, if she could help it! Her father was not so much in awe of the Aldaran Lords as that, and besides, it was only Aldaran of Scathfell, not Aldaran of Castle Aldaran. Scathfell was the richest and most influential of their neighbors, but The MacAran had been an independent landholder since, she had heard, before the raising of Caer Donn city!

Now the set brought her face to face with *Dom* Garris again. He smiled at her and pressed her hand too, and she blushed, holding her own hands cold and stiff against his, just touching as the dance required. She was relieved when the set brought them back to their original places, with Alderic facing her. The musicians swung into a couple-dance, and she saw *Dom* Garris start toward her purposefully; she grabbed at Alderic's sleeve and whispered, "Will you ask me to dance, *Dom* Alderic?"

"To be sure," he said, smiling, and led her out. She said after a moment, returning his smile as they left Garris staring after them, "You are not a clodhopper at all."

"No?" He laughed. "It has been long since I danced, save with the monks—"

"You dance in the monastery?"

"Sometimes. To keep warm. And there is a sacred dance

at some of the services. And some of the students who are not to be of the brethren go into the village and dance at Festival, though I—" it seemed to her that he hesitated a moment, "I had small leisure for that."

"They keep you so hard at your studies? *Domna* Luciella said that Darren looks thin and pale—do they give you enough to eat, and warm clothes?"

He nodded. "I am used enough to hardships," he said, and fell silent, while Romilly enjoyed the dance, the music. He said, as they separated at the end of the music, "You wear my flowers—I hope they pleased you?"

"Very much," she said, then felt shy again; had he put the *dorilys* into her basket as the invitation Mallina said it was, or was it simply a stranger's unfamiliarity with the countryside? She would have liked to ask, but was too bashful. But again it was as if he read her thoughts; he said abruptly, "Darren told me—I meant nothing improper, believe me, Mistress Romilly. In my country—I am a lowlander—the starflower, *dorilys,* it is the gift of the lord Hastur to the Blessed Cassilda, and I meant a courteous compliment in honor of the day, no more."

She said, smiling up at him, "I do not think anyone would believe you capable of any improper innuendo, *Dom* Alderic."

"I am your brother's friend; you need not say *Dom* to me," said Alderic. "After all, we have hunted and flown hawks together—"

"Nor need you call me *damisela,*" she said, "My brothers and sister call me Romy—"

"Good; we shall be even as kinfolk, as I am to Darren," said Alderic. "Will you have some wine?" They had moved close to the refreshment-table. She shook her head and said ingenuously, "I am not allowed to drink wine in company."

"*Shallan,* then?" He dipped her up some of the sweet fruit-drink. She sipped it thirstily. After the romping dance she knew that her hair was beginning to come down, but she did not want to withdraw to the giggling girls in the corner and pin it up.

"You are fond of hawking?" she asked him.

"I am; the women of our family train sentry-birds. Have you ever flown one, *dami*—Romy?"

She shook her head. She had seen the great fierce birds,

but said, "I knew not that they could be tamed! Why, they can bring down a rabbithorn! I should think they were no great sport—"

"They are not flown for sport," Alderic said, "but trained for war, or for fire-watch; it is done with *laran*. A sentry-bird in flight can spy out intruders into a peaceful countryside, or bandits, or a forest-fire. But it is no task for sport, and in truth the birds are fierce, and not easy to handle. Yet I think you could do it, Romilly, if your *laran* was trained."

"It is not, nor likely to be," she said, "and doubtless you know why, if Darren has told you so much. Sentry-birds!" She felt a little shiver, half pleasant, trickle down her spine at the thought of handling the great fierce birds of prey. "I think it would be no harder to train a banshee!"

Alderic chuckled. "I have even heard of that in the far hills," he said, "And banshee-birds are very stupid; it takes little craft to handle them, only to rear them from hatchlings and feed them on warm food; and they will do what you will, spying out game-tracks with he warmth left in the ground, and they make fine watch-birds, for they will scream terribly at any strange smell—"

Now she did shiver; the thought of the great, blind, flightless carnivores trained for watchman-duty. She said, "Who needs a banshee for that when a good Rouser hound is as useful, and much nicer to have around the house?"

"I'll not argue that," said Alderic, "and I would sooner climb High Kimbi in my bare feet than try to train a banshee; but it can be done. I cannot handle even sentry-birds; I have not the gift, but some of the women of our family do so, and I have seen it done in the Tower, where they use them for fire-watch; their eyes see further than any human's." Soft strains of music began again and he asked, "Would you like to dance this one?"

She shook her head. "Not yet, thanks—it is warm, the sun coming in like this."

Alderic bowed to someone behind her, and Romilly turned to see Luciella standing there. She said, "Romilly, you have not yet danced with *Dom* Garris!"

She said scornfully, "It is like him to complain to my stepmother instead of coming like a man to ask me himself."

"Romilly! He is heir to Scathfell!"

"I don't care if he is heir to Cloudland Staircase or to Zandru's ninth hell, if he wants to dance—" she began, but *Dom* Garris appeared behind Luciella and said, with his plump smile, "Will you honor me with a dance, Mistress Romilly?"

There was, after all, no way to refuse without being really rude. He was her parents' guest, even though she felt he should dance with the women his own age and not hang around gawking at the young girls. She accepted his hand on her wrist to lead her out to dance. After all, he could not say or do anything rude in the full view of her father and her brothers, and half the countryside round. His hand on hers was unpleasantly damp, but she supposed that twas not anything he could help.

"Why, you are light as a feather on your feet, *damisela*— quite the young lady! Who would have thought it this morning, seeing you in your boots and breeches like a boy—I suppose all the young lads in the countryside are hanging around you, heh?"

Romilly shook her head silently. She detested this kind of talk, though she knew it would have made Mallina giggle and blush. When they had finished the dance he asked her for another, but she declined politely, saying she had a stitch in her side. He wanted to fetch her wine or a glass of *shallan,* but when she said she only wished to sit down by Darissa for a little he sat beside them and insisted on fanning her. Fortunately, by the time that dance was over, the musicians had struck up another ring-dance and all the young folks were gathering into circles, laughing and kicking up their heels in the rowdy figure. *Dom* Garris finally went away, sulking, and Romilly released her breath.

"You have made another conquest," Darissa teased.

"Not likely; dancing with me is like grabbing at a scullery-girl, something he can do without committing himself to anything," Romilly said. "The Aldarans of Scathfell are too high to marry into our clan, except for their younger sons. Father spoke once of marrying me to Manfred Storn, but he's not fifteen yet, and there's no hurry. Yet, though I am not high enough to marry, I am too well-born for him to seduce without reprisal, and I do not like him well enough for that." She smiled and added, "The worst thing about wedding with Cinhil, should he offer for

me, would be having to call that great fat slug *brother*. Yet
kinship's dues, I dare say, would at least make it unseemly
for him to pay me more than the attention due a brother's wife."

"I would not count on that," said Darissa in an undertone, "When I was pregnant with little Rafael, last year, he
came and sought me out—he said that since I was already
with child I need fear no unseemly consequences, and when
I chided him, he said he looked backward to the old days
in the hills, when brothers and sisters held all their wives
in common . . . and surely, he said, Cathal would pay him
a brother's kindness and not care if I shared his bed now
and again, since his wife was also big with breeding—I
kicked his shins and told him to find a servant-girl for his
bed if he could pay one to overlook his ugliness; and so I
wounded his pride and he has not come near me again. To
tell the truth he is not so bad-looking, only he whines and
his hands are always flabby and damp. And—" she added,
showing the dimples which were almost the only thing un-
changed from the time when she and Romilly had been
girls together, "I love Cathal too well to seek any other
bed."

Romilly blushed, and looked away; reared among animals, she knew perfectly well what Darissa was talking
about, but Luciella was a strictly-observing *cristoforo* and
did not think it seemly to speak of such things among
young girls. Darissa mistook her blush. She said, almost
defensively, "Well, I bear children without much trouble—
I am not like Garris's wife; she left no living children, and
died in childbirth just before Midwinter. He has worn out
three wives, *Dom* Garris, trying to get him an Heir, and I
have marked that all his children die at birth—I have no
wish to get myself with child by *him* or I should follow his
wives into death, no doubt.

"My older sister went for a time to Tramontana Tower
when she was a girl, and she said she had heard there about
the days of the old breeding-program, when the Aldarans
had some strange gifts of *laran,* but they were bound, in
their line, to lethal genes—do you know what those are?
Yes, of course, your father breeds his own horses, does he
not? And Cathal has them not, but I think *Dom* Garris

will leave no heir, so one day my sons by Cathal will inherit Scathfell—" Darissa rattled on.

"And you will rule the roost as their mother," said Romilly, laughing, but then Rael came up and pulled them into the set-dance, saying they had not enough women to make up a second set, and she dropped that line of thought.

The dancing and feasting went on all day, and before midnight The MacAran and Lord Scathfell and the rest of the older people with their ladies, retired to rest, leaving the young people to their dancing and merry-making. Rael was taken away by the governess, also the protesting Mallina, who was comforted only by seeing that her friends Jessamy and Jeralda were also being sent to bed. Romilly was tired, and almost ready to go with the children—she had, after all, been awake before daylight. But Alderic and her brother Darren were still dancing, and she would not admit that her brother could stay awake longer than she could. But she saw, with a little sinking awareness, that Darissa was leaving the hall—pregnant as she was, she said, she needed her sleep.

I will stay close to Darren. In my brother's presence Dom *Garris cannot come too near for comfort . . .* and then she wondered why she was worrying; he had, after all, offered her no word out of the way, and how could she complain, after all, of a mere look? Nevertheless, the memory of his eyes on her made her squirm; and now she thought about it, she realized that all this day and evening she had been somehow, in the back of her mind, aware of his eyes on her.

Is this, then, laran?

I would rather not dance at all, I would rather sit here and talk about hawks and horses with my brother and his friends. . . .

But Cinhil claimed her for a dance, and then she could not in courtesy refuse *Dom* Garris. The dancing was a little wilder, the music faster, now that the elderly and more staid people had left the hall. He whirled her about till she was dizzy, and she was conscious that his hands were no longer decorously on her sleeve but that he was holding her somewhat closer than was comfortable, and when she tried self-consciously to squirm away from them he only chuckled and eased her closer still.

"No, now, you cannot tell me you are so shy as that," he said, and she could tell from the flushed look of his face and the slight slurring of his words that he had drunk over-long of the stronger wine at the high table, "Not when you run about with those lovely long legs showing in breeches, and your breasts showing through a tunic three sizes too small, you cannot play Lady Modesty with me now!" He pulled her close and his lips nuzzled her cheek, but she twisted indignantly away.

"Don't!" And then she said, crossly, "I do not like the stink of too much wine on your breath, and you are drunk, *Dom* Garris. Let me go."

"Well, you should have been drinking more," he said easily, and guided them in the dance into one of the long galleries that led away from the hall. "Here, give me a kiss, Romy—"

"I am not *Romy* to you," she said, and pulled her head away from him, "and if you had not been spying about where you had no right to be, you would not have seen me in my brother's clothes, which I wear only in the sight of my little brothers. If you think I was showing myself to you, you are very much mistaken."

"No, only to that haughty young sprig of the *Hali'imyn* who was squiring you to the hunt and hawking?" he asked, and laughed. She said, twisting her rumpled hair free, "I want to go back to the hall. I did not come out here with you of my own will, I just did not want to make a scene on the dance floor. Take me back to the hall, or I will shout to my brother now! And then my father will horse-whip you!"

He laughed, holding her close. "Ah, on a night like this, what do you think your brother will be doing, then? He would not thank you for calling him away from what ever young man will be about, on Midsummer-Night. Must I alone be refused? You are not such a child as all that. Come, give me a kiss then—"

"No!" Romilly struggled away from his intruding hands, crying now, and he let her go.

"I am sorry," he said gently, "I was testing you; I see now that you are a good girl, and all the Gods forbid I should interfere with you." He bent and dropped a sud-denly respectful kiss on her wrist. She swallowed hard, blinked back her tears and fled from the gallery, back through the hall and upstairs, where she bundled off her festival gown and hid beneath her warm quilts, sobbing.

How she hated him!

Chapter 5

E very year The MacAran held his great Midsummer-
feast as preliminary to a great market in hawks,
trained dogs and horses. On the morning after the Festival,
Romilly wakened to the great bustle in the courtyard, and
men and women thronging, while on the field beyond the
enclosed yard, horses were neighing as men put them
through their paces, and men and women were coming and
going. Romilly dressed quickly in an old gown—there were
still guests, so there could be no thought of borrowing a
pair of Darren's breeches—and ran down. Calinda, meeting
her on the stairs, gave a rueful laugh.

"I knew I should get no work out of Rael this day—he
is beyond me, his father must send him soon to Nevarsin
for teaching by men who can handle him," she said, "But
must you, too, hang around the market, Romilly? Ah
well—" she smiled kindly at her charge, "Go if you will,
I shall have the whole day to work with Mallina on her
penmanship—she takes guidance better when you and Rael
are not there to hear. And I suppose you would not mind
your book if your heart and thoughts were all out in the
courtyard. But you must work all the harder tomorrow,"
she said firmly, and Romilly hugged the older woman with
a vehemence that left her breathless.

"Thank you, Calinda, thank you!"

She picked her way carefully through the trampled mud
of the courtyard and into the field. Davin was displaying
the flight to a lure of one of the best-trained hawks, a great

bird in whose training Romilly had played no small part; she stood watching in excitement till Davin spotted her.

"And this hawk is fierce and strong, but so gentle that even a young maiden could fly her," Davin said, "Mistress Romilly, will you take the bird?"

She slid the gauntlet over her arm and held out her wrist; he set the bird on it, and swirled the lure, and the bird took off, quickly climbing the sky, then, as the whirling leather thong with the meat and feathers came swooping down, striking so quickly that eyes could hardly follow the swift strike. Romilly picked up bird and lure and stood feeding the hawk from her free hand, to the accompaniment of little cries of amazement and delight.

"I shall have that hawk, then, for my lady," said Cathal Aldaran of Scathfell, "She has not had enough exercise since her children were born, and so fine a hawk will encourage her to be out and about, and to ride—"

"No," said the elderly *Dom* Gareth firmly, "No woman shall fly such a hawk as that under my roof; but your training methods are excellent, *messire,* and I will take one of the smaller hawks for Lady Darissa—have you a good lady's hawk? Mistress Romilly, can you advise me, perhaps, as to what hawk my mother-in-law could best fly?"

She said, lowering her eyes modestly, "I fly a *verrin* hawk, *vai dom,* but either of these—" she indicated three of the smaller birds, with wing-spans not much longer than her arm, "are well trained and I think Darissa would have no trouble in handling them. But I give you my word, sir, that if you want to buy the larger bird for her, she is so well trained that Darissa could fly her, and the larger birds are better for hunting for the kitchens; the smaller hawks can bring down nothing bigger than a field-shrew."

He snorted. "The women of my household have no need to hunt for meat for the pot; if they fly hawks, they do so only to have a reason to take air and exercise. And The MacAran still lets a great girl like you hunt with a *verrin* hawk? Disgraceful!"

Romilly bit back the protest on her lip—*Aldaran might not approve of women flying hawks, but perhaps other men were not so stuffy and narrow-minded as he was himself*—realizing that a saucy answer would only alienate a valued

neighbor and customer of her father's. While they produced
most of what they needed on the estate at Falconsward,
still coined money was always in short supply, and most of
her father's ready money came from this sale every year.
She curtseyed to Lord Scathfell and withdrew, handing
back the hawk to Davin. While he haggled with the man,
she cast a quick frightened glance around the field—her
father might have decided to punish her by putting Preciosa
up for sale—but Preciosa was not there, but still safe within
the mews. At the far end, her father was putting one or
two of his best horses through their paces, while the kennel-
man was displaying working dogs trained to obedience to
word or gesture. The high nobility who had danced last
night at their feast rubbed elbows with small-holders and
farmers who had come to pick up dogs for their herding,
or perhaps to trade for a horse rejected by the nobles.
Darren was stationed at the far end, writing down all the
details of the transactions for the steward; Rael was running
in and out of the crowd, playing catch-the-monkey with a
group of small boys his own age, his face and hands already
grubby and his jacket torn.

"Can you take me to see your father's horses?" Alderic
said at her elbow, "I would like to trade my nag for a
somewhat better one; I have not much money, but perhaps
I could work some time for him in return for the difference—do you think he would be interested in a deal like
that? I have marked that your *coridom* is old and feeble--
perhaps I could work for him for forty days or so while he
finds himself a man better suited to the needs of his business, and the old man could be retired to an indoor
steward."

She blinked in surprise—she had begun to be sure that
he was, in fact, the Hastur prince in disguise, and here he
was offering to hire himself, a paid worker, to The Mac-
Aran in return for a horse-trade! But she said politely,
"About the deal, you must ask him yourself; but we have
some good horses which are not good-looking enough to
attract the attention of the highly-born, and must be sold
at a lower cost; perhaps one of them would suit you, if it
was well-trained. That one, for instance—" she pointed out
a great ungainly horse, an ugly color of brown, spotted
unevenly with black, his mane and tail growing somewhat

askew, "He is an ugly raw-boned brute, but if you look carefully at his gait, and the way he carries his tail, you will see that he is a fine strong horse, and spirited too. But he is no ride for a lady, nor for any soft-handed fellow who wants his horse to plod along at a gentle pace; he wants firm hands and good handling. His sire was our best stallion, but the dam was only a cull, so though his blood is not bad, he is an ugly brute and not good-colored."

"His haunches look strong, indeed," said Alderic, "But I would like to look at his teeth for myself. I suppose he is broken to the saddle?"

"Yes, though father was at first intending to make a drafthorse of him; he is too big for most riders," she said, "But you are tall, you would need a large horse. Ruyven broke him to the bridle, but I myself have ridden him— although," she said, with a mischievous smile, "Father does not know it, and you need not tell him."

"And you can handle him, *damisela*?" Alderic looked incredulous.

"I will not ride him before all these people to prove it," she said, "but I would not stoop to lie about it to you, and—" she met his eyes briefly, "I think perhaps you would know if I did."

"That I would, Romilly," he said gravely.

"I give you my word, the horse is good-tempered enough, but he wants firm handling," she said, "I think perhaps he has a sense of humor—if a horse can laugh, I would swear I have seen him laugh at people who think they need only clamber on a horse and let him do all the work, and he had Darren off in two minutes; but my father can ride him without even a bridle, only a saddle and halter; because The MacAran knows how to make him, or any horse, behave."

"Aye, and I am told you have the same gift," he said. "Well, I will make your father an offer for him; would he take my horse in trade, do you think?"

"Oh, yes, he has always need of cheaply-priced horse-flesh, to sell to farmers and such," she said, "Men who will use their horses well, but cannot afford much in the way of stables. One of our old mares, no longer young enough to carry active young folk who would be in the saddle all day, he gave for almost nothing to an elderly man who lives nearby, who was too poor to buy a good horse, just so that the old horse might live out her life in a good home and have only light work. No doubt he would do the same for your horse—is she very old?"

"No," Alderic said, "but I must be into the Hellers when summer comes, and even in summertime it takes a strong horse to ride such trails."

"Into the far Hellers?" She wondered what would take him into the almost-impassable mountain ranges in the summer, but he turned the subject deftly before she could ask.

"I had not expected to find a young woman such a judge of horseflesh—how came you to know so much?"

"I am a MacAran, sir; I have worked at my father's side since I was old enough to follow him about the stables, and when Ruyven left—" she broke off, unable to say to anyone outside the family that her oldest brother's defection had left her father with no one but paid help to share his love of the animals he bred and trained. Yet she sensed that he understood her, for he smiled in sympathy.

"I like your father," Alderic said, "He is harsh, yes, but he is just, and he speaks freely to his children."

"Does not your father?"

Alderic shook his head. "I have hardly had speech with my father half a dozen times since I was out of short dresses. My mother was wedded to him in a dynastic marriage, and there was little love to lose between them; I doubt they have said a civil word to one another since my sister was conceived, and now they dwell in separate houses and meet formally a few times a year, no more. My father is a kindly man, I suppose, but I think he cannot look on my face without seeing my mother's features, and so he has always been ill at ease with me. Even as a babe I called him *sir,* and have hardly spoken with him since I was grown to man's size."

"That cannot have been so long ago," Romilly teased, but he said, with a poignancy that stopped her teasing cold, "Still, I envy you; I have seen Rael climb without fear into his father's lap—I cannot remember that I ever did so with my father, but you can go to your father, speak with him freely, he treats you almost as a friend and listens when you speak. Even though my father is high in—" Alderic stopped himself short, and there was a moment of awkward silence before he finished weakly, "High in station and honor, I wish I need not always address him as *My Lord*. I swear I would trade fathers with you at any moment."

"He might think it a bargain," said Romilly bitterly, but she knew she was not quite truthful; her father loved her, harsh as he was, and she knew it. She said, "Look, there he stands for the moment he has no customer, go now and ask for such a trade for Redwing."

"I thank you," he said, and went; then Davin called to her to show the paces of one of the dogs she had trained, and she forgot Alderic again. She worked all day on the sale fields, displaying the obedience of the dogs, explaining bloodlines and stud-books, exhibiting the hawks; her noonmeal was a mouthful of bread and cheese and a few nuts, swallowed in the enclosure behind the stables among The MacAran's men, and by the time the trading was called to a halt by the evening rain and the guests began to depart, she was famished and filthy, ready for a bath and to be dressed in a comfortable worn tunic and skirt for the family's dinner. A good smell of roasting meat and fresh-baked bread came as she passed the hall, and she went in and took her seat. Rael was still chattering to anyone who would listen about his day spent among the animals, and Luciella finally silenced him with a weary "Hush, Rael, or you shall have supper in the nursery; there are others in this family who would like to speak a word or two without being drowned out! How did it go today, my dear?" she asked The MacAran as he took his seat and picked up his mug. He took a long drink before answering.

"Well enough; I made a good trade for Redwing, who is a fine horse for anyone who has wit to see what lies beneath that ugly coat of his. *Dom* Alderic told me you recommended that sale, Romilly," he said, with a kind glance at his elder daughter.

"Did I well, father? I did not want to interfere, but it seemed to me that he would be a good ride for *Dom* Alderic," she said shyly, "and—" she looked around to see if Alderic had come in, but Darren's place was still empty and his friend was not at table either, "He told me he was short of ready money, so I knew that one of the blacks would be beyond his purse."

"I am grateful to you; I wanted Redwing in good hands," said her father, "and most people could not handle him; but with young Castamir, he was gentle as a child's cagebird. So I thank you, daughter."

"But still," Luciella complained, "this must be the last year she goes out into the fields with the men, showing off hawks and horses—she is a grown woman, Mikhail!"

"No fear of that," said The MacAran, smiling, "other news I have too. Romilly, my dear, you know you are of an age to be married; I had not thought I would have such a good offer for you, but *Dom* Garris of Scathfell has asked me for your hand in marriage, and I have answered him; yes."

Romilly felt as if an ice-cold hand was closing about her throat.

"Father!" she protested, while Luciella beamed and Mallina squeaked with excitement, "Not *Dom* Garris!"

"Come, come," her father said with a genial smile, "Surely you have not set your heart on someone else? Manfred Storn is not yet ready to marry, and I thought you loved Darissa well, and would welcome marrying into that family, so you might be near your best friend."

"I had thought—perhaps Cinhil—"

"If that young man has trifled with your affections," said The MacAran, "I'll turn him over my knee and dust his breeches for him—he's too much a child to be worth calling challenge! Why marry the younger son when you can marry the Heir, my dear?"

Her heart sank as she remembered the moment in the galleries. *I was only testing you. Now I see you are a good girl.* So, she thought, if she had liked *Dom* Garris well enough to kiss him she would have been deprived of marriage, as if it were a prize for good conduct! But since she had showed her loathing, she was then worthy of his attentions? Her eyes burned, but she would not cry here before her father.

"Father, I hate him," she said, pleading, "Please, don't make me marry him!"

"Romilly," said Mallina, "You will be Lady Scathfell! Why, he's Heir to Scathfell, and perhaps even to Aldaran itself some day! Why, the folk of Aldaran were of the Hastur-kinfolk!"

The MacAran gestured the younger girl to silence.

"Romy," he said gravely, "Marriage is not a matter of whim. I have chosen a good young man for you—"

"So young he is not," she flared, "he has buried three wives, and all of them have died in childbirth!"

"That is because he married into Aldaran kindred," her father said, "Any horse-breeder will tell you it is unwise to cross close kindred so often. You have no Aldaran blood and can probably give him healthy children."

She thought of Darissa, not much older than herself, swollen and shapeless with bearing children. Would she be like that, and would those children have been fathered by *Dom* Garris, with his whining voice and damp flabby hands? The thought made her flesh crawl.

"No more talk," said her father firmly, "All silly girls think they know what man they want, but older heads must make the decision as it is best for their lives. I would not have you married before harvest time—I will not have my daughter hustled to marriage—but at the harvest you will marry *Dom* Garris, and that is all I have to say."

"So while I thought you were having a sale of horses and hawks," she said bitterly, "You were also making a sale of your daughters! Tell me, Father, did *Dom* Garris give a good price?"

She knew by the unlovely flush that spread over her father's face that she had caught him on the raw. He said, "I'll hear none of your impertinence, my pert young mistress!"

"I doubt it not," she flung back at him, "You would rather trade in hawks and horses because they cannot talk back—and you can give them what fate you will!"

He opened his mouth to reply; then gave her a heavy glance.

"My lady," he said to Luciella, "it is your task to bring my daughters under control; see to it, will you? I will dine with the steward; I'll not have this brangling at my family table." He rose and strode out of the room.

"Oh, Mother," Romilly wailed, crumpling and throwing her head into Luciella's lap, "do I have to marry that— that—" words almost failed her, but finally she came out with, "that great *slug*? He is like something with a dozen legs that crawled out from under a piece of rotten wood!"

Luciella stroked her hair gently, puzzled. "There, there, child," she murmured, "It will not be so bad as you think; why, didn't you tell *Dom* Alderic that a horse should not be judged by his ugly coat? *Dom* Garris is a good and honorable man. Why, at your age, I had already my first child, and so had your own dear mother, Romy. There, there, don't cry," she added helplessly, and Romilly knew there as no help for it; Luciella would never defy her father. Nor could she. She was only a girl and there was no escape.

Alone in her room, or riding alone over the hills with Preciosa on her saddle, Romilly pondered what she could do. It seemed that she was trapped. She had never known her father to alter a judgment given—he would not hear of forgiveness for Ruyven, for instance—or to change his mind, once made up. He would not break his agreement with *Dom* Garris—or had it been made with Gareth of Scathfell himself?—though the heavens should fall. Her governess, her stepmother even, could sometimes be teased or argued out of a punishment or a judgment; in all the years of her life, her father had never been known to go back on what he had said, even when he knew it was wrong. Far and wide in the Kilghard Hills, the word of a MacAran was like the word of Hastur; as good as another man's signed bond or sworn oath.

What if she should defy him? It would not be the first time. Something inside her quailed at the thought of his rage. But when she countered her father's rage with the thought of the alternative, confronting *Dom* Garris and the memory of lust in his eyes, she realized that she would rather that her father beat her every day for a year than that he should deliver her over to *Dom* Garris. Didn't he *know* what the man was like? And then, with her heart sinking, she realized that The MacAran was a man and would never have seen hat side of Garris of Aldaran; *that, Dom* Garris showed only to a woman he desired.

If he touches me, I will vomit, she thought, and then she knew that whatever her father's anger, she must make a final appeal to him.

She found him in the stable, supervising a stableboy in poulticing the knees of a black pony who had fallen in the yard. She knew it was not an auspicious moment, for he looked cross and abstracted.

"Keep up the poulticing," he directed the boy, "Hot and cold, for at least two hours, and then treat the knees with *karalla* powder and bandage them well. And see he doesn't lie down in the muck— make sure he has fresh straw every few hours. Even with all we can do, he will be scarred and I'll have to sell him at a loss, or keep him for light work on the farm; if his knees get infected, we may lose him altogether. I'm putting you in charge—if anything goes wrong, I'll have it out of your hide, you young rascal, since it was your careless riding let him fall!" The stableboy opened his mouth to protest, but The MacAran gestured him to silence. "And don't give me any back-talk—I saw you running him on the stones! Damned young fool, I ought to put you to mucking-out and not let you exercise any of them for forty days!" He turned his head irritably and saw Romilly.

"What do you want in the stables, girl?"

"I came to find you, father," she said, trying to steady her voice, "I will like a word with you, if you can spare the time."

"Time? I have none this morning, with this pony hurt and perhaps spoilt," he said, but he stepped out of the stable and leaned against one of the rail fences. "What is it, child?"

But she could not speak for a moment, her throat swelling as she looked at the panorama behind her, the mountains that rose across the valley, the green paddock with the brood mares near their time, placidly grazing, the house-folk washing clothes in the yard, over a steaming cauldron poised on the smouldering fire of little sticks . . . this was all so dear to her, and now, whatever came of this, she must leave it . . . Falconsward was as dear to her as to any of her father's sons, yet she must leave her home to be married away, and any of her father's sons, even Ruyven who had abandoned it, could stay here forever, with the horses and the home hills. She swallowed hard and felt tears starting from her eyes. Why could she not be her father's Heir in Ruyven's place, since he cared nothing for it, and bring her husband here, rather than marrying someone she must hate, and living in a strange place.

"What is it, daughter?" he asked gently, and she knew he had seen her tears.

She swallowed hard, trying to control her voice. She said "Father, I have always known I must marry, and I would gladly do your will, but—but—Father, why must it be *Dom* Garris? I hate him! I cannot bear him! The man is like a toad!" Her voice rose, and her father frowned, but quickly smoothed his face into the forced calm she dreaded.

He said reasonably, "I tried to make you the best marriage I could, Romy. He is nearest Heir to Scathfell, and not far from the lordship of Aldaran of Aldaran, should the old man die without children, which now looks likely. I am not a rich man, and I cannot pay much of a marriage-portion for you; and Scathfell is rich enough not to care what you can bring. *Dom* Garris is in need of a wife—"

"And he has worn out three," said Romilly, desperately, "And goes again to marry another girl of fifteen. . . ."

"One reason he asked me for you," her father said, "was that his other wives have been weaklings and too near akin to him; he wanted new blood for the house. If you bear him a healthy son, you will have great honor, and everything you could possibly wish for—"

"And if I do not I will be dead and no one will have a care whether I am happy or not," she cried, her tears starting forth again. "Father, I cannot, I will not marry that—that loathsome man! Oh, Father, I am not trying to defy you, I would willingly marry almost anyone else—Cinhil, or—or *Dom* Alderic—"

"Alderic, hey?" Her father took her chin in his big hand and tipped up her face to look at it. "Tell me the truth, now, child. Have you been playing about in a way you should not? *Dom* Garris will expect to find you chaste; will he be disappointed? Has that arrogant young Castamir sprig been trifling with your feelings, girl? A guest under his roof—"

"*Dom* Alderic has never spoken a word to me, or done anything, which he could not have done in full view of you and Mother," she flared indignantly, "I named him only because I would not find him loathsome, nor Cinhil, nor any healthy kind young man somewhere near my own age! But that—that slimy—" words failed her, and she bit her lip hard so she would not cry.

"Romilly," said her father gently, still holding her face between his hands, "*Dom* Garris not so old as *that*: it is not, after all, as if I had tried to give you to Lord Gareth, or to any man I knew to be evil-tempered, or a drunkard, or a gambler, or one who was a wastrel of substance. I have known Garris all his life; he is a good, honorable and well-born young man, and you should not hold his face against him, since he did not make it. A handsome face will soon be worn away, but honor and good birth and a kindly temper are the things I want for my daughter's husband. You are only a silly young girl, and you can see no further than a man's handsome face and grace at dancing; which is why fathers and mothers make marriages for young girls, so that they can see a man's true worth."

She swallowed, and felt shame overcoming her, to speak of this to her father, but the alternative was worse. She said, "He—he looks at me in such way—as if I were naked—and when we were dancing, he put his hands on me—"

Her father frowned and looked aside and she knew he as embarrassed too. At last he sighed and said, "The man is wanting a wife, that is all; when he is wedded he will not need to do so. And at least you know that he is not a—" he coughed nervously, "he is not a lover of men, and will not desert you to hold hands with one of his paxmen or a pretty young page-boy or Guardsman. I think he will make you a good husband, Romy. He may be awkward and not know how to make himself known to you, but I think he means you well and you will be happy together."

Romilly felt the tears breaking and spilling. She said, feeling her voice break in sobs, "Father—oh, Father, *please* . . . anyone, anyone else, I swear I will obey you without question, but not—not *Dom* Garris—"

The MacAran scowled, biting his lip. He said, "Romilly, this matter has gone so far I cannot honorably draw back. The folk of Scathfell are neighbors, and I am dependent on their good will; to break my word at this point, would be an affront to their honor which I could not recover in a lifetime. If I had had any idea you felt like this, I would never have given my word; but done is done, and I have pledged it in honor. There's no more to be said, child. You are young; you will soon grow used to him, and it will be well, I promise you. Now cheer up, don't cry; I promised you a pair of fine blacks, broken with my own hand, for a wedding-present, and I am going to make over the small farm at Greyrock to you, so you will always have something, a place of your own. And I have told Luciella to send to the markets in Caer Donn for fine stuff for a wedding-dress, so you need not be married in homespun. So cheer up, dry your eyes, and decide for yourself which of the blacks you want for a wedding-present, and you may ask Luciella to have new dresses made for you, three—no, four new outfits and everything to go with them, all kinds of petticoats and feathers and bonnets and gewgaws such as girls like, no girl in the hills will be better outfitted for her wedding."

She bent her head, swallowing hard. She had known it was hopeless, and he had given his word to *Dom* Garris and to Lord Scathfell. He would never draw back now, and it would be useless, no matter what she should say. He mistook her silence for agreement and patted her cheek.

"There's a fine, good girl," he said awkwardly, "I am proud of you, child—would that any of your brothers had your strength and spirit."

"I wish I had been your son," she blurted out, "and that I could stay at home with you always—"

Her father took her gently into his arms. "So do I, girl," he said against her hair, "So do I. But it's for man to wish and Gods to Give, and the Bearer of Burdens alone knows why he gifted only my daughter with those things a man wants from his sons. The world will go as it will and not as you or I would have it, Romy." He patted her, gently, and she cried, holding on to him, cried hopelessly, as if she would never stop.

In a way, she thought desperately later, his sympathy made it worse. If he had stormed and shouted at her, raged and threatened her with a beating, she could at least have felt that she had a right to rebel. Before his kindness she could only see his point of view—that she was a young girl, that her good parents and guardians were doing what they thought best for her, and that she was silly and thoughtless to speak out against their caution for her.

So she tried to seem interested in the preparations for her wedding which, so The MacAran said, would be at the harvest, Luciella sent to Caer Donn for spider-silk for her wedding-gown and fine dyed stuff, crimson and blue and violet, for her new dresses, and had ordered so many petti-

coats and camisoles and fine underthings that Mallina was
openly jealous and sulked while the sewing was being done.

One morning, a rider came from Scathfell, and when he
was welcomed in the courtyard, uncovered a cage before
him on the saddle.

"A message from *Dom* Garris, sir," he said to The Mac-
Aran, "and a gift for Mistress Romilly."

The MacAran took the letter, scowling slightly, and tore
it open. "Your eyes are better than mine, Darren," he said
to his son, "Read it for me."

Romilly thought, annoyed, that if the letter concerned
her, she should have been the one to read it. But perhaps
The MacAran did not want it known that his daughter was
so much a better scholar than his Nevarsin-educated son.
Darren glanced through the letter and frowned, then read
aloud.

"To The MacAran of Falconsward and to my affianced
wife Romilly, greeting from Gareth-Regis Aldaran at
Scathfell. Your daughter informed me that she flies a *verrin*
hawk, which is understandable in the daughter of the finest
hawk-trainer in these hills, but would be unseemly for the
wife of Aldaran's Heir. Therefore I take the liberty of sending her two fine ladybirds which will fittingly adorn the
most beautiful wrist in all of Kilghard Hills, so that she
need not fly a man's hawk. I beg her acceptance of these
fine birds, and I send them now so that she may be accustomed to their flight. Kindly convey my compliments and
respectful wishes to my promised wife, and to you my most
respected greetings, sir." Darren looked up, saying, "It has
Scathfell's own seal affixed."

The MacAran raised his eyebrows, but said, "A courteous latter indeed. Uncover the cage, man."

The cover lifted, two beautiful little hawks were revealed;
their hoods were of fine scarlet-dyed leather with an Aldaran crest worked in gold thread, and the jesses glimmered
with gold threads too. They were tiny brilliant birds, gleaming with gloss and health, and Romilly caught her breath
at the sight of them.

"A beautiful gift," she said, "and most thoughtful. Tell
my—my promised husband," she said, and stumbled over
the words, "That I am most grateful to him and I shall fly
them with all kind thoughts of him." She held out her wrist,

and lifted one of the hawks on to her glove. It sat so quietly that she could tell it was perfectly trained. Never mind that such hawks were no good for anything but flying at field-mice, they were exquisite little birds and for *Dom* Garris to pay so much heed to her known interests was a good sign. For a little while she thought better of her promised husband; but later she began to think it over; was this simply his way of telling her that when she was his wife she would not be allowed to work with a proper hawk at all? From what Gareth of Scathfell—the old man— had said, she was inclined to think so. *It would be unseemly for the wife of Scathfell's Heir.* She made up her mind, firmly, whatever they said, she would never be argued or bullied into giving up Preciosa! The bond between them was too strong for that.

While she was first flying the little hawks—with a guilty thought that she was being disloyal to her beloved Preciosa—she reached out for contact, the strong bond between hawk and flyer. But the tiny birds gave only a faint sense of confusion, exhilaration; there was no close emotion, no sense of rapport and union—the smaller hawks were too lowly organized to have the capacity for *laran.* She knew the cagebirds had no such abilities—she had once or twice tried to communicate with them—in fact, "the mind of a cagebird" was a byword for a stupid woman! Flying the small hawks was dull; she could watch them fly, and they were beautiful indeed, but there was none of the excite-ment, the sense of rapport and completion, she felt with Preciosa. She flew them dutifully every day for exercise, but it was always with relief that she hooded them again with the beautifully worked hoods and cast off Preciosa into the sky, climbing the sky with her in an ecstasy of flight and soaring freedom.

She rode mostly with Darren, now, and Rael; Alderic had been put to the *coridom's* work and was always busy about the place with accounts, arranging the stud-books, supervising the many men about court and stables. She sel-dom saw him, except now and again for a decorous word as he sat by the fire in the evening, or played a game of *castles* or cards with Darren or her father, or sometimes whittled wooden toys to amuse Rael in the long evenings. Her days, too, were filled; her father had said she need do no more lessons, and the plan for her to study ciphering with the old steward had of course been put aside, since she was to be married so soon, so Calinda filled her days with stitching, and taught her how to oversee the kitchen-women and the sewing-women and even the dairies . . . not that there would be so much need for her to do any of these things, but, Calinda said, she must know how to do these things so that she could know whether her servants did them well or not; Lord Scathfell was a widower and she would be the first lady in authority at Scathfell; she must not let them think that Falconsward was a poorly run household, so that the daughter of Falconsward could not fitly supervise her women. Romilly thought she would rather muck out barns and milk dairy-animals and make the butter herself than have to oversee other women doing it; while as for the sewing-women, she was grimly certain that the youngest and least skilled of them would be better than she, so how could she ever presume to supervise or oversee, far less chide or correct? Luciella, too, hunted up one of Mallina's old dolls, and dressed it in Rael's cast-off babyclothes and taught both Mallina and Romilly how to bathe a young baby, how to hold it and support its floppy little head, how to change its napkins and what to do to keep it from having rashes and skin disorders; Romilly could not imagine why, if there were skilled nurses and midwives there, and Darissa with two—no, three children by now—she should have to know how to do all this herself, even before she had any children, but Luciella insisted that it was part of a young wife's proper knowledge. Romilly had no particular objection to having children—Rael as a baby had been adorable—but when she thought of having children, she thought first of Darissa, soft and flabby and fat and sick, and then of the inevitable process by which those children would be gotten. She was farmbred and healthy, and had often thought, with secret pleasure, of the time when she would have a lover, a husband, but when she sought to put *Dom* Garris's face into that place, which (to do her credit) she virtuously tried to do, she only felt sick, and now even when she thought of any man, the very idea made her feel queasy and faint. No, but she *could* not, she would run away, she would join the Sisterhood of the Sword and wear weapons and fight as a mercenary soldier

for one of the kings contending for this land, she would cut
her hair and pierce her ears—and when she got to this
point she realized how foolish she was, for if she ran away
they would only follow her and drag her back. And then
she would make wild plans, a final appeal to her father, to
her stepmother, to Lord Scathfell himself—when they put
the bracelets on her she would scream "No" and tear them
off, when they tried to lead her to the bedding she would
fall on *Dom* Garris with a knife. . . . Surely then he would
put her away, he would not want her . . . she would tell
him how much she loathed him, and he would refuse to
have her. . . .

But she knew in her heart that all this was useless. She
must marry . . . and she could not!

The summer drew on; the evening snow was only a brief
trickle of rain, and the hills were bright with flowers and
budding trees; the nut-bushes were covered with little green
lumps which would ripen into nuts, and almost every day
she and Mallina could cut fresh mushrooms from the sides
of the old trees which had been implanted with fungus-
roots. She picked berries dutifully and helped to stem them
for conserves, helped churn butter in the dairies, and seldom had leisure even for a ride, let alone to give Preciosa
proper exercise; but every day she visited her hawk in the
mews, and begged Darren or Alderic to take her out and
fly her. Darren was afraid of hawks, and still avoided them
when he could, but when Alderic had leisure he would take
out Preciosa on his saddle.

"But she does not fly well for me," he told her one evening, "I think she is pining for you, Romilly."

"And I am neglecting her," Romilly said, with a pang of
guilt. She had herself formed the tie with this wild thing;
now she could not betray it. She resolved that tomorrow,
no matter what duties Luciella laid on her, she would find
some time for a ride, and to take out the hawk.

She flew through her work the next morning with such
speed and willingness that Luciella stared, and said, "Why,
what you can do when you are willing, child!"

"Since I have finished, foster-mother, may I take my
hawk out for a little while?"

Luciella hesitated, then said, "Why yes; you must not

neglect *Dom* Garris's gift. Go then, Romilly, enjoy yourself in the fresh air."

Released, she fled to put on her riding-habit and boots, to order her horse saddled—she supposed it would have to be a lady's saddle, but riding sidesaddle was better than not riding at all—and was swiftly off to the mews. Darren was in the yard, glumly exercising one or two of the hawks; she noted his clumsy movements, and told him she was going hawking—would he come? He went, with relief, and had his own horse saddled. She was taking Preciosa from her block, holding her familiar weight on the gauntlet with pleasure, extending her senses toward the hawk to set up the old contact, when her father stepped into the mews.

"Romilly," he said sharply, "Take your own hawks, not that one. You know what your promised husband said; it is unseemly to fly a *verrin* hawk, and you have hawks of your own. Put her back."

"Father!" she protested, in a sudden flood of anger, "Preciosa is my own hawk, I trained her myself! She is mine, mine! No one else shall fly her! How can it be unseemly for me to fly a hawk I trained? Are you gong to let *Dom* Garris tell you what it is right for your own daughter to do, in your own stable-yard?"

She saw conflict and dismay on his face; but he said sharply, "I told you, put that hawk back on the block and take out your own! I will not have you defy me, girl!" He strode toward her; Preciosa sensed Romilly's agitation and bated wildly, threshing furiously on her wrist, whirling up to the length of the fastened jesses, then settling restively back.

"Father—" she pleaded, lowering her voice not to disturb the easily-frightened birds, "Don't say this—"

The MacAran thrust out his hand and firmly gripped Preciosa's feet. He set her back on the block and said, "I will be obeyed, and that is all there is to it."

"She's not getting enough exercise," Romilly pleaded, "she needs to be flown!"

The MacAran paused. "That's right," he said, and beckoned to Darren.

"Here," he jerked his head to indicate Preciosa on her

block, "Take her; I give her to you. You need a good hawk
to work with, and this is the best we have. Take her out
today, and start getting used to her."

Romilly's mouth fell open in indignant surprise. He could
not do *that* to her—nor to Preciosa! The MacAran grasped
the bird again, held it firmly until the bating quieted, then
set her on Darren's wrist; he jerked back, startled, and Preciosa, even hooded, thrust her head about, trying to peck,
beating her wings; Darren ducked away, his wrist twisting
so that she overbalanced and fell, hanging from her jesses.
He stood holding the wildly bating hawk, and The Mac-
Aran said in a harsh whisper, "Pick her up! Quiet her,
damn you, if she breaks a wing-feather I'll break your
neck, boy!"

Darren made ineffectual movements to quiet the bird,
finally getting her to something like quiet on his glove. But
his voice broke into falsetto as he said, "It's not—not fair,
sir. Father, I beg you—Romilly trained that hawk herself,
and with her own *laran*—"

"Silence, young man! Don't you dare speak that word in
my presence!"

"Refusing to hear it won't make it less true, sir. It's Romilly's hawk, she trained it, she *earned* it, and I don't want
it—I won't take it from her!"

"But you will take it from *me*," said The MacAran, his
jaw thrusting forth, his jutting chin hard with fury, "How
dare you say a hawk trained at Falconsward in my own
mews is not mine to give? Romilly has been given hawks
by her promised husband. She needs not this one, and you
will take it or—" he leaned toward Darren, his eyes blazing, his breath coming and going in rough harsh noises,
"Or I will wring its neck here before you both! I will not
be defied here in my own mews!" He made a threatening
gesture as it to carry out his threat here and now, and
Romilly cried out.

"No! No, Father—no, please! Darren, don't let him—
take the hawk, it's better for you to have it—"

Darren drew a long, shaking breath. He wet his lips with
his tongue, and settled the hawk on his arm. He said shakily, "Only because you ask me, Romilly. Only for that, I
promise you."

Her eyes burning, Romilly turned aside to take up one

of the tiny, useless hawks that had been *Dom* Garris' gift. At that moment she hated them, the little half-brained, stupid things. Beautiful as they were, elegantly trapped, they were only ornaments, pretty meaningless jewels, not real hawks at all, no more than one of Rael's carven toys! But it was not their fault, poor silly little things, that they were not Preciosa. Her heart yearned over Preciosa, perched unsteadily on Darren's awkward wrist.

My hawk. Mine. And now that fool of a Darren will spoil her . . . ah, Preciosa, Preciosa, why did this have to happen to us? She felt that she hated her father too, and Darren, clumsily transferring Preciosa from his glove to the block on the saddle. Tears blurred her eyes as she mounted. Her father had called for his great rawboned grey; he would ride with them, he said wrathfully, to make sure Darren used the hawk well, and if he did not, he would learn it as he had learned his alphabet, beaten into him with The MacAran's own riding-crop!

They were all silent, miserable, as they rode down the pathway from the peaks of Falconsward. Romilly rode last, staring in open hatred at her father, at Darren's saddle where Preciosa perched restlessly. She sent out her consciousness, her *laran*—since the word had been used—toward Preciosa, but the hawk was too agitated; she felt only a blur of confusion and hatred, a reddish-tinged rage that blurred her mind, too, till she had all she could do to sit in the saddle.

All too soon they reached the great open meadow where they had flown their hawks that day—only then it had been Alderic with them, a friendly face and helping hands, not their furious father. Awkwardly, pinching her in his haste, Darren took the hood from Preciosa's head, raised her on his fist and cast her off; Romilly, reaching out her senses to merge with the rising hawk, felt how fury dropped away as Preciosa climbed the sky, and she thought, in despair, *Let her go free. She will never be mine again, and I cannot bear to see her mishandled by Darren. He means well, but he has no hands or heart for hawks.* As she sank into the hawk's mind and heart, her whole soul seemed to go into the cry.

Go, Preciosa! Fly away, fly free—one of us at least should be free! Higher—higher—now, turn and go—

"Romilly, what ails you?" Her father's voice was filled with asperity, "Get your bird out, girl!"

She brought herself painfully back to the moment, her practiced hands loosing the embroidered hood. The little hawk, shining like a jewel in the red sunlight, angled off, high on the wind, and Romilly watched, not seeing—her eyes were blurred with tears, her whole awareness with Preciosa.

Higher, higher . . . now, down the wind, and away, away . . . free on the wind, flying free and away. . . . a last quick sight of the country, spread out below her like a colored picture in one of Rael's schoolbooks, then the frail link snapped asunder and she was alone again, alone in her own mind, her hands and heart empty, and only the shrill tiny screaming of the small hawk striking at some little rodent in the long grass, lifting—the bird lighted on her saddle. With automatic hands she tore at the small carcass, letting the hawk feed from her glove, but her heart was empty.

Preciosa. She is gone. Gone. Never again. . . .

Her father's head was thrown back, scanning the sky where Preciosa had vanished. "She has gone long," he said, "Romilly, do you usually let her fly out of sight?"

Romilly shook her head. The MacAran waited, frozen, and Darren's head was thrown back, his mouth a round 'O' of dread. They waited. At last The MacAran said in a fury, "You have lost her, damn your clumsiness! The best hawk in the mews, and the very first time you fly her, you have lost her, worthless son that you are, worthless brat good for nothing but scribbling. . . ." he raised his riding-crop and the whip came down over Darren's shoulders. He yelped, more from startlement than pain, but the sound galvanized Romilly; she flung herself headlong from her horse and scrambled toward the men, throwing herself between her father and Darren so that the blows fell on her.

"Beat me instead," she cried, "It's not Darren's fault! I lost her, I let her go—I cannot be free, I must be chained inside a house and robbed of my hawk, you damned tyrant, but I will not have Preciosa chained too! I bade her go with my *laran*—with my *laran*—you have given Ruyven away with your tyranny, you have made Darren afraid of you, but I am not afraid of you, and at least you will never mistreat my hawk again, *my hawk, mine*—" and she burst into wild crying. Her father checked a moment as the first blow fell on her shoulders, but as he heard the flood of abuse, as the forbidden words *Ruyven* and *laran* fell on his ears, his face turned furious black, congested with wrath, and he raised the riding-crop and struck her hard. He raised it again and again; Romilly shuddered with the pain, and shrieked at him, incoherently, harder than ever; her father slid from his horse and stood over her, beating her about the back and shoulders with the crop until finally Darren flung his arms around his father, shouting and yelling, and then another voice; *Dom* Alderic, restraining her father with his strong arms.

"Here, here, sir—I'm sorry, but you mustn't beat a girl like that—good God, Romilly, your back is all bloody— look, sir, you've torn her dress!" He wrenched the crop from her father's hands. The man made no protest, letting his arms fall dazed to his sides. Romilly swayed, feeling bloody wetness on her back, numb and smarting, and Alderic shoved her father into Darren's arms, coming to support her with his arm. The MacAran looked dazed, his wrath giving way to numbness; he looked hastily, in dismay, at Romilly's torn dress where the crop had cut the stiff material into ribbons, and then away again.

He said numbly, "I—I did not know what I was doing— I am in your debt, *Dom* Alderic. I—I—" and his voice failed him. He swayed where he stood and would have fallen, but Darren held him upright. The MacAran stared at Romilly, and said harshly, "I lost my temper. I shall not forgive you, girl, that you caused me to forget myself so shamefully! Had you been a boy, I would still beat you senseless! But soon enough your husband will have charge of you, and if you speak to him like that, I doubt it not he will break your head in two! Get out of my sight!"

Romilly stumbled; Alderic pushed her toward her horse. "Can you ride?" he asked in an undertone.

She nodded, numb, tears bursting out again.

"You had better get back to the house," he muttered, "while he is still in shock at what he has done."

The MacAran stood, still shaking his head in dismay and wrath. "In all the years of my life," he said, "Never have

I laid hand on a woman or girl! I shall not forgive myself, nor Romilly for provoking me!" He stared up into the sky where the hawk had vanished, and muttered something, but Romilly, under a push from Alderic, rode away blindly toward Falconsward.

When she stumbled into the house, and into her rooms, her old nurse met her with dismay. "Oh, my lamb, my little one, what has happened to you? Your back—your riding-dress—"

"Father beat me," she mumbled, breaking out into terrible crying, "He beat me because Darren lost my hawk. . . ."

Gwennis soaked the remains of the dress from her back, dressed the broken skin and bruised flesh with oil and herb-salve, put her into an old robe of soft cloth, and brought her hot soup in her bed. Romilly had begun to shiver and felt sick and feverish. Gwennis was grumbling, but she shook her head and demanded, "How did you come to anger your father so much? He is such a gentle man, he must have been beside himself to do something like this!" Romilly could not speak; her teeth were chattering and she kept crying, even though she tried and tried to stop. Gwennis, alarmed, went to fetch Luciella, who cried herself over Romilly's bruises and cuts and her ruined habit, and nevertheless repeated what Gwennis had said— "How in the world came you to anger your father like *this*? He would *never* have done a thing like this unless you provoked him beyond bearing!"

They blame me, Romilly thought, *they all blame me because I was beaten. . . .*

And now there is no hope for me. Preciosa is gone. My father cares more to be on good terms with Aldaran than he cares for me. He will beat Darren ruthlessly into shape because Darren does not have my gifts, but he will not let me be what I am, nor Darren what he is; he cares nothing for what we are, but only for what he would have us be. She would not listen to Luciella's kind words, not to Gwennis's cosseting. She could not stop crying; she cried until her eyes were sore and her head ached and her nose was red-dened and dripping. And at last she cried herself to sleep.

She woke late, when the whole of Falconsward was si-lent, and the great violet face of Kyrrdis hung full and shining in her window. Her head still ached terribly, and her back stung and smarted despite the healing salves Gwennis had put on it. She was hungry; she decided to slip downstairs and find some bread and cold meat in the kitchen.

My father hates me. He drove Ruyven away with his tyranny, but Ruyven at last is free, learning to be what he must be, in a Tower. Ruyven was right; at least, out of range of my father's iron will, he can be what he is, not what Father would have him be. And suddenly Romilly knew that she, too, must be free, as Preciosa was free in the wild to be what she was.

Shaking, she pulled an old knitted vest over her sore back, and put on the old tunic and breeches she had worn. She slipped quietly along the corridor, her boots in her hand. They were women's boots; a woman, she had heard all of her life, was not safe alone on the roads, and after the way *Dom* Garris had looked at her at Midsummer, she knew why. Ruyven's room was shut up, all his things as he had left them; noiselessly she slipped inside, took from a chest one of his plainer shirts and an old pair of leather breeches, a little too large for her, shucked off Darren's too-tight ones and dressed in Ruyven's ample ones; she took a cloak too, and a leather over-tunic, slipped into her room again for her own hawking-glove. Remembering that Preciosa was gone, she almost left it behind, but she thought, *some day I will have a hawk again, and I will remember Preciosa by this.* At the last, before she slid her old dagger into its sheath, she cut her hair short to the nape of her neck, and as she stole outside, thrust the braid deep into the midden, so they would not find it. She had locked Ruyven's door again, and they would never think to look among his old clothes and count the shirts. She would carry her habit with her, so they would be looking for a girl with long hair in a green riding-habit, not a nondescript young boy in plain old clothes. Slipping into the stable, she put an old saddle, dustcovered and hidden behind other discarded bits of harness, on her own horse, then thought better of it and left him in the stall. A black horse, a fine well-bred one, would betray her anywhere as a MacAran. She carried the saddle carefully outside and made a small bundle of

it with her tack and her girl's clothes. She left it there
and slipped quietly into the kitchen—in the summer, all
the kitchen work was done in an outer building so the
building would not be too hot—and found herself meat
and a cut loaf of bread, a handful of nuts and some flat
cakes of coarse grain which the cook baked every day for
the best of the dogs, the breeding bitches and those who
were nursing pups . . . they were palatable enough and
would not be missed as other breads might be, since they
were baked by the dozen, almost by the hundred . . . a
handful would never be counted. She rolled them in a
kitchen towel and tied the neck of the improvised bag,
then put her boots on, went outside and carried bag and
saddle to the outer pasture, where old horses and culls
were left to grass. She scanned them for a horse who
would not be missed for some days—let them think she
had gone afoot. Finally she decided on an elderly hack
who was used only once in a great while, when the old
coridom, now retired and seldom out of doors at all, visited the far pastures. She clucked softly—all the horses
knew her—and he came cantering quietly to the fence.
She murmured to him, fed him a handful of coarse vegetables, then put the saddle on his back, and led him softly
away down the path, not mounting till she as well out of
earshot of the walls. Once a dog began to bark inside the
castle and she held her breath and fiercely *willed* the animal to be silent.

At the foot of the hill, she clambered into the saddle,
wincing as her fresh bruises were jolted, but setting her
teeth against the pain and wrapping herself in her cloak
against the midnight chill. Once she looked up at Falconsward on its crag, high above her.

*Bearer of Burdens! I cannot, I cannot—Father is sorry he
beat me, this is madness, I should go back before I am
missed. . . .*

But then the memory of Darren's face as she gave him
the hawk, of her father's rage, of Ruyven's set, despairing
eyes the last time she had seen him, before he ran away
from Nevarsin. . . . *No, Father will have us what he wishes,
not what we are.* The memory of *Dom* Garris handling her
rudely at Midsummer, the thought of how he would behave

when she was turned over to him, his wife, *his property to do with as he would*—

She set her face like iron. Had there been anyone to see, at that moment, they would have marked; she was very like her father. She rode away from Falconsward without once looking back.

Book Two:

THE FUGITIVE

Chapter 1

On the third day it began to snow. Romilly, who had lived all her life in the foothills of the Hellers, knew that she must find shelter quickly; nothing alive could survive a storm, even at this season, except under cover. The wind whipped like a knife, and howled along the trees lining the path like the voices of ten thousand devils. Briefly she considered retracing her steps to the little hill-farm she had passed early that morning, and asking shelter there . . . but no. The farmers there might have been among those who came, now and again, to Falconsward, and even in her boy's dress might know her for The MacAran's daughter. She did not know them; but she had never been this far from her home, and was not sure where she was.

She knew vaguely that if she followed this trail, keeping to the north, she would come at last to Nevarsin, where she could take the road to Tramontana Tower. There she would find her brother Ruyven—or if he had been sent elsewhere by the *leroni* who ruled in the Towers, she could find news of him. It was in her mind that she might seek the training of her *laran* within the Towers, as the *leronis* Marelie had invited her to do some years ago. Alternatively, she might remain in Nevarsin for the winter—she had lived in the Hellers long enough to know that travelling in the winter, by the roads she must take to Nevarsin, was a dangerous enterprise, undertaken only by the mad or the desperate. Surely in Nevarsin she could seek to find work somewhere as a hawkmaster's apprentice, or with some blacksmith or horsekeeper as a stableboy—for she had no intention of revealing herself as a girl. She had seldom been away from her own home, where even the kitchen-girls and washerwomen were treated kindly and properly supervised by *Domna* Luciella, but the very way they reacted to this treatment told her how rare it was, and one of the women, who had worked as a tavern wench for years, had told many stories of the treatment she was apt to receive. Romilly did not doubt her own ability to care for herself and to keep unwelcome hands off her; but even the lowest stable boy was paid more than any cook-woman or tavern maid, and Romilly had few skills to lift her above the lowest scullery-maid's tasks. All she knew was horses and hawks, and the supervision of servants. Dressmakers and children's nurses, she knew, could earn higher wages, but even the thought of working as a sewing-woman made her smile, remembering the botchery she made of her sewing, and for a child's nurse they would want to know much more about her than she would be willing to tell. No, if she chose to stay in Nevarsin for the winter she would remain a boy to all appearances, and seek work in stables or mews.

And that way, at least, she would be around horses and hawks. She thought with a bitter pang of the lost Preciosa.

But I am glad it happened, she thought fiercely, hunching against the lashing wind and drawing her cloak high over her face, almost to covering her eyes. *Otherwise, I would never have had the courage to break away! I would have remained obedient, perhaps even married* Dom *Garris . .* and a shiver of revulsion went through her. No, she was well out of that, even if she must spend the rest of her life working as a boy in some stranger's stables!

The snow was beginning to turn to a wet, soggy rain; the horse's feet slipped and slithered on the steep trail, and Romilly, sliding into rapport, felt the chill of the wind, the uneasy way the horse shivered and set down his feet with uncertain care on the slippery road. The rain was freezing as it fell; her cloak was stiffening with ice. They must find shelter soon, indeed.

They came to a steep turn in the road, where it forked, one path leading upward through thick trees that lined the trail, the other broader, but steeply downward. Romilly slid off the horse's back and went, craning her neck to stare through the thick misty rain. Downward she could see nothing except a small runnel of water cascading out of sight over the rocks beside the road; but upward, it seemed to her, she could make out the walls of some kind of building, a herder's hut or shelter for animals. The broadening road might lead down to a village or a cluster of valley farms, but she had no assurance, nor did she see any lights in the valley, and the rains were coming ever faster.

Upward, then, it must be, to the shelter, no matter how crude; it would at least be out of the wind or rain. He did not mount again—on a trail as steep as this upward path, the horse would fare better without her weight. She took her horse's bridle, speaking soothingly to the animal as it jerked its head away. She wished she could have had her own horse; this one was a stranger. Yet it was docile enough and even friendly.

The darkness through snow and rain drew darker; it was some building, indeed; not large, but it appeared weather-tight. The door was sagging, half off its hinges, and gave a loud protesting noise when she shoved it and went in.

"Who's there?" a quavering voice cried out, and Romilly felt her heart race rand her throat tighten with fear. Dark as it looked, dilapidated, it was not deserted after all.

She said quickly, "I mean you no harm, ma'am—I was lost in the storm and the rain is freezing. May I come in?"

"Honor to the Bearer of Burdens, and thanks be that you have come," the voice said; a trembling, old voice. "My grandson went to the town and I make no doubt, in this storm he has had to shelter somewhere, I heard your horse's steps and thought for a moment it was Rory comin' back, but he rides a stag-pony and I see you have a horse. I canna' leave my bed; can ye throw a branch on the fire, boy?"

Now her face as beginning to thaw a little she could smell the smoke; groping in the darkness, she went toward the dull embers. The fire was almost out. Romilly stirred the embers, coaxed it alive with small sticks, and when they caught, built it up gain with a bigger branch and then with a log. She stood warming her hands, in the growing light, her eyes made out a few sticks of decrepit furniture, a bench or two, an ancient chest, a box-bed built into the wall, in which lay an old, old woman, propped up against the back of the bed.

As the firelight grew, she said, "Come here, boy. Let me look at you."

"My horse—" Romilly hesitated.

"You can led him round into the stable," said the old voice. "Do that first, then come back."

She had to force herself to wrap the cloak over her face and go into the bitter cold. The stable was deserted, except for a couple of scrawny cats, who whined and rubbed against her legs, and after she had unsaddled her horse and given it a couple of pieces of the dog's bread—the grain would be enough to feed it for tonight—they followed her through the door into the warmth of the now-blazing fire.

"Good, good," said the old woman, in her shaky voice, "I thought of them out in the cold, but I could not get up to let them in. Come here and let me look at you, then, lad." And as Romilly went and stood by the box-bed, she hitched herself up a little further, peering with her face wrinkled up at Romilly's face. "How come ye out in such weather, boy?"

"I am travelling to Nevarsin, *mestra*," said Romilly.

"All alone? In such a storm?"

"I set out three days ago when the weather was fine."

"Are ye from south of the Kadarin? Red hair—ye have a look of the *Hali'imyn* about ye," the old woman said. She was wrapped in several layers of ragged shawls, and three or four threadbare blankets, not much better than horse-blankets, were piled on her bed. She looked gaunt, emaciated, exhausted.

The old woman let out her breath in a trembling sigh. She said, "I hoped he would be back from Nevarsin early this day, but no doubt the snow is worse to the North— well, with you to mend the fire, I will not freeze here alone in the storm. My old bones cannot stand the cold the way I could before, and before he left he built up the fire to last three days, saying he would surely be back before then. . . ."

"Can I do anything else for you, *mestra*?"

"If you can cook a pot of porridge, ye can have a share of it," said the old woman, indicating an empty pot, bowl and spoon at her side, "But get out of your wet things first, lad."

Romilly drew breath; the old woman apparently accepted her as a farm boy. She took off cloak and boots, hanging the cloak near the warmth of the fire to dry; there was a barrel of water near the fire, and she took the empty porridge-pot, rinsed it, and, as the old woman directed her, found a half-empty sack of coarse meal, more ground nuts than grain, and salt, and hung the mixture in the kettle from the long hook over the fireplace. The old woman beckoned her back, then.

"Where are you off to at this bitter time of the year, my lad?"

At that offhand "my lad" Romilly felt a bursting sigh of relief; at least the old woman had accepted her for what she seemed to be, a young boy and not a girl at the edge of being a woman. Then it occurred to her that the deception of an old woman, half-blind, was not so great a matter after all, and people with younger eyes and quicker wits might see through her more easily. And then she realized that the old woman in the box-bed was still peering out at her through those wrinkled eyelids, waiting for her answer.

"I am travelling to Nevarsin," she said at last, "My brother is there."

"In the monastery? Why, you are far off your road for that, youngster—you should have taken the left-hand fork at the bottom of the mountain. But too late now, you must stay till the storm is over, and when Rory is back he will set you on your proper path."

"I thank you, *mestra.*"

"What is your name, lad?"

"Rom—" Romilly hesitated, swallowing back her name, realizing she had not thought of this for a moment. She pondered saying "Ruyven," but then she might not remember to answer to that but would look about for her brother. She swallowed, pretended to have choked for a moment on the smoke of the fire, and said "Rumal."

"And why are you going to Nevarsin all on your own? Are you to become a monk, or being sent there to be taught by the brothers, as they do with the sons of the gentry? You have a look of gentry about you, at that, as if you'd been born in a Great House—and your hands are finer than a stable-boy's."

Romilly almost laughed, thinking of the time when Gwennis, scowling at her calloused hands, worn by reins and claws, had said, reproving, "You will have the hands of a stable-boy if you do not take care!" But once again the old woman was waiting for an answer, and she thought

swiftly of Nelda's son Loran—everyone at Falconsward
knew him to be the MacAran's *nedestro* son, though Luciella liked to pretend she did not know, and refused to admit
the boy existed. She said, "I was brought up in a Great
House; but my mother was too proud to bring me under
my father's eye, since I was festival-got; so she said I could
make more of myself in a city, and I hope to find work in
Nevarsin—I was apprentice to the hawk-master." *And that,
at least, was true; she was more Davin's apprentice than that
worthless Ker.*

"Well, Rumal, you are welcome," the old woman said.
"I live here alone with my grandson—my daughter died
when he was born, and his father's away in the lowlands
in the service of King Rafael, across the Kadarin to the
south. My name is Mhari, and I have dwelt here in this hut
most of my life; we make a kind of living from the nut-
farming, or we did until I grew too old for it; it's hard for
Rory to look after the trees at all seasons, and care for me
too, but he's a good lad, and he went to sell our nuts in
the market at Nevarsin, and bring home flour for porridge,
and herb-medicines for my old bones. When he's a wee bit
older, perhaps, he can find him a wife and they can make
a living here, for it's all I have to leave him."

"I think the porridge is boiling over," said Romilly, and
hurried to the fire, to move the kettle a little further from
the flame. When it was done, she dipped up a bowl for the
old woman, and propped her up to eat it, then shook out
Mhari's pillows and soothed her bedcovers and settled her
down for the night.

"You are neat-handed as a girl," said Mhari, and Romilly's heart stopped till she went on, "I suppose that comes
from handling birds; I never had the hands for that, nor
the patience, either. But your porridge will be cold, child;
go and eat it, and you can sleep there in Rory's pallet by
the fire, since it's not likely he'll be home in this storm."

Romilly settled down by the banked fire to eat her bowlful, then rinsed the bowl in the barrel of water, set it near
the fire to dry and stretched out, wrapped in her cloak, by
the hearth. It was a hard bed, but on the trail she had slept
in worse places, and she lay awake for a time, drowsily
listening to the beating storm outside, and to the occasional
drop of water which made its way down the chimney to

sizzle briefly in the fire. Twice she woke during the night to make certain the fire was still alive. Toward morning the noise of the storm died away a little, and she slept heavily, to be wakened by a great pounding on the door. Mhari sat upright in her bed.

"It is Rory's voice," she said, "Did you draw the bolt, then?"

Romilly felt like a fool. The last thing she had done before settling down to sleep was to lock the inside door—which of course the crippled old woman could never have done. No wonder the voice outside sounded loud and agitated! She hurried to the door and drew the bolt.

She looked into the face of a huge burly young man, bewhiskered and clad in threadbare sacking and a cloak of a fashion which had not been worn in the Hellers since her father was a child. He had his dagger out, and would have rushed at her with it, but he heard old Mhari's cry.

"No, Rory—the boy meant no harm—he cared for me and cooked my supper hot—I bade him sleep here!"

The rough-looking young man let the dagger fall and hurried to the box-bed. "You are really all right, Granny? When I felt the door locked, and then when I saw a stranger within, I was only afraid someone had come, forced his way in and done you some harm—"

"Now, now, now," old Mhari said, "I am safe and sound, and it was well for me that he came, for the fire was near out, and I could have frozen in the night!"

"I am grateful to you, whoever you are, fellow," said the big young man, sliding his dagger into its sheath and bending to kiss his grandmother on the forehead. "The storm was so bad, and all night I could think only of Granny, alone here with the fire burnt out and no way to feed herself. My hearth is yours while you have need of it," he added, in the ancient mountain phrase of hospitality given a stranger. "I left my shelter the moment the rain died, and came home, though my hosts bade me stay till sunrise. And you are well and warm, that's the important thing, Granny dear." He looked tenderly on the old woman. Then, flinging off his cloak on to a bench, he went to the porridge-pot still hanging by the fire, dipped up some with the ladle, thick and stiff after the night by the hearth, and began to munch on the heavy stuff from his fingers. "Ah,

warm food is good—it's cold as Zandru's breath out there
still, and all the rain has frozen on the trees and the road—
I feared old Horny would slip and break a leg. But I traded
for some grain, Granny, so you shall have bread as well as
porridge, and I have dried blackfruits as well in my bag;
the miller's wife sent them for you, saying you would like
the change." He turned to Romilly and asked, "Could I
trouble you to get the saddlebags from my beast? My hands
are so cold they are all but frozen, and I could not unfasten
the tack till they are warm again; and you have spent the
night in the warm."

"Gladly," said Romilly, "I must go out and see to my
horse, in any case."

"You have a horse?" A look almost of greed lighted
Rory's face. "I have always wanted a horse; but they are
not for the likes of me! You must indeed have been
brought up in a Great House."

Romilly went outside, flinging her cloak over her shoulders, and unfastened the heavy saddlebags lying across the
heavy-boned stag-like chervine Rory had ridden. She took
the sack of coarse grain into the byre, and brought the
saddlebags into the cottage, dumping them on the floor
near the fire.

Rory was bending over his grandmother, talking in low
tones; she was sure he had not heard her, so she slipped
out again into the byre, went into her own bags and fed
her horse one or two cakes of the dog-bread, stroking its
muzzle and talking to it. There was an old-fashioned outhouse inside the byre, and she went into it; as she was
readjusting her clothing, she paused, dismayed, at the
bloodstains lining her underwear; because of the storm she
had lost track of the days. *When I thought to pass myself
off as a man,* she said to herself wryly, *I had forgotten
certain very important points which I must remember.* She
had never thought it would be simple, to remember to pitch
her voice at its deepest level and to remember to move
with the free stride for which Luciella and her governess hd
always reproved her, but she had forgotten the inexorable
rhythms of female biology which could have betrayed her
more than any of this.

As she was tearing up one of the old petticoats in her
pack—she could wash it privately by night, perhaps—she

took stock of what she should do now. The old woman had promised that Rory would set her on her road to Nevarsin. Would it be ungracious, she wondered, to insist that she must leave at once? She should have invented someone who was waiting for her in that city and would come to look for her if she did not appear at the appointed time. She made sure that there were no telltale bulges in her clothing, fed the horse and led Rory's stag-pony inside, spreading fresh straw and fodder for it—she did not like the looks of that heavy-set young roughneck, but the riding-animal was certainly not to blame and should not suffer for her dislike of his master's face.

Then she stepped back through the door—and paused, hearing the old woman's voice.

"The youngster was kind to me, Rory. This is an evil thing you do, and a breach of hospitality, which the Gods hate."

Rory's voice was sullen. "You know how long I have wished for a horse, and while I dwell here at the world's end, I shall never have a better chance. If this is a runaway bastard from somewhere, he'll never be missed. Why, did you see his cloak—in all my years I have never even had a chance at such a cloak, and the brooch in it alone would pay a healer to come all the way from Nevarsin to cure your joint-aches! As for your debt to him, well, he had lodging and fire the night—it was not all kindliness on his part. And I can cut his throat quick as a puff of wind, and he'll never have the time to be afeared."

Romilly caught, terrified, at her throat. He meant to kill her! Never had she for a moment thought, even in the poverty of the hut, that her horse and cloak, let alone the copper brooch in its fastening and the money in her small purse, might endanger her very life. She would have turned, noiselessly, to flee; but without cloak or horse, without food, she would die quickly in the bitter cold! She gripped her fingers on the dagger in its sheath at her side. At least, he would find no unaware or easy victim; she would sell her life as dearly as she could. But she must not allow them to know that she knew of their plans, but pretend to suspect nothing till she had her cloak and her pack, and could make a run for the horse. She turned quietly about and went noiselessly back to the byre, where she put her saddle on her horse, and turned him about, ready to flee. Now she must have her cloak, or she would freeze in the hills.

Keeping her hand unobtrusively near the dagger's hilt, she came back to the door, careful to make some noise as she opened it. When she came in, Rory was siting on the bench fiddling with his boots, and old Mhari had laid her head back on the pillow and was asleep, or pretending to be. As Romilly came in, Rory said, "Would you give me a hand wi' my boots, young fellow?"

"Gladly," Romilly said, thinking fast. If he had his boots off, at least he could not pursue her too quickly. She knelt before him, putting both hands to the boot, and hauled it free of his foot; bent forward to the other. She had both hands on it, and was tugging hard, when Rory bent forward, and she saw the glint of the knife in his hand.

Romilly acted without thought; she pushed hard on the leg with the boot, sending it up so that Rory's knee slammed into his chin, with a loud crack. The bench went over backward, with Rory tangled in it, and she scrambled to her feet and ran for the door, snatching up her cloak as she ran. She fumbled at the latch-string, her heart pounding, hearing Rory curse and shout behind her. A quick glance told her; his mouth was bleeding, either the blow had knocked out a tooth or cut his lip. She was swiftly through the door and tried to thrust it shut with shoulder, but he wrestled it open behind her and then he was on her. She did not see the knife; perhaps he had dropped it, perhaps he meant to use only his huge hands closing around her throat; then his eyes widened as he saw the ripped tunic and he tore it all the way down.

"By the Burden! Tits like a very cow! A girl, huh?" He grabbed Romilly's hand, which was clawing at his eyes, and held her immobile; then whirled her about and marched her back into the little kitchen.

"Hey, there! Granny! Look what I found, after all? Hell's own waste to hurt her—haven't I been after a wife these four years, and not a copper for a bride-price, and now one comes to my very door!" He laughed, jubilantly. "Don't be frightened, wench, I wouldn't hurt a hair of your little head now! I've something better to do, hey, Granny? And she can stay with you and wait on you while I'm out at the farming, or away to the mill or the town!" Laughing, the big man squeezed her tight in his arms and mashed a kiss against her mouth. "Runaway servant girl to the gentry, are you, then? Well, pretty thing, here you'll have your own kitchen and hearthfire, what do you say to that?"

Paralyzed by this torrent of words, Romilly was silent, filled with terror, but thinking faster than she had ever thought in her life.

He wanted her. He would not hurt her, at least for a little while, while he still hoped to have her. His mouth against hers filled her with revulsion, but she concealed the crawling sense of sickness and forced herself to smile up at him.

"At least you are no worse than the man they would have had me marry," she said, and realized as she said it that she was telling the absolute truth. "Old, more than twice my age, and always pawing at helpless girls, while you, at least, are young and clean."

He said, contented, "I think we will suit well enough when we are used to each other; and we need only share a bed, a meal and a fireside, and we will be as lawful wedded as if Lord Storn himself had locked the *catenas* on our arms like gentlefolk! I will build up the fire in the inner room where there is a bed, and you can get about cooking a meal for us to share. There is flour in the sacks, and can you make a loaf with blackfruit? I do like a good fruity bread, and I've had nothing but nut-porridge for forty days and more!"

"I will—try my best," Romilly said, forcing her voice to calm, "and if am not sure what to do, no doubt *mestra* Mhari will tell me."

"Ah, you think yourself my old Granny's betters, do you?" Rory demanded truculently, "You will say *Dame Mhari* till *she* gives you leave to say *Granny*, do you hear?"

Romilly realized, abruptly, that she had automatically used the form of a noblewoman speaking to an inferior. She hung head, pretending to be ashamed, and murmured, "I meant no harm—"

"And since you're a girl, it's more suitable for you to wash Granny's face and put her into a clean bedgown, get her ready for the day," Rory said, "D'you think you could sit in the hearth for a little today, Granny? If our fine lady here gets you fresh and ready?"

"Aye, I'll sit in the hearth for your wedding meal, Rory," said the old woman, and Romilly, biting her lip, said meekly that she would be glad to do whatever she could for Dame Mhari.

"I knew she was too fine-handed for a lad," said Mhari, as Romilly bent to lift her, and went to dip hot water from the barrel. As she washed the old woman's face and hands, and brought a clean but threadbare gown from the ancient clothes-press in the corner, she was thinking harder than she had ever done. How could she escape? They would watch her moment by moment until the marriage was consummated; *by which time* she thought grimly, *they would think her too beaten to try and get away.* It made her sick at her stomach to think of that great unwashed lout taking her to bed, but she supposed it wouldn't kill her, and since she was actually in the bleeding part of her woman's cycles, at least he was unlikely to make her pregnant. And then she stopped short in what she was doing, remembering gleefully something Darissa had whispered to her a few months after her marriage. At the time, Romilly had only been embarrassed and giggled about it—what great sillies men were, to be superstitious about such a thing! But now she could make it serve her.

"I am cold, wet and bare like this," the old woman complained, "Wrap me in my gown, girl—what am I to call you?"

Romilly started to tell the woman her name—after all, now they knew she was a girl what did it matter?—but then she thought; her father might seek her even as far as this. She said the first name that came into her head.

"Calinda."

"Wrap me in my gown, Calinda, I am shivering!"

"I am sorry, Mother Mhari," she said, using the meek term of respect for any aging woman, "I had a heavy thought—" and she bent close to the old woman as she wrapped her in gown and woolly shawk and then laid her on her pillows, drying her hands with a towel. "I—I—I will gladly wed your grandson—" and she thought the words would choke her.

"And well you should," said the old woman, "He is a good kind man, and he will use you well and never beat you unless you really deserve it."

Romilly gulped; at least *that* she would never have had to fear from *Dom* Garris. "B-but," she said, pretending to be embarrassed, which was not difficult, "He will be angry with me if he tries to share my bed *this* night, for my—my cycles are on me, and I am bleeding. . . ."

"Ah, well," said the old lady, "You did well to tell me; men are funny that way, he might well have beaten you for it; my man used to thump me well if I did not tell him well before the time, so he could keep away or sleep with the dairy-maid—ah, yes, once I was well off, I had a dairy-maid and a cook-wench at one time, and now look at me. But with a woman's care, I will grow better soon, and Rory will not have to cook porridge and bake bread, which is no work for a man. Look what a fine man you are getting, he never scorned to wash and turn his old Granny in her bed, or bring her food, or even empty my chamberpot. And speaking of a chamberpot—" She gestured, and Romilly fetched the utensil and supported the old woman.

She thinks this life will make me well off; so long as I have a man for husband, I need ask no better than to drudge about barn and byre and kitchen, waiting hand and foot on a bedridden old woman, so long as I have the name of wife. She shivered as she thought, *perhaps some women would truly think themselves well off—a home of their own and a hardworking man, one who was kind to his old grandmother.* She settled the woman in the bed again and went to empty the chamberpot. She was used to working with her hands about animals, and the work itself did not disgust her, but she was frightened of Rory.

I did not refuse Dom *Garris to be married by force to a woodsman, however honest or good. And now I have won myself a few days time. I will pretend to be meek and mild and biddable, and soon or late, they must let me out of their sight.*

When the old woman was washed and dressed in a fresh gown, Romilly went to the pump in the yard to draw water, placing the great kettle over the fire to heat for the washing of linens, then, guided by directions from Dame Mhari, set about mixing and baking a loaf of bread with small lumps of sliced blackfruit in the dough. When the bread was baking in the covered pot in the ashes by the hearth, and Dame

Mhari dozing in her box-bed, she sat down on one of the benches to rest for a moment, and think.

She had gained time. A swift visit to the outhouse showed her that her horse had been unsaddled again and tied with hard knots; well, if a moment served to escape, she must somehow have her dagger ready to cut the knots and flee; choose a moment, perhaps, when Rory had his boots off, and hopefully his breeches too. Her pack she could abandon if she must—the food was gone and she could live without the other things—but her warm cloak she must have, her boots and her saddle . . . though she could ride bareback better than many women could ride saddled. Food, too, she must somehow have; it would not be stealing, she had worked hard and cared for the old woman well, it was but her just due.

Perhaps tonight, when they were all asleep, she thought, and, hauling her weary body up from the bench, set about washing the musty linens from the old woman's bed, and the sheets from the bed in the inner room, which had been long unused—Dame Mhari said that when the weather was warm, Rory slept in there, and only in chilly weather did he sleep on the pallet before the fire. Well, that was something—if she must bed that wretched animal of a man, at least it would not be under the peering eyes of the old grandmother, as it might have been in a poorer cottage with only one room. She shuddered suddenly—was this how folk lived, away from the Great Houses?

Should I give up, flee back to my family, exchange my freedom then for the protected life I would live as the wife of Dom *Garris?* And for a moment, shivering at the thought of what must lie before her, even if she escaped from Rory and his grandmother, she was halfway tempted.

Like a hawk on a block, chained, hooded and dumb, in exchange for being fed and cherished, guarded preciously as a prize possession. . . .

Oh, Preciosa, and that was what I would have brought to you. . . . she thought, and was fiercely glad she had freed the hawk. At least she would never be Darren's possession. She could have kept it clear with her conscience to keep Preciosa herself—the hawk had returned to her of its free will, out of love, after being allowed to fly free. She would never return to Darren.

She is free, she belongs to no man. Nor shall I. Rory might take her—once—as the price of making him think her beaten and submissive. But she would never belong to him; he could not enslave her. Like a hawk badly trained, the moment she was tested in free flight, she would be away into the sky. . . .

She sighed, ferociously sousing the sheets in the harsh soap. Her hands were sore, and ached, but the sheets were clean—at least she would not be taken in that man's dirty bed!

She hung the sheets on a rack near the fire to dry, took the bread from the oven, and hunted in the rickety shelves of the kitchen; she found dried beans and herbs, and put them in the empty kettle to make soup. Rory, stamping in snow-covered from outside, saw her doing this and beamed, flinging down a sack of mushrooms on the table.

"Here; for the soup, girl. For our wedding supper," he said, and stooped to enfold her in an awkward embrace, landing a damp kiss on the back of her neck. She gritted her teeth and did not draw away, and he took her quiet endurance for consent, pulled her round and mashed another kiss against her mouth.

"Tomorrow you will not be so shy, heh, my fine lady— well, Granny, has she taken care of you properly? If she hasn't, I'll teach her." He flung off his own rough cloak and took up hers, slinging it around his shoulders with strutting pride.

"I'll have this; you'll have no need to further out of doors than the outhouse, not till the spring-thaw, and then you'll not need it," he said, and went out again. Romilly swallowed her rage at seeing her brother's well-made, fur-lined cape over his shoulders. Well, if she found a chance to escape, then, she must snatch up Rory's cape; coarse as it was, it was warm enough to shelter her. The few coins in the purse tied at her waist, those she must have too, few as they were, for when she reached Nevarsin. Pitifully small the hoard was—The MacAran was generous with his daughters and his wife, buying them whatever they wished, but he felt they could have small need for ready money, and gave them only a few small silver bits now and again to spend at a fair. But to Rory, she knew, they would seem more; so she found a moment to conceal herself from

Dame Mhari's eyes behind the clothes-press and transfer
the little hoard of coins from the pocket tied at her waist,
into a folded cloth hidden between her breasts; surely, soon
or late, he would take the pocket from her, and she left
one or two small pieces in it to satisfy his greed—maybe
he would seek no further.

As dark closed down from the short gloomy day, she sat
with them at the crude table to eat the soup she had made
and the bread she had baked. Rory grumbled—the bread
was not very good—was this all the skill she had at cooking? But Dame Mhari said peaceably that the girl was
young, she would learn, and the bread, however heavy, was
at least a good change from nut-porridge! When bedtime
came he said sharply, looking away from her, that tonight
she might sleep in the box-bed with Dame Mhari, and that
he would wait four days, no more, for her return to health.

Now she knew the limits of her time. But if she had had
any idea that she might escape while they slept, it vanished
when Dame Mhari said, "Let you sleep on the inside of
the bed, my girl; do you think I don't know you would run
away if you could? You don't know when you are well
off; but when you are Rory's wife you will not wish to
run away."

Oh, won't I? Romilly thought, gritting her teeth, and lay
down fully resolved to try for an escape as soon as the old
woman slept. But she was weary from a day of heavy and
unaccustomed work, and fell asleep the moment she laid
her head on the pillow; and when she woke in the night,
whenever she stirred, she saw by firelight the old woman's
eyes, wide awake and beady as a hawk's, watching her.

Three days passed in much the same way. She cooked
coarse meals, washed the old woman's sheets and gowns,
found a little time to wash her own clothes, including the
torn-up petticoat she had put to use . . . fortunately she
was not too closely observed at the wash-kettle, so she had
a chance to dry the cloths and fold them and hide them
under her tunic.

If she was ever to pass herself off as a boy—and she was
more resolved than ever that she would not travel as a
woman in these mountains—she must find some better way
of concealing this personal necessity. She had heard gossip
about the woman soldiers, the Sisterhood of the Sword,

who were pledged never to wear women's gowns nor to let their hair grow. She had never seen one, only heard gossip, but it was rumored that they knew of a herb which would keep women from bleeding at their cycles, and she wished she knew their secret! She had learned something of herb-lore for doctoring animals, and she knew of herb-medicines which would bring a cow or bitch—or, for that matter—a woman *into* the fertile cycles, but none to suppress it, though there was a drug which would keep a bitch, briefly, from going into heat when it was convenient to breed her. Was that what they used? Maybe she could try it, but she was not a dog, and a dog's cycle of heat was very different from the female human's. It was all theoretical speculation at the moment anyhow, for she had no access to the herb, and would not know how to recognize it in the wild state anyhow, but only when prepared for use by a beast-healer.

On the fourth day, when he rose, Rory said, smirking, "Tonight you shall sleep with me in the inner room. We have shared meal and fireside; it needs only now to bed you, to make the marriage legal in all ways."

And in the mountains, she had heard, *a law would return a runaway wife to her husband.* No matter that she had been wedded without her consent, a woman had small recourse in law; so if she escaped *after* Rory had bedded her, there would be *two* people seeking her, her father and her husband; would a Tower even take her in under those circumstances?

Well, she would ride that colt when it was grown to bear a saddle. But she would try very hard to find a way of escape today.

All day, as she went about the drudgery of the household, she pondered a variety of options. It was possible that she could wait till he had taken her . . . then slip away when he slept afterward, as she had heard that men were likely to do. Certainly the old woman could not follow her—but she might rouse Rory from sleep. Somehow, one way or other, she must manage to prevent Rory from following her. . . .

And if she did that, she might as well have let him take her on that first night. Her throat closed in revulsion at the thought of being a passive victim, letting him take her unchallenged.

Possibly, when they undressed for bed, she might somehow contrive to hide his boots and his leather breeches, so
that he could not at once follow her; barefoot and un-
breeched, would even he manage to chase her, afoot—for
she would also cut loose his riding-chervine and drive it
into the woods. By the time he found boots and breeches,
and rounded up his chervine, she and her horse would be
well on the way to Nevarsin.

But she would have to submit to him first . . .

And then she thought; when we are undressed for bed,
a well-placed knee in the groin would cripple him long
enough to evade pursuit, certainly. Only she must have the
courage to kick hard, and hit her target at the first touch;
otherwise, he would certainly have kill her when he caught
her, and would never trust her again. She remembered
what her own mother had taught her when she and Ruyven
were very small, and she must never hit or kick him there
even in play, because a relatively light blow to that area
would cause serious and possibly permanent damage; if the
parts were ruptured, even death. And that made her stop
and think.

*Was she prepared to kill, if she must, to prevent him from
taking her?*

After all, he had first tried to kill her; if she had truly
been a boy, or if her tunic had not torn, revealing her as
a woman, he would have cut her throat for her horse and
her cloak. Yes, he had been kind to her after his own fashion when he discovered she was a woman, but that was
because he thought that rather than a corpse, he would
prefer to have a slave . . . for surely that was what her life
with him would be, drudging daylong at heavy work and
waiting on the whims of the old woman; he could get more
from her, that way, and have horse and fine cloak too! No,
she would not scruple.

In early afternoon, Rory came in where she was listlessly
kneading bread, and dumped the carcass of a rabbithorn
on the table.

"I have it cleaned and skinned," he said. "Roast a
haunch of it for dinner tonight—I have not tasted meat this
ten-day—and tomorrow we will salt the rest; for tonight,
hang it in the stables, well out of reach of vermin."

"As you wish, Rory," she said, and inwardly she gloated.

The meat, frozen as it would certainly be, would keep her for some time if she could manage to take it with her on her way out. She would be careful to hang it near to her own saddle.

The roast meat soon began to fill the hut with a good smell; Romilly was hungry, but even after she had fed the old woman, wiped her chin and settled her for the night, she found that she could not chew and swallow without choking.

I must be ready. I must be ready. It is tonight or never. She lingered at the table, sipping nervously at a hot cup of bark-tea, until Rory came and wound his arms around her from behind.

"I have built a fire on the hearth in the inner room, so we will not be cold, come, Calinda." She supposed the old woman had told him her assumed name. Certainly she had not. Well, it was upon her; she could delay on longer. Her knees felt weak and wobbly, and for a minute she wondered if she could ever have the courage to carry out her resolve.

She let him lead her into the inner room and close the door and fasten it with a hook from inside. Not good. If she was to make her escape at all, she must have a clear way outside. "Must you lock the door?" she asked. "Certainly Gran—Dame Mhari cannot enter our room at any awkward time, for she cannot walk at all."

"I thought we would be more private this way," he said, smirking again, and she said "But suppose—suppose—" she fumbled a moment, then said, "But suppose Dame Mhari has need of me in the night, and I do not hear her? Leave the door part way open so she can call me if she has a pain or wants me to shift her to her other side."

"You have a good heart, girl," Rory said, and pushed the door open a crack, then sat heavily on the edge of the bed and began to draw off his boots.

"Here, let me help you,' she said, and came to draw them off, then deliberately wrinkled her nose.

"Faugh, how they stink, you must have stepped in the manure pile! Give them to me, my husband," she used the word deliberately, "and I will clean them before you rise in the morning. You might as well give me your leather breeches too," and she stopped, had she gone too far? But Rory suspected nothing.

"Aye, and I will have a clean shirt for the morning if you have one cleaned and dried," he said, and piled his clothes into her arms. "Take them out to the washpot to wait for morning, if they smell of manure they will be better there than in our bridal chamber."

Better and better! But he could still be after her in a flash if he suspected; lingering by the wash pot, half ready to make a dash for freedom then—naked, he could not chase her very far—she heard his suspicious call.

"Calinda! I am waiting for you! Get in here!"

"I am coming," she called, raising her voice, and went back to him. Fate had decided it for her, then. She went back into the bedroom and drew off her own shoes and stockings, her outer tunic and breeches.

He turned back the covers of the bed and got into it. He reached for her as she came and sat on the edge of the bed, and his hand closed on her breast in what was meant, she supposed, for a caress, but his hand was so heavy that she cried out in pain. He twisted his mouth down over hers and wrestled her own on the bed.

"You like to fight, do you? Well, if that's what you want, girl, I'll give it to you that way—" he panted, covering her with his naked body; his breath was hot and sour.

Romilly's qualms were gone. She managed to draw away just a little, then shot out her foot in the hardest kick she had ever given. It landed directly on target, and Rory, with a howl of pain, rolled off the bed, shrieking with fury and outrage, his hands clutched spasmodically between his legs.

"Augh! Augh! Hellcat, tiger, bitch! Augh!"

She heard Dame Mhari's voice anxiously crying out in question; but Romilly scrambled from the bed, clutching her cloak about her, pulling on her tunic with hasty fingers as she fled. She shoved the door open and was in the kitchen, snatching up the remnants of the loaf and the roast meat, grabbing Rory's boots and breeches and her own in an untidy armful, hastily fumbling at the lock of the byre. Behind her Rory was still howling, wordless screams of agony and wrath; they beat out at her, almost immobilizing her, but she fought for breath, thrusting her way into the

byre. With her dagger she slashed through the knots which
tied Rory's riding-chervine and slapped the animal hard on
the rump, driving it with a yell into the courtyard; slashed
at her horse's reins and fumbled to thrust on the bridle.
Rory's howls and Dame Mhari's voice raised in querulous
complaint—she did not know what had happened and Rory
was not yet able to be articulate—blended in a terrifying
duet, it seemed that Rory's agony throbbed painfully in her
own body, but that was *laran,* she thought dimly that it was
a small price to pay for that avenging blow.

*He would have killed me, he would have ravished me—I
need feel no guilt for him!*

She was about to fling his boots and breeches out in the
snow; she fastened her tunic carefully against the cold, bent
to pick up Rory's boots, then had a better thought. She
flung open the door of the small outhouse and thrust them,
with a savage movement, down into the privy, thrust the
breeches down on top of them. Now let him find them and
clean them before he can follow me, she thought, flung
herself on her horse, snatched up the hastily bundled provisions, and dug her heels, with a yell into her horse's side.
The horse plunged away into the woods and she took the
steep path downward, giving her horse his head in her haste
to get away. She had to cling to the horse's neck, so steep
was the road, but there was no horse alive to whose back
she could not stick if she must, and she knew she would
not fall. She remembered Dame Mhari's words, *you should
have taken the left-hand fork at the bottom of the mountain.*
Her heart was pounding so hard she could hardly hear the
sharp clatter of her horse on the path under her feet.

She was free, and for a little time at least, Rory could
not pursue her. No matter that she was abroad on a dark
night, with rain falling underfoot, and with scant provision
and no money except for the few coins in a cloth between
her breasts; she was at least out of the hands of Rory and
the old woman.

*Now I am free. Now I must decide what to do with my
freedom.* She pondered, briefly, returning to Falconsward—
but that would be taken, by her father, as a sign of abject
surrender. *Dom* Garris might give her a slavery more comfortable that she would find with Rory in the woods; but

she had not used all her ingenuity to get free of them, to go back to imprisonment.

No; she would seek the Tower, and training of her *laran*. She told herself, all the old tales of heroism and quests always begin with the hero having to overcome many trials. Now I am the hero—why is a hero always a man?—of my own quest, and I have passed the first trial.

And she shivered at the thought that this might be, not a road to freedom, but only the first of the main trials on her quest.

Chapter 2

Romilly did not slacken her speed till the moon had set; riding in the dark, letting her horse have his head, she finally eased off the reins and let him slow to a walk. She was not sure herself quite where she was; she knew she had not taken the left-hand fork she should have taken at the bottom of the hill, to set her on the way to Nevarsin—it would have been all too easy for Rory to trace her that way. And now she knew that she was lost; she would not even be sure what direction she was riding until the sun should rise and she could get her bearings.

She found an overhanging clump of trees, unsaddled her horse and tied him at the foot of one tree, then wrapped herself in the cloak and the rough blanket she had caught up in her flight, digging into a little hollow at the foot of the tree. She was cold and cramped, but she slept, even though she kept starting out of sleep with nightmares in which a faceless man who was both Rory and *Dom* Garris—no, but he had a look of her father too—came down, at her with inexorable slowness, while she could not move hand or foot. It was certain that if Rory ever set eyes on her again, she had better have her dagger ready. But someone had thrown her dagger down into the privy pit, and she could not look for it because her only clothing was one of her blood-stained rags, and somehow or other they were holding the Festival dance in the meadow where her father had his horse-fair. . . . She was wakened by the horse, restlessly snorting and nuzzling; the sun was up and the ice melting from the trees.

She had been lucky, in her breakneck flight last night, in the dark, that her horse had not broken a leg on the road. Now, soberly, she took stock.

Among the things she had snatched up last night were a frozen quarter of rabbithorn meat, which she could cook and smoke—she had no salt for it, but in this weather it was not likely to spoil. At worst she could slice thin slivers away from the frozen haunch and eat them raw, though she had little liking for raw meat. She had lost flint and steel for firemaking . . . no, what a fool she was, she had her dagger and could search for a flint when the ice was thawed off the road. She had Rory's coarse cloak instead of her own fur-lined one, but that was all to the good; it would keep her warm without exciting the same greed as her finely woven and embroidered one, lined with rich fur. She had boots and heavy leather breeches, her dagger, a few small hoarded coins in their hiding-place between her breasts—she had abandoned the pocket with its few bits; perhaps that an the good cloak would satisfy Rory's greed and he would not pursue her. But she would take no chances, and press on. In her saddle-pack she had still a few pieces of the dog-bread on which she could feed her horse; she got out one of them, and gave it to the horse, letting him chew on the coarse grain while she arranged her clothing properly—she had fled the cottage half-dressed and all put together anyhow—and combed her short, ragged hair with her fingers. Certainly she must look disreputable enough to be a runaway hawkmaster's apprentice! Now the sun was high; it would be a fine day, for already the trees were casting off their snow-pods and beginning to bud again. She shaved a few thin slices of frozen rabbithorn and chewed on them; the meat was tough and unsavory, but she had been taught that anything a bird could eat, a human could digest, and since the hawks were fed on such fare it would certainly not harm her, even if she really preferred cooked food.

She got her bearings by the climbing sun, and set off again toward the north. Sooner or later she must meet with someone who would give her the right road for Nevarsin City, and from there she could inquire the way to Tramontana Tower.

She rode all that day without setting eyes on a single

person or a single dwelling. She was not afraid, for she could find food in this country and while the weather kept fine, she would be safe and well. But before there was another storm, she must find shelter. Perhaps she could sell the horse in Nevarsin, bartering him for a stag-pony and enough in ready money to provide herself with food and a few items of clothing she should have in this weather. She had thrust her feet into her boots in such haste, she had left her warm stockings.

She sighed, put her knife away, and swallowed the last of the tough meat. A few withered winter apples clung to a bush; she pocketed them. They were small and sour, but the horse would like them. High above in the sky she heard the cry of a hawk; as she watched it, circling, she thought of Preciosa. It seemed to her for a moment—but surely it was only memory or imagination?—that she could feel that faint tenuous touch she had felt with Preciosa, as if the world lay spread below her, she saw herself and her horse as tiny specks . . . *Oh, Preciosa, you were mine and I loved you, but now you are free and I too am seeking freedom.*

She slept that night in a long-abandoned travel-shelter, which had not been kept up since the Aldarans declared their independence of the Six Domains of the lowlands; there was not much coming and going across the Kadarin between Thendara and Nevarsin these days. But it kept the rain off, and was better than sleeping under a tree. She managed to make a fire, too, so she slept warm, and roasted some of the rabbithorn. She hoped she would find some nuts—she was tired of meat—but while she was fed, however coarsely, she could not complain. Even the dog-bread she could eat, if she must, but the horse would get more good of it than she would.

So she travelled alone for three or days. By now, she supposed, they must have abandoned the search for her at home. She wondered if her father grieved, if he thought her dead.

When I come to Nevarsin, I will leave a message for him, I will get word to him somehow that I am safe. But no doubt it will be with me as it was with Ruyven, he will cast me off and say I am not his daughter. She felt a tightness in her throat, but she could not cry. She had cried too much already, and had gained nothing from her tears except an aching head and aching eyes, till she left off crying and acted to help herself.

Women think tears will help them. I think men have the right idea when they say tears are womanish; yes, women cry and so they are helpless, but men act on their anger and so they are never without power, not wasting time or anger in tears. . . .

She finished the last of the rabbithorn, and was not sorry—toward the end, she supposed even a dog would have to be fiercely hungry to eat it, and certainly any hawk would have turned up its beak at the stuff. On the fifth night she had only some nuts, found on an abandoned tree, and some woody mushrooms, for her supper. Perhaps tomorrow she could snare some birds, or she would meet with someone who could tell her if she was again on the road to Nevarsin—but she thought not, for this road grew ever poorer and worse-kept, and if she were nearing the biggest city in these hills, she would certainly have come to some travelled roads and inhabited parts before this!

The dog-bread was gone too, and so she stopped several hours before sunset, to let her horse graze for a while. Fortunately the weather kept fine, and she could sleep in the open. She was very tired of travelling, but reflected that she could not now return to her home even if she wished—she had no idea of the road to Falconsward. Well, so much the better; now she could cut all ties with her home.

She slept poorly, hungry and cold, and waked early. The road was so poor . . . perhaps she should retrace her steps for a distance and see if she could come to more travelled parts? She tore some rags and bound her feet with them to ease the chafing of her boots . . . heels and toe were raw and sore. High in the sky, a single hawk circled—why was there never more than one in sight at a single time? Did they keep territories like some other animals for their hunting? And again that strange flash, as if she saw through the hawk's eyes—was it her *laran* again?—and thought of Preciosa. Preciosa, gone, free, lost. *It is strange. I miss her more than father or brothers or home.*

The time for fruiting was past, but she found a few small fruits still clinging to a bush, and ate them, wishing there were more. There was a tree which she knew she could strip the outer bark and eat the soft inner part, but she was not that hungry, not yet. She saddled her horse, weary in spite of her long sleep. Slowly it was beginning to come over her that she could lose herself and even die in these lonely and utterly uninhabited forests. But perhaps today she would meet with someone and begin to find her way to Nevarsin, or some to some little village where she could buy food.

After an hour of riding she came to a fork in the road, and paused there, indecisive, aching with hunger, exhausted. Well, she would let her horse graze for a bit while she climbed to the top of a little knoll nearby and looked about, to see if she could spy out any human habitation, the smoke of a woodcutter's fire, a herder's hut even. She had never felt so alone in her life. *Of course not. I have never been so alone in all my life,* she thought, with wry humor, and clambered up the knoll, her knees aching.

I have not eaten well for days. I must somehow find food and fire this night, whatever comes of it. She was almost wishing she had stayed with Rory and his abominable old grandmother; at least there she had been warm and fed . . . would it really have been so bad, to marry that oaf?

I would rather die in the wilderness, she told herself fiercely, but she was frightened and hungry, and from the top of the knoll she could see only what looked like a wilderness of trees. Far away, at the furthest edge of her sight, a high mountain loomed, to the Northwest, and pale shadows around it which she knew to be snowcapped peaks . . . there lay the Hellers themselves, to which these foothills were only little lumps in the land, and beyond them, the Wall Around the World, which was, as far as she knew from traveller's tales, impassable; at least no one she had ever known had gone beyond it, and on every map she had ever seen, it delimited the very edge of known country. Once she had asked her governess what lay beyond it.

"The frozen waste," her governess told her, "No man knows. . . ." The thought had intrigued Romilly, then. Now she had had enough of wandering in unknown country, and felt that some human company would be welcome.

Although what she had seen already did not make her feel very hopeful about what she would meet with from men on the roads. . . .

Well, she had been unlucky, that was all. She sighed, and

pulled her belt tighter. It would not hurt her to go on fast-
ing another day, though tonight she must find some food,
whatever happened. She looked around again, carefully
taking the bearings of the great peak—it seemed to her
that there was something near the top, a white building,
some kind of manmade structure; she wondered if it was
castle. Great House or, perhaps, one of the Towers. Northwest; she must be careful to keep track of the angle of the
sun and the passage of time so that she would not begin
walking in circles.. But if she followed where the road led,
she would be unlikely to do that.

She should get back to her horse. She glanced up again.
Strange. The hawk still hovered. She wondered, on wild
surmise, if it could be the same hawk . . . no. It was just
that hawks were plentiful in these hills and wherever you
cast your eyes on the sky, there was sure to be some kind
of bird of prey within sight. For an instant it seemed as if
she hovered, seeing the white pinnacle of the Tower and a
faint blue lightning that struck from within . . . she felt faint
and dizzy, not knowing whether it was the hawk or herself
that saw . . . she shook herself and pulled out of the rapport. It would be all too easy to lose herself in that communion with sky and wind and cloud. . . .

She went back to her horse and painstakingly saddled
him again. At least the animal was fed. She said aloud, "I
almost wish I could eat grass as you do, old fellow," and
was startled at the sound of her own voice.

It was answered by another sound; the high, shrill crying
of a striking hawk—yes, the hawk had found some prey,
for she could feel, somewhere in her mind, the flow of
warm blood, a sensation that made her mouth tickle and
flood with saliva, rewakening fierce hunger. The horse startled nervously away, and she pulled on the reins, speaking
softy—and then dark pinions swooped across her vision.
Without thought she thrust out her arm, felt the cruel grip
of talons, and fell blindly into the familiar rapport.

"Preciosa!" She was sobbing as she spoke the name.
How, why the hawk had followed her through her wandering, she would never know. The shrill cry of and the flapping wings roused her from her tears and she was aware
that there was a good-sized bird, still warm, gripped in the
bird's claws. With one hand she gripped the bird's legs,

lifting the claw away from her wrist—it was bleeding a little where the claws had cut, it was her own fault, for she had no proper glove. She set the bird on the saddle, her heart pounding, and pulled out her dagger; gave head and wings to Preciosa, and while the hawk fed—praise to the Bearer of Burdens, the horse knew enough to stand quietly when his saddle was made into an impromptu perch—she plucked what was left of the carcass, struck flint and steel and made a small fire where she roasted the carcass.

She came to me when I was hungry. She knew. She brought me food, giving up her own freedom. The jesses were still clinging to Preciosa's legs. Romilly cut them free with her dagger.

If she wants to stay with me now it shall be of her free will. Never again will I bind her with any mark of ownership. She belongs to herself. But her eyes were still flooding with tears. She met the hawk's eyes, and suddenly awareness leaped between hawk and girl, a strange, fierce emotion flooding her—not love as she knew it, but pure emotion, almost jealousy. *She is not my hawk. I am her girl,* Romilly thought, *she has adopted me, not the other way round!*

The hawk did not stir when she moved toward it; balancing a little by shifting her weight from foot to foot, she stared motionless into Romilly's eyes; then gave a little upward hop and alighted on her shoulder. Romilly caught her breath with the pain as the talons tightened on her flesh, even through tunic and cloak, and immediately the grip slackened, so that Preciosa was holding her just tightly enough to keep her balance.

"You beauty, you wonder, you marvel," Romilly whispered, while the hawk craned her neck and preened the set of her feathers.

Never have I known of such a thing as this, that a hawk once set free should return. . . . and Romilly supposed it was the mark of her *laran* which had brought her close to the hawk.

She stayed quiet, in that wordless communion, for what seemed a long time, while Romilly finished the roasted meat, covered the fire and resaddled the horse; her hands moved automatically about her tasks, but her eyes kept coming back and her mind dropping into silent closeness to the bird.

Will she stay with me now? Or fly away again? It no longer matters. We are together.

At last she cut a branch and trimmed it, fastening it to her saddle behind, as a perch for Preciosa if she chose to stay there, and mounted, setting Preciosa on the improvised perch. Preciosa stayed quiet for a moment, then flapped her wings and rose high, wheeling just at the height of the treetop, hovering near. Romilly drew a long breath. Preciosa would not leave her entirely.

Then she drew on the horse's reins, for she heard voices; a rough man's voice proclaiming, "I tell you, it was smoke I saw," and another one protesting something. There were horse's hooves, too, and somewhere a sharp barking.

Romilly was off her horse, sliding down, leading him into the thickest part of the trees at the edge of the road. She had no wish to met with any travellers before she could get a look at them and see what they were up to and what they looked like.

Another voice spoke, rough and male, but this time in the cultivated accents of an educated man—a lowlander, Romilly thought; he spoke like Alderic. "If anyone else travels on this road, Orain, he is no doubt in our own case, and will be as glad as we are to see another human face." The riders came into sight now, a tall man with flame-red hair, wearing ragged clothing but with a certain look of elegance—this one was no yokel like Rory. Somehow he reminded her of Lord Storn, or the elderly Lord Scathfell, though his dress was as rough as her own, his beard and hair untrimmed. The man at his side was tall too, almost gaunt, wearing a shirtcloak of antique fashion and boots that looked hand-botched together from untanned leather. On a block before him, on his saddle, a huge hooded bird, which did not look like any hawk Romilly had ever seen before, moved uneasily from foot to foot, and Romilly, still partly in rapport with Preciosa at treetop height, felt a little shudder of anger and something like fear. She did not know what sort of bird it was, but she knew instinctively that she did not like to be around it.

Behind the two men in the lead, five or six others rode. Only the two in the vanguard had horses; the others rode an assortment of *chervines,* none of them very large or very good, their coats ill-cared-for and their horns ragged and

rough; one or two of the stag-beasts had been crudely dehorned with lack of skill that made Romilly wince. Her
father would have turned away any hired man who kept
his riding-animals in any such condition, and as for the
dehorning, she could almost have done better herself! She
liked the look of the two men who rode ahead, but she
thought she had never seen such ruffians as the men behind them!

The gaunt, bearded man in the lead, riding at the side
of the red-haired aristocrat (so she immediately styled him
in her mind) got off his horse and said, "Here's trace of
fire; and horse-droppings, too; there's been a rider here."

"And with a horse, in the wild?" the red-haired man
inquired with a lift of his eyebrows. He glanced around, but
it was the gaunt, crudely dressed man whose eyes lighted on
Romilly where she stood by the horse in the thickest part
of the trees.

"Come out, boy. We mean ye' no harm," he said, beckoning, and the red-haired man slid from his horse and stood
by the remains of her fire. He poked about the carefully
covered coals—like everyone brought up in the Hellers,
Romilly was over-cautious about fire in the woods—and
finally extracted a few live sparks; threw in a twig or two.

"You have saved us the trouble of making fire," he said
in his quiet, educated voice, "Come and share it with us,
no one will hurt you."

And indeed Romilly felt no sense of menace from any
of them. She led the horse from the concealed thicket and
stood with her hand on the bridle.

"Well, lad, who are ye and whereaway bound?" asked
the gaunt man, and his voice was kind. He was, she
thought, not quite as old as her father, but older than any
of her brothers. She repeated the tale she had thought of.

"I am a hawkmaster's apprentice—I was brought up in
a Great House, but my mother was too proud to claim me
a nobleman's son, and I thought I could better myself in
Nevarsin; so I took the road there, but I am lost."

"But you have horse and cloak, dagger and—if I make
no mistake—a hawk too," said the redhead, his gray eyes
lighting on the improvised perch, to which Romilly had tied
the cut-away jesses—her whole training had taught her

never to throw away a scrap of leather, it could always be used for something. "Did you steal the hawk? Or what is an apprentice doing with a bird—and where is she?'

Romilly raised her arm; Preciosa swooped down and caught her lifted forearm. She said fiercely, "She is mine; no other can claim her, for I trained her with my own hand."

"I doubt you not," said the aristocrat, "for in this wild, without even jesses, she could fly away if she would, and in that sense at least, you own her as much as anything human can own a wild thing."

He understands that! Romilly felt a sudden extreme sense of kinship with this man, as if he were a brother, a kinsman. She smiled up at him, and he returned the smile. Then he looked around at the men ringing the grove, and said, "We too are on our way to Nevarsin, though the route we travel is somewhat circuitous—for reasons of caution. Ride with us, if you will."

"What *Dom* Carlo means," said the gaunt man at his side, "is that if we rode the main roads, there are those who'd have the hangman on us, quick!"

Were they outlaws, bandits? Romilly wondered whether she had not, in escaping Rory and taking up with these rough-looking men, walked from the trap to the cookpot! But the redhead smiled, a look of pure affection and love, at the other man and said, "You make us sound like a crew of murderers, Orain. We are landless men who lost the estates of our fathers, and some of us lost our kin, too, because we supported the rightful king instead of yonder rascal who thinks to claim the throne of the Hasturs. He assured he would have supporters enough by poison, rope or knife for all those who would not support him, and had enough lands to reward his followers, by murdering, or sending into exile, anyone who looked at him cross-eyed, and did not bend the knee fast enough. So we are bound for Nevarsin, to raise an army there—Rakhal shall not have the Crystal Palace unchallenged! Him a Hastur?" The man laughed shortly. "Ill shall his head rest in that crown while any of us are alive! I am Carlo of Blue Lake; and this is my paxman and friend Orain."

The word he had used for "friend" was on which could

also mean *cousin* or *foster-brother;* and Romilly saw that
the gaunt Orain looked on *Dom* Carlo with a devotion like
that of a good hound for his master.

"But if the lad is a hawk-trainer," Orain said. "I doubt
not he could tell ye what ails our sentry-birds, *Dom* Carlo."

Carlo looked sharply at Romilly. "What's your name,
boy?"

"Rumal."

"And from you accent I can tell you were reared north
of the Kadarin," said he. "Well, Rumal, have you knowledge of hawks?"

Romilly nodded. "I have, sir."

"Show him the birds, Orain."

Orain went to his horse, and took the great bird from
the saddle. He beckoned to two of the other men, who
were carrying similar birds on their saddles; warily, Orain
drew the hood from the head of the bird, being careful to
stay out of reach; it jerked its head around, making pecking
movements, but was too listless to peck. There was a long
feathered crest over the eye-sockets, but the head was
naked and ugly, the feathers unkempt and unpreened, even
the creature's talons scaly and dirty-looking. She thought
she had never seen such ugly fierce-looking birds; but if in
good health they might have had the beauty of any wild
creature. Now they just looked hunched and miserable.
One of them cocked its neck and let out a long scream,
then dropped its head between its wings and looked disreputable again.

Romilly said, "I have never seen birds of this kind."
Though she thought they looked more like *kyorebni,* the
savage scavenger-birds of the high hills, than any proper
hunting-bird of prey.

"Still, a bird is a bird," said Carlo, "We got these from
a well-wisher and we would take them as a gift to Carolin's
armies, in Nevarsin, but they are failing fast and may not
live till we get there—we cannot make out what ails them,
though some of us have trained and flown hawks—but none
of us know how to treat them when they ail. Have you
knowledge of their ills, Master Rumal?"

"A little," Romilly said, trying desperately to muster her
small knowledge of curing sick animals. These were sick
indeed; any bird, from cagebird to *verrin* hawk, who will

not preen its feathers and keep its feet in trim is a sick bird. She had been taught to mend a broken flight feather, but she knew little of medicining sick birds, and if they had molt-rot or something of the sort, she had not the faintest idea what to do about it.

Nevertheless she went up to the strange, fierce-looking birds, and held out her hand to the one Orain held, looking it into the eye and reaching out with that instinctive rapport. A dullness spread through her, a sickness and pain that made her want to retch. She pulled out of the rapport, feeling nauseated, and said, "What have you been feeding them?"

That was a good guess; she remembered Preciosa, sickened by insufficiently fresh food.

"Only the best and freshest food," said one of the men behind Orain, defensively, "I lived in a Great House where there were hawks kept, and knew them meat-eaters; when our hunting was poor, all of us went short to give the damned birds fresh meat, for all the good it did us," he added, looking distressedly at the drooping bird on his saddleblock.

"Only fresh meat?" said Romilly, "There is your trouble, sir. Look at their beak and claws, and then look at my hawk's. That's a scavenger-bird, sir; she should be freed to hunt food for herself. She can't tear apart fresh meat, her beak's not strong enough, and if you've been carrying her on your saddle and not let her free, she's not been able to peck gravel and stones for her crop. She feeds on half-rotted meat, and she must have fur or feathers too—the muscle meat alone, and skinned as well—wasn't it?"

"We thought that was the way to do it," said Orain, and Romilly shook her head. "If you *must* feed them on killed meat, leave feather and fur on it, and make sure she gets a chance to peck up stones and twigs and even a bit of green stuff now and then. These birds, though I am sure you've tried to feed them on the best, are starving because they can't digest what you've given them. They should be allowed to hunt for themselves, even if you have to fly them on a lure-line."

"Zandru's hells, it makes good sense, Orain," said *Dom* Carlo, blinking, "I should have seen it . . . well, now we know. What can we do?"

Romilly thought about it, quickly. Preciosa had wheeled up into the sky, and hovered there; Romilly went quickly into rapport with the bird, seeing for a moment through her eyes; then said, "There is something dead in the thicket over there. I'm not familiar with your—what do you call them—sentry-birds; are they territorial, or will they feed together?"

"We daren't let them too near each other," said Orain, "for they fight; this one I carry near pecked out the eyes of that one on Gawin's saddle there."

Romilly said, "Then there's no help for it; you'll have to feed them separately. There—" she pointed, "is something dead for at least a couple of days—you'll have to fetch it and cut it up for them."

The men hesitated.

"Well," said *Dom* Carlo sharply, "What are you waiting for? Carolin needs these birds, and no doubt at Tramontana they'll have a *leronis* who can fly them, but we've got to get them there alive!"

"Ye squeamish, lily-gutted, cack-handed incompetents," Orain swore, "Afraid to get yer hands dirty, are ye? I'll set an example, then! Where's this dead thing ye spied, lad?"

Romilly began to walk toward the thicket; Orain followed and *Dom* Carlo said with asperity, "Go and help him, you men, as many as he needs! Will you let one man and a child drag carrion for three birds?"

Reluctantly, a couple of the men followed. Whatever animal lay dead in the thicket—she suspected it was one of the small multicolored woods chervines—it announced its presence very soon by the smell, and Romilly wrinkled her nose.

Orain said incredulously, "We're to feed *that* to those fine birds?" He bent down and hauled gingerly at the smelly carcass; a stream of small insects were parading in and out of the empty eye-holes, but it was not yet disintegrated enough to come apart in their hands, and Romilly took one end of the carcass and hoisted, trying to breathe through her mouth so she would not have to breathe in much of the foul smell.

"A *kyorebni* would think it fine fare," Romilly said, "I have never kept a scavenger-bird, but their bellies are not

like those of hawks, and how would you like to be fed
on grass?"

"I doubt not that y're right," said Orain glumly, "But I
never thought to be handling stinking carrion even for the
king's men!" The other men came and lent a hand in the
hauling; Romilly was glad when it was over, but some of
the the men gagged and retched as they handled the stuff.
Orain, however, drew a formidable knife and began hack-
ing it into three parts; even before he was finished the
hooded bird on his saddle set up a screaming. Romilly drew
a long breath of relief. She did not like to think what would
have happened if she had been wrong, but evidently she
had been right. She took up a small handful of fine pebbly
dirt and strewed it over the cut hunk of the carcass, then,
hesitating—but remembering the moment of rapport with
the sick bird—went and unfastened the hood.

Orain shouted, "Hey! Look out there, lad, she'll pick out
yer eyes—"

But the bird, under her light hands, seemed gentle and
submissive. *Poor hungry thing,* Romilly thought, and lifted
the heavy weight—it took all her strength—to set it on the
ground beside the hacked carcass. With a scream, the bird
plunged its beak into the carcass and tore hard, gulping
down fur, pebbles, the smelly half-decomposed meat.

"You see?" said Romilly simply, and went to lift down
the other bird. Orain came to help her, but the strange bird
thrust angry beak at him, and he drew back, letting Romilly
handle it.

When all of the birds had fed and were preening their
feathers, making little croaking sounds of satisfaction, *Dom*
Carlo lifted his eyebrow at Orain, and Orain said, "Ride
with us to Nevarsin, lad, and then to Tramontana to deliver
these birds to Carolin's men; and keep them healthy on the
way. We'll feed you and your horse, and give you three
silver bits for every tenday ye're with us while the birds
stay healthy Your hawk," he added with a droll grin, "can
no doubt hunt for himself."

"Herself," Romilly corrected, and Orain chuckled.

"Be a bird male or female, none cares except another
bird of its own kind," he said. "Otherwise with humankind,
aye, *Dom* Carlo?" And he laughed, though Romilly could

not quite see the joke. "Well, what about it, boy, will ye' have along of us and the sentry-birds?"

Romilly had already made up her mind. She herself was bound, first to Nevarsin and then to Tramontana to seek her brother or news of him. This would give her protection and keep her fed. She said, "Gladly, *Dom* Carlo and Master Orain."

"Bargain, then," said Orain, and stuck out his calloused hand with a grin. "Now the birds have fed, shall we move out of range of the smell of their feeding, and have a bait of vittles for ourselves?"

"Sounds good," Romilly said, and went to unsaddle her horse.

The food was heavy dough, baked by the simple method of thrusting twists of the dough on to sticks and baking over the fire; and a few thick tubers roasted in the ashes. Romilly sat beside Orain, who offered her salt from a little pouch drawn from his pocket. When the meal was done, the birds hooded and taken on their saddles again—Orain asked Romilly for help with getting the hoods back on the birds—she heard one or two of the men grumbling.

"That lad rides a horse when we make do wi' a stag-pony each? What about it—shall we have it from him?"

"Try it," said Orain, turning, "and ye' can ride alone in these woods, Alaric—there are no thieves and bandits in our company, and if ye' lay one finger on the boy's horse, it'll be for *Dom* Carlo to deal with ye'!"

Romilly felt a surge of gratitude; it seemed she had found a protector in Orain, and for the moment, facing the ragged crew, she was a little frightened.

Soon or late, though, she might have to face them on her own, without a protector. . . .

"What are the birds' names?" she asked Orain. He grinned at her. "Does anyone name uglies like these, as if they were a child's cagebird or the old wife's pet cow?"

"I do," Romilly said, "You must give any animal with which you wish to work closely a name, so that he will read it in your mind and know it is of him—or her—that you speak, and to her you are directing your attention."

"Is it so?" Orain asked, chuckling, "I suppose you could call them Ugly-mug One, Ugly-mug Two, and Ugly-mug Three!"

"By no means," said Romilly with indignation. The bird on her fist fluttered restlessly, and she added, "Birds are very sensitive! If you are ever to work with them, you must love them—" before the open derision in the men's eyes she knew she was blushing, but went on nevertheless, "You must *respect* them, and care for them, and feel a real kindness for them. Do you think they do not know that you dislike them and are afraid of them?"

"And you don't?" *Dom* Carlo asked. He sounded genuinely interested, and she turned to him with relief. She said, "Would you mock your best hunting-dog if you wanted to have a good hunt, with him working to your word or gesture? Don't you think he would know?"

"I have not hunted since I was a young lad," *Dom* Carlo said, "but certainly I would not treat any beast I sought to tame to my service, with anything but respect. Listen to what the lad says, men; he's got the right of it. I heard the same from my own hawkmaster once. And surely—" he patted the neck of the superb black mare he rode, "we all have love and respect for our beasts, horse or chervine, who carry us so faithfully."

"Well," said Orain, again with that droll curl of his lip, looking down at the great gross body of the sentry-bird, "We could call this one Beauty, that one Lovely, and that one over there we might call Gorgeous. I doubt not they're beautiful enough to one another—lovesome's as lovesome does, or so my old Ma used to say."

Romilly giggled. "I think that would be overdoing," she said. "Beauty they may not have, but—let me think—I shall call them after the Virtues," she added after a moment. "This one—" she lifted the heavy bird on to its block on Orain's saddle, "Shall be Prudence. This one—" she went, frowned at the dirty perch and thrust the hooded bird on to Orain's gloved fist while she dug out her knife and scraped off a disgusting accumulation of filth and droppings. "This one shall be Temperance, and this one—" turning to the third, "Diligence."

"How are we to tell them apart?" demanded one of the men, and she said seriously, "Why, they are nothing alike. Diligence is the big one with the blue tips on her wings—see? And Temperance—you can't see it now, it's under the hood, but her crest is big and white-speckled. And Prudence

is the little one with the extra toe on her feet—see?" She
pointed out the features one by one, and Orain stared in
amazement.

"Why, so they are different—I never thought to notice."

Romilly climbed into her saddle. She said seriously, "The
first thing you have to learn about birds is to think of each
one as an individual. In their manners and their habits, too,
they are no more alike than you and *Dom* Carlo." She
turned in her saddle to the redhaired man and said, "Forgive me, sir, perhaps I should have consulted you before
naming your birds—"

He shook his head. "I never thought of it. They seem
good names, indeed . . . are you a *cristoforo,* my lad?"

She nodded. "I was reared as one. And you, sir?"

"I serve the Lord of Light," he said briefly. Romilly said
nothing, but was a little startled—the *Hali'imyn* did not
come all that often into these hills. But of course, if they
were Carolin's men in exile, they would serve the Gods of
the Hastur-kindred. And if Carolin's armies were massing
at Nevarsin—excitement caught in her throat. No doubt
this was the reason Alderic was in these hills, to join the
king when the time was ripe. She speculated again, briefly,
about Alderic's real identity. If these were Carolin's men,
perhaps they knew him and were his friends. But that was
not her business and the last thing she should do was to
entangle herself in any man's cause. Her father had said it,
and it was true, why should it matter which rascal sat on
the throne, so long as they left honest folk alone to do
their own business?

She rode in the line of men, keeping rather nervously
close to Orain and *Dom* Carlo—she did not like the way
the man Alaric stared at her, and, no doubt, like the villain-
ous Rory, he coveted her horse. At least he did not know
she was a female and so he did not covet her body; and
she could protect her horse, at least while she had *Dom*
Carlo's protection.

Come to think of it, she hadn't done such a bad job of
protecting her body, at that.

They rode all day, stopping at noon for some porridge
made by stirring cold well-water into finely-ground porridge
powder. This, with a handful of nuts, made a hearty meal.
After the meal they rested for a time, but Romilly busied

herself with her knife, trimming and balancing proper
perches—the sentry-birds were, she could see, in considerable distress from the poorly-balanced saddle-blocks. She
checked the knots in the jesses, too, and found that one of
the birds had a festered place in its leg from too-tight knots,
which she treated with cold water and a poultice of healing
leaves. The other men were lying around in the clearing,
enjoying the sun, but when Romilly came back from checking the birds, she saw that *Dom* Carlo was awake and
watching her. Nevertheless she went on with her work. One
of the men's stag-ponies was poorly dehorned and the
horn-bud trickling blood at the base; she trimmed it and
scraped it clean, drying it with a bit of rag and packing it
with absorbent moss, then went from stag-pony to stag-
pony, checking one which had been limping, and picking,
with her knife-point, a little stone from between the hoof-
segments.

"So," said *Dom* Carlo at last, lazily, opening his eyes,
"You go about your self-appointed tasks well—you are not
lazy, Rumal. Where got you your knowledge of beasts?
You have the skill of a MacAran with them—" and he sat
up and looked at her, "and I would say you had a touch
of their *laran* as well. And now I think of it, you've a look
of that clan, too." His grey eyes met hers, and Romilly felt
a curious sense that he looked at her inside and out, and
she quailed—could he tell, if he was one of the Gifted
Hastur-kinfolk, that she was a girl? But he seemed not to
be aware of her dismay, only went on looking at her—it
was, she thought, as if it never occurred to him that anyone
would refuse to answer him when he asked.

She said, her words stumbling over themselves, "I was—
I said—brought up—I know some of them—"

"Born the wrong side of the bed? Aye, it's an old enough
story in these hills, and elsewhere too," said *Dom* Carlo,
"Which is why that ruffian Rakhal sits on the throne and
Carolin—awaits us in Nevarsin."

"You know the king well, sir? You seem one of the *Hali-
'imyn*—"

"Why, so I am," *Dom* Carlo said easily, "No, Orain,
don't look like that, the word's not the insult in these
mountains that it would be South of the Kadarin. The boy
means no harm. Know the king? I have—not seen him

often," *Dom* Carlo said, "but he is kin to me, and I hold
by him. As I said, a few too many bastards with ambitions
put Carolin in this difficulty—his father was too tender-
hearted with his ambitious kinsmen, and only a tyrant as-
sures his throne by murdering all others with the shadow
of a claim to it. So I have sympathy with your plight, boy—
if the usurper Rakhal laid hands on me, for instance, or
any of Carolin's sons, their heads would soon be decorating
the walls of his castle. I suppose you have some of the
MacAran *donas*, though, or you could not handle beasts as
you do. There is a MacAran *laranzu* in Tramontana—it is
to him and his fellow workers that we mean these birds to
go, in the end. Know you anything of sentry-birds, then,
my boy?"

Romilly shook her head. "Not until today did I ever set
eyes on one, though I have heard they are used for spying—"

"True," said *Dom* Carlo, "One who has the *laran* of your
family or something like to it, must work with them, stay
in rapport as they fly where you wish to see. If there is an
army on the road, you can spy out their numbers and report
their movements. The side with the best-trained spy-birds
is often the side that wins the battle, for they can take the
other by surprise."

"And these are to be trained for this?"

"They must be trained so that they can be handled easily," said Carlo. "A royal gift this was, from one of Carolin's supporters in these hills; but my men knew little of
them, which is why it is as if the very Gods sent you to us,
who can keep them in health and perhaps gentle them a
little to working."

"The one who will fly them at last should do that," Romilly said, "but I will try hard to accustom them to human
hands and human voices, and keep them healthy and properly fed." And she wondered; for Ruyven was at Tramontana, so she had heard, and perhaps he was the *laranzu*
for those hands these birds were destined. How strangely
Fate turned . . . perhaps, if she could make her way to
Tramontana, her gifts could be trained to the handling of
such birds. "If your men have any hunting skills, it would
be well if they could bring down some medium-small game
and feed it to the birds, but not too fresh, unless they can

cut it up very fine and feed them skin and feathers with it. . . ."

"I'll leave their diet to you," *Dom* Carlo said, "And if you have any trouble with them, tell me. These are valuable creatures and I'll not have them mishandled." He looked up into the sky, crimsoning as the great sun began to decline somewhat from noon, where, just at the very edge of sight, Romilly could see Preciosa, a tiny dark speck hovering near. "Your hawk stays near even when she flies free? How did you train her to that? What is her name?"

"Preciosa, sir."

"Preciosa," jeered the man Alaric, coming to saddle *Dom* Carlo's horse, "Like a weak girl naming her doll!"

"Don't mock the lad," *Dom* Carlo said gently, "Till you can better his way with the birds, we need his skills. And you should take better care of your own beast—a chervine can be well-kept, even if he is not a horse. You should thank Rumal for finding the stone in Greywalker's hoof!"

"Oh, an' indeed I do," said Alaric with a surly scowl, and turned away. Romilly watched with a faint frown of distaste. It seemed she already had an enemy among these men, which she had done nothing to deserve. But perhaps she had been tactless in caring for the chervine's hoof— perhaps she should simply have warned Alaric that his beast was going lame. But couldn't he *see,* or feel the poor thing limping? She supposed that was what it was to be head-blind. He could not communicate with any dumb brute. And with the intolerance of the very young, she thought, *if he does not understand animals better than that, he should not try to ride one!*

Soon after, they mounted and rode on through the afternoon. The trails were steeper now, and Romilly began to lag behind somewhat—on these paths and roads, a mountain-bred chervine was better than a horse, and there were places on the narrow mountain paths where Romilly, Orain and *Dom* Carlo had to dismount and lead their horses by the bridle while the men on the sure-footed stag-like riding-beasts stayed in their saddles, secure as ever. She had lived in the hills all her life and was in general not afraid of anything, but some of the steep edges and sheer cliffs over abysses of empty space and clouds made her gasp and catch her breath, biting her lip against showing her fear. Up they went, and upward still, climbing through cold layers of mist and cloud, and her ears began to ache and her breath grew shorter while her heart pounded so loudly in her ears that she could hardly hear the hooves of the horses and stag-ponies on the rocky path. Once she dislodged a stone with her foot and saw it bouncing down the cliffside, rebounding every ten or fifteen feet until it disappeared into the clouds below.

They paused and drew close together in the throat of the pass, and Orain pointed to a cluster of lights against the dusk of the next mountain. His voice was very low, but Romilly lagging with the other horses, heard him.

"There it lies. Nevarsin, The City of Snows, *vai dom*. Two or at the most, three more days on the road, and you will be safe behind the walls of St.-Valentine-of-the-Snows."

"And your faithful heart can rest without fear, *bredu*? But all these men are loyal, and even if they knew—"

"Don't even whisper it aloud, my lord—*Dom* Carlo," Orain said urgently.

Dom Carlo reached out and gave the other man's thin shoulder an affectionate touch.

"You have sheltered me with your care since we were children—who but you should be at my side then, foster-brother?"

"Ah, you'll have dozens and hundreds then to care for you, my—" again he paused, *"vai dom."*

"But none of your faithfulness," said *Dom* Carlo gently. "You'll have all the rewards I can give—"

"Reward enough to see you where you belong again—Carlo," said Orain, and turned back to oversee the descent of the others down through the narrow defile which led away toward the bottom of the ravine.

They camped in the open that night, under a crude tent pitched beneath a tree, just a slanting sheet to keep the worst of the rain from them. As befitted a paxman, Orain kept close to *Dom* Carlo, but as they were spreading their blankets, and Romilly checking the birds and feeding them the last of the carrion—the men grumbled and snarled about the smell, but no one would gainsay *Dom* Carlo—Orain said briefly, "Rumal, you'd better spread your blankets near to us—you haven't much in the way of blankets and even wi' your cloak you'll freeze, lad.''

Romilly thanked them meekly and crawled in between the two men. She had taken off only her boots—she did not want to be seen in fewer clothes than this—but even with cloak and blanket she felt chilled, and was grateful for shared blankets and warmth. She was vaguely aware, at the edge of sleep, when Preciosa swooped down and roosted within the circle of the fires; and beyond that, something else . . . a faint awareness, the touch of *laran*—*Dom* Carlo's thoughts, stirring, circling about the camp to make sure that all was well with men, riding-beasts and birds.

Then she slept.

Chapter 3

In the clear dawnlight, moving around the clearing to fetch water for the birds, and taking stock—one of the men should hunt today, to kill something for the sentry-birds, although already they looked better and were preening their feathers and cleaning their feet—Romilly could see the walls of Nevarsin, clear in the light as if they were made of snow or salt. An ancient city, built into the side of the mountain, just below the level of the eternal snow; and above them, like the very bones of the mountain projecting through the never-ending snow, the gray walls of the monastery, carved from living rock.

One of the men whose name she did not know was fetching water for porridge; another was doling out grain for the horses and *chervines*. The one called Alaric, a heavy glowering man, roughly clad, was the one she feared most, but she could not avoid him completely, and in any case, he must have some feeling for the sentry-birds, he had carried one of them on that crude perch before his saddle.

"Excuse me," said Romilly politely, "but you must go out and kill something for the sentry-birds; if it is killed this morning, by night it will be beginning to decay, and be right for them to eat."

"Oh, so," snarled the man, "So after one night with our good leader you now think yourself free to give orders to men who've been with him this whole hungry year? Which of them had you, or did they take turns at you, little catamite?"

Shocked by the crudeness of the insult, Romilly recoiled,

her face flaming. "You've no right to say that to me: *Dom* Carlo put me in charge of the birds and bade me see they were properly fed, and I obey the *vai dom* as you do yourself!"

"Aye, I may say so," the man sneered, "Maybe you'd like to put that pretty girl-face and those little ladylike hands to—" and the rest of the words were so foul that Romilly literally did not understand what he meant by them, and was perfectly sure she did not want to know. Clinging to what dignity she could—she honestly did not know how one of her brothers would have reacted to such foulness except, perhaps, by drawing a knife, and she was not big enough to fight on even terms with the giant Alaric—she said, "Perhaps if the *vai dom* himself gives you his orders you will take them," and moved away, clenching her teeth and her whole face tightly against the tears that threatened to explode through her taut mouth and eyes. *Damn him. Damn him! I must not cry, I must not. . . .*

"Here, here, what a face like a thundercloud, my lad?" said Orain, his lean face twisted with amusement, "Hurt? What ails ye—"

She clutched at the remnants of self-possession and said the first thing that came into her head.

"Have you a spare glove I can borrow, Uncle?" She used the informal term for any friend of a father's generation. "I cannot handle the sentry-birds with my bare fist, though I can manage a hawk; their talons are too long, and my hand is bleeding still from yesterday. I think I must fly them on a line to try and let them hunt for small animals or find carrion—"

"A glove you shall have," said *Dom* Carlo behind them, "Give him your old one, Orain; shabby it may be, but it will protect his hand. There are bits of leather in the baggage, you can fashion one for yourself tonight. But why must you fly them? Why not give orders to one of the men to catch fresh food for them? We have hunting-snares enough, and we need meat for ourselves too. Send any of the men to fetch fresh food—" and as he looked on Romilly, his reddish eyebrows went up.

"Oh, is that the way of it?" he asked softly, "Which of them was it—Rumal?"

Romilly looked at the ground. She said almost inaudibly

"I don't wish to make trouble, *vai dom*. Indeed, I can fly them, and they should have exercise in any case."

"No doubt they should," Carlo said, "So fly them for exercise, if you will. But I'll not have my orders disobeyed, either. Give her a glove, Orain, and then I'll have a word with Alaric."

Romilly saw the flash of his eyes, like greyish steel striking fire from flint; she took the glove and, head down, went to take down Temperance from her block, attach the lure-lines and set them up to fly. She found a cast feather and used it to stroke the bird's breast, at which the great wicked head bent and dipped with something like pleasure; she was making a good beginning at accustoming the large, savage birds to human touch and presence. When she had flown Temperance and watched her pounce on some small dead thing in the grass, she stood and watched the sentry-bird feed; standing on one foot, tearing with beak and claw. Later she flew Diligence in the same way; then—with relief, for her arm was growing tired—the smaller, gentler Prudence.

They are ugly birds, I suppose. But they are beautiful in their own way; strength, power, keen sight . . . and the world would be a fouler place without birds like this, to clear away what is dead and rotting. She was amazed at the way in which the birds had found, even on lines like the lure-lines, their own food, small carcasses in the grass, which she herself had not seen or even smelled. How had the men managed to ignore their real needs, when it was so clear to her what they wanted and needed?

I suppose that is what it means to have laran, Romilly thought, suddenly humbled. A gift which had been born in her family, for which she could claim no credit because it was inborn, she had done nothing to deserve it. Yet even *Dom* Carlo, who had the precious *laran* too—everything about the man spoke of easy, accustomed power—could not communicate with the birds, though he seemed able to know anything about men. *The gift of a MacAran.* Oh, but her father was so wrong, then, so wrong, and she had been right, to insist on this precious and wonderful Gift with which she had been dowered; to ignore it, to misuse it, to play at it, untrained—oh, that was wrong, wrong!

And her brother Ruyven had been right, to leave Falconsward and insist on the training of his natural Gifts. In the Tower he had found his proper place, *laranzu* for the handling of sentry-birds. One day that would be her place too. . . .

Prudence's scream of anger roused Romilly from her daydream and she realized that the sentry-bird had finished feeding and was tugging again at the lure-line. Romilly let her fly in circles on the line for a few moments, then made contact with the bird and urged her gently back to the ground; she hooded her, lifted her (grateful for the glove Orain had given her, for even through the glove she could feel the fierce grip of the huge talons) and set her back on the block.

As she made ready to ride, she thought soberly of the distance still ahead of them. She would keep as close to Orain as she could; if Alaric should find her alone . . . and she thought, with terror, of the vast and empty chasms over which they had come the day before. A false step there, a slight nudge, and she would have followed that stone down over the cliff, rebounding again and again, broken long before she reached the final impact at the bottom. She felt faint nausea rising in her throat. Would his malice carry him so far as *that*? She had done him no harm. . . .

She had betrayed his incompetence before *Dom* Carlo, whom he evidently held in the highest respect. Remembering Rory, Romilly wondered if there were any men anywhere, alive, who were motivated by anything other than malice and lust and hatred. She had thought, in boy's clothing, she would be safe at least from lust; but even here, among men, she found its ugly face. Her father? Her brothers? Alderic? Well, her father would have sold her to *Dom* Garris for his own convenience. Alderic and her brothers? She really did not know them at all, for they would not have shown their real face to a girl whom they considered a child. No doubt they too were all evil within. Setting her teeth grimly, Romilly put the saddle on her horse, and went about saddling the other horses for Orain and *Dom* Carlo. Her prescribed duties demanded only that she care for the birds, but as things were now, she preferred the company of horses to the company of humankind!

Dom Carlo's kindly voice interrupted her reverie.

"So you have saddled Longlegs for me? Thank you, my lad."

"She is a beautiful animal," Romilly said, giving the mare a pat.

"You have an eye for horses, I can see; not surprising, if you are of MacAran blood. This one is from the high plateaus around Armida; they breed finer horses there than anywhere in the mountains, though I think sometimes they have not quite the stamina of the mountain-bred. Perhaps it does her no kindness, to take Longlegs on these trails; I have often thought I should return her to her native country and get myself a mountain-bred horse, or even a *chervine* for this wild hill country. Yet—" his hand lingered on the glossy mane, "I flatter myself that she would miss me; and as an exile, I have not so many friends that I would be willing to part with one, even if she is a dumb beast. Tell me, my boy; you know horses, do you think this climate is too hard on her?"

"I would not think so," Romilly said after a minute, "Not if she is well fed and well cared for; and you might consider wrapping her legs for extra support on these steep paths."

"A good thought," *Dom* Carlo agreed, and beckoned to Orain; they set about bandaging the legs of their lowlands-bred horses. Romilly's own horse was bred for the Hellers, shaggy-coated and shaggy-legged, with great tufts of coarse hair around the fetlocks, and for the first time since she had fled from Falconsward, she was glad that she had left her own horse. This one, stranger as he was, had at least borne her faithfully.

After a time they set off, winding downward into the valley, which they reached in time for the midday meal, and then along the gradually broadening, well-travelled road which led into Nevarsin, the City of the Snows.

One more night they camped before they came to the city, and this time, noting what Romilly had done the day before, Orain gave orders to the men that they should groom and properly care for their riding-*chervines*. They obeyed sullenly, but they obeyed; Romilly heard one of them grumble, "While we have that damned hawk-boy with us, why can't *he* care for the beasts? Ought to be *his* work, not ours!"

"Not likely, when Orain's already made the brat his own pet," Alaric grumbled. "Birds be damned—the wretch is with us for Orain's convenience, not the birds! You think the Lord Carlo will deny his paxman and friend anything he wants?"

"Hush your mouth," said a third, "You've no call to go talking like that about you betters. *Dom* Carlos a good lord to us all, and a faithful man to Carolin, and as for Orain, he was the king's own foster-brother. Haven't you noticed? He talks all rough and country, but when he wishes, or when he forgets, he can talk as fine and educated as *Dom* Carlo himself, or any of the great Hastur-lords themselves! As for his private tastes, I care not whether he wants women or boys or rabbithorns, so long as he doesn't come after *my* wife."

Romilly, her face burning, moved away out of earshot. Reared in a *cristoforo* family, she had never heard such talk, and it confirmed her opinion that she liked the company of men even less than the company of women. She was too shy, after what she had heard, to join Orain and *Dom* Carlo where they spread their blankets, and spent that night shivering, crouched among the drowsing stag-ponies for their warmth. By morning she was blue with cold, and huddled as long as she dared near the fire kindled for breakfast, surreptitiously trying to warm her hands against the sides of the porridge-pot. The hot food warmed her a little, but she was still shivering as she exercised and fed the birds—Alaric, still grumbling, had snared a couple of rabbithorns, and they were beginning to smell high; she had to overcome surges of nausea as she cut them up, and afterward she found herself sneezing repeatedly. *Dom* Carlo cast her a concerned glance as they saddled and climbed on their horses for the last stage of the ride.

"I hope you have not taken cold, my boy."

Romilly muttered, eyes averted, that the *vai dom* should not concern himself.

"Let us have one thing clearly understood," *Dom* Carlo said, frowning, "The welfare of any of my followers is as important to me as that of the birds to you—my men are in my charge as the birds are in yours, and I neglect no man who follows me! Come here," he said, and laid a concerned hand against her forehead. "You have fever; can you ride? I would not ask it of you, but tonight you shall be warm in the monastery guest-house, and if you are sick, the good brothers there will see to you."

"I am all right," Romilly protested, genuinely alarmed now. She dared not be sick! If she was taken to the monks' infirmary, certainly, in caring for her sickness they would discover that she was a girl!

"Have you warm clothing enough? Orain, you are nearer his size than I—find the lad something warm," said *Dom* Carlo, and then, as he stood still touching her forehead, his face changed; he looked down at Romilly sharply, and for a moment she was sure—she did not know how; *laran?*— that he *knew*. She froze with dread, shivering; but he moved away and said quietly, "Orain has brought you a warm vest and stockings—I saw your blistered feet in your boots. Put them on at once; if you are too proud to take them, we shall have it from your wages, but I'll have no—no one riding with me who is not warm and dry and comfortable. Go round the fire and change into them, this minute."

Romilly bowed her head in acquiescence, went behind the line of horses and stag-beasts, and pulled on the warm stockings—heavenly relief to her sore feet—and the heavy undervest. They were somewhat too big, but all the warmer for that. She sneezed again, and Orain gestured to the pot still hanging over the fire, not yet emptied. He dipped up a ladleful of the hot brew and took some leaves from his pouch.

"An old wives' remedy for the cough that's better than any healer's brew. Drink it," he said, and watched while she gulped at the foul-tasting stuff. "Aye, it's bitter as lost love, but it drives out the fever."

Romilly grimaced at the acrid, musty-tasting stuff; it made her lush with inner heat, and left her mouth puckered with its intense astringency, but, later that morning, she realized that she had not sneezed again, and that the dripping of her nose had abated. Riding briefly at his side, she said, "That remedy would make you a fortune in the cities, Master Orain."

He laughed. "My mother was a *leronis* and studied healing," he said, "and went among the country-folk to learn their knowledge of herbs. But the healers in the cities laugh at these country remedies."

And, she thought, he had been the king's own foster-brother; and now served the king's man in exile, Carlo of Blue Lake. What the men had said was true, though she had not noticed it before; talking to the men, he spoke the dialect of the countryside, while, speaking to *Dom* Carlo, and, increasingly, to her, his accents were those of an educated man. Contrasted to the other men, she felt as safe and comfortable near him as if she were in the presence of her own brothers or her father.

After a time she asked him, "The king—Carolin—he awaits us in Nevarsin? I thought the monks were sworn to take no part in the strife of worldly men? How is it that they take King Carolin's side in this war? I—I know so little about what is going on in the lowlands." She remembered what Darren and Alderic had said; it only whetted her appetite to know more.

Orain said, "The brothers of Nevarsin care nothing for the throne of the Hasturs; nor should they. They give shelter to Carolin because, as they say, he has harmed none, and his cousin—the great bastard, Rakhal, who sits on the throne—would kill him for his own ambition. They will not join in his cause, but they will not surrender him to his enemies while he shelters there, either."

"If Carolin's claim to the throne is so just," Romilly asked, "Why has Rakhal won so much support?"

Orain shrugged. "Greed, no doubt. My lands are now in the hands of the chief of Rakhal's councillors. Men support the man who enriches them, and right has little to do with it. All these men—" he gestured behind them at the followers, "are small-holders whose lands should have been inviolate; they had done nothing but hold loyal to their king, and they should not have been involved in the struggles of the high-born and powerful. Alaric is bitter, aye—know you what was his crime? The crime for which he lost his lands, and was flung into Rakhal's prison under sentence of losing a hand and his tongue?"

Romilly shuddered. "For such a sentence it must have been a great crime indeed!"

"Only before that *cagavrezu* Rakhal," said Orain grimly, "His crime? His children shouted 'Long live King Carolin!' as one of Rakhal's greatest scoundrels passed by their village. They meant no harm—I do not think the poor brats knew one king from the other! So the great scoundrel, Lyondri Hastur, said that he must have taught his little children treason—he took the children from Alaric's house, saying they should be reared by a loyal man, and sent them to serve in his Great House, and flung Alaric into prison. One of the children died, and Alaric's wife was so distraught with what had befallen her man and her babies that she threw herself from a high window and died. Aye, Alaric is bitter, and thinks good of no one, lad; it is not you he hates, but life itself."

Romilly looked down toward her saddle, with a deep breath. She knew why Orain had told her this, and it raised still further her admiration of the man; he had tolerance and sympathy even for the man who had spoken such ugly things of him. She said quietly, "I will try not to think half so evil of him as he thinks of me, then, Uncle."

But still she felt confused. Alderic had spoken of the Hastur-kin as descended from Gods, great and noble men, and Orain spoke as if the very word "Hastur" were an insult.

"Are all the Hastur-kin evil men, then?"

"By no means," Orain said vehemently. "A better man than Carolin never trod this earth; his only fault is that he thought no evil toward those of his kin who were scoundrels, and was all too kind and forgiving toward—" his mouth stretched in what should have been a smile, "bastards with ambition."

And then he fell silent, and Romilly, watching the lines in his face, knew his thoughts were a thousand leagues away from her, or his men, or *Dom* Carlo. It seemed that she could see in his mind pictures of a beautiful city built between two mountain passes, but lying low, in a green valley, on the shores of a lake whose waves were like mist rolling up from the depths. A white tower rose near the shores, and men and women passed through the gateways, tall and elegant as if wrapped in a silken glamour, too beautiful to be real . . . and she could sense the great sorrow in him, the sorrow of the exile, the homeless man. . . .

I too am homeless, I have cast away all my kin .. but it may be that my brother Ruyven awaits me in Tramontana Tower. And Orain, too, is alone and without kin. . . .

They rode through the great, frowning gates of Nevarsin

just as dusk was falling and the swift night of this time of year had begun to blur the sky with rain. *Dom* Carlo rode at their head, his cowled hood drawn over his head concealing his features; along the old cobbled streets of the city, and upward along step paths and narrow winding lanes toward the snow-covered paths that led to the monastery. Romilly thought she had never felt such intense chill; the monastery was situated among the glacier ice, carved from the solid rock of the mountain, and when they paused before the inner gates, under the great statute of the Bearer of Burdens bowed beneath the world's weight, and the smaller, but still larger-than-life image of Saint-Valentine-of-the-Snows, she was shivering again in spite of the extra warm clothing.

A tall dignified man in the bulky brown robe and cowl of a monk gestured them inside. Romilly hesitated; she had been brought up a *cristoforo* and knew that no woman might enter into the monastery, even in the guest-house. But she had chosen this disguise and now could not repudiate it. She whispered a prayer—"Blessed Bearer of Burdens, Holy Saint Valentine, forgive me, I mean no intrusion into this world of men, and I swear I will do nothing to disgrace you here."

It would create a greater scandal if she now revealed her real sex. And she wondered why women were so strongly prohibited. Did the monks fear that if women were there they could not keep to their vows of renunciation? What good were their vows, if they could not resist women unless they never saw any? And why did they think women would care to tempt them anyhow? Looking at the lumpy little monk in the cowl, she thought, with something perilously near a giggle, that it would take more charity than even a saint, to overlook his ugliness long enough to try and tempt *him*!

There were comfortable stables for all their riding-animals, and an enclosed stone room where Romilly found blocks and perches for her birds.

"You can go into the city and buy food for them," Orain said, and handed her some copper rings, "But be back in good time for supper in the guest-house; and if you will, you may attend the night prayers—you might like to hear the choir singing."

Romilly nodded obediently, inwardly delighted; Darren had spoken once of the fine singing of the Nevarsin choir, which he had not, in his days as a student, been musical enough to join; but her father, too, had spoken of one of the high points of his life, when he had attended a solemn service in the monastery and heard the singing of the monks. She hurried out into the city, excited and a little scared by the strange place; but she found a bird-seller, and when she made her wants known to him, he knew at once the proper food for the sentry-birds; she had half expected to have to carry a stinking, half-rotted carcass back through the city, but instead the seller said that he would be pleased to deliver the food to the guest-house stables. "You'll be lodged in the monastery, young man? If it is your will, I can have proper food delivered every day for your birds."

"I shall ask my master," she said, "I do not know how long they propose to stay." And she thought this was a fine thing, that such services should be provided; but when he told her the price she was a little troubled. Still, there was no way she could go outside the walls and hunt for food for them herself; so she arranged for the day and for tomorrow, and paid the man what he asked.

Returning through the city streets, grey and old, with ancient houses leaning over the streets and the walls closing around her, she felt a little frightened. She realized that she had lost contact with Preciosa before they entered the gates of Nevarsin; the climate here was too cold for a hawk . . . had Preciosa turned back to a more welcoming climate? The hawk could find no food in the city . . . there was carrion enough in the streets, she supposed from the smell, but no fresh living food for a hawk. She hoped Preciosa was safe. . . .

But for now her charge was the sentry-birds; she saw to their feeding, and there was a large cobbled court where she could exercise them and let them fly. At the edge of the court while she was flying them in circles on the long lines—they screamed less, now, and she realized they were becoming accustomed to her touch and her voice—she saw, crowded into the edges of the court, an assembly of small boys. They all wore the bulky cowled robes of the monastery. But surely, Romilly thought, they were too young for monks; they must be students, sent as Ruyven, then Dar-

ren, had been sent. One day, perhaps, her brother Rael
would be among them. *How I miss Rael!*

They were watching the birds with excited interest. One,
bolder than the rest, called out, "How do you handle the
birds without getting hurt?" He came to Romilly, leaving
the clustered children, and stretched out his hand to Temperance; Romilly gestured him quickly back.

"These birds are fierce, and can peck hard; if she went
for your eyes, she could hurt you badly!"

"They don't hurt *you*," the child protested.

"That is because I am trained to handle them, and they
know me," Romilly said, Obediently, the boy moved out
of reach. He was not much older than Rael, she thought;
ten or twelve. In the courtyard a bell rang, and the children
went, pushing and jostling, down the hallway; but the boy
who was watching the birds remained.

"Should you not answer that bell with your fellows?"

"I have no lesson at this hour," the boy said, "Not until
the bell rings for choir; then I must go and sing, and afterward, I must go to arms-practice."

"In a monastery?"

"I am not to be a monk," the boy said, "and so an arms-
master from the village comes every other day to give lessons to me and a few of the others. But I have no duties
now, and I would like to watch the bids, if you do not
mind. Are you a leronis *vai domna,* that you know their
ways so well?"

Romilly stared at him in shock. At last she asked, "Why
do you call me *domna*?"

"But I can see what you are, certainly," the boy answered, "even though you wear boy's clothes." Romilly
looked so dismayed that he lowered his voice and in a
conspiratorial whisper, "Don't worry, I won't tell anyone.
The Father Master would be very cross, and I do not think
you are harming anyone. But why would you want to wear
boy's clothes? Don't you like being a girl?"

Would anyone? Romilly wondered, and then asked herself why the clear eyes of this child had seen what no one
else could see. He answered the unspoken thought.

"I am trained to that as you are trained to handle hawks
and other birds: So that, one day, I may serve my people
in a Tower as a *laranzu.*"

"A child like you?" Romilly asked.

"I am twelve years old," he said with dignity, "and in only three years more I shall be a man. My father is Lyondri Hastur, who is a Councillor to the king; the Gods have given me noble blood and therefore I must be ready to serve the people over whom I shall one day be placed to rule."

Lyondri Hastur's son! She remembered the story Orain had told her, of Alaric and the deaths of his family. She pretended to be fussing over the bird's line; she had never had to conceal her thoughts before, and knew only one way to do it—with quick random speech.

"Would you like to hold Prudence for a little while? She is the lightest of the birds and will not be too heavy for your arm. I will keep her quiet for you, if you like." He looked excited and pleased. Carefully hooding Prudence, and sending out soothing thoughts—*this little one is a friend, he will not harm you, be still*—she slipped the glove over the boy's arm with her free hand, set the bird on it. He held her, struggling to keep his small arm from trembling, and she handed him a feather.

"Stroke her breast with this. Never touch a bird with your hand; even if your hands are clean, it will damage the set of their feathers," she said, and he stroked the bird's smooth breast with the feather, crooning to it softly.

"I have never been so close to a sentry-bird before," he murmured, delighted. "I heard they were fierce and not to be tamed—I suppose it is *laran* which keeps her so calm, *domna*?"

"You must not call me *domna* here," she said, keeping her voice low and calm so as not to disturb the bird, "The name I use is Rumal."

"Is it *laran*, then, Rumal? Do you think I could learn to handle a bird like this?"

"If you were trained to it, certainly," said Romilly, "but you should begin with a small hawk, a ladybird or sparrow hawk so that your arm will not tire and your fatigue trouble the bird. I had better take Prudence now," she added, for the small arm was trembling with tension. She set the bird on a perch. "And *laran* can do nothing but help you to make your mind in tune with the bird's mind. But the cli-

mate here is too cold for ordinary hawks; for that you must
wait till you return the lowlands, I think."

The boy sighed, looking regretfully at the bird on the
perch. "These are hardier than hawks, are they not? Are
they akin to *kyorebni*?"

"They are not dissimilar in form," Romilly agreed,
"though they are more intelligent than *kyorebni,* or than
any hawk." It seemed disloyal to Preciosa to admit it, but
after the few days rapport with the sentry-birds, she knew
these were superior in intelligence.

"May I help you, *dom*—Rumal?"

"I have mostly finished," Romilly said, "but if you wish,
you can mix this green stuff and gravel with their food. But
if you touch the carrion, your hands will stink when you go
to choir."

"I can wash my hands at the well before I got to the
choir, for Father Cantor is very fat and always late to practice," said the boy solemnly, and Romilly smiled as he
began portioning the gamy-smelling meat, sprinkling it with
the herbs and gravel. The smile slid off quickly; this child
was a telepath and the son of Lyondri Hastur, he could
endanger them all.

"What is your name?" she asked.

"I am called Caryl," the boy said. "I was named for the
man who was king when I was born, only Father says that
Carolin is not a good name to have now. Carolin was king,
but he abused his power, they said, and was a bad king, so
his cousin Rakhal had to take the throne. But he was kind
to *me*."

Romilly told herself; the child was only repeating what
he had heard his father say. Caryl finished with the bird-
food, and asked if he might give it to one of the birds.

"Give that dish to Prudence," said Romilly, "She is the
gentlest, and already, I can see you have made friends."

He carried the dish to the bird, stood watching as she
tore greedily into it, while Romilly fed the other two. A
bell rang in the outer court of the monastery, muted softly
by the intervening walls, and the boy started.

"I must go to choir," he said, "and then I must have my
lesson. May I come tonight and help you feed the
birds,—Rumal?"

She hesitated, but he said earnestly, "I'll keep your secret, I promise."

At last she nodded. "Certainly, come whenever you like," she said, and the boy ran away. She noticed that he wiped his hands on the seat of his breeches, like any active youngster, quite forgetting his promise to wash at the well.

But when he was out of sight, she sighed and stood motionless, ignoring the birds for the moment.

Lyondri Hastur's own son, here in the monastery—and it was here that *Dom* Carlo was to meet with King Carolin, with his gift of valuable sentry-birds, and to raise an army in the city. It was not impossible, she supposed, that he might know the king by sight, so if Carolin was in the city in disguise and came near the monastery, he might recognize him, and then. . . .

What do I care which rogue keeps the throne? Her father's words echoed in her mind. But Alderic, who seemed quite the best young man she had ever known beside her own brothers, was Carolin's sworn man, perhaps even his son. Carlo and Orain, too, were loyal to the exiled king. And his councillor, Lyondri Hastur, whatever his son might say, seemed to be one of the worst tyrants she had ever heard about—or so the story of what he had done to Alaric's children seemed to indicate.

And she was *Dom* Carlo's man, at least while she took money in his service. He should know of the danger to the man he called his rightful king. Perhaps he could warn Carolin not to come near the monastery, while there was a child there who would recognize him and penetrate whatever disguise he might wear. Sharp indeed were the boy's eyes and his *laran* . . . he had seen that Romilly was a woman.

Though I cannot tell Dom Carlo, nor his friend how I know the child has laran. . . .

She went to the tables attached to the monastery, finding the horses in good hands; spoke briefly to the stablemen about care for their horses, and tipped them, as was proper, with the generous amount of silver and copper Orain had given her for their expenses. After the encounter with young Caryl, she was on her guard, but none of the stablefolk paid any attention to her; one and all they accepted her as what she was, just another apprentice in the train of the young nobleman staying in the monastery. Then she went in search of *Dom* Carlo, to deliver her warning. In the rooms assigned to them in the guest-house, however, she found only Orain, mending his crudely-sewn boots.

He looked up as she came in.

"Is anything gone wrong with birds or beasts, then, lad?"

"No, they are all doing well," Romilly said, "Forgive me for intruding in your leisure, but I must see *Dom* Carlo—"

"You can't see him now, or for some time," said Orain, "for he's closeted with Father Abbot, and I don't think he's confessin' his sins—he's no *cristoforo*. Can I do anything for ye', boy? There's not great urgency to work, now the birds are cared for and in good health—take time to see some of the city, and if ye need an excuse, I'll send you out on an errand; you can take these boots to be mended." He held them out to her, saying with a droll grin, "They're beyond my skill."

"I will do your errand gladly," Romilly said, "but indeed I have an important message for *Dom* Carlo. He—you—you are Carolin's men, and I have just heard that—that someone who knows the king by sight, and might also know some of his Councillors, is here, in the monastery. Lyondri Hastur's son, Caryl."

Orain's face changed and his lips pursed in a soundless whistle. "Truly? The whelp of that wolf is here, poisoning their minds against my lord?"

"The boy is but twelve," protested Romilly, "'and seems a nice child; he spoke well of the king, and said he had always been kind—but he might know him—"

"Aye," said Orain grimly, "No doubt; a new-hatched serpent can sting like an old snake. Still, I know no evil of the child; but I'll not let Alaric know he is here, or he might let son pay for son—if he saw the Hastur-Lord's son, I doubt he could keep his hands from his throat, and I know well how he feels. My lord must know of this, and quickly—"

"Would Caryl recognize *Dom* Carlo, too? Was he around the court so much? *Dom* Carlo is—" she hesitated, "Is he not one of Carolin's kin?"

"He's of the Hastur-kin," said Orain, nodding. He sighed. "Well, I'll keep an eye out for the child, and put a word in *Dom* Carlo's ear. It was thoughtful of you to warn

me, Rumal, lad; I owe you one for that." As if dismissing
the thought deliberately, he bent and picked up the much-
patched boots. "Take these into the city—and lest you get
lost, I'll come along and show you the way."

He linked his arm carelessly through Romilly's as they
went out of the monastery guest-house and down through
the streets of the old town. The mountain air was biting
and cold, and Romilly drew her cloak tighter about her,
but Orain, though he wore only a light jacket, seemed comfortable and at ease.

"I like the mountain air," he said, "I was born in the
shadow of High Kimbi, though I was fostered on the shores
of Hali; and still I think myself a mountain man. What
of you?"

"I was born in the Kilghard Hills, but north of the Kadarin," Romilly said.

"The country around Storn? Aye, I know it well," Orain
said, "No wonder you have hawks in your blood; so have
I." He laughed, ruefully. "Though you're my master at that;
I had never held a sentry-bird before, nor will I think myself ill-used if I never set hand on one again." They
turned into the doorway of a shop, smelling strongly of leather
and tanbark and rosin. The bootmaker raised supercilious
eyebrows at the patched old boots in Orain's hand, but
quickly changed his tone when Orain took out his pocket
and laid down silver and even copper.

"When would the *vai dom* be wanting these back?"

"I think they're past mending," Orain said, "But they fit
well; make me a pair of the measure of these, for I may
be going high into snow country. Have you boots for the
far Hellers, Rumal? Ye'll be riding with us to Tramontana,
I doubt not—"

Why not, after all? Romilly thought. *I have nowhere else
to go, and if Ruyven is there, or I can get news of him there,
Tramontana is my best path.*

"Those boots the younger sir is wearing, they will never
hold up on the path across the glaciers," said the shoe-
maker, with an obsequious look at Orain, "I can make your
son a stout fine pair for two silver bits."

Only now did Romilly realize how generously *Dom*
Carlo had arranged to pay her for her care and knowledge
of hawks and birds. She said quickly, "I have—"

"Hush, boy, *Dom* Carlo told me to see you had what you needed for the journey, as I do for all his men," Orain said, "Let you sit there, now, and let him measure your foot . . . son," he added, grinning.

Romilly did as she was told, thrusting out her slender foot in its shabby too-large stocking. The bootmaker hummed, whistling a little tune, as he measured, scrawling down cryptic notes and numbers with a stump of chalk on the board by his bench. "When d'you want these ready?"

"Yesterday," growled Orain, "We may have to leave the city at a moment's notice."

The bootmaker protested; Orain haggled a few minutes, then they agreed on a price and the day after tomorrow.

"Should be tomorrow," Orain said scowling as they left the shop, "but these workmen have no more pride in their craft these days. Humph!" He snorted as Romilly turned. "In a hurry to get back to the monastery, Rumal lad, and dine on cold boiled lentils and smallbeer? After all these days on the road, living on porridge-powder and journey-cake not much better than dogbread, I'm for a roast fowl and some good wine in a cookshop. What reason have ye to get back? The birds won't fly away, now, will they? The horses are warm in their stable, and the monks will give them some hay if we don't get back. Let's walk through the town, then."

Romilly shrugged and acquiesced. She had never been in a city the size of Nevarsin before, and she was afraid she would be lost if she explored alone, but with Orain, she might learn her way about the confusing streets. In any case she could hardly fail to find the way back to the monastery, she need only follow any street straight up the mountain—the monastery was high above the town.

The short winter day brightened, then faded again as they walked through the city, mostly in a companionable silence; Orain did not seem inclined to talk much, but he pointed out various landmarks, the ancient shrine of Saint-Valentine-of-the-Snows, the cave high on the mountain where the saint was said to have lived and died, a forge which, he said, did the best horse-shoeing north of Armida, a sweetshop where, he said with a grin, the students at the monastery chose to spend their pocket money on holidays. It was as if she was one of her own brothers, here and free,

unconstrained by any of the laws which governed the behavior of women; she felt as easy with Orain as if she had
known him all her life. He had quite forgotten the country
accent, and talked in a pleasant, well-bred voice, with only
the faintest trace, like Alderic's, of a lowland accent.

She could not guess his age. He was certainly not a young
man, but she did not think he was as old as her father. His
hands were rough and calloused like a swordsman's, but
the nails were clean and well-cared-for, not grimy or broken like the other men who followed *Dom* Carlo.

He must be well-born enough, anyhow, if he had been
foster-brother to the exiled Carolin. Her father, she knew,
would have welcomed him and treated him with honor as
a noble, and though *Dom* Carlo did not quite treat him as
an equal, he showed him affection and respect and sought
his advice in everything.

As the twilight gathered, Orain found a cookshop and
commanded a meal. Romilly felt inclined to protest.

"You should not—I can pay my share—"

Orain shrugged. "I hate to dine alone. And *Dom* Carlo
made it clear he has other fish to fry this night. . . ."

She bent her head, accepting graciously. She had never
been in a public tavern or cookshop before, and she noted
there were no women present except for the bustling fat
waitress who came and slapped crockery in front of them
and fussed away again. If Orain had known her true sex
he would never have brought her here; if a lady, unimaginably, came in here, there would have been all sorts of deferential fuss made, they would never have taken her quite
simply for granted. Far less would she be able to lounge
here at ease, her feet propped on the bench across from
her, sipping from a tankard of cider, while the good smell
of cooking gradually filled the room.

No, it was better to remain a boy. She had respectable
work, three silver bits for a tenday; no cook-women or
dairy-maid could hope to command such pay for any work
she could do, and she remembered that Rory's grandmother, telling of her lost affluence, had spoken of the fact
that when her husband did not seek her bed, he was sent,
quite without worrying about what the dairymaid thought
about it, to sleep with the dairymaid as a matter of course.

Better to spend all her life in breeches and boots than have that added to the regular duties of a dairymaid's work!

She found herself wondering if Luciella made such routine demands of her women. Well, she must at some times—there was Nelda's son. It made Romilly uncomfortable to think of her father that way, and she reminded herself that he was a *cristoforo* . . . but would that make such a difference? In the world where she had been brought up it was taken for granted that a nobleman would have bastards and *nedestro* sons and daughters. Romilly had never really thought about their mothers.

She shifted uneasily in her seat, and Orain said with a grin, "Getting hungry? Something smells good in the kitchen yonder." Half a dozen men were flinging darts at a board hung at the back of the tavern, a few others playing dice. "Shall we have a game of darts, lad?"

Romilly shook her head, protesting that she did not know the game. "But don't let me stop you."

"You'll never learn younger, then," Orain said, and Romilly found herself standing, urged to fling the darts.

"Hold it this way," Orain instructed, "and just let it go—you don't have to push it."

"That's the way," said one of the men standing behind her in the crowd, "Just imagine the circle painted on the wall is the head of King Carolin and you have a chance at the fifty copper *reis* offered for his head!"

"Rather," said a bitter voice somewhere behind the first speaker, "that the head is of that bloodthirsty wolf Rakhal—or his chief jackal Lyondri, the Hastur-Lord!"

"Treason," said another voice and the speaker was quickly hushed, "That kind o' talk's not safe even here beyond the Kadarin—who knows what kind of spies Lyondri Hastur may be sending into the city?"

"I say, may Zandru plague'em both with boils and the bald fever," said another, "What matters it to free mountain men which great rogue plants his backside on the throne or what greater rogue tries to pry his arse loose from the seat? I say Zandru take'em both off to his hells and I wish 'im joy of their company, so that they stay south o' the river and leave honest men to go about their business in peace!"

"Carolin must ha' done something or they'd never o' kicked him off the throne," someone said, "Down there, the *Hali'myn* think the Hastur are kin to their filthy Gods— I've heard some tales when I travel down there, I could tell you—"

The darts had been forgotten; no one came to take a turn from Romilly. She whispered to Orain, "Are you going to let them talk that way about King Carolin?

Orain did not answer. He said, "Our meat's on the table, Rumal. Neighbors, maybe we'll have another round later, but the dinner's getting cold while we stand here gabbing," and gestured to Romilly to put down the darts and go to their seat. When the food arrived, and Orain was cutting the meat into portions, he muttered under his breath. "We're here to serve Carolin, lad, not defend him to fools in taverns. Eat your dinner, boy." And after a moment, he added, still in a half-whisper, "Part of my reason for walking about town is to hear how the folk think—see how much support there is here for the king. If we're to raise men for him here, it's urgent there must be popular support so no one will betray us—a lot of things can be done in secret, but you can't raise an army that way!"

Romilly put her fork into the roast meat, and ate in silence. She noted that when he spoke to her, Orain had, without thinking, dropped the rough up-country accent and spoken again like an educated man. Well, if he was the king's foster-brother, as she had heard, that was not surprising. Carlo too must have been high in those councils and one of his loyal men—no doubt he too had lost lands and possessions when Carolin was deposed and fled to the hills. Which reminded her again—

I do not know if Carolin has enemies in the city, but he certainly has at least one in the monastery. I do not think a child like Caryl would do him any great harm, he said the king had shown him kindness; but if Carlo and Orain are expecting to meet the king within monastery walls, there is at least one pair of eyes who would recognize him. They must prevent him from coming there. And Romilly wondered why it should matter to her what happened to the exiled king. As her father had said so often, what did it matter what great rogue sat on the throne, or what worse rogue tried to unseat him?

Orain and Carlo could not follow an evil master. Which-ever king they follow, he is my king too! And the story she had heard of the evil Hastur-Lord Lyondri had filled her with revulsion. She thought, wryly that without knowing it, she had somehow become a partisan of Carolin.

"Take that last cutlet, lad; you're a growing boy, you need your food," Orain said, grinning, and called to the serving-woman for more wine. Romilly reached for another cup, but Orain slapped her hand away.

"No, no, you've had enough—bring the boy some cider, woman, he's too young for your rotgut here! I don't want to have to carry you home," he added, good-naturedly, "and lads your age have no head for this kind of thing."

Her face burning, exasperated, Romilly took the huge mug of cider the woman set before her. Sipping it, she acknowledged to herself that she liked it better than the strong wine, which burned her mouth and her stomach and made her head swim. She muttered, "Thank you, Orain."

He nodded and said, "Think nothing of it. I wish I'd had a friend to knock my head out of the winepot when I was your age! Too late now," he added with a grin, and lifting his tankard, drank deep.

Romilly sat listening, full and sleepy, as Orain went back to the dart board; when asked to join him, she shook her head, feeling drowsy, listening to the talk around the bar.

"Well thrown! Whang in the eye of whichever king you don't favor!"

"I heard Carolin's in the Hellers because the *Hali'myn* are too soft to search for him up here—they might freeze their dainty tailbones!"

"Whether Carolin's here or no, there are enough sup-porters for his rule—he's a good man!"

"Whatever Carolin's like, Ill join anything which gets that bastard Lyondri the rope's end he deserves! Did ye' hear what he did to old Lord Asturien? Burned over his head, poor old man, and him and the old lady by the side of the road in their night-gear and bedslippers, if one of their woodsmen hadn't taken 'em in and given 'em a place to lie down in. . . ."

After a time Romilly fell into a doze, in which Carolin and the usurper Rakhal wandered in dreams with the faces of great mountain cats, slinking through the woods and tearing at one another, and the shrill cry of hawks, as if she were soaring far above and watching the battle. She flew over a white Tower, and Ruyven was waving to her from the summit, and then he somehow took wing and was flying beside her, telling her gravely that Father would not approve of it. He said solemnly "The Bearer of Burdens said that it is forbidden for man to fly and that is why I have no wings." and saying it, he fell like a stone; Romilly started awake, to feel Orain lightly shaking her.

"Come, lad, it's late, they're closing the doors—we must go back to the monastery!"

His breath was heavy with wine, his speech slurred; she wondered if he was able to walk. However, she laid his cloak over his shoulders, and they went out into the crisp, frosty darkness. It was very late; most of the houses were dark. Somewhere, a dog barked in a frenzy, but there was no other sound, and little light in the street; only the pale and frosty light of blue Kyrrdis, low on the rooftops of the city. Orain's steps were unsteady; he walked with one hand on the nearest house-wall, steadying himself, but when the narrow streets opened into a stair, he tripped on the cobbles and went flailing down full-length on the stone, howling with drunken surprise. Romilly helped him up, saying in amusement, "You had better hold on to my arm." Had he made certain his companion would stay sober, so that he would have someone to guide him back to the monastery? Romilly was fairly good at finding a path she had once travelled; she managed to direct their steps upward into the shadow of the monastery.

"Do you know if Carolin is truly in the city, Orain?" she asked at last in a low voice, but he peered with drunken suspicion into her face and demanded, "Why d'ye ask?" and she shrugged and let it go. When he was sober she would talk to him about that; but at least the wine he had drunk would not unseal his mouth and he would not babble of his mission or plans. As they climbed the last steep street, which led into the courtyard of the monastery guest-house, he held tightly to her arm, sometimes putting a drunken arm around her shoulders, but Romilly edged away—if he held her too close he might, as Rory had done, discover that she was a woman beneath the heavy clothes she wore.

*I like Orain, I would rather respect him, and if he knew
I were a woman he would be like all the others. . . .*

As they climbed he leaned on her arm more and more
heavily. Once he turned aside from her, and, unbuttoning
his trousers, relieved himself against a house wall; Romilly
was, not for the first time, grateful for her farm upbringing
which had made this something she could accept unblush-
ing—if she had been a housebred woman like Luciella or
her younger sister, she would have been outraged a dozen
times a day. But then, if she had been a housebred woman,
she would probably never have thought to protest the marriage her father had arranged, and she would certainly
never have been able to travel with so many men without
somehow revealing herself.

At the monastery gates Orain tugged at the bell-pull
which announced their presence to the porter at the guest-
house. It was very late; for a moment Romilly wondered if
they would be admitted at all, but finally the Brother Porter
appeared at the gates and, grumbling, let them inside. He
frowned and sniffed disapprovingly at the reek of wine
which hung around them, but he did let them in, and shook
his head when Orain offered him a silver bit.

"I am not allowed, friend. I thank you for the kind
thought. Here, your door is this way," he said, and added
audibly to Romilly, "Can you get him inside?"

"This way, Orain," said Romilly, shoving him to the door
of his room. Inside, Orain looked around, fuzzily, like an
owl in daylight. "Whe'—"

"Lie down and go to sleep," Romilly said, pushed him
down on the nearer of the two beds and hauled at his heavy
boots. He protested incoherently—he was drunker than she
had realized.

He held her by one wrist. "You're a good boy," he said,
"Aye, I like you, Rumal—but you're *cristoforo*. Once I
heard you call on the Bearer of Burdens . . . damn . . ."

Gently Romilly freed her hand, pulled his cloak around
him, went quietly away, wondering where *Dom* Carlo was.
Not, surely, still closeted with the Father Master? Well, it
was none of her affair, and she must be up early to care
for the animals and the sentry-birds. She shrank from sharing the sleeping quarters of the men who attended on Carlo
and Orain, so she had chosen to sleep on the hay in the

stables—it was warm and she was unobserved; she need not be quite so careful against some accidental revealing of her body. She had not realized, until she was alone again, quite what a strain it was to be always on guard against some momentary inadvertent word or gesture which might betray her. She pulled off her boots, glad of the thick stockings under them, rolled herself into a bundle in the hay and tried to sleep again.

But she found herself unexpectedly wakeful. She could hear the stirring of the birds on their perches, the soft shifting hooves of horses and chervines; far away inside the depths of the monastery she heard a small bell and a far-away shuffle of feet as the monks went their way to the Night Offices, when all the world around them slept. Had Orain some feud with the *cristoforos* that he would say he liked her, *but* she was *cristoforo*? Was he bigoted about religion? Romilly had never really thought much about it, she was *cristoforo* because her family was, and because, all her life, she had heard tales of the good teachings of the Bearer of Burdens, whose teachings had been, so the *cristoforos* said, brought from beyond the stars in days before any living man could remember or tell. At last, hearing the muffled chanting far away, she fell into a restless sleep, burrowing herself into the hay. For a time she dreamed of flying, soaring on hawk-wings, or on the wings of a sentry-bird; not over her own mountains, but over a lowland country, green and beautiful, with lakes and broad fields, and a white tower rose above a great lake. Then she came half awake as a bell rang somewhere in the monastery. She thought, a little ruefully, that if she had had supper within the monastery she would have heard the choir singing— perhaps the only woman who would ever do so.

Well, they would be there for days, it seemed; there would be other nights, other services to hear. How lucky Darren was no longer here at the monastery—even from his seat within the choir, he would have seen and recognized her.

If King Carolin comes to the monastery, young Caryl will recognize him—Dom *Carlo must warn him.* . . .

And then she slept again, to dream confused dreams of kings and children, and someone at her side who spoke to her in Orain's voice and drowsily caressed her. At last she slept, deep and dreamlessly, waking at fist light to the screams of the sentry-birds.

Life in the monastery quickly fell into routine. Up at early light to tend the animals, breakfast in the guest-house, occasionally an errand to be done for *Dom* Carlo or Orain. Two days later she had her new boots, made to her own measure, and with the pay they gave her—for now she had been in their service ten days—she found a stall where warm clothing was sold, and bought warm stockings so that she could wash and change the ones she had been wearing since Orain had given them to her. In the afternoon she wandered alone around the city of Nevarsin, enjoying a freedom she had never had in the days when she was still the ladylike daughter of The MacAran; in the evenings, when the birds had been tended and exercised again, after a frugal supper in the guest-house, she would slip into the chapel and listen to the choir of men and little boys. There was one soprano among the boys, with a sweet, flutelike voice; she strained her eyes to see the singer and realized at last that it was small Caryl, the son of Lyondri Hastur.

He wished King Carolin no ill. Romilly hoped that Orain had passed along his message to *Dom* Carlo and that he, somehow, had gotten word to the king, that Carolin had not come to the city.

Once or twice during the tenday that followed, she went again with Orain to the tavern, or to another, though never again did he drink more than a mug or two of the local wine, and seemed not even a little befuddled by it. *Dom* Carlo she had not seen again; she supposed he was about whatever business for King Carolin had brought him to this city. For all she knew to the contrary, he had left Nevarsin and gone to warn Carolin not to come here—there was one who would recognize him. She did not think the child would betray Carolin—he had said the king had been kind to him—but his loyalties, naturally, would be to his own father. She did not question Orain. It was none of her business, and she was content to have it that way.

Shyly, she began to wonder; if her father had chosen to marry her to one like Orain, would she have refused him? She thought not. But that was conflict too.

For then would I have stayed at home and been married,

and never known this wonderful freedom of city and tavern, woods and fields, never have worked free and had money in my pockets, never really known that I had never been free, never flown a sentry-bird.

She was growing fond of the huge ugly birds; now they came to her hand for their food as readily as any sparrow-hawk or child's cagebird. Either her arm grew stronger or she was more used to it, for now she could hold them for a considerable time and not mind the weight. Their docility and the sweetness she felt when she went into rapport with them, made her think with regret of Preciosa; would she ever see the hawk again?

She seldom saw the other men; she slept apart from them, and encountered them only morning and night, when they all came together for meals in the monastery guest-house. She was quite content that it should be so; she was still a little afraid of Alaric, and the others seemed strange and alien too. It seemed sometimes that the only person to whom she spoke these days, aside from the man who delivered the bird-food and fodder for horses and *chervines,* was young Caryl, who came whenever he could escape for a few minutes from his lessons, to look at the birds, hold them, croon lovingly to them. With Caryl she was always a little troubled, lest he should forget and thoughtlessly address her again as *vai domna*—it was a heavy weight of secrets for a child to bear. Once Orain came to the chapel to hear the singing; he took a seat far back and in the shadows, and she was sure that the little boy, in the lighted choir, could not see the face of a solitary man in the darkest part of the chapel, but she remembered that the child knew Carolin and would certainly recognize one of the king's men; she was so agitated that she rose quietly and went out, afraid that the telepathic child would sense her agitation and know its cause.

Midwinter-night was approaching; stalls of spicebread trimmed with copper foil, and gaily painted toys, began to appear in the marketplace, and sweet-sellers filled their displays with stars cut from spicebread or nut-paste. Romilly, homesick at the smell of baking spicebread—Luciella always baked it herself, saying that the servants should not be given extra work at this season—almost regretted leaving her home; but then she remembered that in any case she would not have spent this holiday at her home, but at Scathfell as the wife of *Dom* Garris—and by now, no doubt, she would have been like Darissa, swollen and ugly with her first child! No, she was better here; but she wished she could send a gift to Rael, or that he could see these bright displays with her.

On the morning before the Festival, she woke to snow blowing into the cracks of the room where she slept, though she was warm in the deep-piled hay. A midwinter storm had blown down, wailing, from the Wall Around the World, and the monastery courtyard was knee-deep in fresh powdery snow. She put on both pairs of warm stockings when she dressed, and her extra tunic, and even so she shivered as she went out into the yard to wash at the well; but the little novices and students were running about barefoot in the snow, and she wondered how they could do it, laughing and gossiping and tossing snowballs at one another. They looked rosy and warm, whereas her own hands were blue with cold!

She went in to care for the riding-animals, and stopped in dismay; *Dom* Carlo's horse was not in the stable! Had it been stolen? Or had *Dom* Carlo gone out, into this bitter storm? It was still snowing, a few flakes drifting down now and again from the overburdened sky. As she was lifting forkfuls of fragrant hay to the beasts, Orain came in, and she turned to him in distress.

"*Dom* Carlo's horse—"

"Hush, lad," he said in a low tone, "Not even before the men. His life could be in your hands; not a word!"

Romilly nodded, and he said, "Good boy. After mid-day, walk to the town with me; perhaps, who knows, I shall have a Midwinter gift for you, away as you are from home and family— "

It seemed as if he must be reading her mind, and she turned away. "I expect no gifts, sir," she said stiffly. Did he know, had he guessed? But he only grinned and said, "Mid-day, remember." and went away.

At mid-day Romilly was trying, in the deep snow, to get the sentry-birds to fly a little—they got little enough exercise, in this weather—before they were fed. They screamed rebelliously as she snapped them on lure-lines, and tried to encourage them to fly—they were temperamental and did

not like the still-falling snow. The snow in the cobbled
court, too, was so deep that it came over her boot-tops and
trickled down inside, and her feet were cold and her fingers
stiff. She was chilled and cross, and even little Caryl's
cheerful face could not lighten her mood. She thought, *it
might, in this weather, be just as well to be a lady by the
fire, with nothing to do but make embroidery stitches and
bake spicebread!* Caryl was wearing only a thin tunic, his
arms bare, and his feet were in the snow, and she asked
crossly, "Aren't you freezing?"

He shook his head, laughing. "It is the first thing the
monks teach us," he said, "How to warm ourselves from
within, by breathing; some of the older monks can bathe
in the water of the well and then dry their clothes by their
body heat when they put them on, but that seems a little
more than I would want to try. I was cold for the first
tenday before I learned it, but I have never suffered from
the cold since then. Poor Rumal, you look so cold, I wish
I could teach it to you!" He held out his arm to take Prudence, saying seriously, "Come birdie, you must fly, I know
you do not like the snow, but it is not good for you to sit all
the time on your perch, you must keep your wings strong."

Prudence flapped away and circled at the end of the line,
while Caryl cast out the lure, watching her swoop down.
"See, she likes to play with it, even in the snow! Look
at her!"

"You are happy," Romilly said sourly, "Do you like the
storm as much as that?"

"No, I would like to go out, but in this weather I have
to stay indoors, and the arms-master cannot come, so I will
miss my lesson at sword-play," said the boy, "but I am
happy because tomorrow is a holiday, and my father will
come here to visit me. I miss my father and my brothers,
and father is sure to bring me a fine gift—I am twelve years
old and he promised me a fine sword, perhaps he will give
it to me for a Midwinter-gift. And he always takes me walking in the town so that I can buy spicebread and sweets,
and my mother always sends me a new cloak at Midwinter.
I have been working very hard at all my lessons, because
I want him to be pleased with me."

Lyondri Hastur? Here in the monastery? Her first thought
was of Orain and *Dom* Carlo; the second of their king.

Quieting her thoughts carefully, she asked, "Is you father here now?"

"No, but he will come for the holiday, unless this weather should keep him housebound a day's journey away," the boy said, "and Father is never afraid of storms! He has some of the old Delleray Gift, he can work a little on the weather; you'll see, Father will make it stop snowing before it is night."

"That is a *laran* of which I have not heard," Romilly said, keeping her voice steady, "Do you have it?"

'I don't think so," the child said, "I have never tried to use it. Here, let me fly Temperance while you take Diligence, will you?"

She handed the lure-line to the child, trying to conceal her agitation. Alaric, too, should be warned—or would he try to take vengeance on his enemy, whom he regarded as murderer of his wife and child? She could hardly make conversation with the little boy. And halfway through feeding the birds, she saw the door from the stables open and Orain came into the court. She tried to motion to him to withdraw, but he came into the courtyard, saying, "Not finished with the birds yet, my boy? Make haste, I want your company for an errand in the town," and Caryl turned and saw him. His eyes widened a little.

"My lord," he said, with a courtly little bow, "What are you doing here?"

Orain flinched, and for a moment did not answer. Then he said, "I have come here for sanctuary, lad, since I am no longer welcome at the court where your father rules the king. Will you give the alarm, then?"

"Certainly not," said the boy with dignity, "Under the roof of Saint Valentine, even a condemned man must be safe, sir. All men are brothers who shelter here—this much the *cristoforo* have told me, Master Rumal, if you wish to go with your master, I will put the birds on their perches for you."

"Thank you, but I can manage them," said Romilly, and took Temperance on her fist; Caryl trailed her with the other bird on his two hands. He said in a whisper, "Did you know he was one of Carolin's men? They are really not safe here."

Romilly pretended gruffness and said, "I don't ask questions about my betters. And you should run along to choir, Caryl.''

He bit his lip, flushing, and turned away, dashing barefoot through the snow. Romilly drew a long breath; she would have turned and spoken to Orain, but his hand closed with an iron grip on her shoulder.

"Not here," he said. "Outside these walls; I am not sure, now, that they have not ears, and the ears are those of a certain lord."

Silent, Romilly finished her work with the sentry-birds and followed Orain through the gates of the monastery. The street was white and silent, muffled with the thick snow. At last Orain said, "The Hastur-whelp?"

She nodded. After a moment she said in an undertone, pitching her voice so that Orain had to lean close to listen, "That's not the worst of it. His father—Lyondri Hastur— is outside the city and will be visiting him for the holiday."

Orain's clenched fist drove into his other hand. "Damnation! And Zandru knows, *he's* not one to observe sanctuary-law! If he sets eyes—" Orain fell silent. "Why did *Dom* Carlo have to go away at *this* time of all times—" he said at last. "I;ll-luck dogs us! I'll try and get a message to him—"

Silence; even their footsteps were silent in the snow-muffled street. At last Orain said, dismissing it, "Let's go down to the tavern. With such news as this I need a drink, and they have spiced cider in honor of the holiday, so you may drink too."

Romilly said soberly, "Shouldn't Alaric and the others be warned to watch themselves, if the Hastur-Lord is likely to be about?"

"I'll pass a word to them," Orain said, "But for now, no more talk—"

In the tavern where Orain had taught her, some days ago, to play at darts, he commanded wine, and hot cider for Romilly; it smelled sweet with spices, and she drank it gratefully and accepted his offer of a second mug. He said, "I have a gift for you—that filthy cloak you wear is hardly worthy of a stable-man's son. I found this in a stall—it's old and worn but suits you, I think." He beckoned to the serving-woman, said "Bring me the bundle I left here yesterday."

He tossed it across the table at her. "A good Midwinter-night to you, and Avarra guard you, son."

Romilly untied the strings; took out a green cloak, spun of rabbithorn-wool, finely embroidered and trimmed with clasps of good leather. It must have been very old, for it had sleeves cut in one with the cape, in a fashion she had seen in portraits of her great-grandsire in the Great Hall at Falconsward; but it was richly lined and comfortable. She flung aside the shabby old cloak she had taken when she fled from Rory's house in the woods, and put on the new one, saying after a moment, embarrassed, "I have no gift for you, Master Orain."

He put his arm round her shoulders. "I want nothing from you, son; but give me the hug and kiss you'd give your father if he were here today."

Bushing, Romilly embraced him, and touched her lips gingerly to his cheek. "You are very good to me, sir. Thank you."

"Not at all—now you are dressed as befits your red hair and the manner you have of a nobleman's son," he said. There was just enough irony in the words that Romilly wondered; did he *know* she was a woman? She had been sure, at one time, that *Dom* Carlo knew.

"That old thing, you can make into a horse-blanket," said Orain, motioning the tapster's boy to make it up into a bundle. Romilly would rather had thrown it away where she need never touch it again, but in this weather horses could not go un-blanketed, and the horse-blanket she had had been meant for warmer climates. Her horse would be grateful for the extra warmth, with this midwinter storm.

There were but few patrons in the tavern this evening; the approaching storm, and the morrow's holiday, contrived to keep most of the men at home, Romilly supposed, by their own hearths.

Orain asked, when she had finished her meal, "Will we have a game of darts, then?"

"I am not a good enough player to make it worth your trouble," she said, and Orain laughed. "Who cares? Come along, then."

They stood, alternately flinging the darts and sipping from their tankards, as the evening passed. Suddenly Orain stiffened, went silent.

"Your turn," Romilly said.

"You throw—I'll be back in a moment," Orain said, his speech slurred, and Romilly thought, *he cannot possibly be drunk so early.* Yet as he walked away he reeled drunkenly, and one of the sparse patrons of the tavern yelled jovially "Drunk so early on Midwinter-night? You'll not hold your wine on the holiday, then, man!"

She wondered; *is he sick? Should I go and help him?* One of the things Romilly had carefully avoided, during her weeks in the town, was going inside the common latrine behind any of the taverns—it was the one place where she might possibly be discovered. Yet Orain had been good to her, if he was in trouble, surely he deserved help—

A small voice in her mind said; *No. Stay where you are. Act as if everything were normal.* Since Romilly was not yet accustomed to the use of her own *laran*—and it was rare for her to be so much in touch with the feelings of any human, though she now took rapport with her birds for granted—she was not sure whether this were actually a message reaching her, or her own projected feelings; but she obeyed it. She called out, recklessly drawing attention to herself, "Who'd like a game, then, since my friend's overcome with drink?" And when two townsmen came up to her, she challenged them, and played so badly that she soon lost and had to pay the forfeit of buying them a round of drinks. It seemed that at the very edge of the room she could see movement in the shadows—had Orain not left the room after all, but only withdrawn? Who was he talking to? She kept the game going, and by a great effort did not turn to try and see the other figure, tall and graceful, a hood shrouding face and head, moving softly near Orain. But as if she had eyes in the back of her head, it seemed that she could see it, hear whispers . . . her spine prickled and at every moment she thought she would hear an outcry, voices, shouts. *Holy Bearer of burdens, whose day this is, tell me, how did I become entangled in this intrigue, as if it mattered to me which king sat on the throne of the Hali'i-myrn? Damn them both, outcast king and usurper king. Why should a good man like Orain risk a noose for his neck because one king or another holds the throne of the Hasturs?*

If any harm comes to my friend, I will . . . and she

stopped there. What could she do? Unlike her brothers, she had no knowledge of arms, she was defenseless. *If I escape this night's intrigue,* she thought, *I will ask Orain to teach me something of the arts of fighting . . .* but she laughed and shouted, "Well thrown, whang in the cat's eye," and flung her own dart almost at random, surprised when it landed anywhere near the target.

"Drink up, young'un," said the man who had lost, setting a mug of wine before her, and Romilly drank recklessly. Her head felt fuzzy, and she stopped halfway through the mugful, but they were all looking at her, and against her better judgment, she finished the drink.

"You'll have another game? My turn to win," said one of the men, and she shrugged and gave up the dart. Her neck felt that cold, vulnerable prickle that she knew meant she was being watched, somewhere undercover. *What is going on in that room? Damn these intrigues!*

Then Orain was at her side again, clapping her on the shoulder. "Aye, now you have the way of it, but you can't yet teach an old dog how to gnaw a bone—gi'me the darts, lad." He took the feathered darts, poised them, called for wine all around; she saw the exited glitter of his eyes. When the nest pair took the darts, he muttered next her ear, "Next round we must get away; I've a message—"

She nodded to let him know she understood. The next moment Orain shouted, "What in nine hells do you there, man, your big feet halfway over the line—I won't play darts with a cheating bastard like that, not even at Midwinter— gifts I will make but not be cheated out of a drink or a silver bit!" and shoved angrily against the man who was throwing. The man whirled drunkenly and swung at him.

"Here, you lowland bugger, who do you call cheat? You'll swallow those words with your next drink or I'll ram them down your throat—" He connected with Orain's chin, and Orain's head went back with a crack; he staggered against the wall, came out swinging furiously. Romilly flung her dart, and it landed in the man's hand as he swung again at Orain; the attacker turned, howling, and barged toward her, hands out as if to strangle her. She moved away, tripped on a barrel and went sprawling in the sawdust. Orain's hand grabbed her, pulled her upright.

"Here, here—" the barman came over, scowling, separating them with rough hands. "No brawling, friends! Drink up!"

"The rotten little bastard threw a dart at me," growled the man, shoving up his sleeve to reveal a red mark.

"You're a baby to bawl at a bee-sting?" demanded Orain, and the barman shoved them apart.

"Sit down! Both of you! The penalty for fighting is a drink for the house, from each of you!"

With a show of reluctance, Orain pulled out his purse, flung down a copper piece. "Drink up and be damned to you, and I hope you all choke on it! We'll be off to a quieter place for drinking!" he snarled, grabbed Romilly's elbow and steered a drunken path toward the door. Outside her straightened up and demanded in a low, quick voice, "Are you hurt?"

"No, but—"

"That's all right, then. Let's make tracks!" He set a pace up the hill that Romilly could hardly follow. She knew she had had too much to drink and wondered, as she staggered dizzily after him, if she was going to throw it up. After a moment he turned and said, gently, "Sorry—here, lad, take my arm," and supported her. "You shouldn't have drunk that last cup."

"I couldn't think of anything else to do," she confessed.

"And you saved my neck by it," he said in a whisper. "Come, perhaps you can get a bit of rest at the monastery before—look," he gestured at the clearing sky, "The snow's stopped. We'll be expected to show at the Midwinter-eve service, any guest at the monastery who's not abed with a broken leg is expected to be there for heir damned hymn-singing! And with the weather cleared that rat Lyondri—" he clenched his fists. "He may well be there, large as life and twice as filthy, sitting smug in the choir and singing hymns like a better man."

Romilly asked, troubled, "Would he recognize you, then, Uncle?"

"That he would," said Orain grimly, "and others than me."

She wondered; *can it be that Carolin himself is somewhere in the monastery?* Or did he speak of Alaric, whose family had been condemned to death by the Hastur-lord? Or of

Carlo, who was certainly an exiled man and high in Carolin's confidence? Orain's hand was beneath her arm.

"Here, lean on me, lad—I'd pretend to be sick and hide in the guest-house, but then they'd hale me off to the infirmary, and find out soon there's nothing wrong with me but a cup too many of their wine."

She looked at the settled snow, cringing in the keen wind that came as the snow had quieted. "Is there truly a *laran* which can work sorcery on the weather?"

"So I have heard," Orain muttered, subsiding into gloom again. "Would that you had some trace of it, son!"

Chapter 4

The Midwinter-night service in St. Valentine-of-the-Snows was famous throughout the Hellers; people came from all through Nevarsin, and from the countryside round, to hear the singing. Romilly had heard some of the music before this but never sung so well, and she would have enjoyed the service, had she not been so troubled by Orain's obvious worried state. He insisted that they should sit at the back, and when she asked where *Dom* Carlo was, and why he had not come to the service, scowled and refused to answer. He had cautioned Alaric, too, not to enter the chapel at all. But toward the end of the service, when there was a moment's lull, he whispered "No sign yet of Lyondri Hastur. We may be lucky." His face twisted and he muttered, "We'd be luckiest if he fell off a cliff somewhere and never made it to Nevarsin at all!"

And, as Caryl said, some weather magic has been done. I did not think the weather would clear so quickly.

She saw Caryl, scrubbed and shining, in the front row of the choir, his mouth opening like a bird as he sang; it seemed to Romilly that his voice soared out over all the choir. It was as well, perhaps, that *Dom* Carlo was not here, except for Orain's dread; it seemed that the big gaunt man could hardly sit still, and no sooner was the service ended than he was up and out of his seat, pushing for the back of the chapel. He walked with her to the stable, and busied his hands checking on the sentry-birds, so that Romilly would have been annoyed—did he think she could not care for them properly, then? Later she knew what he had been looking for, why he had arranged everything close together so that they could be snatched up and ready to ride at a moment's notice, but at the moment she was only exasperated and wondered if he was still drunk, or believed *she* was too drunk to handle them properly. He checked on the *chervines* and horses too, turning up each hoof, arranging saddle-blankets and saddles, until she thought she would scream with nervousness at his fiddling. Or was he lingering so that he would see it, if Lyondri Hastur actually arrived at the monastery?

But at last he sighed and turned away. He said, "A good Festival to you, lad," and gave Romilly a rough hug. "If it's too cold here in the stable, you can sleep in *Dom* Carlo's bed, no one will know the difference—"

"I think I should stay near the birds," Romilly said, avoiding his gaze. It was not that she did not trust him, exactly; she had lived in camp among them, and if her real sex had not yet been discovered, he was unlikely to discover it now, even should they share a sleeping room. And if he should—she discovered that she felt shaky and weak when she thought about that—Orain was not a *cristoforo* and would not be bound by their Creed of Chastity—she had heard stories all her life, of how licentious were the lowlanders and the *Hali'imyn*—but somehow she could not imagine that he would attempt to force himself upon her. Still, she was uncomfortable at his touch, and pulled away as quickly as she could, remembering the dream she had had . . . in the dream he had held and caressed her as if she was the woman he did not know her to be. . . .

She burrowed into the hay, still a little dizzied with the wine she had drunk, and after a time she slept. She dreamed, as she had dreamed before, that she was flying on the wings of hawk or sentry-bird, that there was someone flying at her side, who spoke to her in Orain's voice, and drowsily caressed her . . . she sank into the dream, never thinking to resist. . . .

She came abruptly awake in the half-light, hearing the clamor of bells—was it some observance of the *cristoforo* monks for the Festival? She sat up to see Orain, white as death, standing at the door of the little chamber.

"Rumal, lad! Is *Dom* Carlo with you? This is no time for modesty—"

"*Dom* Carlo? I have not seen him in days! What do you mean, Orain?"

"There was a time—no, I see you know not even what I mean. Damnation!" He staggered, reeled against the wall. I hoped against hope—it cannot be that he has been taken! Aldones grant he has already been warned and made his escape—listen!" He gestured and again she heard the alarm-bell ringing. "We have been betrayed, someone has recognized him, or recognized me—I knew he should not have ventured down there today!" He swore, striking the wall with his fist. "Quick, up, boy, search the guest-house! They know that where I appear, Carolin—or his men— cannot be far away! And while the Father Master might not violate sanctuary, I would not trust the Hastur-lord to keep it, not if the Lord of Light appeared before his nose and bade him—"

Orain was dead sober now; he looked ill and haggard, his gaunt face sunken, but his eyes blazing with anger.

"That child of Lyondri's—did he babble, do you think, to his playfellows? Lyondri's son—like dog, like pup! I'd run the boy through with my skean and think the world a safer place lest the whelp grow up like his abominable father!"

Romilly shrank back and Orain scowled. "No, I'd not harm a child, not even Lyondri's, I suppose—get your boots on, boy! We must make haste out of here, out of the city— if we are caught here, none of our lives are worth a feather's weight! Go and call—no, I will rouse Alaric and the others! You make the horses ready—"

It seemed suddenly as if *Dom* Carlo's face swam in the air before her—but he was not there! Still it seemed she could hear him saying to her, *Bring the birds, go through the monastery to the highest gate, to the secret pass above the hidden cells on the glacier.*

"Move, lad!" Orain snarled, "What are you staring at?"

Her voice shaking, Romilly repeated *Dom* Carlo's words. "He was here, I heard him; his very voice—"

"Dreams," Orain said, jerking his head impatiently, and it seemed that Carlo's voice said in Romilly's mind, *Bid him remember a certain belt of red leather over which we fought and bloodied both our noses.*

Romilly caught at Orain's sleeve as he turned to go. "I

swear, Orain, I heard *Dom* Carlo—something of a red leather belt over which you both bloodied your noses."

Orain blinked. He made a quick, superstitious gesture. Then he said, "You have *laran;* no? I thought as much. Aye, that belt was a jest between us for a hand-span of years. I will go rouse the men. Make ready, as quick as you can."

Romilly found that her hands were steady as she got the saddles on the animals, wrapped herself in the cloak that had been Orain's Midwinter-gift—grateful for the fur lining—and stuffed a couple of saddlebags with grain and fodder for the riding-beasts and another with the smelly food for the sentry-birds. She hooded them—it would have been impossible to handle them in the middle of the night this way without rousing the whole monastery, but hooded they would at least be quiet—and fastened their blocks to her own saddle and to Orain's, and gave the third to Alaric's *chervine.*

After a bit she looked up and found Alaric working at her side. "Some bastard betrayed us," he said shakily, listening to the distant clamor of bells—it was growing nearer and nearer now, "They're searching the city house to house, when the time comes they reach the monastery, they'll search every cranny, the monk's cells, the very chapel! What is it, lad, you know Orain's counsel—are we to ride them down at the gates?"

"I am not in their counsels," Romilly said, "But something of a secret gate at the highest part—"

"And while we waste time looking for the secret paths, Lyondri's men find us and I dance on a rope's end?" demanded Alaric. Romilly said steadily, "I do not think *Dom* Carlo will abandon us like that. Trust him."

"Aye; but the *vai dom* is Hastur, when all's done, and blood's thicker than wine, they say. . . ." Alaric grumbled.

"Alaric!" she turned round to him, shocked beyond speech. After a moment she found her voice and said, "Surely you can't believe Carlo would side with the Hastur-lord against—well, against us, and Orain—"

"Well, not against Orain," he said, "Get that saddle on, boy, if there's a chance—but how do I know? Likely ye're of the gentlefolk yourself. . . ." his voice trailed away, uncertain.

"Finish with the saddling, and don't talk nonsense," she said sharply. "Will you lift that grain-bag to the saddle? I can't lift it alone—"

He helped her to hoist the heavy pack to the back of the chervine, and led the beast out of the stable. A hand seized her wrist in a hard grip and she started to cry out before, not knowing how, she recognized Orain's grip, even in the darkness.

"This way," he whispered, and, knowing his voice even in the silenced whisper, she relaxed and let him lead them into the dark passageway. She heard the other men, trying to move silently, only small creaks and rustles; someone bashed a toe against a rock wall and cursed softly. Then, she heard a soft childish voice.

"My lord Orain—"

"Ah—it's you, ye devil's pup—"

Caryl cried out, a muffled squeak. "I won't hurt you," he said, gasping—Romilly could not see in the dark, but sensed, from the pain in the small voice, that Orain had grabbed him harshly. "No, I only—I meant to guide you on the secret path—I *don't* want my father to find—find the *vai dom*—he will be angry, but—"

"Let him go, Orain," Romilly muttered, "he's telling the truth!"

"Ah—I'll trust your *laran*, boy," said Orain, and she heard a little whimper of relief as, evidently, he loosed his punishing grip on the child. "A path you know? Lead us. But if you play us false—" he added through clenched teeth, "Child or no, I'll run my skean into you—"

They followed through the narrow passage, crowding together, bumping, the sentry-birds making uneasy squealing noises in the darkness. Someone cursed in an undertone and Romilly saw the flash of flint on steel, but Orain commanded harshly, "Put that out!" and the light subsided, with someone grumbling and swearing.

"Silence," Alaric commanded harshly, and there was no sound except the uneasy sounds of animals crowded in the narrow stone passages. There was a place where they had to go single file in the dark and one of the loaded chervines stuck between the stone walls. Alaric and one of the other men had to off-load the beast, hastily, swearing in whispers, while they hauled and shoved. Later they came to a place where the air was bad, coming up as if from the sulphurous center of the earth, and even Romilly could not stifle her coughing. Caryl murmured, "I am sorry—this is only a little bit, but watch your steps here, there are cracks and fissures, someone might break a leg."

Romilly groped her way along in the dark, scuffling her feet slowly against the possibility of an unseen crack underfoot. At least they were all through, and there was a breath of icy air from the glacier, a little riffling wind, and they stood out of doors in chilly starlight. The pallid face of a single moon, the tiny pearl-colored Mormallor, hung just above the hill, hardly bright enough to lighten the darkness at all; and underfoot was pale slippery ice.

"No one travels this path," whispered Caryl, "except for a few of the brothers who practice their mastery of the ordeals by living here, naked, and even if they knew you were here, they would not know or care who you were, they think only of the things of the heavenly realms, not of kings and wars. But oh, go carefully, my lords—there are dangers—"

"What dangers?" demanded Alaric, grabbing his throat. Caryl squeaked softly, but did not cry out.

"No dangers of man; banshee-birds live here, though our Brothers have a pact with them, as they say the holy Saint Valentine-of-the-Snows had a pact when he preached to them and called them God's little brothers—"

"You led us into a nest of banshee-birds, ye devil's pup?" Alaric demanded, but Orain said, "Let him go, damn you, man; touch the boy again and I'll give you something you'll remember! The banshees are not of his calling, he thought to warn us, which is more than even the Father Master thought to do!"

"Take your hands from the boy, Alaric! Are you mad?" demanded a new voice, and *Dom* Carlo stood among them. Romilly did not see from whence he had come; he was simply there. Later she realized he must have come through another secret tunnel or path, but at the moment it was as if he jumped up among them like magic. Caryl gave a little startled cry; Romilly's eyes were adjusting to the darkness now, and she could see the child's face. He held out his arms to *Dom* Carlo for a kinsman's embrace, saying simply, "Uncle. I am glad you are safe."

"It makes my heart glad to know you are not my enemy," said Carlo, not as if he spoke to a child, but as if he spoke to another noble, his equal in rank and age. He kissed the boy on either cheek. "Walk in the Light, lad, till we meet again."

"Vai dom—" Caryl's young high voice suddenly wavered, "I am your friend, not your enemy. But—I beg you—if my father is in your hands—spare him for my sake—"

Dom Carlo held Caryl's shoulders gently between his hands. He said, "I wish I could promise you that, son. I do swear this, by the Lord of Light, whom I serve as you the Bearer of Burdens; I will make no quarrel with Lyondri while he makes none with me. For the rest, I will hope with all my heart that Lyondri stays afar from me; I wish him far less ill than he wishes me. He was once my friend, and the quarrel was none of my making." He kissed Caryl again, and released him. "Now get you back to your bed, child, before your father hears that you have been abroad this night, or Father Master seeks to punish you. May the Gods walk with you, *chiyu*."

"And with you, my lord." Caryl turned and started back into the dark mouth of the passage. Then Alaric grabbed him around the waist. He struggled, but one quick blow from Alaric sent him sagging softly, with a little sigh, into the man's arms.

"Are you mad, *vai dom'yn*?" he demanded, "Lyondri's own son in our hands for hostage, and you'd let him free? With this whelp in our hands, we could bargain our way out of Rakhal's very clutches, to say nothing of being secure against Lyondri Hastur!"

"And you would reward him like this for guiding us to safety?" Romilly cried in outrage, but Alaric's face was hard and set.

"You're a fool, boy. And you too, under favor, my lords," he said to Orain and *Dom* Carlo. "The boy may have led us honestly—who'd seek to distrust a little one with angel face like this? But his elders have *laran*—even if *he* means us no harm, how do we know *they* haven't trailed us through the boy's *laran*? I won't hurt the least hair on his head, but he stays with us till we're safe from glacier and Lyondri's men! We can leave him in Caer Donn, or some such place!"

"If you've hurt him—" *Dom* Carlo said with soft menace, and Romilly hoped his wrath would never be turned on *her*. He felt the boy's forehead. "I wouldn't reward the child's loyalty like this! But we can't leave him here unconscious, to die of the cold," he added. "Bring him with you, then, if you must; we dare not delay for him to recover. But you'll hear of this after, Alaric," he said angrily, and turned his back on the man. "Set the boy on one of the horses, and you, young Rumal," he added, beckoning to Romilly, "Ride behind him, for he cannot keep his saddle as he is now, and I am reluctant to tie him as if he were a prisoner. Now come, make haste!"

The limp unconscious form of Caryl was lifted into the saddle and Romilly, mounting behind him, had all she could do to hold the child from falling on the uneven, icy path. They went upward and upward in silence, with no sound but the small, uneasy cries of the hooded sentry-birds. Riding in the dark, holding Caryl, small and limp, in her arms, Romilly thought of Rael, sleeping against her shoulder; missed him, sharply and with bitterness. Would she ever see her little brother again?

The narrow path was steep, so steep that Romilly had to lean forward in the saddle as they climbed; it was narrow, and icy underfoot, and it was all she could do to hold Caryl's unconscious weight against her so that he would not fall from the saddle. But the men, too, had all they could do to manage the nervous chervines and the sentry-birds, who were uneasy, and, even hooded, kept making little squealing sounds and trying to flap their wings and hop around restlessly on their blocks. This made horses and chervines even more nervous; she wondered what their sharper senses saw, and would have tried rapport to find out, but it was all she could do, on the steep path, to hold herself and the unconscious child in the saddle without falling.

Once there sounded a high screaming wail, a paralyzing sound that seemed to turn Romilly's blood to ice. Her horse started and snorted nervously under her, and she fought to control it. The sentry-birds fidgeted on their blocks, flapping their wings in panic. Romilly had never heard such a cry before, but she needed no one to tell her what it was; the cry of a banshee, the huge flightless birds who lived above the snow-line; all but blind, but sensing the body warmth of anything that lived, and their powerful claws that could disembowel horse or man with a single stroke. And it was night, when they actually could see a little, blind as they were in the light of the red sun. Their terrible cries, she had heard, were intended to paralyze prey with fright; hearing it now in the distance, she hoped she would never actually *see* one.

At the sound Caryl made a small pained noise and stirred, his hands going up to feel the lump on his head. The movement made the horse startle; his hooves all but slipped on the icy path. Romilly bent forward and whispered urgently, "It's all right, but you must be quiet; the road is dangerous just here, and if you frighten the horse, he may fall—and so would we. Be still, Caryl."

"Mistress Romilly?" he whispered, and she said crossly *"Hush!"* He subsided, looking up at her. Her eyes had adjusted now to the darkness so that she could see his small frightened face. Still gingerly feeling the lump at his temple, he blinked and she hoped he would not cry.

He whispered, "How did I get here? What happened?" And then, remembering, "Someone *hit* me!" He sounded more surprised than angry. She supposed that he, a pampered lowland child, had never been struck before, that no one had spoken to him other than gently. She held him tight in her arms.

"Don't be afraid," she whispered, "I won't let them hurt you." She knew, as she said it, that if Alaric offered any further violence to the child she would set herself between them. He wriggled himself into a more comfortable position on the saddle; now that he could sit upright, and was no longer a dead weight who must be held to keep him from falling, it was easier to control her horse.

"Where are we?" he whispered.

"On the road to which you guided us; *Dom* Carlo brought you with us because he could not leave you lying unconscious to die of the cold, but he means you no harm. Alaric wanted you as a hostage; but Orain won't let him hurt you again."

"Lord Orain has always been kind to me," said Caryl after a moment, "even when I was very small. I wish my father had not quarreled with him. And Father Master will be very angry with me."

"It wasn't your fault."

"Father Master says whatever happens to us is always our fault, one way or another," said the child, keeping his voice low, "If we have not deserved it in this life, we have certainly done so in another. If it is good we have earned it and may enjoy it, but if it is bad, we must also believe that somehow we have deserved the bad too, and it is not always easy to know which is which. I am not sure what that means," he added naively, "but he said I would understand when I was older."

"Then I must be very young too," said Romilly, unable to keep back a laugh—talking elevated *cristoforo* philosophy on this dangerous road, with the king's men, for all they knew, hard at their heels! "For I confess I do not understand it at all."

Orain heard the laugh; he pulled his horse aside and waited for them to come up with him, where the path widened just a fraction. "Are you awake, young Caryl?"

"I wasn't asleep," the boy protested, scowling, "Somebody hit me!"

"True," said Orain seriously, "And he has heard about it, believe me, from *Dom* Carlo. But now, I fear, you must ride with us to Caer Donn; you cannot possible return alone over this road. I would have trusted you not to betray us willfully, but I know from old that Lyondri had *laran* and might read in your thoughts which way we had gone. I give you my word, which, unlike your father, I have never broken, that when we reach Caer Donn you will be sent back to him under a flag of truce. He—" with an eloquent shrug of his caped shoulder, he indicated *Dom* Carlo, riding ahead, "wishes you no ill. But in this company I should warn you to guard your tongue."

'My lord—" Caryl began, but Orain gave a slight, warning shake of his head, and said quickly, "If you would be more comfortable riding behind me, you may, when we have gotten through this path; this is no place to stop and change horses. Or if you will give me the word of a Hastur that you will not try to flee from us, I will arrange it that one of the pack-animals can carry you, and you may ride alone."

"Thank you," the boy said, "but I would rather stay with—" he paused and swallowed and said, "with Rumal." She was astonished at his presence of mind; no other youngster, she was sure, could have remembered, even in this extremity, not to blurt out her secret.

"Ride carefully, then," Orain said, "and guard him well, Rumal." He turned back to his own riding, and Romilly, settling Caryl as comfortably as she could in front of her— it would indeed be easier if he could sit behind her and hang on, but there was no way to stop and change now— reflected that he had protected her even when he had noting to gain by keeping her secret, and when he might have made trouble among his captors. An unusual youngster indeed, and cleverer than Rael, disloyal as she felt to her own little brother think so.

He knew she was a woman. Though, she had thought sometimes that *Dom* Carlo knew and kept his counsel for his own reasons, whatever they were. And then, for the first time—so swiftly had affairs moved since she was awakened—she remembered Orain's exact words when he came seeking her. *Is Carlo with you? This is no time for modesty!* Had Carlo, then, confided to Orain—or been told by him, perhaps?—that he knew her a woman, and, knowing that, did he think her such a woman as might be free of her favors, so that he might have found Carlo in her bed? Even in the bitter cold, Romilly felt the hot flush of shame on her cheeks. Well, riding with them in men's clothes, what sort of woman *could* he think her?

"Well, if he knew, he knew, and if he thought *that* of her, he must think what he liked. At least he had been gentleman enough not to spread it among these roughnecks. But she had begun to like Orain so much!

Again from the crags above them came the eerie scream of a banshee; it was closer now, and Romilly felt the throbbing, eldritch wail going all through her, as if her very bones were shuddering at the sound. She knew how the natural prey of the bird must feel; it seemed to stop her in her tracks, to wipe out the world around so that there was nothing except that dreadful vibration, which seemed to

make her eyes blur and the world go dark around her.
Caryl moaned and dug his hands over his ears with an
agonized shiver, and she could see the men ahead of them
fighting to control their terrified horses while the sentry-
birds flapped, and the chervines made their odd bawling
cry and stepped around, almost prancing with terror, on
the icy path. One of them stumbled and went down and
the rider fell, sliding some way before he could dig his heels
into the ice and stand up, scrambling to catch his riding-
animal; another beast piled into him and there was a clumsy
sprawling collision. Swearing, they fought with the reins.
The screaming of the hooded sentry-birds, their bating
wings, added to the dismay, and again the eerie terror-filled
banshee scream shuddered out from the crags above, and
was answered by yet another.

Romilly gave Caryl a little shake. "Stop that!" she demanded furiously. "Help me, help me quiet the birds!" Her
own breath was coming ragged, she could see it steaming
in the icy air, but she put her mind swiftly to reaching out
with that special sense of hers, and sending thoughts of
calm, peace, food, affection. She could reach them still; as
she felt Caryl's thoughts join with hers, one after another
the great birds quieted, were still on their blocks on the
saddles, and Carlo and his men could get the riding-animals
under control again. Carlo gestured to them to gather
close—the path widened here just enough that three or four
of the animals could stand abreast, and they gathered in a
little bunch.

The crags above them were beginning to stand out stark
against the paling sky; pink and purple clouds outlined the
blackness of the rocks of the pass. Dawn was near. The
trail above them narrowed and led across the glacier; and
even as they looked, a clumsy shadow moved on the face of
the rocks, and again there came the terrible wailing scream,
answered by another from higher up. Orain compressed his
narrow lips and said wryly, "Just what we needed; two of
the damned things! And daylight still a good hour away—
and even when the sun comes up, we might not escape
them. And we can't wait anyway; if there's pursuit we
should be away and across the path before full daylight,
and well to the other side where the woods will conceal

our traces! A blind man would be able to read our tracks
on ice, and Lyondri's sure to have half a dozen of his
damned *leroni* with him!"

"We're in the very mouth of the trap," Carlo muttered,
his face going silent and distant. He said at last, into the
silence, "No pursuit, at least not yet—I need no *leronis* to
tell me so much. You were a damned fool to bring the boy,
Alaric—with him to follow, Lyondri will follow us through
the track led through all nine of Zandru's hells! Now he
has a second and personal grudge!"

"If the boy's with us,' Alaric said, his teeth set tight, "we
can buy our lives, at least!"

Caryl drew himself upright on the saddle and said angrily, "My father would not compromise his honor for his
son's life, and I would not want him to!"

"Lyondri's honor?" growled one of the men, "The sweet
breath of the banshee, the welcoming climate of Zandru's
ninth hell!"

"I will not hear you say—" Caryl began, but Romilly
caught him around the waist before he could physically
climb down the saddle and attack the speaker, and Carlo
said quietly, "Enough, Caryl. A sentiment seemly for Lyondri's son, lad, but we have no time for babble. Somehow
we must get across the path, and though I have no will to
hurt you, if you can't keep your tongue behind your teeth,
I fear you must be gagged; my men are in no mood to hear
a defense of one who has set a price on our heads. And
you, Garan, and you, Alaric, you shut your faces too; it's
not well done to mock a child about his father's honor, and
there's harder work ahead of us than quarreling with a little
boy!" He looked up again as the shrilling shriek of the
banshee drowned their voices, and Romilly saw his whole
body tense in the effort to conquer the purely physical, fear
that screaming cry created in their minds. Romilly hugged
Caryl tight, not sure whether it was to comfort the child or
to still her own fears, whispering, "Help me quiet the animals." It was well to give him something to think about
except his own terror.

Again the soothing vibration spread out, and he knew
her own talent, *laran* or whatever they called it, enhanced
by the already-powerful gift of the young Hastur child. As
it died into silence, Alaric said, his hand on his dagger,

"I have hunted banshees before this, *vai dom,* and slain them too."

"I doubt not your courage, man," said Carlo, "but your wit, if you think we can face two banshees in a narrow pass, without losing man or horse. We have no deaf-hounds, nor nets and ropes. Perhaps, if we keep between the horses and chervines, we may manage to escape with a horse for each, but then would we be afoot in the worst country in the Hellers! And if we stand here, we will be taken in the jaws of the trap."

"Better the beak of the banshee than the tender mercies of Lyondri's men," said one of the riders, edging uneasily away from his place at the head of the little cavalcade. "I'll face what you face, my lord."

"Too bad your skill with birds extends not to such creatures as *those,*" said Orain, looking at Romilly with a wry grin, "Could you but calm *those* birds as you worked with hawk and sentry-bird, then should we be as well off as any Hastur-lord with his per *leronis!*"

Romilly shuddered at the thought . . . to enter into the minds of those cruel carnivores, prowling the heights? She said weakly "I hope you are joking, *vai dom.*"

"Why should that *laran* not be as workable against banshee as against sentry-bird, or for that matter, barnyard fowl?" asked Caryl, sitting upright on the saddle, "They are all creatures of Nature, and if Rom—Rumal's Gift can quiet the sentry-birds, with my own *laran* to help, why, perhaps we can reach the banshees too, and perhaps convince them that we are not destined for their breakfast."

Romilly felt again a perceptible shudder run through her. But before young Caryl's eager eyes, she was ashamed to confess her fear.

Carlo said quietly, "I am reluctant to leave our safety in the hands of two children, when grown men are helpless. Yet if you can help us—there seems no other way, and if we delay here, we are dead men, all of us. Your father would not harm you, my young Carolin, but I fear the rest of us would die, and not too quickly or easily."

Caryl was blinking hard. He said, "I do not want any harm to come to you, sir. I do not think my father understands that you are a good man; perhaps *Dom* Rakhal has poisoned his mind against you. If I can do anything to help, so that he may have time to think more sensibly about all this quarrel, I will be very glad to do what I can." But Romilly noticed that he too looked a little frightened. And as they moved slowly forward he whispered, "I am afraid, Rumal—they look so fierce it is hard to remember that they too are the creations of God. But I will try to remember that the blessed Valentine-of-the-Snows had a pact of friendship with them and called them little brothers."

I do not think I truly wish to be brother to the banshee, Romilly thought, urging her horse forward with a little cluck and the pressure of her knee, trying to throw out soothing thoughts to calm the animal's fear. But she must not think that way. She must remember that the same Force which created the dogs and horses she loved, and the beloved hawks, had created the banshee for its own purposes, even if she did not know what they were. And the sentry-birds, who looked so fierce, were gentle and loving as cagebirds, when she had gotten to know them; she truly loved Prudence, and even for Temperance and Diligence she felt a genuine affection.

If the banshee is my brother . . . and for a moment she felt an amusement bubbling up that she recognized as all but hysterical. Her gentle brother Ruyven, timid Darren, dear little Rael, in the same breath with the screaming horrors on the crag?

She heard Caryl whispering to himself; the only words she caught were, *Bearer of Burdens* and *Blessed Valentine* . . . and she knew the child was praying. She caught him tight against her, burying her face against his caped shoulder, closing her eyes. Was this true goodness, or a mad presumption, to think that somehow their minds could reach the mind of a banshee—*if the banshees have any mind,* she thought, and again forced the rising hysteria down. No one knew she was a girl, she could not cry and scream with terror! She thought, grimly, that both Orain and *Dom* Carlo looked frightened too; where they were afraid, she had no need to feel shame for her fear!

She shut her eyes again and tried to form a prayer, but could not remember any. *Bearer of Burdens, you know what I want to pray, and now I have to try and do what I can to save us all,* she said in a half-voiced whisper, then sighed and said, "We will try, Caryl. Come, link with me—"

Her mind reached out, just aware enough of her body to
keep it upright in the saddle, moving with the horse's uneasy step. Reached out—she was aware of the horses, shuddering inwardly yet moving on, step by slow step, out of
loyalty to their riders; of the sentry-birds, frightened at the
noise, but calm because she and Caryl, whose mental voices
they trusted, had bidden them be calm. She reached farther,
felt something cold and terrifying, felt again the shrilling
scream, shuddering through all creation, but, her hands
clasped tightly in Caryl's, she stayed with it, moved into
the alien mind.

At first she was conscious only of tremendous pressures,
a hunger so fierce that it cramped her belly, a restless cold
driving toward warmth, that seemed like light and home
and satisfaction, the touch of warmth driving inward and
flooding her whole body with a hunger almost sexual, and
she knew, with a tiny fragment that was still Romilly, that
she had reached the mind of the banshee. *Poor hungry,
cold thing . . . it is only seeking warmth and food, like the
whole of Creation. . . .* Her eyes blotted out, she could not
see, only feel, she *was* the banshee and for a moment she
fought a raging battle, her whole mind alive with the need
to fling herself upon the warmth, to rend and tear and feel
the exquisitely delicious feel of warm blood bursting . . .
she felt her own hands tighten on Caryl's warmth, and then
with a leftover part of herself she knew she was human, a
woman, with a child to protect, and others dependent on
her skill. . . .

Linked tightly to Caryl, she felt his soothing mental
touch, like a soft murmur, *Brother banshee, you are one
with all life and one with me. The Gods created you to rend
and tear at your prey, I praise and love you as the Gods
made you, but there are beasts in this wilderness who know
not fear because the Gods have given them no consciousness.
Search for your prey among them, my little brothers, and let
me pass. . . . In the name of the blessed Valentine, I bid
you, bear your own burdens and seek not to end my life
before the time appointed. Blessed is he who prays and
blessed is he who gives life to another. . . .*

I mean you no harm, Romilly added her quiet mental
appeal to the child's, *seek elsewhere for your food.*

And for a moment, in the great flooding awareness that

she, and the horse she rode, and the child's soft body in her arms, and the banshee's wild hunger and seeking for warmth, were all one, a transcendent wave of joy spread through her, the red streaks of the rising sun filled her with heat and wonderful flooding happiness, Caryl's warmth against her breast was an overflow of tenderness and love, and for a dangerous moment she thought, *even if the banshee takes me for its prey, I shall be even more one with its wonderful life-force. But I too want to live and rejoice in the sunlight.* She had never known such happiness. She knew that there were tears on his face, but it did not matter, she was part of everything that lived and had breath, part of the sun and the rocks, even the cold of the glacier was somehow wonderful because it heightened her awareness of the heat of the rising sun.

Then somehow the magical link shattered and was gone. They were on the downward side of the pass, and high above them, the lumbering form of a banshee was shambling toward a cavemouth in the rocks, without paying them the slightest heed. Caryl was crying in her arms, hugging her tight. "Oh, it was hungry and we cheated it out of its breakfast."

She patted him, too shaken to speak, still caught up in the experience. Carlo said huskily, "Thank you, lads. I don't really want to be the banshee's breakfast, so even if the poor thing was hungry, it can take its breakfast elsewhere."

The men were looking at them in awe. Orain said shakily, trying to break the spell, "Ah, you're too big and tough a boy for a banshee's delicate appetite—it would rather have a tender young ice-rabbit, I'm sure," and they all guffawed. Romilly felt weak, still under the spell of the wide-ranging enchantment they had woven with their *laran*.

Dom Carlo rummaged in his saddle-bags. He said roughly, "I can't say what I owe you two. I remember the *leroni* were starving after they did such work—here." He thrust dried meat, dried fruit, wafers of journey-bread at them. Romilly began to sink her teeth into the meat, and then somehow her gorge rose.

Once this was living, breathing flesh, how can I make it

my prey? Or I am no better than the banshee. Once this dried flesh was the living breath of all my brothers. She gagged, thrust the meat from her and thrust a dried fruit into her mouth.

This too is of the life of all things, but it had no breath and it does not sicken me with the consciousness of what once it was. The Bearer of Burdens created some life with no purpose but to give up its life that others might feed . . . and as she felt the sweetness of the fruit between her teeth, briefly, the ecstasy returned, that this fruit should give up its sweetness so that she might no longer hunger. . . .

Caryl, too, was chewing ravenously at a hunk of the hard bread, but she noted that he, too, had put the meat away, though a piece had small sharp toothmarks in it. So he had shared her experience. Distantly, like something she might have dreamed a long time ago, she wondered how she could ever again eat meat.

Even when they made brief camp, with the sun high in the sky, to give grain to the horses and meat to the sentry-birds, she ate none of the dried meat, but only fruit and bread, and stirred some water into the dried porridge-powder, eating a bowlful. Yet, to her own surprise, it did not trouble her when the sentry-birds tore greedily at the somewhat gamy meat they carried for them; it was their nature, and they were as they were meant to be.

She noticed that the men still kept a wary distance. She was not surprised. If she had seen two other people quiet an attacking banshee, she would have been silent in awe, too. She still could not believe she had done it.

As they finished their meal and resaddled the horses, she looked at *Dom* Carlo, standing straight and tall at the edge of the clearing, with his face distant and listening. She was now skilled enough in the use of *laran* to know that he was extending his mental awareness along the trail behind them, toward the pass.

"So far we are not pursued," he said at last, "And the paths are so many, unless Lyondri has a horde or *leroni* with him, I do not truly think he will be ale to pick up our trail. We must keep ordinary caution; but I think we can ride for Caer Donn in safety now." He held out his arms to Caryl.

"Will you ride behind my saddle, kinsman?" he asked, as if he spoke to a grown man and his equal, "There are things I would say to you."

Caryl glanced at Romilly, then collected himself and said courteously, "As you wish, kinsman." He scrambled up into the saddle. As they rode away, she could see that they were talking together in low tones, and Romilly found that she missed the child's warm weight in front of her. Once she saw Caryl shaking his head, seriously, and a word or two reached her ears.

". . . oh, no, kinsman, I give you my word of that. . . ."

Suddenly jealous of this closeness, Romilly wished she could hear what they were saying. So near, now, was her *laran* to the surface, that it occurred to her;

Perhaps I need only reach out and know.

And then she was shocked at herself. What was she thinking, she who had been reared in a Great House and taught proper courtesy toward both equals and inferiors? Why, that would be worse than eavesdropping at doors, snooping like a nasty child, that would be completely unworthy of her.

Having the power of *laran,* certainly, did not mean that she had a right to know what did not concern her! And then, frowning as she fell into line—she had taken the sentrybird Prudence on her own saddle, so that *Dom* Carlo could carry Caryl behind him—she found herself pondering the proper manners associated with *laran.* She had the power, and perhaps the right, to force her will on the hawks she trained, on the horses she rode, even, to save her life, on the wild banshee of the crags. But how far did this power go? How far was it right to use it? She could urge her horse to bear saddle and bridle, because he loved her and willingly learned what would bring him closer to his master. She had felt Preciosa's deep love, so that the hawk returned of her free will when Romilly had set her free.

(And that was pain. Would she ever see Preciosa again?)

But there were limits to this power. It was right, perhaps, to quiet the dogs who loved her, so they would not awaken the household to her going.

But there was trouble, too, and a deep conflict. She could urge the prey into the beak of the hawk she hunted, she could perhaps force the young and stupid ice-rabbit into

the waiting mouth of the dogs . . . surely that was not
intended, that was not part of nature, that was a distinctly
unfair advantage to have in hunting!

Her eyes stinging, she bent her head, and for the first
time in her life found herself sincerely praying.

*Bearer of Burdens! I did not ask this power. Please,
please, help me use it, not for wrong purposes, but only to
try and be one with life. . . .* Confusedly, she added, *As I
was, for a little while, this morning, when I knew that I was
one with all that lived. As you must be, Holy one. Help me
decide how to use this power wisely.* And after a moment
she added, in a whisper. *For now I know I am a part of
life . . . but such a small part!*

Chapter 5

All the long road to Caer Donn, it continued to trouble her. When she hunted meat for the sentry-birds, she thought of her *laran* and feared to use the power for evil, so that sometimes she let game escape them and was roundly scolded by the men. She did use her awareness to seek out dead things in hill and forest which she could use to feed the birds—they had no further use for their bodies, surely it could not be wrong to use a dead creature to feed a living one. She felt as if she wanted to close up her new skill where it would never be touched again, though she had to use it in handling the birds—surely it could not be wrong to show her fondness for them? Or was it, since she used it to keep them quiet for her own convenience?

There were times when she tried to handle them without calling on the MacAran Gift which she now knew to be *laran,* and when they screamed and rebelled, *Dom* Carlo demanded, "What's gotten into you, youngster? Do the work you're paid to do, and keep those birds quiet!" She had to use her *laran* then, and again suffer the conflicts as to whether she did right or wrong.

She wished she could talk to *Dom* Carlo; he had *laran* and had perhaps suffered some of these same worries when he was her age and learning to use it. Was this what Ruyven had had to overcome? No wonder he fled from a horse-training estate and took refuge behind Tower walls! She found herself envying Darren, who had none of the Mac-Aran Gift and though he feared and hated hawks and horses, at least he was not tempted to meddle with their

minds in order to show his power over them! She could
not talk to Caryl, he was only a child, and used his power
with pleasure, as she had always used it since she found
out she had special skill with horses and used it in training
them. And whenever she tried to eat fresh-killed game, it
seemed that she could feel the life and the blood of the
dead animal pounding through her mind, and she would
gag and refuse to eat; she made her meals of porridge and
fruit and bread, and was fiercely hungry in the bitter, aching
cold of the mountain trails, but even when *Dom* Carlo commanded her to eat, she could not, and once when he stood
over her until she reluctantly swallowed part of a haunch
of the wild chervine they had killed for their meal, she felt
such terrible revulsion that she went away and vomited it
up again.

Orain saw her coming back from the thicket, white and
shaking, and came over to where she was, with fumbling
hands, trying to cut up offal and remainder of the chervine for the sentry-birds. It was hard to find gravel in this
snowy country, and so she had to mix skin and slivers of
bone with the meat, or they would have further trouble
in digesting. He said, "Here, give me that," and carried
the mess over to the birds where they were fastened on
their blocks, safely above the snow. He came back leaving
them to tear into it, and said, "What's the matter, lad?
Off your feed, are you? Carlo means well, you know, he
just was worried that you weren't eating enough for this
rotten climate."

"I know that," she said, not looking at him.

"What's ailing you, youngster? Anything I can do to
help?"

She shook her head. She did not think anyone could
help. Unless she could somehow talk to her father, who
must somehow have fought this battle himself in his youth,
or how could he have come to terms with his own Gift?
He might hate the very word *laran* and forbid anyone to
use it in his hearing, but he possessed the thing, whatever
he chose to call it or not to call it. With a sudden, homesick
force, she remembered Falconsward, the face of her father,
loving and kindly, and then his contorted, wrathful face as
he beat her. . . . She put her face in her hands, trying
desperately to stifle a fit of sobs which must surely reveal

her as a girl. But she was so tired, so tired, she could hardly keep back her tears. . . .

Orain's hand was gentle on her shoulder. "There, there, son, never mind—I'm not one to think tears all that unmanly. You're ill and tired, that's all. Bawl if you want to, I'll not be telling on you." He gave her a final reassuring pat, and moved back to the fire. "Here; drink this, it'll settle your stomach," he said, sifting a few of his cherished herbs into a cup of hot water, and shoving the mug into her hand. The drink was aromatic, with a pleasant faint bitterness, and indeed made her feel better. "If you can't eat meat just now, I'll bring you some bread and fruit, but you can't go hungry in this cold." He gave her a chunk of hard bread, liberally spread with the fat of the *chervine;* Romilly was so hungry that she gulped it down, chewed on the handful of fruits he gave her as they were settling the horses for the night. He spread their blanket rolls side by side; Caryl had none, so he had been sleeping in Romilly's cloak, tucked in her arms. As she was pulling off her boots to sleep, she felt an ominous dull pain in the pit of her belly, and began secretly to count on her fingers; yes, it had been forty days since she had escaped from Rory's cabin, she must once again conceal this periodic nuisance! Damn this business of being a woman! Lying awake between Caryl and Orain, still shivering, she wondered grimly how she could manage to conceal it in this climate. Fortunately it was cold enough that nobody undressed at all in the camp, and even to sleep piled on all the clothes and blankets they had. Romilly had been sleeping, not only in the fur-lined cloak Orain had given her, but in the rough old one she had taken from Rory's cabin, rolling herself up in them both, with Caryl in her arms.

She must think. She had no spare rags, or garments which could be made into them. There was a kind of thick moss, which grew liberally all through the higher elevations, here as well as at Falconsward; she had seen it, but paid no attention—though she knew the poorer women, who had no rags to spare, used this moss for babies' diapers, packing them in it, as well as for their monthly sanitary needs. Romilly's fastidious soul felt a certain disgust, but it would be easier to bury moss in the snow than to wash out rags in this climate. Tomorrow she would find some of it; here in snow country it would, at least, not be covered with mud or dirt and need not be washed. What a nuisance it was, to be a woman!

It was so bitterly cold that they all rolled close together, like dogs sleeping in heaps; when the camp was awakening in the morning, Alaric jeered, as Orain unrolled himself from Caryl and Romilly, "Hey, man, are you running a nursery for the children?" But Orain's presence was comforting to her, and, she felt, to Caryl as well; he was gentle and fatherly, and she was not afraid of him. In fact, if it came to necessity, she did not doubt she could confide in Orain without real danger; he might be shocked at finding she was a girl in this rough country and climate, but he would not make that kind of trouble for her, any more than her own father or brothers. Somehow she *knew*, beyond all doubt, that he was not the kind of man ever to ravish or offer any offense to any woman.

She went away to attend to her personal needs in private—she had been jeered at, a bit, for this, they said she was as squeamish as a woman, but she knew they only thought it was because she was a *cristoforo;* they were known to be prudish and modest about such things. She was sure none of them suspected, and Caryl, who know— and *Dom* Carlo, who, she felt, knew perfectly well—chose to say nothing.

But she would keep her secret as long as she could. When she came to Caer Donn, it might not be so easy as in Nevarsin to find work as hawk-keeper or horse-trainer, but certainly it could be done, and certainly Orain, or *Dom* Carlo himself, could give her a good reference as a willing and skilled worker.

She still felt a certain revulsion against eating meat, though she knew it was foolish—it was in the way of nature that some animals were prey to others, but though she knew the intense immediacy of her revulsion was beginning to fade a little, she still preferred porridge and bread to the meat, and Carlo, (she wondered if Orain had spoken to him about?) no longer urged her to eat it, but simply gave her a somewhat larger ration of porridge and fruit. Alaric jeered at her once, and *Dom* Carlo curtly bade him be silent.

"The less there is of meat for him, the more for the rest of us, man. Let him have such food as he likes best, and you do the same! If all men were alike, you would long since have been meat for the banshee; we owe it to him to let him have his way."

They had been, she thought, nine days on the road from Nevarsin when, circling high above them, they saw a bird winging from the range of hills. Romilly was feeding the sentry-birds, and they strained at their jesses as the small bird flew down into their camp; then she saw *Dom* Carlo standing motionless, his arms extended, his face the blank, silent stare of *laran*-focused thoughts. The bird darted down; alighted and stood quivering on his hand.

"A message from our folk in Caer Donn," Carlo said, sought for the capsule under the wing and tore it open, scanning the finely-written lines. Romilly stared—she knew of message-birds who could fly back to their own loft across trackless wilds, but never of one which could see out a particular man whose whereabouts were unknown to the sender!

Carlo raised his head, smiling broadly.

"We must make haste to Caer Donn, men," he cried out, "A tenday hence we will gather beneath Aldaran, and Carolin will be at the head of the great army which is massing there, to march on the lowlands. Now let Rakhal look to himself, my faithful fellows!"

They cheered, and Romilly cheered too. Only Caryl was silent, lowering his head and biting his lip. Romilly started to ask what was wrong, then held her tongue. He could hardly rejoice at an army massed against his father, who was Rakhal's chief advisor. It would be unfair to expect it. Yet she had seen that he loved *Dom* Carlo as a kinsman—in fact, she was sure they were kinsmen, though perhaps distant; she had heard that all of the lowland Hasturs were kin, and she was sure now, recalling Carlo's red hair, the look he had which reminded her of Alderic, that he was one of the Hastur-kinfolk, and higher in rank than any of his men knew. If Orain, who was the king's foster-brother, treated him with such deference, he must be noble indeed.

They rode into Caer Donn late in the evening, and *Dom* Carlo turned, just inside the gates of the city, to Orain.

"Take the men and the birds to a good inn," he said, "and command all my faithful people the best dinner money can buy; they have had a hard journey and paid dearly for their following of the exiles. You know where I must be going—"

"Aye, I know," said Orain, and Carlo smiled faintly and gripped his hand. He said, "A day will come—"

"All the Gods grant it," said Orain, and Carlo rode away through the streets of the city.

If she had never seen Nevarsin, Romilly might have thought Caer Donn a big city. High on the side of the mountain above the town, a castle rose, and Orain said as they rode, "The home of Aldaran of Aldaran. The Aldarans are Hastur-kin from old days, but they have no part in lowland strife. Yet blood-ties are strong."

"Is the king there?" asked Romilly, and Orain smiled and drew a deep breath of relief. "Aye, we are back in country where that beast Rakhal is not admired, and Carolin is still true king of these lands," he said. "And the birds we've brought will be in the hands of the king's *leroni* in a few days. Pity you've not the training of a *laranzu,* lad, you have the touch. You've done Carolin's men a service, believe me, and the king will not be ungrateful when he comes to his throne."

He looked down the streets. "Now, if memory fails me not, I recall an inn near the city wall, where our birds may be housed and our beasts fed, and that good meal Carlo commanded may be found," he said, "Let's go and find it."

As they rode through the narrow street, Caryl pushed close to his side.

"Lord Orain, you—the *vai dom* pledged me I should be sent back to my father under a truce-flag. Will he honor that pledge? My father—" his voice broke, "My father must be wild with fear for me."

"Good enough!" Alaric said harshly, "Let him feel some o'what I feel, with my son and his mother dead—at your father's hands—"

Caryl stared at him with his eyes wide. Finally he said, "I did not recognize you, Master Alaric; now I recall you.

You wrong my father, sir; he did not kill your son, he died of the bald fever; my own brother died that same summer, and the king's healer-women tended them both as carefully. It was sad that your son died away from his father and mother, but on my honor, Alaric, my father had no hand in your son's death."

"And what of my poor wife, who flung herself from the window to death when she heard her son had died far away from her—"

"I did not know that," Caryl said, and there were tears in his eyes, "My own mother was beside herself with grief when my brother died. I was afraid to be out of my mother's sight for fear she would do herself some harm in her grief. I am sorry—oh, I am sorry, Master Alaric," he said, and flung his arms around the man, "If my father had known this, I am sure he would not pursue you, nor blame you for your quarrel with him!"

Alaric swallowed; he stood without moving in the boy's embrace and said, "God grant my own son would have defended me like to that. I canna' fault you for your loyalty to your father, my boy. I'll help Lord Orain see ye get back safe to him."

Orain heaved a great sigh of relief. He said, "We'll not send you into danger in the lowlands without an army behind you, Alaric; ye'll stay here with the army. But here in this city is a hostel of the Sisterhood of the Sword; my cousin is one of the swordswomen, and we can hire two or three of these women to go south to Thendara and take the lad safe there. I'll speak to *Dom* Carlo about it, Caryl, and perhaps you can leave day after tomorrow. And perhaps a message-bird could be sent to your father at Hali, to tell him you are well and safe, and to be escorted safe back to him."

"You are kind to me, Lord Orain," said Caryl simply. "I have enjoyed this trip, but I do not like to think of my father's grief, or my mother's if she knows I am not safe in Nevarsin where she thought me."

"I'll see to it, soon as we reach the inn," said Orain, and led the way toward a long, low building, with stables at the back, and a sign with a crudely painted hawk. "Here at the Sign of the Hawk we can dine well and rest after that miserable trip through the snows. And how many of you would like to order a bath, as well? There are hot springs in the city and a bath-house not ten doors away."

That roused another cheer, but Romilly thought, a little glumly, that it did her no good; she certainly could not risk a man's bath-house, though she felt grubby and longed to be clean! Well, there was no help for it. She saw the horses and chervines properly stabled, cared for the sentry-birds, and after washing her face and hands as well as she could, went in for the good meal Orain had commanded in the inn. He had ordered rooms for them all to sleep, saying that he had taken the best room the inn offered for young Caryl, as his rank demanded.

"And you are yourself welcome to share my own quarters, Rumal, lad."

"It is kind of you," Romilly said warily, "but I will stay in the stable with my charges, lest the sentry-birds be restless in a strange place."

Orain shrugged, "As you will," he said. "But another thing I would ask you over dinner."

"What you wish, sir."

They went in to the dining-room; there was fresh-baked bread and baked roots, plump and golden, as well as some roasted birds and a stew of vegetables; everyone ate hugely after the long spartan fare of the travelling, and Orain had commanded plenty of wine and beer as well. But he refused Caryl wine, in a kind and fatherly way, and frowned at Romilly when she would have taken her second mug of it.

"You know very well you've no head for it," he scolded, "Waiter! Bring the boys some cider with spice-root in it."

"Aw," Alaric teased good-naturedly, for once, "Old Mammy Orain, will ye put them to bed and sing 'em a lullabye, while the rest of us are all off to soak out our long travel in the bath-house?"

"Nay," said Orain, "I'm for the baths with the rest of you."

"And for a house of women soon after that," called out one of the man, taking a great spoonful of the stewed fruits that had finished the meal, "I haven't looked at a woman for Zandru knows how long!"

"Aye, and I mean to do more than look," called another one, and Orain said, "Do what you like, but this is no talk before the children."

"I hope for a bath too," said Caryl, but Orain shook his head.

"The bath-house here in the city is not like the one in the monastery, my boy, but a place of resort for whores and such like as well; I can take care of myself, but it's no place for a respectable lad of your years. I'll order you a tub of water in your own room, where you may wash and soak and then to bed and rest well. You too," he said, scowling faintly at Romilly, "You're young for the rough folk at the bath-house; see you that the lad here washes his feet well, and then call for a bath for yourself; you'd be too easy prey for the lowlife folk who hang about such places, as much so as if you were a young and respectable maiden."

"Why coddle the boy?" demanded Alaric, "Let him see something of life, as no doubt you did when you were of his years, Lord Orain!"

Orain scowled. "What I may have done is not to the point; the boy's in my charge, and so is Lyondri's son here, and it's not fit a Hastur should go without service. You stay here, Rumal, and look after the lad, see him into his bed. You'll get a bath to yourself then."

"Stand up to him for your rights, lad, you don't have to be treated like a child," said one of the men, who had drunk more than enough wine, "You're no servant to the Hastur-pup!"

Romilly said, relieved at this solution, "Indeed I would as soon stay here; I am a *cristoforo*. and have no taste for such adventures."

"Oh ah, a *cristoforo* bound to the Creed of Chastity," jeered Alaric, "well, I did my best for ye, boy, if ye'd rather be a little boy hiding behind the skirts of the holy Bearer of Burdens, that's for you to say! Come along! Who's for the bath-house, men?"

One after another, they rose and went, not too steadily, into the street. Romilly took Caryl upstairs and sent for the promised bath; when the serving-women brought it, she would have bathed him as she had done with Rael, but he turned on her, his face pink.

"I won't say anything before the men," he said, "but I know you're a girl, and I'm too big for my mother or my sister, even, to wash me, and I can bathe myself! Go away! mistress Romilly. I'll have them send you a bath too, shall I? Lord Orain is away and doubtless he'll be at the baths half the night, he may be looking for a woman too—see, I'm old enough to know about such things. So you can bathe in his room and go to your own bed afterward."

Romilly could not help but laugh. She said "As you will, my lord."

"And don't make fun of me!"

"I wouldn't dream of it," Romilly said, trying to keep her face straight. "But Lord Orain charged me with the task of seeing that you wash your feet well."

"I have been bathing myself in the monastery for more than a year," said Caryl, exasperated, "Go away, mistress Romilly, before my bath water gets cold, and I will have them send a bathtub to you in Lord Orain's room."

Romilly was grateful for this solution—indeed she had longed for a hot bath, and went to the stable for her saddle-bags while the bath-women were hauling the wooden tub into the room and pouring out steaming water into it, laying out great fluffy towels and a wooden cask of soapweed. One of the bath-women lingered, widening her eyes at Romilly and saying in a suggestive voice, "Would you like me to stay and help you, young sir? Indeed, it would be a pleasure to wash your feet and scrub your back, and for half a silver bit I will stay as long as you like, and share your bed as well."

Romilly had to struggle again to hide a smile; this was embarrassing. Was she such a handsome young man as that, or was the woman only looking for her silver bit? She shook her head and said, "I am tired with riding; I want to wash and sleep."

"Shall I send you a masseur, then, young sir?"

"No, no, nothing—go away and leave me to bathe," Romilly said sternly, but she gave the woman a small coin and thanked her for her trouble. "You can come and take the tub away in an hour."

Assured at last of privacy, she stripped and climbed into the tub, scrubbing herself vigorously with soapweed, lying back in the hot water with a sigh of luxurious content. She had last washed herself all over in the old woman's cabin, when she was pretending she would be married to Rory. At Nevarsin she had washed as best she could, but had not, of course, dared to use the bath-house in the monastery, nor had she dared to try and find a woman's bath-house in Nevarsin, though there must have been some of them, lest she be seen coming from the place.

What a splendid thing a bath was! She lay in the hot water, soaking and enjoying it, till the water finally cooled and she got out, dried her hair carefully, and put on her cleanest underclothing. She looked longingly at Orain's bed, spread up for him by the maids; no doubt he was finished at the bathhouse and had found a woman somewhere for the night, and this good bed would be wasted, while he slept in some street-woman's bed. She realized that she felt a twinge of jealousy—she remembered her dream, where Orain had caressed her, sleeping, and she had been happy that he should touch her—did she really envy the unknown woman in whose bed he was spending this night?

Well, she should ring for the bath-woman to take away the tub and go to her own quarters in the stables; there was plenty of hay to keep her warm, and blankets, and she could even command hot bricks and more blankets if she wished. She pulled on her breeches and rang for the bath-woman, and went, knocking softly at Caryl's door He was in bed and already half asleep, but he sat up in bed to hug her as if she were his own sister, wishing her a good night, and slid down, asleep already in the big bed. It *was* a big bed, big enough for three or four, she was tempted to lie down and sleep beside the child, they had slept curled up together often enough on the road. But she realized that he would be embarrassed if he found her there in the morning—he was just old enough to be aware that she was a woman. It would not matter so much, she thought, yawning and reluctant to go out to the stable, if she lay down to sleep a little—no doubt Orain would not return home before morning, and if he did he would be so drunk that he would not notice her there, nor care whether she was a boy or a dog; he would never know she was a woman, if he had travelled with her all this time and not known, and he had none of the inconvenient *laran* which had betrayed her to Caryl and perhaps to *Dom* Carlo.

She would sleep here a little, at least—she could wake and be away to the stable if she heard Orain coming up the stairs. The bed looked so good, after all this time on the road. The bath-woman, when she took the tub away, had warmed the sheets with a pan of hot coals, and they smelled fresh and inviting. Romilly hesitated no more, but lay down in her tunic and drawers, pulling up the covers and drowsing. At the edge of her mind, wary, she thought, *I must not entirely go to sleep, I should go out to the stable, Orain may be coming back before I expect him . . .* and then she was asleep.

The door creaked, and Orain, stepping quietly, was in the room, throwing off his clothes and yawning, sitting on the edge of the bed. Romilly sat up, shocked and startled that she had slept so long. He grinned at her.

"Ah, stay where you are, boy," he said drowsily. "Bed's big enough for two." He had been drinking, she could tell, but he was not drunk. He reached out and ran his hand lightly across her hair. "So soft, you must ha' had a nice bath too."

"I will go now—"

He shook his head. "The outside door o' the inn's locked; ye couldn'a get out." His voice was again overlaid with the soft low-country accent. "Stay here, lad—I'm half asleep a'ready." He drew off his boots and outer garments; Romilly, rolling to the far edge of the bed, tucked her head down under the blanket and fell asleep.

She never knew what waked her, but she thought it was a cry: Orain tossed, turned over, cried out, and sat bolt upright. "Ah—Carolin, they will have ye'—" he cried, staring into the empty room, his voice so full of terror that Romilly knew he dreamed. She tugged at his arm and said, "Wake up! It's only a nightmare!"

"Ah—" he drew a long breath and sanity came into his face again. "I saw my brother, my friend, in the hands of Rakhal, Zandru send him scorpion whips—" His face was still troubled, but he lay back down, and Romilly, curling her feet up, sought to go back to sleep. After a time, however, she was aware that Orain's arm was around her, that he was gently drawing her to him.

She pulled away, frightened. He said in his gentlest voice, "Ah, lad, don't you know how I feel? You're so like Carolin, when we were boys together—red hair—and so timid and shy, but so brave when there's need—"

Romilly thought, shaking, *but there's no need for this, I am a woman—he does not know, but it's all right, I will tell him it's all right—* She was trembling with embarrassment, shy, but still the very real warmth and kindness she felt for Orain made her feel, this was not at all as it had been when *Dom* Garris sought to paw her, nor when Rory thought to force himself on her—

She sat upright and put her arms around him, laying her head on his shoulder. "It's all right, all right, Orain," she whispered, close to his cheek. "You knew all the time, didn't you? I—I—" she couldn't say it. She took his hand and put it inside her tunic, against her breast.

He sat upright, jerking away, his face flaming.

"Hell's fire," he whispered, in incredulous embarrassment, shock, and, Romilly realized with horror, real dismay, "Hell's fire, you're a girl!" And he actually leaped out of bed and stood staring at her, pulling his nightshirt together over his body with shock and modestly looking away from her.

"Mistress—*damisela,* a thousand pardons, I most humbly beg your pardon—never, never, I did not guess for a moment—Avarra's mercy, mistress, I cannot believe it! Who are you?"

She said, shaking with cold and her whole body trembling with the shock of the rejection, "Romilly MacAran," and burst into tears.

"Oh, blessed Gods," Orain implored, bending to wrap the blanket round her, "I—don't cry, someone will hear you, I wouldna' hurt you for the world, lady—" and he gulped and stood back, shaking his head in dismay.

"What an unholy mess this is and what a damnable fool I've made of myself! Forgive me, lady, I wouldn't lay a finger on you—" Romilly cried harder than ever, and he bent, urgently hushing her.

"Ah, don't cry, little lady, there's nothing to cry about— look, hush, we're friends anyway, aren't we, I don't care if ye're a girl, you must have some reasons—" and as she sought to stifle her weeping, he wiped her nose gently with the sheet and sat down beside her. "There now, there now, that's a good girl, don't cry—sweeting, I think you'd better tell me all about it, hadn't you?"

Book Three:

SWORDSWOMAN

Chapter 1

Snow had fallen toward morning, and the streets of Caer Donn were piled high with trackless white. All the same, there was a softness in the air which told the country-bred Romilly that the spring thaw was nearing and this was the last blow of the winter.

Father always said that only the mad or the desperate travel in the winter; now I have crossed the worst of the Hellers after Midwinter-night. Why am I thinking of that now?

Orain patted her shoulder with the same clumsy deference he had shown since last night. It made her want to weep for the old, lost, easy companionship. She should have known he would not have liked her half so well as a woman; it was, when she really took thought, written clear all over him and must have been evident to everyone in the company except herself.

"Here we are, *damisela*," he said, and Romilly snapped, raw-edged, "My name is Romilly, Orain, and I have not changed so much as all *that*."

His eyes, she thought, looked like a dog's that had been kicked. He said, "Here is the hotel of the Sisterhood," and went up the steps, leaving her to follow.

Once he knew—certainly he could not allow her to face the dangers of life in camp and trail. He would always be aware, now, of her unwelcome womanhood. This was, after all, the best answer.

A hard-faced woman, with heavy hands which would have seemed more appropriate holding a hayfork, welcomed them to the front hall—or, Romilly thought, welcome was not quite the right word, but she did let them in. Orain said, "Kindly inform Mistress Jandria that her cousin has come to visit her." His voice was again the im-

peccably courteous, well-bred voice of the courtier, with
the last trace of the soft country accent carefully hidden.
The woman stared suspiciously, and said, "Sit there," pointing to a bench as if they were a pair of street urchins come
a-begging. She went away down the hall and Romilly heard
women's voices at the far end of the building. Somewhere
there was the noise of a hammer on an anvil—at least that
was what it sounded like—and the small, familiar, friendly,
chink-chink-chinking sound made Romilly a little less rigid
with apprehension. All the doors along the hallway were
closed, but as they sat there, two young women, wearing
crimson tunics, their hair all tucked under red caps, went
through the hallway arm in arm. They were obviously not
what Romilly's stepmother would have called ladies: one
of them had great red hands like a milkmaid's, and were
wearing loose long trousers and boots.

At the back of the hall another woman appeared. She
was slender and pretty, and Romilly thought, about Orain's
own age, forty or more, though her dark, close-cropped
hair had faded, with streaks of gray at the temples.

"Well, kinsman," she said, "what's that ye've got wi'
ye'"? She had the country accent Orain had learned to
conceal. "And what brings ye' into this country in winter?
King's business, I hear—and how's himself?" She came and
gave him a quick, breezy embrace and a haphazard kiss
somewhere on the side of his face.

"The king is well, Aldones be praised," said Orain quietly, "and with the Aldarans at the moment. But I have
two charges for you, Janni."

"Two?" Her salt-and-pepper eyebrows went up in a comical grimace. "First of all, what's this, boy or girl or hasn't
he or she made up its mind?"

Romilly, with a scalding blush, bent her eyes on the floor;
the woman's good-natured mockery seemed to take her in
and sort her out and discard her as useless.

"Her name is Romilly MacAran," said Orain quietly,
"Don't mock her, Janni, she travelled with us through the
worst climate and country in the Hellers and not one of us,
not even myself, knew her for a girl. She did her full share
and cared for our sentry-birds, which I'd never known a
woman could do. She brought them through alive and in
good condition, and the horses too. I thought she was a

capable lad, but it's even more extraordinary than I thought. So I brought her to you—"

"Having no use for her once ye' found she wasna' one of your lads," said Jandria, with an ironical grin. Then she looked straight at Romilly.

"Can't you speak for yourself, girl? What led you into the mountains in men's clothes? If it was the better to seek a man, take yerself off again, for we want no girls among us to give us the name of harlots in disguise! We travel with the armies, but we are not camp-followers, be that understood! Why did ye' leave home?"

Her sharp tone put Romilly on the defensive. She said, "I left my home because my father took the hawk I trained myself, with my own hands, and gave it to my brother; and I thought that not fair. Also, I had no will to marry the Heir to Scathfell, who would have wanted me to sit indoors and embroider cushions and bear his ugly children!"

Jandria's eyes were sharp on her. "Afraid of the marriage-bed and childbirth, hey?"

"No, that's not it," Romilly said sharply, "but I like horses and hounds and hawks and if I should ever marry—" she did not know she was going to say this until she said it, "I would want to marry a man who wants me as I am, not a pretty painted doll he can call wife without ever thinking what or who she is! And I would rather marry a man who does not think his manhood threatened if his wife can sit in a saddle and carry a hawk! But I would rather not marry at all, or not now. I want to travel, and to see the world, and to do things—" she broke off. She was saying this very badly. She sounded like a discontented and disobedient daughter, no more. Well, so she was and no otherwise, and if Mistress Jandria did not like her, well, she had lived as a man before in secret and could do so again if she must! "I am not asking charity of you, Mistress Jandria, and Orain knows me better than that!"

Jandria laughed. "My name is Janni, Romilly. And Orain does not know anything about women."

"He liked me well enough till he found out I was a woman," Romilly said, prickled again by that thought, and Janni laughed again and said, "That is what I mean. Now that he knows, he will never see anything about you except that you should be wearing skirts and sending out signs, so that he will not be led unwitting into trusting you. He let down his guard before you, I doubt not, thinking it safe, and now he will never forgive you for it—isn't that it?"

"You are too hard on me, Janni," said Orain uneasily, "But sure you must see that Mistress MacAran cannot travel with men and live rough in a camp with hard men such as I command!"

"In spite of the fact that she has done so for a span of tendays," said Jandria, with that flicker of a wry grin, "Well, you are right, this is the place for her, and if she is good with horses and birds, we can always make use of her, if she is willing to live by our rule."

"How do I know until I know what that is?" demanded Romilly, and Jandria laughed. "I like her, cousin. You can go and leave her to me, I won't bite her. But wait, you said you had another charge for me—"

"Yes," Orain said, "Lyondri Hastur's son; Carolin. He was a student in Nevarsin monastery, and he came into our hands as a hostage—never mind how, it's better if you don't know. But I have given my word I will have the boy sent back to Thendara under truce-flag when the passes are open, and unharmed. I cannot go myself—"

"No," Jandrai said, "You certainly cannot; for all your head's stuffed with old rubbish and ugly as sin, it adorns your shoulders better than it would adorn a pike outside Lyondri's den! Yes, we'll take the lad to Thendara for you; I may even go myself. Lyondri has certainly not seen my face since we danced together at children's parties and would not remember it without long curls and bows in my hair." She chuckled as at a secret joke. "How old is young Carolin now? He must be eight or nine—"

"'Twelve, I think," Orain said, "and a nice child; it's pity he got himself mixed up in this, but he saved my neck and my men's and Carolin has cause to be grateful to his godson, so guard him well, Janni."

She nodded. "I'll take him south as soon as the passes are open, then; you can send him to me here." She chuckled and gave Orain another of her quick, offhand hugs. "And now you must go, kinsman—what of my reputation, if it is known I entertain a man here? Worse, what of yours, if it is found out you can speak civilly to a woman?"

"Oh, come, Janni—" protested Orain, but he rose to take his leave. He looked, embarrassed, at Romilly, and stuck out his hand. "I wish you well, *damisela.*"

This time she did not bother to correct him. If he could not see that she was the same whether in boy's clothes or the name of a Great House, well, so much the worse for him; he did not sound like her friend Orain at all, and she could have cried again, but she did not, for Janni was staring appraisingly at her.

After the door closed behind Orain, she said, "Well, and what happened? Did he try and lure ye' to bed, and recoil in unholy horror when he found out you were a woman?"

"That's not quite how it happened," said Romilly, moved to defend Orain without knowing why, "It was—he had been kind to me, and I thought he knew I was a woman, and wanted me so—I am not a wanton," she defended herself, "Once I came near to killing a man who would have had me against my will." She shivered and shut her eyes; she had thought she was free of the nagging horror of Rory's attempted rape, but she was not. "But Orain was good, and I—I liked him well, and I only thought to be kind to him, if it was what he wanted so much."

Janni smiled, and Romilly wondered, defensively, what was funny. But the older woman only said, quite kindly, "And you are a maiden still, I doubt not."

"I am not ashamed of it," Romilly flared.

"How prickly you are! Well, will you live by our rule?"

"If you will tell me what it is, I will answer you," she said, and Janni smiled again.

"Well then; will you be sister to all of us, whatever rank we may bear? For we leave rank behind us when we come into the Sisterhood; you will not be *My Lady* or *damisela* here, and no one will know or care that you were born in a Great House. You must do your share of whatever work falls to us, and never ask quarter or special consideration because you are a woman. And if you have love affairs with men, you must conduct them in decent privacy, so that no man can ever call the Sisterhood a company of camp-followers. Most of us are sworn to live celibate while we follow the armies and the sword, though we do not force it upon anyone."

It sounded exactly like what Romilly would have wished for. She said so.

"But will you swear it?"

"Gladly," Romilly said.

"You must swear, as well, that your sword will always be ready to defend any of your sisters, in peace or war, should any man lay a hand on one who does not wish for it," said Jandria.

"I would be glad to swear to that," Romilly said, "but I do not think my sword would be any good to them; I know nothing about swordplay."

Now Janni smiled and hugged her. She said, "We will teach you that. Come, bring your things into the inner room. Did that dolt Orain remember to give you breakfast, or was he in so much of a hurry to hustle you away from the camp that he forgot that women get hungry too?"

Romilly, still sore with rejection and pain, did not want to join Janni in making fun of Orain, but it sounded so much like what had actually happened, that she could not help but laugh. "I am hungry, yes," she confessed, and Janni hoisted one of her bundles.

"I have a horse in the stable of the inn," Romilly said, and Janni nodded. "I will send one of the sisters for it, in your name. Come into the kitchen—breakfast is long over, but we can always find some bread and honey—and then we will pierce your ears so that you can wear our sign and other women will know that you are one of us. Tonight you may take the oath. Only for a year at first," she warned, "and then, if you like the life, for three; and when you have lived among us for four years, you may decide if you wish to pledge for a lifetime, or if you wish to go on your own, or to return to your family and marry."

"Never!" Romilly said fervently.

"Well, we will fly that hawk when her pinions are grown," said Janni, "but for now you may take the sword with us, and if you have some skill with hawks and horses, we will welcome you all the more; our old horse-trainer, Mhari, died of the lung-fever this winter, and the women who worked with her are all away with the armies to the south. None of the girls in the hostel now are even much good at riding, let alone for breaking them to the saddle—can you do that? We have four colts ready to be saddle-broken, and more at our big hostel near Thendara."

"I was raised to it at Falconsward," Romilly said, but Janni raised a hand in caution.

"None of us have any family or past beyond our names; I warned you, you are not *my lady* or *Mistress MacAran* among us," she said, and, rebuked, Romilly was silent.

Yet, whatever I call myself, I am Romilly MacAran of Falconsward. I was not boasting of my lineage, only telling her how I came to be so trained—I would hardly have learned it at some croft in the hills! But if she chooses to think I was boasting, nothing I would say can change it, and she must think what she likes. Romilly felt as if she were old and cynical and worldly-wise, having arrived at this much wisdom. She followed Janni silently along the corridor, and through the large double doors at the end of the hall.

Her lineage too must be good, for all her refusal to speak of it, since she spoke of dancing with Lyondri Hastur at children's parties. Maybe she too has been warned against speaking of her past.

It was a long and busy day. She ate bread and cheese and honey in the kitchen, was sent to practice some form of unarmed combat among a group of young girls, all of whom were more adept than she—she did not understand a single movement of the ones they were trying to teach her, and felt clumsy and foolish— and later in the day, a hard-faced woman in her sixties gave her a wooden sword like the ones she and Ruyven had played with when they were children, and tried to teach her the basic defensive moves, but she felt completely hopeless at that too. There were so many women—or it seemed like many, though she found out at dinner-time that there were only nineteen women in the hostel—that she could not even remember their names. Later she was allowed to make friends with the horses in the stable, where her own was brought—she found it easier to remember *their* names—and there were a few *chervines* too. Then Janni pierced her ears and put small gold rings into them. "Only while they are healing," she said, "Later you shall have the ensign of the Sisterhood, but for now you must keep twisting the rings so that the holes will heal cleanly, and bathe them three times a day in hot water and thornleaf." Then, in front of the assembled women, only a blur of faces to Romilly's tired eyes, she prompted her through the oath to the Sisterhood, and it was done. Until spring-thaw of the next year, Romilly was oath-bound to the Sisterhood of the Sword. That finished, they crowded around and asked her questions, which she was hesitant to answer in the face of Janni's prohibition that she must not speak of her past life, and then they found her a much-patched, much-worn nightgown, and sent her to sleep in a long room lined with half-a-dozen beds, tenanted by girls her own age or younger. It seemed that she had hardly fallen asleep before she was wakened by the sound of a bell, and she was washing her face and dressing in a room full of half a dozen young women, all running around half-dressed and squabbling over the washbasins.

For the first few days it seemed to Romilly that she was always gasping behind a group of girls who were running somewhere just ahead of her and she must somehow keep up. The lessons in unarmed combat frightened and confused her—and the woman who taught them was so harsh and angry of voice. Although, one afternoon, when she had been sent to help in the kitchens, where she felt more at home, the woman, whose name was Merinna, came in and asked her for some tea, and when Romilly brought it, chatted with her so amiably that Romilly began to suspect that her harshness in class was assumed to force them all to pay strict attention to what they were doing. The lessons in swordplay were easier, for she had sometimes been allowed to watch Ruyven's lessons, and had sometimes practiced with him—when she had been eight or nine, her father had been amused by her handling of a sword, though later, when she was older, he forbade her even to watch, or to touch even a toy sword. Gradually those early lessons came back to her, and she began to feel fairly confident at least with the wooden batons which served in practice.

Among the horses in the stable, she felt completely at home. This work she had done since she was old enough to rub soapweed on a saddle and polish it with oil.

She was hard at work polishing saddle-tack one day when

she heard a noise in the street outside, and one of the youngest girls in the house ran in to call her.

"Oh, Romy, come—the king's army is passing by at the end of the street, and Merinna has given us leave to run out and see! Carolin will march southward as soon as the passes are open—"

Romilly dropped the oily rag and ran out into the street with Lililla and Marga. They crowded into an angle of the doors and watched; the street was filled with horses and men, and people were lining the streets and cheering for Carolin.

"Look, look, there he goes under the fir-tree banner, blue and silver—Carolin, the king," called someone, and Romilly craned her neck to see, but she could catch only a glimpse of a tall man, with strong ascetic profile not unlike Carlo's, in the instant before his cloak blew up and she could see only his russet hair flying.

"Who is the tall skinny man riding behind him?" someone asked, and Romilly, who would have known him even in darkness with his face hidden, said, "His name is Orain, and I have heard he is one of Carolin's foster-brothers."

"I know him," said one of the girls, "he came to visit Jandria, someone told me that he was one of her kin, though I don't know whether to believe it or not."

Romilly watched the horses, men, banners moving by, with detachment and regret. She might still have been riding with them, had she gone to her own bed in the stable that night, still at Orain's side, still treated as his friend and equal. But it was too late for that. She turned about sharply and said, "Let's go inside and finish our work—I have seen horses enough before this and a king is am an like other men, Hastur or no."

The armies, she heard, were being moved to a great plain outside Caer Donn. A few days later, she was summoned to Janni, and when she went out into the main room where she had met Janni first, she saw Orain again, with Caryl at his side.

Orain greeted her with some constraint, but Caryl rushed at once into her arms.

"Oh, Romilly, I have missed you! Why, you are dressed like a woman, that is good, now I will not have to remember to speak to you as if you were a boy," he said.

"*Dom* Carolin," Janni said formally, and he turned his attention respectfully to her.

"I listen, *mestra*," he said, using the politest of terms for a female inferior in rank.

"The Lord Orain has commissioned me to escort you to Hail and return you, under safe-conduct, to your father," she said, "and there are two choices before you; I am prepared to treat you as a man of honor, and to ask your preferences, instead of making the decision for you. Are you old enough to listen to me seriously, and to answer sensibly and keep your word?"

His small face was as serious as when he had sung in the chapel at Nevarsin. "I am, *mestra* Jandria."

"Well, then, it is simple. Shall I treat you as a prisoner and have you guarded—and, make no mistake, we are women, but we shall not be careless with you and allow you to escape."

"I know that, *mestra*," he said politely, "I had a governess once who was much harsher with me than any of the masters and brothers in the monastery."

"Well, then," said Janni, "Will you be our prisoner, or will you give us your parole, not to attempt to escape our hands, so that you may ride beside us and take such pleasure in the trip as you can? It will not be an easy journey, and it will be simpler if we can allow you to ride without watching you every moment of the night and day, nor have you tied up at night. I will have no hesitation in taking the word of a Hastur, if you give me your parole of honor."

He did not answer at once. He asked, "Are you my father's enemies?"

"Not particularly," said Janni, "Of your father, my lad, I know only what I have been told; but I am Rakhal's enemy, and your father is his friend, so I trust him not. But then, I have not asked for his word of honor, either. I am dealing with you, *Dom* Carolin, not with him."

He said, "Is Romilly coming with us?"

"I thought to put you in her charge, since she has travelled with your before, if that is agreeable to you, young sir."

He smiled then, and said, "I would like to travel with Romilly. And I will gladly give you my word of honor not to try and escape. I could not travel through the Hellers

alone, whatever happened. I promise you, then, *mestra,* to
be at your orders until I am returned to my father's hands."

"Very well," Janni said, "I accept your word, as you may
accept mine, that I will treat you as I would one of my own
sisters, and offer you no indignity. Will you give me your
hand on it, *Dom* Carolin?"

He held out his hand and took hers. Then he said, "You
need not call me *Dom* Carolin, *mestra.* That is the name
of the former king, who is my father's enemy, though he is
not really mine. I am called Caryl."

"Then you shall call me Janni, Caryl," she said, smiling
at last, "and you shall be our guest, not our prisoner.
Romy, take him to the guest-room and make him comfortable. Orain—" she raised her eyes to her cousin, "we shall
set out tomorrow, if the weather allows."

"I thank you, cousin. And you," he added, turning to
Romilly, bending ceremoniously—like a courtier, she
thought—over her hand. She thought, heart-sore, that a few
days before, he would have taken leave of her with a rough
hug. She hoped, suddenly and passionately, that she and
Orain would never meet again.

They rode out of Caer Donn very early in the morning,
and had been more than an hour on the road before the
red sun rose, huge and dripping with mist. Caryl rode on
the pony Jandria had found for him, side by side with Romilly's horse; behind them were six women of the Sisterhood,
leading, on long pack-reins, a dozen good horses which,
they said, were for the armies in the South. They did not
say *which* armies, and Romilly carefully did not ask.

It was good to be riding free again in the sunlight, without the cold and storms of her earlier journey through the
Hellers. They stopped at noon to feed the horses and rest
them for a little, then rode on. In late afternoon they made
camp, and at Jandria's command, one of the pack-horses
was off-loaded, and as two women sat about making fire,
Janni called to Romilly.

"Come here and help me, Romy, with this tent—"

Romilly had no notion to how to set up a tent, but she
obediently hauled ropes and drove in pegs where Janni
ordered, and within a minute or two a large and roomy
shelter of waterproof canvas was ready for them. Blanket-

rolls were spread out within it, and under its hanging flap the evening drizzle could not dampen their fire or their supper. Very soon porridge was cooked, hot and savory with sliced onions frizzled in the fat of a roast fowl, and the women sat cross-legged on their bed-rolls, eating their food out of wooden bowls which had come out of the same pack.

"This is nice," said Caryl admiringly, "Men never make a camp as comfortable as this."

Janni chuckled. "There is no reason they should not," she said, "They are as good at cookery and hunting as we women are, and they would tell you so if you asked them; but maybe they think it unmanly to seek for comfort in the fields, and enjoy hard living because it makes them feel tough and strong. As for me, I have no love for sleeping in the rain, and I am not ashamed to admit I like to be comfortable."

"So do I," said Carl, gnawing on the ends of his bone, "This is good, Janni. Thank you."

One of the women, not one that Romilly knew well, whose name was Lauria, took a small hand-harp from her pack and began to play a tune. They sat around the fire, singing mountain ballads, for half an hour or so. Caryl listened bright-eyed, but after a time he fell back, drowsily, half asleep.

Janni signed to Romilly, and said, "Take off his boots, will you, and get him into his sleeping-roll?"

"Of course," Romilly said, and began to pull off Caryl's boots. He sat up and protested sleepily. Lauria said, grumbling, "Let the boy wait on himself, Romy! Janni, why should one of our sisters wait on this young man, who is our prisoner? We're no subjects or servants to the Hastur-kind!"

"He's only a boy," Janni said, placatingly, "and we're being well-paid to care for him."

"Still, the Sisterhood are no slaves to one of these men," grumbled Lauria, "I wonder at you, Janni, that for money you'd take a commission to escort some boy-child through the mountains—"

"Boy child or girl, the boy cannot travel alone," said Janni, "and needs not be drawn into the quarrels of his elders! And Romilly is willing to care for him—"

"I doubt not," said one of the strange women with a sneer, "One of those women who still think her duty in life is to wait on some man, hand and foot—she would disgrace her earring—"

"I look after him because he is sleepy, too sleepy to wait on himself," Romilly flared, "and because he is about the age of my own little brothers! Didn't you look after your own little brother if you had one, or did you think yourself too good to look after anyone but yourself? If the Holy Bearer of Burdens could carry the World-child on his shoulders across the River of Life, shall I not care for any child who comes into my hands?"

"Oh, a *cristoforo*," sneered one of the younger women, "Do you recite the Creed of Chastity before you sleep, then, Romy?"

Romilly started to fling back an angry retort—she made no rude remarks about the Gods of others, they could keep their mouths off her own religion—but then she saw Janni's frown and said, mildly, "I can think of worse things I might be saying." She turned her back on the angry girl, and went to spread out Carly's blanket beside her own.

"Are we to have a male in our tent to sleep with us?" the girl who had protested asked angrily, "This is a tent for women."

"Oh, hush Mhari, the boy can hardly sleep out in the rain with the horses," Janni said crossly. "The rule of the Sisterhood is intended for common sense, and the boy's no more than a baby! Are you fool enough to think he'll come into our blankets and ravish one of us?"

"It is a matter of principle," said Mhari sullenly, "Because the brat is a Hastur, are we to let him intrude into a place of the Sisterhood? I would feel the same if he were no more than two years old!"

"Then I hope you will never have the bad taste to bear a son instead of a daughter," said Janni lightly, "or will you, out of principle, refuse to feed a male at your breast? Go to sleep, Mhari; the child can sleep between me and Romilly, and we'll guard your virtue."

Caryl opened his mouth; Romilly poked him in the ribs, and he subsided without speaking. She saw that he was trying not to giggle aloud. It seemed a little silly to her, but she supposed they had their rules and principles, just as the brothers of Nevarsin did. She lay down beside Caryl, and slept.

She found herself dreaming, clear vivid dreams, as if she flew, linked in mind with Preciosa, over the green, rolling hills of her own country. She woke with a lump in her throat, remembering the view of the long valley from the cliffs of Falconsward. Would she ever see her home again, or her sister or brothers? What had they to do with a wandering swordswoman? Her ears ached where they had been pierced. She missed Orain and Carlo and even the rough-tongued Alaric. As yet she had made no friends among these strange women. But she was pledged to them for a year, at least, and there was no help for it. She listened to Caryl, sleeping quietly at her side; to the breathing of the strange women in the tent. She had never felt so alone in her life, not even when she fled from Rory's mountain cabin.

Five days they rode southward, and came to the Kadarin river, traditional barrier between the lowland Domains and the foothills of the Hellers. It seemed to Romilly that they should make more of it, going into strange country, but to Janni it was just another river to be forded, and they crossed with dispatch, at a low-water ford where they hardly wetted their horses' knees. The hills here were not so high, and soon they came to a broad rolling plateau. Caryl was beaming; all the trip he had been in good spirits, and now he was ebullient. She supposed he was glad to be coming home, and glad of the long holiday that had interrupted his studies.

Yet Romilly felt uneasy without mountains surrounding her; it seemed as if she rode on the flat land, under the high skies, like some small, exposed thing, fearfully surveying the skies here as if some bird of prey would swoop down on them and carry her away with strong talons. She knew it was ridiculous, but she kept uneasily surveying the high pale skies, filled with rolling violet cloud, as if something there was watching her. At last Caryl, riding at her side, picked it up with his sensitive *laran*.

"What's the matter, Romy? Why do you keep looking at the sky that way?"

She really had no answer for him and tried to pass it off. "I am uneasy without mountains around me—I have al-

ways lived in the hills and I feel bare and exposed
here. . . ." she tried hard to laugh, looking up into the
unfamiliar skies.

High, high, a speck hovered, at the edge of her vision.
Trying to ignore it, she bent hr eyes on the rough-coated
grass, only lightly frosted, at her feet.

"What sort of hawking is there on these plains, do you
know?"

"My father and his friends keep *verrin* hawks," he said,
"Do you now anything of them? Do they have them across
the river, or only those great ugly sentry-birds?"

"I fly a *verrin* hawk," Romilly said, "Once I trained
one—" and she looked uneasily around again, her skin
prickling.

"Did you? A girl?"

The innocent question rubbed an old wound; she
snapped at him, "Why should I not? You sound like my
father, as if because I was born to wear skirts about my
knees I had neither sense nor spirit!"

"I did not mean to offend you, Romy," said Caryl, with
a gentleness which made him seem much older than his
years. "It is only that I have not known many girls, except
my own sister, and she would be terrified to touch a hawk.
But if you can handle a sentry-bird, and calm a banshee as
we did together, then surely it would take no more trouble
to train a hawk." He turned his face to her, watching with
his head tilted a little to one side, something like a bird
himself with his bright inquisitive eyes. "What are you
afraid of, Romy?"

"Not afraid," she said, uneasy under his gaze, then,
"Only—as if someone was watching me," she blurted out,
not knowing she was going to say it until she heard her
own words. Realizing how foolish they were, she said defensively, "Perhaps that is only because—the land is so
flat—I feel—all exposed—" and again her eyes sought the
sky, dazzled by the sun, where, wavering at the very edge
between seen and unseen, a speck still hovered . . . *I am
being watched!*

"It is not uncommon, that," said Janni, coming up beside
them, "when first I rode into the mountains, I felt as if
they were closing in, as if, while I slept, they might move
in and jostle my very skirts. Now I am used to them, but

still, when I ride down into the plains, I feel as if a great weight has been lifted and I can breathe more easily. I think *that,* more than all kings or customs, divides hillman from lowlander; and I have heard Orain say as much, that whenever he was away from his mountains, he felt naked and afraid under the open sky. . . ."

She could almost hear him say it, in that gentle, half-teasing tone. She still missed Orain, his easy companion-ship, it seemed she was like a fish in a tree among all these woman! Their very voices grated on her, and it seemed to her sometimes that in spite of their skill with sword and horsemanship, they were far too much like her sister Mal-lina, silly and narrow-minded. Only Janni seemed free of the pettiness she had always found in women. But was that only because Janni was like Orain and so less like a woman? She did not know and felt too sore to think much about it.

Yet, she thought with annoyance at herself, forty days ago I was thinking that I liked the company of men even less than that of women. Am I content nowhere? Why can't I be satisfied with what I have? If I am going to be always discontented, I might as well have stayed home and married *Dom* Garris and been discontented in comfort among fa-miliar things!

She felt the gentle, inquiring touch of the boy's *laran* on her mind; as if he asked her what was the matter. She sighed and smiled at him, and asked, "Shall we race across this meadow? Our horses are well-matched, so it will only be a matter of which is the better horseman," and they set off side by side, so rapidly that it took all her attention not to tumble off headlong, and she had to stop thinking about what troubled her. She reached the appointed goal a full length ahead of him, but Janni, coming up more slowly, scolded them both impartially—they did not know the ter-rain, they might have lamed their horses on some unseen rock or small animal's burrow in the grass!

But that night, as they were making camp—the days were lengthening now perceptibly, it was still light when they had eaten supper—she had again the sharp sense that she was being watched, as if she were some small animal, prey huddling before the sharp eyes of a hovering hawk—she scanned the darkening sky, but could see nothing. Then, incredulous, a familiar sense of wildness, flight, contact, rapport—hardly knowing what she did, Romilly thrust up her hand, felt the familiar rush of wings, the grip of talons.

"Preciosa!" she sobbed aloud, feeling the claws close on her bare wrist. She opened her eyes to look at the bluish-black sheen of wings, the sharp eyes, and the old sense of closeness enveloped her. Against all hope, beyond belief, Preciosa had somehow marked her when she came out of the glacier country, had trailed her even through these unfamiliar hills and plains.

She was in good condition, sleek and trim and well-fed. Of course. There was better hunting on these plains than even in the Kilghard Hills where she was fledged. Wordless satisfaction flowed between them for a long space as she sat motionless, the hawk on her hand.

"Well, will you look at that!" the voice of one of the girls broke through the mutual absorption, "Where did the hawk come from? She is bewitched!"

Romilly drew a long breath. She said to Caryl, who was watching silently, rapt, "It is my hawk. Somehow she has followed me here, so far from home, so far—" and broke off because she was crying too hard to speak. Troubled by the emotion, Preciosa bated, trying to balance on Romilly's fist; flapped her wings and flew to the branches of a nearby tree, where she sat looking down at them without any sign of fear.

Mhari demanded, "Is it your own hawk—the one you trained?" and Janni said in a quiet voice, "You told me your father took her from you, and gave her to your brother—"

With an effort, Romilly controlled her voice. She said, "I think Darren found out that Preciosa was not my father's to give." She looked up through her tears to the tree branch where Preciosa sat, motionless as a painted hawk on a painted tree, and again the thread of rapport touched her mind. Here, among strange women in a strange country, with all she had ever known behind her and past the border of a strange river, as she looked at the hawk and felt the familiar touch on her mind, she knew that she was no longer alone.

Chapter 2

Three days more they rode, and came into a warm country, green, rolling hills and the air soft, without the faintest breath of frost. To the end of her life Romilly remembered that first ride across the Plains of Valeron—for so Caryl told her they were called—green and fertile, with crops blooming in the field and trees without even snow-pods for their night-blossoms. Along the roadside, flowers bloomed, red and blue and silver-golden, and the red sun, warm and huge in these southern skies, cast purple shadows along the road. The very air seemed sweet, euphoric.

Caryl was ecstatic, pointing out landmarks as he rode beside Romilly. "I had not expected to be home before mid-summer after this! Oh, I am so glad to be coming home—"

"And your father sent you from this warm and welcoming country into the snows of Nevarsin? He must indeed be a good *cristoforo*."

Caryl shook his head, and in that moment his face looked distant, closed-in, almost adult. He said quietly, "I serve the Lord of Light, as fits a Hastur best."

Then why—Romilly almost burst out with the question, but she had learned not to speak any question of his father to the boy. But he picked up the question in her mind.

"The *cristoforos* at Nevarsin are learned men, and good men," he said at last. "Since the Hundred Kingdoms were made, there has been war and chaos in the lowlands, and such learning as can be gotten is small indeed; my father wished me to learn in peace, away from the wars and safe from the feuds that beset the Hastur-kinfolk. He does not share the worship of the Brotherhood, but respected their religion and the knowledge that they are men of peace."

He fell silent, and Romilly, respecting that silence—what scenes of war and pillage had that child seen, far from the sheltering hills which keep men safe in their own fortressed homes?—rode on, thoughtfully. She had heard tales of war, far away in her own peaceful mountains. She called to mind the battles by which this green and peaceful country had been laid waste. It now seemed, to her hypersensitive consciousness, bestrewn with the black of blood under the crimson sun, all dark, the very ground crying out with the slaughter of innocents and the horrors of armies treading the crops into the soil from which they sprung. She shuddered, and abruptly the whole scene winked out and Romilly knew she had been sharing the child's consciousness.

Indeed his father did well to send his son to safety among the cold and untroubled crags of the City of Snows; a time of rest, a time to heal the wounds of a child with laran, *sensitive and aware of all the horrors of war.* With sudden passionate homesickness, Romilly was grateful for her childhood of peace and for the stubbornness that had kept The MacAran his own man, taking no part in the factions that swept the land with their lust to conquer. What was his watchword? *To their own God Zandru's deepest forges with both their households. . . .*

Oh, Father, will I ever see you again?

She looked up at Caryl but he rode silent beside her, unseeing, and she knew he rode enclosed in his own pain, unable to see hers, or at least blinded with the effort to block it away from himself. *Have I come to this, then, that I would turn to a child of twelve, a baby no older than my little brother, for comfort when I cannot suffer my own lot, which I chose for myself?* She rode among strangers, and wondered for a moment if each of the women around her rode like this, each closed in with her own weary weight, each bearing her share of the burdens laid upon mankind. *Is this why men call upon the Bearer of Burdens as if he were not only a great teacher of wisdom, but also a God— that we may have Gods to bear our burdens because otherwise they are too heavy for mankind to bear?*

She could not endure the sorrow in Caryl's small face. She at least was a woman grown and could bear her own burden, but he was a child and should not have to. She broke in upon him, gently, asking, "Shall I call Preciosa from the sky to ride with you? I think she is lonely—" and as she whistled to the hawk, and set her upon Caryl's saddle she was rewarded by seeing the unchildlike weight disappear from the childish face, so that he was only a boy again, gleefully watching a hawk fly to his hand.

"When this war is over, Romy, and the land is at peace again, shall I have you for my hawkmaster, and will you teach me all about training hawks? Or no, a girl cannot be a hawk*master,* can you? You will then be hawkmistress to me, one day?"

She said gently, "I do not know where any of us will be when this war is over, Caryl. It would be a pleasure to teach you what I know about hawks. But remember that much of what I know cannot be taught. You must find it somewhere within you, your heart and your *laran*—" and at the edge of her consciousness she realized that now she felt quite comfortable with that alien word—"to know the birds and to love them and to be aware of their ways."

And she found it easy to believe that this small wise boy, with his sensitive awareness of men and beasts, the gravity of the monks among whom he had been reared and the charm of the Hastur-kin, would perhaps one day be king. It seemed for a moment that she could see the luminous glimmer of a corona about his reddish curls—and then she shut away the unwanted sight. She was learning fast, she reflected, to handle the Gift given to her, or to shut it away.

Was this how her father had learned to survive, outside a Tower, she wondered, by closing away all the *laran* he could not use in his work of training horses? And could she stand to shut away all this new part of herself? Could she bear to have it—or *not* to have it, now? It was a terrifying gift and bore its own penalties. No wonder, now, that there were old tales in the mountains of men driven mad when their *laran* came upon them. . . .

And how could Caryl be a king? His father was no king but sworn liegeman to *Dom* Rakhal, and whether Rakhal won this war, or Carolin, Lyondri Hastur was no king. Or would he prove false to Rakhal as he had been false to

Carolin, in the ambition to form a dynasty of his own blood?

"Romilly—Romy! Are you asleep riding there?" Caryl's merry voice broke in on her thoughts. "May I see if Preciosa will fly for me? We should have some birds for supper—should we not?"

She smiled at the boy.

"If she will fly for you, you shall fly her," she agreed, "though I cannot promise that she will fly for anyone but me. But you must ask Dame Jandria if we have need of birds for supper; she, not I, is in charge of this company."

"I am sorry," Caryl said, unrepentant, the words mere formality, "But it is hard to remember that she is a noblewoman, and it does not come naturally to me to remember to ask her, while when I am with you I am always aware that you are one of the Hastur-kind."

"But I am not," said Romilly, "and Janni is Lord Orain's own cousin, if you did not know, so her blood is as good as mine."

Suddenly Caryl looked scared. "I wish you have not told me that," he blurted out, "for that makes her one of my father's greatest enemies and I do not want him to hate her. . . ." Romilly berated herself; he looked stricken. She said quickly, "Rank has no meaning among the Sisterhood, and Jandria has renounced the privileges brought with noble birth. And so have I, Caryl." And she realized that he looked relieved, though she was not sure why.

"I will ask Jandria if we have need of game for the pot," she said quickly, "and you shall fly Preciosa if she will fly at your command; surely Jandria could not object if you want to get a bird for your own supper, unless you try to make one of us pluck and cook it for you."

"I can do that myself," Caryl said proudly, then grinned, lowering his eyes. "If you will tell me how," he said in a small voice, and Romilly giggled, Caryl giggling with her.

"I will help you cook the bird for a share of it—is that a bargain, then?"

Three nights later they began to ride along the shore of a lake, lying in the fold of the hills, and Caryl pointed to a great house, not quite a castle, situated at the head of the long valley.

"There lies Hali, and my father's castle."

Romilly thought it looked more like a palace than a fortress, but she said nothing. Caryl said, "I shall be glad to see Father again, and my mother," and Romilly wondered; how glad would his father be, to see a son held hostage by his worst enemy's men, and taken from the safety of Nevarsin, whence he had sent him? But she said nothing of this. Only that morning, flying through Preciosa's eyes, she had seen out over the whole vast expanse of the Plains of Valeron, armies massing and moving on the borders. The war would soon be upon the green lowlands again.

And all that day they rode through a country scoured clean by war; farmsteads lay in ruins, great stone towers with not one stone left upon another, only scattered rubble as if some monstrous disruption like an earthquake had shaken them from their very foundations; what army, what dreadful weapon had done that? Once they had to turn aside, for as they came to the top of the rise, they saw in the valley before them a ruined village. A strange silence hung over the land, though houses stood undamaged, serene and peaceful, no smoke rose from the chimneys, no sound of horses stamping, children playing, hammers beating on anvils or the worksongs of women weaving or waulking their cloth. Dread silence lay over the village, and now Romilly could see a faint greenish flickering as if the houses were bathed in some dreadful miasma, an almost tangible fog of doom. They lay, pulsing faintly greenish, and she knew suddenly that when night fell the street and houses would glow with an uncanny luminescence in the dark.

And even as she looked, she saw the lean, starved figure of a predator slinking silently through the streets; and while they looked, it moved more slowly, subsided, lay down in its tracks, still stirring feebly, without a cry.

Jandria said curtly, "Bonewater-dust. Where that stuff's been scattered from the air, the land dies, the very houses die; should we ride through there, we would be in no better case than that woods-cat before many nights. Turn about—best not come too near; this road is closed as if a nest of dragons guarded it; or better, for we might somehow manage to fight even dragons, but against this there's no fighting, and for ten years or more this land will lie accursed and the very beasts of the forests be born awry. Once I saw a mountain-cat with four eyes and a plains chervine with toes for hooves. Uncanny!" She shuddered, pulling her horse around. "Make as wide a circle as we can around this place! I've no wish to see my hair and teeth fall out and my blood turn to whey in my veins!"

The wide detour added two or three days to their ride, and Janni warned Romilly not to fly Preciosa.

"Should she eat of game tainted by that stuff of war, she would die, but not soon enough to save her great suffering; and should we eat of it, we too might lose hair and teeth if no worse. The taint of the foul stuff lingers long in all the country round, and spreads in the bodies of predators and harmless beasts who wander through the blighted countryside. She can fast for a day or two more safely than she can risk hunting too close to that place."

And so for two days Romilly carried Preciosa on her saddle, and, though she had sworn to herself that she could never again confine her freed bird, she yielded to fear at last and tied jesses about her legs.

I dare not let you fly or you would eat of game which would kill you, she tried miserably to form a picture in her mind which the hawk could clearly see, of the game glowing with that unhealthy and poisonous glow, and although she was not sure she had made contact with the bird's mind, for the hawk sulked and brooded on the saddle, she did not fight the bonds, and rode with her head tucked under her wing; Romilly could feel the fierce hunger pulsing within her, but she seemed willing to ride thus chained for her own protection.

At last it seemed that they were out of danger, though Janni warned all the women that if they should begin to comb out handfuls of hair, or their teeth should loosen, they should tell her at once; she thought they had made a wide enough circle around the tainted land; "But none can be sure with that deadly stuff," she warned, and rode on, her jaw clenched hard. Once she said to Romilly, with a brief glance that made Romilly think of her hawk, closed-in and brooding her eyes swiftly hooded, "Orain was fostered in that village. And now no man will be able to live in it for a span of years and perhaps more. All the Gods blast Lyondri and his devil weapons!"

Romilly cast a quick glance at Caryl, but either he had

not heard, or concealed it. How heavy a weight the boy must carry!

They camped a little early that night, and while the women were setting up the tent, Janni called Romilly away from the camp.

"Come with me, I need to talk to you. No, Caryl, not you," she added, sharply, and the boy fell back like a puppy that had been kicked. Janni led Romilly a little away from the camp, and motioned to her to sit down, lowering herself crosslegged to the rough soft grass.

"Any sign of loosening teeth, falling hair?"

Romilly bared her teeth in a smile, then raised her hand and tugged graphically at her short hair. "Not a bit of it, Janni," she said, and the woman breathed a sigh of relief.

"Evanda be praised," she said, "who has guarded her maidens. I found some loose hair this morning when I combed my hair, but I am growing old and must look to falling hair as a woman's lot in age. Still I could not help fearing that we had not ridden wide enough round that cursed site. What madman will destroy the very land of his own vassals? Oh, yes, I have ridden to war, I can see burning a croft—though I like it not to kill the humble folk because of the wars of the great and mighty—but a croft, burned, can be rebuilt; and crops trampled down can be grown again when the land is at peace. But to destroy the very land so no crops will grow for a generation? Perhaps I am too squeamish for a warrior," she said, and fell for a moment into silence. At last she asked, "Have you had trouble with your prisoner?"

"No," said Romilly, "he is glad to be coming home, but he has scrupulously minded his parole."

"I thought as much, but I am glad to hear you say it," said Jandria. She loosened the cheap silver buckles on her cloak and flung it back, sighing as the wind ruffled her thick hair. Her face seemed lined and weary. Romilly said with swift sympathy, "You are so tired, Jandria. Let me take your part in the camp work tonight, and go to rest in your tent now. I will bring your evening meal to you in your blanket-roll."

Janni smiled. "It is not weariness which weighs on me, Romilly; I am old and hardened to travel and camp, and I have slept in places far more comfortless than this without

a whimper. I am troubled, that is all, for good sense tells
me one thing and honor tells me another.''

Romilly wondered what trouble lay on Janni, and the
woman smiled and reached for her hand. She said, ''Young
Carolin is in my care, and honor bids that I be the one to
convey him to his father. Yet I thought perhaps I would
send you to deliver the lad within the walls of Hali city to
the hands of the Hastur-lord.''

Romilly's first thought was that she would have a chance
to see within the walls of the great lowland city; her next,
that she would be very sorry to part with Caryl. Only after
that did she realize that she would also have to meet with
that great rogue Lyondri Hastur.

''Why me, Janni?''

Jandria's heavy sigh was audible. ''Something you know
of courtly ways and the manners of a Great House,'' she
said. ''I feel traitor to the Sisterhood to say as much, having
sworn to leave rank behind me forever. Mhari, Reba,
Shaya—all of them are good women, but they know no
more than the clumsy manners of their fathers' crofts, and
I cannot send them on such a mission of diplomacy. More
than this, for the safety of all of us.'' Her strained smile
was faint, hardly a grimace. ''Whatever I said to Orain,
Lyondri Hastur would know me if I wore banshee-feathers
and did the dance of a Ya-man in a Ghost Wind! I have
no wish to hang from a traitor's gallows. Carolin, and Orain
too, were among those Lyondri loved best, and those whom
he pursues with the greater fury now. Carolin, Orain, Lyondri and I—we four were fostered together.'' She hesitated,
sighed again and at last said, ''Orain does not know this;
he never wished to see what befell between man and
maiden, and he did not know— hell's fire,'' she burst out,
''Why does it shame me to say that Lyondri and I lay together more than once, before I was even fully a woman.
Now I have turned from him to my own kindred, I think
it would give him pleasure to hang me, if my death would
give pain to Carolin or to Carolin's sworn man! Nor can I
bear to meet him—Avarra comfort me, I cannot but love
him still, almost as much as I hate!'' She swallowed and
looked at the ground, holding tight to Romilly's hand. ''So
now you know why I am too cowardly to meet with him,

however sworn he may be with his flag of truce—he might spare me for our old love, I do not know. . . ."

"It is not needful, Janni," said Romilly gently, feeling the woman's pain, "I will gladly go. You must not risk yourself."

"Seeing you—do you understand this, Romilly?—Lyondri and Rakhal see only a stranger, and more than that, one Caryl loves well, someone who has been kind to his son; and they know only that you are an envoy of the Sisterhood, not a rebel or one sworn to Carolin: Be clear, Romilly, I send you into danger—it may be that Lyondri will not honor his pledged word of safety for the courier who brings his son; but you may risk nothing worse than imprisonment. Lyondri *may* kill you; he would certainly lose no chance for revenge against me."

Danger for her, against certain death for herself? Romilly hesitated just a moment, and Janni said wearily, "I cannot command you to this risk, Romilly. I can only beg it of you. For I cannot send Caryl alone into the city; I pledged he should be safely delivered into his father's very hands."

"I thought he had sworn safe-conduct—"

"Oh, and so he has," said Janni, "But I trust that no further than Lyondri sees his advantage, which he saw ever. . . ." and she covered her face with her hands. Romilly felt weak and frightened. But the Sisterhood had taken her in when she was alone, sheltered and fed her, welcomed her with friendliness. She owed them this. And she was a sworn Swordswoman. She said, tightening her hand on Janni's, "I will go, my sister. Trust me."

Before they rode into the city, Caryl washed himself carefully at a stream, begged a comb from one of the women and carefully combed his hair and trimmed his nails. He dug from his saddlebags his somewhat shabby clothes—for the last few days he ha been wearing bits and pieces, castoff trousers and tunic of one of the women, so that he could wash his own in one of the streams and have them clean for his return to court, though nothing could make them look like proper attire for a prince.

He said with regret, "Father sent me a new festival costume before Midwinter-night, and I had to leave it in the monastery when I left so suddenly. Well, it can't be helped, this is the best I have."

"I will cut your hair if you like," Romilly offered, and trimmed his curling hair to an even length, then brushed it till it shone. He laughed and told her he was not a horse to be currycombed, but he looked at himself with satisfaction in the stream.

"At least I look like a gentleman again; I hate to be shabby like a ruffian," he said. "*Mestra* Jandria, will you not come with us? My father could not be angry with anyone who had been so kind to his son."

Jandria shook her head. "There were old quarrels between Lyondri and me before you were hatched or Rakhal sought out Carolin's throne, dear boy; I would rather not come under your father's eye. Romilly will take you."

"I will be glad to ride with Romilly," said Caryl, "and I am sure my father will be grateful to her."

"In the name of all the Gods of the Hasturs, boy, I hope so," said Jandria, and when Caryl bent over her hand in his courtly manner, she pressed it. "*Adelandeyo,*" she said after the manner of the hill women, "Ride on with the Gods, my boy, and may They all be with you, and with Romilly."

Only Romilly, seeing the tensing in Janni's jaw, the tremble in her eyes, knew that Janni was thinking, *Gods protect you, girl, and may we see you again safe out of Lyondri Hastur's hands.*

Romilly clambered into her saddle. With a clarity not usual to her unless she was in rapport with her hawk and seeing all things through her *laran* and not he eyes, she saw the clear pale sky, the tent of the Sisterhood; heard thwacks where Mhari and Lauria were practicing with the wooden batons they used for swords, saw two other women slowly working through the careful training moves of unarmed combat, the dancelike ritual which trained their muscles to work without thought in defensive movement. She could still see smoke from the breakfast fire and felt alerted and frightened—smell of smoke when no food was cooking?—before she remembered that they were not now in the forest and there was, in this green meadow, no chance of wildfire.

She had made herself tidy, with her best cloak, the one Orain had bought for her in the Nevarsin market—though now she felt sore and raw-edged about his gift, she had nothing else nearly so good or so warm—and had borrowed the cleanest tunic she could find in the camp from one of the sworsdwomen. She was conscious of the still-stinging earrings in her ears, mercilessly revealed by her short hair. Well, she told herself defensively, I am what I am, a woman of the Sisterhood of the Sword—even though I am not very good with it yet—and Lyondri Hastur can just accept me as an emissary under safe-conduct; why should I worry about whether I look like a lady? What is Lyondri to me? And yet a little voice that sounded like Luciella's was saying in her mind, with prim reproach, *Romy, for shame, boots and breeches and astride like a man, what would your father say?* Mercilessly she commanded the voice to be quiet.

She clucked briefly to her horse and nodded to Caryl, who drew his horse into an easy trot beside her own.

Hali was an unwalled city, with broad streets which were uncannily smooth under foot; at her puzzled look, Caryl smiled and told her they had been laid down by matrix technology, without the work of human hands. At her skeptical glance he insisted, "It's true, Romy! Father showed me, once, how it can be done, laying the stones with the great matrix lattices under ten or twelve *leroni* or *learanzu'in*. One day I will be a sorcerer as well and work among the relays and screens!"

Romilly was still skeptical, but there was no use at all in challenging what a child's father had told him, so she held her peace.

He directed her through the streets, and it was all she could do to keep from staring about her as if she were the freshest of country bumpkins, hardly away from the farmyard; Nevarsin was a fine city, and Caer Donn as well, but Hali was wholly different. In place of steep, cobbled streets and stone houses crowded together as if huddling under the great crags of the Hellers or of Castle Aldaran, there were broad streets and low open dwellings—she had never seen a house which was not built like a fortress to be defended, and wondered how the citizens could sleep secure in their beds at night; not even the city was walled.

And the people who walked in these streets seemed a different race than the mountain people—who were strongly built, clad in furs and leather against the bitter chill, and seemed hard and fierce; here in this pleasant lowland city, finely dressed men and women strolled the broad streets, wearing colorful clothing, embroidered tunics and brightly dyed skirts and veils for the women, colorful long coats and trousers for the men, and thin cloaks of brilliant colors, more for adornment than for use.

One or two of the people in the streets paused to stare at the blazing red head of the boy, and the slender, trousered, earringed young woman who rode at his side in the scarlet of the Sisterhood and the old-fashioned mountain-cut cloak of fur and homespun. Caryl said under his breath, "They recognize me. And they think you, too, one of the Hastur-kind because of your red hair. Father may think so too. You must be one of our own, Romilly, with red hair, and *laran* too. . . ."

"I don't think so," Romilly said, "I think redheads are born into families where they have never appeared before, just as sometimes a bleeder, or an albino, will appear marked from the womb, and yet no such history in their family. The MacArans have been redheads as far back as I can remember—I recall my great-grandmother, though she died before I could ride, and her hair, though it had gone sandy in patches, was redder than mine at the roots."

"Which proves that they must at one time have been kin to the children of Hastur and Cassilda," the boy argued, but Romilly shook her head.

"I think it proves no such thing. I know little of your Hastur-kind—" tactfully she bit back the very words on her tongue, *and what little I know I do not much like.* But she knew that the boy heard the unspoken words as he had heard the spoken ones; he looked down at his saddle and said nothing.

And now, as they roe toward a large and centrally situated Great House, Romilly began to be a little frightened. Now, after all, she was to meet that beast Lyondri Hastur, the man who had followed the usurper Rakhal and exiled Carolin, killed and made homeless so many of his supporters.

"Don't be frightened," said Caryl, stretching out his hand

between their horses, "My father will be grateful to you because you have brought me back. He is a kind man, really, I promise you, Romy. And I heard that he pledged a reward when the courier from the Sisterhood should bring him to me."

I want no reward, Romilly thought, *except to get safe away with a whole skin.* Yet like most young people she could not imagine that within the hour she might be dead.

At the great doors, a guard greeted Caryl with surprise and pleasure.

"*Dom* Caryl . . . I had heard you were to be returned today! So you've seen the war an' all! Good to have you home, youngster!"

"Oh, Harryn, I'm glad to see you," Caryl said with his quick smile. "And this is my friend, Romilly, she brought me back—"

Romilly felt the man's eyes travel up and down across her, from the feather in her knitted cap to the boots on her trousered legs, but all he said was "Your father is waiting for you, young master; I'll have you taken to him at once."

It seemed to Romilly that she sensed a way of escape now. She said, "I shall leave you, then, in the hands of your father's guardsman—"

"Oh, no, Romilly," Caryl exclaimed, "You must come in and meet father, he will be eager to reward you. . . ."

I can just imagine, Romilly thought; but Janni had been right. There was no real reason for Lyondri Hastur to violate his pledged word and imprison a nameless and unknown Swordswoman against whom he ha no personal grudge. She dismounted, saw her horse led away, and followed Caryl into the Great House.

Inside, some kind of soft-voiced functionary—so elegantly clothed, so smooth, that calling him a *servant* seemed unlikely to Romilly—told Caryl that his father was awaiting him in the music room, and Caryl darted through a doorway, leaving Romilly to follow at leisure.

So this is the Hastur-lord, the cruel beast of whom Orain spoke. I must not think that, like Caryl himself he must have laran, *he could read it in my mind.*

A tall, slightly-built man rose from the depths of an armchair, where he had been holding a small harp on his knee;

set it down, bending forward, then turned to Caryl and took both his hands.

"Well, Carolin, you are back?" He drew the bouy against him and kissed his cheek; it seemed that he had to stoop down a long way to do it. "Are you well, my son? You look healthy enough; at least the Sisterhood has not starved you."

"Oh, no," said Caryl, "They fed me well, and they were quite kind to me; when we passed through a town, one of them even bought me cakes and sweets, and one of them lent me a hawk so I could catch fresh birds if I wanted them for my supper. This is the one with the hawk," he added, loosing his father's hands and grabbing Romilly to draw her forth. "She is my friend. Her name is Romilly."

And so at last Romilly was face to face with the Hastur-lord; a slight man, with composed features which, it seemed, never relaxed for a second. His jaw was set in tight lines; his eyes, grey under pale lashes, seemed hooded like a hawk's.

"I am grateful to you for being good to my son," said Lyondri Hastur. His voice was composed, neutral, indifferent. "At Nevarsin I thought him beyond the reach of the war, but Carolin's men, I have no doubt, thought having him as hostage was a fine idea."

"It wasn't Romilly's idea, father," said Caryl, and Romilly knew that he had thought about, and rejected, telling his father that Orain had been angry about it; it was no time to bring Orain's name up at all. And Romilly knew, too, from the almost-imperceptible added clenching of the Hastur-lord's jaw, that he heard perfectly well what his son had not said, and it seemed that a shadow of his voice, faraway and eerie, said almost aloud in Romilly's mind, *Another score against Orain, who was my sworn man before he was Carolin's.*

I should keep this woman hostage; she may know something of Orain's whereabouts, and where Orain is, Carolin cannot be far.

But by now the boy could read the unspoken thought, and he looked up at his father in real horror. He said in a whisper, "You pledged your word. The word of a Hastur," and she could almost see his shining image of his father crack and topple before his eyes. Lyondri Hastur looked from his son to the woman. He said, in a sharp dry voice,

"Swordswoman, know you where Orain rides at this moment?"

She knew that with his harsh eyes on her she could not lie, he would have the truth from her in moments. With a flood of relief she knew that she need not lie to him at all. She said, "I saw Orain last in Caer Donn, when he brought Caryl—*Dom* Carolin—to the hostel of the Sisterhood. And that was more than a tenday ago. I suppose by now he is with the army." And, though she tried, she could not keep from her mind the picture of the army passing at the end of the street, the banner of the Hasturs, blue and silver, and Orain riding at the side of the unseen king. Lyondri would not consider him king but usurper. . . .

I have made promises I could not keep . . . I knew not what manner of man I served, that I have become Rakhal's hangman and hard hand . . . and with shock, Romilly realized that she was actually receiving this thin trickle of thoughts from the man before her; or was this true at all, was she simply reading him as she read animals, in the infinitesimal movements of eyes and body, and somehow co-ordinating them with his thoughts? She was acutely uncomfortable with the contact and relived when it stopped abruptly, as if Lyondri Hastur had realized what was happening and closed it down.

I have read thoughts, more or less, much of my life, why should it disturb and confuse me now?

The Hastur-lord said with quiet formality, "I owe you a reward for your care of my son. I will grant anything save for weapons which might be used against me in this unjust war. State what you wish for his ransom, with that one exception."

Jandria had prepared her for this. She said firmly, "I was to ask for three sacks filled with medical supplies for the hostels of the sisterhood; bandage-linen, the jelly which helps the clotting of blood, and *karalla* powder."

"I suppose I could call those weapons, since no doubt they will be used to aid those wounded in rebellion against their king," Lyondri Hastur mused aloud, then shrugged. "You shall have them," he said, "I will give my steward the orders, and a pack-animal to take them back to your camp."

Romilly drew a soft sigh of relief. She was not to be imprisoned, then, or held hostage.

"Did you believe that of me?" asked Lyondri Hastur aloud, dryly, then gave a short, sharp laugh. She saw it in his mind again, two telepaths could not lie to one another. She was fortunate that he did not wish his son disillusioned about his honor.

Romilly found herself suddenly very grateful that she had not encountered Lyondri Hastur when Caryl was not by, and when he did not wish to keep his son's admiration.

"But, father," Caryl said, "This is the woman with the hawk, who let me fly her—can I have a hawk of my own? And one day, I wish Mistress Romilly to be my hawk-mistress—"

Lyondri Hastur smiled; it was a dry, distant smile, but nevertheless, a smile, and even more frightening than his laugh. He said, "Well, Swordswoman, my son has taken a fancy to you. There are members of the Sisterhood in my employment. If you would care to stay here and instruct Carolin in the art of falconry—"

She wanted nothing more than to get away. Much as she liked Caryl, she had never met anyone who so terrified her as this dry, harsh man with the cold laughter and hooded eyes. Grasping for an honorable excuse, she said, "I am— I am pledged elsewhere, *vai dom.*"

He bowed slightly acknowledging the excuse. He knew it was an excuse, he knew what she thought of him, and he knew she knew. He said, "As you wish, *mestra.* Carolin, say good-bye to your friend and go to greet your mother."

He came and gave her his hand in the most formal way. Then, impulsively, he hugged her. He said, looking up to her with earnest eyes, "Maybe when this war is over I will see you again, Romilly—and your hawk. Give Preciosa my greetings." Then he bowed as if to a lady at court, and left the room quickly, but she had seen the first traces of tears in his eyes. He did not want to cry in front of his father; she knew it.

Lyondri Hastur coughed. He said, "Your pack-animal and the medical supplies will be brought to you at the side door, near the stable. The steward will show you the way," and she knew that the audience with the Hastur-lord was over. He gestured to the functionary, who came and said softly, "This way, *mestra.*"

Romilly bowed and said, "Thank you, sir."

She turned, but as she was about to follow the steward, Lyondri Hastur coughed again.

"Mistress Romilly—?"

"Via dom?"

"Tell Jandria I am not quite the monster she fears. Not quite. That will be all."

And as she left the room, Romilly wondered, shaking to her very toenails, *what else does this man know?*

Chapter 3

When Romilly delivered the message from Lyondri Hastur to Janni—"Tell her I am not the monster she thinks me, not quite," Jandria said nothing for a long time. Romilly sensed, from her stillness, (although she made a deliberate effort, her first, not to use her *laran* at all) that Jandria had several things she would have said; but not to Romilly. Then, at last, she said, "And he gave you the medical supplies?"

"He did; and a pack animal to carry them."

Janni went and looked them over, saying at last, tight-lipped, "He was generous. Whatever Lyondri Hastur's faults, niggardliness was never one of them. I should return the pack animal—I want no favors from Lyondri—but the sober truth is that we need it. And it is less to him than buying his son a packet of sweets in the market; I need suffer no qualms of conscience about that." She sent for three of the women to look over the medical supplies, and told Romilly she might return to her horses. As an afterthought, as Romilly was going out the door, she called her back for a moment and said, "Thank you, *chiya*. I sent you on a difficult and dangerous mission, where I had no right at all to send you, and you carried it off as well as any diplomatic courier could have done. Perhaps I should find work better suited to you than working with the dumb beasts."

Romilly thought; *I would rather work with horses than go on diplomatic missions, any day!* After a minute or two she said so, and Jandria, smiling, said, "Then I will not keep you from the work I know you love. Go back to the horses, my dear. But you have my thanks."

Freed, Romilly went back to the paddock and led out the horse she was beginning to break to the saddle. But she had not been at the work very long when Mhari came out to her.

"Romy," she said, "saddle your own horse and two pack animals, at once, and Jandria's riding-horse. She is leaving the hostel tonight, and says you must go with her."

Romilly stared, with one hand absent-mindedly quieting the nervous horse, who did not at all like the blanket strapped to his back. "To leave tonight? Why?"

"As for that, you must ask Janni herself," said Mhari, a little sullenly, "I would be glad to go wherever she would take me, but she has chosen you instead, and she bade me make up a packet of your clothes, and four days journey-rations too."

Romilly frowned with irritation; she was just beginning to make some progress in gentling this horse, and must she interrupt the work already? She was sworn to the Sisterhood, but must that put her at the mercy of some woman's whim? Nevertheless she liked Jandria very much, and was not inclined to argue with her decisions. She shrugged, changed the long lunge-line for a short leading-rope and took the horse back into the stable.

She had finished saddling Jandria's horse, and was just putting a saddle-blanket on her own, when Jandria, cloaked and booted for riding, came into the stable. Romilly noticed, with shock, that her eyes were reddened as if she had been crying; but she only asked "Where are we going, Janni? And why?"

Jandria said, "What Lyondri said to you, Romy, was a message; he knows that I am here; no doubt he had you followed to see where the Sisterhood's hostel was located outside the walls of Hali. Simply by being here, I endanger the Sisterhood, who have taken no part in this war; but I am kin to Orain and he might somehow think to trace Orain through me, might think I know more of Orain's plans—or Carolin's—than I really do. I must leave here at once, so that if Rakhals men under Lyondri come here to seek me, they can say truthfully, and maintain, even if they should be questioned by a *leronis* who can read their thoughts, that they have no knowledge of where I have gone, or where Carolin's men, or Orain, may be gathered. And I am taking you with me, for fear Lyondri might try to lay hands on you, too. These other women—he knows nothing of them and cares less; but you have come under his eyes, and I would just as soon you were out of his field of notice . . . I would rather not have you at the very gates of Hali. Besides—" her smile was very faint, "Did you not know? A woman of the Sisterhood does not travel alone, but must be companioned by one, at least, of her sisters."

Romilly had not thought of that—Jandria was Orain's kin, and Lyondri Hastur could use her for hostage, too, even if he did not, as Jandria had feared, mean to put her to death. She said formally, *"A ves ordes, mestra,"* and finished saddling her horse.

"Go into the hostel and get yourself some bread and cheese," Jandria said, "We can eat as we ride. But be quick, little sister."

Is there need for such haste as that, or is Jandria afraid without reason? But Romilly did not question her; she did as she was told, returning with a loaf of bread and a great hunk of coarse white new cheese, which she stowed in her saddlebag—she was not hungry now, Jandria's message had effectively destroyed her appetite, but she knew she would be glad of it later. She had a bag of apples, too, which the cook had given her.

She did ask, as they led out their horses to mount, "Where are we going, Janni?"

"I think it would be safer if you did not know that, not just yet," said Jandria, and Romilly saw real fear in her eyes. "Come, little sister, let us ride."

Romilly marked that they rode northward from the city, but the trail soon curved, and Jandria took a small, little-travelled road, hardly more than the track left by mountain *chervines,* which wound upward and upward into the hills. Before long Romilly had lost all sense of direction, but Jandria seemed never to hesitate, as if she knew precisely where she was going.

Before long they began to ride under the cover of heavy forested slopes, and Jandria seemed to relax a little; after an hour or so she asked for some of the bread and cheese, and ate it with a good appetite. Romilly, chewing on the coarse crust, began to wonder again, but did not ask.

At last Jandria said, mounting again and taking the lead-rope of the pack animal, "Even a sentry-bird cannot spy us out here. I know not if Lyondri has such birds trained to his use—they are not really all that common—but I thought it better to keep under cover till the trail was well and truly lost; all Gods forbid I should lead him straight to Carolin armies."

"Is *that* where we are going?"

The Sisterhood has a cohort of soldiers there," said Jandria, "and your skills may be needed to train horses for the army. And I doubt not that the Sisterhood with Carolin's army can make use of me, somehow or other. If Lyondri knew I was in the hostel—as he must have known or he would not have sent that message—then he might think, or Rakhal might think for him, that if he kept watch on me, I might lead him straight to Carolin's rendezvous; even if he could not tear the knowledge of that rendezvous straight from my mind without even a *leronis* to aid him. So I hastened to get out of there, and into the cover of the forest, so that he could not set watch on the hostel and give orders to have me followed. I may possibly have moved faster than he, for once; and it may be that we are already safe." But she glanced apprehensively down the trail where they had come, and then, even more apprehensively, at the sky, as if even now Lyondri's sentry-birds could be hovering there to spy them out. And her fear made Romilly frightened too.

That night they camped still within the shelter of the forest, and Jandria even forbade a cooking-fire; they ate the cold bread and cheese, and tethered the animals under a great tree. They spread their blankets beneath another, doubled for warmth (although the mountain-bred Romilly found it reasonably warm) and Romilly slept quickly, tired from riding. But she woke once in the night to hear soft sounds as if Jandria was crying. She wished, wretchedly, that she could say something to comfort the other woman, but it was a trouble far beyond her comprehension. At last she slept again, but woke early to find Jandria already up and saddling the horses. Her eyes were dry and tearless, her face barricaded, but the eyelids were red and swollen.

"Do you think we can risk a fire this morning? I would like some hot food, and if we are not pursued by now, surely we must have gotten away," Romilly said, and Jandria shrugged.

"I suppose it makes no difference. If Lyondri truly wishes to find me, I am sure he would not need trackers, seeing that he read my thoughts of him so far away. It would not be Lyondri who pursued us, but Rakhal, in any case." She was silent, sighing. "Build us a fire, and I will cook some hot porridge, little sister. I have no right to make this trip harder for you with my causeless fears and dreads; you have travelled so long and hard already, Romy, and already I have you off again when you thought you had found a place of repose."

"It's all right," Romilly said, not knowing what to say. She would rather travel with Jandria than remain in the hostel with the strange women among whom she had made no friends as yet. She knelt to kindle a fire. But when they were eating hot porridge, and their horses munching at ease in the grass, Romilly asked, hesitantly, "Do you grieve for—for Lyondri?" What she was wondering, was this; Lyondri had been her lover, was she still bound to him? Jandria seemed to know what she meant, and sighed, with a small sad smile.

"My grief, I suppose, is for myself," she said at last. "And for the man I thought Lyondri was—the man he might have been, if Rakhal had not seduced him with the thought of power. That man, the man I loved, is dead—so long dead that even the Gods could not recall him from whatever place our dead hopes go. He still wants my good opinion—so much the message, or warning, meant—but that could be no more than vanity, which was always strong in him. I do not think he is—is all evil," she said, and stumbled a little over it, "The fault is Rakhal's. But by now he must know what Rakhal is, and still follows after him. So I cannot hold him guiltless of all the atrocities done in Rakhal's name."

Romilly asked, shyly, "Did you know them both—Carolin and Rakhal? How did Rakhal come to seize his throne?"

But Jandria shook her head. "I do not know. I left court when Rakhal still professed to be Carolin's most loyal follower, accepting all the favors Carolin showered on him as his dearest cousin who had been fostered with him."

"Carolin must be a good man," said Romilly at last, "to inspire much devotion in Orain. And—" she hesitated, "in you."

She said, "But surely when you were with Orain, you met with Carolin?"

Romilly shook her head "I understood the king was at Nevarsin; but I did not meet with him."

Jandria raised her eyebrows, but all she said was, "Finish your porridge, child, and rinse the dish in the stream, and we shall ride again."

Silently, Romilly went about her work, saddling the horses, loading what was left of their food. But as they mounted, Jandria said, so long after that Romilly had almost forgotten what she asked, "Carolin is a good man. His only fault is that he trusts the honor of the Hasturs without reason; and he made the mistake of trusting Rakhal. Even Orain could not tell him what Rakhal was, nor could I; he thought Orain was only jealous. Jealous—Orain!"

"What is Rakhal like?" asked Romilly, but Jandria only shook her head.

"I cannot speak of him fairly; my hate blinds me. But where Carolin loves honor above all things, and then he loves learning, and he loves his people, Rakhal loves only the taste of power. He is like a mountain-cat that has had a taste of blood." She climbed into her saddle, and said, "Today you will take the pack-animal's leading-rope, and I will ride ahead, since I know where we are going."

When they had come out from under the cover of the forest, Romilly had again the faint far sense of being watched; that trickle of awareness in her mind that told her Preciosa was watching her; the hawk did not descend to her hand, but once or twice Romilly caught a glimpse of

the bird hovering high in the sky, and knew she was not
alone. The thought warmed her so deeply that she was no
longer aware of fear or apprehension.

She and I are one; she has joined her life to mine. Romilly
was dimly aware that this must be something like marriage,
indissoluble, a tie which went deep into the other's body
and spirit. She had no such tie for instance with her present
horse, though he had carried her faithfully and she wished
him well and thought often of his welfare.

The horse is my friend. Preciosa is something else, something like a lover.

And that made her think, shyly and almost for the first
time, what it might be like to have a lover, to have a
bond with someone as close to her as the hawk, tied in
mind and heart and even in body, but someone with
whom she could communicate, not as the MacArans did
with their horses and hounds and hawks, across the vast
gulf that lay between man and horse, women and hawk,
child and dog, but with the close bonding of species. *Dom*
Garris had wanted her, but his lecherous glances had
roused nothing in her but revulsion; revulsion doubled
when it was Rory, who would as soon have cut her throat
for her horse and cloak and a few coppers, but had wished
to bed her as well.

Orain had wanted her—at least while he still believed
her to be a boy. And . . . deliberately facing something
she had not even clearly understood at the time . . . she
had wanted him. Although, when it was happening, she
had not realized what her own strange feelings meant.
Even so, she would rather have had Orain as a friend
than a lover; she had been willing to accept him as a
lover, when she thought he knew her a woman and
wanted her, in order to keep him as a friend. But had
she never seriously thought of any man in that way? Certainly none of the boys she had grown up knowing, her
brothers' friends—she could no more envision them as
lovers than as husbands, and a husband was the last thing
she would have wanted.

*I think I could have married one like Alderic. He spoke
to me as a human being, not only as his friend Darren's
silly little sister. Nor was he the kind of man who would
feel he must control me every moment, fearing I would fly*

*away like an untamed hawk if he let go of the jesses for
a moment.*

*Not that I wanted him as a husband, so much. But per-
haps I could make up my mind to marry if the husband had
first been my friend.*

All during that day and the next, whenever she took her
eyes from the trail, she could see, at the furthest range of
her vision, that Preciosa still hovered there, and feel the
precarious thread of communication from the hawk, strange
divided sight, seeing the trail under her feet, aware of her
own body in the saddle, and yet some indefinable part of
her flying free with the hawk, far above the land and hillside slopes. Jandria had told her that they were travelling
now in what were called the Kilghard Hills.

They were not like her home mountains—bleak and bare
with great rock cliffs and poor soil of which every arable
scrap must be carefully reclaimed and put under cultivation
for food; and even less were they like the broad and fertile
Plains of Valeron which they had crossed enroute to Hali.
These were hills, high and steep and with great deserted
tracts of wild country set with virgin forest and sometimes
overgrown in thick brush-tangles so that they must cut their
way through or, sometimes, retrace their steps tediously
and go round. But there was no lack of hunting. Sometimes,
before sunset, drowsing in her saddle, Romilly would feel
something of her fly free with the hawk, stoop down and
feel, sharing with Preciosa, the startle of the victim, the
quick killing stroke and the burst of fresh blood in her own
veins. . . . Yet every time it came freshly to her as a new
experience, uniquely satisfying.

Once, she thought it was the sixth day of their journey,
she was flying in mind with the hawk when her horse
stepped into a mudrabbit-burrow and stumbled, fell; lay
thrashing and screaming, and Romilly, thrown clear of the
stirrups, lay gasping, bruised and jarred to the bone. By
the time she was conscious enough to sit up, Jandria had
dismounted and was helping her to rise.

"In the name of Zandru's frozen hells, where was your
mind, you who are so good a horseman, not to see that
burrow?" she demanded crossly. Romilly, shocked by the
horse's screams, went to kneel by is side. His eyes were
red, his mouth flecked with the foam of agony, and, quickly

sliding into rapport with him, she felt the tearing pain in her own leg, and saw the bare, white, shattered bone protruding through the skin. There was nothing to be done; weeping with horror and grief, she fumbled at her belt for her knife and swiftly found where the great artery was under the flesh; she thrust with one fast, deep stroke. A final, convulsive struggle, a moment of deathly pain and fear—then it was quiet, all around her stunned and quiet, and the horse, with his fear, was simply gone, gone from her, leaving her empty and cold.

Stunned, fumbling, Romilly wiped her knife on a clump of grass and put it again into its sheath. She could not look up and meet Jandria's eyes. Her damned *laran* had cost the horse his life, for had she been attending to her riding, she would surely have seen the burrow. . . .

Jandria said, at last, "Was it necessary?"

"Yes." Romilly did not elaborate. Jandria did not have *laran* enough to understand, and there was no reason to burden her with all Romilly's own feelings of guilt, the rage at her own Gift which had tempted her to forget the horse beneath her in straining for the hawk above. Swallowing hard against the tears still rising and making a lump in her throat, she cursed the Gift, "I am sorry, Janni. I—I should have been more careful—"

Jandria sighed. "I was not reproaching you, *chiya;* it is ill fortune, that is all. For here we are shy of a horse in the deepest part of the hills, and I had hoped we could reach Serrais by tomorrow's nightfall."

"Is that where we are going? And why?"

"I did not tell you, in case we were followed; what you did not know, you could not tell—"

So Jandria does not trust me. Well enough; it seems I am not trustworthy . . . certainly my poor horse did not find me so. . . . yet she protested. "I would not betray you—"

Gently, Jandria said, "I never thought of that, love. I meant only—what you did not know could not be wrung from you by torture, or ravished from your mind by a *leronis* armed with one of their starstones. They could find out quickly that you knew nothing. But now you would know in a day or two, anyhow."

She knelt beside Romilly and began to tug at the saddle straps. "You can ride one of the pack chervines; they cannot travel at the speed of your horse, but we can put both the packs on the back of the other. We will travel less swiftly by chervine-pace than we would with two good horses, but it can't be helped."

She began to off-load the nearer of the chervines, saw Romilly standing stone-still and snapped, "Come and help me with this."

Romilly was staring at the dead horse. Insects were already beginning to move in the clotted blood around the smashed leg. "Can't we bury him?"

Jandria shook her head. "No time, no tools. Leave him to feed the wild things." At Romilly's look of shock she said gently, "Dear child, I know what your horse meant to you—"

No you don't, Romilly thought fiercely, *you never could.*

"Do you think it matters even a little to him whether his body is left to feed the other wild things, or whether he had a funeral fit for a Hastur-lord? He is not *in* his body any more."

Romilly swallowed hard. "I know it—it makes sense when you say it like that, but—" she broke off, gulping. Jandria laid a gentle hand on her arm.

"There are beasts in this forest who depend on the bodies of the dead things for their food. Must they go hungry, Romy? This is only sentiment. You feel no pain when your hawk kills for her food—"

To Romilly's sore senses it seemed that Jandria was taunting her with her inattention, that she was away somewhere sharing the kill with her hawk and thus leading her horse to its death. She wrenched her arm free of Jandria's and said bitterly, "I don't have any choice, do I? *A ves ordres, mesra,*" and began wrenching at the pack-loads of the other cherivine. In her mind, aching, accusing, was the memory of the sentry-birds for whom she had spied out carrion. Now her horse would fall prey to the *kyorebni,* and perhaps that was as it should be, but she felt she could not bear to see it, knowing her own carelessness had cost the faithful creature his life.

As if for comfort she looked into the sky, but Preciosa was nowhere in sight.

Perhaps she too has left me. . . .

*　　*　　*

Toward nightfall the land Sisterhood changed; the green fields gave way to sandy plateaus, and the roads were hard-baked clay. The chervines were forest and hill creatures, and walked laggingly, little rivulets of sweat tracing vertical lines down their thick coats. Romilly wiped her forehead with her sleeve and took off her thick cloak and tied it in a bundle on her saddle. The sun was stronger here, it seemed, and blazed with cloudless intensity from a clear, pale sky. Twilight was beginning to fall when Jandria pointed.

"There lies Serrais," she said, "and the hostel of the Sisterhood where we shall sleep tonight, and perhaps for a span of ten days. I shall be glad to sleep in a proper bed again—won't you?"

Romilly agreed, but secretly she was sorry that the long journey was coming to an end. She had grown fond of Jandria, and the thought of living in a houseful of strange women really frightened her. Furthermore, she supposed, now she was in a regular dwelling-place of the Sisterhood, she would be required to go back to the frightening lessons in swordplay and unarmed combat, and she dreaded it.

Well, she had chosen to swear to the Sisterhood, she must do her best in that place in life to which she had been guided by providence. *Bearer of Burdens, help me to bear mine then as you bear the world's weight!* And then she felt surprised at herself. She could not remember, before this, thinking much about prayer, and now it seemed that she was forever turning to such little prayers. *I wonder, is this what the Book of Burdens calls* Dhe shaya, *a grace of God, or is it only a kind of weakness, a sense born of loneliness, that I have nowhere else to turn?* Jandria was her friend, she thought, but she would not share her fears, Janni enjoyed the life of the Sisterhood and was not terrified at the very thought of wars and battles; such things as the village blighted with bonewater-dust enraged and horrified her, but they did not fill her with that kind of terror; Janni seemed quite free of that kind of personal fear!

They rode into the city when dusk had already fallen, and made their way through the strange wide street, the old houses of bleached stone that shone with pallid luminescence in the moonlight. Romilly was almost asleep in her saddle, trusting the path to the steady plodding pace of her chervine. She roused up a little when Jandria stopped before a great arched gate with a rope and bell hanging from it, and pulled on it. Far away inside, she heard the sound, and after a time a drowsy voice inquired, "Who is it?"

"Two women of the Sisterhood come from Hali," Janni called, "Jandria, Swordswoman, and Romilly, apprentice Swordswoman, oathbound and seeking shelter here."

The door creaked open, and a woman peered out into the street.

"Come in, Sisters," she said. "Lead the beasts into the stable there, you can throw them some fodder if you wish. We are all at supper." She pointed to a stable inside the enclosure, and they dismounted, leading the tired animals into the barn. Romilly blinked when she saw the place by the faint lanternlight; it was not large, but in a couple of loose-boxes at the back she saw crowded horses, some of the finest horses she had ever seen. What was this place, and why did they crowd so many horses into so small a stable? She felt full of questions, but was too shy to speak any of them. She put her chervine into one of the smaller stalls, led Jandria's horse into another, then shouldered her pack and followed the strange woman into the house.

There was a good smell of fresh-baked bread, and the spicy, unfamiliar smells of some kind of cooking food. In a long room just off the hall where they left their packs, at a couple of long tables, what looked like four or five dozen women were crowded together, eating soup out of wooden bowls, and there was such a noise of rattling bowls and crockery, so much shouting conversation from one table to another and from one end to the other of the long tables that Romilly involuntarily flinched—after the silence of the trails through forest and desert, the noise was almost deafening.

"There are a couple of seats down there," said the woman who had admitted them. "I am Tina; after supper I will take you to the housemother and she can find you beds somewhere, but we are a little crowded, as you can see; they have quartered half the Sisterhood upon us here, it seems, though I must say they're good about sending

army rations here to feed them. Otherwise we'd all be living on last year's nuts! You can go and sit down and eat—
you must be wanting it after that long ride."

It did not seem that there was any room at all at the
table she indicated, but Jandria managed to find a place
where the crowding was a little less intense, and by dint of
some good-natured pushing and squeezing, they managed
to wriggle into seats on the benches, and a woman, making
the rounds of the tables with a jug and ladle, poured some
soup into their bowls and indicated a couple of cut loaves
of bread. Romilly pulled her knife from her belt and sawed
off a couple of hunks, and the girl squeezed in next to
her—a good-natured smiling woman with freckles and dark
hair tied back at her waist—shoved a pot of fruit spread at
her. "Butter's short just now, but this goes pretty good on
your bread. Leave the spoon in the jar."

The spread tasted like spiced apples, boiled down to a
paste. The soup was filled with unidentifiable chunks of
meat and strange vegetables, but Romilly was hungry and
ate without really caring what it was made of.

As she finished her soup, the woman next to her said,
"My name is Ysabet; most people call me Betta. I came
here from the Tendara hostel. And you?"

"We were in Hali, and before that, in Caer Donn," Romilly said, and Betta's eyes widened. "Where the king fled?
Did you see his army there "

Romilly nodded, remembering Orain and a banner in a
strange street.

"I heard Carolin was camped north of Serrais," Betta
said, "and that they will march, before snow falls, on Hali
again. The camp is full of rumors, but this one is stronger
than most. What is your skill?"

Romilly shook her head. "Nothing special. I train horses
and sometimes hawks, and I have handled sentry-birds."

Betta said, "They told us that an expert in horse-training
was to come from Hali! Why, you must be the one, then,
unless it is your friend there—what is her name?"

She is Jandria," Romilly said, and Betta's eyes widened.
"Lady Jandria! Why, I have heard of her, if it is the same
one, they said she is cousin to Carolin himself—I know we
are not supposed to think of rank, but yes, I see she has
red hair and a look of the Hasturs—well, they said they

would send a Swordswoman from Hali, and a woman adept at horse-training. We will need it—did you see all the horses in the stable? And there are as many more in the paddock, and they were taken as a levy from the Alton country in the Kilghard Hills . . . and now they are to be broken for Carolin's armies, so that the Sisterhood will ride to battle for Carolin, our true king . . ." Then she looked at Romilly suspiciously. "You are for Carolin, are you not?"

"I have ridden from before day light till after dark, today and for the last seven days," Romilly said, "By now I hardly know my own name, let alone that of the king." It seemed very hot in the room, and she could hardly keep her eyes open. But then, remembering that they had fled from the possibility of being followed by Lyondri Hastur, she added, "Yes; we are for Carolin."

"As I said, half the Sisterhood seems to be quartered on us here," Betta said, "and there are so many rumors in this place. Two nights ago we had women sleeping on the tables in here, and even under them, even though we who live here in the hostel slept two to a bed and gave up the emptied beds to the newcomers."

"I have slept on the ground often enough," Romilly said, "I can sleep somewhere on the floor." At least this was out of the rain, and under a roof.

"Oh, I am sure that for the Lady Jandria they can find a bed somewhere," Betta said. Are you her lover?"

Romilly was too tired and confused even to know for certain what Betta meant. "No, no, certainly not." Although, she supposed, the question was reasonable. Why would a woman seek the life of a Swordswoman, when she could just as well marry? There had been a time or two, since she had come among the Sisterhood, when she had begun to wonder if her constant rejection of the idea of marriage meant that at heart she was a lover of women. She felt no particular revulsion at the thought, but no particular attraction to it either. Fond as she had grown of Jandria during these days, it would never have occurred to her to seek her out as she had sought Orain. But now her attention had been forcibly drawn to the subject, she wondered again. *Is this why I have never really wanted a man, and even with Orain, it was a matter of liking and kindness, not any real desire?*

I am too tired to think clearly about anything, let alone anything as important as that! But she knew she must consider it some day, especially if her life was to be spent among the Sisterhood.

One by one, or in little groups of three and four, the women of the Sisterhood were leaving the table and going to seek their various beds. Blanket rolls stowed in a corner of the big room were unrolled on the floor, with some good-natured bickering for places near the log-fire; Tina came and found them and led them to a room with three beds, two of which were already occupied.

"You can sleep there," she told them, "And the House-mother wants to see you, Lady Jandria."

Janni said to Romilly, "Go to bed and sleep; I will be along later." Romilly was so tired that, although she told herself it would be difficult to sleep in a room with four other women, some of whom were certain to snore, she was fast asleep even before her head hit the pillow, and did not remember, afterward, at what hour Jandria had come in.

But the next morning, when they were dressing, she said to Jandria, "They seemed to know who you were, and to be expecting us. How could you send a message that would come faster than we did ourselves?"

Jandria looked up, a stocking in her hand. She said, "There is a *leronis* of my acquaintance with Carolin's army; this is why I dared not fall into the hands of Lyondri. I know too much. I sent word, and asked that news be sent to the hostel of the Sisterhood; so that they were ready to admit us. Do you really think they would open their doors after dark in a city full of soldiers, and readying for war?"

It seemed to Romilly that every day she learned something new about Jandria. So she had *laran* too? *Laran* of that curious kind which could link to send messages over the trackless miles? She felt shy and confused again—could Janni read what she was thinking, know all her rebellion, her fears? She kept her mind away from the implications of that.

"If I am to break horses here," she said, "I suppose I should go at once to the stables and begin."

Jandria laughed. "I think there will be time to have

breakfast first," she said, "The Housemother told me to sleep as long as I could after the long ride; and I think we have slept long enough that we can find someplace to eat in the dining-room without kicking the sleepers off tables. That was the only reason I did not want to sleep on the floor there—I knew the cooks and servers for this tenday would come in and rouse us at daybreak so they could get to their breakfast kettles!"

And indeed by the time they were dressed, the dining-room was empty, with only a few old women lingering over cups of hot milk and bread soaked in them. They helped themselves to porridge from the kettle and ate, after which Betta came in search of them.

"You are to go to the Housemother, Lady Jandria," she said, "And Mistress Romilly to the stables—"

Jandria chuckled good-naturedly and said, "Just Jandria or Janni. Have you forgotten the rule of the Sisterhood?"

"Janni, then," Betta replied, but she still spoke with residual deference. "Practice in unarmed combat is at noon in the grass-court; swordplay at the fourth hour after. I will see you there."

In the stables and paddock, Romilly found a number of horses; black horses from the Kilghard Hills, the finest she had ever seen. It would be, she thought, a pleasure and a privilege to train these to the saddle.

"They are needed by the Army, in as much haste as possible," said Tina, who had brought her here, "And they must be trained to the saddle, to a steady pace, and to stand against loud noises. I can get you as many helpers as you need, but we have no expert, and Lady Jandria told us that you have the MacAran Gift. So you will be in charge of the work of training them."

Romilly looked at the horses; there were a good two dozen of them. She asked, "Have any of them been trained to pacing on a lunge-line?"

"About a dozen," Tina said, and Romilly nodded.

"Good; then find a dozen women who can try their paces, and take them out in the paddock," she said, "and I will begin getting to know the others."

When the women came she noticed that Betta was among them, and greeted her with a nod and smile. She sent them out to work for a few minutes at running the horses in circles on the lunge-lines, steadying their paces, and went into the stable to choose the horse which she would herself work with.

She decided to give each horse into the charge of the woman who had exercised it today; it was easier if they formed a close tie with the horse.

"For then the animal will trust you," she told them, "and will do things to please you. But it cannot be a one-way connection," she warned, "Even as the horse loves and trusts you, you must love him—or, if it is a mare, love *her*—and be completely trustworthy, so that the horse can read in your mind that you love; you cannot pretend, for he will read a lie in moments. You must be open to the horse's feelings, too. Another thing—" she gestured to the short training-whips which were in their hands, "You can snap the whips if you like, to get their attention. But if you hit any horse enough to mark it, you are no trainer; if I see a whip in serious use, you can go and practice your swordplay instead!"

She sent them to work and listened for a moment to the chattering as they went out.

"Not to use our whips? What are they for, then?"

"I don't understand this woman. Where is she from, the far mountains? Her speech is so strange. . . ."

Romilly would have thought it was *their* speech which was strange, slow and thoughtful, as if they chewed every word a dozen times before speaking; while it seemed to her that she talked naturally. Still, after she had heard a dozen women say that they could not understand her, she tried to slow her own speech and speak with what seemed to her an affected, unnatural slowness.

If they were at Falconsward, everyone would think their speech silly, foreign, affected. I suppose it is a matter of what they are used to.

She turned to the horses with definite relief. At least, with them, she could be herself and they, at any rate, would not be critical of her speech or manners.

The horses, at least, speak my language, she thought with pleasure.

There were so many of them, and of all kinds, from sturdy shaggy mountain ponies like the one she had killed on the way here, to sleek blacks such as her own father bred. She went into the loose-box among them (to the distinct horror of Betta, who seemed as troubled as if she had gone into a cage full of carnivorous mountain-cats) and moved through them, trying to find the right horse to begin with. She must do a splendid job of training, because she knew that there was some grumbling—she looked so young, they said, and they would be quick to spot any mistakes.

I am not so young, and I have been working among horses since I was nine years old. But they do not know that.

As she moved through the box, one horse backed up against the wooden rails and began kicking; Romilly noticed the wide rolling eyes, the lips drawn back over the teeth.

"Come out and away from that one, Romilly, he's a killer—we are thinking of returning him to the Army, who can turn him out to pasture for stud; no one will be able to ride that one—he's too old for breaking to saddle!" Tina called it anxiously, but Romilly, lost and intent, shook her head.

He is frightened almost to death, no more. But he won't hurt me.

"Bring me a lead-rope and bridle, Tina. No, you needn't come into the box if you are afraid, just hand it to me across the rails," she said. Tina handed it through, her face pale with apprehension, but Romilly, rope in hand, had her eyes only on the black horse.

Well, you beauty, you, do you think we can make friends, then?

The horse backed nervously, but he had stopped kicking. *What fool put him into this crowded box, anyhow? Softly, softly, Blackie, I won't hurt you; do you want to go out in the sunshine?* She formed a clear image of what she meant to do, and the horse, snorting uneasily, let him pull her head down and slip bridle and lead-rope over it. She heard Tina catch her breath, amazed, but she was so deeply entwined now with the horse that she had no thought to spare for the woman.

"Open the gate," she said abstractedly, keeping close contact with the mind of the stallion. "That's wide enough. *Come along now, you beautiful black thing. . . .* See, if you handle them right, no horse is vicious; they are only afraid, and don't know what's expected of them."

"But you have *laran*," said one of the watchers, grudgingly, "We don't; how can we do what you do?"

"*Laran* or no," Romilly said, "if your whole body and every thought in it is stiff with fear, do you expect the horse not to know it, to smell it on you, even? Act as if you trusted the animal, talk to him, make a clear picture in your mind of what you want to do—who knows, they may have some kind of *laran* of their own. And above all, let him know absolutely that you won't hurt him. He will see and feel it in every movement you make, every breath, if you are afraid of him or if you wish him ill."

She turned her attention back to the horse.

"So, now, lovely fellow, we're going into the sunshine in the paddock . . . come along, now . . . no, not that way, silly, you don't want to go back in the stable," she said half aloud, with a little tug on the ropes. In the paddock half a dozen women were running horses in circles on the long lunge-lines, calling to them, and in general keeping the pace smooth. Romilly made a quick check of what was going on—none of them were doing really badly, but then no doubt they had chosen the more docile animals for training first—and found a relatively isolated place of paddock; one or more of the mares might be in season and she did not want him distracted. She backed away on the lunge-line and clucked to him.

He was strong, a big, heavy horse, and for a moment Romilly was almost jerked off her feet as he began to lope, found the line confining him, then explored its limits and began to run in a circle at its limit. She pulled hard and he slowed to a steady walk, around and around. After a little, when she was sure he had the idea, she began to let him move a little faster.

His paces are beautiful; a horse fit for Carolin's self. Oh, you glorious thing, you!

She let him run for almost an hour, accustoming him to the feeling of the bridle, then called for a bit. He fought it a little, in surprise—Romilly half sympathized with him; she did not much blame him, she did not think she would care to have a cold metal thing forced into her mouth, either.

But that's the way it is, beauty, you'll get used to it, and then you can ride with your master. . . .

At noon she led him back, suggesting to one of the

women that they put her more docile horse into the loose-box and leave her own small stall for the black stallion. Already, it seemed, she could see the nebulous figure of King Carolin riding into Hali on this splendid horse.

From this work, which she found easy—well, not exactly easy, but familiar and pleasant—she was sent to practice unarmed combat. She did not especially mind having to learn to fall without hurting herself—she had, after all, fallen from a horse more times than she could remember while she was learning to ride, and she supposed the skill was similar—but the series of holds, thrusts, jabs and throws seemed endlessly complex, and it seemed that every woman there, including the beginners with whom she was set to practice basic movements, knew more of it than she did. One of the older women, watching her for a moment, finally motioned her away, signalled to the others to go on, and said. "How long have you been pledged to the Sister-hood, my girl?"

Romilly tried to remember. Things had been happening so swiftly in the last few moons that she really had no notion. She shrugged helplessly. "I am not sure. Some ten days—"

"And you do not see much cause for this kind of training, do you?"

She said, carefully trying to be tactful, "I am sure there must be some reason for it, if it is taught in every hostel of the Sisterhood."

"Where were you brought up—what's your name?"

"Romilly. Or I'm called Romy sometimes. And I was brought up in the foothills of the Hellers, near Falcon-sward."

The woman nodded. "I would have guessed that much from your speech; but you grew up in outland country, then, not near to a big city, where you never met a stranger?"

"That's true."

"Well, then. Suppose you are walking down a city street, one of the more crowded and dirty sections." She beckoned and the girl who had sat next to Romilly at supper last night, Betta, came and joined them.

"You are walking along a dirty street where thieves cluster and men think all women like the doxies of the taverns," the older woman said. Betta shrugged, began to walk along the wall and the older woman suddenly leaped at her with a strangling grip. Romilly gasped as Betta twisted her upper body, jerked the woman forward and flung her to her knees, her arm immobilized behind her back.

"Ow! Betta, you are a little rough, but I think Romy sees what is meant. Now, come at me with a knife—"

Betta took up a small wooden stick, about the size of a clasp-knife, and came at the woman with 'knife' lowered to stab. So rapidly that Romilly could not see what happened, the 'knife' was in the other woman's hands and Betta lying on her back on the floor, where the older woman pretended to kick her.

"Careful, Clea," Betta warned, laughing and moving out of the way, then suddenly jerked at the woman's foot and pulled her down.

Laughing in her turn, Clea scrambled up. She said to Romilly, "Now do you see what good this might be to you? Particularly in a city like this, where we are at the edge of the Drylands, and there are likely to be men who think of women as possessions to be chained and imprisoned? But even in a civilized city like Thendara, you are likely to meet with those who will have neither respect nor courtesy for man or woman. Every women taken into the Sisterhood must learn to protect herself, and—" her laughing face suddenly turned deadly serious, "When you are life-pledged to the Sisterhood, like myself, you will wear this." She laid her hand on the dagger at her throat. "I am pledged to kill rather than let myself be taken by force; to kill the man if I can, myself if I cannot."

A shiver ran down Romilly's back. She did not know whether she would be able to do that or not. She had been prepared to injure Rory seriously, if she must. But to kill him? Would that not make her as bad as he was?

I shall face that if, and when, I am sworn for life to the Sisterhood, should that day ever come. By then, maybe, I will know what I can do and what I cannot.

Clea saw her troubled look and patted her shoulder. "Never mind, you will learn. Now get over there and practice. Betta, take her and show her the first practice moves so she won't be so confused; time enough later to throw her into a group of beginners."

Now that somebody had bothered to inform Romilly what they were doing and why, it went better. She began to realize, then and in the days that followed, that when she faced another woman in these sessions, she could read, by following tiny body and eye movements, precisely what the other was going to do, and take advantage of it. But knowing was not enough; she also had to learn the precise movements and holds, jabs and thrusts and throws, the right force to use without actually damaging anyone.

And yet, in men's clothing, I travelled all through the Hellers. I would rather live in such a way that I need not be prey to any man.

Yet there was pride, too, in knowing that she could defend herself and need never ask for mercy from anyone. Later the lessons in swordplay seemed easier to her, but they brought another fear to the surface of her mind.

It was all very well to practice with wooden batons where the only penalty for a missed stroke was a bad bruise. But could she face sharp weapons without terror, could she actually bring herself to strike with a sharp weapon at anyone? The thought of slicing through human flesh made her feel sick.

I am not a Swordswoman, no matter what they call me. I am a horse trainer, a bird handler . . . fighting is not my business.

The days passed, filled with lessons and hard work. When she had been there for forty days, she realized that Midsummer was approaching. Soon she would have been absent from her home for a whole year. No doubt her father and stepmother thought her long dead, and Darren was being forced to take his place as Heir to Falconsward. Poor Darren, how he would hate that! She hoped for her father's sake that little Rael was able to take her place, to learn some of the MacAran gifts,—if Rael was what her father would have called "true AmacAran", perhaps Darren would be allowed to return to the monastery. Or perhaps he would go as she had done, without leave.

A year ago her father had betrothed her to *Dom* Garris. What changes there had been in a year! Romilly knew she had grown taller—she had had to put all the clothes she had worn when she came here, into the box of castoffs, and find others which came nearer to fitting her. Her shoul-

ders were broader, and because of the continuous practice
at swordplay and her work with the horses, her muscles in
upper arms and legs were hard and bulging. How Mallina
would jeer at her, how her stepmother would deplore it—
You do not look like a lady, Romilly. Well, Romilly silently
answered her stepmother's imagined voice, I am not a lady
but a Swordswoman.

But all her troubles disappeared every day when she was
working with the horses, and especially for the hour every
day when she worked with the black stallion. No hand but
hers ever touched him; she knew that one day, this would
be a mount fit for the king himself. Day followed day, and
moon followed moon, and season followed season; winter
closed in, and there were days when she could not work
even with the black stallion, let alone the other horses.
Nevertheless, she directed their care. Time and familiarity
had changed the strange faces in the hostel to friends. Midwinter came, with spicebread, and gifts exchanged in the
hostel among the Sisterhood. A few women had families
and went home to visit them; but when Romilly was asked
if she wished for leave to visit her home, she said steadily
that she had no kin. It was simpler that way. But she wondered; how would her father receive her, if she came home
for a visit, asking nothing, a professional Swordswoman in
her tunic of crimson, and the ensign of the Sisterhood in
her pierced ear: Would he drive her forth, say that she was
no daughter of his, that no daughter of his could be one
of those unsexed women of the Sisterhood? Or would he
welcome her with pride, smile with welcome and even approve of her independence and the strength she had shown
in making a life for herself away from Falconsward?

She did not know. She could not even guess. Perhaps
one day, years from now, she would risk trying to find out.
But in any case she could not travel into the depths of the
Hellers at the midwinter-season; most of the women who
took leave for family visits lived no further away than
Thendara or Hali, which was, perhaps, seven days ride.

In this desert country there were few signs of spring. One
day it was cold, icy winds blowing and rain sweeping across
the plains, and the next day, it seemed, the sun shone hot
and Romilly knew that far away in the Hellers the roads
were flooding with the spring-thaw. When she could work

the horses, she took off her cloak and worked in a shabby, patched tunic and breeches.

With the spring came rumors of armies on the road, of a battle far away between Carolin's forces and the armies of Lyondri Hastur. Later they heard that Carolin had made peace with the Great House of Serrais, and that his armies were gathering again on the plains. Romilly paid little heed. All her days were taken up with the new group of horses brought in to them early in the spring—they had put up a shelter for them and rented a new paddock outside the walls of the hostel, where Romilly went with the women she was training, every afternoon. Her world had shrunk to stables and paddock, and to the plain outside the city where they went, two or three days in every ten, to work and exercise the horses. One afternoon when they left the city and went out through the gates, leading the horses, Romilly saw tents and men and horses, a bewildering crowd.

"What is it?" she asked, and one of the women, who went out every morning to shop for fresh milk and fresh fruits, told her, "It is the advance guard of Carolin's army; they will establish their camp here, and from here they will move down again across the Plains of Valeron, to give battle to King Rakhal—" her face twisted with dislike, and she spat.

"You are a partisan of Carolin, then?" Romilly asked.

"A partisan of Carolin? I am," the woman said vehemently, "Rakhal drove my father from his small-holding in the Venza Hills and gave his lands to a paxman of that greedy devil Lyondri Hastur! Mother died soon after we left our lands, and Father is with Carolin's army—I shall ride out tomorrow, if Clea will give me leave, and try to find my father, and ask if he has word of my brothers, who fled when we were driven from our lands. I am here with the Sisterhood because my brothers were with the armies and could no longer make a home for me; they would have found a man for me to marry, but the man they chose was one Lyondri and his master Rakhal had left in peace, and I would not marry any man who sat snug in his home while my father was exiled!"

"No one could blame you, Marelie," said Romilly. She thought of her travels in the Hellers with Orain and Carlo and the other exiled men; Alaric, who had suffered even more from Lyondri Hastur than Marelie's family. "I too am a follower of Carolin, even though I know nothing about him, except that men whose judgment I trust, call him a good man and a good king."

She wondered if Orain and *Dom* Carlo were in the camp. She might go with Merelie, when she went to seek her father in the camp. Orain had been her friend, even though she was a woman, and she hoped he had come safe through the winter of war.

"Look," said Clea, pointing, "There is the Hastur banner in blue with the silver fir-tree. King Carolin is in the camp—the king himself."

And where Orain is, Carolin is not far away, Romilly remembered. That night in the tavern, when he had wanted her to make a diversion—had that shadowy figure to whom he spoke, been Carolin himself?

Would he welcome a visit from her? Or would he only find it an embarrassment? She decided that when next Jandria visited the hostel—she had been coming and going all year, on courier duty between Serrais and the cities to the south, Dalereuth and Temora—she would ask what Jandria thought.

She should have remembered that when a telepath's mind was drawn unexpectedly to someone she had not seen for a time, it was not likely to be coincidence. It was the next day, when she had finished working with the black stallion, and finally led him back into the stable—after a year of work, he was perfectly trained, and docile as a child, and she had spoken to the housemother of the hostel about, perhaps, presenting him to the king's own self—she saw Jandria at the door of his stall.

"Romy! I was sure I would find you here! He has come a long way from that first day when I saw you bridle him, and we were all sure he would kill you!"

Jandria was dressed as if she had just come from a long journey; dusty boots, dust-mask such as the Drylanders used for travel hanging unfastened at the side of her face. Romilly ran to embrace her.

"Janni! I didn't know you were back!"

"I have not been here long, little sister," Jandria said, returning her hug with enthusiasm. Romilly smoothed back her flying hair with grubby hands, and said, "Let me unsaddle him, and then we will have some time to talk before supper. Isn't he wonderful? I have named him Sunstar—that is how he thinks of himself, he told me."

Jandria said, "He is beautiful indeed. But you should not give the horses such elaborate names, nor treat them with such care—they are to go to soldiers and they should have simple names, easy to remember. And above all you should not grow so fond of them, since they are to be taken from you very soon—they are for the army, though some of them will be ridden by the women of the Sisterhood if they go with Carolin's men when they break camp. You have seen the camp? You know the time is at hand when all these horses are to go to the army. You should not involve yourself so deeply with them."

"I can't help growing fond of them," Romilly said, "It is how I train them; I win their love and trust and they do my will."

Jandria sighed. "We must have that *laran* of yours, and yet I hate to use you like this, child," she said, stroking Romilly's soft hair. "Orain told me, when first he brought you to us, that you have knowledge of sentry-birds. I am to take you to Carolin's camp, so you can show a new handler how to treat them. Go and dress yourself for riding, my dear."

"Dress for riding? What do you think I have been doing all morning?" Romilly demanded.

"But not outside the hostel," Jandria said severely, and suddenly Romilly saw herself through Janni'a eyes, her hair tangled and with bits of straw in it, her loose tunic unfastened because it was hot and sweaty, showing the curve of her breasts. She had put on a patched and too-tight pair of old breeches she had found in the box of castoffs which the Sisterhood kept for working about the house. She flushed and giggled.

"Let me go and change, then, I'll only be a minute or so."

She washed herself quickly at the pump, ran into the room she shared now with Clea and Betta, and combed her tousled hair. Then she got swiftly into her own breeches and a clean under-tunic. Over her head she slipped the crimson tunic of the Sisterhood and belted it with her dagger. Now she looked, she knew, not like a woman in men's clothes, nor yet like a boy, or a street urchin, but like a member of the Sisterhood; a professional Swordswoman, a soldier for Carolin's armies. She could not quite believe it was herself in that formal costume. Yet this was what she was.

Jandria smiled with approval when she came back; Janni too wore the formal Swordswoman tunic of crimson, a sword in her belt, a dagger at her throat, her small ensign gleaming in her left ear. Side by side, the two swordswomen left the gates of the hostel and rode toward the city wall of Serrais.

Chapter 4

Now Romilly had a closer look at the encampment of Carolin's men, the silver and blue fir-tree banner of the Hasturs flying above the central tent which, Romilly imagined, must be either the king's personal quarters or the headquarters of his staff. They rode toward the encampment, past orderly stable-lines, a cookhouse where army cooks were boiling something that smelled savory, and a field roped off, where a Swordswoman Romilly knew only slightly was giving a group of unshaven recruits a lesson in unarmed combat; some of them looked cross and disgruntled and Romilly suspected that they did not like being schooled by a woman; others, rubbing bumps and bruises where she had tossed them handily on the ground, were watching with serious attention.

A guard was posted near the central part of the camp, and he challenged them. Jandria and Apprentice Romilly," she said, "and I seek the Lord Orain, who has sent for me."

Romilly tried to make herself small, supposing that the guard would say something sneering or discourteous, but he merely returned her salute and called a messenger, a boy about Romilly's age, to request Lord Orain's attention.

She would have recognized the tall, gaunt figure, the lean hatchet-jaw, anywhere; but now he was dressed in the elegant Hastur colors and wore a jewelled pendant and a fine sword, and Romilly knew that if she had met him first like this, she would have been too much in awe of him to speak. He bowed formally to the women, and his voice was the schooled accent of a nobleman, with no trace of the rough-country dialect.

"*Mastra'in,* it is courteous of you to come so quickly at my summons," he said, and Jandria replied, just as formally, that it was her pleasure and duty to serve the king's presence.

A little less formally, Orain went on "I remembered that Romilly was schooled in the training, not only of hawks but of sentry-birds. We have a *laranzu* come with us from Tramontana, but he has had no experience with sentry-birds, and these are known to you, *damisela.* Will it please you to introduce the skills of handling them to our *laranzu?*"

"I'd be glad to do it, Lord Orain," she said, then burst out, "but only if you stop calling me *damisela* in that tone!"

A ragged flush spread over Orain's long face. He did not meet her eyes. "I am sorry—Romilly. Will you come this way?"

She trailed Jandria and Orain, who walked arm in arm. Jandria asked, "How's Himself, then?"

Orain shrugged. "All the better for the news you sent ahead, love. But did you see Lyondri face to face?"

Romilly saw the negative motion of the older woman's head. "At the last I was too cowardly; I sent Romilly in my place. If I had met them then—" she broke off. "I do not know if you saw those villages last year, along the old North road. Still blighted, all of them . . ." she shuddered; even at this distance, Romilly could see. "I am glad I am an honest Swordswoman, not a *leronis!* If I had had to have a part in the blighting of the good land, I know not how I could ever again have raised my eyes to the clean day!"

Was this, Romilly wondered, the reason why The Mac-Aran had quarreled with the Towers, why Ruyven had had to run away, and he had driven the *leronis* from his home without giving her leave to test Romilly and Mallina for *laran? Laran* warfare, even the little she had seen of it, was terrifying.

Orain said soberly, "Carolin has said he will not fight that kind of war unless it is used against him. But if Rakhal has *laranzu'in* to bring against his armies, then he must do what he must; you know that as well as I, Janni." He sighed. "You had better come and tell him what you learned in Hali, though the news will make him sorrowful. As for Romilly—" he turned and considered her for a moment, "The bird-handlers' quarters are yonder," he said, pointing. "The bird-master and his apprentice have that tent there, and no doubt you will find them both around behind it. This way, Janni."

Jandria and Orain went off arm-in-arm toward the central tent where the banner flew, and Romilly went on in the indicated direction, feeling shy and afraid. How was she to talk to a strange *laranzu*? Then she straightened her back and drew herself up proudly. She was a MacAran, a Swordswoman, and a hawkmistress; she need not be afraid of anyone. They had summoned her to their aid, not the other way round. Behind the tent she saw a roughly dressed lad of thirteen or so, carrying a great basket, and if she had not seen him she could have smelled him, for it stank of carrion. On heavy perches she saw three familiar, beautiful-ugly forms, and hurried to them, laughing.

"Diligence! Prudence, love!" She held out her hands and the birds made a little dipping of their heads; they knew her again, and the old, familiar rapport reached out, clung. "And where is Temperance? Ah, there you are, you beauty!"

"Don't get too close to them," a somehow-familiar voice said behind her, "Those creatures can peck out your eyes; the apprentice there lost a finger-nail to one of them yesterday!"

She turned and saw a slight, bearded man, in the dark robes not unlike those of a monk at Nevarsin, scowling down at her; then it seemed as if the strange bearded face dissolved, for she knew the voice, and she cried out, incredulous.

"Ruyven! Oh, I should have known, when they said it was a *laranzu* from Tramontana—Ruyven, don't you know me?"

She was laughing and crying at once, and Ruyven stared down at her, his mouth open.

"Romy," he said at last. "Sister, you are the last person in the world I would have expected to see *here*! But—in this garb—" he looked her up and down, blushing behind the strangeness of the beard. "What are you doing? How came you—"

"I was sent to handle the birds, silly," she said, "I bore them all the way from the foothills of the Hellers into Nevarsin, and from Nevarsin to Caer Donn. See, they know me." She gestured, and they made little clucking noises of pleasure and acknowledgement. "But what are you doing here, then?"

"The same as you," he said. "The Lord Orain's son and I are *bredin*; he sent word to me, and I came to join Carolin's army. But you—" he looked at the dress of the Sisterhood with surprise and distaste, "Does Father know you are here? How did you win his consent?"

"The same way you won consent from him to train your *laran* within the walls of Tramontana Tower," she said, grimacing, and he sighed.

"Poor father. He has lost both of us now, and Darren—" he sighed. "Ah, well. Done is done. So you wear the earring of the Sisterhood, and I the robes of the Tower, and both of us follow Carolin—have you seen the king?"

She shook her head. "No, but I travelled for a time with his followers, Orain and *Dom* Carlo of Blue Lake."

"Carlo I know not. But you handle sentry-birds? I remember you had always a deft hand with horses and hounds, and I suppose hawks as well, so the MacAran Gift should fit you to handle these. Have you had *laran* training then, Sister?"

"None; I developed it by working with the beasts and the birds," she said, and he shook his head, distressed.

"*Laran* untrained is a dangerous thing, Romy. When this is ended, I will find a place for you in a Tower. Do you realize, you have not yet greeted me properly." He hugged her and kissed her cheek. "So; you know these birds? So far I have seen none but Lord Orain who could handle them. . . ."

"I taught him what he knows of sentry-birds," Romilly said, and went to the perches, holding out her hand; with her free hand she jerked the knot loose, and Prudence made a quick little hop to sit on her wrist. She should have brought a proper glove. Well, somewhere in Carolin's camp there must be a proper falconer's glove.

And that made her think, with sudden pain, of Preciosa. She had had no sight of the hawk since they came into this drylands country. But then, Preciosa had left her before they came to the glaciers, and rejoined her again when she had returned to the green hills. It might be that Preciosa would return to her, some day . . .

. . . and if not, she is free . . . a free wild thing, belonging to the winds of the sky and to herself. . . .

"Can you get me a glove?" she asked, "I can, if I must, handle Prudence with my bare hands, because she is small and gentle, but the others are heavier and have not such a delicate touch—"

"That creature, delicate?" Ruyven said, laughing, then the smile slid off as he saw how serious she was. "Prudence, you call her? Yes, I will send my helper for a glove for you, and then you must tell me their names and how you tell them apart."

The morning passed quickly, but they spoke only of the birds; not touching at all on their shared past, or on Falconsward. At midday a bell was rung, and Ruyven, saying that it was dinnertime in the army mess, told her to come along.

"There are others of the Sisterhood in the camp," he said, "They sleep in their hostel in the city—but I dare say you know more about them than I. You can eat at their table, if you will—and I suppose it would be better, since they do not mix with the regular soldiers except when they must, and you cannot explain to the whole army that you are my sister."

She joined the long lines of the army mess, taking her bread and stew to the separate table with the seven or eight women of the Sisterhood who were employed with the army—mostly as couriers, or as trainers of horses or instructors in unarmed combat—one, in fact, as an instructor in swordplay. Some of the women she had met in the hostel and none of them seemed even slightly surprised to see her there. Jandria did not appear. Romilly supposed that she had been kept with Lord Orain and the higher officers, who evidently had their mess apart.

"What are you doing?" one asked her, and she replied briefly that she had been sent for to work with sentry-birds.

"I thought that was work for *leronyn*," one of the women remarked, "But then you have red hair, are you too *laran*-gifted?"

"I have a knack for working with animals," Romilly said, "I do not know if it is *laran* or something else." She did not want to be treated with the distant awe with which they regarded the *leroni*. When she had finished her meal she rejoined Ruyven at the bird-handlers' quarters, and by the end of the day he was handling the birds as freely as she did herself.

Dusk was falling, and they were settling the birds on their perches, to be carried in under the tent-roof, when Ruyven looked up.

"King Carolin's right-hand man," he said briefly, "We see Carolin's self but seldom; word comes always through Lord Orain. You know him, I understand."

"I travelled with him for months; but they thought me a boy," Romilly said, without explaining. Orain came to them and said to Ruyven, ignoring Romilly, "How soon will the birds be ready for use?"

"A tenday, perhaps."

"And Derek has not yet arrived," said Orain, scowling. "Do you think you could persuade the *leronis* . . ."

Ruyven said curtly, "The battlefield is no place for the Lady Maura. Add to that, Lyondri is of her kin; she said she would handle the birds but she made me promise to her that she would not be asked to fight against him. I blame her not; this war that sets brother against brother, father against son, is no place for a woman."

Orain said, with his dry smile, "Nor for a man; yet the world will go as it will, and not as you or I would have it. This war was not of my making, nor of Carolin's. Nevertheless, I respect the sentiments of the Lady Maura, so we must have another to fly the sentry-birds. Romilly—" he looked down at her, and for a moment there was a trace of the old warmth in his voice, "Will you fly them for Carolin, then, my girl?"

So when he wants something from me, he can be halfway civil, even to a woman? Anger made her voice cold. She said, "As for that, *vai dom,* you must ask my superiors in the Sisterhood; I am apprentice, and my will does not rule what I may do."

"Oh, I think Jandria will not make trouble about that," Orain said, smiling. "The Sisterhood will lend you to us, I have no doubt at all."

Romilly bowed without answering. But she thought, *not if I have anything to say about it.*

They rode back to the hostel in the light of the setting sun, the sky clear and cloudless; Romilly had never ceased to miss the evening rain or sleet in the hills. It still seemed to her that the country here was dry, parched, inhospitable. Jandria tried to talk a little of the army, of the countryside, to point out to Romilly the Great House of Serrais, perched on the low hillside, where the Hastur-kind had established their seat, as at Thendara and Hali and Aldaran and Carcosa in the hills; but Romilly was silent, hardly speaking, lost in thought.

Ruyven is no longer the brother I knew; we can be friendly now but the old closeness is gone forever. I had hoped he would understand me, the conflicts that drove me from Falconsward—they are like his own. Once he could see me simply as Romilly, not as his little sister. Now—now all he sees is that I have become a Swordswoman, hawkmistress . . . no more than that.

Even when I lost Falconsward, father, mother, home—I thought that when I again met with Ruyven we would be as we were when we were children. Now Ruyven too is forever gone from me.

I have nothing now; a hawk and my skills with the sword and with the beasts. They reached the hostel, where supper was long over, but one of the women found them something in the kitchens. They went to their beds in silence: Jandria, too, was wrapped in thoughts which, Romilly thought, must be as bitter as her own.

Damn this warfare! Yes, that is what Ruyven said, and Orain too. It may be that father was right . . . what does it matter which great rogue sits on the throne or which greater rogue seeks to wrest it from him?

Every day, Romilly worked first with the other horses, who were simpler to handle because they were less intelligent; they seemed to have less initiative. Sunstar she saved as a reward for herself at the end of a long morning of working with the other horses, directing her assistants in exercising them and personally supervising their gaits and the speed with which they had been broken to saddle and riding gear. She knew that she was only one of the army horsetrainers in Serrais who had been engaged by Carolin to produce the cavalry for his armies—she saw some of the others, sometimes, come out from the city of Serrais and working on the plains. But she would have been a fool not to know that her horses were trained fastest and best.

Now, at the near end of a long morning, she walked around her little domain, with a pat and a touch on the nose and a long, blissful moment of emotional rapport with each of her horses. She loved every one, she felt the bitter-sweet knowledge that soon she would have to part with them; but every one of them would carry some of herself wherever Carolin's armies might ride. Touch after touch, a hug around a sleek neck or a stroking of a velvety nose, and each moment of rapport building her awareness higher, higher yet, till she was dizzied with it, with the sense of racing in the sun, the awareness of running at full stretch on four legs, not two, the mastery of the burden of the rider with its own delight, and somewhere at the back of her mind Romilly felt as if each of these beasts bearing its rider knew something of the inward rightness of the Bearer of Burdens who, said in the writings of the sainted Valentine, bore alone the weight of the world. She *was* each horse in turn, knowing its rebellions, its discipline and sub-mission, the sense of working in perfect unity with what was allotted to it.

Blurrily, she thought, *perhaps only horses know what true faith may be as they share with the Bearer of Burdens . . . and yet I, only human, have been chosen to share and to know this. . . .* it was easier to be carried away in union and rapport with the horses than with hawks or even the more brilliant sentry-birds, because, she thought, horses had a keener intelligence. The birds, sensitive as they were, blissful as it was to share the ecstasy of flight, still had only limited awareness, mostly focused in their keener eyesight. The sensual awareness was greater in the horses because they were more organized, more intelligent, a human *style* of awareness and yet not quite human.

And now at the end of her morning, when the other horses had been led away, she brought out Sunstar from his place. He worked so closely with her now that a bare word summoned him, and a part of her flooded out in love, she *was* the horse, she felt the saddle slipped over her own back as she caressed the leather straps of it, she was in a strange doubled consciousness.

She did not know whether she climbed into the saddle

or accepted the grateful weight on her own back. Part of her was sunk joyously into her own body awareness, but that was all swallowed up in the larger consciousness of striding free, racing with the wind . . . so balanced, so fused into the horse that for a long time she was hardly aware of which was herself, which Sunstar. Yet for all the blurring she felt she had never been so precisely and wholly herself, flooded with a kind of reality she had never known. The heat of the sun, sweat streaming down her flanks, her exquisite leaning to balance from above the weight she felt from below, from *within*. Time seemed divided into infinitesimal fragments, to each of which she gave its true weight, with no thought of past or future, all gathered up into the absolute present.

And, then, regretfully, she came back and separated herself from Sunstar, sliding down at the paddock rail, falling against him and flinging against him and flinging her arms around his glossy neck in an absolute ecstasy of love, wholly giving, wholly aware. It needed no words. She was his; he was hers; even if they never again knew this ecstasy of consummation, this delicious flooding delight, if she never mounted him again nor he raced with her toward an endless plain of oblivious pleasure, they would always, in some part of their being, be fused together; this moment was eternal and would go on happening forever.

And then, with faint regret—but only faint, for in her exalted state she knew that all things had their proper moment and this one could not be prolonged too far—she let herself slide down another level of awareness and she was Romilly again, giving the horse's silken shoulders a final pat of love and leading him, separate now but never far, to his own paddock. She could hardly feel her feet beneath her as she walked back toward the hostel, but she felt distinct annoyance at Clea's friendly voice.

"How beautiful he is—is that is the black stallion they told me about? Is he too fierce, will they have to turn him out to stud again?" Then alerted by something in Romilly's face, she asked, "You—you've been riding him?"

"He is gentle as a child," said Romilly absently. "He loves me, but a child could ride him now." Absurdly, she wished she could give this beautiful creature over to Caryl, who would surely love him as she did, for he had

more than a trace of her own kind of *laran*. Since she
could not keep this imperial creature herself, it would be
finest if he could go to that sensitive boy. Who was, she
reminded herself with a sharp coming-down-to-earth, the
son of Lyondri Hastur and her sworn enemy. "What did
you want, Clea?"

"I was coming to speak to you about your unarmed-
combat lesson," the other woman said, "but on the way I
met with Jandria, who says that you have been sent for
again to the king's camp; you are to work with sentry-birds,
I hear. You are to take all your things; you will not be
coming back here, I understand."

Not coming back? Then she must say farewell to Sunstar
even sooner than she had believed. But in her aware state
she knew it really did not matter. They would always be
part of one another. For now she was to be mistress of
hawks to Carolin's armies—she did not stop to think how
she knew that—and she, like Sunstar, must carry her appointed share of the world's weight. She said, "Thank you,
Clea. And thank you for everything, all you have taught
me—"

"Romy, how your eyes shine! It has been a pleasure to
teach you; it is always a pleasure to teach anyone who is
so apt and quick to learn," Clea said, and hugged her with
spontaneous warmth. "I am sorry to lose you. I hope you
come back to our hostel some day, but if not, we will meet
at another. Swordswomen are always travelling and we are
sure to come across one another somewhere on the roads
of the Hundred Kingdoms."

Romilly kissed her with real warmth and went into the
hostel to pack her few possessions.

By the time she was finished, she found Jandria in the
hallway ready to ride, she too bearing a rolled pack with
all her possessions.

"I had Sunstar brought out," Jandria said, "The other
horses are being brought along later in the day; but you
have spent so much time, and so much love, on this one,
that I thought you should have the privilege of handing
him over yourself to King Carolin."

*So it has come quicker than I thought. But after this morn-
ing, Sunstar and I will always be one.*

He did not take kindly to the leading rein; Romilly wished that she could ride him herself, but that was not suitable for a horse to be presented to the king. She soothed him in soft words with her voice, and even more, with the outreaching of contact, so that, guided by her soothing flood of tenderness and reassurance, he came along, docile, feeling her concern and her touch guiding him.

You are to be a king's mount, did you know that, my beauty?

The contact between them needed no words; it meant nothing to Sunstar, who knew nothing of kings, and Romilly knew that while he might, and probably would, come to love and trust Carolin, no other would ever ride Sunstar with that same sense of close oneness with the horse. Suddenly she felt sorry for Carolin. The beautiful black stallion might be his. But she, Romilly, would always own him in both their hearts.

Chapter 5

There was a subtly different feel to the army camp today. The great central tent where the Hastur banner had flown was being pulled down by what looked like a horde of workmen, there was confusion coming and going through the length and breadth of the camp. Leaving Sunstar with Jandria and the others who had come to help her with the stallion, Romilly hurried off to the bird-handlers quarters. She found Ruyven there, fussing with the perches installed for the sentry-birds atop pack-animals. The chervines, disliking the carrion smell that clung to the birds, were stamping restlessly and moving around with little, troubled snorts and pawings.

"I imagine," Romilly said, "that this all means that the army is about to move southward and I am to go with you."

He nodded. "I cannot handle or fly three birds alone," he said, "and there is not another qualified handler for these sentry-birds within a hundred leagues, except, God help us, for the ones who may be among Rakhal's scouts or advance guard. We have had intelligence from Hali that Rakhal is massing his own armies under Lyondri Hastur, and if he moves as we think—and that will depend to some degree upon how well you and I use the eyes of our birds—we will meet him near Neskaya in the Kilghard Hills. In fact, Lord Orain has asked if we can fly the birds out today and see what we can spy out."

"And, of course, when Orain speaks, all the army jumps to attention," said Romilly dryly. Ruyven stared at her.

"What is the matter with you, Romy? Lord Orain is a

good and kindly man, and Carolin's chief adviser and friend! Do you dislike him? And with what reason?"

That recalled Romilly to herself. It was only wounded vanity; while he thought her a boy, Orain had admired her and trusted her, and when he knew her a woman, all that went into discard and she was just another nonentity, another woman, perhaps a danger to him. But that was Orain's problem and not hers; she had done nothing to deserve being ruthlessly cast out of his affections like that.

And he is the loser by it. Not I.

She said steadily, "I value Orain's gifts better than you know; I travelled with him and worked close to him for many moons. I do not think he should look down on me simply because I am a woman; I have shown I can do my work as well and skillfully as any man."

"No one doubts that, Romy," said Ruyven, in a note so conciliating that Romilly wondered how much of her hidden anger had actually shown in her face, "But Orain loves not women, and he has not had Tower teachings—we know in Tramontana that women's strengths and men's are not so different, after all. We are the first Tower who experimented with a woman for Keeper in one of our circles, and she is as skillful with the work as any man, even a Hastur. I think you, too, could benefit by such training."

"I used to think so," said Romilly, "But now I know what my *laran* is and my Gift. Father too must have some of this Gift, or he could not train horses as he does, and now I know how well I have inherited it."

"I would not be too quick to decide against Tower training," said Ruyven, "I too thought I had mastered my *laran* even in Nevarsin, but I discovered that while I kept all at bay on the front lines of the war with self, I had left undefended fortresses at my back, and through these I was almost conquered."

Romilly made an impatient gesture; the symbolism of the warrior struck her as far-fetched and unnecessary. "If we are to take the birds out and fly them, let us be about it, then. After all, if Lord Orain has given orders, Carolin's chief adviser cannot be kept waiting."

Ruyven seemed about to protest the sarcasm, but he sighed and was still. In his black robe he looked very much like a monk, and his narrow face had the detached, impas-

sive look she associated with the Nevarsin brothers. "They
will come for us when they want us. Will you make sure
that Temperance's jesses are not too tight? I was afraid
they were tearing an old scar on her leg, and Orain said
that before you came to them, she had suffered some damage. I think your eyes are keener than mine."

Romilly went to examine the bird's leg, soothing Temperance with her ready thoughts. She found no serious
trouble, but she did shift the location of the jesses around
the bird's leg; the old scar did indeed look red and raw.
She sponged it with a solution of *karalla* powder as a precaution, then turned the three hoods inside out and dusted
them lightly inside with the same powder as a preventive
against any dampness or infection, or the tiny parasites
which sometimes got on birds and caused trouble at
molting.

Ruyven said at last, "I am sorry to use my talents this
way, at war, when I would rather stay peacefully in the
Tower and work for our own people in the hills. But otherwise, all the Kingdoms may fall, one by one, to the tyranny of Lyondri Hastur and that wretch Rakhal, who has
neither honor nor *laran* nor any sense of justice, but only
a vicious will to power. Carolin, at least, is an honorable
man."

"You say so and Orain says so. I have never seen him."

"Well, you shall see him now," said Orain, standing at
the back of the enclosure; he had evidently heard the
exchange. "Jandria told me of your hostel's gift to the
king, and she thought it only right, Mistress Romilly, that
you should present it with your own hands, so come
with me."

Romilly glanced at Ruyven, who said, "I will come too,"
and, replacing his glove, came after them.

*Why is Ruyven the king's hawkmaster and I regarded only
as his helper? I am a professional Swordswoman and it is I
who have the greater skill. Ruyven would rather be in his
Tower, and this work is life to me. He says himself that in
the Tower women are allowed to hold high offices, yet it
never seems to occur to him that I, his little sister, should be
treated with that kind of fairness. Carolin's armies, then, are
ruled by the old notion that a man must always do any work
better than the most skilled of women?*

But her rebellious thoughts were interrupted by the sight of Jandria, who stood holding Sunstar by the reins. He was saddled and bridled, and as he raised his silken nose and whickered softly in recognition of Romilly, she reached out again to touch the horse's mind in greeting and love.

Jandria said, "It is an honor to the Sisterhood that we can make this splendid gift to the king, and for their sake I thank you."

"I am the one who is honored," Romilly answered in a low voice, "It has been a pleasure to work with Sunstar."

"There he is, with Lord Orain," said Jandria, and Romilly saw Orain, dressed for riding, next to a hooded and cloaked man who was walking toward them. She gripped Sunstar's reins in excitement.

"High-lord, you lend us grace," Jandria began with a deep bow. "The Sisterhood of the Sword is honored and pleased to present you with this magnificent horse, trained by our finest horse-woman, Romilly."

She did not raise her eyes to the king's, though she was conscious of Orain's glance. She said, looking only at the horse's sleek nose, "His name is Sunstar, Your Majesty, and he is trained to all paces and gaits. He will carry you for love; he has never felt whip or spur."

"If you had his training, Mistress Romilly, I know he is well trained," said a familiar voice, and she looked up at the hooded form of the king, to look into the eyes of *Dom* Carlo of Blue Lake. He smiled at her surprise. "I am sorry to have the advantage of you, Mistress MacAran; I knew who you were long ago. . . ." and she remembered the moment when she had felt the touch of his *laran*.

"I wish you had told *me, vai dom*," said Orain, "I had no notion she was a girl and I made a precious fool of myself!"

Dom Carlo—*no*, Romilly reminded herself, *King Carolin, Hastur of Hastur, Lord of Thendara and Hali*—looked at Orain with open, warm affection. He said, "You see only what you want to see, *bredu*," and patted Orain's shoulder. He said to Romilly, "I thank you, and the Sisterhood, for this magnificent gift, and for your loyalty to me. Both are precious to me, believe me. And I have heard, too, that you are to continue with your handling of the sentry-birds whose lives you saved when we met with you on the trail to Nevarsin. I shall not forget, my—" he hesitated a moment, smiled and said, "Swordswoman. Thank you—thank you all."

Romilly touched Sunstar again, a loving and final gesture of leave-taking. "Serve him well," she whispered, "Carry him faithfully, love him as I—as I love you." She moved away from the animal, watching as the king gathered up the reins and mounted.

He has some touch of that gift. I remember well. Sunstar, then, does not go to a brutal or insensitive man, but to one who will reckon him at his true worth.

Still she was troubled. *Dom* Carlo had known she was a girl and had not betrayed her among the men; but he might have spared her humiliation at Orain's hands, too, by warning his friend. But then, remembering to be fair, she told herself that he might have had no notion of her feelings for Orain, and he certainly could never have guessed that she would throw herself at Orain's head—or into his bed—in that way.

Well, it did not matter; done was done. Ruyven came toward her and she presented him to Jandria.

"My brother Ruyven; the Lady Jandria."

"Swordswoman Jandria," corrected the older woman, laughing. "I have told you; rank we leave behind us when we take the sword. And your brother is—"

"Ruyven MacAran," he told her, "Fourth in Tramontana, Second Circle. Have you finished with my sister, *domna*?" Romilly noted that, as if automatically, he called Jandria by the formal title given an equal or superior, *domna*—Lady—rather than the simpler *mestra* which he would have used to a social inferior.

"She is free to go," Jandria said, and Romilly, frowning, followed Ruyven.

She had hoped that some time that day it would seem natural to speak to Ruyven of her departure from Falconsward. She had intended, then—how long ago it seemed!—to seek the Tower where he had taken refuge. Somehow she had expected that he would welcome her there. But this quiet, monkish stranger seemed to bear no relation whatever to the brother who had been so close to her in childhood. She could not imagine confiding in him.

She felt closer now to Jandria, or even to Orain, stranger that he had now become!

She looked back briefly at Sunstar, pacing along at a stately gait with *Dom* Carlo—no, she must remember, King Carolin—in the saddle. A brief mental touch renewed the old communication, and she felt herself smile.

I am closer to that horse than to anything human; closer than I have ever been to anything human.

When they had done for the day, Jandria came for her.

"At the edge of the camp, there is a tent where the Swordswomen who follow Carolin are to sleep," she said. "Come with me, Romilly, and I will show you."

"I should sleep here with the birds," Romilly said with a shrug, "No hawkmaster goes out of earshot of his trained birds—I will roll myself in my cloak, I need no tent."

"But you cannot sleep among the men," said Jandria, "it is not even to be thought of."

"The king's hawkmaster is my own brother born," said Romilly, impatient now, "Are you saying that he is likely to be any damage to my virtue? Surely the presence of my older brother is protection enough!"

Jandria said with a touch of sharpness, "You know the rules for Swordswomen outside their hostels! We cannot tell everyone in the army that he is your brother, and if it becomes known that an oath-bound Swordswoman has slept alone in the tent with a man."

"Their minds must be like the sewers of Thendara," aid Romilly angrily. "I am to leave my birds because of the dirty minds of some soldiers I do not even know?"

"I am sorry, I did not make the rules and I cannot unmake them," said Jandria, "but you are sworn to obey them."

Fuming with wrath, Romilly went along with Jandria to supper and to bed in the tent allotted to the dozen women of the Sisterhood who were assigned to Carolin's army. She found Clea there, along with a strange woman from another hostel; the two were to train Carolin's men in close-quarters unarmed combat. The others were not well known to Romilly; they were among the women who had been quartered in the hostel but did not really belong to it. They were horsehandlers, quartermasters and supply

clerks, and one, a short, sturdy, dark woman who spoke
with the familiar mountain accent of the Hellers, was a
blacksmith, with arms like whipcord, and great swelling
muscles across back and shoulders that made her look almost like a man.

*I cannot believe that one's virtue would be in danger if she
slept naked among a hundred strange soldiers—she looks as
if she could protect herself, as the Hali'imyn here say, against
all the smiths in Zandru's forges!*

And then she thought, resentfully, that she had been
more free when she travelled in men's clothes through the
Hellers with Orain and Carlo—*Carolin*—and their little
band of exiles. She had worked along with the men, had
walked alone in the city, drunk in taverns. Now her movements were restrained to what the rules of the Sisterhood
thought suitable to avoid trouble or gossip. Even as a free
Swordswoman, she was not free.

Still grumbling a little, she made ready for bed. It struck
her again; even these free women, how petty their lives
seemed! Jandria she loved, and she could speak freely with
Jandria without stopping to censor her thoughts; but even
Jandria was trammeled by the question of, what would the
men in the army think, if the Swordswoman were not
bound by their rules to be as proper and ladylike as any
marriageable maiden in the Hellers? Clea, too, she respected and genuinely liked, but still she had few friends
in the Sisterhood. *Yet when I came among them, I though
I had found, at last, freedom to be myself and still let it be
known that I was a woman, not the pretense of male
disguise.*

*I do not want to be a man among men, and hide what I
am. But I do not care much for the society of women—not
even Swordswomen—either. Why can I never be contented,
wherever I am?*

Nevertheless, at last she was doing work for which she
was fitted, and if any man offered her any insult she need
not fear him as she had feared Rory. And the king himself
had complimented her work with horses. Before she
climbed into her bedroll, she reached out drowsily, as she
had done every night of her year in the hostel, and sought
for Sunstar's touch. Yes, he was there, and content. King
Carolin would be good to him, certainly, would appreciate

his intelligence, his wondrous speed, his beauty. She reached out again, a little further, seeking for the sentry-birds on their perches. Yes, all was well with them, too, and if it was not, Ruyven at least slept near them as a proper hawkmaster should. Sighing, Romilly slept.

She had returned to the bird-handlers's tent the next morning, and with Ruyven's young apprentice, a boy of fourteen or so called Garen, they set about feeding the birds. As she was examining the bandaged spot on Temperance's leg, she sensed a stranger's presence, and in the next moment, confirming it, the birds set up the high shrilling sound they had to indicate uneasiness in the presence of a stranger.

It was a young officer, in a green-gold cape; his hair was a light strawberry-blonde, his face narrow and sensitive.

"You are the hawkmaster?"

"Do I look like it?" Romilly snapped, "Swordswoman Romilly, *para servirte.* Carolin's hawkmistress."

"Forgive me, *mestra,* I meant no insult. I am Ranald Ridenow, and I came to give orders from His Majesty; I am to lead the detachment which will move ahead of the main army this morning." His voice was crisp, but without arrogance, and he smiled a little nervously. "I was also to seek my kinswoman, *Domna* Maura Elhalyn." He had to raise his voice over the shrilling noise the sentry-birds were making.

"As you can see, the lady is not in my pocket," said Romilly tartly, "Nor, as far as I know, abed with my brother, but you can ask him. Now, *Dom* Ranald, if you would kindly move away from the birds, since they will keep up this god-forgotten noise until you are out of their sight. . . ."

He did not move. "Your brother, *mestra*? Where will I find him?" He managed to sound anxious even while he was yelling to make himself heard over the noise of the nervous birds, and Romilly came and physically shoved him out of range. The sound slowly quieted to soft churring noises, then silence.

She said, "Now that we can hear ourselves think, I know nothing about your kinswoman, though my brother, the hawkmaster, spoke of a Lady Maura, now I come to think of it. I will go and—no, I need not, for here he is."

"Romy? I heard the birds—is someone bothering them?" Ruyven suddenly sighted the Ridenow officer.

"*Su serva, Dom* . . . may I help you?"

"Lady Maura—"

"The lady sleeps in that tent yonder," said Ruyven, indicating a small pavilion nearby.

"Alone? Among the soldiers?" Ranald Ridenow's nostrils narrowed in distaste, and Ruyven smiled.

"Sir, the lady is better chaperoned by these birds than by a whole school of lady-companions and governesses," he said, "for you yourself have heard that any stranger coming near will rouse them, and if I heard them aroused, I would come to her aid, and could rouse the camp if there was danger."

Ranald Ridenow looked at the young man in the ascetic dark robe, and nodded with approval. "Are you a *cristoforo* monk?"

"I have not that grace, sir. I am Ruyven MacAran, Fourth in Tramontana, Second circle," he said, and the young officer in the green and gold cloak acknowledged him with another nod.

"Then my cousin is safe in your hands, *laranzu*. Forgive my question. Do you know if the lady is yet awake?"

"I was about to awaken her, sir, as she asked, or better, send my sister to do so," said Ruyven. "Romy, will you tell Lady Maura that a kinsman seeks her?"

"It is not urgent, not at this moment," said the Ridenow lord, "But if you could awaken her, Carolin has sent orders that we are to ride as soon as possible. I have orders—"

"I will need no more than thirty minutes to be ready," said Ruyven, "Romy, you are ready for riding? Awaken the Lady Maura that a kinsman seeks her?"

His offhand assumption of authority nettled Romilly; so, for this arrogant lowland lordlet, she was to become errand-girl to some plains lady? "It's not that easy," she snapped, "the birds must be fed, and I'm nae servant to the lady; if ye' want her fetched and carried for, me lord, ye' can even do it yerself." She realized with horror that her strong mountain accent was back in her speech when her year in the plains had almost smoothed it away. Well, she was a mountain girl, let him make of it what he wanted. She was a swordswoman and no lowlander to bow and scrape before the *Hali'imyn*! Ruyven looked scandalized, but before he could speak a soft voice said;

"Well spoken, Swordswoman; I, even as you, am servant to Carolin and to his birds." A young woman stood at the door of the small tent, covered from neck to ankle in a thick night-gown, her flame-red hair loose and curling halfway to her waist. "I did not have the pleasure of meeting you yesterday, Swordswoman; so you are our bird-handler?" She bowed slightly to Ranald. "I thank you for your concern, cousin, but I need nothing, unless Carolin has summoned me—no? Then, unless you wish to lace up my gown for me as you used to do when you were nine years old, you may tell Carolin that we will be ready to ride within the hour, as soon as the birds are properly fed and tended. I will meet you in good time, kinsman." She nodded in dismissal, and as he turned away, she laughed gaily.

"So you are Romy?" she said, "Ruyven spoke to me of you on the way here, but we had no idea you would be our handler. Perhaps while we are on the road, you can get leave from your Swordswoman company to share my tent, so that we can both be near the birds at night? I am Maura Elhalyn, *leronis,* monitor in Tramontana to the Third Circle, and my mother was a Ridenow, so that I have some of the Serrais Gift . . . do you know that *laran*?"

Romilly said, "I do not. I know little of *laran*—"

"Yet you must have it, if you can handle sentry-birds," Lady Maura said, "for they can be handled only with *laran;* they are almost impossible to work with otherwise. You have the old MacAran Gift, then? In which Tower were you trained, *mestra*? And who is your Keeper?"

Romilly shook her head silently. She said, "I have never been in a Tower, *domna*."

She looked surprised, but her manners were too good to show it. She said, "If you will excuse me for five minutes, I will go and put on my gown—I was only teasing my cousin Ranald, I can perfectly well dress myself—and I will do my part in tending the birds, as I should do; I had no intention of leaving all their care to you, Swordswoman."

She went quickly to the tent, her fingers already busy at the fastenings of her night-gown, and pushed it shut behind her. Romilly went to examine the bandages of Temper-

ance's leg, seeing with approval that the sore spot was
smooth and not at all festered. While Ruyven went to tend
Diligence she said, with a frown, "Are we to have this lady
to rule over us, then?"

Ruyven said, "The *leronis* knows better than that, Romilly. She is not familiar with sentry-birds, so she told me;
yet you noted that they did not scream at her approach
either. She helped to care for them on the trip from the
mountains—surely you did not think I handled three
birds alone?"

"Why not?" Romilly asked, "I did." Yet Maura's frank
friendliness had disarmed her. "What is this Serrais *laran*
of which she spoke?"

"I know very little about it," said Ruyven, "even in the
Towers it is not common. The folk of Serrais were noted,
in the days of the breeding-program among the Great
Houses of the Hastur kinfolk, because they had bred for a
laran which could communicate with those who are not
human . . . with the trailfolk, perhaps, or the catmen, or . . .
others beyond them, summoned from other dimensions by
their starstones. If they can do that, communicating with
sentry-birds should be no such trouble. She said to me once
that it was akin to the MacAran Gift, perhaps had been
bred from it."

"You knew her well in the Tower?" Romilly asked with
a trace of jealousy, but he shook his head.

"I am a *cristoforo*. And she is a pledged virgin. Only
such a one would come among soldiers with no more fuss
or awareness than that."

He might have said more, but Lady Maura came from
her tent, dressed in a simple gown, her sleeves rolled back.
Without a moment's hesitation she took the smelly basket
of bird-food and took a handful, without any sign of distaste, holding it out to Prudence, crooning to the bird.

"There you are, pretty, there is your breakfast—speaking
of which, Romilly, have you breakfasted? No, you have
not, like a good handler, you see to your beasts first, do
you not? We need not exercise them, they will have exercise enough and more today. Ruyven, if you will send an
orderly to the mess, we should have breakfast brought to
us here, if we are to ride as soon as all that." As she spoke,
she was feeding the bird tidbits of carrion, smiling to it as

if they were fragrant flowers, and Prudence churred with pleasure.

Well, she is not squeamish, she does not mind getting her hands dirty.

Ruyven picked up the thought and said in an undertone, "I told you so. In Tramontana she flies a *verrin* hawk and trained it herself. To the great dismay, I might add, of Lady Liriel Hastur, who is highest in rank there, and of her Keeper, Lord Doran; who both love hawking but would rather leave their training to the professional falconer."

"So she is not some soft-handed lady who wishes to be waited on hand and foot," Romilly said, grudgingly approving. Then she went to finish her work with Temperance, and when she had done, an orderly had brought food and small-beer from the mess, and they sat on the ground and breakfasted, Lady Maura, with no fuss, tucking her skirt under her and eating with her fingers as they did.

When they had finished, Ranald Ridenow appeared with half a dozen men, and the three of them loaded the sentry-birds on to blocks on their horses; the little detachment moved through the just-wakening camp, and took the road east across the desert lands toward the Plains of Valeron.

The Ridenow lord set a hard peace, though Romilly and Ruyven and the soldiers had no trouble keeping up with them. Lady Maura was riding on a lady's saddle, but she did not complain and managed to keep up. Although she did say to Romilly, at one stop to breathe the horses, "I wish I could wear breeches as you do, Swordswoman. But I have already scandalized my friends and my own Keeper, and I should probably not give them more cause for talk."

"Ruyven told me you trained a *verrin* hawk," Romilly said.

"So I did; how angry everyone was," Maura said, laughing, "but now, knowing you, Swordswoman, I know I am not the first nor yet the last woman to do so. And I would rather have her trained to my own hand than to a strange falconer's and then try to transfer her loyalty to me. Sometimes I have actually felt that I *am* flying with the bird; though perhaps it is my imagination—"

"And perhaps not," Romilly said, "for I have had that experience." Suddenly, and with poignant grief, she remembered Preciosa. It had been more than a year that she had dwelt in that damned desert town, and Preciosa had no doubt gone back to the wilds to live, and forgotten her.

Yet, even if I see her no more in life, the moments of closeness we have known are part of me now as then, and there is no such thing as future or past. . . . For a moment her head swam, and she confused the moment of ecstasy with Preciosa's flight with that all-consuming moment in which she had ridden Sunstar, joined absolutely with the horse, she flew, she raced, she was one with sky and earth and stars. . . .

"Swordswoman—?" Lady Maura was looking at her, troubled, and Romilly swiftly jerked her awareness back to the moment. She said the first thing that came into her head.

"My name is Romilly, and if we are to work together you need not say *Swordswoman,* so formally, every time . . ."

"Romilly," Maura said with a smile, "and I am Maura; in the Tower we do not think of rank separating friends, and if you are a friend to these birds I am your friend too."

Then the Towers have something in common with the Sisterhood, she thought, but then Ranald called the men together and they rose to ride again. She wondered why they were going so far ahead of the main army.

All day they rode, and at night made camp; the men and Ruyven slept under the stars, but there was a little tent for Lady Maura, and she insisted that Romilly must share it. They were tired from riding at a hard pace all day, but before they slept, Lady Maura asked quietly, "Why did you never go to a Tower for training, Romilly? Surely you have *laran* enough—"

"If you know Ruyven, and how he had to come there," said Romilly, "then you will know already why I did not."

"Yet you left your home, and quarreled with your kin," said Maura, quietly insistent, "After that, I should think you would have come at once—"

And so I had intended, Romilly thought. *But I made my way on my own, and now have no need of the training the* leronis *told me I must have. I know more of my own* laran *than any stranger.* She fell into a stubborn silence, and Lady Maura forbore to question her further.

Two days they rode, and they came out of the desert land and into green country; Romilly breathed a sigh of relief when they were able to see hills in the distance, and

the evening breath of cool rain. It was high summer, but
at this season frost lay on the ground at morning, and she
was glad of her fur cloak at night. On the third day, as the
road led over a high hill which commanded a view for many
leagues around, Ranald Ridenow drew them to a halt.

"This will be the right place," he said, "Are you ready
with the birds?"

Maura evidently knew what was wanted, for she nodded,
and asked, "Who will you link with? Orain?"

"Carolin himself," said the Ridenow lord quietly. "Orain
is not head-blind, but has not *laran* enough for this. And
they are his troops."

Maura was blinking rapidly and looked as if she was
about to cry. She said in an undertone, more to herself
than Romilly, "I like this not at all, spying upon Rakhal's
movements. I—I swore not to fight against him. But Lyondri has brought all this upon himself, for he too is oath-
foresworn! After what he has done . . . kinsman or no . . ."
and she broke off, pressing her lips tight together and saying, "Romy, will you fly first?"

"But I know not what to do," Romilly said.

"Yet you are hawkmistress . . ."

"I know the sentry-birds habits, diet and health," said
Romilly, "I have not been schooled to their use in warfare.
I do not know—"

Maura looked startled, but quickly covered it, and Romilly was amazed; *she is being polite to me?* She said quietly,
"You need only fly the bird and remain in rapport with
her, seeing what she sees through her eyes. Ranald will
make the link with you and so relay what you have seen
to Carolin, so that he can spy out the land ahead and know
what are Rakhal's movements in the land."

The name *sentry-birds* suddenly made sense to her; she
had never really thought about it before. She took Prudence from the block, loosing with one hand the knots
which secured her jesses, and lifted her free; watched her
soar high into the sky. She arranged her body carefully in
the saddle, leaving a part of her consciousness . . . a very
small part . . . to make certain she did not fall from the
saddle, and then. . . .

   *. . . high into the sky, on long, strong winds, rising higher
and higher. . . .*

All of the land lay spread out below her, like a map. She could see the curve of water below, and was dimly aware of a presence within her mind, seeing what she saw through her link with the bird. Through this mind, which she recognized as Carolin's, she began to make sense out of what she saw, although this was very distant and almost unconscious ... most of her was soaring with the bird, seeing with keen sharpness everything which lay below.

. . . There the shores of Mirin Lake, and beyond that, Neskaya to the north, at the edge of the Kilghard Hills. And there ... ah, Gods, another circle of blackness, not the scar of forest-fire, but where Rakhal's men have rained clingfire from the sky from their infernal flying machines! My people and they burn and die beneath Rakhal's fires when it was given to me and I swore with my hand in the fires of Hali that I would protect them against all pillage and rapine while they were loyal to me, and for that loyalty they burn ...

. . . Rakhal, as Aldones lives, I shall burn that hand from you with which you have sown disaster and death on my people ... and Lyondri I shall hang like a common criminal for he has forfeited the right to a noble death; the life he now lives as Rakhal's sower of death and suffering is more ignoble than death at the hands of the common hangman. . . .

Over the Kilghard Hills now, where the hills lie green with summer, and the resin-trees blaze in the sun ... there again a Tower rises ... quickly, fly to the North, little bird, away from the spying eyes of Lyondri's own forsworn laranzu'in. . . .

And there they lie, Rakhal's armies, where I an march to the East and take them unawares, unless they can spy with eyes like mine ... and I think there are no sentry-birds now except in the far Hellers. . . .

Romilly heard the shrill crying of the bird as if from her own throat; the contact melted and for a moment she sat on her horse again, Carolin gone from her mind, Ranald Ridenow suddenly jolted out of contact, staring at her. She lurched in the saddle, swayed, and Maura said quietly, "Enough. Ruyven, your turn, I think. . . ."

Romilly had not noticed; Ruyven had loosed Temperance at the same time as Prudence. Diligence, too, was gone from Maura's saddle. She saw Ruyven slump ... *as she had done?* ... and for an instant she was part of Ruy-

ven/Ranald/Carolin flying in rapport with the bird, swooping low over the armies, something inside her *counting . . .*

Horsemen and foot soldiers, so many . . . wagons of sup-
plies, and archers, and . . . ah Gods . . . Evanda guard us,
that smell I know, somewhere within their ranks they are
again making clingfire *. . .*

By sheer force of will Romilly tore herself, exhausted,
from the rapport. She was not interested in the details of
Rakhal's armies. She would rather not know; the horror
she had felt in Ruyven's mind, or was it Carolin's, made
her feel dizzy and sick. Spent, she collapsed in her saddle,
almost asleep where she sat, weak, light-headed. She noticed at the edge of her consciousness that the sun was
substantially lowered, almost at the edge of the horizon,
and the light was dimming enough so that the great violet
disk of Liriel could be seen rising from the eastern horizon,
a few nights before its full. Her mouth was dry, and her
head ached and throbbed as if a dozen tiny smiths were
beating on their forge-anvils inside it.

Darkness descended so swiftly that Romilly wondered if
she had been asleep in her saddle; it seemed to her that
one moment she looked on sunset and the next, on violet
moonlight, with Liriel floating in the sky. As she came
aware, she realized Ruyven was looking at her anxiously.

"You're back?"

"For some time," he said, surprised. "Here, the soldiers
have food ready for you," He gestured, and she slid from
her horse, aching in every muscle, her head throbbing. She
did not see Maura at all, Ranald Ridenow came and said,
"Lean on me, if you wish, Swordswoman," but she straightened herself proudly.

"Thank you, I can walk," she said, and Ruyven came
and motioned her to sit beside them on the grass. She protested "The birds—"

"Have been seen to; Maura did it when she saw the state
you were in," he said. "Eat."

"I'm not hungry," she said, shrugging it off, and rose
swiftly to her feet. "I had better see to Prudence—"

"I tell you, Maura has the birds and they are perfectly
all right," Ruyven said impatiently, and thrust a block of
sticky dried fruit into her hand. "Eat this."

She took a bite of it and put it aside with a grimace.

She knew that if she swallowed it she would be sick. From somewhere her little tent had been put up, the one she shared with Maura, and she shoved into it, aware from somewhere of Ranald Ridenow's face, white and staring, troubled. Whey should he care? She flung herself down on her pallet in the tent and fell over the edge of a dark cliff of sleep.

She knew she had not really wakened, because she could somehow see through the walls of the tent to where her sleeping body lay, all thin like gauze so that she could see through it to beating heart and pulsing veins. She waved a hand and the heart speeded up its beat slightly and the veins began to go in swirling circles. Then she flew away and left it behind her, rising over plains and hills, flying far away on long, strong wings toward the Hellers. Ice cliffs rose before her, and beyond them she could see the walls of a city, and a woman standing on a high battlement, beckoning to her.

Welcome home, dear sister, come here to us, come home . . .

But she turned her back on them too, and flew onward, higher and higher, mountain peaks dropping away far below, as she flew past the violet disk . . . no, it was a round ball, a sphere, a little world of its own, she had never thought of the moon as a world. Then a green one lay beneath her, and the peacock crescent of Kyrris, dark, lighted only at the rim by the red sun, which somehow was still shining at midnight. She flew on and on, until she left the blazing sun behind and it was only a star among other stars, and she was looking down from somewhere on the world with four moons like a jeweled necklace, and someone said in her mind, *Hali is the constellation of Taurus, and Hali the ancient Terran word for necklace in the Arabic tongue,* but the words and the worlds were all meaningless to her; she dropped down, down slowly, and the great ship lay smashed against the lower peaks of the Kilghard Hills, and a Ghost wind blew across the peaks . . . and a little prim voice in her mind remarked, *racial memory has never been proven, for there are parts of the brain still inaccessible to science* . . . and then she began to fly along the rim of the Hellers. But the glaciers were breathing their icy breath at her, and her wings were beginning to freeze, the dreadful cold was squeezing her heart, slowing the wingstrokes, and then one wing, hard like ice, broke and splintered, with a dreadful shock of pain in her head and heart, and the other wing, white and frozen and stiff, would no longer beat, and she sank and sank, screaming. . . .

"Romilly! Romilly!" Lady Maura was softly slapping her cheeks. "Wake up! Wake up!"

Romilly opened her eyes; there was a soft lantern-glow in the tent, but through it she was still freezing among the glaciers, and her wings were broken . . . she could feel the sharp jagged edges near her heart where they had shattered in the cold and splintered away. . . .

Maura gripped her hands with her own warm ones, and Romilly, confused, came back to her own body's awareness. She felt the unfamiliar, intrusive touch . . . somehow Maura was *within* her body, touching it with mental fingers, checking heart and breathing . . . she made a gesture of refusal, and Maura said gently, "Lie still, let me monitor you. Have you had many attacks of this kind of threshold sickness?"

Romilly pushed her away. "I don't know what you're talking about; I had a bad dream, that is all. I must have been tired. I've never done that before with the birds, and it was exhausting. I suppose the *leroni* are accustomed to it."

"I wish you would let me monitor you and be sure—"

"No, no. I'm all right." Romilly turned her back to the other woman and lay still, and after a moment Maura sighed and put out the lantern, and Romilly picked up a fragment of her thought, *stubborn, but I should not intrude, she is no child, perhaps her brother* . . . before she slept again, without dreams this time.

In the morning she still had a headache, and the smell of the carrion for bird-food made her as queasy—she told herself impatiently—as if she were four months pregnant! Well, whatever ailed her, it was not that, for she was as virgin as any pledged *leronis*. Perhaps it was her woman's cycles coming on her—she had lost track, with the army coming and her intense work with Sunstar. Or perhaps she had eaten something that did not agree with her; certainly she had no mind for breakfast. After caring for the birds, she got into her saddle without enthusiasm; for the first time in her life she thought it might be rather pleasant to sit inside a house and sew or weave or even embroider.

"But you have eaten nothing, Romilly," Ruyven protested.

She shook her head. "I think I caught a chill yesterday, sitting so still after sunset in my saddle," she said. "I don't want anything."

He surveyed her, she thought, as if she were Rael's age, and said, "Don't you know what it means when you cannot eat? Has Lady Maura monitored you?"

It was not worth arguing about. She said sharply, "I will eat some bread in my saddle as we ride," and took the hunk of bread, smeared with honey, that he handed her. She ate a few bites and surreptitiously discarded it.

Ranald was riding with the blank look Romilly knew enough, now, to associate with a telepath whose mind was elsewhere. At last he came out of it and said, "I should know how far it is to the main branch of the armies; Carolin will join with us sometime today, though they are some way behind us. Romilly, will you take our bird and see if you can spy out Carolin's armies, and see how far they are behind us?"

She felt some qualms after her last experience with the flight with birds. Yet when she flung the bird in the air and followed it with her linked mind, she found that there was none of the disquieting disorientation; to her intense relief, it was only like flying Preciosa; she could see with a strange doubled sight, but that was all. The bird's sight, keener than her own a hundred times, told her that Carolin's armies lay half a day's ride behind where she rode with their little advance party, and she could sense, but with no sense of intrusion, that Ranald had picked up their position and relayed it to Carolin himself.

"We will camp here and wait for them," Maura said with authority, "We are all weary, and our hawkmistress needs rest."

I should not let them pamper me. I do not want Ruyven, nor Orain, nor Carolin himself, to think that because I am a woman I must be favored. Orain will respect me if I am as competent as a man. . . .

Lord Ranald yawned. He said, "I too feel as if I had

been dragged backward over a waterfall, after these days
of hard riding. I shall be glad of the rest. And the birds
need not be moved more." He gestured to the soldiers to
set up the camp.

Chapter 6

Romilly knew the main army was approaching, not from what she heard—though, when she listened quietly, where she lay inside the tent she shared with *Domna* Maura, she could hear a soft distant sound in the very earth which she knew to be the noise of the great column of men on the march. But what really told her of Carolin's approach was a growing awareness within her mind, a sense of oneness, an approaching that she knew. . . .

Sunstar. Her mind was within and surrounded by the black stallion, it seemed that it was not on his but her back that the king rode, surrounded by his men, and for a moment her mind strayed to touch his too, to see Orain for a moment through his eyes, with love and warmth. Once she had seen them together, unguarded, wishing somehow that she had such a friend. Now she shared, for a moment, the quick unconscious touch between the king and his sworn man, something not sexual but deeper than that, a closeness which went back through their lives, mind and heart and somehow encompassed even a picture of their first meeting as young children, not yet in their fourth year . . . all three dimensions of time as somehow she was aware of Sunstar as a colt running in the hills of his native country. . . .

She jerked herself away from the extended contact and back into her own body, shocked and startled. She did not know what was happening, but she supposed it was some new dimension of her *laran,* opening of itself—what did she need, after all, of a Tower?

But the first person who came to her, when she was

working around the birds, picking up little tags and fringes of the sight-awareness she had known yesterday when she flew them, was Jandria. After the two Swordswomen had greeted one another with a hug, Jandria said, "We had your message through the birds; it was Himself who told me." Romilly remembered that this was always how she spoke of King Carolin when he was not actually present. "You are doing well, Romy. And I have permission from the Swordswomen here for you to go on sharing Lady Maura's tent, if you will. I will go and speak to her; we were girls together."

Romilly held her peace—she had long known that Jandria was of higher rank than she had ever realized, though she had left it behind her when she took the oath of the Sisterhood. She turned her attention to the birds, though she could hear, with a tiny pang she recognized as jealousy, the two women talking behind her somewhere.

And I have no friend, no lover, I am alone, alone as any monk in his solitary cell in the ice caves of Nevarsin . . . and wondered what she was thinking about, for even now her mind was filled with the awareness of the great stallion racing in the sun, and Carolin with him, riding. . . .

She made her reverence before she ever looked up at the king's face and then was not really sure whether she had bowed to Carolin or to Sunstar, his black mane disordered with the hill-country wind. Carolin slid from his back and greeted her graciously.

"Swordswoman Romilly, I came myself to bring you my thanks for your message; you and your companions with the sentry-birds. We are to march tomorrow on Rakhal's armies and you and the *laranzu* must do this, for I have pledged to my kinswoman Maura that she need not take part in any battle against her kinsman." He smiled at her. "Come, child, you were not so tongue-tied when you rode with me to Nevarsin. You called me 'Uncle' then."

Romilly blurted, "I did it in ignorance, sir. I meant no disrespect, I thought you were only Carlo of Blue Lake—"

"And so I am," said Carolin gently, "Carlo was my childhood nickname, as my little cousin is called Caryl. And my mother gave me the country estate called Blue Lake when I was a boy of fifteen. And if I was not what you thought me, why, neither were you, for I thought you a stable boy, some MacAran's bastard, and not a *leronis,* and now I find you."

She remembered that he had seen her in boy's clothes, and she sensed that he had known her a girl quite soon, and for his own reasons had kept silent. That silence had allowed Orain to befriend her, and for that she was grateful. She said, "Your Majesty—"

He waved that aside. "I stand on no ceremony with friends, Romilly, and I have not forgotten that if it had not been for you, I would have been the banshee's breakfast. So; you will fly the sentry-birds to keep my advisers ahead of Rakhal's—or Lyondri's—movements into battle?"

She said, "I shall be honored, sir."

"Good. Now I must speak with my kinswoman and relieve her fears," he said. "Dame Jandria, too, I think, still has enough love for Lyondri—"

"For what he was," said Jandria quietly, standing in the door of Maura's tent, "not for what he is, Carlo. It goes against me to raise my own hand to him, but I will not lift a single hand to hold back his fate. If I had *laran* enough, I would be among your *leroni* today, to hold back what he has become. If he still holds enough of what he was to know what he is now, he would pray for clean death."

Maura's eyes were wet with tears. She said, "Carlo, I swore I would never raise hand or *laran* against my Hastur kin. I am Elhalyn, and they are blood of my blood. But like Jandria, I will not hinder you from what you must do, either." She went to the perch where Temperance sat and bent her head before the bird, and Romilly knew it was because she was crying.

This war that sets brother against sister and father against son . . . what matters it which rogue sits on the throne or which greater rogue seeks to wrest it from him . . . ? she was not sure whether it was Ruyven's thought she heard, or whether her father spoke in her memory, for it seemed that time had no more existence. . . .

Carolin said, looking at them sadly, "Still, I swore to protect my people, even if I must protect them from the Hastur kin who are unmindful of that oath. I wish you could know how little I want Rakhal's throne, or how gladly would I cede it to him if only he would treat my people as a king must, respecting them and protecting them. . . ." But it seemed he spoke to himself, and afterward Romilly was not sure whether he had spoken aloud or if she had imagined it all. Her *laran,* it seemed, was playing strange tricks on her, it seemed as if her mind was too small to enclose everything that wanted to crowd into it, and she felt somehow stretched, violated, crammed with strangenesses, as if her head were bursting with it. She said to Carolin, "May I greet my good friend, your horse, my lord?"

"Indeed, I think he is missing you," Carolin said, and she went to Sunstar, where Carolin had flung his reins around a rail when he dismounted, and flung her arms around the horse.

You are a king's mount but still are you mine, she said, not in words, and felt Sunstar in her mind, reaching out, *mine, love, together, sunlight/sunstar/always together in the world. . . .*

She discovered that she was clinging to the rail alone; Sunstar was gone and Ruyven was touching her hesitantly. "What ails you, Romy? Are you sick?"

She said brusquely, "No," and went to the birds. Again, somehow, it seemed, she had lost track of time. Could this be some new property of her *laran* that she did not understand? Maybe she should ask Maura about it. She was a *leronis* and would certainly be willing to help. But she could hear Maura in her mind now, weeping for Rakhal who had once sought her hand, so that afterward Maura had become *leronis* and a pledged virgin . . . mourned for Rakhal as Jandria mourned for Lyondri . . . and she for Orain's old comradeship . . . no, that was gone, what was *wrong* with her mind these days?

There was no need of the sentry-birds this day, and Romilly, still weak and confused after yesterday's fierce effort and the evil dreams of the night, was glad of it. Yet as she rode, in the favored place near Carolin and his advisers, she was not really conscious of herself or of her own horse, so much was she riding with Sunstar at the head of the troops. Orain was riding near them, and she heard him talking easily and as equals with Lady Maura and Lord Ranald.

"You have the Serrais *laran,* Ranald, it would be no trouble to you, I dare say, to learn to handle the birds; it is near enough the MacAran Gift, which I saw in Mistress Romilly all those weeks when we travelled together." From her distance Romilly could sense the memory of how Orain had watched her, with tenderness not unmixed with something else, something akin to love. She knew now why Orain avoided her, because he could not see Romilly now without the painful memory of the boy Rumal who he had thought he knew, and he felt like a fool, layers of awareness overlapping and blurring.

Ranald said, "I am willing to try. And perhaps Mistress Romilly would be willing to school me. Though like all Swordswomen she is arrogant and harsh of tongue—" and Maura's merry laughter, saying that he was not used to women who did not regard him, a Ridenow lord, as a special creation for their delight.

"Oh, come, Maura, I am not all that much of a womanizer, but if women were made by the Goddess Evanda for the delight of men, why should I refuse the Lady of Light her due by failing to worship Her in her creation, the loveliness of women?" he laughed. "No doubt She will punish *you,* one day, Orain, that you deny her due." And Orain's good-natured laughter, and Romilly knew that she was listening to a conversation not meant for her ears. She tried to shove it away but she did not know how, except by turning her attention elsewhere, and then she was riding again with Sunstar and too aware of Carolin. It was not a comfortable day, and when that evening Ranald came and asked if he could assist her to dismount, and said that he wished to learn the ways of the birds, so that he could fly one while Lady Maura was oath-bound not to do so, she was short with him.

"It is not so simple as all that. But you may try to approach them; however, do not complain to me if you should lose a fingernail or even an eye!"

She did not like the way he looked at her. It reminded her all too much of *Dom* Garris, or even Rory, as if he had physically fingered her young breasts with rude hands; she was painfully aware of his look—*I have never felt this way before*—and of the open desire in it. But he had done nothing, said nothing, how could she make any objection to it? She drew her cloak about her as if she was cold, and gestured him toward the birds.

He lowered his eyes and she knew he had picked up some sense of her unease. He said quietly, "Forgive me, *mestra,* I meant no offense." No more than Carolin could he seek to force any attentions on a woman unwilling, since he would share the victim's shock and distress, her sense of violation even at a rude look. But he was not used to women who were not of his own Hastur-kind who would be aware of this sensitivity.

Yet a woman who has not laran—*it is like coupling with a dumb beast, hardly alive* . . . she saw the scalding crimson on his turned-away neck and wished she knew how to tell him that it was all right. He approached the birds; she sensed the way in which he reached out to them, trying to echo the sense of harmlessness; to extend his senses toward the birds with nothing but the friendliest feelings. For a moment Romilly waited . . . then Temperance lowered her head and rubbed it against the scratching-stick in the Ride-now lord's hand.

So he will be flying them, and he will be one with us, as Maura was . . . she did not know why the thought troubled her.

Maura must be still with the army, Romilly thought, they could not have left her behind, with the country alive with war; but Romilly had not seen her that day. When they rode out ahead with the birds, it was Lord Ranald who came with them, Temperance on his saddle; Romilly had yielded her own favorite, Prudence, to Ruyven, so that she could take Diligence, who was the most difficult of the birds to handle, on her own saddle. Diligence fussed and shrilled restlessly, but quieted when Romilly touched her mind.

Yes, you're a beauty too, Romilly told the bird, and saw nothing incongruous in so addressing the huge, ugly creature.

But there was no call for their services that day, and Romilly was glad, for it would give Lord Ranald extra time to be completely familiar with the bird, to create close rapport with her. After an hour or so, when Romilly felt sure there would be no trouble and no need for her service, Romilly let her mind drift again into close contact with Sunstar, where he rode with Carolin at the head of the army.

Now it seemed that the countryside was deserted, with

great open tracts of deserted lands, and now and again a quiet farmstead lying empty, wells broken, houses burst or fallen away with time. Romilly, riding with Sunstar, was really not aware that she was eavesdropping on Carolin and Orain, riding together with Lady Maura close to them. Maura was wrapped in her cloak and spoke little, but Carolin said, looking at the deserted country, "When I was a child I rode through here and this was all settled land with farmers and crops. Now it is a wasteland."

"The war?" Maura asked.

"War in my father's time, before I was old enough to hold a sword—still I remember how green and fertile was this country. And how the settled lands are nearer to the edge of the hills; in the aftermath of war there are always bandits, men made homeless by war and conscienceless by the horrors they have seen; they ravaged this country, what the war had left of it, until the folk settled nearer to the protection of the forts and soldiers near Neskaya."

But Romilly, her mind submerged in Sunstar, thought only, how green and fertile were the fields, how lovely the pastures. They camped that night by a watercourse, a narrow brook which rolled and tumbled down a cascade of old piled rocks, then flowed smooth and lovely across a fertile meadow starred with little blue and golden flowers.

"It will be a perfect night in High Summer," said Carolin lazily, "Before the night is past, three of the moons will appear in the sky, and two of them near the full."

"What a pity we will not have Midsummer-Festival here," Maura laughed, and Carolin said, suddenly sober, "I vow to you, Maura—and to you, *bredu*," he added, turning to Orain with a smile of deep warmth, "that we shall hold our Midsummer-Festival within the walls of Hali, at home. What say you to that, cousins?"

"Evanda grant it," Maura said seriously, "I am homesick—"

"What, none of the young men in that faraway tower beyond the mountains—" lightly, Carolin punned on the name of Tramontana—"have shaken your resolve to remain maiden for the Sight, Maura?"

Maura laughed, though the sound was strained.

"On the day when you invite me to be queen at your side, Carolin, I shall not send you away disappointed."

Sunstar jigged sidewise, restlessly, as Carolin leaned from his saddle to touch Maura's cheek lightly with his lips. He said, "If the Council will have it so, Maura, so be it. I had feared your heart was dead when Rakhal turned away from you—"

"Only my pride was wounded," she said quietly. "I loved him, yes, as cousin, as foster-brother; but his cruelty slew my heart. He thought he could come to me over the bodies of my kinfolk, and I would forgive him all when I saw the crown he offered, like a child forgetting a bruise when she is given a sweetnut. I would not have it said that I turned from Rakhal to you because I would have the one who could bring me the crown—" her voice faltered, and Sunstar tossed his head indignantly at the jerk on the reins which brought him to a halt so that Carolin could lean again toward Maura's saddle; but this time he felt it as his rider lifted the slight from of the *leronis* bodily from her saddle to his own, and held her there. There were no more words, but Sunstar, and Romilly with him, sensed an outflow, an outpouring of emotion that made him restless, made him prance until Carolin chided him with a tug on the reins, and in Romilly's mind were flooding images of sleek flanks and satiny bodies, of swift running in moonlight, which made her rub her head as if she were feverish, with unfamiliar sensations flooding her whole body, so that she retreated abruptly into herself, away from the great stallion's unfamiliar emotions and touch.

What has come over me, that I am so filled with emotion, that I laugh and cry without a word spoken or a touch?

Carolin said in her mind, and she was not conscious that he was not at her elbow, *We can leave the horses for tonight in this field; you are a* leronis, *can you keep them there without fencing, which we have no time to set up?* And Romilly was about to answer when she heard Maura's voice as clear as if spoken aloud, *I have not Romilly's gift, but if you will summon her to help me, I will do what I can.*

Romilly tugged the reins a little and pulled her own horse to a stop. Ruyven turned startled eyes on her, but she said, "We are to stop here for the night and I am summoned to the king and the *leronis*."

It was Orain who brought her the word, riding through the mass of men and horses and equipment flowing along the road, calling out, "Where are you off to, Romilly? The *vai dom* has requested you to attend him!"

"I know," said Romilly, and went on toward the king, leaving Orain staring and surprised behind her.

Carolin extended his arm toward the broad field. He said, "We are to make camp here for the night. Can you help Maura to set pastures here for the horses so that they will not stray?"

"Certainly," she said, and the men set about making camp, turning the best horses into the field, Sunstar among them.

Maura said, when they were done, "Now we shall set a chasm across which they will see, though we cannot; horses are afraid of heights, so we need only make them see it."

Romilly linked minds with the young *leronis,* and together they wove an illusion; a great chasm between horses and men, surrounding the pasture . . . Romilly, still partly linked in mind with Sunstar and her senses extending to her own horse and to the others in the field . . . and aware with them of the great black stallion—saw it and physically flinched, great spaces down which she might fall, shrinking back. . . .

"Romilly," said Maura seriously, breaking away from the link, "You are what we call a wild telepath, are you not?"

She turned, filled with a prickly awareness of the critical sound in Maura's voice. "I don't know what you mean," she said stiffly.

"I mean, you are one whose *laran* has been developed of itself, without the discipline of a Tower," Maura said. "Do you know that it can be dangerous? I wish you would let me monitor you, and make certain that you are under control. *Laran* is no simple thing—"

She said, even more stiffly, "The people of MacAran have been animal trainers, working with birds and horses and dogs, since time unknown; and not all of them have been supervised by the Towers either." A trace of the mountain accent crept back in her speech, as if the echo of her father's voice, saying, "The *Hali'imyn* would have it that a man's own mind must be ruled over by their *leronyn* and their Towers!"

Maura said placatingly, "I have no wish to rule over you, Romilly, but you look feverish, and you are still of an age where you might be subject to—to some of the dangers of *laran* improperly supervised and developed. If you cannot allow me to monitor you and see what has happened to you, your brother—"

Still less, Romilly thought, could she allow her stern and ascetic brother, so like a *cristoforo* monk, to read the thoughts she hardly dared acknowledge to herself. She twisted away impatiently, fumbling at a barrier against Maura. "It is generous of you, *vai domna*, but truly you need not concern yourself about me."

Maura frowned a little, and Romilly sensed that she was weighing the ethics of a Tower-trained telepath, never to intrude, against a very real concern for the girl. It annoyed Romilly—Maura was not *so* much older than she was herself, why did she think she was needed to straighten out Romilly's *laran*?

I was left on my own with it, and now when I need it no longer they are eager to offer help! I was not offered help when my father would have sold me to Dom *Garris, and there was none to help me when I would have been raped by Rory, or when I made an idiot of myself forcing my way into Orain's bed. I have won these battles alone and unhelped, what makes them think I need their damned condescension now?*

Maura still looked at her uneasily, but at last, to Romilly's relief, she sighed and turned away.

"Look," Carolin said, and pointed, "Are you sure that your illusion has worked?"

Romilly looked up, her breath almost stopping; Sunstar was rushing toward them, his head flung up, his legs seeming hardly to touch the ground as he bolted. Maura lifted her hand. "Wait," she said, and as Sunstar reached the corner of the meadow he stopped short, placing all four feet together as if truly on the edge of a cliff, his head lowered, foam dripping from his teeth as if in mortal terror. He shuddered with fear, then snorted, backed away, tossed his head and raced away in the other direction.

"The illusion will hold them tonight, at least," Maura said.

"But he is so frightened," Romilly protested; she was dripping with the stallion's sweat of fear.

"Neither memory nor imagination," said Maura quietly.

"You have both, Romy, but look at him now." And, indeed, Sunstar was quietly cropping grass; he stopped,
sniffed the wind and began to move closer to a group of
mares silently grazing in the meadow.

"He will improve the quality of your royal stables," said
Orain jocularly, "and any mare he covers tonight will have
a foal worthy of those same stables, I doubt not."

Carolin chuckled. "He is welcome to his sport, old friend.
We who are responsible for this war—" he touched Maura
gently, only on the shoulder, but the look that passed between them made Romilly blush, "must wait for a while
for our satisfactions; but they will be all the dearer for that,
will they not, my love?"

She only smiled, but Romilly physically turned her eyes
from the intensity of that smile.

That night Jandria came and asked Romilly if she wished
to join the Swordswomen's mess again, now that she was not
riding ahead of her special detachment with the birds. It was
evident from Jandria's voice that she expected Romilly to be
overjoyed at being allowed again to join her sisters, but Romilly was too weary and raw-edged for the chatter, the noise
and giggling of the young women of the Sisterhood, eager to
sleep away from their communal tent. She made the excuse
that she was still needed among the birds.

"And you need not fear that I am improperly guarded,"
she said sourly, "for between the Lady Maura and my
monkish brother, I might as well be a priestess of Avarra
on her guarded isle where no man may come without the
Dark Mother's death-curse!"

she could see that Jandria was still troubled, but the older
woman only embraced her. She said, "Rest well, then, little
sister. You look so weary; they have demanded much of
you in very little time, and you are still young. Be sure to
eat a good supper; I have known *leroni* before this, and to
replenish their energies after their work, a fragile little girl
will eat enough to satisfy three wood-cutters! And sleep
long and soundly, my dear."

She went away; Romilly fed the birds, with Ruyven's
help, and even Lord Ranald, she noted with satisfaction,
did not shirk his share of the tending. But the smell of their
carrion food which the army hunters had brought her, made
her feel queasy again, and although Carolin had sent a good

haunch of roast *chervine* from his own tables, with his compliments to his bird-handlers, she could hardly eat and only shoved the food around on her plate.

By the time the camp was completely settled for the night, it was well past sunset, but the night was lighted with three full moons, and the fourth was a half-filled crescent.

"Four moons," said Lord Ranald, laughing, "What madness shall we do? They say in Thendara, *What is done under four moons need not be remembered or regretted . . .*

Ruyven said with frozen courtesy, "Such nights are sacred, friend; I shall spend much of my night in sacred silence and meditation, if Carolin's soldiers—" he gestured to where, faintly and downwind, he could hear the sound of a *rryl* and loud, untuneful voices all shouting the chorus of a popular drinking song, "will allow me a little peace."

"The king's quartermasters have given the soldiers an extra ration of wine," Lord Ranald said, "but not enough to make them drunk; they will sit round their fires and sing in the moonlight, that is all." He offered Romilly his arm. "Shall we join them at their fires? There are three or four in my old unit who have fine voices and sing together in taverns: they sing well enough to get all the beer they want, and more. And be assured they will offer a Swordswoman no discourtesy, but be pleased to know you have come to hear their music."

"They sound not like such fine voices," said Romilly, listening to the discordance of the faraway song, and Ranald laughed.

"They are but amusing themselves; it would not be worth the trouble of the Windsong Brothers—for so they call themselves, though they are not brothers but four cousins— to sing before all are assembled and calling for entertainment. We will be in plenty of time to hear them, and the soldiers like it if the gentry come to their fires to hear their amusements."

Put like that, Romilly could not refuse, though she felt dull and headachy and wished she could go quietly to bed. But with the camp filled with song and laughter she knew she would not sleep anyhow; perhaps Ruyven had the discipline for quiet meditation in such a racket, but she did not. She took his offered arm.

The moonlight made it almost as bright as day—well,

perhaps a grey and rainy day; she did not think she could
have read print, and the colors of Ranald's garish cloak
and her own crimson tunic, were indistinct, but there was
plenty of light to make out where they were going A part
of Romilly, unawares, was cropping grass in the meadow
with Sunstar, and yet she was filled with a strange restlessness. As they neared the fires they could hear the soldiers
roaring out a song whose words were far from decorous,
about some scandalous goings-on among the nobility.

"O, my father was the Keeper of the Arilinn Tower,
He seduced a chieri with a kireseth flower;
From this union there were three;
Two were *emmasca* and the other was me . . ."

"That song," said Ranald, "would have them torn to
pieces if they sang it anywhere on the Plains of Arilinn.
Here it is different, there is an old rivalry between Arilinn
and Neskaya Towers . . ."

"Curious goings-on for a Tower," said Romilly, whose
picture of a Tower was still colored by what she had seen
in Ruyven's disciplined and austere thoughts.

He chuckled. "I spent a few years in a Tower—just
enough to learn control of my *laran*. You must know how
it is. When it began, when I was thirteen, I sometimes could
hardly tell myself from a *cralmac* in rut, or from going into
heat with every bitch on the farm! It was very upsetting to
my governess—I was still in the schoolroom then. Of
course, she was a frozen-faced old viper—I won't insult my
favorite dog by calling the lady a bitch! I am sure she often
wished she could have had me gelded like the pack chervines, so she could go with my lessons!"

Romilly giggled uneasily. He sensed her unease and said
kindly, "I am sorry—I had forgotten you were a *cristoforo*
and brought up to their ways. I had thought girls were
different, but I had four sisters, and if I had ever enter-
tained any feelings that girls were different and more delicate, I got over them soon enough—and I won't apologize,
you are a woman from the mountains and I know from
your work with the birds that you have been around animals enough to know what I mean."

Romilly blushed, but the feeling was not unpleasant, and

she remembered the high summer in her own hills near Falconsward, the world flowing with life, cattle and horses mating, so that she too had unashamedly shared the flow of nature all round her, even though, with her child's body, it had been an undifferentiated awareness, sensual but never personal. She knew he was teasing her, but she did not really care.

"Listen," said Ranald, "There are the singers."

They were all in the uniform of common soldiers; four men, one tall and burly, another with shaggy, reddish-brown hair and an untrimmed patch of beard, one short and fat with a round, rosy face and a lopsided smile, and the fourth tall and gaunt, with a scrawny face and big red hands; but from his throat came the most exquisite tenor she had ever heard. They hummed a little together to find their pitch, then began to sing a popular drinking song which, Romilly knew was very old.

"Aldones bless the human elbow.
May he bless it where it bends:
If it bent too short, we'd go dry, I fear,
If it bent too long, we'd be drinking in our ear . . ."

They finished the catch by up-ending their tankards with a flourish to show them empty, and the soldiers roared approval and poured them all brimming mugfulls, which they drank and then began another song.

Their songs were rowdy but not indelicate, mostly concerned with the pleasures of drink and women, and their voices were splendid; with the rest, Romilly cheered and sang along on the choruses till she was hoarse. It made her forget her own strange feelings, and she was grateful to Lord Ranald for suggesting this. At one point someone thrust a mug into her hand—it was the strong, fragrant lowlands beer, and she felt a little tipsy from it; her voice sounded good to herself—usually she had no singing voice to speak of—and she felt pleasantly dizzied and yet not drunk enough to be off her guard. At last, it grew later and the men sought their beds, and the Windsong Brothers, full of wine and yet walking steadily, sang their last song to wild cheers and applause. Romilly had to lean on Ranald as she sought her tent.

He drew her close to him in the bright moonlight. He whispered, "Romy—what is done under the four moons need not be remembered or regretted—"

Half-heartedly she shoved him away. "I am a Swords-woman. I do not want to disgrace my earring. You think me wanton, then, because I am a mountain girl? And Lady Maura shares my tent."

"Maura will not leave Carolin this night," Ranald said seriously, "They cannot marry, till the Council had agreed, and will not while she is needed as his *leronis,* but they will have what they can; do you think she would blame you? Or do you think me selfish enough to make you pregnant, while we are in the middle of this war and your skills are as valuable as mine?" He tried to pull her into his arms again, but she shook her head, wordless, and he let her go.

"I wish—but it would be no pleasure to me if it was none to you," he said, but he pressed a kiss into her palm. "Perhaps—never mind. Sleep well, then, Romilly." He bowed again, and left her; she felt empty and chill, and almost wished she had not sent him away. . . .

I do not know what I want. I do not think it is that.

Even in her tent—and Ranald had been right, Lady Maura was not within, her blanketroll was tossed empty on the floor of the tent—she felt that the moonlight was flood-ing through her whole body. She crawled into her blankets, pulling off her clothes; usually she left on her undertunic at night, but tonight she felt so heated in the moonlight that she could hardly bear the touch of cloth on her fever-ish limbs. The music and the beer were still pounding in her head, but in the dark and silence, it seemed that she was outside in the moonlight, that she was somewhere paw-ing at the grass, a sweet, heady smell arising from the earth and somewhere a frantic restlessness everywhere within her.

Sunstar, too, seemed flooded with the restlessness of the four moons and their light . . . now she was linked deep in rapport with the stallion . . . this was not new to her, she had sensed this before, in begone summers, but never with the full strength of her awakened laran, her suddenly wake-ful body . . . the scent of the grass, the flooding of life through her veins till she was all one great aching tension . . .

sweet scents with a tang of what seemed to her shared and doubled senses a tang of musk and summer flowers and something she did not even recognize, so deeply was it part of herself, profoundly sexual, sweeping away barriers of thought and understanding . . . at one and the same time she was one with the great stallion in rut, and she was Romilly, frightened, fighting to break out of the rapport which she had, before this, shared so unthinking, it was too much for her now, she could not contain it, she was bursting with the pressure of the raw, animal sexuality under the stimulating light of the moons. . . . She felt her own body twisting and turning as she fought to escape, hardly knowing what it was she dreaded, but if it should happen she was terrified, she would not bear it she would be drawn in forever and never get back never to her own body what body she had no idea it was too much unendurable . . . PASSION, TERROR, RUT . . . NO, NO. . . .

Blue moonlight flooded the tent as the flap was drawn back . . . but she did not see it, she was beyond seeing, only the moonlight somehow reached her fighting body, tossing head. . . .

She was held gently in gentle arms; a voice was calling her name softly. Gentle hands were touching her.

"Romilly, Romy . . . Romy, come back, come back . . . here, let me hold you like this, poor little one . . . come back to me, come back *here* . . ." and she saw Ranald's face, heard his voice softly calling her; she felt as if she was drowning in the flood of what she was not, came back gratefully to awareness of her own body, held close in Ranald's arms. His lips covered hers and she put up her arms and drew him down wildly to her, anything now, anything to keep her here safely within her own body, shut out the unendurable overload of emotion and physical sensation; Ranald's arms held her, Ranald caressed her, she was herself, she was Romilly again, and she hardly knew whether it was fear, or gratitude, or real desire, that locked her lips to his, flung her into his arms, thrusting away all the unwanted contact with the stallion, reminding her that she was human, human, she was real, and this, this was what she wanted. . . . She could read in his mind that he was startled and delighted, even if a little overcome, by her violent acceptance, and more startled yet to find her virgin, but it did not, in that shared violence of that moment, matter to either of them at all.

"I knew," he whispered afterward, "I knew it would be too much for you. I do not think it was to me you were calling, but I was here, and I knew. . . ."

She kissed him thankfully, astonished and delighted. It had happened so naturally, it now seemed so sweet and right to here. A random thought, as she floated off into sleep, touched her mind at the edge of laughter.

It would never have been like this with Dom *Garris! I was perfectly right not to marry him.*

Chapter 7

Carolin's army remained encamped in the watercourse for three days. On the third day, Romilly went out to fly the sentry-birds again, Ranald at her side. She was quite aware that she must somehow shield her thoughts from Ruyven; he would not understand at all what had happened. He would see only that his young and innocent sister had shared her bed with a Ridenow lord, and to do her justice, Romilly was more worried that this might spoil the ability of the three of them to work together, than she was troubled by any sense of shame or regret for what she had done. Ruyven would be certain to think that Ranald had played the seducer, and it was not like that at all; he had simply pulled her free from something she had found herself quite unable to tolerate. Even now, Romilly did not know why she had found it unendurable.

"Remind me not to look at you and smile like that," Ranald said, picking up her concern lest Ruyven should know, and she smiled back. She felt soothed and happy, able to look into the pasture by the watercourse where Sunstar and the horses were grazing and pick up her old, close communion with the stallion, with no sense of distaste or unease, no break in her warm sense of unity with Sunstar.

Ranald made it so easy for me.

Maura told me, about something else; *horses have neither memory nor imagination.* That is why I can pick up where I left off.

Twice during these days she went and joined the Swordswomen's mess, sharing her meal with the women of the Sisterhood. Clea jeered a little at her.

"So you are still one of us, in spite of hob-nobbing with the nobility and all?"

"Be fair," said Jandria, "she has her work to do just as we do, and Lady Maura is as good a chaperon as a whole hostel full of our sisters. One of the handlers is her own brother, too. And if rumor tells true—" but she looked inquisitively at Romilly, "that same Lady Maura will one day be our queen—what do you know of that, Romy?"

Romilly said, "I know no more than you. And King Carolin cannot marry until the Council gives him leave—a noblewoman of Lady Maura's station cannot marry without parental consent, and how much more if the king comes wooing? But certainly, if they have their will, there will be a marriage made."

"And if there is not, the king will get him a bastard to make as much trouble in the kingdom as that *gre'zuin* Rakhal," said Tina scornfully. "Nice behavior for a *leronis*—I know from her waiting-woman that she spent two nights in the king's tent; what sort of chaperon is she for Romy, then?"

Ranald had taught her to shield herself a little; so Romilly managed neither to blush nor turn away her eyes. "Between three ugly birds and my brother, do you truly think I need a chaperone, Tina? As for Maura, I have heard she is kept virgin for the Sight, and I cannot believe she would endanger that, even in a king's bed, while the war still rages; but I am not the keeper of her conscience; she is a grown woman and a *leronis,* and need account to no man."

Clea made a contemptuous sound. "So she might sell her maidenhood for a crown, but not for love? Bravely done, *leronis!*" she made an applauding gesture. "See that you profit by her example, Romy!"

She had thought that among these women, who were free to follow their own wills, she might have been able to speak of this thing that had happened to her; even now, she felt, if she could speak with Jandria alone, she would like to tell her . . . but Jandria was already rising to attend on Carolin's advisers, and there was no other, not even Clea, whom she had thought her friend, to whom she felt she could talk freely. Not after their scornful words. No, she would not speak of Ranald. They would not understand at all.

She knew that she had not disgraced her earring, nor brought the Sisterhood into contempt. Her oath bound her to nothing more; and at least she had not sold herself to that elderly lecher *Dom* Garris in return for riches and the prospering of her father's horse-trade with Scathfell!

So on the third day, when she went out to fly the birds, with Ruyven and Ranald, her spirits were high. The day was grey and drizzly, with little spats and slashes of gusty rain coming across the plains, and even when a rare break came in the clouds, the wind was high. The sentry-birds huddled on their perches, squalling with protest when they were put on their blocks; they did not like this weather, but they needed exercise after two days of full fed rest, and Carolin needed to know where Rakhal's armies moved in the countryside.

"Somehow we must keep them low enough to spy through the mists," Ranald said, and Romilly protested, "They will not like that."

"I am not concerned with their liking or the lack of it," Ranald said curtly, "We are not flying the birds for our own pleasure nor yet theirs—have you forgotten that, Romy?"

She had, for a moment, so close she felt to the great birds. As she tossed Diligence free of her gloved hand, she went into rapport with the winged creatures, flying on strong pinions, high over the ranges, then remembered, forced it into flying lower, hovering, guiding the bird eastward to where they had last seen Rakhal's armies.

Even so, and with the bird's extra keen sight, she could not see very far; the drizzle clouded vision, so that she had to fly the bird low enough to see the ground, and the rain, slanting in from the northeast, dimmed sight further. This kind of flight bore no relationship to what she had known last time they flew, soaring in headlong flight, hovering high and letting the picture of the ground be relayed through Ranald to Carolin. Now it was slow, sullen effort, forcing the bird's will against the stubborn wish to turn tail and fly home to huddle on the perch till fine weather, then forcing it down against the instinct to fly high above the clouds.

Sentry-birds; spy-birds. Like all of us I am a tool for

Carolin's army to strike. How angry her father would be! Not only the runaway son he had disowned, but the daughter he had thought compensation for one runaway son and one worthless bookish one . . . how was Darren managing, she wondered, had he resigned himself to handling hawks and horses now?

She had lost track of the bird, and a sharp sense of question from Ruyven recalled her to the flying in the rain, chilled and battered by the icy gusts of sleet which buffeted her . . . or Diligence? She must risk flying lower, for they could see nothing through the thick curtain of wet. They were linked three ways, and now she set herself to follow Temperance, flying ahead strongly toward a break in the clouds. Below them the land lay deserted, but low on the horizon she could see smoke which she knew to be Rakhal's army where it waited out the rain. Behind her she could actually feel the displacement in the air where Prudence flew at her tail. At the same time a part of her was Romilly, balanced carefully in her saddle, and a part of her still Carolin, waiting for intelligence through the minds of bird-handlers and birds.

A speck against her sight, swiftly growing larger and larger . . . of course, she should have known that they too would have had spy-birds out in this weather! She—*or was it Diligence?*—shifted course ever so slightly, hoping to miss unseen the oncoming bird. Was it Rakhal himself, or one of his advisers, behind the hovering wings of that bird, poised to intercept. . . .

Would it come to a fight? She could not hope to control the bird if raw instinct took over; there was not much difficulty in controlling the mind of the bird if all was well, but in danger instinct would override the shared consciousness. Temperance was still flying well ahead, and through the link with Ruyven's mind she too could see the outskirts of the enemy camp, and a wagon about which something black and sinister was hovering . . . she was not sure she saw it with her eyes; was she perceiving something through Ruyven's mind or the bird's? Birds—Maura's phrase echoing in her mind, *neither memory nor imagination*—could only see with their physical sight, and could not interpret what they saw unless it concerned them directly, as food or threat.

It was taking all of her strength to hold Diligence on course. The wagon was there, and a curious, acrid smell which seemed to sting her, whether her own nose or the bird's she was not sure; but the blackness was something she must be perceiving through one of the minds linked in rapport with the sentry-birds spying. She was vaguely curious, but so sunk in the bird's consciousness that she was content to leave it to Carolin to interpret.

Something was in the air now . . . danger, danger . . . as if a red-hot wire had seared her brain, she swerved, shrieking and then there was a slicing pain in her heart and Romilly came with a cry out of the rapport, fighting to hold to it . . . *pain . . . fear . . .* somewhere, she knew, Diligence was falling like a stone, *dizzy, consciousness fading out, dying. . . .* Romilly, seated on her horse, physically clutched at her breast as if the arrow which had slain the sentry-bird had penetrated her body as well. The pain was nightmarish, terrifying, and she stared wildly around her in anguished disorientation. Then she knew what must have happened.

Diligence! She had flown her bird deliberately into the danger of those arrows, over-riding the bird's own sense of caution, its instinct to fly high and away from danger. Guilt and grief fought within her for dominance.

Someone very far away seemed to be calling her name . . . she came up out of grey fog to see Ranald looking at her, with deep trouble in his face. She said, strangled, "Prudence . . . Temperance . . . get them back . . ."

He drew a long breath. "They are away from the soldiers' I sent them high up, out of range . . . I am sorry, Romy; you loved her—"

"And she loved life!" she flung at him wildly, "And died because of you and Carolin— ah, I hate you all, all you men and kings and your damned wars, none of them are worth a feather in her wing-tip—" and she dropped her head in her hands and broke into passionate crying.

Ruyven's head was still flung back, his face glazed with intent effort; he sat unmoving until a dark form dropped from the clouds, sank down to his gloved hand.

"Temperance," Romilly whispered, with relief, "but where is Prudence—"

As if in answer from the clouds came a shrilling cry, answered by another; two dark forms burst through the layers of mist and rain, locked together, falling joined in battle; feathers fell, and the screaming and shrilling died. A small dark limp body dropped at their horses' feet; another sped away, screaming in triumph.

"Don't look! Ranald, hold her—" Ruyven began, but Romilly was off her horse, crying wildly, catching up the small blood-spattered form of Prudence, still limp and warm with recently-departed life. She clutched it against her breast, her face wet and furious. "Prudence! Ah, Prudence, love, not you too—" she cried, and the bird's blood smeared her hands and her tunic. Ranald dismounted, came and gently took it from her.

"No use, Romilly; she is dead," he said quietly, and his arms caught her to him. "Poor little love, don't cry. It can't be helped; that is war."

And that is supposed to be the excuse for all! Romilly felt fury surging within her. *They play with the lives of the wild things and hold themselves harmless, saying it is war . . .I question not their right to kill themselves and one another, but what does an innocent bird know or care of one king over another?*

Ruyven was gentling Temperance on his fist, sliding the hood over her restless head. He said, "Romilly, try to be calm, there is work to do, Ranald—you saw—"

"Aye, I saw," Ranald said shortly, "Somewhere in Rakhal's train there is *clingfire* and I know not where he means to use it, but Carolin must know at once! Time may be short, unless we want to burn beneath the stuff, and I for one want none used against me, or any of the lands hereabout—"

"Nor I. I saw what clingfire can do, in Tramontana," said Ruyven, "Though not in war. Carolin has pledged he will not use it against folk who must live in his lands. But if it is used against us, I know not how he can fight it."

Romilly, still standing silent, demanded, "What is clingfire?"

"The very breath of Zandru's forges," said Ranald, "Fire flung which burns and keeps on burning as long as there is anything to feed it, through skin and bone and into the very stone . . . fire made by wizardry and *laran*."

I doubt it not. Folk who would kill an innocent bird for some king's claim, why should they stop at killing people too?

"You must come with us." Ranald gently urged her into her saddle. "Carolin must know of this and he will need all of his *leronyn*—Maura has sworn not to fight against Rakhal, but I do not think she will hesitate to stop the use of clingfire against her own people, no matter what she may still feel for Rakhal!"

But Romilly rode blind, tears still streaming from her eyes. She knew nor wished to know nothing of the weapons these men and their kings and their *leroni* used. Dimly she knew that Ranald rode away from her, but she reached out blindly for contact with Sunstar, feeling, in the reassuring strength of the great stallion, an endless warmth and closeness. He was in her and she was in him, and drawn into the present, with neither memory nor anticipation, without imagination or emotion save for the immediate stimuli; green grass, the road under foot, the weight of Carolin, already beloved, in the saddle. She rode unseeing because the best part of her was with Sunstar, loss and grief wiped out in the unending present-moment of timelessness.

At last, comforted somewhat, she came out of the submersion in the horse's world, half aware that somewhere they spoke of her.

She was very fond of the sentry-birds, she is very close to them. It was so from the moment we first saw her, we spoke of how ugly they were, and it was she who pointed out to us that they had their own kind of beauty. . . .

. . . her first experience with this kind of loss, she must learn how to keep herself a little separate. . . .

. . . what can you expect, then, of a wild telepath, one who has tried to learn without the discipline of the Towers. . . .

She thought, resentfully, that if what they taught in the Towers would teach her to be complacent about the deaths of innocent beasts who had no part in men and their wars, she was glad she had not had it!

"Please understand," Carolin said, looking at the three bird-handlers, "No blame attaches to any one of you, but we have lost two of our three sentry-birds, and the remaining one must be sent out at once, danger or no. Which of you will fly her?"

"I am willing," said Ruyven, "My sister is new to this work and she is deeply grieved—she has handled these birds since they were young and was very close to them. I do not think she is strong enough to work further now, Sire."

Carolin glanced at Ranald and said, "I shall need all my *leronyn* if we are to destroy the clingfire in Rakhal's hands before he can manage to use it. As for Romilly—" he looked at her, compassionately, but she bristled under his sympathy and said, "None but I shall fly Temperance. I know enough now not to take her into danger—"

"Romilly—" King Carolin dismounted and came toward the girl. He said seriously, "I am sorry, too, about the birds. But can you look at this from my point of view, too? We risk birds, and beasts too, to save the lives of men. I know the birds mean more to you than they can to me, or to any of us, but I must ask you this; would you see me die sooner than the sentry-birds? Would you risk the lives of the birds to save your Swordswomen?"

Romilly's first emotional reaction was, *the birds at least have done Rakhal no harm, why cannot men fight their battles without endangering the innocent?* But she knew that was irrational. She was human; she would sacrifice bird or even horse to save Ranald, or Orain, or Carolin himself, or her brother. . . . She said at last, "Their lives are yours, your Majesty, to save or spend as you will. But I will not run them heedless into danger for no good reason, either."

She saw, and wondered, that Carolin looked so sad. He said, "Romilly, child . . ." and broke off; finally, after a long pause, he said, "This is what every commander of men and beasts must face, weighing the lives of some against the lives of all. I would like it better if I need never see any of those who have followed me die—" and sighed. "But I owe my life to those I am sworn to rule . . . in truth, sometimes I think I do not rule but serve. Go, send your bird," he added, and after a time Romilly realized, in shock, that only the last four words had been spoken aloud.

I read his thoughts, and he knew I would read them . . . he would not have spoken such things aloud before his armies, but he could not hide his thoughts from anyone with laran. . . .

It was bad enough that such a king must lead his people to war. She should have known that Carolin would waste no life, needless. And if by sending sentry-birds into danger he thus could spare the lives of some of his followers, he would do so, there must be responsible choice; as when she had chosen to let the banshee go hungry, because for it to feed would have meant death for all of them. She was human; her first loyalty must always be to her fellow men and women. She bowed, rode a little away from Carolin with Temperance on her saddle, and raised a gloved fist to send the bird into the rainy sky again.

She was flying, hovering over the field . . . and not far away, she heard the thunder of charging horses, as Rakhal's army swept down over the brow of the hill and the troops charged toward one another. There was a tremendous shock, and Romilly saw through the bird's eyes. . . .

Horses, down and screaming, sliced open by swords and spears . . . men lying on the ground, dying . . . she could not tell whether Carolin's men or Rakhal's, and it did not matter. . . . A picked group of men swept down toward where the blue fir-tree banner flew over Carolin's guard . . . *Sunstar! Carry my king to safety . . .* and a part of her rode with the great black stallion, thundering away with the king, to form a compact group, awaiting the charge again.

Flames seemed to sear the air; it was filled with the acrid smell of burning flesh, men and horses shrieking, and death, death everywhere. . . .

Yet through it all Romilly kept still, hovering over the field, bringing the bird's-eye picture of the battle to Carolin's eye so that he could direct his men where they were most needed. Hours, it seemed, dragged by while she swept over the field, sated with horrors, sickened with the smell of burning flesh. . . .

And then Rakhal's men were gone, leaving only the dead and dying on the field, and Romilly, who had been in rapport with the remaining sentry-bird (she knew now that it was Ruyven who had seized her bridle and led her horse to safety atop a little hill overlooking the field, while she was entranced in rapport with the bird) returned to her own awareness, sick and shocked.

Dying horses. Seven of them she had trained with her own hands in the hostel . . . dead or dying, and Clea, merry Clea who had talked so lightly of death, lying all but dead on the field, her blood invisible on the crimson tunic of the Swordswoman. . . . Clea, dying in Jandria's arms, and an

*empty place, a vast silence where once had been a living,
breathing, human being, beloved and real. . . .*

There was no rejoicing on this battlefield; Carolin had
felt too many deaths that day. Soberly, men went to bury
the dead, to give the last few dying horses the mercy-stroke,
Ruyven went with the healers to bind up the wounds of
those who had been struck down. Romilly, shocked beyond
speech, set up the tent aided only by Ruyven's young apprentice, who had a great burn on his arm from the *clingfire*
that had rained down on the army. Three perches were
with the baggage, but only one bird perched alone, and
Romilly felt sick as she fed her . . . the carrion smell was
now all around them. She could not bring herself to sleep
in the little tent she had shared with Lady Maura; she
searched through the camp at the edge of the battlefield
till she found the rest of the Sisterhood, and silently crept
in among them. So many dead. Horses, and birds, who had
been part of her life, into whom she had put so much time
and strength and love in their training . . . the Sisterhood
had set her to training these horses, not that they might
live and serve, but that they might die in this senseless
slaughter. And Clea, whom Jandria had carried dead off
the field. Two of the Sisterhood called to Romilly.

"Sister, are you wounded?"

"No," Romilly said numbly. She hardly knew; her body
was so battered with the many deaths which had swept over
her wide-open mind, which she had felt in her very flesh;
but now she realized that she was not hurt at all, that there
was not a mark anywhere on her flesh.

"Have you healing skills?" And when Romilly said no,
they told her to come and help in the digging of a grave
for Clea.

"A Swordswoman cannot lie among the soldiers. As she
was in life, so in death she must be buried apart."

Romilly wondered, with a dull pain in her head, what it
would matter now to Clea where she lay? She had defended herself well, she had taught so many of her sisters
to defend themselves, but the final ravishment of death had
caught her unaware, and she lay cold and stiff, looking very
surprised, without a mark on her face. Romilly could hardly
believe that she would not laugh and jump up, catching
them off guard as she had done so many times before. She

took the shovel one of the Swordswomen thrust into her hand. The hard physical labor of digging the grave was welcome; otherwise she caught too much pain, too many wounded men, screaming, suffering, in silence or great moans, their pain racking her. She tried to shut it all out, as Ranald had taught her, but there was too much, too much. . . .

Out on the field, dark flapping forms hovered, waiting. Then one swept down to where a dead horse lay, already bloating, and thrust in his beak with a great raucous cry of joy. Another flapped down and another, and then dozens, hundreds . . . feasting, calling out joyously to one another. Romilly picked up a thought from somewhere, she could not tell whether from one of the Swordswomen beside her at the grave, or someone out of sight on the dark camp-ground, *the defeat of men is the joy of the carrion-bird, where men mourn the kyorebni make holiday* . . . and dropped her shovel, sickened. She tried to pick it up, but suddenly doubled over, retching. She had not eaten since morning; nothing came up but a little green bile, but she stayed there, doubled over, sick and exhausted, too sick-ened even to weep.

Jandria came and led her silently inside the tent. Two Swordswomen were tending the wounds of three others, one woman with a clingfire burn on her hand which was still burning inward, another unconscious from a sword-cut across her head, and still another with a leg broken when her horse fell and rolled on her. One looked up, frowning, as Jandria led Romilly inside and pushed her down on a blanket.

"She is unwounded—she should be helping to bury our dead!"

Jandria said gruffly, "There is more than one kind of wound!" She held Romilly close, rocking her, stroking her hair, soothing her, but the girl was unaware of the touch, lost in a desperate solitude where she sought and sought for the dead. . . .

Romilly wandered in a dark dream, as if on a great grey plain, where she saw Clea before her, laughing, riding on one of the dead horses, and Prudence perched on her fist . . . but they were so far ahead, no matter how she raced, her feet were stuck as if she waded through thick syrup and she could not catch up with them, never, never. . . .

Somewhere Romilly heard a voice, she felt she ought to know the voice but she did not, saying, *She has never learned to shut it out. This time, perhaps, I can give her barriers, but there is really no remedy. She is a wild telepath and she has no protection.*

Romilly only knew that someone . . . *Carolin? Lady Maura?* . . . touched her forehead lightly, and she was back in the tent of the Swordswomen again, and the great desolate grey plain of death was gone. She clung to Jandria, shuddering and weeping.

"Clea's dead. And my horses, all my horses . . . and the birds . . ." she wept.

Jandria held and rocked her. "I know, dear. I know," she whispered, "It's all right, cry for them if you must, cry, we are all here with you." And Romilly thought, in dull amazement, *She is crying too.*

And she did not know why that should seem strange to her.

Chapter 8

Romilly woke, on the morning after the battle, to a grey and dismal day of heavy rain. On the field nothing stirred except the omnipresent carrion-birds, undaunted by the downpour, feeding on the bodies of men and horses.

It makes no difference to her now, Romilly thought, but even so she was grateful that Clea lay in the earth, her body guarded from the fierce beaks of the quarreling *kyorebni.* Yet one way or another, her body would return to its native elements, food for the small crawling things in the earth, to feed grasses and trees. She had become part of the great and endless cycle of life, where those who fed on the earth became in turn food for the earth. *Why, then, should I grieve?* Romilly asked herself, but the answer came without thought.

Her death did not come in the full course of time, when she had lived out her days. She died in a quarrel between kings which was none of her making. And yet, troubled, she remembered how she had met with Lyondri Hastur. Lyondri's cruelties were many, while Carolin at least seemed to feel that it was his duty to serve and protect those who lived in the lands he had been born to reign over.

Carolin is like a horse . . . with her love of Sunstar and of the other horses, it never occurred to Romilly that she was being offensive to the king. . . . *While Rakhal and Lyondri are like banshees who prey on living.* Suddenly, for the first time in the year she had been among the Swordswomen, Romilly was glad that Preciosa had abandoned her.

She too preys on the living. It is her nature and I love her but I could not, now, endure to see it, to be a part of it!

She dressed herself, drew the hood of her thickest cloak over her head, and went to tend Temperance. Her first impulse was to leave her to Ruyven; she felt that the sight of the empty perches of Prudence and Diligence would re-waken all the horror and dread of their deaths. But she was sworn to care for them, she was the king's hawk-mistress, and Ruyven, though he cared dutifully for the birds, did not love them, as she did.

Temperance sat solitary on her perch, huddled against the chilly dampness; the perches were sheltered but there was no protection against the wind, and Romilly decided to move the bird inside the tent in which neither she nor Maura had slept now for several nights; Temperance was the only remaining sentry-bird with Carolin's armies, and if she took cold in this damp and drizzly weather, she could not fly. Romilly shrank from the memory of her last flight, but she knew that she would, as her duty commanded, fly the bird again, even into danger. Not gladly; that gladness had been a part of innocence and it was gone forever. But she would do it, as duty demanded, because she had seen warfare and known a hint of what would befall the folk of these hills under Lyondri Hastur's harsh rule.

Lyondri did not wish—she knew this from her brief con-tact with him—to be only Rakhal's executioner. *Tell Jan-dria,* he had said, *that I am not the monster she thinks me.* Yet, he believed that this was his only road to power, and therefore he was as guilty as Rakhal.

He is Carolin's kinsman. How can they be so unlike?

As she was caring for Temperance, there was a step out-side the tent, and she turned to see a familiar face.

"*Dom* Alderic," she cried, but before he had more than a moment to stare at her in surprise, Ruyven hurried to greet Alderic with an enthusiastic kinsman's embrace.

"*Bredu!* I should have known you would hurry to find us here—does your father know?"

Alderic Castamir shook his head and smiled at his friend. He said, "I am recently come from Falconsward; your fa-ther gave me leave to go, though not willingly; you should know that Darren has returned to the monastery."

Ruyven sighed and shook his head. "I would so willingly

have yielded my place as Father's heir to Darren, and hoped, when he was not in my light, that Father would come to see his true worth. . . ."

"His *own* worth," Alderic said quietly. "Darren has small love for horses or hawks, and no trace of the MacAran Gift. He cannot be blamed for what he is not, any more than you for what you are, *bredu*. And I think The MacAran has had to grant that you cannot forge a hammer from featherpod fluff, nor spin spider-silk even from precious copper. Darren's skills are otherwise, and The MacAran has sent him to Nevarsin, to complete his schooling; one day he shall be Rael's steward, while Rael—I have already begun to teach him to work with horses and hawks."

"Little Rael!" marvelled Ruyven, "When I left Falconsward he was still at Luciella's knee, it seemed! Yet I knew he would have the MacAran Gift; I think I was blinded about Darren because I love him and I wanted so much for him to have the Gift, that I might be free. Well, Darren has found his place, as I mine."

Alderic came and bent over Romilly's hand. "Mistress Romilly," he said gently, and Romilly corrected him:

"Swordswoman Romilly—and I know what my father would say to that; he shall have no chance."

"Under favor, Romy," said Alderic, looking directly into her eyes, "Your father loves you and mourns you as dead; and so does your stepmother. May I beg you as your friend—and theirs, for your father has been more than kind to me—to send them word that you live."

She smiled wryly. "Better not. I am sure my father would rather think of me dead than earning my bread by the sword, or wearing the earring of the Sisterhood."

"I would not be quick to be too sure of that. I think, when you left Falconsward, he changed; it was not long after that, that he bowed his head to the truth and gave Darren leave to return where he was happy. You must have been blind, deaf and dumb, Romilly, if you did not know that you were the favorite of all his children, though he loves you all."

"I know that," Ruyven said, lowering his eyes, and his voice was strangled and harsh, "I never thought he would bend so far. I too have been harsh and stiff-necked. If we come alive from this war—*Bearer of Burdens, grant that!*—" he interjected in that stifled voice, "I shall go to Falconsward and be reconciled to him, and beg him to make his peace with the Towers, so that Rael may have proper training for his *laran* before it is too late. And if I must abase myself to him, so be it. I have been too proud."

"And you, Romilly?" asked Alderic. "He has grieved for you so terribly that he has grown old in this single year."

She blinked tears from her eyes. It tore at her heart to think of her father grown old. But she insisted, "Better he should think me dead, than that a daughter of his should disgrace him by wearing the earring—"

Alderic shook his head. "I cannot persuade you, but would it ease your heart to know that Mallina was married to *Dom* Garris at Midwinter?"

"Mallina? My little sister? To that—that disgusting lecher?" Romilly cried, "and you say my father has changed?"

"Be not too quick to judge," Alderic cautioned, "Garris dotes on her, and she, to all appearances, on him—even before they were wedded, she confided to me that Garris was not so bad at all, when she came to understand him; she said, the poor fellow has been so lonely and unhappy that his wretchedness drove him to all kinds of things, and now he has someone to love him and care about him, he is completely changed! You should see them together!"

"God forbid," Romilly said, shaking her head, "but if he makes Mallina happy, better her than me!" She could not imagine how anyone could tolerate that man, but Mallina had always been something of a fool, perhaps they deserved one another! "Anyhow, Mallina would be the kind of docile and obedient wife that Garris wanted."

Ruyven said, "You are so fond, you say, of my father; but have you yet gone to greet your own?"

"My father can willingly dispense with my company," Alderic frowned stubbornly. "He has never sought it; he sees only my mother in my face."

Romilly remembered what she had guessed before she left Falconsward; Alderic was Carolin's son! And therefore, rightfully heir to all these lands. . . .

She bowed and said, "Let me take you to your father, my prince."

Alderic stared and laughed. "Romilly, Romilly, my young

friend, if you have believed me the king's son, better than you know now how you have misjudged me! Carolin's sons are safely in the care of the Hastur of Carcosa, and I have heard rumors that Carolin is courting a certain *leronis* of Tramontana—" he smiled at Ruyven and said, "That was in the air even before you left the Tower, my friend."

"And *Domna* Maura has promised to wed him, if the Council gives leave," said Ruyven, adding grimly, "Providing any of us escape this war. Rakhal fell upon us with *clingfire*-arrows; we managed to fight him away, but he will rally and be upon us again, and the Bearer of Burdens knows alone what devilry of *laran*-work he will fling against us when next he comes! So make haste to greet your father, 'Deric, for this is but the lull before the storm, and by this time tomorrow we may be fighting for our lives! Would you greet your Gods after death with the stain of kin-strife still upon you? For it is most likely you have come only to die at your father's side."

"As bad as that?" Alderic asked, searching Ruyven's face. Ruyven nodded, grimly.

"We are, as I said, at the center of the storm; at peace for a moment, no more. Carolin has need of all the *leronyn* he can summon to his side, 'Deric."

Romilly interrupted, "What is this? If you are not Carolin's son—"

Alderic said quietly, "My father is called Orain, and he is foster-brother and friend of Carolin. I was reared at Carolin's court."

She reached for his hand with sudden confidence. She should have guessed, when he had spoken of the way in which his father could not endure to look on him. Carolin, even in an unwanted dynastic marriage, could have shown courtesy and kindness to a woman; but, as reward for her moment of foolishness, she had seen straight into Orain's heart. She was sorry for Alderic that he had not known a father's love; for now she knew how blessed she had been in that love.

"I am the king's hawkmistress," she said, "and he will have need of my bird soon, if we are to meet Rakhal again on the field of war. And, no doubt, your father is with him."

"I doubt it not at all," Alderic said, "He is never far

from the side of his king. When I was younger, I hated him
for that, and resented it because he cared more for Carolin's sons, and even Lyondri Hastur's little son, than for
me." He shrugged and sighed. "The world will go as it will;
love cannot be compelled, even within kin, and to such a
man as my father, my very existence must have been a
painful reminder of an unhappy time in his life. I owe Orain
a son's duty—may I never fail in it—but no more. Kinship,
I sometimes think, is a joke the gods play, to bind us to
those we do not love, in the hope we can somehow be
reconciled to them; but friends are a gift, and your father
has been a friend, almost a foster-father to me. When we
are free of this war—" he touched her hand lightly. "We
need not speak of that now. But I think you know what I
would say."

She did not look at him. There had been a time, indeed,
when she had thought she would willingly have married
this man. But much had happened to her in the year since
then. She had desired Orain himself, even though he had
not wanted her. And Ranald . . . what had happened with
Ranald was not the sort of thing which led to marriage,
nor would a Drylands lord be likely to marry a mountain
Swordswoman; indeed, she did not think she would marry
him if he asked, and there was no reason he should. Their
bodies had accepted one another joyfully, but that was
under unusual conditions; she would have accepted any
man she supposed, who had come to her and offered sur-
cease from what was so tumultuous within her. But apart
from that, they knew little of one another. And if Alderic
knew she was not the virtuous maiden she had been a
Falconsward, would he even want her?

She said, "When this war is done, Lord Alderic—"

"Call me Deric, as your brother does," he interrupted
her. "Ruyven and I are *bredin,* and as friend to both your
brothers, I owe you always a brother's protection, even if
no more."

"I am a Swordswoman—Deric," she said. "I need no
man's protection, but I will gladly have your friendship.
That, I think, I had, even at Falconsward. As for anything
more than friendship, I think—" uncontrollably, her voice
was shaking. "We should not even speak of that, until we
are free of this accursed war!"

"I am grateful for your honesty, Romilly," he said. "I would not want a woman who would marry me just because I am the son of Carolin's chief counselor and friend. My father married because the old king wished to honor his son's foster-brother by giving him in marriage to a high-born lady; they despised one another, and I have suffered for that; I would not wish my own children torn by hatred between their parents, and I have always sworn that I would marry no woman unless we were, at least, friends." His eyes, levelled and gentle, met hers, and for some reason the kindness in them made her want to cry.

"For anything more we can wait—Swordswoman."

She nodded. But all she said was, "Let us go, then, and greet your father."

But they did not reach Carolin's tent before they met Orain, hurrying toward the place where the birds were kept. He said, "Mistress Romilly, your sentry-bird is wanted—" and stopped, blinking, at the sight of her companion.

"Father," Alderic said, and bowed.

Orain took him, for a moment, in a brief, formal embrace. The sight hurt Romilly; she was so accustomed to Orain's rough affection. She thought, he would have greeted *me* with more kindness than that! He said, "I did not know you had come, my boy. Carolin has need now of any who are skilled at *laran;* perhaps you have heard that he came down on us with clingfire."

"I heard it when I came to camp, Father," Alderic said, "and I was making haste to offer such small skill as I have to Carolin's service; but I came first to greet you, sir."

Orain said, with constraint, "For that I thank you in his name. The king's *leronyn* are gathered there—" and he gestured. "Mistress Romilly, bring your bird; we must know how long we have before Rakhal falls on us again."

"Are we to march out on Rakhal, then?" Alderic asked, and Orain said, with his mouth set in a grim line,

"Only to get free of the bodies here, so that we can maneuver if we must. If Rakhal has clingfire at command, we dare not meet him in the woods, or all this land will be burned over between here and Neskaya!" And as Romilly looked toward Carolin's headquarters she saw the tent struck, and the Hastur banner taken out by his guardsmen. Alderic glanced once at Romilly, but all he said was, "I

must join the others, then. Guard yourself well, Romilly,"
and hurried away.

She went back swiftly to prepare herself for riding, and
set Temperance on her saddle, leaving it to Ruyven's young
assistant to strike the tent and pack it for moving with the
army. Could Rakhal indeed be so thoughtless of the land
as to send fire-arrows in forested country, at this season,
and risk fire? Well, it was like what she had heard of the
man. For that reason, if for no other, somehow they must
defeat that unprincipled man who called himself king!

Now that she knew what she was seeking, it proved easier to send up the sentry-bird. Because of the rain, Temperance was reluctant to fly, but this time Romilly did not
hesitate to send the bird up, almost to the bottom of the
low-lying clouds. She flew her slowly in circles, gradually
widening, so that she could see Rakhal's army on the move.
As she rode, half of her mind on the bird, she joined Carolin and his array of skilled *leronyn*, men and women; it
crossed her mind, briefly, that she was one of them, that
perhaps at last, she had found her true place.

*I am Swordswoman still. But I am grateful that I need
not bear a sword in this combat. If I must, I think I could
do so, but I am glad that my skills lead me elsewhere. I do
not want to kill . . .* and then, grimly, she forced herself to
be realistic. She was a part of this killing, as much as if she
bore sword or bow into the battlefield; more, perhaps, for
her sentry-bird's eyes directed the killing. She took her
place, resolutely, between Lady Maura and Ranald. One or
both of them would remain in rapport with her, to relay
the information to the ears of Carolin and his general.

*It cannot be easy for Jandria, to go against Lyondri this
way, and know that she will be instrumental in his death—
and now there is no help for him but death.* She was not
sure at that moment whether the thought was hers, or Lady
Maura's, or even, perhaps, Lord Orain's. They were all in
a tight little group, clustered around Carolin, and Alderic
was among them. At the edge of her awareness she saw
Alderic greet Jandria kindly, and call her "My lady Aunt."
As if it were something she had dreamed a long time ago,
it crossed her mind that if she married Alderic, she would
be kinswoman to Jandria.

But we are sworn to one another in the Sisterhood, any-

way, I need not that to be her kin. Alderic said it so; kinsmen are born, but friendship is a gift of the Gods. . . .

Maura looked at her meaningfully, and Romilly remembered her work; she went swiftly into rapport with Temperance, who was still flying in widening circles over the great
plain. At last she spotted, through the keen eyes of the
bird, a darkening cloud of dust on the horizon. . . .

Rakhal's army, on the move, and riding swiftly toward
the forested cover of the hills. As she saw, and as this
information was relayed swiftly to Carolin, she caught the
thought of the king, *So he would hide within the cover of
the trees, for he knows I am unwilling to use* clingfire, *or
even ordinary fire-arrows, where there is danger that the
resin-trees may bring on wildfire. Somehow we must over-
take him before he reaches the forest, and do battle on
ground of my choosing, not his.* And Romilly sensed the
touch of his mind on Sunstar's;

Lead my men, then, great horse. . . .

She saw with a strange widening consciousness, linked to
Carolin, to Sunstar, to all the men around her. She knew
that Ranald had seized her horse's rein and was guiding
him, so that she could ride safely even while she was in
rapport with the sentry-bird, and spared him a quick
thought of gratitude. The rain was slowing, and after a time
a strange, low, watery sunlight came through the clouds.
She flew Temperance lower, over the armies, trying to fly
high enough that she could not be seen, yet dipping in
and spying . . .

Rakhal's armies seemed shrunken in size, and off to the
north she saw another body of men and horses. Were they
coming to Rakhal's aid, now that the first battle had
thinned his ranks? No; for they were riding away from Rakhal's main army as swiftly as they could. And Carolin's
thoughts were jubilant.

*Rakhal's men are deserting him, now they know what he
is . . . they have no more stomach than I for this kind
of warfare. . . .*

But the main body of men was still formidable; they had
come to a halt at the brow of a little hill, and Romilly
knew, being in communication with the minds of Carolin's
men, that Rakhal had seized the most advantageous terrain,
and would make a stand there and defend it.

This, then, would be the decisive battle. Under urging from Carolin, she flew the bird down closer, so that through her eyes, Carolin's advisers might take stock of the size of the forces arrayed against them. Rakhal had the advantage, it seemed, in numbers, and in terrain.

Somehow we must lure Rakhal from that hill. . . .

Alderic rode toward his father and spoke to Orain urgently for a few moments, and Romilly, what small part of her mind was not with the bird, heard Orain say to Carolin, "By your leave, my lord. My son has put me in mind of an old trick in the mountains, and we have *leronyn* enough to make it effective. Let me lead a dozen or two of your men, with the *leronyn,* to cast an illusion as if there were four times as many of us, to force Rakhal to charge down upon us; then you can come and take him on the flank."

Carolin considered for a moment. "It might work," he said at last, "but I'll not send your *leronyn* into danger; most of them do not even wear swords."

Ranald Ridenow said, "My *laran* as well as my sword are at your service, my King. Let me lead these men."

"Pick your men, then—and Aldones ride with you, all of you!" Carolin said, "but pick your moment carefully—"

"Mistress MacAran shall do that for us," said Ranald, with his hand on Romilly's bridle.

Orain said, "Would you take a woman into battle?" and Romilly, pulling herself free for a moment of the rapport with the bird-mind, said, "My lord Orain, I am a Swordswoman! Where my brother will go, I shall go with him!"

Ruyven did not speak, but she felt the warmth that said, not in words, *Bravely spoken, sister,* and with it a touch from Alderic. Somehow it reminded her of the day when they had flown hawks at Falconsward, at Midsummer-festival.

When I am free of this war, I shall never again hunt for pleasure, for I know now what it is to be hunted . . . and with amazement, she knew that the mind which held this thought was Orain's.

How near to my own thought! Romilly felt again the bitter regret for the distance that had fallen between Orain and herself. *We were so close in so many ways, so much alike!* But the world would go as it would, and Orain was as he was and not as she would have him. She threw herself back into rapport with the sentry-bird, letting Ranald see through her mind, and relay to Orain and Alderic, what she saw in Rakhal's army.

Horsemen were drawn up at the perimeter of his army, surrounding foot-soldiers and bowmen, and at the center, a number of great wagons, with the acrid smell she knew now to be the chemical smell of *clingfire*. They ringed the brow of the little hill completely while they took their stand there, it would be impossible to breach their defenses.

But that is precisely what we must do, it was Alderic's thought, and he rode the company of two dozen men, headed by the small band of *leronyn,* breakneck toward the hill; suddenly stopped them.

Now!

And suddenly it seemed to Romilly that a great cloud of dust and fire moved on the hill, with a racing and a pounding of hooves, and cries . . . *what soldiers are these?* And then she knew that she had seen these men, the men who had deserted Rakhal and were riding away . . . it was like a great mirror, as if the image of this separate army were thrown straight at Rakhal's men . . . for a little they held firm, while a cloud of arrows came flying down toward the close-clustered band of soldiers and *leronyn* at the foot of the hill . . . but they were shooting short, at the image of the racing *soldiers* . . .

Join with us! In the name of the Gods, everyone who has laran, *join us to hold this image* . . . on and on the racing cloud of dust, in which Romilly could now see indistinct shapes, horses' heads like great grey skulls, the burning visages of skeletons, glowing with devil-fire inside the hidden cloud of dust and sorcery. . . .

She heard a voice she had never heard before, reverberating within her mind, bellowing; "Stand firm! Stand firm!" But that could not stand against the assault of the ghostly army; Rakhal's men broke and charged down the hill, riding straight into the cloud of magical images, screaming in terror, and their line faltered, broke in a dozen places. Fire struck up through the ground, licking, curling, green and blue flames rising . . . then it was as if a river of blood flowed up the hill, through the horses' feet, and they stopped short, snorting, screaming in terror, stamping. Some of their riders fell, a few men held their ground, crying out, "No smell of blood, no smell of burning, it's a trick, a trick—" but the line was broken; horses stampeded, colliding with one another, trampling their riders, and the officers struggled wildly to rally the broken line, to gather the men into some semblance of order.

"Now! Carolin!"

"A Hastur! A Hastur!" Carolin's men charged, the main body of the army, flowing like water up the hill and into the broken ranks of the horsemen. Right over Rakhal's outer defenses they flowed, and then they were fighting at close quarters, but Ranald and Alderic broke and dashed right through to the center of the armies, where the guarded wagon stood with the *clingfire*. Men were gathered, hastily dipping their arrows in the stuff, but Alderic and Orain and their little band rode right over them and toward the wagon. Swiftly, like a running tide of energy, they linked minds, and a band of blue fire rolled out toward the wagon with the clingfire. It struck, blazed upward, and then a roaring column of fire burst skyward, blazing so fiercely that Rakhal's men scattered and ran for their lives. Burning droplets fell on some of them and they blazed up like living torches and died screaming; the fire ran through Rakhal's own armies, and, panicked, they ran, scattered, and ran right on Carolin's spears and swords.

Although a part of Romilly was still linked with the bird, she knew there was no more need of it. She found herself closely linked in mind with Sunstar, as Carolin urged him forward; she knew the terror of fire, shuddering with the smell of burning grass and burning flesh; even in the rain which had begun to drizzle down again in the fitful sunlight, the *clingfire* burned on. But the great stallion, bravely overcoming that inborn fear, carried his rider forward . . . or was it Romilly herself, bearing the king into the heart of the fleeing enemy.

"See where Rakhal flies with his sorcerers!" cried out Orain, "After them, men! Take them now!"

Romilly let Temperance fly upward out of range of the fire; it was burning inward now, with a ring round it where there was nothing left to burn—so much had the *leronyn* of Carolin's armies accomplished; but she, with Carolin, was away with the stallion Sunstar, forging to the heights, where the last remnant of Rakhal's men, cut off between

Carolin and the raging remnant of clingfire, fought with their backs to the fire. Sunstar seemed to fly forward with Carolin's own will to take the height, and Romilly felt that it was she herself who bore him on to the last moment of success. . . .

Then she stumbled—for a moment Romilly was not sure it was not she herself who had stumbled—recovered, and reared high in the air, Carolin's hand guiding him up, then down, to trample the man who had risen, sword in hand, before him. His great hooves were like hammers pounding the man into the ground. Romilly felt the man go down, his head splitting like a ripe fruit beneath her hooves— Sunstar's hooves—felt Carolin fighting for balance in the saddle. And then another man reared up with a lightning-flash of steel, she felt Carolin slip back in the saddle and fall, and in that moment Romilly felt sharp shearing pain as the sword sliced through neck and throat and heart, and blood and life spurted away. . . .

She never felt herself strike the ground.

. . . rain was falling, hard cold rain, pounding down; the ground was awash with it, and even the smell of the *clingfire* had been washed away. The sky was dark; it was near nightfall. Romilly sat up, dazed and stunned, not even now fully aware that it was not she who had been felled by the sword.

Sunstar! She reached out automatically for his mind, found—

Found nothingness! Only a great sense of vacancy, emptiness where he had been. Wildly she looked around and saw, lying not far away the stallion's body, his head nearly severed, and the man he had killed lying beneath his great bulk. The rain had washed the blood clear so that there was only a great gaping wound in his neck from which the blood had soaked into the ground all around him. *Sunstar, Sunstar—dead, dead, dead!* She reached out, again, dazed, to nothingness. Sunstar, whose life she had shared so long. . . .

And whom she had betrayed by leading him to death in a war between two kings . . . *neither of them is worth a lock of his black mane . . . ah, Sunstar . . . and I died with you* . . . Romilly felt so empty and cold she was not sure that she was still alive. She had heard tales of men who did not know they were dead and kept trying to communicate with the living. Dazed, drained of all emotion except fury and grief, she managed to sit up.

Around her lay the bodies of the dead, Rakhal's men and Carolin's; but of Carolin himself there was no sign. Only the body of Sunstar showed where Carolin had once been. Vaguely, not caring, she wondered if all Carolin's men were dead and Rakhal victor. Or had Orain's party captured or killed Rakhal? What did it matter?

What matters it which great rogue sits on the throne. . . .

She began to get her bearings a little. As before the previous battle, the field was covered with the dark shapes of *kyorebni,* hovering. One lighted, with a harsh scream, on Sunstar's head, and Romilly rushed at it, flapping her arms and crying out. The bird was gone, but it would come back.

Sunstar is dead. And I trained him with my own hands for this war, betrayed him into the hands of the one who would ride him into this slaughter, and the noble horse never faltered, but bore Carolin to this place and to his death. I would have done better to kill him myself when he ran joyously around our green paddock behind the hostel of the Sisterhood. Then he would never have know fire and fear and a sword through his heart.

Dark was falling, but far away at the edge of the battlefield, a lantern bobbed, a little light wandering over the field. Grave-robbers? Mourners seeking the slain? No; intuitively Romilly knew who they were; the women of the Sisterhood, seeking their fallen comrades, who must not lie in the common grave of Carolin's soldiers.

As if it mattered to the dead where they lay. . . .

They would come here soon, thinking her dead—when she had fallen from her horse, stricken down by Sunstar's death, no doubt they had left her for dead. Now they would come to bury her, and find her living, and they would rejoice. . . .

And then Romilly was overcome with rage and grief. They would take her back to themselves, reclaim her as a warrior-woman. She had fled from the company of men, come among the Sisterhood, and what had they done? Set her to training horses, not for their own sake or for the service of men, but to be slaughtered, slaughtered senselessly in this strife of men who could not keep their quarrels to themselves alone but involved the innocent birds and horses in their wars and killings. . . .

And I am to go back to that? No, no, never!

With shaking hands, she tore the earring of the Sisterhood from her ear; the wire caught and tore her ear but she was unconscious of the pain. She flung it on the ground. *An offering for Sunstar, a sacrifice offered to the dead!* She could hardly stand. She looked around, and saw that riderless horses were wandering here and there on the battlefield. It took only the slightest touch of her *laran* to bring one to her, his head bent in submission. It was too dark now to see whether it was mare or gelding, grey or black or roan. She climbed into the saddle, and crouched over the pommel, letting the horse take his own way . . . *where? It matters not. Away from this place of death, away, friend. I will serve no more, not as soldier nor Swordswoman nor leronis. From henceforth I shall serve no man nor woman.* Blindly, her eyes closed against streaming hot tears, Romilly rode alone from the battlefield and into the rain of the night.

All that night, she rode letting the horse find his own pathway, and never knew where she went or what direction she took. The sun rose and she was still unaware, sitting as if lifeless on the animal's back, swaying now and again but always recovering herself before she quite fell. It did not seem to matter. Sunstar was dead. Carolin and Orain had gone she knew not where, nor did it matter, Orain wanted nothing of her . . . she was a woman. Carolin, like the Sisterhood, sought only to have her use her *laran* to betray other innocent beasts to the slaughter! Ruyven . . . Ruyven cared little for her, he was like a monk from the accursed Tower where they learned devilry like *clingfire.* . . .

There is no human who shall mean anything to me now.

She rode on, all day, across a countryside ravaged and deserted, over which the war had raged. At the edge of the forest, she slid from her horse, and set him free.

"Go, my brother," she whispered, "and serve no man or woman, for they will only lead you to death. Live free in the wild, and go your own way."

The horse stared down at her for a moment; she gave it a final pat and pushed it away, and, after a moment of motionless surprise, it turned and cantered awkwardly

away. Romilly went quietly into the darkness of the forest.
She was soaked to the skin, but it seemed not to matter,
any more than the horse minded his wet cloak of hair. She
found a little hollow between the roots of a tree, crawled
into it, drew her cloak tightly around her, covering her face;
curled herself into a ball and slept like the dead.

At dawn she woke to hear birds calling, and it seemed,
mixed with their note, she could hear the harsh screams of
the *kyorebni,* still feeding on the waste of the battlefield.
She did not know where she was going; somewhere away
from the sound of those screams. She got numbly to her
feet and walked, not caring in which direction, further into
the wood.

She walked most of that day. She was not conscious of
hunger; she moved like a wild thing, silently, avoiding what
was in her path and whenever she heard a noise, freezing
silently in her tracks. Late in the day she nearly stumbled
into a small stream, and cupping her hands, drank deeply
of the clear sweet water, then laid herself down in a patch
of sunlight that came between the leaves and let the sun
dry the remaining damp from her clothes. She was still
numb. As darkness fell, she curled up under a bush and
slept. Some small thing in the grasses brushed against her
and she never thought to turn aside.

The next morning she slept late and woke with the sun's
heat across her back. Before her, a spider had spun its web,
clear and jewelled with the dew; she looked on its marvel-
ous intricacy and felt the first pleasure she had felt in many
days. The sun was bright on the leaves; a bushjumper suddenly bolted on long legs, followed by four miniature babies, their bushy tails standing up like small bluish flags
riding high. Romilly heard herself laugh aloud, and they
stopped, tails quivering, dead silent; then, as the silence fell
around them, with a burst of speed all four of the tiny flags
popped down a hole in the grass.

How quiet it was within the woods! There could certainly
be no human dwelling nearby, or nothing could have been
so peaceful, the wild things so untroubled and unafraid.

She uncurled herself from sleep, lazily stretching her
limbs. She was thirsty, but there was no stream nearby; she
licked the dew from the low leaves of the tree over her
head. On a fallen log she found a few old woody mush-

rooms, and ate them, then found some dried berries hanging to a stem and ate them too. After a little while, as she wandered lazily through the wood, she saw the green flags of a root she knew to be edible, grubbed it up with a stick, rubbed off the dirt on the edge of her tunic, and chewed it slowly. It was stringy and hard, the flavor acrid enough to make her eyes water, but it satisfied her hunger.

She had lost the impetus that had kept her moving restlessly from place to place; she sat in the clearing of the fallen log most of the day, and when night fell again she slept there.

During her sleep she heard someone calling her name; but she did not seem to know the voice. Orain? No, he would not call her; he had wanted her when he thought her a boy, but had no use for the woman she really was. Her father? He was far away, across the Kadarin, safe at home. She thought with pain of the peaceful hills of Falconsward. Yet it was there she had learned that evil art of horse-training by which she had betrayed the beloved to his death. In her dream she seemed to sit on Sunstar's back, to ride like the wind across the grey plain she once had seen, and she woke with her face wet with tears.

A day or two later she realized that she had lost shoes and stockings, she did not remember where, that her feet were already hardening to the dirt and pebbles of the forest floor. She wandered on aimlessly, ever deeper into the forest, eating fruits, grubbing in the earth for roots; now and again she cooled her feet in a mountain stream but she never thought of washing. She ate when she found food; when once for three days together she found nothing edible, she was dimly aware of hunger, but it did not seem important to her. She no longer troubled to rub the dirt from the roots she ate; they seemed just as good to her in their coats of earth. Once she found some pears on an abandoned tree and their taste was so sweet that she felt a rush of ecstasy. She ate as many as she could but it did not occur to her to fill her pockets or to tie them into her skirt.

One night she woke when the purple face of Liriel stood over her in the sky, seeming to look down and chide her, and thought, *I am surely mad, where am I going, what am I going to do? I cannot go on like this forever.* But when she woke she had forgotten it again. Now and again, too, she heard, not with her ears but within her mind, voices that seemed to call, *Romilly, where are you?* She wondered faintly who Romilly was, and why they were calling her.

She came to the end of the woods, the next day, and out into open plains and rolling hills. Waving grasses were covered with seeds . . . all this country must once have been settled and planted to grain but all around the horizon which stretched wide from west to east, from the wall of the forest behind her to the mountains which rose greyish-pink in the distance, there was no human dwelling. She picked a handful of the seeds, rubbed their coats from them, and chewed them as she walked.

High in the sky, a hawk soared, a single hawk, and as she watched, it dropped down, down, down, falling toward her with folded wings, it alighted on her shoulder. It seemed to speak in her mind, but she did not know what it was saying, yet it seemed that once she had known this hawk, that it had a name, that once she had flown beside it in the sky . . . no, that was not possible, yet the hawk seemed so sure that they knew one another. She reached out to touch it, then stopped, there was some reason she should not touch it with her finger . . . she wished she could remember why. But she looked into the hawk's eyes, and wished she knew where she had seen the hawk before this.

She woke again that night, and again she was aware that she was certainly quite mad, that she could not wander forever like this. But she had no idea where she was, and there was no one to ask. She knew who she was, now, she was Romilly, and the hawk, the hawk which had perched on the low limb of a nearby tree, the hawk was Preciosa, but why had she sought her out here? Did she not know that she, Romilly, set the touch of her mind on bird or horse only to train it to follow humankind meekly to its own death?

It took her five days to cross the plain; she counted them, without thinking, as the face of Liriel grew toward full. When last the moon was full, she had followed Sunstar— she slammed the memory shut; it was too painful. There were plenty of the grainlike seeds to eat, and water to drink. Once the hawk brought a bird down from the sky and lighted on her shoulder, screaming in frustration; she looked at the dead bird, torn by the hawk's beak, and shuddered. It was the hawk's nature, but the sight of the blood made her feel sick, and at last she flung it to the ground and walked on.

That night she came beneath the edges of another patch of forest. She found a tree heavy with last year's nuts, and by now she had sense enough to fill her pockets with them. She was still not certain where she was going, but she had begun to turn northward when there was a choice. She moved noiselessly now through the woods, driven restlessly onward . . . she did not know why.

Overhead, toward evening, she heard the cry of waterfowl, flying toward the south. She looked up, soaring with them in their dizzy flight, seeing from afar where a tall white tower rose, and the glimmer of a lake. Where was she?

The moons were so bright that night, four of them shining down on her, Liriel and Kyrrdis round and full, and the other two shining pale and gibbous, that she could not sleep. It seemed to her that when last she had seen four moons in the sky, something had happened . . . no, she could not remember, but her body ached with desire and hunger unslaked, and she did not know why. After a time, lying in the soft moss, she began to range outward, feeling hungers like her own all round her. . . .

A cat crawled along a branch, and she felt the tug of the light within her, too, the flow of the life of the world, and herself with it. She could see the gleam of the great eyes, followed it with her mind while she prowled around the foot of the tree. There was a sweet, sharp, musky scent in the air now and, in the mind of the cat, she followed it, not knowing whether or not she moved or whether only the cat moved . . . closer and closer she came, and heard herself make a small snarling, purring cry of hunger and need . . . turned with a lashing of the great tail as the cat's mate pounced down the tree trunk, with cries and frisking sounds. Her body ached and hungered and as the cat seized her mate, Romilly twisted on the moss of the ground and dug her hands into the ground, gasping, crying out . . .

Ranald . . . she whispered, in the moment before she was lost in the wild surge of heat. The night seemed filled with the snarling, purring sound of the great cats in their mating, and she lay silent, battered down beneath it, and at last, her senses and *laran* overloaded, she lost consciousness.

The next morning she woke, hardly aware what had happened, feeling sick and exhausted. She did not know why, but her aimless moving through the forest had quickened pace. She must get away, get away . . . a nameless apprehension was on her, and when she heard, above her, the same snarling cry of the great cat, she was too numbed to be afraid. And then there was a dark flash as it slithered to the ground and stood facing her, mouth drawn back in a snarl over sharp fanged teeth. Behind it she sensed the presence of the little balls of brownish fur, hidden in the hollow tree. . . .

The cat was protecting her young! And, she, Romilly, had blundered into the proximity of the cat's protected territory . . . she blundered backward, fighting the temptation to turn and run, run away . . . if she did, she knew the cat would be on her in a moment! Slowly, stealthily, she drew backward, backward, trying to catch the animal's eyes, to press on it with her *laran* . . .

Peace, peace, I mean no harm, not to you, not to your little ones. . . . At some time, she had done this before, something which menaced her, cold, fierce in the snows. . . .

Silently, silently, step after step, withdraw, withdraw . . . *peace, peace, I mean you no harm, your cubs no harm.* . . .

Then, when she was almost at the edge of the clearing, the cat moved like a streak, with a single long leap, and landed almost at Romilly's feet.

Peace, peace . . . The cat bent her head, almost laid it at Romilly's feet. Then shock struck through her.

No, no! I betrayed Sunstar to death, I swore I would use that laran *no more, never, never . . . no more of the innocent to die* . . .

One paw lashed out like a whip; claws raked Romilly's face, and the weight of the arm stretched her sprawling and gasping with pain; she felt blood break from her cheek and her lip. *Now she has spilled my blood, will she kill me now as sacrifice to her cubs, in expiation for the death of Sunstar.* . . .

The hoarse, soft snarling never stopped. Romilly rolled herself into a ball, to protect her face. Then, as the cat sprung again, a fury of wings lashed down, and the hawk's claws raked at the eyes of the great cat, beating wings flapping around the cat's muzzle.

Preciosa! She has come to fight for me!

Romilly rolled free, springing up and climbing into a nearby tree. Preciosa hovered, just out of reach of the deadly claws, flapping and striking with beak and talons, until the cat, snarling softly, turned her back and vanished into the long grasses where her cubs were hidden. Her breath catching in her throat, Romilly slid down the tree and ran as far as she could in the opposite direction, Preciosa close behind her; she heard the sound of the wings and the little shrilling sound of the hawk. When she was out of range, she stopped, turned, thrust out her fist, in a gesture so familiar that she did not even make it consciously.

"*Preciosa!*" she cried, and as the hawk's talons closed, gently, on her arm, she remembered everything, and began to cry.

"Oh, Preciosa, you came for me!"

She washed in a stream, that night, and shook the leaf-mold and dirt from her cloak. She took off her tunic and trousers, and shook them out to air, and put them on again. She had lost, somewhere, her Swordswoman's earring—she never knew where. With the hawk riding on her shoulder, she tried to orient herself.

She supposed the white Tower nearby must be Neskaya, but she was not certain. A day's walk should bring her there, and perhaps she could send a message somewhere, and know what had befallen Carolin, and what the armies did. She still flinched from the thought of joining them again, but she knew someday she must return to her own kind.

Late that night, as she was looking for a dry place to sleep, and wondering how she had managed all these days alone—she thought she must have been in the woods all of three days, perhaps—it seemed that she heard someone calling her name.

Romilly! Romilly!

Search for her with laran, *only so we can find her, she is hiding . . .*

She cannot be dead. I would know if she was dead. . . .

She recognized, vaguely, some of the voices, though it was still not clear.

If you can find her, bid her come back to us. This was a voice she knew, a voice she loved; Jandria, mourning. And although she had never done it before, somehow Romilly knew how to reach out with her mind.

Where are you? What has happened? I thought the war was over.

It is ended, and Carolin is encamped before the walls of Hali, came the answer. *But it is stalemate, for Lyondri has Orain as hostage somewhere within the city.*

And Romilly did not even stop to remember her grudge, or what it had been.

I will come as swiftly as I can.

Chapter 9

She slept only a little that night, and was awake and walking by daylight, sending out her *laran* to spy out a dwelling of men. Once in the village she sought out a man who had horses for hire.

"I must have a fast horse at once. I am of the Sisterhood of the Sword, and I am on an urgent mission for King Carolin; I am needed at once at Hali."

"And I am His Majesty's chief cook and bottle-washer," jeered the stableman. "Not so fast, *mestra;* what will you pay?" And Romilly saw herself reflected in his eyes, a gaunt scarecrow of a woman in a tattered tunic and breeches, barefoot, her face savagely clawed and bleeding where the mountain-cat had swiped at her, the unkempt hawk riding on her shoulders.

"I have been through the war and worse," she said. She had dwelt among animals so long she had forgotten the need of money. She searched the deep pockets of tunic and breeches and found a few coins forgotten she spilled them out before him.

"Take these as earnest," she said, not counting them, "I swear I will send the rest when I reach a hostel of the Sisterhood, and twice as many if you will find me a pair of boots and some food."

He hesitated. "I will need thirty silver bits or a copper *royal*," he said, "and another as token that you will return the horse here—"

Her eyes glittered with rage. She did not even know why she was in such need of haste, but she was sought for at

Hali. "In Carolin's name," she said, "I can take your horse if I must—"

She signalled to the nearest horse; he looked fast, a great rangy roan. A touch of her *laran* and he came swiftly to her, bowed his neck in submission. His owner shouted with anger and came to lay his hand on the horse's lead-rope, but the horse edged nervously away, and lashed out, kicking; circled, and came back to rub Romilly's head with his shoulder.

"*Leronis . . .*" he whispered, his eyes widened, staring.

"That and more," said Romilly tartly.

A young woman stood watching, twisting her long apron. At last she whispered, "My mother's sister is of the Sisterhood, *mestra*. She has told me that the Sisterhood will always pay debts incurred by one of them, for the honor of them all. Let her have the horse, my husband, and—" she ran into the house, brought back a pair of rough boots.

"They were my son's," she said in a whisper, "Rakhal's men came through the village and one of them killed him, cut him down like a dog, when they seized our plow-beast and slaughtered it for their supper, and he asked them for some payment. Carolin's men have done nothing like this."

Romilly slipped the boots on her feet. They were hillmen's boots, fur-lined, soft to her toes. The woman gave her half of a cut loaf of bread. "If you can wait, *mestra*, you shall have hot food, but I have nothing cooked. . . ."

Romilly shook her head. "This is enough," she said. "I cannot wait." In a flash she was on the horse's back, even while the man cried, "No lady can ride that horse—he is my fiercest—"

"I am no lady but a Swordswoman," she said, and suddenly a new facet of her *laran* made itself clear to her; she reached out, as she had done to the mountain cat, and he backed away before her, staring, submissive.

The woman cried, "Do you not want saddle—bridle—let me bind up your wounds, Swordswoman—"

"I have no time for that," Romilly said, "Set me on the road to Hali."

The woman stammered out directions, while the man stood silent, goggling at her. She dug her heels into the horse's back. She had ridden like this, with neither saddle nor bridle, when she was a child at Falconsward, just learning her *laran*, guiding the horse with her will alone. She felt a brief, poignant regret; *Sunstar!* Sunstar, and the nameless unknown horse she had ridden away from the battle and turned loose to wander in the wild. She had surely been mad.

The horse moved swiftly and steady, his long legs eating up the road. She gnawed at the hard bread; it seemed that no fine meal had ever been quite so delicious. She needed fresh clothes, and a bath, and a comb for her hair, but nightmare urgency drove her on. *Orain, in the hands of Lyondri!* Once she stopped to let the horse graze a little and rest, and wondered, *What do I think I can do about it?*

The Lake at Hali was long and dim, with a Tower rising on the shore, and pale waves lapping like stormclouds at the verge; at the far end Carolin's army encamped before a city whose walls were grey and grim. And now she was sure enough of her *laran* to reach out and feel for the presence of the man she had known as *Dom* Carlo, and to know that he was her friend, king or no. He was still the man who had welcomed her, protected her among his men even when he knew she was a woman, kept her secret even from his dearest friend and foster-brother.

She made her way through the staring army, hearing one of the Swordswomen call her name in amazement. She knew how she must look to them, worn and gaunt, her tunic and breeches filthy, her hair a ragged and uncombed mop, the cat-claw marks still bloody across her face, riding a countryman's horse with neither saddle nor bridle. Was this any way to present herself to a king?

But even as she slid from her horse, Jandria had her in a tight embrace.

"Romilly, Romy, we thought you were dead! Where did you go?"

She shook her head, suddenly too exhausted to speak.

"Anywhere. Everywhere. Nowhere. Does it matter? I came as swiftly as I could. How long since the battle? What is this about Orain being held hostage for Lyondri?"

Alderic and Ruyven came to stare, to clasp her in their arms. "I tried to reach you, with Lady Maura," Alderic said, "but we could not—" and Jandria cried out, "What happened to your face—your earring—?"

"Later," she said, with an exhausted shake of her head,

and then Carolin himself was before her; he held out both his hands.

"Child—" he said, and hugged her as her own father might have done. "Orain loved you, too—I thought I had lost both of you, who followed me not as a king but as an outlaw and fugitive! Come in," he said, and led the way into his tent. He gestured, and Jandria poured her a cup of wine, but Romilly shook her head.

"No, no, I have eaten almost nothing, I would be drunk if I drank half a cup now—I would rather have some food," she said. The remnants of a meal were laid around the rough table inside, and Carolin said, "Help yourself." Jandria cut her a slice of meat and bread, but Romilly laid the meat aside—she knew she would never taste it again—and ate the bread, slowly. Jandria took the rejected wine and washed the deep claw-marks on her face.

"Why, how came you to have these? The healer must tend them, a cat's claw-wounds always fester; you could lose the sight of an eye if they spread," she said, but Romilly only shook her head.

"I hardly know. Some day I will tell you all I can remember," she promised, "But Orain—"

"They have him somewhere in the city," Carolin said. He had been pacing the tent but now he dropped wearily into one of the folding camp-chairs. "I dare not even enter to search for him, for they have warned me . . . yet it might give him an easier death than what Lyondri plans for him. Rakhal's army is cut to pieces; most of them have made submission to me, but Rakhal himself, with a few of his men, and Lyondri, took refuge here . . . and they have Orain captive; he has been in their hands since the battle. Now they are using him to parley—" she could see his jaw move as he swallowed and said, "I offered them safe-conduct across the Kadarin, or wherever they wished to go, and both their lives, and to leave Lyondri's son safe in Nevarsin, and have him reared as kinsman at my court, with my own sons. But they—they—" He broke off, and Romilly saw that his hands were trembling.

"Let me tell her, Uncle," Alderic said gently. "I sent word I would surrender myself in exchange for my father, and go with them where they wished across the Kadarin to safety, to whatever place they should appoint for refuge; I also made offer of copper and silver—"

"The long and short of it is," Jandria said, "that precious pair have demanded that Carolin surrender *himself* to them for Orain's life. I, too, offered to exchange myself—I thought Lyondri might agree to that. And Maura said she would give herself up to Rakhal, even go with him into exile if that was what he wished, so that Carolin might have his paxman. But—" her face was grim, "Let her see what answer they sent us."

Ruyven fumbled with a little package wrapped in yellow silk. His hands shook dreadfully. Carolin took the silk from him and tried to unwrap it. Maura laid her hands over his, stroked them for a moment, then opened the bloodstained cloth.

Inside—Romilly thought that she would retch—was a calloused finger. Clotted blood caked the end where it had been cut from the hand; and the horror was, that one finger bore a copper ring, set with a blue stone, which she had seen on Orain's hand.

Carolin said, "They sent word—they would return Orain to me—a little piece at a time—unless I surrendered myself to them, and made complete submission of my armies." His hands were shaking, too, as he carefully wrapped up the finger again. "They sent this two days ago. Yesterday it was—it was an ear. Today—" he could not go on; he shut his eyes, and she saw the tears squeezing from his eyes.

"For Orain I would give my life and more, and he has always know it," Carolin said, "but I—I have seen what Rakhal has done to my people—how can I give all of them over to him and his butcher Lyondri?"

"Orain would let himself be cut into little pieces for you, and you know that—" Maura said, and Carolin lowered his head and sobbed. "Lyondri knows that, too. Damn him! Damn him waking and sleeping—" His voice rose, almost in hysteria.

"Enough." Maura laid a gentle hand on his, took the horrid silk package from him and set it aside.

Jandria said grimly "I swear, I shall not sleep nor drink wine till Lyondri has been flayed alive—"

"Nor I; but that will not save Orain from his fate," said

Carolin. "You come when we have lost hope, and are almost ready to storm the city, so that Orain may have a death that is swift and clean. Yet somehow we must find out where they are keeping him, and he has managed to shield the city against *laran*. But we still have one sentry-bird, and we thought, perhaps—we could fly her; she has not been manageable since the battle, Ruyven could not handle her—"

Maura said, "And Ranald was killed in the final charge, where we thought you too had died. But Ruyven said you were not dead, that he would have felt you die—and the Swordswomen could not find your body. But we knew not where you had gone. Yet perhaps, if we can find out in what part of the city they have kenneled for their filthy work—if we enter the city, they have threatened, they will start to cut him to pieces at that moment, and we may have what is left by the time we have searched long enough to find him." Her face twisted with dread and horror. "So we cannot search at random, and—and somehow his *leronyn* have guarded the city—but perhaps they would not notice a bird— "

"They would see a sentry-bird at once," said Romilly. "Their *leronyn* would be aware of just such a plan—"

"That is what I told them," Ruyven said, "but it seemed a chance—if you can handle Temperance—"

"Better that I should send Preciosa," said Romilly. "She would not come into the army with me, but flew away—but I can call her." Had she ever believed that she would not use her *laran* again? It was, like her body and her life, at Carolin's service. No land could survive with a mountain-cat like Lyondri at its head. No; the cat killed because it was its nature, from hunger or fear, but Rakhal and Lyondri kill for power alone.

"That might do," said Carolin, "They might think her only a wild hawk—the Gods know there are enough of them in the country round Hali, and you might spy out where Orain is being held, so that we can make directly for that place, and they will have to surrender Orain or kill him quick and clean."

Somewhere a horn blew; Carolin started and cringed. "That is their accursed summons," he said weakly, "It was at this hour—just before sunset—that they came on the

other two days, and while I sit here trying to summon courage to storm the city, Orain—" his voice failed again. Again
the horn sounded, and Carolin went out of his tent. A
common soldier came toward him, with insolent bearing.
In his hand he bore a little packet of yellow silk. He bowed,
and said, "Carolin, pretender to the throne of the Hasturs,
I have the honor to return another portion of your faithfully sworn man. You may take pride in his bravery."

He laughed, a jeering, raucous laugh, and Alderic
leaped forward.

"Wretch whom I will honor by calling *dog,* I will at least
rid you of that laugh—" he shouted, but Jandria flung her
arms round him.

"No, Deric, they will only revenge themselves on
Orain—"

The soldier said, "Do you not want to see what token they
have sent you of your paxman's bravery and devotion?"

Carolin's hands were shaking. Jandria said, "Let me,"
released Alderic and unwrapped the horrid packet. Inside
there was another finger. The soldier said, "This is the message of Lyondri. We weary of this play. Tomorrow it will
be an eye; the next day, the other eye; and the day after
that, his testicles. Should you hold out beyond that, it will
be a yard of skin flayed from his back—"

"Bastards! Sons of bastards!" cursed Carolin, but the soldier turned his back and, to the sound of the trumpet again,
walked within the gates of the city.

"Follow him with *laran!*" commanded Carolin, but although Ruyven, Maura and Alderic all sought to do so—
Romilly could sense it, tried to follow the man with her
special senses—it was as if her body rammed against an
impregnable wall of stone; as soon as the man was inside
the gates, she could not reach him. Carolin was shaking
with horror, unable to even shed tears; Maura held him
tightly in her arms.

"My dearest, my dearest, Orain would not have you surrender—"

"Avarra protect me, I know that—but ah, if I could only
kill him quickly—"

Inside the tent again he said with implacable fury, "I
cannot let them blind him, geld him, flay him. If we can
think of nothing this night, tomorrow at dawn I storm the

city with everything I have to throw at them. I will send word that no citizen will be harmed who does not raise hand against me, but we will search every house till we find him; and at least there will be a swift end to his torment. And then the tormenters will come into *my* hands."

Yet Romilly knew, watching him, that Carolin was a decent man; he would do nothing worse, even to Lyondri Hastur, than to kill him. He might hang him, ignobly, and expose his corpse for a warning, rather than giving him a nobleman's swift death by the sword; yet Lyondri would still be in better case than Orain, should it go on so far. Carolin sent word quietly through the army to make ready to storm the gates at dawn.

"Can your hawk see well enough in the dark to lead us to where Rakhal hides with his torturers? I do not think he did this by himself, alone—" he gestured weakly at the little packet.

"I do not know," said Romilly quietly, but while they spoke, a plan had been maturing in her.

"How many men watch the city walls?"

"I do not know; but they have sentry-birds all along the wall, and fierce dogs, so that if anyone tries to sneak into the city by breaking the side gates—we tried that once— the birds and the dogs set up such a racket that every one of Rakhal's men is wakened and rallies to that spot," he said despondently.

"Good," said Romilly quietly. "That could hardly be better."

"What do you say—"

"Think, my lord. My *laran* is of small use against men. And you say Rakhal's *leronyn* have guarded the city against our *laran*—*laran* such as your men use. But I fear no bird, no dog ever whelped, nothing that goes on four legs or flies on a wing. Let me go into the city alone, before dawn, and search that way, my lord."

"Alone? You, a girl—" Carolin began, then shook his head.

"You have proved again and again that you are more than a girl, Swordswoman," he said quietly. "It is worth a risk. If it fails, at least we will have some notion before dawn where to strike first, so they will have to give him a quick death. But let the night fall first; and you have had a long ride. Find her some proper food, Jandria, and let her go and sleep a little."

"I could not sleep—" Romilly protested.

"At least, then, rest a little," Carolin commanded, and Romilly bent her head.

"As you will."

Jandria took her to the tent of the Swordswomen, then, and found her food and fresh clothing.

"And washing-water and a comb," Romilly begged, so Jandria brought her hot water from the army's mess fires, and Romilly washed, combed out her tangled hair—Jandria, who helped her, finally had to cut it very short—and climbed gratefully into the clean soft underlinen and fresh tunic and breeches. She had no boots except the country-woman's, but she put clean stockings on her feet under them. What a relief it was, to be clean, dressed, to eat cooked food, to be human. . . .

"And now you must rest," Jandria said, "Carolin commanded it. I promise you, I will have you called at the midnight hour."

Romilly lay down beside Jandria on the blanket roll. The light of the waning moon came into the tent, and Romilly thought, with a great sadness, of Ranald lying beside her when last the moons were full. Now he was dead, and it seemed so bitter, so useless. She had not loved him, but he had been kind to her, and she had first accepted him as a man, and she knew she would remember him and mourn for him a little, forever. Jandria lay silent at her side, but she knew that Jandria, too, mourned; not only because of Orain's peril, but for Lyondri Hastur who had once been to her what Ranald was to Romilly herself, the first to rouse womanhood and desire. And she could not even think of him with the sweet sadness of the dead; he had gone further from her, become a monster—she put her arms around Jandria, and felt the woman shaking with grief.

There has been so much sorrow, all useless. In my pride, I too have brought grief on those who have done me no harm. I will do my uttermost to save Orain from the fate they have measured for him; it looks hopeless, but not all porridge cooked is eaten. But whichever way it goes, if I am alive at dawn I shall send word to Father and Luciella that I live and they must not grieve for me.

Jandria's sorrow is worse than mine. Orain, if he dies, I will mourn, because he was my friend and because he died nobly for Carolin, whom he loves. But who could mourn, or have any feeling except relief, if Lyondri can do no more evil?

She held Jandria's sobbing body in her arms, and at last felt her drop away into sleep.

She had slept for an hour or two, when Jandria shook her shoulder softly.

"Get up, Romilly. It is time."

Romilly splashed her face with cold water, and ate a little more bread, but she refused wine. For this she must be perfectly alert. Carolin was waiting for her in his tent, his face composed and grim. He said, "I hardly need tell you that if you free Orain—or save him any more suffering, even if you must put your own dagger through his heart— you may name your own reward, even if you wish to marry one of my own sons."

She smiled at the thought; why should she wish to do that? She said, speaking as if he were the *Dom* Carlo she had first known, "Uncle, I will do what I can for Orain because he was kind to me beyond all duty when he thought me only a runaway hawkmaster's apprentice. Do you not think a Swordswoman and a MacAran will risk herself as well for honor as from greed?"

"I know it," Carolin said gently, "but I will reward you for my own pleasure, too, Romilly."

She turned to Jandria. "The boots will make too much noise. Find me a pair of soft sandals, if you will." When Jandria had brought a pair of her own—they were too big, but Romilly bound them tightly on her feet—she tied her hair into a dark cloth, so that no stray gleam would give her away, and smeared her face with dirt so that it would not shine in a watchman's lantern. Now she could go noiselessly into the city, and she feared no sentry-bird nor dog. At this hour, certainly, all but a few men would be sleeping.

Alderic said in a tone that brooked no denial, "I will go with you to the side gate."

She nodded. He too had a touch of this *laran*. She held his hand, silently, as they stole on their soft shoes away from Carolin's tent, making a wide circle away from the gates. Somewhere a dog barked; probably, she thought, sending out a questing tendril of awareness, at a mouse in the streets; but she silenced him anyway, sending out thoughts of peace and drowsiness . . .

"The gate will creak if you try to open it, even if you can quiet the sentry-birds," whispered Alderic, and without a word, made a stirrup of his hand as if he helped her to mount a tall horse; she caught at the top of the small side-gate and climbed to the top, looking down on the sleeping city by moonlight.

She sent out her thoughts to the sentry-birds, sending out peace, quiet, silence . . . she could see them on the walls now, great ugly shapes with their handlers, like statues against the sky. A disturbance and they would scream, awakening all of Rakhal's armies. . . .

Peace, Peace, silence . . . through their eyes she looked down at the moon-flooded streets, which lay dark, with only, now and again, a single lighted window . . . one after another she reached out to investigate them. Ordinary *laran* was clouded, but reaching into the minds of animals, she could feel silence . . . behind one lighted window, a woman struggled to give birth to a child and a midwife knelt, holding her hands and whispering encouragement. A mother sat beside a sick child, singing in a voice hoarse with worry and weariness. A man wounded somewhere in the war tossed with the fever in the stump on his leg. . . .

A dog snarled from a side street, and Romilly knew it would burst into a frenzy of barking . . . she reached out, silenced it, felt its bewilderment, where had the disturbing one gone . . . ? She crept silently past.

Now she was far from the walls, the sentry-birds silent. Would they have thought to guard the rest of the city against *laran*? Or had it stretched the few *leronyn* at Rakhal's command, to guard the gates, so that they were open inside the city?

Carefully, ready to retreat at a moment's touch, she reached out. . . . Orain had little *laran*, she knew, but he was not head-blind and she could *feel* him somewhere; he lay wakeful with the pain of his injuries . . . she must not let him feel her presence; he might be monitored by Rakhal's or Lyondri's sorcerers. Yet she moved, softly, nearer to him, block by block of the ancient city, and as she stole quietly through, no dog barked, no mouse in the walls squeaked aloud. *Silence, silence, peace on the city.* Horses drowsed in their stables, cats left off chasing mice and dozed before hearths, restless babies quieted under the powerful spell; from one end to the other of the ancient city of Hali, no living soul felt anything but peace and silence. Even the woman in labor fell into a peaceful sleep, and the midwife dozed at her side.

Peace, calm, silence. . . .

Outside a silent house near the opposite wall—she had traversed the whole city in her entranced spell—Romilly became aware of the two minds she had touched before. Orain; Orain lay within, somnolent under the sleep-spell that she had put on all things, but through it she could feel pain, fear, despair, a hope that perhaps he could somehow manage to die. Carefully, carefully, she thrust out a tendril of thought. . . .

Keep silence, do not move or stir lest someone be alerted when you wake. . . .

The door creaked, but so still was all within that the sleeping man outside Orain's door did not stir. Beyond him, in an inner room, she sensed the stony wall of Lyondri Hastur's thoughts—he too was deeply troubled. *The dreadful thing is that Lyondri is not a cruel man by nature. He will not even watch the torturer who does his beastly work. He does this only for power!*

His thoughts seemed to quest out, seeking an intruder . . . Romilly quickly submerged her own mind in that of a cat, sleeping across the hearth, and after a moment Lyondri Hastur slept . . . the watchman drowsed . . .

Even if I kill him too swiftly for him to cry out—Romilly's hands tightened on the dagger in her belt, *his death-cry even in thought will waken Lyondri! But perhaps he would stop at killing Orain with his own hands. . . .*

She must. There was no help for it. Then she realized that the watchmen was more deeply asleep than she, with her soothing consciousness extended throughout the whole city, could have managed; and felt another mind touch hers. Then there was a soft movement behind her, and she whirled, alert, dagger in hand—

"Don't kill me, Romilly," Caryl whispered. He was wearing a child's white night-gown, and his fair hair was tousled as if he had come from his bed. He reached out and gripped her in a great hug . . . *but not for one moment did the spell relax. . . . .*

"Oh, Romilly, Romilly—I pleaded with my father, but he would not hear me—I cannot bear it, what they are doing to Orain—it—it hurts me too—have you come to take him away?" His whisper was all but inaudible. If Lyondri Hastur stirred in his sleep, and touched his son's mind, he would think him gripped in nightmare.

And Lyondri Hastur did this where his son could know of it, feel it. . . .

"He said it would harden me to the necessity of being cruel sometimes, when the good of the realm demands it," Caryl whispered almost inaudibly, "I am—I am sickened—I did not think my father *could* do this—" and he struggled to hold back tears, knowing that would waken his father too . . .

Romilly nodded. She said, "Help me quiet the dogs as I go . . ."

But she could not take Orain sleeping. Silently, she stole past the sleeping watchman.

The torturer. He is worse than any brute; his mind is an animal's mind, otherwise I could not so easily enspell him. . . .

"Orain—" she whispered, and her hand went out to grip his mouth silent against an involuntary cry. *Remember you are dreaming this. . . .*

Orain knew instantly what she meant; if Lyondri wakened or his slumber lightened, he would think he wandered in dreams. . . . Softly, moving as noiselessly as Romilly herself, he drew himself to his feet. One of them was bleeding through a rough bandage. She had not seen the cut-off finger. But she fought to suppress her horror, to keep the sleep-spell strong, as he moved softly across the room, forced his feet, wincing, into his boots.

"I would not leave that man alive—" he whispered, glancing with implacable hate at his jailer, but he sensed, so close they were in rapport, Romilly's reason for not killing him, and contributed a single wry thought:

When Lyondri wakes and finds me escaped while he slept, what he will do to the man will be worse than your dagger through his heart; for mercy I should kill the man! But I am not kind enough for that.

The smell of the air told Romilly that dawn was nearing; she would soon have to contend with dogs waking all over the city, with the sentry-birds on the wall rousing, and if they did *not* waken at the proper time, that too would alert their handlers; they must be free of the city before then. She took Orain's shoulder. His hand, too, was wrapped in rough bandages, and there was a patch over the cut-off ear which had bled through. But he was not seriously harmed, and came silently after her. Now they were outside the house and she came aware that Caryl was following them on noiseless feet, in his nightgown.

"Go back!" She whispered, and shook the boy's shoulder. "I cannot be responsible—"

"I will not return!" His voice was stubborn and set. "He is no longer my father; I would be worse than he is, to stay with him." She saw that great silent tears were rolling down his face, but he insisted, "I can help you quiet the guards."

She nodded and signalled him to steady Orain, who was limping. Now she must quiet pain, keep the tumult of his thoughts and emotions under her own, and . . . yes, she must let the birds wake normally, with ordinary cries, elsewhere in the city, while keeping those near here safely entranced until they had somehow made their escape—

They had reached the side gate. Caryl set a hand on the latch and the lock gave way and swung open. There was a horrendous creaking from the broken lock, a sound of tortured metal and wood that rent the sky; everywhere, it seemed, there was an uproar from the walls, but they dropped all caution and ran, ran hurriedly through the camp and the forming army, ran toward Carolin's tents . . . and then Carolin caught Orain in his arms, weeping aloud in relief and joy, and Romilly turned and hugged Caryl tight.

"We're safe, we're safe—oh, Caryl, we could never have done it without you—"

Carolin turned a little and opened his arms to clasp Romilly and Caryl in the same hug that encircled his friend.

"Listen," Orain said, "The racket—they know I am gone—"

"Yet our army is here to guard you," said Carolin quietly. "They shall not touch you again, my brother, if our lives answer for it. But now, I think, they will have to surrender; I will not burn my people's city over their heads, but I will spare any man who makes his submission and swears loyalty to me. I think Rakhal and Lyondri will find few partisans this morning." He felt Orain flinch as the embrace touched the bandage over his ear.

"My brother, let me have your wounds tended—"

He brought him into the tent, and Maura and Jandria hastened to attend Orain. While the hacked fingers and ear were bandaged, Carolin sat blinking back tears in the lamplight.

"How can we reward you, Romilly?"

"There is no need of reward," she said. Now it was over, she was shaking, and glad to feel Alderic's arm supporting her, holding a wine-cup to her lips. "It is enough that now my lord Orain knows—" she did not know what she was going to say until she heard herself saying it, "that even though I am only a girl, I have no less courage or worth than any boy!"

Orain's arms swept out and he hugged her close, knocking the bandage loose and bleeding all over her. "Sweetheart, sweetheart," he whispered, holding her tight and crooning to her like a child, "I did not mean—I could not want you that way, but always I wanted to be your friend . . . only I felt such a fool—"

She knew she was crying too as she hugged him and kissed his cheek. She found herself in his lap like a child, while he stroked her hair. Orain held out his free hand to Alderic and said, "They brought me news that you had offered to exchange yourself for me, my son—what have I done to deserve that? I have never been a father to you—"

"You gave me life, sir," said Alderic quietly. "I owe you that, at least, since you have had nothing else from me of love or respect."

"Perhaps because I have not deserved it," Orain said, and Caryl came to his knees and hugged Orain too, and Romilly who was still in his lap. Carolin said, finding his voice through thickness in his throat, "You are all here and safe. That is enough. Caryl, I swear I shall be a father to you, and you shall be brought up with my own sons. And I will not kill Lyondri if I can help it. He may leave me no choice, and I cannot now trust his oath or his honor; but if I can, I shall let him live out his life in exile."

Caryl said shakily, "I know you will do what is honorable, Uncle."

"And now if you are all done with your love-feast," said Jandria, waspishly, "I would like to bandage this man up again so he will not be bleeding into our breakfast!"

Orain grinned at her and said, "I'm not hurt as badly as that. The man knew his business as well as any army surgeon. He made it quick, at least. They told me, though—" and suddenly he shuddered, and said, shaking, "You came just in time, Romilly."

He took her hand in his undamaged one. He said gently, "I cannot marry you, child. It is not in my nature. But if Carolin gives leave, I will betroth you to my son—" and he looked up at Alderic. "I can already see that he is willing."

"And nothing would please me better," said Ruyven, coming to smile at Alderic.

"Then that's settled," Orain said, smiling, but Romilly pulled loose in outrage.

"And am I to have nothing to say about this?" she demanded, and her hand went to her ear where the earring had been torn loose. "I am not free of my vows to the Swordswomen until the year has ended. And then—" she grinned a little nervously at Alderic and Ruyven, "I know now that however good my *laran,* it is still not properly trained, or I could have done better with it. It betrayed me on the battlefield, when Sunstar was killed . . . I came near to dying with him because I did not know how to keep myself clear. If they will have me—" she looked from Ruyven to Alderic, "I will go to a Tower, and learn what I must do to master my *laran* so that it will not master me. And then I must make my peace with my father and stepmother. And then—" she smiled now, waveringly, at Alderic, "Then, perhaps, I will know myself well enough to know if I want to marry you—or anyone else, my lord."

"Spoken like a Swordswoman," Jandria said approvingly, but Romilly hardly heard, Alderic sighed, then took her hand.

"And when that is done," he said quietly, "I shall await your decision, Romilly."

She clasped his fingers, but only for a moment. She was not sure; but she was no longer afraid.

"My lord," she said to Carolin, "Have I leave to take

your kinsman to the tent of the Swordswomen and find him some breeches?" She looked at Caryl, who flushed with embarrassment and said, "Please, Uncle. I—I cannot show/ myself to the army in a night-gown."

Carolin laughed and said, "Do as you wish, hawk-mistress. You have been faithful to me, and to those I love. And when you have done your duty to your *laran* and to your parents and to the one who would marry you, I shall expect you to come back to us in Hali." He turned and took Maura's hand, saying, "I pledged to you that we would celebrate our Midsummer-festival in Hali, did I not? And the next moon will see us at Midsummer. If it will please you, Lady—I had thought to make the hawk-mistress's marriage at the same time as her Queen's. But we can wait for that." He laughed aloud and said, "I am not so much of a tyrant as that. But one day, Romilly, you will be hawkmistress to the reigning king as you were in exile."

She bowed and said, "I thank you, sir." But her mind, ranging ahead, was already seeking the walls of Tramontana Tower.

MARION ZIMMER BRADLEY

THE DARKOVER NOVELS

EXILE'S SONG

A Novel of Darkover

by Marion Zimmer Bradley

Margaret Alton is the daughter of Lew Alton, Darkover's Senator to the Terran Federation, but her morose, uncommunicative father is secretive about the obscure planet of her birth. So when her university job sends her to Darkover, she has only fleeting, haunting memories of a tumultuous childhood. But once in the light of the Red Sun, as her veiled and mysterious heritage becomes manifest, she finds herself trapped by a destiny more terrifying than any nightmare!

- A direct sequel to *The Heritage of Hastur* and *Sharra's Exile*
- With cover art by Romas Kukalis

☐ **Hardcover Edition**   UE2705-$21.95

MERCEDES LACKEY
& LARRY DIXON

The Novels of Valdemar

DARIAN'S TALE
☐ OWLFLIGHT   0-88677-804-2—$6.99
☐ OWLSIGHT   0-88677-803-4—$6.99
☐ OWLKNIGHT (Hardcover)   0-88677-916-2—$6.99
Two years after his parents' disappearance, Darian has sought refuge and training from the mysterious Hawkbrothers. Now he has
opened his heart to a beautiful young healer. Finally Darian has
found peace and acceptance in his life. Until he learns that his parents may still be alive—and trapped behind enemy borders . . .

THE MAGE WARS
☐ THE BLACK GRYPHON   0-88677-804-2—$6.99
☐ THE WHITE GRYPHON   0-88677-682-1—$6.99
☐ THE SILVER GRYPHON   0-88667-685-6—$6.99

Mercedes Lackey

The Novels of Valdemar

"Please, Fausto, don't feel guilty on my account. I was a full participant in this." She gestured to the expanse of sand between them. **"You don't need to have any regrets."**

And yet he did. In that moment he felt swamped by them—by his own lack of self-control, by the desire that still coursed through him. By the sure and certain knowledge that he'd hurt a woman he admired and respected, and yet still knew he could never marry.

But why couldn't he?

The question, so unexpected, suddenly seemed obvious. Why shouldn't he marry Liza Benton? Admittedly, she would not be his family's first choice by any stretch. His mother would be disappointed and hurt. His father would never have countenanced such a choice.

He acknowledged she would struggle to fit into his world, both here and even more so in Italy. She was not from one of Lombardy's ancient families, not by any means. Not even close.

Yet he wanted her. He cared about her. He didn't love her, not yet, and that could only be a plus. She wouldn't be able to hurt him. And, of course, she was lovely and gracious and kind.

And, he realized hollowly, she could at this moment be carrying his child.

Dear Reader,

I fell in love with Jane Austen's *Pride and Prejudice* when I first watched the 1995 BBC adaptation with Colin Firth. I read the book afterward and then watched the program again with my teenage daughters. Whose heart doesn't beat a little faster at the sight of Mr. Darcy's stern countenance? When my editor asked if I'd be willing to write a Harlequin Presents version of this classic, I was beyond thrilled. Mr. Darcy—so cold, so autocratic, so gorgeous and with a steely core of honor—is, in my opinion, the ultimate Presents alpha male and the perfect hero!

Pride and Prejudice is, in some sense, a dryly clever comedy about manners and society, but in order to turn it into a Presents with all the necessary high-stakes emotion, I really needed to dig deeper into the characters. Why is Mr. Darcy—my Fausto Danti—so arrogant? Why is Lizzy Bennet—my Liza Benton—so quick to judge? Exploring the emotions beneath the witty, charming surface of the story was both challenging and fun, and I fell in love with *Pride and Prejudice* all over again, just as I hope you will!

Happy reading!

Kate

Kate Hewitt

———

PRIDE & THE ITALIAN'S PROPOSAL

HARLEQUIN®
PRESENTS®

Recycling programs
for this product may
not exist in your area.

ISBN-13: 978-1-335-40348-3

Pride & the Italian's Proposal

Copyright © 2021 by Kate Hewitt

This edition published by arrangement with Harlequin Books S.A.

For questions and comments about the quality of this book,
please contact us at CustomerService@Harlequin.com.

Harlequin Enterprises ULC
22 Adelaide St. West, 40th Floor
Toronto, Ontario M5H 4E3, Canada
www.Harlequin.com

Printed in U.S.A.

After spending three years as a die-hard New Yorker, **Kate Hewitt** now lives in a small village in the English Lake District with her husband, their five children and a golden retriever. In addition to writing intensely emotional stories, she loves reading, baking and playing chess with her son— she has yet to win against him, but she continues to try. Learn more about Kate at kate-hewitt.com.

Books by Kate Hewitt

Harlequin Presents

Claiming My Bride of Convenience
Vows to Save His Crown

Conveniently Wed!

Desert Prince's Stolen Bride

One Night with Consequences

Princess's Nine-Month Secret
Greek's Baby of Redemption

Secret Heirs of Billionaires

The Secret Kept from the Italian
The Italian's Unexpected Baby

Visit the Author Profile page
at Harlequin.com for more titles.

Dedicated to all the *P&P* fans out there—may you find your Mr. Darcy!

CHAPTER ONE

'YOU'LL NEVER GUESS who just walked in!'

Liza Benton looked at her younger sister's flushed face and laughed. 'I'm sure I won't,' she returned with a smile. 'Considering I don't know a single person in this place.' She glanced around the busy bar in Soho, its interior all sleek wood and chrome stools, pounding music and bespoke cocktails. Right now it was full of glamorous people who had a lot more money and fashion sense than she did, and they seemed to be taking delight in showing both off.

Liza had only moved to London from rural Herefordshire six weeks ago and she was still feeling a bit like a Country Mouse to a whole load of sleek Town Mice. But her younger sister Lindsay, visiting for the weekend with their mother Yvonne, was determined to be the belle of whatever ball—or bar—they frequented.

It had been Lindsay who had assured Liza and their older sister Jenna that Rico's was the place to be. 'Everyone who's anyone goes here,' she'd said with a worldly insouciance that belied her seventeen years. Considering she'd hardly ever left their small village in Herefordshire save for a few school trips, Liza wasn't sure how her sister would know such things, but she seemed confident that she did. Of course, Lindsay was confident—perhaps a bit too confident—about everything, including her own youthful charms.

Looking around Rico's now, Liza didn't think it looked all that special, although she acknowledged she didn't know much about these things. She hadn't been to many bars, and hadn't particularly wanted to. Her twenty-three years had been spent helping out with her large family and then getting her degree; socialising or romance hadn't played much part at all, save for one unfortunate episode she had no desire to dwell on.

'So who walked in?' her older sister Jenna asked with a little laugh as Lindsay collapsed breathlessly onto the banquette next to her, determined to maximise the melodrama. Their mother took a sip of her violently coloured cocktail, eyes wide as she waited for her youngest daughter to dish. She loved a bit of gossip as much as Lindsay did.

'Chaz Bingham,' Lindsay announced triumphantly. Liza and Jenna both stared at her blankly but Yvonne nodded and tutted knowingly.

'I saw him in a gossip magazine just last week. He's recently inherited some sort of business, hasn't he? Investments, I think?' Her mother spoke with the same worldly air as her daughter, although she left Herefordshire even less than Lindsay did. All her knowledge was gained from TV chat shows and tabloid magazines, and treated as gospel.

Lindsay shrugged, clearly not caring about such details. 'Something like that. I know he's loaded. Isn't he *gorgeous*?'

Liza met Jenna's laughing gaze as they both silently acknowledged how their younger sister's excited voice carried. The sophisticated occupants of the table next to theirs exchanged looks, and Liza rolled her eyes at Jenna. She'd never had time for snobs, and she'd encountered a few over the years, people who thought her family was a little too different, a little too loud—her lovably eccentric father, her exuberantly over-the-top mother, and the four Benton girls—pretty Jenna, smart Marie, fun Lindsay...and Liza. Liza had no idea what her sobriquet would be. Quiet, perhaps? Normal? *Dull?* She knew she possessed neither Jenna's looks nor Marie's brains, and definitely not Lindsay's vivacity. That had been made apparent to her on more than one occasion, often by well-meaning people, but once...

She really had no desire to dwell on that now, when they were having so much fun and apparently someone exciting had walked into the bar, even if she'd never heard of him.

'Where is he?' their mother asked, her eyes on stalks as she rubbernecked for a glimpse of the mysterious but apparently impressive Chaz Bingham.

'There.' Lindsay pointed towards the entrance of the bar, and Liza muffled a chuckle.

'Shall we make an announcement on the Tannoy system?' she asked wryly, and her sister gave her a blank look.

'Liza, a bar like this isn't going to have a *Tannoy.*'

'Silly me,' she murmured, and Jenna smiled before she suddenly let out a soft, wondering gasp that had Liza curious enough to see who all the fuss was about. She glanced towards the entrance of the bar and her breath caught as her gaze snagged on the man who had just come in. Now that she'd seen him, it was impossible *not* to notice him. Not to feel as if he took up all the space and air in the place.

He was half a head taller than anyone else in the room, with ink-black hair pushed away from a high aristocratic forehead. Steel-grey eyes under hooded brows scanned the room dismissively, a cynical twist to his sculpted mouth that Liza could see all the way from across the room. Cheekbones like blades and a hard chiselled jaw worthy of any of the steamy novels that Lindsay loved to read.

His powerful physique was encased in a snowy-white dress shirt, unbuttoned at the neck to reveal a bronzed, alluring column of throat—how a *neck* could be sexy, Liza had no idea, and yet it was—and narrow black trousers, an outfit that would suit a waiter, and yet such a thought was laughable when it came to this man.

Everything about him exuded power, wealth, influence and, most of all, arrogance. He looked as if he not only owned this bar, but the entire world. Normally Liza hated conceit of any kind—and she had good reason for it—but this combination of blatant sex appeal and innate arrogance was both compelling and disturbing and, unable to make sense of her thoughts, she forced herself to look away.

'Did you see him?' Lindsay demanded, and Liza jerked her head in a nod. How could she *not* have seen him? Even now, looking away, she could still visualise him perfectly—from that twist of his lips to the powerful shrug of his shoulders. He was emblazoned on her mind's eye, which was another disturbing thought. Why had she reacted so viscerally to a stranger?

'Jenna, I think he's noticed you,' Yvonne whispered excitedly, although her whisper was as loud as Lindsay's, especially after two of her fancy cocktails. Jenna smiled and flushed.

Liza glanced up; the dark-haired Adonis wasn't looking anywhere near her sister, but a friendly-looking man with rumpled blond hair and ruddy cheeks was, with obvious interest. *This* was Chaz Bingham? Then who was the other man?

Unthinkingly, she looked for him, only to find herself suddenly speared on his sardonic gaze for a terrible second, his steely eyes blazing into hers and branding her with their knowledge before, indifferently, he looked away.

'He's coming closer!' Lindsay squealed and, turning away from the man who had so casually dismissed her, Liza wished her sister wasn't *quite* so loud.

Amazingly, Chaz really was coming closer to their table. Liza braced herself, wondering if he was going to ask them to lower their voices, or maybe if he could have the chair they'd piled all their coats on, but he did nothing of the kind. He gave Jenna an immensely appealing smile before turning to them all, including them easily in his friendliness.

'I say, may I buy you a drink?'

'Oh...' Jenna was blushing prettily, and Liza smiled at the man's gentlemanly charm, as well as his obvious interest in her beautiful sister. With her long, tumbling blonde hair and vivid blue eyes, not to mention her curvy figure, Jenna had never been without admirers. Amazingly, her beauty hadn't made her vain in the least; she'd barely had a boyfriend, and she always seemed surprised by the attention she received. Liza, however, was not, and she had never resented her sister's popularity…even when it had caused her pain.

'Yes, *please*,' Lindsay said, elbowing Jenna meaningfully, and the man—Chaz—smiled and took their orders.

'Of all the women in the whole room,' their mother whispered triumphantly when he'd gone to the bar, 'he chose you!'

'Mum, he's just buying me a drink,' Jenna protested, but Liza saw how her gaze tracked Chaz as he headed towards the bar. Her own gaze moved instinctively to the *other* man in the room, a man who created a tingling awareness all through her body even when he wasn't looking at her. He was clearly with Chaz, for he'd joined him at the bar, propping one elbow upon it as he talked to him, his bored, sardonic gaze moving slowly and disinterestedly around the room.

Really, the look on his face was rather ridiculously arrogant, almost a parody of what Liza imagined some lord of the manor would look like as he gazed down upon his peasants. She felt a thorny spike of annoyance pierce her; why did such a good-looking man have to be so *proud*? Looks weren't everything and yet, Liza acknowledged with an inward sigh, in this world they certainly counted for a lot. She'd discovered that to her detriment—plain Liza compared to pretty Jenna for most of her childhood—and when it had mattered.

'When he comes back,' their mother instructed Jenna, interrupting Liza's thoughts, 'for heaven's sake, invite him to sit down.'

'*Mum*—'

'Of course she's going to invite him to sit down,' Lindsay interjected with a scoffing laugh. 'And if she won't, I will. I tell you, he's *loaded*.'

'I don't think he'll appreciate the invitation quite as much, coming from you,' Liza interjected with a smile, and her sister gave her a fulminating look. Liza reached for her white wine, which only had one sip left in the glass; she'd declined Chaz Bingham's offer of a top-up. Would Chaz sit down with them if he was asked? she wondered. And if he did, would his dark, proud friend join him? Her heart tumbled over at the thought, and she decided she needed to fortify herself with more wine.

'Liza, where are you going?' her mother demanded, pulling on her sleeve. 'Chaz will be coming back any second—'

Already it was Chaz, she thought wryly. He hadn't even introduced himself yet. 'I've decided I want a glass of wine after all,' Liza said, and with her heart fluttering a little she headed towards the bar—and the intriguing man leaning against it.

'Why on earth did you choose this place?' Fausto Danti glanced around the crowded bar with a grimace of distaste. Having arrived in London from Milan only that afternoon, he'd been hoping for a quiet dinner in a discreet and select club with his old university friend, not a booze-up in a bar that looked like it was full of tourists and college students.

Chaz glanced at him, full of good humour as always. 'What, you don't like it?' he queried innocently. Fausto did not dignify his question with a reply. 'You've always been something of a snob, Danti.'

'I prefer to consider myself discerning.'

'You need to loosen up. I've been telling you that since our uni days. And come on.' He nodded meaningfully towards the table with its bevy of squawking women. 'Isn't she the loveliest creature you've ever seen?'

'She's nice enough,' Fausto allowed, because he had to admit the woman Chaz had set eyes on the second they'd walked through the door was really rather beautiful. 'She's the only pretty one among them.'

'I thought her sisters were nice enough.'

'Sisters?' Fausto arched an imperious eyebrow. 'How do you know they're not all just friends?'

Chaz shrugged. 'They all have a similar look about them, and the older one is clearly their mother. Anyway, I intend to get to know them all. And you can do the same.'

Fausto snorted at such an unlikely suggestion. 'I have no desire to do any such thing.'

'What about the one with curly hair?'

'She looked as plain and boring as the other, if not more so,' Fausto replied. He'd barely glanced at any of the women; he had no intention of picking someone up in a place like this, or even picking up someone at all. His stomach tightened with distaste at the thought.

He'd left such pursuits behind him long ago… and for good reason. He was here in England to deal with the fallout of the London office only, and then he was returning to Italy, where his mother was hoping he would soon announce his choice of bride. His stomach tightened again at *that* thought, although he knew there was no question of not fulfilling his duty.

'Oh, come on, Danti,' Chaz insisted. 'Relax, if you can remember how. I know you've been working hard these last few years, but let's have some fun.'

'This is generally not how I amuse myself,' Fausto replied as he took the tumbler of whisky from the bartender with a terse nod of thanks. 'And certainly not with a couple of obnoxious, gold-digging women who look poised to fawn over your every word.' He'd heard the younger one jabber about how much money Chaz had, not even caring who might be listening.

'Fawning over my every word? That's more

your style, mate.' Chaz patted him on the arm and Fausto gave him a tight-lipped smile, even as he felt an uncanny frisson of—something— ripple through him, an awareness he didn't understand, but certainly felt.

He turned swiftly, expecting someone to be standing right next to him, but no one was. He scanned the crowded room but saw only the dull mix of middle class Londoners out for an evening of cocktails and fun.

'Come on,' Chaz said as he hoisted the drinks he'd bought for the motley crew of women, including a revolting-looking cocktail that was garnished with a pink umbrella and no less than three maraschino cherries.

With the utmost reluctance, Fausto followed his friend towards the table of eagerly waiting women. The blonde Chaz had set his sights on was indeed attractive, if in a rather simple way. There was no guile in her clear gaze, no depths to discover in her open face. Yet, Fausto concluded fairly, he would not necessarily consider her looks insipid.

The second sister, who looked to be still in her teens, was all flash and flare, her make-up overdone, her light brown hair pulled into a high, tight ponytail, a tight cropped top emphasising her curvy figure. The look in her eyes was what Fausto could only call avaricious, and his stomach tightened once more in sour anticipation of a most unpleasant evening.

The mother, he saw, was cut from the same cloth as the sister, and dressed in almost as revealing an outfit—but hadn't there been another at the table? Briefly Fausto recalled curly chestnut hair, a pair of glinting hazel eyes. They were no more than vague impressions, but he held the distinct certainty there had been a fourth woman at the table. Where was she?

Chaz set the drinks down with a gentlemanly flourish and, predictably, the pretty blonde stammered an invitation for him to join them, which Chaz did, sliding into the booth next to her. Fausto was left with no choice of seating other than next to the teenager with a lusty look in her eye, and so he coolly informed them he would prefer to stand.

'I'm sure you would,' a voice quipped near his ear, as the woman he realised he'd been looking for walked briskly by and slid into the booth next to her sister. 'To tell the truth, you seem as if you couldn't get out of here fast enough.'

Fausto locked gazes with the hazel eyes he'd recalled, and they were just as glinting as he remembered. Even more so, for right now they were flashing fire at him, and he wondered why on earth this Little Miss Nobody was looking at him with such self-righteous anger.

'I admit this was not my first choice of establishment,' he returned with a long, level look at this slip of a woman who dared to challenge him.

Her hair was the colour of chestnuts and tumbled over her shoulders in a riot of corkscrew curls.

Large hazel eyes were framed with lush chocolate-coloured lashes, and her mouth was a ripe cupid's bow. She wore a plain green jumper and jeans and, all in all, Fausto decided after a moment's deliberate perusal, she was nothing remarkable.

The woman raised her eyebrows as he held her gaze, her angry expression turning to something more mocking, and with a disinterest that was not as legitimate as Fausto would have wished, he flicked his gaze away.

Chaz was making introductions and Fausto turned to listen, although he doubted he would ever have the need to address any of these women by name.

'Jenna… Lindsay… Yvonne… Liza.' Chaz looked as delighted as if he'd just done an impressive sum in his head, and Fausto shoved his hands in the pockets of his trousers. So now he knew her name was Liza, not that it mattered.

'And your name?' the mother, Yvonne, trilled. It was obvious she already knew who he was—Chaz graced enough of the gossip rags and society pages, with his pedigree, wealth and cheerful attendance at many social occasions.

'Chaz Bingham, and this is my good friend from university, Fausto Danti. He's here from Milan to head up his family's London office for a few months.'

Fausto gave him a coldly quelling look; he did not need these people knowing his business. Chaz smiled back, completely unrepentant as always.

'What do you think of our country, Mr Danti?' the mother asked in a cringingly girlish voice. Fausto gave her a repressive look.

'I find it as well as I did when I was here for university fifteen years ago,' he answered coolly, and she gave an uncertain laugh and then blushed, before gulping down her ridiculous cocktail.

Instinctively, unwillingly, Fausto glanced at the woman—Liza—and saw she was glaring at him with unbridled fury. This time she was the one to look away, a deliberate snub which he found both irritating and unsettling. It wasn't as if he *cared*.

Chaz was chatting animatedly to Jenna, which left the four of them—Fausto and these three tedious women—to sit through an insufferable silence. At the start Lindsay attempted a few flirtatious forays of conversation which Fausto shot down unreservedly. He was tired, out of sorts, and he had absolutely no interest in getting to know these people, not to mention a seven a.m. start tomorrow. After fifteen excruciating minutes, he looked pointedly at his watch. Chaz caught his eye and then blithely ignored him. Fausto ground his teeth.

He didn't want to be here, but neither did he wish to be unapologetically rude and leave his friend flat—although perhaps that was what Chaz wanted, all things considered. Fausto glanced at his watch again, even more pointedly this time.

'I'm so sorry we're keeping you,' Liza remarked acidly, and Fausto glanced at her, unperturbed.

'Actually, Chaz is keeping me,' he returned, and she let out a huff of indignation.

'He seems like he's having a good time,' she said with a nod towards Chaz and Jenna, their heads bent together. 'I'm sure he wouldn't mind if you chose to leave.' Her eyebrows lifted and Fausto saw a definite spark of challenge in her eyes that caused a ripple of reluctant admiration to pass through him. Here was a woman with a bit more fire than her beautiful sister, a few more depths to discover. Not that it mattered even remotely to him.

'I'm inclined to agree with you,' he replied with a short nod. 'And so, in that case, I will make my goodbyes.' He gave another nod, this one of farewell, his impassive glance taking in all three women before he nodded at Chaz, who gave him a shamefaced grin and kept talking to Jenna.

Fausto couldn't keep from giving Liza one last glance before he left, and as their eyes met something shuddered through him—and then, as dismissive as he had been at the start, she looked away.

CHAPTER TWO

LIZA STARED AT her bedroom ceiling as the autumn sunlight filtered through the curtains and lit her tiny room with gold. She didn't take any notice of it, however, because in her mind she was picturing Fausto Danti, with his steel-grey eyes and his sculpted mouth, his midnight hair and his disdainful look.

Jerk. Rude, arrogant, irritating *boor*.

Her fists clenched on the duvet as she remembered his aristocratic drawl. *'She looked as plain and boring as the other, if not more so.'* She'd heard his damning statement, so indifferently given, when she'd gone to the bar, and the words had scorched through her, branding her with their carelessly cruel indictment. Reminding her that she wasn't anything special—something she'd always felt, had been told to her by someone she'd thought she'd cared about, but to have it confirmed so ruthlessly, and by a *stranger*…

It felt as if Fausto Danti had ripped off the barely healed scab covering the wound she'd done her best to hide from everyone, even herself. She'd always known she wasn't beautiful like Jenna, or intelligent like Marie, or spirited like Lindsay. But to have it confirmed *again*…

After Fausto's callous comment, Liza had raced back to her table, furious and hurt, before he could see her. It wasn't as if she cared or even knew the man, she told herself, and he obviously didn't care at all. The way he'd looked down his nose at them all…as if they were so uninteresting that he simply couldn't be bothered even to make the most basic of pleasantries for a few minutes.

And the way he'd looked at *her*… Liza's fists clenched harder and her stomach did too. There had been something simmering in his iron-coloured eyes that had made everything in her seem to both shiver and heat. As much as she wanted to hate him, and she did, of *course* she did, that look had created a sweet, surprising longing in her she couldn't deny even as she strived to, because she knew it couldn't lead to anything good.

Yet, based on what he'd said, she'd obviously misread that look completely, which added another humiliation to the whole sorry story. Of course he hadn't looked at her like *that*. She wouldn't even know what *that* kind of look was like. She had certainly misread one before.

As for her own humiliating reaction, all heat and awareness…so the man was attractive. Any woman with a pulse would respond to his looks, that much was certain, although after Chaz had left, having exchanged mobile numbers with Jenna, the excited chatter between her mother and sisters had all been about him rather than Fausto Danti.

Would he call? Would he ask Jenna out? When? Where? The deliberations had gone on for half the night, until Liza had finally retreated to bed, unable to contribute to the excitement but not wanting to lower the mood.

She had no doubt that all the conversation today would continue to be about Chaz. No one had even mentioned Fausto Danti last night, which seemed rather incredible considering both his undeniably good looks as well as his undeniably bad manners. But no, her mother and sisters had only wanted to talk about Chaz. Handsome, polite, perfectly nice Chaz Bingham, who was clearly halfway to being head over heels in love with Jenna. And meanwhile Liza couldn't stop thinking about Fausto Danti.

With a sigh she rose from her bed. She had a feeling it was going to be a long day.

By Sunday night, when she said goodbye to her mother and sister who were heading back to Herefordshire, Liza felt it had been a very long two days. They'd shopped on Oxford Street, had tea at The Ritz and seen a West End musical. They'd gone out for curry, strolled through Hyde Park and had makeovers at Selfridge's, and all the while they'd talked of Chaz, Chaz, Chaz.

How rich was he? How many houses did he have? Where had he gone to school? Lindsay had done countless searches on her phone, trumpeting every gleaned fact with triumph while Jenna had murmured something appropriately modest and blushed.

By the end of it all, Liza was heartily tired of even thinking about Chaz Bingham—as well as Fausto Danti. She'd thought about him far too much while her family wittered on about his friend. Why had he been so rude? Who did he think he was? Had she been imagining some sort of…spark…in the look he'd given her? She must have, based on what he'd said to Chaz about her. Of course she had. She was ridiculous to think— *hope*—she hadn't, even for a second. Ridiculous and pathetic.

In any case, they were all futile questions because Liza knew she'd never see him again. In fact, she thought he'd most likely make sure of it, and if he didn't, she would. She *would*.

Still, thoughts of the irritable and inscrutable man dogged her as she headed to work on Monday. Although her position as an assistant to the editor of a tiny, obscure publisher of poetry paid peanuts, Liza loved it.

She loved everything about her job—the elegant, high-ceilinged office in Holborn, with its many bookcases and tall sashed windows over-looking Russell Square. She loved her boss, an elderly man named Henry Burgh, whose grand-father had founded the business a hundred years ago. He was holding onto it now by the skin of his teeth—as well as his generous but dwindling inheritance.

Liza had no idea who bought the slender vol-umes of poetry with their silky pages and ink-drawn illustrations, but she thought they were the most beautiful books she'd ever seen, and she loved the combination of older canonical poetry with works by refreshingly modern poets.

It annoyed her that as she worked at her desk in that beautiful room, she was *still* thinking about Fausto Danti. Wondering why he was so arro-gant—and if there was any chance whatsoever that she might see him again. She really needed to stop.

'You seem a bit distracted,' Henry commented as he came out of his office to give her some man-uscripts to copy edit. As usual he was wearing a three-piece suit in Harris tweed, a gold pocket watch on a chain in his waistcoat pocket. For a man nearing eighty, Henry Burgh certainly had style.

'Sorry.' Liza ducked her head in apology. 'Busy weekend. My family visited.'

'Ah, and how did they find the city?' He raised

shaggy grey eyebrows as he gave her a kindly smile.

'They loved it, but I knew they would.' Liza thought Lindsay had been waiting all her life to get to London, to the business of living among fashionable people, socialites and YouTubers and the wealthy elite. A school trip to Paris at age twelve was the furthest adventure Lindsay had had so far, and she was most certainly ready for more when she started university next September.

'I'm pleased,' Henry told her. 'The next time they come, you must bring them here to meet me.'

Liza murmured her agreement, although privately she doubted her mother or sisters would want to visit her workplace. None of them, not even Marie, were interested in reading poetry. Her father would, she thought, but he was reluctant to leave the former vicarage in Little Mayton that he'd bought for a song thirty years ago and done up slowly. He loved his home comforts—his study, his workshop, his garden. Unlike his daughters, he had no hankering for adventures outside the home.

What would Fausto Danti think of the place where she worked? Liza wondered after Henry had gone back into his office. Was he a man who liked books? Poetry? Of course she had no idea, and yet somehow she suspected he might. There had been a quiet, contained intensity about him that suggested a man with at least some kind of an inner life, although perhaps that was stupidly wishful thinking on her part. Why should she think the man had depths, just because he had a sexy scowl? No, of course he didn't. He was just a jerk.

Smiling to herself at the thought, Liza reached for the stack of manuscripts.

'Liza!'

Jenna threw open the door of their tiny flat as soon as Liza had reached the top of the stairs, causing her to put her hand to her heart in alarm.

'What's wrong—?'

'Nothing's wrong,' Jenna declared with a chortle. 'Everything is wonderfully right. Or at least— I think it might be! *Look.*' She thrust her phone so close to Liza's face that the screen blurred and she had to take a step back. 'It's from him,' Jenna explained, although Liza had already figured that out.

'If you're free this weekend,' she read, 'I'd love for you to come to a little house party I'm having in Surrey.' She glanced up at Jenna. 'A house party? Really?'

Jenna bit her lip, doubt flickering in her blue eyes. 'Why not?'

'You've met him once, Jen. And now he wants you to go to his house? Doesn't it seem…' Liza struggled for a way to explain her concerns that didn't sound too harsh '…a bit much, a bit too soon?' she finished helplessly.

'There will be loads of other people there. And it's only for the weekend.'

'I know, but…'

'This is what people like him do, Liza. Just because we've never been to house parties doesn't mean it isn't the usual thing.'

'I suppose.' Liza handed back the phone as she headed into their flat. She was tired and her feet ached from her walk from the Tube. She was looking forward to an evening of ice cream and maybe some Netflix, but it was clear her sister wanted to talk about Chaz. Again. Not that she'd begrudge Jenna anything, because her sister was her best friend and just about the most genuinely sweet person in the world. She was the one with the attitude problem.

'Do you think I shouldn't go?' Jenna asked as Liza opened the fridge to peruse its meagre contents. 'I won't if you don't think I should.'

'It's not for me to say…'

'But I need your input,' Jenna protested. 'I trust you, Liza. Do you think it's a crazy idea? I barely know him. It's just he seems so *nice*.'

'He does,' Liza admitted, because that much was certainly true.

'And I do like him.' Jenna bit her lip. 'More than I probably should, considering how little I know him.'

'There's no reason not to go, really,' Liza said as she closed the fridge and started examining the contents of their cupboards. 'We came to London for adventure, after all. Now you're having one.'

'Yes…' Jenna still looked uncertain. The truth, Liza knew, was that her older sister had never been particularly adventurous. It had been more Liza's idea than Jenna's to come to London, desperate for a new start, after she'd been offered the job of editorial assistant. Jenna had found a position as a receptionist at an accountancy firm, and Liza had bowled them both along. It wasn't like her older sister to step out on her own. It never had been. 'I know,' Jenna said suddenly. 'What if you go with me?'

'What?' Liza turned from her disappointing perusal of the cupboards. 'Jenna, I can't just show up without an invitation.'

'I'm sure I could bring a plus one.'

'I'm sure Chaz Bingham is counting on you *not* bringing a plus one,' Liza returned dryly. 'There's no way I can just turn up like a spare part and act as if I was invited.'

'Please, Liza.' Jenna's eyes widened appealingly as she gave Liza a pleading look. 'You know how nervous I get on my own. I'm no good at these kinds of things…'

'We've never *been* to this kind of thing—'

'Parties. Social events. You *know*. I never know

what to say, and I go all shy and silent. I need your support.'

Liza shook her head resolutely. 'Jenna, if you're too nervous to go on your own, you shouldn't go at all. You could always go and then leave if you really don't like it. But I cannot, and will not, turn up uninvited.' She suppressed a shudder at the thought. If Chaz Bingham was having a house party, there was a chance Fausto Danti would be there and she could only too well imagine the incredulous and disdainful look on his face if she appeared unexpectedly, an obvious hanger-on. He might think she was trying to attract his attention, *and* she'd be seeming to confirm the unkind remark he'd made about them being gold-diggers. No, thank you!

'I don't know...' Jenna murmured, fiddling with her phone, and Liza reached for a packet of pasta, realising this conversation might take the entire evening and she was going to need sustenance for it.

It took three days of deliberation, but on Thursday morning Jenna finally decided to accept the invitation. Liza helped her word a polite but reserved text back to Chaz.

By Friday afternoon Jenna was packed, and Liza saw her off on the train to Chaz's family estate in Surrey, trying to squelch that treacherous flicker of envy that Jenna was going somewhere exciting and she wasn't. Of course Chaz wouldn't have invited *her*, and Fausto Danti wouldn't have extended an invitation either. The idea was utterly ludicrous; it wouldn't have even crossed his mind, and it was shaming that it had crossed hers, even for an instant.

Besides, Liza reminded herself as she headed back to her flat for a quiet weekend alone, she wouldn't have wanted to go anyway. If either man had invited her, she would have refused. Politely, but most definitely firmly. The last thing she needed was a man in her life making her feel inferior, unwanted. Undesirable.

Although, to be fair, Fausto Danti hadn't been quite that bad. No, she was projecting onto him the feelings she still had about being so thoroughly rejected by Andrew Felton. Liza closed her eyes, determined not to think of the man she'd convinced herself she'd been love with, only to have him laugh at her, and worse.

It had been a long time ago now—well, eighteen months—and she hadn't been that hurt. She hadn't even loved him, not really, even if at the time she thought she had.

It was stupid to think of Andrew just because Fausto Danti had been similarly snide. Fausto Danti, Liza acknowledged, was a million times more attractive—and therefore a million times less likely to be interested in her. The sooner she got that through her head, the better.

As one of four sisters, Liza was used to being around people, but she had never minded her own company and she would normally be perfectly content to spend a weekend alone, even if the weather was dire—as cold and rainy an October as there had ever been.

This weekend, however, the hours seemed to drag and drag. There were no texts from Jenna even though she'd promised to tell her how she was getting on and, with the weather so miserable, Liza decided to stay inside. On Saturday afternoon, with little else to do, she began to blitz clean the flat; two hours into her efforts, when she was sweaty and dirty and covered in dust, her phone finally buzzed with a text from Jenna.

Liza, HELP! I've come down with the worst cold and everyone here is such a snob. I'm soooo miserable. Please, please come and rescue me.

'Check.'

Chaz let out a groan as he looked down at the chessboard. 'How did I not even see that?'

'You never see it,' Fausto remarked dryly. 'In all the times I've played you in chess.'

'Too true. I think we should try another game.'

'Go Fish?' Fausto suggested and Chaz laughed.

'That's about my speed.' He glanced out of the window at the rain streaking relentlessly down the long diamond panes, the view of Netherhall's park shrouded in gloom. 'This weather is horrendous.' He rose from the unfinished game and began to prowl about the elegant confines of the study.

'If you're going to have a house party in October,' Fausto remarked, 'you should expect rain.'

'It's not that.'

Fausto leaned back in his chair as he surveyed his old friend. 'Let me guess,' he said. 'It's the fact that your so-called guest of honour is currently laid up in bed.'

Chaz turned to him with his usual ready smile, eyebrows raised. 'So-called?'

Fausto lifted one shoulder in a negligent shrug. 'Did you *meet* her mother?'

Chaz did not bother to defend the woman in question, which did not surprise Fausto. The woman had been too appalling, with her breathy voice and her avaricious manner, not to mention her revolting cocktails. The same with the younger sister. Gold-diggers, the pair of them, and he certainly knew how to recognise one. Admittedly, he couldn't fault either Liza or Jenna, although he still had his suspicions. A woman could seem sweet on the outside and be thinking only about money and prestige.

Look at Amy…

But he refused to think of Amy.

'So?' Chaz answered with a shrug, drawing

Fausto out of his grim recollections. 'I didn't invite her mother.'

'Still, it's telling.'

'Of what?'

Fausto toyed with the queen he'd taken off Chaz a few moments earlier, his long fingers caressing the smooth white marble, memories of Amy still haunting his mind like ghosts. 'They're not exactly people of…class.'

Chaz let out a huff of disbelieving laughter. 'You sound about a hundred years old. This isn't the eighteen-hundreds, Danti.'

It was an accusation Fausto had heard before from his friend. People weren't supposed to talk about class any more, or the fact that someone with a position in society had a duty to uphold it.

But it had been drilled into him since he was a child, by both his parents—ideas about respect, and dignity, and honour. Family was everything, and always came first—above happiness, pleasure, or personal desire. He'd rebelled against it all once, and it had cost both him and his family greatly. He had no desire to do it again.

For a second he saw his father Bernardo's proud and autocratic face, turned haggard and wasted by disease. Fausto could almost feel his father's claw-like fingers scrabbling for his own. *'Family, Fausto. Family always comes first. The Dantis have been the first family of Lombardy for three hundred years. Never forget that. Never dishonour it. You carry our name. You represent it everywhere...'*

It was a responsibility he'd shirked once and now took with the utmost seriousness, a burden he was glad to bear, for the sake of his father's memory. It defined who he was, how he acted, what he believed. He would never forget he had a duty to his father, to his family, to himself. A duty to act honourably, to protect the family's interests, to live—and to marry—well, to carry on the Danti name, to run the vast estates that bore his name.

Chaz, he knew, did not feel the same sense of responsibility that he did. His friend wore his wealth and privilege lightly, carelessly, and he did not let himself be weighed down by expectation or tradition—not, Fausto acknowledged, that his parents, currently living in the south of France, cared too much for either. They were new money, a family of socialites, eager to enjoy their wealth. Yet, for all that, Chaz was as friendly and unpretentious a person as any Fausto had ever met.

'In any case, you're not serious about this woman, are you?' he asked.

'I don't know,' Chaz returned thoughtfully. 'I might be.'

Fausto chose not to reply. He couldn't see his friend marrying such a nobody, beautiful though she might be, but if he wanted to amuse himself with an affair, that was his own business.

'Hopefully she'll take some paracetamol then,' he remarked. 'So you can at least see her before she has to go home.' Jenna Benton had shown up at the house late on Friday afternoon, soaking wet and sneezing. She'd barely said a word at dinner, shooting Chaz beseeching looks, and had been holed up in her room ever since.

The other guests Chaz had invited—the usual tedious selection of socialites and trust fund babies—had been as insipid as Fausto had expected. He should have stayed in London and worked through the weekend, but he'd allowed Chaz to convince him to come. Clearly a mistake.

'Perhaps I'll check on her now,' Chaz said, brightening at the thought. 'Make sure she has tea and toast and whatever else she needs.'

'By all means, go and play nursemaid.' Fausto replaced the queen piece on the chessboard before gesturing to the door.

Chaz smiled wryly. 'Are you going to closet yourself in here all weekend? You could have gone into Guildford with everyone else, you know.'

'In the pouring rain?' Fausto shook his head. That afternoon the other three guests had gamely gone into town, but Fausto had refused.

'I know my sister in particular is hoping you'll venture out,' Chaz remarked slyly. 'She was the one to insist you come along.'

'I'm sorry to disappoint her.'

Chaz let out a laugh. 'I don't think you're sorry at all.'

Fausto decided in this case discretion was the better part of valour. As much as he liked Chaz, he had very little patience with his twittering and vapid sister, Kerry. Chaz laughed again, and shook his head.

'All right, suit yourself. I'm going to check on Jenna.'

'Good luck.'

As Chaz headed upstairs, Fausto rose from his chair by the fire and walked about the room, as restless as Chaz had been a moment ago. Perhaps he would make his excuses and return to London tonight.

Danti Investments' London office had been in lamentable shape when he'd arrived last week, a fact which still made him burn with futile fury for its cause. It would take all his time and effort to get it to the productive place it needed to be before he returned to Milan. He didn't have time to waste enduring the company of people he actively disliked.

For a second an image flitted in his mind of someone he didn't actively dislike…someone he didn't actually *know*. Corkscrew curls, hazel eyes, a mocking smile, a willowy figure. Jenna's sister Liza had been occupying too many of his thoughts since he'd first laid eyes on her last weekend.

It was absurd, because she was of absolutely no importance to him, and yet he kept thinking about her. Remembering the pointed sweetness of her tone as she'd sparred with him, the lively intelligence in her face, the sweetly enticing curves of her slender figure. It was aggravating in the extreme that he kept thinking about her, especially when he had no desire to.

When he married, it would have to be to a woman of appropriate status and connections back in Italy, from one of the ancient families he'd known for many years, who held the same values of honour and respect that he did, who knew how to be his partner in running the vast Danti empire. That had been the promise he'd made to his dying father, and he intended to keep it.

As for other, less honourable, possibilities…he had no desire to get caught up in some run-of-the-mill affair that would undoubtedly run its short and predictable course, and in doing so become messy and time-consuming. Sexual gratification could be delayed. Work—and family—were far more important than such base needs.

The sonorous chimes of the house's doorbell echoed through the hall and Fausto stilled, wondering what unexpected guest might be making such a late appearance. He waited, but no one came to answer the door; Chaz had to be busy with Jenna, and the staff were no doubt occupied elsewhere. The doorbell rang again.

With a hurried exhalation of annoyance, Fausto strode out of the study. It was most likely only a delivery man or some such, but he hated rudeness or impunctuality, and not answering the door was both.

The large entrance hall was empty as he walked through it, towards the front door. Rain streamed down the windows; it really was a deluge out there. Barely reining in his impatience, Fausto threw open the door with a scowl—and then blinked at the bedraggled figure standing there, looking woebegone and forlorn and very, very wet.

He gaped for a second before his mouth snapped shut and he stared at her, eyebrows creasing together, his mouth drawn down into a disapproving frown.

'Liza Benton,' he stated coolly. 'What on earth are you doing here?'

CHAPTER THREE

OF ALL THE people to answer the door. Liza blinked through the rain streaming down her face at the sight of Fausto Danti glaring at her so predictably. He didn't seem like the kind of man who lowered himself to answer doors, so Liza had no idea why he was standing here before her, looking down his nose at her just as he had before.

What she did know was that she was freezing cold and dripping wet, her clothes sticking to her skin, her hair in rat's tails about her face as she shivered visibly. When she'd answered Jenna's summons and arrived in the village of Hartington by train, she'd been told Netherhall was only five minutes' walk from the station. It was more like fifteen, and thirty seconds after she'd started it had begun to bucket down with rain. So here she was, soaking wet and staring at Fausto Danti. Perfect.

'I'm here to see Jenna,' she said with as much dignity as she could muster, which she feared wasn't all that much. 'She texted me and asked me to come because she wasn't feeling well.' It sounded lame to her own ears. *Why* had she hared off so impetuously after receiving Jenna's text?

She'd grabbed her purse and coat and been at the train station in less than twenty minutes, without a thought or care in the world. It was only now, as Fausto Danti regarded her with such chilly hauteur, that she realised how ridiculous—and possibly scheming—she must seem. It wasn't as if Jenna was at death's door. She had a *cold*. Did Danti think she'd come here for him? Liza squirmed inwardly at the humiliating possibility.

'By all means, come inside,' Fausto said and he stepped aside so Liza could enter, dripping muddy water all over the entrance hall's gleaming parquet floor. She felt entirely at a disadvantage—wet, cold, dirty and, worst of all, uninvited. And all the while Fausto Danti lounged there, his hands in his pockets, his expression one of unveiled incredulous condescension.

'I'm sorry to come unannounced like this,' Liza said stiffly. 'But Jenna sounded completely miserable, and I didn't want her to be alone.'

'She is hardly alone.'

Any other man, Liza reflected, any normal, polite, kind, well-brought-up man at least, would have graciously dismissed her apology and insist that she needn't have made it. He would have ushered her in, offered her a cup of something warm and told her she could stay as long as she liked. She was quite sure that was what Chaz Bingham would have done. Why couldn't *he* have answered the door? Or his blasted butler? Surely he had one.

Anyone but Danti. *Anyone.*

'You are very wet,' Fausto observed.

'It's raining.'

'You didn't take a cab?'

'It wasn't raining when I left the station,' Liza returned with some asperity. 'And I was told it was a five-minute walk. And,' she flung at him for good measure, sensing it would annoy him somehow, 'I'm not in the habit of wasting money on cabs.'

'It would have been five pounds, at most,' her adversary returned mildly, 'but I take your point. Why don't you come into the study? There's a fire in there and you can dry off.'

This unexpected kindness appeased Liza somewhat, but she was still miffed by his high-handed manner and, moreover, stepping into a study with him felt a bit like entering the lion's den without either weapon or armour. Besides, she wanted to see her sister.

'I'm here to see Jenna,' she said, aware that an irritating note of petulance had entered her voice. Fausto raised his eyebrows, his mobile mouth quirking in the smallest of mocking smiles.

'You can hardly see her sopping wet. Besides, Chaz is with her now, and I'm quite sure you don't want to interrupt whatever *tête-à-tête* they might be having.'

Liza frowned at him, trying to gauge his tone. No, she didn't want to interrupt them, but the sharpness in Fausto's voice made her feel uneasy and defensive. What was he implying? Another stupid antiquated reference to gold-digging?

'Very well,' she said, not wanting to pursue the point, and she followed him into a pleasant wood-panelled room where a fire was burning cheerily. Fausto gestured her towards the blaze and as she started towards it, anticipating its wonderful warmth, his hands came to rest on her shoulders.

She stiffened in shock as an electric awareness pulsed through her, starting from the warmth of his hands on her shoulders and racing to every extremity with disturbing force and speed.

'Your coat,' he murmured after an endless unsettling moment, and Liza closed her eyes in mortification. He just wanted her *coat.* What had she been thinking—that he was making a move on her? As if...! Surely she knew better than to think such a thing. She prayed he hadn't noticed her humiliating reaction.

'Thank you,' she muttered, and she shrugged out of the wet garment. She turned, and the sight of Fausto Danti with her battered, sopping jacket in his hands, his expression rather bemused, made her suddenly laugh out loud, that moment of unsettling awareness thankfully dissipated.

He raised his eyebrows in query. 'What's so funny?'

'The sight of you with my poor coat in your hands. It just looks rather…incongruous.'

He glanced down at her coat, five years old and bought off the bargain rack, and then with a shrug draped it over a chair. His hooded gaze swept over her, his face as inscrutable as ever, but all the same Liza was conscious of her very wet clothes; without the protection of her coat, she realised they were clinging rather revealingly to her body, and she plucked uselessly at her sodden jumper.

'You should change,' Fausto said abruptly. 'Did you bring any spare clothes?'

'No,' Liza admitted. 'I—we—won't be staying.'

His eyebrows lifted once more. 'It's already six o'clock in the evening. You can hardly be returning to London tonight.'

Liza shrugged, defensive again. 'Why not? It's not as if we're in the sticks out here. There are trains running to London all the time.'

'Not from Hartington. They stop at four in the afternoon. And in any case I'm sure Chaz won't hear of it. He hasn't spent any time with Jenna yet.'

'If she has a cold…'

'I have no doubt some paracetamol and a bit of TLC will perk her right up,' Fausto replied, his tone so dry that Liza prickled again. Why did he have to sound so cynical? What was he accusing Jenna of—just wanting Chaz for his money? It was an ugly idea, as well as a ludicrous one if he'd spent two minutes with her sister. 'I'll fetch you some clothes,' he stated, and turned towards the door.

'I can borrow Jenna's—' she protested, but Fausto silenced her with a look.

'Nonsense. You can't remotely be the same size.'

Liza blushed at that, for the truth was Jenna was far curvier than she was, as well as a good four inches taller. Still, it annoyed her that Fausto presumed to know their sizes. Before she could make any further protest, however, he was already gone, the door clicking decisively shut behind him and leaving Liza alone in the room.

Restless and edgy, she paced the study, glancing at the leather-bound books lining the walls—all very distinguished tomes—and then at the chessboard set in front of the fire, clearly an unfinished game, with black at a distinct advantage.

She was still studying the board when Fausto returned with a bundle of clothes under his arm.

'Do you play?' he asked, sounding so sceptical that some sudden contrary instinct made Liza widen her eyes innocently.

'Sometimes. Do you?'

He gave a terse nod, and that impish instinct

inside her gave voice once more. 'Perhaps you would give me a game?'

Fausto looked startled, and then he thrust the clothes at her. 'Perhaps you should get dressed first.'

'Very well.' Of course he wasn't going to play a game of chess with her. She'd only asked to tease him, which had been stupid of her. Fausto Danti did not seem like a teasing sort of person. Flushing from the humiliating ridiculousness of it all, Liza turned away.

Everything about this situation was so very *odd*, she reflected rather grimly as she took the clothes and Fausto gave her directions to a powder room down the hall. It didn't seem to be much of a house party since the house, enormous as it was, appeared empty.

She found the powder room, which was as big as her flat's living room, without trouble and groaned at the sight of her reflection in the gilt-edged mirror—hair in a frizzy mess, cheeks and nose reddened with cold and the jumper and jeans which had been perfectly respectable when she'd put them on this morning now clinging to her like a second skin. No wonder Fausto Danti had been looking at her so disdainfully.

With a dispirited sigh Liza peeled off the wet clothes and hung them on the towel rail to dry. Dubiously she inspected the outfit she'd been given—a modest yet clinging dress in cranberry-coloured cashmere.

It slid over her chilled skin as soft as a whisper, making her wonder whose it was. She scrunched her hair and blotted her face, knowing there was little else she could do to repair the damage wrought by the rain. She still looked very much like a drowned rat, if a little less so than before. She supposed it didn't really matter. She could hardly hope to impress him, and she certainly wasn't going to humiliate herself by trying. She knew how that would go.

As Liza headed back to the study, she wondered yet again where everyone was. She felt like Goldilocks stumbling upon a castle rather than a cottage, and instead of three bears there was merely one incredibly intimidating—and attractive—man.

Having no idea what to expect of this encounter, Liza pushed open the door of the study and peeked in. To her surprise, Fausto was sitting at the chessboard in front of the blazing fire. He'd set the board up for a new game, and he gestured to it as she entered the room.

'Well?' His heavy-lidded gaze swept over her figure, clad in the clinging red dress, her feet bare, but he made no further remark. Liza pushed her damp hair away from her face.

'You want to play?' she asked incredulously.

'I believe you asked for a game.'

'So I did.' Her stomach fizzed with sudden expectation and excitement. She hadn't thought Fausto would humour her in such a way, and she had no idea why he was, but as she took her seat across from him she realised in a scorching instant why she'd come all the way to Netherhall in the pouring rain. It hadn't been to rescue her sister, as much as she loved her. It had been to see *him*—the incredibly attractive, arrogant, frustrating and fascinating Fausto Danti.

Fausto studied his opponent from under his lashes as she considered the board. They'd played the first moves in silence, and he'd noted her predictable use of the Spanish Opening, attacking his knight on the third move. Basic but acceptable, and about what he'd expect from someone who played chess but was still a beginner. At least she didn't call the knight a horse.

He was reflecting on whether to put her out of her misery right away or prolong the game simply for the pleasure of seeing her sitting across from him—the dress he'd taken from Chaz's sister's wardrobe fitted her just as he'd hoped it would, skimming her slender curves with an enticing delicacy, making her look warm and so very touchable.

Her legs were bare, slim and golden, one foot tucked up under her, her hair, as it dried from the warmth of the fire, curling up into provocative ringlets about her heart-shaped face. Everything about her was utterly delectable.

Fausto didn't wish to consider what contrary impulse had led him to agree to her suggestion of a match, but he suspected it was a rather base one. The sight of the firelight glinting on her still-damp curls, the pretty flush on her face as well as the gentle rise and fall of her breasts…it was all a distraction he did not need, and yet even so he found he was enjoying it immensely and he could not be sorry.

'I've never been to a house party,' Liza remarked as she unexpectedly—and, Fausto thought, amateurishly—moved her bishop, 'but I always assumed there would be guests involved.' She looked up at him with laughing eyes. 'Where is everybody?'

'They've all gone to Guildford,' he replied as he moved his knight. 'Since they were so bored here, with the rain.'

'Except for Jenna and Chaz?'

'Jenna stayed because of her purported cold, and Chaz stayed because of Jenna.' Fausto spoke tonelessly, refusing to let his own suspicions colour his words, but Liza frowned anyway, her eyes crinkling up as she cocked her head.

'Purported?' she repeated a bit sharply.

'I have not seen her, so I cannot judge for myself.'

'And yet you judge no matter what,' she returned tartly as she flicked her hair over her shoulders and moved her queen. 'Regardless of the situation.'

'I judge on what I see,' Fausto allowed as he captured her queen easily. She looked unfazed by the move, as if she'd expected it, although to Fausto's eye it had seemed a most inexpert choice. 'Doesn't everyone do the same?'

'Some people are more accepting than others.'

'Is that a criticism?'

'You seem cynical,' Liza allowed. 'Of Jenna in particular.'

'I consider myself a realist,' Fausto returned, and she laughed, a crystal-clear sound that seemed to reverberate through him like the ringing of a bell.

'Isn't that what every cynic says?'

'And what are you? An optimist?' He imbued the word with the necessary scepticism.

'No, that's Jenna. I'm the realist. I've learned to be.' For a second she looked bleak, and Fausto realised he was curious.

'And where did you learn that lesson?'

She gave him a pert look, although he still saw a shadow of that unsettling bleakness in her eyes. 'From people such as yourself.' She moved her knight—really, what was she thinking there? 'Your move.'

Fausto's gaze quickly swept the board and he moved a pawn. 'I don't think you know me well enough to have learned such a lesson,' he remarked.

'I've learned it before, and in any case I'm a quick study.' She looked up at him with glinting eyes, a coy smile flirting about her mouth. A mouth Fausto had a sudden, serious urge to kiss. The notion took him so forcefully and unexpectedly that he leaned forward a little over the game, and Liza's eyes widened in response, her breath hitching audibly as surprise flashed across her features.

For a second, no more, the very air between them felt tautened, vibrating with sexual tension and expectation. It would be so very easy to close the space between their mouths. So very easy to taste her sweetness, drink deep from that lovely, luscious well.

Of course he was going to do no such thing. He could never consider a serious relationship with Liza Benton; she was not at all the sort of person he was expected to marry and, in any case, he'd been burned once before, when he'd been led by something so consuming and changeable as desire.

As for a cheap affair…the idea had its tempting merits, but he knew he had neither the time nor inclination to act on it. An affair would be complicated and distracting, a reminder he needed far too much in this moment.

Fausto leaned back, thankfully breaking the

tension, and Liza's smile turned cat-like, surprising him. She looked so knowing, as if she'd been party to every thought in his head, which thankfully she hadn't been, and was smugly informing him of that fact.

'Checkmate,' she said softly and, jolted, Fausto stared at her blankly before glancing down at the board.

'That's impossible,' he declared as his gaze moved over the pieces and, with another jolt, he realised it wasn't. She'd put him in checkmate and he hadn't even realised his king had been under threat. He'd indifferently moved a pawn while she'd neatly spun her web. Disbelief warred with a scorching shame as well as a reluctant admiration. All the while he'd assumed she'd been playing an amateurish, inexperienced game, she'd been neatly and slyly laying a trap.

'You *snookered* me.'

Her eyes widened with laughing innocence. 'I did no such thing. You just assumed I wasn't a worthy opponent.' She cocked her head, her gaze turning flirtatious—unless he was imagining that? Feeling it? 'But, of course, you judge on what you see.'

The tension twanged back again, even more electric than before. Slowly, deliberately, Fausto knocked over his king to declare his defeat. The sound of the marble clattering against the board was loud in the stillness of the room, the only other sound their suddenly laboured breathing.

He *had* to kiss her. He would. Fausto leaned forward, his gaze turning sleepy and hooded as he fastened it on her lush mouth. Liza's eyes flared again and she drew an unsteady breath, as loud as a shout in the still, silent room. Then, slowly, deliberately, she leaned forward too, her dress pulling against her body so he could see quite perfectly the outline of her breasts.

There were only a few scant inches between their mouths, hardly any space at all. Fausto could already imagine the feel of her lips against his, the honeyed slide of them, her sweet, breathy surrender as she gave herself up to their kiss. Her eyes fluttered closed. He leaned forward another inch, and then another. Only centimetres between them now...

'Here you are!'

The door to the study flung open hard enough to bang against the wall, and Fausto and Liza sprang apart. Chaz gave them a beaming smile, his arm around a rather woebegone-looking Jenna. Fausto forced a courteous smile back, as both disappointment and a very necessary relief coursed through him.

That had been close. Far, far too close.

CHAPTER FOUR

LIZA'S SENSES WERE still swimming as she blinked her sister and Chaz Bingham into focus. Had that really happened? Had Fausto Danti almost *kissed* her?

She touched her tongue to her lips, as if she could feel the press of his lips against hers still, even though he hadn't actually touched her at all.

She had been able to imagine it so thoroughly, even as she recognised she could not truly envision it at all. In her twenty-three years, Liza had had a handful of casual dates, and one total disaster. None of it had, thankfully, gone too far, although she was still reeling from the emotional fallout of her almost-fling with Andrew Felton, even if she pretended otherwise.

Still, none of her experience, those few kisses, had been as memorable, as mind-blowing, as she was sure Fausto Danti's would be. As even the *possibility* of his had been.

But he hadn't kissed her and, looking at him

now standing in front of the fire, his expression as austere as ever, she thought he never would.

She had a sudden, awful certainty that she'd imagined the whole thing; it had been a fabrication of her fevered mind, of the utterly inconvenient longing she'd felt for this man since she'd first stepped into Netherhall. Even now she felt overwhelmed by the height and breadth and power of him, the sight and sound, even the *smell* of him, a sharp, woodsy aftershave that made her senses tingle, along with everything else.

But of course he wasn't interested in her. He couldn't be. Realisation scorched through her. He must have been teasing her, toying with her, and she'd fallen for it completely.

'Liza!' Jenna exclaimed, and started towards her.

Feeling clumsy and stiff, Liza hugged her sister. 'Are you okay?' she asked.

Next to her, Fausto drawled, 'It *was* just a cold, wasn't it?'

Liza threw him a glare that was meant to be mocking. Jenna let out a wobbly laugh.

'I think I've made a fuss over nothing. Chaz gave me some paracetamol and a cup of tea and I feel *so* much better.'

Jenna smiled adoringly at Chaz, who puffed his chest out as if he'd scaled Mount Everest rather than doled out a couple of tablets. Liza could not keep from glancing again at Fausto, whose inscrutable expression still managed to relay his arrogant assurance that he had been entirely correct about the nature of Jenna's *purported* cold, and she fumed inwardly. How could she dislike a man and yet want him to kiss her so much? *So much she'd imagined the chemistry that she'd felt pulsing between them?*

'I'm sorry I made you come all this way,' Jenna said with a guiltily apologetic look for Liza. 'I was just feeling so low.'

'I'm sure you were,' Liza murmured. She could not deny the awkwardness she felt now at having gate-crashed, and she felt it most from Fausto, even though he didn't say a word. When she dared look at him again he looked so severe and unimpressed that she felt quite overwhelmingly that she could not continue to stay there. She would not fulfil Fausto Danti's obviously low expectations of her and her family; she would not let him tease her for another instant with his mocking looks and his almost-kisses.

'Then it looks like I don't need to be here at all,' she said in a voice of patently false brightness. 'I'll call a cab to take me to Guildford—the trains will still be running from there.'

'Oh, no,' Chaz exclaimed, just as she'd feared he would. 'We can't send you away now. Stay the weekend, along with Jenna. I'm sure we could all use the company.'

'I can't…' Liza began. She knew insisting on

leaving now would be rude, but she was frustratingly, furiously aware of Fausto's fulminating silence, and she wondered if he thought she and Jenna had orchestrated the whole thing, for some nefarious, mercenary purpose, no doubt. *Gold-diggers*, the pair of them. How she disliked the man, even if she *still* wished he'd kissed her.

'You can certainly stay,' Chaz insisted, and then, to Liza's humiliation, he turned to Fausto. 'Can't she, Danti?'

'Liza must do as she pleases,' Fausto replied with a shrug. Inwardly, everything in Liza writhed with humiliation at his dismissive tone.

'Then it's settled. You'll stay.'

'I don't have any clothes or toiletries,' Liza protested, determined to make one last attempt at departure.

'That's no trouble.' Chaz airily waved away her concern. 'We've got loads of extra shampoos and things like that, and you look about the same size as my sister Kerry. In fact, I think she has a dress just like that one.' He smiled easily, as carefree as a little boy, while Liza flushed. So that was where Fausto had found the dress.

'Thank you, this is really kind of you,' she said dutifully, because she knew she could give no other response.

'I'll show you to our room,' Jenna suggested, and Chaz nodded.

'Yes, we're eating at eight—not too long now.

I'll see you then?' He smiled hopefully at them both, and Liza nodded.

'Thank you,' she said again, and she turned away, making sure not to catch Fausto Danti's eye.

As soon as they were upstairs, Jenna launched into a glowing description of all Chaz had done for her. 'He's so nice, Liza, I mean really nice. You don't often meet people who are good all the way through.'

'You are,' Liza said with a smile. Her sister was so big-hearted, so generous with her time and talents, that Liza felt small for ever having resented her for a millisecond. Andrew Felton was *not* Jenna's fault.

Jenna had ushered her into a room that was twice as big as their flat, with huge windows overlooking a terraced garden, the kind you'd normally have to pay to look at.

'I mean it, though,' Jenna insisted, as if Liza had contradicted her. 'He really is a good person.'

'I believe you.' Liza reached for her sister's toiletries bag and started to tend to her frizzing hair. 'That being the case, though,' she asked mildly, 'why did you send me that text?'

Jenna had the grace to grimace guiltily. 'I'm sorry. I don't think I should have, really. It's just I was feeling so low. My head was aching and everyone besides Chaz seems so…well, I don't like to criticise, but they're…'

'Snobs?' Liza filled in succinctly and Jenna shrugged.

'I suppose, although they're all very nice on the surface, Chaz's sister Kerry in particular. She was cosying up to me right from the beginning, acting *so* sweet, but I had the feeling she'd talk behind my back the second I was out of the room.'

'She probably would,' Liza agreed.

'You've never even met her,' Jenna couldn't help but protest, and Liza sighed.

'I don't need to, but you're right, I should reserve judgement until I do.' Not that Fausto Danti ever did. Checkmating him had been one of the greatest pleasures of her life, although in truth she would rather he'd kissed her.

The thought appalled Liza as soon as it had formed in her head. No, of course she wouldn't have wanted *that*. She couldn't. She actually loathed the man, even if she was helplessly attracted to him.

And if he'd kissed her it would have been either to toy with her or mock her, not out of genuine desire. Of that she was sure. He liked her even less than she did him, and worse, he made her feel so *small*, and she hated that most of all. She had vowed never to feel like that again, and yet here she was.

'You'll meet them all at dinner, anyway,' Jenna said. 'And then you can see for yourself.'

'Do you have anything I can wear? This dress

belongs to Chaz's sister, and I really don't feel
like turning up in it.'

'I only brought one dress,' Jenna said apologetically. 'And I think it's going to pale in com-
parison to what everyone else is wearing. They're
all millionaires, Liza. They all went to the same
private schools, and know the same small group
of people. Some of them have such toffee-nosed
accents I can barely understand them.'

'Oh, *deah*,' Liza mocked, putting on a drawl-
ing aristocratic accent as she planted one hand
on her hip. '*Howevah* will we manage?'

Jenna smiled and then let out a giggle, and Liza
rolled her eyes. 'Honestly, I think these people
are ridiculous, looking down their noses at us just
for being *normal*. They're the odd ones, really.'
She gestured to the enormous bedroom with its
sumptuous silk hangings and ornate furniture.
'Who really lives like this any more?' She wasn't
going to be cowed by all the money. She didn't
care about it. And she certainly wasn't going to
let Fausto Danti think she or her sister were gold-
diggers…not that she could do anything about
that, unfortunately.

'They do, obviously.' Jenna narrowed her eyes
as she regarded her shrewdly. 'These people,' she
repeated, 'or just one man in particular?'

Liza stilled, willing herself not to blush, but
she did anyway. 'I don't like Fausto Danti,' she
said frankly as she turned away to focus on her

hair, and hide her flushed face from her sister. 'He's an arrogant snob.'

'A *gorgeous* arrogant snob. When we came into the study, it almost looked as if he was about to kiss you.'

'He wasn't!' Liza exclaimed, her face ever hotter. She scrunched her curls with firm, hard hands. 'We were just looking at the chessboard. I'd checkmated him.'

'That's no surprise,' Jenna answered. 'I can't remember the last time you lost a game.'

'He's annoying,' Liza declared. 'I suspect he thinks we're here as gold-diggers or something like that.'

'Gold-diggers!' Jenna sounded horrified at the prospect. 'He didn't actually say that, did he?'

Liza decided not to mention the comment she'd heard last week at the cocktail bar. She knew it would only distress her sister. 'He didn't have to.'

'Oh, Liza.' Jenna shook her head. 'Sometimes I think you're as snobby as him, only in reverse.'

'I'm not,' Liza insisted. 'I just want to take people as they truly are.' Not, she thought darkly, as someone like Fausto Danti saw them. She didn't judge the way he did, and she wasn't nearly as proud. She wasn't proud at all. In fact, quite the reverse. She knew she struggled with her self-esteem, not that she'd ever apprise Fausto of that fact.

'Well, take them as they are in an hour,' Jenna

said with a sigh. 'We'll have to face everyone at dinner and even though I feel better now I'm glad you're with me. It's like going into the lion's den sometimes.'

Just as she'd felt with Fausto. Liza continued to fluff her hair as she met her sister's gaze in the mirror and smiled with determination. 'I'm glad I'm here too,' she said, and she hoped she meant it.

Fausto sipped the pre-dinner sherry one of Netherhall's staff had served as he observed the other guests circulating in the drawing room before dinner was called. Chaz was talking to Oliver, one of his rather bumbling friends from prep school, a keen cricketer who had far more money than sense. Chaz's sister Kerry was whispering with her friend Chelsea, a hotel heiress in a slippery gold sheath dress. Both of them kept shooting him coquettish looks which Fausto chose to ignore. Where were Jenna and Liza? It was three minutes past eight. They were late.

Not, Fausto told himself as he tasted the sweet sherry with a slight grimace, that he was eagerly awaiting their arrival. Of course he wasn't. The afternoon with Liza had been surprisingly pleasant, and he'd spent the intervening hours thinking far too much about her—from that electric almost-kiss that had been, in its own way, a more satisfying and passionate experience than the last time he'd actually been with a woman—to the fact that she'd trounced him in chess in just a few short minutes. She was, he admitted reluctantly, a superior sort of woman. Sadly, that still didn't make her suitable for a man in his position, with his responsibilities, his expectations. *His past.*

'Jenna!' Chaz sprang away from his friend as the sisters came into the drawing room. Jenna was wearing a rather worn-looking black dress, the kind a hostess at a restaurant might wear, and Liza was still in the cranberry knit dress Fausto had given her, although at least she'd found a pair of flats and styled her hair into a loose knot. Compared to the other women in their designer cocktail dresses and stiletto heels, the Benton sisters looked woefully underdressed, and yet he still found he preferred Liza's unadorned simplicity to the other women's obvious attempts.

Chaz had put his arm around Jenna as he ushered her into the room, and Liza came in behind them, head held high, gaze averted from Fausto's in what he suspected was a deliberate snub, a fact which both amused and annoyed him.

'Goodness,' Kerry remarked in a clipped, carrying voice. 'You aren't wearing my dress, are you?' She let out a tinkling little laugh, like the breaking of glass.

Liza flushed and lifted her chin another inch; any further and she'd be staring at the ceiling. 'I think I probably am,' she admitted with stiff dignity. 'I'm afraid I arrived without a change of clothes, and I was caught in the rain.'

'I gave it to her, Kerry,' Fausto interjected in a deliberately bored drawl. 'I didn't think you'd mind.'

Kerry could hardly say she did mind, and so she contented herself with merely raising her eyebrows and giving Chelsea a disbelieving look. Chelsea tittered, and Liza flushed harder but to her credit said nothing. Fausto realised afresh how much he disliked Chaz's sister.

'Perhaps you should consider giving it to her,' he remarked. 'I think it suits her colouring far more than yours.'

'I'm sure it doesn't,' Liza intervened quickly. 'But thank you, Kerry, it's very kind of you to lend your clothes to a stranger.'

'We're not strangers now,' Chaz insisted in a jolly voice. 'Since we're spending the rest of the weekend together. Now that we're all here, let's eat!'

The dinner was, as Fausto had expected, quite interminable, save for the pleasure of looking upon Liza when he could. She'd purposely seated herself as far from him as possible, which again gave him that push-pull sensation of both annoyance and amusement. Was she putting herself out of the way of temptation, or did she really dislike him that much? What he knew she didn't feel was indifference, and that knowledge satisfied in a deep and primal way.

The chatter and gossip during the meal bored him completely, however, and he stayed silent through it all, despite Kerry's obvious attempts to engage him in flirtatious conversation. He hoped his silence was discouragement enough, but he suspected with a woman like Kerry it would not be. Still, that was a problem for another day.

As for Liza…she ate her meal quietly, gaze lowered and yet alert, and he sensed she was listening to every word and finding it all as tedious as he was, a thought that gave him unexpected pleasure.

After dinner they all retired to the house's high-tech media room, where Chaz put on music and Kerry mixed cocktails. Chelsea draped herself over a leather sofa as artfully as possible, and Oliver sprawled on another as he scrolled through his phone. Jenna was chatting to Chaz, and Liza sat alone, looking serenely composed. Fausto walked over to her.

'How are you finding the company?' he asked, and she looked up at him, hazel eyes wide and clear, her mouth curving into a slight smile.

'I find them as I see them.'

'A scathing indictment, then.'

'Actually, I've found the whole evening quite entertaining. You all live in your cosy little world, don't you?'

Fausto drew back at that matter-of-fact remark. 'What is that supposed to mean, exactly?'

Liza shrugged slim shoulders. 'Only that this is quite a rarefied way of living. You don't seem to have any of the paltry concerns most people do.'

'Is that a criticism?'

'Merely an observation.'

'I suppose you're right, in a way,' Fausto said after a moment. He didn't know whether he felt glad or irritated that she'd chosen to highlight their differences. It was a needed reminder, in any case. As much as he enjoyed Liza's company, he could never consider her seriously. His family obligations as well as his own history made sure of that.

'You certainly don't seem to be enjoying the evening,' Liza told him with a laugh. 'I've been watching you scowl. Do you find everyone disagreeable, Mr Danti?'

'You should call me Fausto.'

'I've been calling you Fausto in my head,' she admitted blithely, 'but you seem like the sort of person who would want everyone to address you appropriately.'

'I don't need people to bow and scrape, if that's what you mean,' Fausto said sharply. He might have ideas about his position, and of respect and honour, but he had absolutely no need for people to be servile. The thought was repugnant to him. 'But if you really do want to get it right, it's Conte, not Mr.'

She looked startled, but then her expression cleared and she smiled and nodded. 'Of course it is,' she said, and Fausto felt frustratingly inferior for having mentioned his title. He hadn't intended to; he rarely used it. 'In future I shall address you as such. Is that Conte Danti, or the Conte of Something-or-Other?'

'Conte di Palmerno,' he bit out. 'But, as I said, there is no need. I am not accustomed to being addressed that way and, in any case, it's a courtesy title only. Officially, nobility was abolished in Italy in 1946.'

'In that case, it's Fausto all the way,' Liza quipped, and Fausto gave a tight-lipped smile. He could not help but feel she'd somehow got the better of him in the conversation.

'What I really want to know,' he said as he stepped closer to her, 'is how did you get so good at chess?'

Her eyebrows raised as her smile widened. 'You weren't expecting it.'

'You led me to believe you were a beginner.'

'I did not,' she returned. 'You assumed it.'

He paused, and then realised she was right. He *had* assumed it, but it had seemed like a very justifiable assumption to make. 'You're very good,' he remarked.

'Better than you,' Liza agreed, her eyes sparkling, and Fausto let out an unwilling laugh.

'Perhaps we should have a rematch.' He hadn't meant those words to be so laden with innuendo…had he? Because now he wasn't thinking about the pieces on the board, but the kiss that had so very nearly happened over it. The kiss he wanted—*needed*—to happen again.

This rematch, he realised, was merely a pretext to get her alone, and as Liza looked up at him, eyes wide, lips slightly parted, he thought she must know it.

'Are you sure you're up for a rematch?' she asked softly, and there was no mistaking the subtext in the tremble of her voice, the way her gaze lowered and her chocolate-coloured lashes skimmed her cheeks. He ached to touch her.

'Quite sure,' he said, his low voice husky. 'Quite, quite sure.'

'What on earth are you two talking about?' Kerry called from the cocktail bar. 'You look *awfully* serious.'

'We were talking about chess,' Liza called back lightly, although her voice wavered a little. 'Fausto is insisting on a rematch after I trounced him.'

'You did not *trounce*,' Fausto felt compelled to point out.

She turned back to him with glinting eyes. 'Oh,

no? You thought I'd lost my queen for no good reason.'

That much was true, and he could not deny it. He inclined his head in acknowledgement instead, and Liza laughed out loud.

'Come have a cocktail, Fausto,' Kerry said petulantly. 'I've made you a gin sling.'

'I only drink whisky and wine,' Fausto replied. 'But thank you anyway.'

'I'll drink it, if you like,' Liza offered, and with a challenging spark in her eyes she walked over to the bar, her gaze meeting Fausto's as she tossed back the cocktail. He watched her, caught between admiration, amusement and an overwhelming, heady desire. He didn't care whether she was suitable or not. He just wanted to be with her alone.

'Delicious,' Liza pronounced to Kerry, but she was still looking at Fausto. He nearly groaned aloud at the invitation in her eyes. Did she even know it was there? How did everyone in the room not see and feel what was practically pulsing between them?

'That rematch,' he said, the words bitten out. 'Now.'

'For heaven's sake, it's only chess,' Chaz interjected with a laugh.

Kerry was regarding them both with narrowed eyes. 'Why don't you bring the board in here?'

she suggested all too sweetly. 'We can all play, have a tournament.'

'You don't play, Kerry,' Chaz pointed out, and Kerry shrugged impatiently.

'I know the rules, at least.'

Fausto didn't think Kerry had any interest whatsoever in playing chess, but he wasn't about to belabour the point. 'As you wish,' he said instead, and then he turned to Liza. 'Will you help me fetch the board and pieces?'

A flush rose on her cheeks as she nodded. At last they would have a few minutes alone.

With eyes only for Liza, Fausto left the room, his breath coming out in a relieved rush when she followed.

CHAPTER FIVE

THEY WALKED IN silence from the media room, down a long, plushly carpeted hall towards the study. The house yawned darkly in every direction, silent and empty. Liza wondered if Fausto could hear the thudding of her heart.

She couldn't believe how flirtatious she'd seemed, how confident. Something about Fausto's manner, his undivided attention, had made her sparkle, and she relished the feeling even as she tried to caution herself. Not to read emotions into a conversation where there weren't any, because heaven knew she'd done that before.

'Why on earth would you think I was interested in you, even for a second?'

She banished the mocking voice of memory as she focused on the present. She didn't think she'd been imagining the undercurrent of sexual innuendo in her and Fausto's conversation. At least, she hoped she wasn't. Every time Fausto looked at her, her whole body tingled. She felt as if she were electrically charged, as if sparks might fly from her fingers. If Fausto touched her, she'd burn up.

And yet he *had* to touch her. She couldn't bear it if he didn't. She might dislike the man, but she needed him in a way she had never needed anyone before—elementally, at the core of her being. And he seemed to need her in the same way, at least in this moment. And being needed, even if just for now, just for *this*, was a powerful aphrodisiac. She wouldn't let herself think about anything else.

Finally they were at the study, and Fausto pushed the door open so Liza could step first into the darkened room, her shoulder brushing his chest as she passed him. She heard him inhale sharply, and she thrilled to the sound. She felt dizzy with desire, and yet he hadn't even touched her yet.

But he would…wouldn't he? He *had* to.

She walked towards the table in front of the fire where the chessboard lay, Fausto's king still toppled from their match. Unthinkingly, she picked it up, the marble cool and smooth in her fingers. She felt Fausto standing behind her, a powerful, looming presence, and then she turned.

She could barely see him in the shadowy room, but oh, she could feel him. The chess piece fell from her fingers with a clatter as Fausto laid one hand against her cheek. His palm was warm and rough and frankly wonderful.

For a suspended moment they were both silent and still, his hand on her cheek, his gaze burning into hers. Silently asking her permission. And she gave it, leaning her face into his palm for a millisecond before his lips came down hard on hers. Finally, *finally*, he was kissing her.

And what a kiss it was. Hard and soft, demanding and pleading, taking and giving. Liza had never, ever been kissed like this. She backed up against the table, and then Fausto hoisted her right onto the chessboard, scattering the pieces as he deepened the kiss, plundering her mouth and claiming her as his own.

Her hands fisted in the snowy white folds of his dress shirt as he pressed his hard, powerful body against hers and the kiss went on and on. She tilted her head back as he began to kiss her throat, his hands sliding down her body to fasten on her hips.

Her breath came out in a shudder as his lips moved lower, to the V-neck of her dress. Everywhere his lips touched her, she burned. Her whole body felt as if it were on fire, as if she had only just finally come wonderfully, twangingly alive.

And then a voice, as petulant as always, floated down the hall. 'Fausto? Where *are* you?'

They both froze for a millisecond and then Fausto stepped quickly away, pushing his hair back from his forehead as he strove to control his breathing. Liza leapt off the chessboard, humiliatingly conscious of her dishevelled clothes, her flushed face and swollen lips, not to mention the fact that she'd been sprawled across a chessboard of all things, ripe for the taking.

'Forgive me,' Fausto said in a low voice as he stooped to gather the chess pieces, and Liza realised that wasn't at all what she'd wanted him to say in such a moment.

She began to gather some of the fallen pieces as well, and just a few seconds later the light flicked on and Kerry was standing in the doorway, her hands fisted on her hips.

'Well.' She let out a high, false laugh. 'If I didn't know any better, I'd think something had been going on here.'

'Don't be ridiculous,' Fausto said shortly, and Liza did her utmost to school her expression into something bland. *Don't be ridiculous*?

Of course it was ridiculous, for something to have been *going on* between them. Ridiculous to him. She didn't have the space or time to be hurt by Fausto's instantaneous denial, and so she focused on gathering up the pieces while he grabbed the chessboard. No one spoke, but the air felt thick with tension.

Liza's body still tingled everywhere. Her lips both trembled and stung. She'd never been kissed like that in her life. She felt as if she'd been changed for ever, branded somehow, and the intensity of her reaction scared her.

I don't even like him, she reminded herself rather frantically, but the words seemed hollow even in the privacy of her own mind.

'So, a tournament,' Fausto said without any enthusiasm, and Kerry gave him a narrow look while Liza looked away. She wanted this evening to be over.

Unfortunately, it wasn't; the three of them trooped back to the media room where everyone was swilling cocktails. Chaz had put on a film that no one seemed to be watching, and the prospect of a chess tournament was dismissed without a word. Fausto stood in the back of the room, his hands in his pockets, while Liza went over to Jenna.

'I think I'll go upstairs,' she whispered. 'It's been a long day.'

'Oh, but...' Jenna glanced at Chaz, and Liza patted her arm.

'You stay. I don't mind an early night.' It wasn't even that early by her standards, already nearly eleven, and she felt more than ready for bed.

She said her goodnights to everyone, ignoring Fausto, who was scowling by the door; she had no choice but to walk by him on her way out. She tensed as she passed him and for a second she thought he'd speak, but he didn't, and neither did she.

Liza walked out of the room and upstairs on unsteady legs. Her whole body felt like a bowlful of jelly, wobbly and weak. As she closed her door and then collapsed onto the king-sized bed, she had an urge both to laugh wildly and burst into tears. *What had just happened?*

Well, she knew what had happened, of course. Fausto Danti had kissed her senseless. And while it would be a wonderful memory to hold onto, she was sensible enough to realise—at least she hoped she was—that it hadn't *meant* anything. Fausto disdained her as much as he ever did, and she disliked him. Mostly. Flirting a little over chess of all things certainly didn't change that.

And yet…and yet…the feel of his lips on hers, his *hands* on her…the wild passion and yet the surprising tenderness…

'Oh, come *on*,' Liza muttered to herself as she punched her pillow. 'Don't be like this again. Get a grip.'

She wasn't going to fall for the first pair of pretty eyes that made her feel special. Not like she had with Andrew, when she'd believed his flattery and made a fool of herself. She had promised herself she wouldn't fall for that again, and so she hadn't.

She knew very well that Fausto wasn't interested in her, not really, and in any case there hadn't been any simpering compliments involved, not like there had been with Andrew.

Just overwhelming mutual physical attraction…

With a groan, determined to put it all out of her head, Liza got ready for bed. She folded up Kerry's dress and took a T-shirt of Jenna's to sleep in, the excitement of the kiss draining out of her like flat champagne as she realised all the awkwardness that would likely ensue as a result. Fausto's 'Forgive me' most certainly meant he'd regretted his actions almost immediately; tomorrow he would apologise again, if he didn't just ignore her completely. Both prospects made Liza feel miserable, and she wished, quite desperately, to go home.

Eventually she fell asleep, barely stirring when Jenna came in several hours later, and then waking up a little after dawn, a feeling like lead in her stomach. She did not want to see Fausto Danti again. She had an awful feeling when she did he would be colder than ever, as disdainful and dismissive as he'd been that first night at Rico's, only this time, instead of annoying her a little, it would actually hurt.

She knew she wasn't particularly desirable or interesting; she'd already felt a bit lost in the shuffle even before Andrew had dealt her self-confidence its seeming death blow. To think, even for a moment, that she could hold the interest of a man like Fausto Danti…

Of course she couldn't. And she wouldn't let herself want to.

In any case, none of it turned out as Liza had expected. Jenna was brimming with shy excitement about her evening with Chaz, and his promise to take her out to dinner when they were back in London, and no mention was made of Fausto at all.

By the time Liza headed downstairs, dressed in an outfit of Jenna's that swam on her smaller frame, her stomach was seething with nerves and she only picked at the generous buffet that had been laid out for breakfast. She jumped every time someone spoke or came to the door; Kerry strolled in, yawning and bored, and Chelsea and Oliver were both clearly hung over, although Chaz was in as good spirits as ever.

Liza wasn't brave enough to ask where Fausto was, and it was only as they were planning their activities for the day that she learned the truth.

'It's too bad that Danti had to leave this morning,' Chaz said with unaccustomed gloominess. 'He promised me he'd stay until tonight.'

'Why did he leave in such a rush?' Kerry asked with a pout, and Liza stared down at her plate. Chaz mentioned something about him needing to work but she was afraid she knew the truth. Fausto Danti had left because he couldn't bear to see her again.

Fausto shrugged off his coat as he strode through the office of Danti Investments, located in a beautiful Georgian building overlooking Mayfair. It was empty on a Sunday morning, which suited him perfectly because he wanted to work. He wanted to work and forget a beguiling sprite named Liza Benton even existed.

It had been, Fausto had ample time to reflect on the journey back to London, utterly foolish to have kissed her, and kissed her so thoroughly at that. In the moment he'd been inflamed by his desire and he'd completely lost any power of rational thought. It was only afterwards, when Kerry had come in looking so suspicious, and Liza had looked so dazed and overwhelmed, that he'd realised what a mistake he'd made.

The last thing he needed was gossip—or any kind of attachment, physical or otherwise. He didn't want to act dishonourably, and neither did he wish to hurt Liza, and he feared he had by sending out an entirely wrong signal. He wasn't interested in her, didn't care about her, and had no desire to make it seem as if he did.

And yet... Fausto sat back in his desk chair, his unseeing gaze on the gracious view of Mayfair out of the window; his mind's eye was occupied entirely by one woman.

Perhaps he was attributing too much tender feeling on Liza's part. Heaven knew he'd made that mistake before, with Amy.

Amy... For a second he pictured her laughing eyes, her long golden hair, the way she'd smiled and teased and made him feel so light-hearted, as if anything was possible, as if for once the weight of his world and all the responsibility he bore didn't rest so heavily on his shoulders.

Then he thought of her look of regret when

she'd said goodbye to him, with his father's cheque in her hand. Yes, he knew about gold-diggers, and how guileless they could seem. Look at Jenna, with that overblown cold she'd dreamed up to take Chaz's attention. It had, to his mind, been glaringly obvious. Was Liza's response to him some of the same? Were both sisters hoping to snag rich husbands, or perhaps just rich benefactors?

Maybe all these tender feelings he feared she had for him were nothing more than a blatant ruse to keep him dangling on the hook so she could reel him in. Maybe he didn't need to worry about Liza Benton's feelings at all.

The prospect brought both a necessary relief and an unsettling irritation. He didn't like the thought that Liza was mercenary, and deep down he didn't truly believe she was. Yet the alternative was to think she might care about him, and that was just as unwelcome a thought. He never should have kissed her, even as he was thinking about doing it again.

What he should do, Fausto acknowledged irritably, was forget the whole episode completely, and yet somehow that seemed impossible. With a grimace of disgusted impatience, he pulled his laptop towards him and started to work.

Fausto managed to convince himself that he hadn't thought of Liza for an entire fortnight— almost. The energy and thought he expended in *not* bringing her to mind might have told another story, if he cared to listen to it. He did not.

He worked long hours that precluded thought about anything other than the business at hand, and he returned home to the townhouse that had been in the Danti family for over a hundred years with nothing in mind except food and sleep. And so two weeks passed well enough.

In fact, Fausto kept Liza Benton so well out of mind that when he stopped by his godfather's business one Friday afternoon in mid-November to fulfil a promise of saying hello, he stared in complete and utter incomprehension as Liza herself looked up from her desk and stared back at him in the same way.

'What...?' Her voice was a faint thread of sound. 'What on earth are you doing here?'

She looked so achingly beautiful, and he thought he saw a spark of hope in her eyes, but the feeling of being completely wrong-footed in the moment had him retreating into chilly reserve.

'I'm here to see my godfather, Henry Burgh. I had no idea you worked here.'

Something flashed across Liza's face—Fausto thought it was hurt—and then she drew herself up. 'And I had no idea you were his godson,' she answered. 'How did that come to be?'

'Henry was my father's tutor in university,' Fausto said, his voice decidedly cool. 'They were very close. I've known him all my life.'

'I see.' She rose from behind her desk, slim and elegant in a navy pencil skirt and ivory blouse, her usually wild hair pulled up into a neat chignon, although a few wayward curls escaped to frame her lovely face. 'I'll let him know you've arrived.'

Fausto watched in frustrated silence as she crossed the room, the only sound the click of her heels on the parquet floor, and knocked on the door of Henry's office. As she opened the door he turned away, determined to act uninterested. He *was* uninterested. He hadn't thought of her once these last few weeks, after all, and it was far better that they resorted to being nothing more than acquaintances, which was in fact all they were.

He was studying the volumes on the floor-to-ceiling shelves when Liza returned. 'He's on a telephone call, but he'll see you shortly. He said to make yourself comfortable.' She gestured to one of the two leather settees facing each other, her face blank and composed.

Fausto resumed his deliberation of the shelves for a few more moments before he took a seat. 'How long have you been working here?' he asked as he sat down.

Liza had retreated behind her desk and made a great show of getting on with her work, pulling a pile of papers towards her and studying them intently. 'About two months.'

'That's not very long.'

'It's when I moved to London.'

'From Herefordshire, as I recall?'

'Yes, a small village in the middle of nowhere.' She lifted her head to look at him, her chin raised a little, a spark in her eyes that was definitely not hope. Was she angry with him? He supposed leaving so abruptly from the house party might have been construed as rude. He hadn't meant it as some sort of snub, not exactly. He'd just needed to get away. Not, of course, that he had any intention of explaining his reasons to her, or how much of a temptation she had been.

'Have you been very busy with work?' Liza asked after a moment, all frosty politeness, and Fausto gave a terse nod.

'Yes.'

'Chaz and Jenna have seen quite a bit of each other in the last few weeks. I suppose you know?'

He shrugged indifferently. 'I don't keep tabs on all my friends, and in any case I've been too busy to go out these last few weeks, but he did mention that he'd seen her.' And rhapsodised about how much he liked her, while Fausto had made no response.

'I think it might be serious,' Liza flung at him like a challenge.

He glanced at her, noting the steely glint in her eyes. 'I'm sure Chaz is well on his way to falling in love with her,' he agreed coolly. 'It's his habit, after all.'

Liza pursed her lips. 'Does he fall in love very often?'

'More than I do.'

'Ah.' She sat back, her arms folded, eyes still flashing. 'Is that a warning?'

Startled, he spared her a wary glance. He didn't trust her in this mood. 'It wasn't meant to be,' he said, although he realised as he answered that it wasn't exactly true. It had been, at least in part.

'Don't worry,' Liza assured him. 'I'm not in any danger of falling in love with you.'

Fausto stiffened in both surprise and affront. 'I was under no illusion that you were.'

'Well, that's a relief,' Liza drawled. 'Here I was, worried you'd raced away from Netherhall because you were heartbroken.'

He didn't know whether to feel amused or outraged by her absurd statement. 'Trust me, that was not the case.'

'No,' Liza said softly, and for a moment the mask dropped, her face fell, and she looked unbearably sad, which was even worse than her anger. 'I didn't think it was.'

The door to Henry's office opened and the older man emerged, his wrinkled face wreathed in smiles. 'Fausto! What a delight to see you after so long.'

Fausto rose and they shook hands while Liza watched, narrow-eyed, although she managed a smile when Henry turned towards her.

'Liza, I insist you take the rest of the afternoon

off. I've made a reservation for afternoon tea for the three of us at The Dorchester.'

'What…?' There was no disguising Liza's shocked alarm. 'Oh, Henry, I don't think…'

'Nonsense,' her employer answered with a smile. 'You're on the clock for another hour anyway. I really do insist.' Henry's smile was both genial and steely and, managing a lukewarm smile, Liza murmured her assent.

Fausto knew better than to object to any of it, and in any case he could certainly suffer through an hour's conversation with Liza. Perhaps it would go some way to smoothing things over between them. If the opportunity arose, he decided, he would apologise for the kiss. That was the honourable thing to do, and then they could both put it firmly behind them—not that it was entirely necessary, since he didn't think they would ever see each other again. Still, it was the right decision, and one he felt satisfied with.

Yet as Henry locked up the office and they headed outside into the chilly dusk of a late autumn afternoon, Fausto was honest enough to acknowledge he was deceiving himself if he thought that was the only reason he'd agreed to this afternoon. The truth was, he was simply enjoying being with Liza again…far too much.

CHAPTER SIX

LIZA WALKED WITH Henry and Fausto towards The Dorchester in a daze. This was the last thing she'd expected. The very last thing! For Fausto to walk into her office…and now to be taking tea with him… She didn't know whether it was the stuff of dreams or nightmares.

Certainly he'd featured in her thoughts, both waking and sleeping, far too much these last few weeks. She'd tried not to think about him at all, but it was hopeless. A girl couldn't be kissed like that and then just forget about it. At least, Liza couldn't.

Still, she'd managed to give herself a very brisk and practical talking-to about the nature of that kiss, and how it had, of course, been only physical attraction, nothing more. Base and animalistic and easily dismissed on both sides. Or so she'd kept telling herself and she was almost convinced, until Fausto had walked through the door.

Now, sliding sideways glances at him walking down the street, she remembered how powerful his shoulders had felt under her questing hands, how hard and strong his chest was, how soft and warm his lips…

Everything about him made her buzz and come alive. *Still.* Just thinking about that kiss had her tautening like a bow as yearning arrowed through her. Two weeks of disciplined thought flew right out of the window, and she feared she was setting herself up for disappointment and hurt—again.

Henry was chatting with Fausto, which made it easy for Liza to lag behind and say nothing. She'd stay for an hour, no more, and then make her excuses. After that she'd never have to see Fausto Danti again.

Why did that thought make her feel so depressed? She couldn't deny that seeing him again had lit her up inside like a firework, even though she hadn't wanted it to. She glanced at his profile—the hard, smoothly shaven jaw, the straight nose, those sculpted lips. He was like a Roman bust come to life, all aristocratic angles and sharp lines. *And just as cold.*

They arrived at the hotel and a tuxedoed waiter ushered them to a private parlour off the main dining room, already set with silver, crystal and linen for a high tea.

Liza took her seat, trying to quell the nerves fluttering in her stomach. She had a feeling the next hour was going to be unbearable.

'Fausto runs Danti Investments, out of Milan,'

Henry explained to her as they all placed their napkins in their laps and the waiter brought a fresh pot of tea.

Liza glanced at Fausto, unsure how to handle the conversation. Was he going to pretend he'd never met her before? Why did that thought hurt her so much?

'Liza and I met a few weeks ago,' Fausto said smoothly, answering her silent question. 'At a house party. She trounced me in chess.'

'I thought I *didn't* trounce you,' she said before she could think better of it, and Fausto smiled faintly.

'I must give credit where it is due. But we haven't had our rematch.'

Liza stared at him in confusion, unsure if he was flirting or not. His voice was so light, his expression so bland, it was impossible to tell, although she told herself as sensibly as she could that of course he wasn't flirting. He couldn't be. She was just misreading signals—again—because she wanted to. The realisation shamed her although she did her best to rally.

'If you hadn't had to leave early, perhaps we could have,' she said after a pause, and he inclined his head in acknowledgement.

'Unfortunately, I really had no choice.'

What was *that* supposed to mean? Liza's head was spinning from the subtext, even as she wondered if she was reading too much into everything Fausto said. Discomfited, she reached for her teacup while Henry watched them both in smiling bemusement.

'It's always delightful,' he pronounced, 'when people I enjoy spending time with have already become acquainted with one another. Sandwich, Liza?'

Liza nibbled a cucumber sandwich while Henry and Fausto caught up on all their mutual friends, thankful not to have to contribute to the conversation. She'd barely had that thought when Henry turned to her with a smile.

'Have you ever been to Italy, Liza?'

'No, I'm afraid not.' She hadn't been anywhere. With four children and a large house, her childhood had been happy and full, but money had always been tight, trips abroad out of the question. 'I haven't really travelled,' she admitted with a rather defiant look at Fausto. She had a sudden contrary urge to remind him of how different they were, before he did. 'Or done much of anything. There hasn't been the money or opportunity, I'm afraid, but I've never minded. I've lived a very quiet life, really.'

'Perhaps that will change,' Henry suggested, and Liza gave him a small smile.

'Perhaps,' she allowed with another glance at Fausto's inscrutable face. 'Although I don't think so.'

The conversation moved on, thankfully, and

Liza did her best to contribute as little as possible without seeming rude. Finally, after an hour, she rose from the table and made her apologies.

'This has been so lovely, Henry, but Jenna and I have plans tonight and I really should get back. Thank you.' She spared Fausto the briefest glance possible. 'It was nice to see you again.'

She barely listened to his murmured reply before she hurried out of the room, a breathy sigh of relief escaping her as soon as the door shut behind her.

When she got back to the flat, Jenna was already dressed to go out.

'Get your dancing shoes on,' she told Liza gaily. 'We're meeting Chaz at a new bar in Soho, and it has live music.'

'We are?' Liza couldn't help but sound unenthused. When Jenna had asked her to go out tonight she'd been hoping for a sisterly chat over a glass of wine at their local.

'Yes, and I really do want you to come. You've been moping for the last two weeks, Liza. It's time to have some fun.'

'I haven't been *moping*.' At least, she thought she'd been doing a better job of hiding the fact.

'It'll be fun,' Jenna insisted, and reluctantly Liza went to change. At least she didn't think Fausto would be there. He hadn't mentioned anything that afternoon and he'd made a point of saying how little he'd seen of Chaz, and how busy he was with work. She was safe on *that* score, even if the realisation brought its own treacherous flicker of disappointment.

The bar was pulsing with music and people as Fausto pushed through the door, blinking in the neon-lit gloom of a place that was too trendy for its own good. He hadn't wanted to come, telling Chaz he needed to work, but once again his friend had insisted and after keeping his nose to the grindstone for the last few weeks Fausto had decided it might be enjoyable to relax for one evening, even if it was in a place like this.

The fact that Liza had mentioned she had plans and could very well be here tonight naturally had nothing whatsoever to do with his decision.

He forced himself not to look around for her as he made his way to the bar and ordered a double whisky. The afternoon with Henry and Liza had been, to his own annoyance, both unbearable and invigorating.

He'd done his best not to look at her, and yet even so his gaze had been drawn to her again and again, as helpless as a hapless moth to the habitual dangerous flame. With her hair pulled up, he hadn't been able to help noticing how slender and delicate her neck was. He hadn't been able to help imagining kissing the nape of it either.

He'd barely been able to conduct a conversation with his godfather with Liza seated across from him; every time he drew a breath he'd inhaled her perfume, a light floral scent that teased his senses with its subtly sweet notes.

Somehow, through it all, the conversation had got away from him. He'd intended to make some sort of apology to Liza for their kiss, but the words wouldn't come, especially with Henry present. While he'd done his best to be friendly, she'd done her best to ignore him. The hour had been endless and yet when she'd left in such a hurry he'd felt a deep sense of disappointment as well as frustration. He wanted to make things right between them, but he was uncertain as to how—or if Liza would even let him.

Perhaps tonight, if he saw her, he'd have a chance.

'Danti!' Chaz clapped him hard on the shoulder. 'Good to see you.'

'You're looking cheerful,' Fausto remarked as he leaned against the bar and took a sip of his drink. Chaz grinned.

'I am! You remember Jenna?' He ushered forth Liza's sister, who gave him a perfunctory smile.

'I do.'

'Jenna has given me the brilliant idea of having a Christmas ball at Netherhall,' Chaz declared. 'Wouldn't that be a laugh? Fancy dress, dancing, the works. We'll all pretend we're straight out of Charles Dickens or something.'

'More like Jane Austen.' Fausto glanced coolly

at Jenna, who fidgeted and avoided his gaze. So she'd suggested Chaz host a ball? Already practising at playing Lady of the Manor, it seemed. The suspicions he hadn't wanted to give voice to began to harden into certainty. He knew how women like this worked—was Liza one of them too? He didn't like to think of it, and yet he'd been duped before.

'You'll come, won't you?' Chaz asked. 'I'm inviting everyone. All of Jenna's family too.'

'All of them?' Fausto glanced again at Jenna, who flushed. She really was shamelessly inserting herself into Chaz's circle if she was asking him to invite her ridiculous mother and sister along with the rest of her relatives.

'I'll invite yours too,' Chaz declared grandly. 'What about that lovely little sister of yours, Francesca?'

'She's in Italy,' Fausto stated coolly. 'Thank you for the invitation, though.'

'She could hop over on a flight…'

'I don't think so.' The last thing he needed was seventeen-year-old Francesca having her head turned by some useless lout she met at a ball. Again.

'Well, you'll come, at least,' Chaz insisted, and Fausto gave a tight-lipped nod. He wouldn't be so rude as to refuse, although he was tempted to, especially if he had to deal with the other members of the Benton family shamelessly promoting themselves as they had when he'd first met them. Chaz clapped him on the back again before moving on with Jenna, leaving Fausto to drink his whisky in peace.

His gaze moved slowly, inexorably, over the crowded room, looking for those bright laughing eyes and that wild tumult of curly hair. He wasn't going to bother with the paltry pretence of trying to convince himself he wasn't looking for her; he was. He wanted to see her. He would apologise for the kiss, find a way to start afresh, as friends. She deserved that much. He did too. Liza Benton had caused him far too much aggravation and uncertainty. It was high time to put the whole thing to rest and prove to himself that he was master of his own mind, or at least his libido.

He did another sweep of the room, fighting an alarmingly fierce sense of disappointment, only to have his heart skip and his stomach tighten when he suddenly caught a glimpse of her in the corner of the bar, perched on a stool. Her head was tilted to one side, her hair wild and loose, and even from across the crowded space Fausto could see the sparkle in her eyes, the teasing curve of her lips. She looked as if she was *flirting*.

Instinctively, needing to know, he craned his neck to catch sight of whomever she was talking to, and then everything in him turned to incredulous ice when he saw the man in question—his smoothed-back blond hair, his easy manner, the open-necked polo shirt and expansive gestures so irritatingly familiar. *Jack Wickley*. What the hell was that bastard doing here? And why was he talking to Liza?

Fausto's fingers tightened on his tumbler and he tossed down the last of his whisky, appreciating its burn all the way to his gut. He could hardly approach Liza now. He couldn't come within ten feet of Wickley without wanting to punch the man. He turned back to the bar and ordered another double.

An endless hour passed with Liza talking to Wickley for most of it, before she left the corner she'd been perched in and came to the bar with her empty wine glass. Fausto, who had been tracking her every move, saw when she caught sight of him—her eyes widened as her gaze locked with his and her step faltered before she determinedly started forward again, her gaze skimming over him as if he wasn't there.

As she approached the bar she angled herself away from him, and incredulous indignation fired through him. Was she actually going to *ignore* him?

He leaned forward and he caught the scent of her perfume, which made him dizzy. 'I thought you'd be here tonight.' She gave a brief nod without looking at him, and resentment flared hotly. How dare she ignore him? 'Have you been enjoying yourself?' he asked, hearing the aggressive tone in his voice and wondering at it, but he *felt* too much to care.

'Yes, as a matter of fact I am.' Liza turned, and Fausto started at the obvious derision he saw in her eyes. Why was she looking at him as if she loathed him? She'd been sharp with him that afternoon, yes, but she hadn't looked at him like *that*.

She reached for the fresh glass of wine the bartender had poured for her. 'I hope you are as well,' she said in a final-sounding tone, clearly ending the conversation.

'I wanted to talk to you.' Liza raised her eyebrows, and Fausto struggled to find the right words, hardly able to believe that he—*he*—was being put at such a disadvantage. 'I wanted to apologise,' he said stiffly.

'For what, exactly?' she asked, looking distinctly unimpressed.

'For kissing you. It shouldn't have happened.'

'Noted.'

'I trust we can move beyond it.'

Her smile widened as she informed him with acid sweetness, 'I already have.'

And then, while Fausto could do nothing but gape and fume, she took her wine back to Jack Wickley, who was waiting for her with an all too smug smile.

Fausto swore under his breath. From the moment he'd laid eyes on Liza Benton he had not been himself—acting on impulse, saying and doing things he continued to regret. Acting the way he had with Amy, or even worse, which was utterly appalling. No more. For the sake of his family, for the sake of his own pride, not to mention his sanity, it was time to finally forget Liza Benton ever existed.

CHAPTER SEVEN

'Liza, hurry or we'll be late.'

Liza glanced at her reflection one last time in the hotel room mirror as nerves zoomed around in her belly. Her family had taken temporary residence in a small hotel outside Hartington, for tonight was Chaz's Christmas ball.

Tonight she'd see Fausto Danti again and even though she'd come to despise the man she couldn't deny some contrary part of her was looking forward to seeing him once more—and she definitely wanted to look her best when she did.

Her unease around Fausto had deepened considerably over a month ago, when she'd met Jack Wickley at the evening out with Chaz and his friends. She'd been sitting in the corner of the bar sipping wine when he'd come in with Chaz's group and, seeing she was alone, he'd approached her.

Liza had been wary of him at first; he'd looked too slick and assured for her taste, and there was something a bit too brash about his manner. She'd learned not to trust men like that. Men like Andrew.

Yet after a few minutes of chatting she'd thawed a bit; he had known Chaz from some party or other, and he was funny and charming and it was rather nice to talk to someone who wasn't giving her coldly disapproving looks half the time.

Then, after about twenty minutes of aimless chitchat, he'd stiffened, and Liza had followed his gaze to the sight of Fausto Danti glowering by the bar. Her heart had lurched towards her throat at the sight of him, even as an undeniable pleasure unfurled inside her like a flower.

'Do you know him?' she'd asked, and Jack had let out a humourless laugh.

'Fausto Danti? I should say so.' She'd waited for more, and he'd given it immediately. 'I grew up with him. My father was his father's office manager in Milan.' He'd paused, his lips twisting. 'We went to the same boarding school, in fact.'

'Oh.' She'd eyed him uncertainly for there could be no disguising the bitterness twisting his features. 'I only met him recently.'

He'd turned to her with an ugly sort of smile. 'And what did you think of him?'

Liza had hesitated. 'He can be a bit cold, I suppose,' she'd said, and then felt oddly disloyal for the remark.

'Cold?' Jack had sounded as if he wanted to say much more. 'Yes, I suppose you could say that.'

'Why do you sound as if you don't like him?'

Jack had thrown back the rest of his drink, and then shrugged. 'I don't. I don't want to bias you against the man, but you sound as if you already dislike him.'

'I do,' Liza had said, and then felt even worse.

'Not as much as I do,' Jack had stated grimly. 'Fausto Danti cheated me out of my inheritance. Our fathers were great friends—mine died, and then his did, and it had always been an understanding between them that I would inherit part of the estate, and be given a senior position with Danti Investments. I staked my future on it— and Fausto refused to honour either agreement, even though he knew, as I did, that his father wanted nothing more than to see me take over at least part of the family firm.' He put his glass down with a final-sounding clink. 'He's also bad-mouthed me to everyone he knows, so I haven't been able to be hired by anyone decent, even in an introductory role.'

Liza had stared at him, horrified. 'But why?' She might have disliked the man, but she'd thought he possessed a fundamental core of honour, even if it was of his own particular brand.

Jack had shrugged. 'Because he was always jealous of the way his father preferred me. They never had a close relationship. And because he's petty and mean-spirited, but I'm sure you can find that out for yourself.' He'd smiled at her, shrugging aside all the bitter words. 'But never mind about all that. He's the last person I want to talk or even think about. Another drink?'

Liza had insisted she'd get it herself, mainly because she wanted to see Fausto up close, even if she didn't speak to him, and judge for herself what sort of man he was, after all that Jack had told her. She'd faltered when they'd locked gazes and he'd glowered at her, but then she'd continued on.

To her surprise, he'd apologised for their kiss, which had both irritated and gratified her. She supposed he thought he was being kind, but was a kiss something to apologise for, especially when they'd both so clearly enjoyed it? Or was he apologising because he regretted it so much, since she was so clearly not the sort of woman he'd ever kiss, never mind actually date or marry? He'd certainly made that obvious.

In any case, she'd chosen to end the conversation; Jack's words were still echoing in her ears and she'd realised that everything he had said had confirmed her own instinct about Fausto Danti—he was a thoroughly arrogant and unpleasant man.

'Liza? Come *on*!'

Taking a deep breath, Liza turned away from the mirror. She was worried her dress was a bit over-the-top, but her mother had taken everyone to Hereford for a shopping trip, and all her sisters had insisted she try this one on. Crimson in colour, it had a bodice of ruched satin before it fanned out in a full-length skirt that made her feel like Cinderella at the ball. But if every other woman was wearing a cocktail dress she'd feel a bit ridiculous.

As Liza joined them in the hallway she tried not to let her alarm show at her mother's dress—a perfectly nice evening gown in royal blue, except Yvonne had insisted she was still a size fourteen when she hadn't been for at least twenty years. She looked like a tube of toothpaste that had been well and truly squeezed.

Lindsay's dress was even more alarming—a long slinky skirt of silver lamé with a double slit nearly up to her crotch and a matching bikini top. She'd insisted it was the latest fashion, and that her favourite YouTuber had worn something similar, but to Liza it just looked inappropriate.

As she gazed at them both she realised she was thinking like Fausto Danti, all coldly disapproving—and of her family! Who cared if her mother's dress was too tight, or Lindsay's too sexy? They thought they looked beautiful, and so did Liza. She hated how Fausto had somehow wormed his way into her thoughts, changed the way she looked at her family, even for a moment.

'And now to the ball!' Yvonne declared grandly.

She'd been so thrilled to have the invitation from Chaz that she'd talked about nothing but the ball since. When Liza had come home for Christmas she'd listened to her mother's plans for dresses, hotel rooms, and her hopes that every single one of her daughters might find true love in Netherhall's ballroom.

Jenna, at least, was almost a certainty; she and Chaz had been practically inseparable for the last month and Liza didn't think she'd ever seen her sister look so happy, elegant in her ice-blue off-the-shoulder dress. Lindsay would no doubt be on the lookout, but Liza wouldn't be surprised if Marie spent the whole evening in the corner with a book.

As for herself…? True love, she was quite sure, would be nowhere to be found.

As she followed her family outside the hotel, Liza did a double take at the sight of the white stretch Hummer her mother had ordered for the occasion, complete with champagne and Christmas carols blasting.

She knew she should get into the fun festive spirit of the thing, but once again she imagined Fausto's look of disdain and she could only cringe. Why was she letting him affect her this way, even when he wasn't here? She had to stop it.

'Oh, isn't everything beautiful!' Jenna exclaimed as they entered Netherhall a short while later. A twenty-foot Christmas tree decorated tastefully with silver and blue glass baubles stood between the double staircases in the house's main hall. Ropes of evergreen and branches of holly decorated every available surface, while a string quartet played Christmas carols in the ballroom and members of staff handed out crystal goblets of mulled wine. It was all incredibly elegant, and her family, Liza couldn't help but feel, stuck out like a lamentably sore thumb.

Well, who cared about that? She straightened her shoulders as she gazed around the crowded ballroom with determined defiance. She didn't care what these people thought. They were ridiculous themselves, caught up in their own privileged little world, just as she'd told Fausto back in October. They liked to look down at people who hadn't been born into the kind of society and money that they had, and the whole thing was utterly absurd. Who even cared?

She was, she decided, going to have a lovely evening dancing and chatting and having fun, and she wouldn't care what anyone else thought…especially Fausto Danti.

He knew the moment Liza entered the ballroom, even though he didn't see her. He felt her, like a frisson in the air, and he broke off his conversation with an acquaintance of Chaz's to look around the ballroom with an almost hungry air.

Fausto hadn't seen Liza since the night in the

bar over a month ago, and while he'd been determined to banish every thought of her from his mind, he'd failed. He'd thought about her all too often in the nearly six weeks since he'd seen her, and he was certainly thinking about her now. *Where was she?*

His gaze snagged on the sight of a young woman in the most absurd outfit he'd ever seen—a skin-tight silver two-piece ensemble that looked as if it belonged in a strip club rather than a ballroom. With a jolt, he realised it belonged to Liza's sister Lindsay. Amazingly, he'd managed to forget just how obvious and showy she really was. His gaze moved further to Liza's mother, who was looking both uncomfortable and excited in a dress that was far too tight for her. Fausto's mouth thinned. But where was Liza?

Then he saw her, standing slightly apart, holding a glass of mulled wine and looking a little wistful. Looking utterly *beautiful*. Her dress was nothing like those of her sister or mother—a princess-like confection of crimson satin, it flowed over her in a simple river of fabric. Her hair had been pulled up into an elegant chignon, but a few curls fell artfully about her shoulders; another brushed her cheek. Fausto started walking towards her without even realising he was doing so.

Liza remained where she was, looking around the ballroom, until she turned slightly and her eyes flared as she caught sight of him walking straight towards her. Fausto didn't know if he saw it or simply felt it, but a tremble went through her. Her fingers tightened on the stem of her glass. He kept walking.

The whole room seemed to fall away—the crowds, the music—as she remained steadily in his sights. Her eyes were fixed on him, seeming huge in her pale face, and yet she was so very lovely. Always so lovely.

Weeks of not seeing her had only sharpened his hunger, given focus and piquancy to the desire he'd done his best to banish. He stopped and stood before her, his gaze sweeping over her in silent admiration. She looked up at him, waiting.

'Dance?' he queried softly, and her eyes widened further, lush lashes sweeping her cheeks as she looked down for a moment to compose herself.

The animosity he'd felt from her the last time they'd met—the kiss, the apology, the unsuitability and the desire, the sparring and the wanting— all of it seemed to matter both more and less in this moment. Right now it felt amazingly simple and yet infinitely complicated—he wanted to dance with her. He wanted to take her in his arms and feel her body against his. Everything else could wait.

Finally, wordlessly, she nodded. Fausto took her half-drunk glass of mulled wine and handed it to a passing staff member. As if on cue, the string quartet struck up a sonorous tune. And as he'd been wanting to do all evening, all *month*, he took her into his arms.

Her dress seemed to enfold him as she swayed lightly against him, one slender hand resting on his shoulder, another clasped in his. They moved to the music, but only just. Fausto was conscious of nothing but her.

They moved together, unspeaking, needing no words. At least Fausto didn't need them. It was enough to hold her in his arms, press his cheek against her hair and feel her lean into him.

The song ended and another began, and still they danced. If people noticed or cared, Fausto wasn't aware. They hadn't said a word to one another, but he felt speaking might break the web they'd woven around themselves, a fragile cocoon of silent intimacy.

Desire flowed through him, but also something deeper. Something more elemental and yet more profound. He realised in this moment that he *cared* about Liza Benton—cared about her more than he had ever cared about any other woman.

The thought was utterly alarming. He couldn't care about her, not like that. Not like he had for Amy, when his honour, along with his heart, had been smashed. He couldn't give in to emotion or desire, not with so much at stake. Besides, his mother was expecting him to marry someone suitable from home, someone his family had known for decades if not centuries, someone capable and assured who could manage his estates and appear at his side without a qualm.

And yet, despite all that, or perhaps because of it, he knew he wanted simply to treasure this moment—the feel of her against him, the sight and sound of her, even the smell of her. His senses reeled.

Then the music stopped and they were forced to come to a standstill. Fausto kept his arms around her for a moment longer before he felt compelled to drop them. She stared at him uncertainly, and he realised he was scowling. He hadn't wanted the dance to end.

'May I get you a drink?'

'Since you took my last one off me,' she answered with a small smile, 'yes, you may. Thank you.'

The mulled wine had been replaced by champagne, and Fausto fetched two flutes. 'You seem in a better temper with me tonight,' he remarked as he handed Liza one, then wished he hadn't said anything.

'It's a ball, and it's almost Christmas,' she answered after a moment. 'I'm in a good temper with everyone.'

'That's a relief to hear.'

'You have been busy working this last month, I suppose?' He nodded and she continued. 'I don't actually know what you do. You're a Count, I know that much, but you have a business as well?'

'Yes, Danti Investments. It is one of the oldest banks in Italy.'

'Ah, yes, Henry said. Very noble.' She nodded, and he couldn't decide if her tone was genuine or not.

'How is Henry?' he asked. 'I haven't seen him since that afternoon at The Dorchester.'

'He's very well.'

'Good.'

They both lapsed into silence as the music struck up again; the spell that had been cast over them during the dance seemed to entirely be at an end. Fausto wished he could dispense with these meaningless pleasantries. There was so much he wanted to say, and yet all of it remained unformed, vague thoughts and feelings he could not give words to, no matter how much he wished it.

He was more than half inclined to take her by the arm and steer her out of the ballroom, back to the study, which would be quiet and dark. There he'd forget about the mere ruse of the chessboard and any possibility of a rematch—he'd take her in his arms and kiss her even more thoroughly than he had before. Kiss her, and then lead her upstairs...

'You're very quiet,' Liza remarked, and Fausto blinked at her, the fantasy he'd been constructing in his head falling to pieces.

'I have never been inclined to idle chatter.'

'Sometimes idle chatter can be pleasant,' she returned. 'Where will you spend Christmas?'

'In London.'

'By yourself?'

He shrugged. 'My family is in Italy.'

'You don't want to see them?'

'I need to sort out matters here. The London office has needed some attention since my father's passing.'

She raised her eyebrows. 'Don't you have an office manager?'

'I did, but he left a year ago. Where are you spending Christmas?' He did not want to talk about business matters with her, or even inadvertently allude to the disaster that had unfolded in the London office, thanks to his father's blind faith and old age—and one man's egotistical evil.

'I'll be in Herefordshire, with my family.'

'Ah, your family.' He couldn't keep his tone from sharpening slightly, even though he hadn't meant it to. His gaze roved around the ballroom and came to rest on Lindsay, who was holding a glass of champagne aloft as she twerked to the sounds of the string quartet.

Liza followed his gaze and blushed at the sight of her sister dancing with a suggestiveness that looked unbearably obscene from afar. Even from across the ballroom, it was clear that people standing nearby were either laughing at her or making shocked faces of disapproval.

'She's young,' she murmured, her face almost as scarlet as her dress, and pity stirred inside him.

'So were you once, but I doubt you ever behaved like that.'

'You sound so judgemental,' she flashed, and then strove to lighten her tone. 'Are you implying I'm not young any more?'

'How old are you?'

'Twenty-three.'

'And I'm thirty-six. So if anyone is to accuse anyone of being old...' He smiled, hoping to lessen any tension and also simply because he wanted her to smile back. She did, after a moment, and he was about to ask her to dance again, already imagining holding her and having the whole world fall away once more, when a carrying voice had them both stiffening.

'Liza, there you are! And oh, it's that Italian. Donato, isn't it—'

'Danti,' Fausto said as he turned to Yvonne Benton with a cool smile. 'It's Fausto Danti. So lovely to see you again.'

CHAPTER EIGHT

LIZA WATCHED HER mother eye Fausto with blatant curiosity—there were practically pound signs in her eyes—and she tried not to squirm. Fausto's lips quirked, and she couldn't tell if he was amused or annoyed by her mother's blatant scrutiny. He arched an eyebrow in silent enquiry, inclining his head, but her mother didn't notice.

Several glasses of mulled wine and a generous helping of hors d'oeuvres had not helped her dress situation, Liza noticed. Her mother looked as if it wouldn't take more than one deep breath to have her popping out, something she seriously hoped wouldn't happen. As she glanced at Fausto she saw his brows draw together in a frown and she suspected he was thinking the same thing—and hoping it wouldn't happen even more than she was.

'I've seen so many interesting people here,' Yvonne declared as she fanned her flushed face. 'So many *names*. I've recognised several people from *You Too!*.' She turned to Fausto. 'Do you ever read that magazine?'

He kept his face straight as he answered, 'I do not.'

'Well, you should. You'd recognise so many people if you did! Lindsay told me there was some YouTuber here, but I'm not sure if I believe her. There are some people with titles—proper titles! You know, Lord or Lady This or That.' Yvonne sounded breathlessly impressed. 'Liza, did you see the Farringdons? He used to be a footballer and they have a gorgeous house up in Yorkshire. *You Too!* did a whole spread on it a few months ago—the most enormous kitchen with a beautiful family room, everything in white leather. Just amazing.'

'I must have missed that one,' Liza murmured. She wished she could find some way to steer her mother away from Fausto, or at least away from talking about all the guests as if they were celebrities to be gawked at. Had her mother's voice always been so *loud*? It seemed ridiculously so right now, and yet she felt ashamed that she cared. Still, anyone in a twenty-foot vicinity could hear them. Easily.

And, judging from the either amused or disapproving glances that were being slid their way, people were listening. And judging, just as Fausto was. Just as *she* was.

'And I must say,' Yvonne continued without

a care for who was around, 'I think things are looking very promising for Jenna and Chaz. *Very* promising.'

'Mum…' The last thing Liza wanted was for her mother to start talking about wedding bells for Jenna and Chaz. She dreaded to imagine what Fausto would think about *that*. She tried to give her mother a pointed look but Yvonne just smiled.

'They've been in each other's pockets for two months now, haven't they? And don't tell a soul—' a rather ridiculous request considering how loudly she was speaking '—but I caught Jenna looking at bridal magazines the other day.'

'Mum!' Liza shook her head. She was quite sure Jenna had been doing no such thing but, even if she had, she would not want the news trumpeted about the ballroom.

'Just a peek, but still. Won't she have a lovely time doing this place up? It *is* looking a bit shabby, I have to admit. Some of the furniture is so old.'

'I believe it's called antique,' Fausto interjected politely.

'Oh, yes, antiques. They're all well and good, but everyone likes a bit of modern, don't they? So bright and clean.'

'There's nothing modern in our house, Mum,' Liza said a bit desperately. Their home was a hodgepodge of car boot sale and charity shop chic, with a few battered family heirlooms thrown in.

'Oh, yes, but if I had the choice I'd do it all up properly. Get everything modern. Of course I don't have the money Chaz has.'

'Where's Dad?' Liza blurted. Surely her father would put a stop to her mother's runaway tongue. She knew her mum meant well, and she might have had a little bit too much to drink, but the conversation, with Fausto listening to every word in that disdainful way of his, was beyond humiliating.

'He's dancing with Marie,' Yvonne said. 'He managed to get her on the dance floor, although she's got a face like a sour lemon. Why can't she have fun the way Lindsay does?'

Which made them all turn to Lindsay, who had her hands in the air as if she was at a rave, her champagne glass tilted at an angle that caused drops to spray anyone who was standing nearby.

'Your daughter does seem to be enjoying herself,' Fausto remarked.

'Lindsay's always known how to have a good time.'

'Indeed.'

Liza could take no more. She hated that her family was embarrassing themselves, but even more she hated that she cared so much. She hated that Fausto was looking down on them, and she hated herself for minding something she'd never even considered before.

'I'm going to get some air,' she said, turning

away from them both, although what her mother might say to Fausto when she got him alone Liza did not dare to think.

She slipped through the crowd of guests, barely aware of her surroundings—the gorgeous Christmas decorations, the sharp scent of evergreen, the candlelight and the elegant antiques her mother had called shabby. *Shabby.* Liza let out a huff of despairing laughter.

The entrance hall was as crowded as the ballroom and, mindful that she should hardly be snooping about the house, Liza went into the one room she was most certainly familiar with—the study.

It was dim inside, the chessboard still on the table by the now-empty grate, the room blessedly quiet. Here she could collect herself, but she couldn't, because when she looked at that blasted chessboard all she thought about was Fausto.

Fausto kissing her with thrillingly urgent passion…

Liza turned away from the board and went to the window. As she laid one hand upon the glass she realised it was actually a French window that led out onto a terrace that wrapped around the entire back of the house, and with one wrench of the handle she opened the window and stepped outside into the cold, clear evening.

Her breath came out in frosty puffs as she stood

on the terrace under a sky full of stars and tilted her head to take in the slender crescent of moon.

In the distance she could hear the strains of the string quartet, the sound of chatting and laughter, but it felt thankfully far away. She wanted to be alone. Tears of shame stung her eyes, although she wasn't even sure what they were for. Lindsay's dancing? Her mother's blabbing? Or the fact that Fausto had been standing there, looking down his nose at them all, silently judging them as somehow unworthy. Judging her.

Or maybe she was crying for herself, for feeling so ashamed and disloyal. She loved her family. Yes, they could be a bit OTT, she'd always known that, but they had *fun*. She thought back to camping trips when they were little, and how her mother had washed all their underclothes and draped them over the trees and bushes, heedless of the nearby campers inspecting their rather raggedy pants.

The annual tradition of the Christmas quiz at the pub in Little Mayton—they were the loudest, most raucous team, and no one minded *there*. Yvonne always brought a big bottle of pink champagne as a thank you to Darren, the pub's landlord.

Countless family dinners or chaotic barbecues in the garden, impromptu singalongs and games of rounders—she'd had a happy childhood in a busy home, and right now she felt ashamed of it all and she absolutely hated the feeling.

It was all Fausto's fault.

'Liza.'

His voice, a low thrum in the darkness, made her start and she wondered if she'd imagined it because she'd been thinking about him. Cursing him.

But no, she hadn't been imagining it, for as she turned around he stepped towards her from the study door, a dark figure in his tuxedo, the moonlight casting his features into silver.

'What are you doing here?'

His mouth quirked slightly. 'Talking to you.'

'How did you find me?'

'I followed you.'

She huffed impatiently, turning around so her back was to him as she stared out at the darkened garden. 'I came out here to be alone.'

'You're shivering.'

She was, because it was freezing and her arms were bare, but she simply shrugged off his words. She felt too muddled up in her head, too tangled in her heart, to offer any sort of coherent reply, never mind have an entire conversation.

Then she heard his footsteps behind her and his jacket dropped over her shoulders, enveloping her in his woodsy scent. He rested his hands on her shoulders, just as he had before, and just as before a pulse of longing raced through her, nearly made her shudder.

'You didn't need to do that,' she said quietly and he dropped his hands and stepped back.

'You were clearly freezing.'

Liza shook her head, closing her eyes against the night. Against him. 'Why are you really here, Fausto?'

It was a question he couldn't answer. *Why* had he followed her out onto the terrace? It wasn't like him at all, but since meeting Liza Benton he hadn't acted anything like his usual self—calm, reserved, *controlled*. He lost it all when it came to this woman.

'I wanted to speak to you,' he said finally.

'What about? My ridiculous mother? Or my worse sister? Or the fact that you think Jenna is some absurd gold-digger? I know you still do—I saw it in your eyes. Maybe you think I am one too.' She let out a little cry as she shrugged impatiently. 'Oh, it doesn't matter. I don't want to talk to you.'

'I have not said a word against your family.'

'You didn't need to! I saw you looking down your long aristocratic nose at them all. You think we're so beneath you.'

Fausto clenched his fists as he fought a rising frustration. He might not have known why he'd come out here, but it certainly wasn't to talk about the less salubrious members of the Benton family.

'I admit I find the behaviour of some of your family members to be...' he paused, wanting to be honest but not unduly hurtful '...questionable.' Liza let out another choked cry. 'That does not, however, reflect on my feelings for *you*.'

'Oh?' she flung at him. 'And what feelings do you have for *me*?'

The question seemed to hover in the air between them before falling to the ground, silent and unanswered—because he *couldn't* answer. He didn't have any feelings for her, at least any that he wanted to admit to, even in the privacy of his own mind.

Yes, while they were dancing he'd admitted to himself that he cared about her—against his will—but a relationship between them was still impossible and although part of him contemplated the idea of an affair with longing he knew he wouldn't lower himself or Liza to suggest such a thing. He knew she would take offence at the idea, as would he.

'Well?' she demanded, and then she let out a harsh laugh. 'Why am I not surprised that you won't—can't—answer? Because you can't bear to admit that you might like me at all, or find me interesting or attractive or anything else!'

'I—'

'From the moment you met me you've struggled against feeling anything for me, even if it's just basic physical attraction. Well, let me relieve you of that struggle, Fausto Danti. *I* don't have any feelings for you!'

She shrugged out of his jacket, flinging it towards him, and as he caught it he found himself catching her as well, taking her by the arms and drawing her towards him.

'Don't,' she said, a jagged edge of despair in her voice, and he looked down into those hazel eyes, now possessing a sheen of tears.

'Do you really not want me to?' he asked in a low voice, and with a cry of defeat she stood on her tiptoes and pressed her lips against his. The shock of the kiss was like tumbling down a hill, or missing the last step in a staircase. Everything felt jolted and off-kilter for a heart-stopping second, and then it all felt amazingly right.

His arms came around her, his jacket falling to the ground as he drew her closer to him, her breasts pressed to his chest, her body trembling and slender against him. Her mouth opened under his as he took the clumsy kiss she'd started with and made it his—their—own.

Once again the world fell away and the stars above them seemed to sparkle with an intensity no person had surely ever seen before; the universe possessed a brilliance it hadn't a moment ago, and he saw and felt it all in one simple kiss that blew his mind apart and overwhelmed his body.

And then Liza wrenched away with a gasp, one hand to her mouth as if she'd been hurt—wounded—by him.

'Don't,' she said savagely. 'Don't...don't kiss me like that when... Don't kiss me at all!'

'Liza—'

But it was too late; she was already stumbling past him, back into the house, away from him.

Fausto stood out in the cold, still air for several moments while he tried to calm his thudding heart, his whirling mind. *What had just happened?*

Well, he'd kissed Liza Benton—and she'd stopped it. She'd rejected him! Sheer incredulity had him emitting a sound that was meant to be a laugh but most certainly wasn't. Slowly, Fausto shook his head. Of course he knew he shouldn't have kissed her. Never mind that she'd kissed him first, he'd certainly taken mastery of it. And considering that he'd apologised for the last time he'd kissed her, a second round was definitely not a good idea.

But damn it, he could not get the woman out of his mind.

He needed to, though, that much was obvious. She obviously wanted him to! Shaking his head again, he walked slowly inside. The party was still in full swing as he came into the ballroom, feeling as flat as the champagne would be tomorrow morning, should any be left undrunk.

Judging by the way Lindsay Benton was swilling it, he doubted it. His mouth twisted in a grimace as he watched Lindsay still twerking away by the string quartet. The party was over as far as he was concerned.

He scanned the crowded room for Chaz, finally finding his friend at the buffet table. He started forward, determined to make his apologies.

'Danti! Where have you been?' Chaz greeted him with his usual good cheer.

'Around,' Fausto answered brusquely. 'But I'm going to bow out now.'

'What? Oh, no, old man, you can't do that. It isn't even eleven yet.'

Fausto shrugged his words aside. 'I'm tired.'

'Tell me, though,' Chaz said, slinging his arm around Fausto's shoulders. 'What do you think of Jenna? Seriously now, because you know how much I value your opinion.'

Fausto hesitated, knowing absolutely he was not in the right frame of mind for this conversation. And yet… Jenna's planning this ball, looking at bridal magazines, seeming so restrained with Chaz… Lindsay's regrettable behaviour… Liza's abandoned kiss…not to mention his past with Amy, the way she'd taken that cheque, the smile of regret she'd given him as she'd walked away…

It all felt tangled up in his mind, a pressure in his chest. 'I have some concerns,' Fausto said shortly, and Chaz's face fell.

'Seriously?'

'Yes, seriously. Serious concerns. About her family. Surely you do as well.'

'I don't care about her family—'

'And concerns about her.' Fausto realised he meant it. He'd been duped once; he wouldn't let his friend be. 'Are you sure she feels the same way about you? Because from everything I've seen of her, she seems…unenthused.'

'Do you really think so?' Chaz looked as if he'd been kicked, and Fausto felt a flicker of remorse. But it was true, he reasoned; he'd seen nothing of Jenna Benton that made him believe she was as head-over-heels about Chaz as he obviously was about her…and too many warning signs that indicated the opposite.

And if her sister's behaviour was anything to go by, the Benton women blew hot and cold.

'I think,' he said carefully, 'that you need to think long and hard before you proceed with a woman like Jenna Benton. She might like the thrill of the chase, the heat of the moment, and of course all the advantages you might give her…' He paused, wanting to choose his words with care even as part of him resisted saying anything at all. 'But in the end, does she care about *you*, Chaz Bingham, and not everything that you might offer her?'

The words seemed to reverberate between them as Chaz regarded him unhappily. 'I suppose…' he answered slowly. 'I suppose I never thought about it quite like that before.'

'Then perhaps you should,' Fausto said, clapping his friend on the shoulder before he walked away, wondering if he'd just done his friend the biggest favour he could have—or orchestrated the worst betrayal.

CHAPTER NINE

CHRISTMAS WAS QUIET, and only kept from being completely miserable by the fact that it was in fact Christmas and Liza was at home with her family whom she loved. She did her best to take part in all the family traditions that she so enjoyed—stockings and carols around the piano, glasses of sherry while listening to the Queen's speech and hilarious charades. Throughout it all she felt a shadow of her usual self—and all because of Fausto Danti.

Drat the man. Drat him for being so arrogant, so cold...so *gorgeous*. Drat him for kissing her, and drat him for when he didn't kiss her. Liza's mind and heart were both in a ferment as she considered the damning things Jack Wickley had told her, and then the incredible way Fausto kissed. The two together were positively insupportable, and she returned to London just before New Year as miserable as she'd been before.

Jenna was miserable as well, although in a

quiet way; Liza could tell her sister was flagging and she soon found out why.

'Chaz said he'd take me out for New Year's Eve,' Jenna explained with a sad smile. 'But he hasn't called or texted me once since the Christmas ball.'

A quiver of trepidation went through Liza at this revelation. 'Have you been in touch with him?'

'I couldn't. I've always waited for him to contact me first.'

'Surely you can send him a text, Jenna! It's the twenty-first century, after all. We don't have to wait by the phone any more.'

'I know, but...' Jenna nibbled her lip, her big blue eyes full of unhappiness. 'If he wanted to be in touch, he would.'

'Maybe he lost your number.'

'It's programmed into his phone.'

'Still, who knows? In any case,' Liza insisted staunchly, 'you deserve an answer. You've been seeing him several times a week for two months.'

It took several days of convincing, but Jenna finally decided to send a text. Then it took several hours of deliberating to compose all six words of it.

Haven't seen you around. Everything okay?

The reply, when it came three days later, was unhappily short.

Sorry. Been busy.

'He's gone off me,' Jenna said with a sound that was far too close to a sob. She flung her phone onto the sofa and tucked her knees up to her chest. 'I knew he would.'

'I knew no such thing! He was crazy about you. He still is.'

Jenna looked at her sceptically. 'Then why wouldn't he have called me?'

Liza didn't reply as her mind raced. She could think of no reason why Chaz would have gone off Jenna. Unless…surely, surely Fausto wouldn't have interfered? He'd been disapproving enough of her family at the ball, and he certainly hadn't denied her gold-digger remark, but even so…

Had he said something? Could he have been that judgemental, that arrogant, that low?

'Give him some time,' Liza suggested feebly, and Jenna gave her a sad smile.

They spent New Year's Eve at home, eating ice cream and watching Netflix while swearing off all men for ever.

'I always wondered if there was something between you and Fausto Danti,' Jenna said as she dug out the last of her Rocky Road. 'Things always seemed a bit intense there.'

'Intense?' Liza scoffed. 'Intensely unpleasant. I never liked him, not even one bit.'

Jenna raised her eyebrows. 'I think the lady doth protest too much.'

'No, really,' Liza insisted. She could and would not mention the two scorching kisses she'd shared with him. 'I learned some things about him... Well, I already knew he was rude and arrogant—'

'I never thought he was rude,' Jenna interjected. 'Reserved, perhaps. Distant, but maybe he's just shy.'

'Shy—?' Liza repeated in disbelief.

Jenna shrugged. 'Some people are. I am. Why not Fausto Danti?'

Because he was rich and arrogant and titled and gorgeous, and people like that tended not to be *shy*.

'What else have you learned about him?' Jenna asked.

'It's not worth repeating,' Liza said after a moment. She felt a strange reluctance, even now, to relate what Jack Wickley had said to her. She was unlikely to see him—or Fausto—again, so it hardly mattered, and yet something still made her stay silent.

'Well, I say we need more ice cream,' Jenna said with a brave attempt at a smile, and she headed to the freezer.

January felt endless to Liza—a long, dull, dark month, where all she did was go to work and go home again. The dubious highlight was a visit from Lindsay in the middle of the month; she insisted on them all going out, this time to a nightclub in Islington. Liza didn't think she could have been less in the mood for such a thing, but for Lindsay's sake she went. She was hardly likely to run into Fausto Danti at a place like that, and she didn't.

By mid-February her employer began to show concern. 'You seem to have lost your sparkle,' Henry commented wryly as he signed some letters and handed them to her for mailing. 'Although admittedly it's difficult for anyone to retain good humour at such a dull time of year.'

Liza managed a rather wan smile. 'I'm all right,' she said. She *had* been dragging, but she was reluctant to admit it. Henry gave her a small encouraging smile that suggested he didn't believe her but was too polite to say so.

A few days later, however, he did say something. 'Sometimes it takes a new perspective,' he announced.

'What does?' she asked a bit warily.

'To regain one's sparkle. I'm planning to go to my cottage in Norfolk this weekend. My grandniece is joining me with her family. Why don't you come too?'

It was the last thing Liza had expected 'Oh...'

'The weather is meant to be good, if a bit bracing, and I promise you the walks on the beach are quite restorative. It won't be fancy—whatever kitchen suppers we can throw together, and most likely fish fingers and chips for the little ones.' He pretended to shudder but he was smiling.

Liza was on the cusp of saying no out of habit more than anything else when she remembered that Jenna was going back to Hereford for the weekend to visit some school friends. Why shouldn't she get out of the city, see something different?

For a second she wondered if Fausto might be there, but Henry would surely have mentioned it if he was. Besides, he might be back in Italy by now. He probably was—a prospect that did not make her feel sorry in the least. Or so she insisted on telling herself more than once.

'All right, then,' she told Henry, injecting as much cheer into her voice as she could. 'That's very kind of you. Thank you.'

Three days later she was taking the train to King's Lynn, and then the bus to Hunstanton, where Henry's cottage was located. He'd decamped there the day before, but Liza had chosen to come on Friday afternoon, so as not to take up all of Henry's time with his family.

'It's so good to see you,' Henry said warmly when he picked her up from the station, as if he hadn't seen her yesterday at the office.

It was a short ride through the falling dusk out of Hunstanton to his 'cottage', which Liza quickly discovered wasn't a cottage at all, but an eight-bedroom manor house with a garden rolling down to a private beach. As Henry pulled into the sweeping drive he nodded to a navy blue BMW parked next to a battered estate.

'Ah, we have a visitor,' he said cheerfully, and Liza gave him a sharp look. *A visitor...?*

'You mean besides your family?' she ventured, even though that much was already obvious.

She told herself a visitor could be anyone, from a kindly neighbour to a distant relative, but her stomach was fluttering, her heart starting to pound, as if her body *knew*. Her heart knew.

Fausto Danti stepped out of the car.

He should have known Henry was up to something. Fausto kept his expression carefully bland as Henry parked the car and Liza slowly emerged from the passenger side, her face pale as she tried not to look at him.

It had been two months since he'd seen her, and he thought she looked a bit wan. No less lovely, but there was a certain weariness to her features that made him want to comfort her, surely a ridiculous notion. She as good as hated him, it seemed, no matter that she'd been the one to kiss him last—and if two months had thawed her dislike, surely this weekend would renew it.

When Henry had called to let him know he'd be at his country house this weekend, Fausto had decided to accept the obvious invitation. The last two months had been both dreary and exhausting, and he'd found himself increasingly occupied with work—and increasingly restless. He'd told himself he'd forgotten about Liza Benton, because he certainly hadn't been thinking of her, but as he looked at her now he realised just how much effort it had taken to keep her from his mind.

'Fausto,' Henry said as he came forward to shake his hand, 'I'm so glad you could make it.' Liza stiffened and Fausto knew for sure that she'd had no idea he would be here. 'Liza, you remember Fausto Danti?'

'I do,' she said coolly, and moved past him towards the house. Henry smiled easily, and Fausto wondered if the older man could not sense the tension simmering between them, or if he knew the nature of it and that was why he'd invited Fausto along.

It was, Fausto thought grimly, going to be a long weekend—and yet he could not deny that he was glad to see her again, if just for the sheer pleasure of looking at her.

An hour after they'd arrived, they were all in the drawing room with a roaring fire and glasses of sherry; Liza had met Henry's grand-niece, Alison, and her two young children, who were involved in a game of draughts. She stood by the fire, her hair wild and curly about her face, her hazel eyes pensive as she sipped her sherry.

She'd changed from her travelling clothes into a simple knit dress of moss green that skimmed her curves and reminded Fausto of how lovely she had felt in his arms. He nodded towards the chessboard that was set up in an inviting alcove.

'We could have that rematch now.'

She let out a huff of laughter that held no humour and shook her head. 'I'm afraid I'm too out of practice.'

'You beat me easily enough last time.' She looked away without replying and Fausto stepped closer to her. Alison and Henry were having an involved discussion, catching up on their various relations, and he didn't think they would be overheard.

'I didn't know you would be here,' he said in a low voice.

'Nor I you.' She slanted him a challenging look. 'Although you probably think I've orchestrated the whole thing.'

Startled, Fausto drew back. 'I do not.'

'You reserve that judgement just for my sister, then?' she replied, and then took a gulp of sherry.

'I have never judged you in that way,' Fausto said. He had wondered, but he hadn't judged.

Liza turned back to him, eyes flashing, eyebrows raised. 'Never?'

Compelled, as always, to both honour and honesty, he answered, 'A few doubts, I admit, but that is all.' And he could admit now—mostly—

that they had been unfounded doubts. Liza had never pursued him the way Amy had. Quite the opposite.

'Oh, what a *relief*,' she drawled.

'You did ask.'

'And now I know.'

He paused, sorting through the tangle of his own feelings as well as hers. 'You're angry with me for thinking you might have been after my money?'

She huffed and looked away. 'I don't like you enough to be angry with you.'

'You hardly sound indifferent.' She didn't reply. 'Is it because of that—or something else?'

'It is a whole range of things,' Liza snapped. 'But, more to the point, why do you care? You have made it clear that you're not interested in me, not really.' He was silent and she threw him a challenging look. 'You don't deny it?'

'No,' he said after a moment. 'I cannot.'

'And why is that?' Her voice trembled with the force of her feeling and she moved away from him, feigning interest in a book of photographs of the Norfolk beaches on display on a side table.

Fausto watched her, trying to school his expression into something neutral. He did not want to hurt her, but perhaps it was best if he stated his case plainly. 'I am thirty-six. I need to marry.'

She stiffened, her gaze still on the books. 'And?'

'And when I do it must be to a woman of whom

my family approves, someone who is capable of managing my household, standing by my side.'

'How unbelievably quaint,' Liza said after a moment. 'How absolutely *archaic.*'

'I admit it is an old-fashioned view, but it is the one I hold. My position is demanding, and would be so for my wife.'

'And obviously I'm not even in the running.'

Again he hesitated, and then decided truth was best. 'No.'

She turned to him, a wild glint in her eyes. 'Because of my family, whom you obviously find embarrassing? Or because of me?'

Fausto stared at her in miserable discomfort, not knowing how to respond. Both—and yet neither. *Because of him*, he almost said, but he couldn't have explained that answer even to himself.

'Your silence is answer enough,' Liza said quietly, and she brushed past him as she walked out of the room.

He saw her again at dinner and, although Henry gave him a concerned look, Fausto brushed off his godfather's remarks. He was in no mood to explain the complicated dynamics between him and Liza Benton.

He determined that avoidance was the only sensible option for them both, and that proved easy enough to do—Liza had already had breakfast when Fausto came downstairs the next morn-

ing, and she was nowhere to be found when he set
out on a bracing walk down the stretch of private
beach belonging to Henry's property, hoping the
brisk sea air would improve his mood.

It did not. As he walked along with his hands
deep in his pockets, his head lowered against the
wind, the confusion he'd been feeling gave way to
a despondency he did not want to acknowledge.

He hated the quandary he found himself in,
fighting an affection for a woman who thought he
considered her not worthy of it. He didn't doubt
Liza—not really—but he doubted himself. Love
was a fickle emotion; he knew Amy had loved
him once, and then been persuaded to change her
mind. He hadn't realised she had, and he did not
know if he would be able to discern Liza's feelings either. She certainly seemed one thing then
another already, and who was he to know the difference? He hadn't before.

And then there was the fact that love was a
dangerous emotion as well. He had been hurt
before; he did not care to repeat the lamentable
experience. Reminding himself that Liza really
wasn't suitable felt like the sanest, safest option,
even if it filled him with frustration.

And yet he could not deny, at least to himself,
that he had come to care for her—her fire, her
wit, the kindness and sensitivity she'd shown to
everyone, even the children last night. After dinner she'd engaged them in a game of charades,

and the sight of her being silly would have made him smile if he hadn't still been feeling so conflicted.

He wasn't in love with her, he decided with some relief; they didn't know each other well enough for that. But the depth of his feeling was clearly not reciprocated in the least, and that knowledge was both humiliating and hurtful.

Of course it was all for the best, since they could have no formal relationship. And yet… Fausto fumed. He did not want to end things this way. He did not want to be so unfairly disliked, and for what?

He lifted his head from his rather grim perusal of the damp sand beneath his feet to gaze out at the rippleless surface of the sea, glinting like a mirror under the wintry sun. Then he tensed as that old instinct took over; when he turned his head he saw a speck in the distance, a hunched figure on the sand that he simply knew had to be Liza.

He walked slowly towards her; her head was bent so she did not see him coming, and the wind carried away the sound of his footsteps.

Her knees were drawn up to her chest, her arms wrapped around them, her hair whipped in a wild tangle around her face. As he came closer, Fausto realised with a jolt that she was crying—and he hated that thought.

'Liza,' he said quietly and she looked up, her eyes red, her face tear-streaked.

'Of course you would find me like this,' she said with a wobbly laugh, and then sank her chin back onto her knees.

'Why are you crying?'

'It doesn't matter. You don't care, anyway.'

'I do care,' he insisted quietly, and then he decided not to qualify that statement any further.

Liza looked up at him, pushing her hair out of her lovely tear-stained face. 'Well, if you must know,' she said in a wobbly voice that still managed to sound reckless, 'I'm crying about you.'

CHAPTER TEN

LIZA DIDN'T KNOW what had made her decide in that moment to be honest. Perhaps it was because she was so tired of feeling sad. Or maybe she was just trying not to care any more, when it had become so very hard to keep disliking Fausto, no matter how many reasons he gave her.

Either way, for the last two months she'd had to drag herself through every day, and all because of this man. Even before that she'd been out of sorts, everything a tangle of longing and outrage and uncertainty. She was tired of feeling so much, and yet she felt the recklessness of her words, their implicit challenge. She stared at him now, daring him to reply.

'About me,' he repeated in that voice of cool reserve she knew so well that gave nothing away, and she let out a half wild laugh.

'Yes, *you*. Are you outraged, Fausto? Disgusted? Or is it just par for the course that a woman would shed tears over you?'

'I would never wish any person to cry over

me,' he said stiffly, and she sighed wearily and wiped her face.

'No. Of course not.'

He sat down next to her, his elbow resting on one drawn-up knee. The nearness of him brought a tingle of awareness, even in her teary state, along with a rush of longing *still*.

'Last night you acted as if you hated me,' he said after a moment, sounding cautious. 'Yet it seems unlikely you would cry for someone you hate.'

'That's just the problem. I want to hate you. I want to dismiss you from my mind, and instead I let myself be hurt. Again.' Her heart tumbled over at the blatant confession. What would he do with it? Why was she making herself so vulnerable, when she already felt so low? She didn't think she could bear his disdain now.

Fausto was silent for a moment and Liza risked a look at him, sitting so near to her. His brows were drawn together, his eyes so dark they looked nearly black. He looked so troubled and yet so handsome, and her heart ached because she knew she was halfway to falling in love with him, and the thought was terrifying.

No, she told herself rather frantically, she *couldn't* actually be anything close to in love with him. It had to be infatuation. That was all it could be, surely, considering how little they knew each other, how difficult every encounter between them had been...

'Again?' Fausto asked after a moment, and Liza shrugged.

'It was a long time ago, with someone else.' Even that was putting too much emphasis on what hadn't even been anything close to a relationship. 'Stupid of me to still be hurt, but it seems I never get these things right.'

'I have never wanted you to hate me,' Fausto said after a moment, his voice low, his head bent.

'I don't,' Liza confessed.

'And that is why you were crying? Because you *can't* hate me?' There was a lilt of humour in his voice as well as a flicker of sadness in his eyes, and both made her ache.

'It's most irritating, not to be able to do it,' she said with a desperate attempt at levity, and his lovely mobile mouth quirked in the tiniest of smiles.

'I can well imagine.'

'I have been trying so hard.'

'Indeed.' He turned his head so his face was an inch or two closer to hers, and her heart skipped a wonderful, terrifying beat. If he was toying with her now, she didn't even care. She just wanted to *feel* again—to feel that lovely, consuming desire, the wonderful certainty of *being* desired, and how together both sensations were enough to overwhelm her completely.

'And yet I keep failing,' she said, and she leaned a little towards him, both daring and pleading with him to close the small space between their mouths. Her heart was thudding now, with hard, heavy intent. 'I absolutely cannot hate you, no matter how hard I try,' she confessed in a breathless whisper.

'Perhaps you should stop trying,' Fausto murmured, leaning even closer, and then, finally, wonderfully, he kissed her.

His lips were as sweet as she remembered— as soft and hard, his kiss the most wonderful demand, the most urgent plea. Oh, she'd missed this. She'd needed it. Having it again felt as if the gates of heaven were opening. She was drowning in sunlight, overwhelmed with joy. Never mind it wouldn't last, or that he fought against his feelings even more than she did. This—this alone— was enough.

He deepened the kiss as her mouth opened under his and she scrabbled at his coat to keep her balance, and failed. They fell backward in a tangle of limbs, the sand cold and hard beneath them, their mouths still locked.

The weight of Fausto's body on top of hers was glorious, thrilling—Liza put her arms about him and drew him even closer. She felt as if she couldn't get enough of him; she wanted to infuse herself with him, solder their bodies together as if they were made of one pure metal.

He slid his hand under her coat and jumper as their kiss went wonderfully on, and she jolted at the feel of it on her bare skin.

Fausto immediately stilled. He broke the kiss, which made her frantic, as he looked down at her with dark, troubled eyes. 'Liza…?'

'It's just your hand is *cold*.' She let out a trembling laugh; she couldn't bear it if he stopped now. She might spontaneously combust if he did—or cry. She put her hand on top of his own and, daringly for her, moved it up higher on her body.

Fausto's eyes flared hotly as his hand covered her breast. It felt intimate and terrifying and so very wonderful, and Liza knew she didn't want him to stop. She arched her body upward to kiss him again, and with a groan Fausto surrendered, deepening their kiss as his hands freely roved over her body, creating fire wherever they touched. There was nothing cold about either of them now.

The wind whipped around them but Liza felt as if they were in their intimate cocoon, their own sacred world. In one sinuous movement Fausto shrugged out of his coat and she slipped her hands under his jumper to thrill at the hard planes of his chest.

Somehow their clothes were rucked aside, their breathing laboured and ragged as their kisses became more urgent and passionate, as if already they sensed the moment was slipping away from them and they were both desperate to hold onto it, to give it its full importance.

Liza sank her hands into his crisp, dark hair as his mouth moved lower on her body, tantalising her hidden places and making everything in her ache for more.

Her hands clenched his shoulders as she urged him on, wanting and needing even more. And he gave it—her body thrilling to every intimate touch even as the very core of her cried out for yet more still.

She reached for him, pressing one trembling hand against the arousal straining his jeans, and Fausto let out a choked laugh, his face buried in her neck.

'We should stop.'

'No.'

He raised his head. 'If we don't stop now...'

She pressed her hand against him again, letting her fingers tease, amazed at her own daring and yet knowing how much she longed for this. 'I don't want to stop.'

'*Liza...*'

'I don't want to stop. Please, Fausto.'

The moment was charged with silence, importance; Fausto lay above her, braced on his forearms, his face flushed with both desire and torment. Liza hooked her arms around his neck and did her best to draw him towards her, but his body was like a band of iron.

'Give me this, at least,' she whispered, 'if nothing else.' With a muttered oath in Italian, he surrendered to her, and she to him, as his body enfolded hers and he kissed her again. She lost herself to all of it—to his kiss, his touch, his very self.

The future fell away along with the past; she wanted nothing but this moment in all of its glory—even with the wet sand, the icy wind, the roaring waves. She was overwhelmed by it all, but most of all by him, his arms wrapped around her, his mouth on hers, his hard body pressed along her whole length and yet still, *still* not close enough.

She tried to unbutton his jeans and her fingers fumbled on the snap. Fausto wrapped his hand around hers.

'You are sure about this…?'

'Yes, I am sure,' she cried, half wild, and finally, thankfully, he unbuttoned his jeans himself. Then he reached for hers, and she wriggled out of them as best she could, barely conscious of the damp sand beneath her, the awkwardness and incongruity of the moment right here on the beach—none of it mattered.

'*Liza…*' Fausto said, his voice a groan, her name a plea.

She pulled him towards her. For a second he

hesitated again, poised above her, their worlds and selves about to collide in the most intimate and sacred way possible.

Then Liza arched up and with a low, guttural moan of both surrender and satisfaction Fausto sank inside her.

He'd tried to resist. He wanted no regrets for either of them, but Liza—her body, her *self*—proved impossible to resist. Fausto buried his face in the sweet curve of her neck as he waited for her to adjust to the feel and weight of him.

He knew from that first incredible moment that she had to be a virgin, but he couldn't think further than that as the siren song of pleasure drove everything else out.

'Are you all right?' he managed after a moment, his voice strangled, and she let out a breathless laugh.

'For heaven's sake, yes—*yes.*'

Then, amazingly, he was laughing too, amazed to share such joy in this moment, until laughter was replaced by something far, far sweeter as he found a rhythm and Liza matched it, clumsily at first but then with greater assurance and fluidity, until they were both moving as one. They *were* one.

Fausto had never felt so attuned, so fulfilled and unified and utterly complete. It was beyond the physical, even beyond the emotional; to say it was sacred would have felt, out of the moment, absurd, and yet it was. It *was*.

Higher and higher they moved and strove, each stroke unified and glorious, until their oneness was made even more complete as their bodies crashed together in the final cymbal note of pleasure, before Fausto rolled over onto his back, breathing heavily, taking Liza with him.

His vision cleared and his heart began to beat more slowly as he became aware, in increments, of the cold, damp sand beneath him and something sharp poking into his back. Liza's hair was spread across his face, tickling his nose, and he felt her heart thudding against his like a bird trapped in a cage.

His jeans were rucked, rather ridiculously, about his knees, as were hers. He had a terrible suspicion that if they were to be observed from afar they would look not only absurd, but obscene. The sand really did feel very cold.

He didn't know which of them moved first, if Liza stirred or if he tensed, but as one—and yet now utterly *not* as one—they separated. Liza sat up, wriggling back into her jeans, her head bent, her hair falling forward so Fausto could not see her face.

Fausto did the same, straightening his jumper and buttoning his jeans. Neither of them spoke, and the longer the silence stretched between them the worse it felt.

Fausto tried to examine his own mind, but his feelings were so jumbled—a vague self-loathing mixed with a soul-deep satisfaction—that he did not think he could utter a single coherent syllable.

Never, not once in his life, had he lost control the way he had with Liza Benton. Not even with Amy, not with *anyone*. He'd tried, heaven knew, to keep his head—and his body—but he hadn't. In the moment he'd been more than happy to sweep aside every concern, every second for pause, every perfectly good reason not to rut like a sheep on a beach in winter where anyone could happen by!

At least it was a private beach, but *still*. What if Alison's children had run up to them? Or even Henry? Fausto could not bear to think of such horrifying possibilities, and yet he had to now, as he hadn't then.

And that, he acknowledged grimly, was just considering the *appearance* of the whole thing. What about his motive, his *honour*? Liza was— *had been*—a virgin, something he thought he could have surmised before this morning, and yet he'd felt no compunction at taking her virginity on a cold, hard beach, with little romance and even less tenderness. His stomach roiled with disgust at himself and his actions. This was not who he was. This was not who his father had taught him to be.

He glanced at Liza, who was running her fingers through her hair, trying to untangle the knots. Her expression seemed composed, and yet he still sensed a fragility about her, a vulnerability that made him long to reach out and take her in his arms—yet he knew where that would go, and he had no desire to go there again.

Although the truth, Fausto reflected, was that he *did*, far too much, and that was why he stayed where he sat.

'I'm sorry,' he said at last. She let out a huff of sound that he suspected was meant to be a laugh but wasn't.

'That's about as bad as "Forgive me".'

It took him only a few seconds to remember that was what he'd said the first time they'd kissed. 'I should have acted with more restraint,' he said. 'For that I am sorry.'

She turned to look at him, her hair still in tangles about her face, her lips swollen from his kisses. 'Do you regret it?' she asked baldly, and he heard a challenge in the question. He didn't know what answer she wanted him to give, but in any case he knew he could only give an honest reply.

'Yes—I never would have chosen this.' She looked away. 'And I can't imagine you would have either—especially for your first time.' He paused, half hoping she would deny it, but she didn't. 'It was your first time?'

'Yes.' Her voice was wooden, her face still turned away from him.

'Then I truly am sorry.'

'Is that the only reason you're sorry?' she asked after a moment, her fingers plucking at a frayed thread on her jumper. 'Because it wasn't candle-light and roses and a king-sized bed?'

A more pointed and dangerous question. Fausto sighed. 'No, it's not.'

'I didn't think so.'

'Liza—please believe me, I've never wanted to hurt you.'

'You haven't,' she shot back, her voice brittle. 'Please, Fausto, don't feel guilty on my account. I was a full participant in this.' She gestured to the expanse of sand between them. 'You don't need to have any regrets.'

And yet he did. In that moment he felt swamped by them—by his own lack of self-control, by the desire that still coursed through him. By the sure and certain knowledge that he'd hurt a woman he admired and respected, and yet still knew he could never marry.

Yet why couldn't he?

The question, so unexpected, suddenly seemed obvious. Why shouldn't he marry Liza Benton? Admittedly, she would not be his family's first choice, by any stretch. His mother would be disappointed and hurt. His father would never have countenanced such a choice.

And, he acknowledged, she would struggle to fit into his world, both here and even more so in Italy. She was not from one of Lombardy's ancient families, not by any means. Not even close.

And yet…he wanted her. He cared about her. He didn't love her, not yet, and that could only be a plus. She wouldn't be able to hurt him. And, of course, she was lovely and gracious and kind.

And, he realised hollowly, she could at this moment be carrying his child. He hadn't used protection. Amazingly, he hadn't even *thought* about protection. And he had a feeling it was far too much to hope for that she might already be on the pill.

'We should get back,' Liza said in that same toneless voice that hinted at despair. She struggled to get up from the sand, and Fausto reached out a hand to help her rise. She jerked away from him.

'Liza, please.'

'I'm… I'm sorry.' She drew a hitched breath. 'I can't. I'm trying to be sanguine and sophisticated about this, but I'm finding it hard.' Another hitched breath, this one more revealing. 'I know that's not what you want to hear.'

'This isn't about what I want to hear,' Fausto insisted. 'We need to talk about this. Properly.'

'We already have, at least as much as I want to.' She buttoned up her coat with trembling fingers. Fausto rose easily from the ground as he gazed at her frustration. Only moments ago she'd been eminently touchable; now she seemed entirely unreachable.

'We haven't,' he declared firmly. 'Not in the least. There's the matter of birth control, for a start—'

She let out a ragged laugh that was lost to the wind. 'Of course that's what you'd be concerned about. Heavens, a baby born on the wrong side of the blanket! Common enough these days, but it's the stuff of your nightmares, I'm sure.'

Irritation warred with sympathy; he could see how much she was hurting and yet he couldn't comfort her. She wouldn't let him. 'That's not what I meant—'

'Then what did you mean?' She flung up a hand. 'No, don't tell me. I don't want to know. Every time you've told me what you've been thinking it's been the worse for me, and I really don't think I can handle what you're thinking right now.'

'Liza—'

'No, Fausto, please. Let's leave it at this.' She forced herself to look at him, her face heartbreakingly lovely, her expression one of both courage and fragility. 'You don't need to feel any regrets. I won't. What happened here was—well, it was amazing.' She let out a trembling laugh. 'The most amazing experience of my life, so thank you, actually.' Another laugh, this one full of tears. 'And that's…that's all I'm going to say about it.' She started walking, hurrying past him, her head tucked low. Fausto tried to catch her arm but she shrugged away from him.

'Liza!' he called, but she shook her head and started running. Fausto knew he could have caught up with her easily enough, but that hardly seemed to be a wise course of action. And so, even though everything in him resisted, he simply stood there and watched her go.

CHAPTER ELEVEN

SHE HAD SPENT the last four hours hiding in her room and Liza knew her unsociability was bordering on rude. Thankfully, she hadn't seen anyone when she'd come back to the house; she didn't think she'd have been able to give an answer if she had.

She'd hotfooted it to her room and stripped off her rumpled clothing, trying not to burst into tears. She wasn't even sure why she felt like crying; she'd meant what she'd said when she'd told Fausto it had been the most amazing experience of her life. Perhaps that was the cause for her tears. It certainly wasn't going to happen again, and it had left her in a state of both wonder and longing.

She'd hoped half an hour standing under a near-scalding spray would have helped balance her mood but she'd felt even more despondent when she'd emerged, as pink as a boiled crab. She'd wrapped herself in the dressing gown that had been provided on the back of the bathroom door and curled up in bed while a bittersweet montage of moments played relentlessly through her head.

She knew she was tormenting herself by reliving those sweet, sweet moments with Fausto—as well as the unbearably awkward and painful moments after. She'd so wanted to be sophisticated and unruffled, as if she had sandy trysts all the time, but she hadn't been. She hadn't been at *all*. She'd been gauche and prickly and so very hurt. And now Fausto Danti had yet another reason to regret her very being.

The thought of having to see him for the rest of the weekend was unbearable. To stumble through pleasantries as if they were merely acquaintances—she couldn't do it. She wouldn't. And yet to run away the first chance she got would be rude to Henry, and too revealing to Fausto. She wanted to show him she didn't care, even if she very much did.

Even if there had been a large, sorry part of her that had been hoping—waiting, even—for him to take her in his arms afterwards and kiss her tenderly and tell her he'd fallen in love with her. As if...! When would she learn? When would she remember that no man had ever remotely wanted to do such a thing?

Fausto had looked horrified afterwards. He'd acted as if he regretted absolutely everything about their encounter. He'd even said as much.

And meanwhile she'd felt as if the universe had unveiled its secrets, as if the very atoms of her being had shifted and reformed. She was absurd, the very parody of a naïve, stupid virgin with stars in her eyes and hope in her heart.

With a groan Liza pressed her face into the pillow, wanting only to will it all away—even though she never actually would want such a thing. She wanted to hold onto all the memories even as she despised them. Oh, why did Fausto Danti provoke such a maelstrom of contradictory emotions within her? The sooner this weekend ended, the better.

And yet then she'd most likely never see him again...

Liza groaned again.

Eventually, knowing she needed to show herself, she rose from the bed, aching and weary, and dressed. She took pains with her appearance—fluffing her curls and applying understated make-up, even though she hated the thought of Fausto knowing she'd gone to such pains. Still, at a time like this make-up felt like armour.

Downstairs, the house was strangely quiet; when she ventured into the drawing room, Henry put down his newspaper to give her a charming smile.

'How lovely to see you! Did you enjoy the beach? The wind does take it out of one, I find.'

'It was lovely,' Liza murmured, unable to look

him in the eye. She glanced around the empty room. 'Where is everyone?'

'Alison has taken the young ones into Hunstanton. Fausto was taking some business calls—but I'm sure he'll be here shortly. Perhaps he'll give you that game of chess?'

Henry raised his eyebrows while Liza blushed and mumbled something mostly unintelligible. A few moments later Fausto appeared, checking his step as he caught sight of Liza before he assumed that oh, so bland expression and came into the room.

'Fausto, I was just saying you and Liza should have that rematch.' He gestured to the board while Liza fidgeted. She had never hated chess so much in her life.

'If she wants a game, I'd be happy to play,' Fausto replied after a beat. He had showered since their beach interlude; his hair was dark and damp, brushed away from his freshly shaven face, and Liza was drawn to the clean, strong lines of him, remembering exactly how he'd felt against her. She *had* to stop thinking like that.

'It's not necessary,' Liza said.

Fausto turned to her. 'You never told me how you came to be so good at chess.'

'My father is a grandmaster,' she said, unable to look him in the eye. She moved her gaze rather wildly around the room, finally letting it rest on the chessboard. 'We played all through my childhood. I competed in junior tournaments when I was young.'

'I had no idea,' Fausto said, and she threw him a challenging look.

'Why would you?'

He acknowledged her point with an inclination of his head. 'Shall we play?'

She swallowed. The last thing she wanted to do was play a game of chess with Fausto Danti. Considering their history, it felt far too intimate—every word, every move loaded with both innuendo and memory.

'Yes, why don't you?' Henry said. Liza looked Fausto full in the face and, to her shock, his returning smile was full of sympathy. There was no mockery there, no icy hauteur, just kindness, and that nearly undid her.

'All right,' she said, her voice little more than a whisper. 'Let's play.'

Her fingers trembled as she picked up her knight to make the opening move. She could feel Fausto across the table from her—his presence, his power, the overwhelming *force* of him. It was like an undertow, pulling her down, drowning her. She could barely form a coherent thought, much less plan strategic chess moves.

They played in silence for a few minutes, the tension ratcheting up with every move, and any neat tricks Liza had been planning were just as neatly avoided by Fausto. Halfway through the game, both of them down several pieces, the game suddenly turned into something bigger, something far more important. Winning felt crucial. To lose was not to be contemplated. Defeat would be an emotional disaster, and one she didn't think she would ever recover from.

Slowly but surely, Liza felt the tide turning in Fausto's favour and she knew the game was slipping out of her control. Then, in a foolish error, she lost her queen and she bit her lip hard enough to taste blood.

'Draw?' Fausto suggested softly, and she shook her head.

'Let's play to the end.'

He won in just a few short moves, and somehow Liza managed a stiff nod. 'Well done. Good game.' She rose unsteadily from the table, feeling as if she could break. It was only a stupid game, she reminded herself fiercely, and yet it felt like just another reminder that she wasn't good enough for Fausto Danti in any way. That she never would be.

'It was a very good game,' Fausto said, rising from his chair as Liza moved blindly past him.

'I think I'll get some air,' she managed, and walked quickly from the room. She weaved through the house, finally ducking into a small morning room decorated in soothing blues and greys, although little did they help her mood. She let out a shuddering breath, willing the tears back.

It was so ridiculous to cry over a chess game, and yet she knew it was more than that. So much more.

'Liza.'

Fausto's voice had her groaning aloud. 'Can you *never* let me have a moment's peace?' she demanded raggedly.

'Not when there is unfinished business between us, no.'

She took a deep breath and turned around, willing herself to have enough strength for one more conversation. 'What is it, then?'

Fausto regarded her quietly for a moment and then he closed the door behind him. 'I want to ask you something,' he said.

Liza shrugged, spreading her hands helplessly. 'What? What could you possibly want to ask me?'

'I want,' Fausto said, his voice low and firm with purpose, 'to ask you to marry me.'

As soon as he said the words, Fausto realised how much he meant them—and how shocking they sounded. He'd been thinking of proposing to Liza since their interlude on the beach, but it hadn't crystallised into both fact and desire until now. Until he'd said it out loud.

Liza's mouth dropped open and she gaped at him soundlessly for a few seconds before she shook her head. 'I was so not expecting you to say that.'

'I've said it, and I mean it.'

'Why?'

Her incredulity was understandable, and so Fausto sought to explain as clearly and concisely as he could. 'First, because I care about you. Second, because we have an undeniable physical chemistry. And third, because you could be carrying my child.'

Liza pressed her lips together, her eyes flashing. 'Why do I think it's the last one that has forced your hand?'

He inclined his head. 'Perhaps it has, but I mean it no less.'

She let out a huff of disparaging sound. 'Why not just wait a couple of weeks, Fausto? Make sure I am pregnant, because I'm probably not.'

'You have no way of knowing and, in any case, possible pregnancy aside, I still wish to marry you.'

Liza shook her head again. She still looked winded and dazed by his offer. 'You cannot possibly want to marry me.'

'It is true, I have fought against it,' Fausto said steadily. 'Considering the differences in our life situations, and the expectations my own family has for my bride, I didn't want to feel anything for you, and I did my best to avoid you.'

'Oh, you did, did you?' Liza stated with a broken laugh.

'There are obvious disadvantages to our union,'

Fausto continued. He would not shirk away from mentioning the unfortunate and the obvious.

'Oh?' Liza's body tensed and her eyes flashed again. 'And what are those, exactly?'

Fausto exhaled impatiently. 'Surely they're apparent.'

'I'd still like you to say them,' she snapped, looking angrier by the second, but Fausto was no longer in any mood to appease her.

'I am the Conte di Palmerno,' he said, only to have her interject,

'I thought it was a courtesy title only.'

'Perhaps you are not aware of my position,' Fausto said after a moment, willing to give her the benefit of the doubt. 'And what it would mean to be my Contessa. The duties and responsibilities—'

'Oh, I'm sure it would be a great privilege,' Liza drawled, sounding as if it would be anything but. 'But since I didn't ask to be your Contessa, and have no desire to be your Contessa, this whole conversation is pointless!'

Fausto stared at her for a moment, shocked by her outrage as well as her defiance. He realised he had expected neither. Surprise, yes, a certain amount of caution. But to act insulted? When he was offering such a compliment and yes, indeed, a privilege? It could not be denied. 'You…you are refusing me?' he asked slowly.

She let out a hard, ugly sort of laugh. 'Is that so very hard to believe?'

'As it happens, yes.'

She let out another laugh, the sound just as unforgiving. 'Your arrogance knows no bounds.'

'I don't believe it is arrogant to be aware of all I can offer you, especially considering your own situation, and the disadvantage your family might bring—'

'*My* family!' Liza practically shouted. 'A disadvantage to you? Just because they're normal?'

'Liza, you know as well as I do—'

'And if I cared about money, perhaps—' she cut across him furiously '—perhaps I would want you to list all those obvious advantages. But, as it happens, I don't. When I marry it will be for love—because someone loves me. *Me*, and no one else, no matter where I come from or what my family is like, or whether I'll make a good *Contessa*.'

'I told you I care for you—' Fausto protested.

'Against your will! You have fought against feeling anything for me. If I were to agree to marry you, I'd be as good as dragging you to the altar with a gun to your head!'

Her theatrics annoyed him, although he strove to stay calm. 'I assure you, I would go there of my own free will.'

'Stop, Fausto, these sweet nothings are really too much,' Liza retorted sarcastically, her tone like acid. 'The answer is, and always will be, no. Absolutely, unequivocally no.'

He could hardly believe she was saying such a thing—and he was hearing it. In all his deliberations about whether to propose, he'd never once considered that Liza would refuse him. Perhaps that *had* been arrogance, but even now he considered it justified.

'May I know why?' he asked coldly.

For a second Liza looked as if she might burst into tears—her lips trembled and she blinked rapidly, drawing a shuddering breath before she stated staunchly, 'Because you are not the kind of man I wish to marry.'

'And why is that?'

'Do you find it so hard to believe? Do you think so highly of yourself that you can't imagine a woman refusing you?'

'I would not put it in such terms, of course—'

'Well, think again,' Liza cried, her voice trembling on a high, wild note. 'Everything you have ever said or done has shown me that you are a snobbish, arrogant, rude and unlikeable person, and I have absolutely no desire to spend another minute with you, never mind the rest of my life!'

Fausto stared at her, anger warring with a deep, terrible hurt. He had known Liza was fighting her feelings, just as he was, but to impugn him so thoroughly...

'In every instance I have tried to act honourably,' he said in a low voice, a thrum of fury vibrating through it.

'Then your sense of honour is very different from mine, as well as most people's.'

Anger—and that damnable hurt—pulsed through him. He'd been called old-fashioned, standoffish and, yes, proud, mostly by people who didn't know him very well. At home, with people he knew and loved, he could be comfortable and relaxed, but a need to be formal and set apart had been ingrained into him since he was child. He was a Danti. He had to be an example. And yet Liza seemed to think he was an example of everything bad, and nothing good.

'I did not realise you held me in such low esteem,' he said after a moment. For a second Liza looked again as if she were about to cry. 'Is there something in particular that has caused you to think of me with so little regard?' he asked, and she drew a hiccuppy breath.

'Jack Wickley, for one.'

'Jack *Wickley*?' He stared at her in disbelief, hardly able to credit that she'd believed that amoral chancer over him. 'You are accusing me—judging me—based on the word of Wickley?'

She tilted her chin up, her eyes flashing fire. 'Why shouldn't I?'

Fausto could not bring himself to reply. The idea that Liza would believe every word that slimy worm had said—that, after knowing him, Fausto, more than a little, she would still judge him so unfairly and harshly…

'Well?' Liza demanded, and Fausto simply shook his head. He would not stoop to defend himself against Wickley. He could not lower himself so.

'You deny what you did?' she challenged, and he stared at her coldly.

'What is there to deny?'

'That you deprived him of his inheritance and the job your own father promised him, and spread rumours about him that he wasn't trustworthy, so no one would hire him.'

He pressed his lips together as a white-hot rage threatened to consume him. 'That is what he told you?'

'Yes.'

'And you believed him?'

'Why would I have any reason to doubt him?' Liza flung at him. 'In any case, it's not just that. What about Jenna and Chaz?'

'What about them?' Fausto asked, his voice toneless, the words clipped. Fury beat through his blood but he held it in check.

'Did you warn Chaz off Jenna? I didn't want to believe it, but I know how you were looking at us all at that Christmas ball, and he dropped her like a hot potato right after.'

'I told him to proceed carefully,' Fausto conceded after a brief, heightened pause. 'And that I questioned her feelings for him, as well as her intentions.'

Liza's face flushed as she glared at him, her hands clenched into fists at her sides. 'You had no right!'

'He asked my opinion, and I gave it,' Fausto stated. 'He is a grown man, and he acted accordingly. I exerted no pressure, if that is what you're implying.'

'Your opinion is pressure enough!'

'That is hardly my fault.'

She glared at him for a full thirty seconds, her face full of hurt and anger, her eyes flashing fire and yet possessing a sheen of tears. 'I loathe you,' she choked. '*Loathe* you. And nothing would ever induce me to accept your horrible, half-hearted proposal.'

'Never fear,' Fausto returned in the iciest tones he'd ever used. 'Nothing would ever induce me to repeat it.' Not trusting himself to say any more, he inclined his head and then left the room as quickly as he could.

Unable to face Henry or his family, he went up to his bedroom and started to pack. He would not stay another moment under the same roof as Liza Benton. He could not believe she had treated his proposal—made in good faith and with honour—with such scorn and derision. And all because of a single word to his good friend—and Jack Wickley's damning recounting.

Fausto swore under his breath as he considered that wretch of a man. He had not wanted to stoop to justify himself to Liza, but he was sorely tempted. She thought him so proud? So snobbish and arrogant and rude and *unlikeable*? Perhaps he would show her otherwise.

Before he could think better of it, he stormed back downstairs, barely conscious of Henry peering out from the drawing room, and flung open the door to the little sitting room where he'd found Liza before.

She was still there, collapsed into a chair, her head cradled in her arms. She lifted her tear-stained face, her expression incredulous, as the door banged against the wall and he came into the room, fists clenched, chest heaving.

'You called me proud—well, I am not so proud as all that. I resisted telling you the truth about Jack Wickley because I had hoped that it would be enough for you to know the kind of man I was, rather than a stranger you met once in a bar.' Belatedly registering her tears, he realised she must have been crying, but he had no time to wonder at it as he continued steadily, 'Jack Wickley was the son of my father's office manager in Milan— a good man, who died when Jack was only sixteen. My father took him under his wing, brought him into our house and paid for his education through university, promising him a position with the company after he graduated.'

Liza, looking dazed, nodded slowly and, as the old hurt and bitterness coursed through him, Fausto made himself continue. 'I have known Jack since I was a child myself, and I have never liked him. Not because I am proud, but because he seemed crafty and sly. He cheated on his exams in school, and I discovered during university he was a terrible playboy and womanizer. Despite all that, I honoured my father's word and will, and I gave Jack the position of office manager here in London, over three years ago now. My father was ill, and unable to run the company, and I was consumed with family matters. However, upon my father's death, it became clear to me over time that Jack Wickley had terrorized the office staff, made unwanted advances to female employees and embezzled from the company to the tune of several hundred thousand pounds.'

Liza's eyes widened and a soft gasp escaped her, which was gratifying enough but, now that he had started, Fausto knew he had to continue. 'Moreover,' he said, 'I discovered that he had attempted to seduce my sister Francesca at a family party two years ago, when she was only fifteen. So if I dislike and distrust the man, surely you can understand why. I had no idea he was spreading the story you told me, so I can add deceit to his ever-growing list of sins.' He drew a breath and let it out, half relieved he'd told her everything, and half ashamed that he'd had to. 'If you doubt my story you can talk to Henry, who knows most of it, except about my sister, or Chaz. Or, for that matter, anyone in the London office of Danti Investments. The whole reason I have been here these last months is to repair the damage Jack Wickley wrought upon my company and my family.' He stared at her, his fury still pulsing through him. 'As for the matter of Jenna and Chaz, it is true I have had reservations about your sister. Perhaps they were unwarranted, but I have been fooled by a woman before.' He paused before making himself continue. 'I thought I loved her, and I brought her home to meet my family. Her true colours soon became all too clear.' And that was all he would say about that. 'I advised Chaz to be cautious, no more, and I still believe I was justified. If I was not, and your sister truly has feelings for Chaz, then I am sorry.' He let out a low breath before giving a terse nod of farewell. 'And now I will say goodbye.'

Without waiting for her reply, not trusting himself to say or do something he knew he would later regret, Fausto left the room. He made his apologies to Henry, finished his packing and had left the house before Liza had even stirred from her chair.

CHAPTER TWELVE

LIZA SPENT THE next two months in a daze. Days passed, grey and alike, and she was barely aware of their coming or going. She worked, ate, slept, and thankfully neither Henry nor Jenna nor anyone else pressed her on any point, or asked her why she seemed so very miserable.

Perhaps, she reflected, she was doing a better job than she thought at seeming normal, even happy. She went out at the weekends with Jenna; she went home to Hereford twice, and had Lindsay come to stay. She even accompanied Lindsay and Jenna to a nightclub, but she didn't dance and she left when she glimpsed Jack Wickley, of all people, come through the door. That was one person she could not bear to talk to, or even to see.

And of course there was another person she couldn't bear even to think about—although for entirely different reasons. Ever since Fausto had proposed, and then explained so much to her, Liza's emotions had been in an utter tangle. Her mind went round and round in circles as she tried to make sense of what Jack Wickley had told her, to what Fausto had told her, to what she had seen—and felt—herself. The result was a very uncomfortable ferment of uncertainty, followed by a far worse sweeping sense of desolation.

What if she'd been wrong? What if, to guard her own heart and for the sake of her own pride, she'd turned Fausto Danti into someone he never had been—someone like Andrew Felton, whom she couldn't trust and had come to dislike? Yet Fausto was no Felton, and she should have been smart and sensitive enough to see that. Yes, he was proud, but he was also honourable.

Wasn't he?

In any case, Liza reminded herself more than once, it was all too late now. As Fausto had said himself, he was never going to repeat his proposal. Not that she would accept it, anyway. She might have been wrong in her assumptions about who he was as a man, but that didn't mean she wanted to *marry* him. Even if he was an honourable man, he still had old-fashioned notions of suitability and position, and he'd made it clear he was expected to marry some Italian socialite or other, from a family he'd known for about a million years. She was not remotely in the running, for so many reasons.

Besides, the possibility of her being pregnant had evaporated within a week; there was nothing, absolutely nothing, to draw them together again.

And that prospect was not something, she told herself again and again, to feel downcast about, never mind heartbroken. Her heart was not broken at *all*.

Jenna and Henry might have acted as if they didn't notice her doldrums, but someone unexpected did. At the end of April, more than two months after that weekend in Norfolk, Yvonne called her with a proposition.

'I know you must have some holiday to take, and your nan has got it in her head to go travelling. You know as well as I do that she can't go alone, so I said you'd go with her.'

'Me...?' Liza loved her nan, her father's mother, a gentle, cheerful woman with a spine of steel. 'But I don't even know if I can take time off, Mum...'

'I'm sure you can and, in any case, it's only for a week in May. I can't go, with Lindsay's exams and Marie still at home, and besides, your nan can only stand me for about ten minutes. I know I'm too silly for her.'

Her mother spoke in her usual matter-of-fact way, but this time it made Liza's eyes fill with tears. 'You're not silly, Mum.'

'Oh, yes, I am. I'm a silly old bird, all right, and I don't mind. But your nan likes your company, and you've always wanted to see something of Europe. Now's your chance.'

'Europe? Where is she going?'

'A tour of Italy. She's got it all arranged and booked. All we need to do is book you a ticket, and make sure your passport hasn't expired. I know you haven't had any real cause to use it, but now's your chance.'

Italy… It was ridiculous to think she'd bump into Fausto in all of Italy, and yet still the prospect made her heart beat faster. 'I don't know, Mum…'

'You're going,' Yvonne said firmly. 'It'll be good for you, Liza. A change of scenery from all the grey we've been having. You need your spirits lifting.'

It was all arranged within a matter of days, and just a few weeks later Liza found herself on a flight to Milan with her nan, and then booked into a lovely little *pensione* on the shores of Lake Maggiore.

It was all so beautiful—the bougainvillea tumbling from pots on the little wrought iron balcony outside her window, the lake a deep, dazzling blue-green in the distance, the air warm and scented with lavender and thyme.

Her nan, Melanie, had informed her on the flight over that they would not be having a tour of the entire country, but rather one just of the Italian lakes.

'I've always wanted to see them, and as we only have a week we can hardly see everything in all of Italy.'

'I suppose not,' Liza agreed as a wave of trepidation—and surely not anticipation or even
hope—went through her. Fausto's estate was, she
knew, in the lakes region. Still, it was very, very
unlikely that she would stumble upon him during their week-long stay. So unlikely it bordered
on absurd, if not downright fantastical.

'So,' Melanie announced as she came into Liza's room, 'I thought we'd have dinner at the little
restaurant down the street, and then tomorrow I
want to take a tour of one of the estates nearby—
some of its gardens are open to the public, along
with a few of its main rooms. It's meant to be
one of the most impressive properties in all of
Europe.'

'Oh?' Liza asked. Then some towering sense
of inevitability prompted her to go on, even while
she already felt she knew, 'Who does it belong
to?'

'The Conte di Palmerno,' Melanie said with a
grand flourish. 'Apparently, he's someone quite
important.'

The next morning dawned bright and sunny, and
Liza tried to still the swarm of butterflies that
had taken residence in her stomach as she took
particular care with her appearance.

'You are not going to see him,' she scolded her
reflection. 'He's probably not even in Italy, or if
he is he'll be in Milan, working.' She took a deep

breath as she smoothed her hands down the daisy-sprigged sundress she'd chosen to wear. 'Even if he's on the estate, it's completely unlikely that he'll be out wandering in the gardens when we are. So stop worrying.'

Except she didn't think she was worrying, precisely. *Hoping* was closer to the mark, which was an alarming realisation. Worry would be far more reassuring.

It was a twenty-minute cab ride to Villa di Palmerno, a beautiful drive along the shores of Lake Maggiore, with villas perched on the verdant hillsides and motorboats speeding along the calm blue waters.

'Stop fidgeting,' Melanie said with a laugh as next to her Liza shifted nervously and then checked her hair. 'We're just going to see some gardens.'

'I know,' Liza murmured, flushing, and once again she had to give herself a stern mental talking-to.

A few minutes later the taxi turned into the impressive wrought iron gates that led to the Palmerno estate. Liza drew her breath in at the sight of the endless smooth green lawns, the extensive gardens behind high stone walls and then the house—oh, the house.

She stared in wonder at the villa, with its balconies and balustrades, its turrets and terraces. Well over two dozen windows sparkled in the sunlight as the cab pulled up in front of the separate entrance to the vast gardens.

'Isn't it magnificent?' Melanie exclaimed, and Liza could not find it in herself to reply. When Fausto had been asking her to marry him, he'd been asking her to be mistress and chatelaine of all this. It was too awesome a thought to comprehend and in fact she hadn't comprehended it at all when she'd thrown his proposal back in his face.

She cringed now as she remembered just how thoroughly and thoughtlessly she'd refused him. *Absolutely, unequivocally no.* She closed her eyes and her heart against the memory as she got out of the car on weak, wobbly legs.

The gardens were beautiful, each one perfectly landscaped and surrounded by a high hedge to give privacy. They wandered through rose gardens and wildflower meadows, gardens with marble fountains and benches and gardens with trellises of wisteria and beds of lavender. They found a kitchen garden that was an acre at least, full of vegetables and seedlings. There was an orchard with every kind of fruit tree imaginable and half a dozen greenhouses where, a gardener informed them, the estate produced all sorts of tomatoes, melons and other fruits, including a unique orange that the Conte had helped to develop.

'What sort of man is the Conte?' Liza forced herself to ask in as casual a tone as she could, and the elderly gardener's lined face crinkled into a smile.

'He is *bene—molto bene!*' He kissed his fingers and then laughed. 'A very good master of the house, *signorina*. Truly the best. Some say he can be a bit reserved, but only those who do not know him truly. He is as kind and generous a man as anyone could wish.'

'I see,' Liza said, the words practically choking her, and she turned away.

Everything about the place, from the beautiful, endless gardens to the villa perched above them as gracious and lovely a building as one could ever imagine, not to mention utterly enormous, made Liza ache—not with longing for the material wealth she saw all around her, although it was unbelievably impressive.

She ached because of how quickly and completely she'd dismissed Fausto's claims about his family, his position. She'd considered them utterly unimportant, a matter not worth spending a second of thought on, and yet now she saw how understandable his concerns were.

He was lord of this place, responsible for hundreds, if not thousands, in his employ. He had a reputation to uphold, people's livelihoods to support, and naturally he would want a woman at his side who was capable of helping him shoulder such a huge responsibility, who could offer advice and welcome people from all walks of life, attend dinner parties and charity galas and press conferences and who knew what else. Of course he had to be cautious when thinking of his bride, his wife.

Yet she'd scorned it all in a moment of prideful pique. She'd scorned *him*, and now she found she deeply regretted it—regardless of his proposal or whatever future they might have had together, Fausto had deserved her to take him and his concerns seriously, rather than scornfully, and now it was too late. The bitter regret she felt was enough to choke her. She could have lain down right there in the garden and wept.

Fausto drove up and parked his navy sports convertible in front of the villa, the wind ruffling his hair as he gazed at his family home. It was good to be back; it was good to be away from London.

The last two months had crawled by, as he'd pulled sixteen-hour working days, returning to his Mayfair townhouse to simply eat and sleep. Even then he had not been able to banish thoughts of Liza—Liza, who had yielded so sweetly to him, who had rejected him so utterly. *Liza.* Why could he not forget her?

He wanted to, heaven knew. He'd even sent a reckless email to Gabriella Di Angio, a member of another of Lombardy's noble families, in order to re-establish an old connection. When she'd emailed back a blithe reply to tell him of her recent engagement to a French CEO, he'd only felt relieved. He did not want to renew his acquaintance with such a suitable woman. And yet he needed to stop thinking about a woman who was most unsuitable—a woman who didn't want him.

There had been plenty of opportunity to forget Liza in London. He'd gone out with Chaz several times, but his friend had been as dour as he was and neither of them had had any interest in the many women who'd sent all the right signals, and received none in reply.

With a sigh, Fausto stepped out of the car. Perhaps things would be better here, at Villa di Palmerno. At least he was further away from Liza, from temptation, from terrible, tempestuous memory.

He turned, and his heart seemed to still in his chest as he saw Liza herself walking through the garden gates with an older woman. For a few seconds he couldn't make any sense of it. How on earth could she be here? It was a figment of his imagination, a fantasy of his fevered mind...

But then she looked up and her eyes widened with shock and he knew it was her. She was here in the flesh, at Villa di Palmerno, just as he'd once imagined, bringing her back as his bride.

Slowly, wonderingly, Fausto took a step towards her. Liza froze where she stood, her gaze transfixed on his face, her expression wary, even frightened. Considering how they'd last parted, he could understand her uncertainty and yet suddenly, amazingly, it all seemed so simple to him, so very easy. She was here; he wanted her here. That was all that mattered.

'Liza.' He walked towards her, both hands extended, and she stared at him in blank wonder as he took her hands in his, gave them a light squeeze and then kissed her cheek. He inhaled her light floral fragrance and it reminded him of so much—but he couldn't think about all that now.

'Fausto,' she said faintly, 'I had no idea you would be here…'

'And I had no idea you would be here,' he returned with a smile. 'How did it come to pass?'

'You know him?' the older woman said in surprise, and then recollected herself. 'But obviously you do.' She held out her hand. 'Melanie Benton. I am Liza's grandmother.'

'Fausto Danti, Conte di Palmerno. Charmed to meet you,' Fausto said, and took her hand.

'Likewise.' Melanie looked both intrigued and pleased. No doubt she was wondering just what the nature of Fausto's relationship was with her granddaughter—as was he.

'My nan wanted to…to do a tour of the lakes,' Liza explained, stammering a little. 'And I came along to accompany her. I really had no idea you'd be here. I didn't even know we were coming here to the villa until last night…'

'It's a delightful surprise.' She looked shocked as well as dubious at his pronouncement, but Fausto meant every word. He was so very glad to see her. And she looked wonderful—her wild curls pulled back with a green ribbon, her sunglasses pushed up on her head. The sundress she wore was covered in daisies and her bare shoulders were tanned and sprinkled with golden freckles. He wanted to kiss every one. He wanted to kiss her—to take her in his arms, to feel her body against his, to tell her he didn't care about anything that had happened before.

The last two months had not lessened his feelings for Liza Benton in the least, he realised. They'd only grown stronger. And yet…he knew he needed to caution himself. As pleased as he was to see her, he had no intention of repeating his marriage proposal. One scorching rejection was certainly enough, if not one too many, especially considering he'd thought he'd already learned that unpleasant lesson before.

No, Fausto decided as he met Liza's enquiring gaze, he would have to proceed very cautiously—for his own sake as well as hers. He was glad she was here, but that was all. He wasn't ready to let it be more.

'We were actually about to leave,' Liza said,

brandishing her phone. 'I was just going to call a cab.'

'Have you seen inside the house yet?' Fausto asked.

'No, I was hoping to see some of the rooms you have open to the public,' Melanie interjected, 'but I think Liza is a bit tired.'

Liza slid her gaze away from Fausto's and did not reply.

'Why don't you come into the house?' he suggested. 'I'll show you the public rooms myself, and then we can have some refreshments in the private apartments afterwards.'

'We couldn't—' Liza began, but Melanie was already nodding her vigorous acceptance.

'That is so very kind of you, Conte—'

'Please, call me Fausto.'

'Fausto.' She looked delighted. 'I really did want to see those rooms.'

Smiling at them both, Fausto ushered them into the villa. His mother was in Milan on a shopping trip, and Francesca was visiting friends. They had the house to themselves, and he was glad.

'Oh, lovely,' Melanie breathed as they stepped into the enormous entrance hall, with its black and white marble floor and skylight three storeys above. Liza regarded her surroundings silently, making no comment. Fausto couldn't keep from glancing at her, wanting to know what she thought. How she felt.

'Come this way,' he murmured, and he dared to put his hand on Liza's lower back for a brief instant before he removed it and ushered them towards the villa's main drawing room, a chamber of impressive proportions, with many antiques and rare works of art.

Melanie exclaimed over everything as he took them through the drawing room, dining room, ballroom and library, but Liza said not a word. Fausto kept glancing at her to gauge her reaction, but her face was utterly expressionless. What was she thinking? And, more importantly, what was she feeling? He longed to know.

Having finished with the public rooms, he led them back to a sun-filled conservatory filled with plants and flowers that overlooked a wide terrace that led down to the villa's more private gardens.

'Oh, what a view!' Melanie exclaimed, for the shores of Lake Maggiore were glinting at the bottom of the gardens, jewel-bright. Villa di Palmerno had more lake frontage than any other lakeside property in Italy.

Fausto had rung for refreshments as soon as they'd started their tour, and they had only just sat down in comfortable rattan chairs in the conservatory when a maid brought in a tray with fresh lemonade, a selection of Italian pastries and a bowl of fresh fruit.

'Oh, you're so kind,' Melanie exclaimed. 'Really, Conte—Fausto. And I haven't yet asked...'

She glanced thoughtfully at her granddaughter. 'How is it that you two know each other?'

Fausto leaned back in his chair, crossing one leg over the other as he glanced at Liza's sudden expression of alarm. After her deliberately blank looks all through their tour, it felt as if her careful veneer was finally cracking.

'Yes, Liza,' he said pleasantly. 'Why don't you explain to your grandmother how it is we know each other?'

CHAPTER THIRTEEN

LIZA FELT AS if she'd stumbled into some incredible alternate reality. Surely she couldn't be here, sipping lemonade and nibbling delicious pastries in Fausto Danti's amazing villa, while the man himself sat across from them, looking mind-bogglingly relaxed and acting so very charming? It felt impossible and yet it was happening, and she was here, and so was Fausto.

When she'd seen him step out of his car, some part of her hadn't even been surprised. Some part of her—a hopeful, desperate, wanting part—had *known* she would see him here. That secret part of her had been waiting for him all along and when she'd seen him a voice inside her had whispered thankfully, *At last*.

But what she hadn't expected was for Fausto to be so welcoming. His smile was easy, his manner assured, every word and gesture nothing but friendly. Yet the last time they'd met he'd been in a fury—and so had she.

What had changed? Why had he? Was it that

he didn't care any more, and so such kindness was easy? Liza had no answers to any of it, but as she took a small sip of lemonade she knew she felt very, very cautious.

'Liza, aren't you going to explain?' Melanie asked with a laugh. 'How did you and Con— Fausto meet?'

'Well…' Liza licked dry lips as she took another nibble of her pastry, simply to stall for time. Outside, the verdant gardens tumbled down to the shining lake; she didn't think she'd ever seen anything so beautiful before. 'We met in a bar, actually.' Melanie's eyebrows rose and Liza clarified quickly, 'It was when Mum and Lindsay were visiting. Fausto was there with his friend and we all got to talking.' She glanced at him to see how he would take this explanation, and he nodded and smiled.

'Yes, and we met a few more times after that, didn't we?' His grey, glinting gaze met hers in laughing challenge, and in a panic she wondered why he was doing this. *Taunting* her.

'Yes, a few times,' she murmured. 'At a party…'

'And in Norfolk,' Fausto supplied. 'At the house of a mutual friend. My godfather, in fact. We had a lovely walk on the beach.' When Liza risked a glance at him she found he was gazing straight at her, and there was knowledge in his eyes. She felt herself flush as memories she'd been doing her best not to think about rose up in a rush. The kiss that had gone on and on...the feel of him against her...his body pressed to hers...

'I'm amazed you never said a word, Liza,' Melanie scolded. 'Considering you knew where we were going.'

'It...er...didn't seem relevant,' Liza said. She knew she sounded ridiculous. If she'd been more sophisticated and sanguine, she would have mentioned to her grandmother before about knowing Fausto in a careless manner, but she'd known she couldn't talk about him without revealing the depth of her emotion. It was hard enough now to act indifferent. In fact, it was impossible.

She didn't think she could sit here a moment more, pretending she and Fausto were nothing but casual acquaintances. She lurched upright, spilling a bit of her lemonade as she replaced it on the tray. 'It's getting late, Nan, and I'm sure the Conte is busy. We should get going.' She fumbled for her phone. 'I'll call a cab.'

'Nonsense, I'll have one of my staff drive you,' Fausto replied. 'It is no trouble. But I insist you return for dinner. Tomorrow night?'

Liza gaped at him while Melanie smoothly accepted the invitation. 'That would be lovely, thank you.'

'I don't think...' Liza began helplessly, knowing it was already too late. *Why are you doing this?* She tried to form the question in her eyes but Fausto either didn't see it or chose to ignore it.

'Let me arrange your transportation,' he said, and rose fluidly from his seat. As he left the room Melanie leaned towards Liza.

'What a lovely man,' she said in a hushed voice. 'I can't help but feel there's more to your knowing each other than you're willing to admit.'

'There isn't,' Liza replied woodenly. Nothing she wanted to relate to her grandmother, in any case.

'The car will be ready shortly,' Fausto said as he returned to the room. 'While we wait, perhaps I can show you the villa's private gardens?'

'That would be lovely,' Melanie said before Liza could frame a response.

Fausto opened the French windows that led onto a wide marble terrace. Silently, Liza followed him, while Melanie exclaimed over everything.

Steps lined with flower pots ran all the way down the landscaped hill to the lake, and Fausto led them down while Liza trailed a little behind.

As they progressed down the hill he urged Melanie forward to look at the rose bushes while he dropped back a little to walk with Liza.

'I trust you are well?' he asked quietly.

'Yes.' Liza didn't trust herself to say anything else. Having him standing so close to her, looking so unbearably handsome in his navy blue suit, was just about all she could handle. Had his hair always been so dark, his jaw so hard, his body so powerful? Yes, she was sure it all had, and yet she felt herself responding in such an overwhelmingly visceral way to him now that it took all her strength not to reach out and touch him.

'I spoke to Henry back in March,' Fausto continued, his voice pitched low so Melanie wouldn't overhear their conversation. 'I wanted to make sure you were…well.'

It took her a moment to realise he meant *not pregnant*. She swallowed. 'That must have put your mind at ease.'

'It did, for your sake.'

She glanced at him sharply; as usual she couldn't tell anything from his expression. 'And not yours?'

'Such an…occurrence would have complicated matters, undoubtedly,' he replied after a brief pause. 'But I would not have regretted it.'

Which made her feel more confused than ever. 'That wasn't the impression you gave me the last time we met.'

'The impressions we gave each other were both unfavourable,' Fausto replied and Liza fell silent. She could not make sense of him at all. As they came onto the shore of the lake she realised she would have preferred him to be his usual self—cold and autocratic.

It would have made it so much easier for her

heart to heal. As it was, she felt only confused and unhappy by his seeming solicitude. It didn't make *sense*. She'd thought him one sort of man, and now she was realising more and more that he might be another, and she did not know how to deal with either. Part of her wished she had never seen him again, even as another, far greater part yearned for him still.

'This is so very beautiful,' Melanie exclaimed yet again as they came onto the wide dock where a top-of-the-line speedboat was moored. 'I don't think I've ever seen such a pretty spot.'

'It is lovely,' Liza said, because she felt she had to say something. All of it—the blue, blue lake, the fringe of grey-green mountains on the horizon, the gracious villa and its gardens—was stunning, and looking at it all made her ache in a way she didn't want to examine too closely.

'Perhaps tomorrow we could go out in the boat,' Fausto said with a nod towards the craft in question. 'Then you would be able to see the lake properly.'

'I'm afraid I'm not one for being out on the water,' Melanie answered with a laugh. 'But I know Liza would enjoy it.'

'Then it shall be done,' Fausto said, and Liza gave him a quick, sharp look.

'I'm not one for boats either,' she said quickly. 'And Nan and I were going to tour one of the other lakes tomorrow.'

'We don't—' Melanie began, but Liza shook her head.

'I want to.'

Fausto slanted her a wry, knowing look. 'Perhaps another time,' he said.

They walked back up to the villa and Liza made sure to walk ahead with her grandmother so Fausto couldn't speak to her again. His veiled references to their past stirred up far too much inside her. She didn't know how to respond to any of it. Was he being genuine? Or was he taunting her, showing her all that she could have had, but refused? She wouldn't even blame him if he was.

Perhaps he was doing both. One thing Liza knew was that Fausto's motives weren't clear, perhaps not even to himself. Perhaps he was, as he always was, fighting his attraction to her, because of her glaringly obvious unsuitability. At this point Liza didn't know if she could fault him for it. *She* didn't think she was suitable.

A few minutes later Fausto was escorting them out to the waiting luxury sedan, and he shook Melanie's hand before turning to Liza with an inscrutable smile.

'Until tomorrow evening.'

Was that a promise—or a threat? *What did he want from her?* Liza merely nodded, not trusting herself to speak. She got in the car and as it sped down the drive she forced herself not to look back, as much as she wanted to.

* * *

'So who is this woman, Fausto?'

Francesca's smile was teasing as she came into Fausto's bedroom. He was standing in front of the mirror, adjusting the cuffs of his dress shirt, frowning slightly at his reflection.

'She's an acquaintance—a friend—from London.'

'A *friend*? She sounds rather special.'

Fausto spared his sister a smiling glance. 'You have always been a romantic, Chessy,' he said, using the nickname he'd given her in her childhood. Although she was nineteen years younger than him, an unexpected blessing after years of infertility for his parents, they'd always been close. Francesca had looked up to him, and he had doted on her. He didn't think that would ever change.

'I am a romantic,' Francesca allowed, 'but, you know, your voice changes when you speak of her.'

Fausto regarded his sister with a frown. 'It does not.'

'It does, Fausto,' she answered with a laugh. 'And the fact that you don't even know it, *and* that you deny it, makes me think she must be *really* special.'

Fausto decided not to deign his sister's observation with a reply. She was always seeing hearts and flowers where there were none, and in the case of Liza Benton…

What did he feel? Nothing as uncomplicated as simple romance or affection, he acknowledged as he turned away from the mirror. In fact, he had no idea what had motivated his extraordinary invitation yesterday. Yes, it had been the simple pleasure of seeing her again—but had there been something more? A desire to deepen their so-called friendship, or a more unflattering compulsion to let her see the full extent of all she'd missed out on?

Everything felt tangled, and yet nothing had really changed. He still meant what he'd told her back in Norfolk—he had no intention of repeating his proposal. He would not risk the kind of blistering rejection she'd given him the first time around. If that made him as proud as she'd accused him of being, then so be it.

'We should go downstairs,' he told Francesca. 'Our guests will be here soon.' His mother was in Milan until the weekend, which was just as well because he knew she would not find Liza suitable in the least. His mother was inherently proud, her dignity bordering on a reserve far chillier than anything Fausto had ever shown Liza or anyone else. He did not look forward to the two of them ever meeting, and perhaps they never would.

Downstairs, Fausto paced the drawing room, feeling more restless than he wished as he anticipated Liza's arrival. Already he was more than half regretting his invitation. How would they bridge the tension and awkwardness that existed between them? Francesca was sure to guess something of what had happened, if Liza's grandmother hadn't already. She'd seemed like a rather shrewd woman.

More importantly, he wished he had an understanding in his own mind of his feelings towards Liza Benton. As always, he felt pulled in two very different directions—a deep and even consuming desire to be with her, and a compulsion to push her away. She was not a suitable bride for him or his family, a fact that seemed even more obvious now that she was in his surroundings.

And yet…and yet…she was lovely, and kind, and gracious and smart—all very *suitable* qualities.

None of that mattered, however, Fausto reminded himself, because Liza had refused him once and he would not risk such a bitter refusal again. A man could take only so much rejection, especially when it had been given with such scathing vehemence. So, really, all of this was utterly moot, and he'd treat her as he saw her—a casual acquaintance, someone he might call a friend. That was all. That was all it ever could be.

'I think they're here,' Francesca said excitedly, and Fausto felt his heart flutter, a most unusual and irritating sensation. He straightened, eyes narrowing as Paolo, the villa's butler, went to answer the door. A minute later he was ushering

Liza and her grandmother into the private drawing room reserved for family and guests.

The first thing Fausto noticed was how sophisticated she looked. She wore a flowing jumpsuit in emerald-green silk and her hair was pulled back in an elegant up-do, a few curls escaping to frame her lovely face. She'd paired the outfit with a pair of chandelier earrings and high heeled sandals and he realised, with a warm glow of masculine admiration, that she could rival any of the socialites in his circle for both sophistication and beauty.

'Thank you for having us,' Melanie said, while Fausto found he could not tear his gaze away from Liza.

'It is my pleasure, I assure you,' he promised Melanie as he continued to look upon Liza. Under his lingering gaze a blush touched her cheeks and made her only look lovelier. Then he felt someone else's eyes on him and he turned to see Francesca looking at him with avid interest. 'Let me introduce my sister,' he said, and made the necessary introductions.

Soon Melanie was asking about the history of some of the artwork and while Fausto answered he saw, out of the corner of his eye, that Francesca and Liza were chatting away. A burst of laughter emerged from their bent heads and he wondered what on earth they were talking about. They were certainly getting along, and that knowledge was both unsettling and gratifying, giving him even more of a sense of the push-pull he'd always felt with Liza.

Dinner passed more easily and with more enjoyment than Fausto had expected. Liza was a sparkling conversationalist and although she mostly addressed her comments to Melanie or Francesca she would occasionally favour him with a remark or cautious smile.

Melanie asked about various aspects of the estate, which Fausto was happy to give. 'In fact,' he said halfway through the meal, 'you are drinking Danti wines. We have a vineyard as part of the estate, a few miles away.'

'What don't you have?' Liza said with a hint of laughter in her voice, although there was a serious question in her eyes that Fausto didn't know how to answer.

You, he thought unwillingly. *I don't have you.*

After dinner they retired to the drawing room for coffee, and Liza had just sat down when Francesca asked Melanie if she'd like to see the portrait gallery upstairs.

'You've been asking about our ancestors,' she said with a smile, 'so let me show you their faces.'

'Oh—' Liza started to get up but Francesca waved her aside. 'Why don't you stay here and keep Fausto company, Liza? He doesn't want to see those fusty old portraits again.'

And before Liza could even manage a reply

they were gone. Fausto smiled in bemusement; his sister's ploys were all too obvious. He glanced at Liza, who met his enquiring look with a wry smile of her own. Then she laughed.

'Are you thinking what I'm thinking?' he asked as he handed her a coffee.

'That your sister likes to play matchmaker?'

'She is a romantic. She can't help herself.'

'Does she know—about us?' Liza asked abruptly, the smile dropping from her face. 'I mean...what happened?'

Fausto took a sip of his coffee as he watched her expression turn wary and guarded. 'No, she does not. I have not told anyone about that.'

'Of course you haven't,' Liza agreed, and he raised his eyebrows.

'Your meaning...?'

She shook her head. 'Only that you wouldn't want people to know.'

'Only because I would not want anyone to know my private business, or yours, for that matter.' He searched her face, trying to discern her mood, but she rose from her seat and paced the room, her back to him as she sipped her coffee and looked out at the darkened gardens.

'Your villa—the whole estate—is very beautiful.'

'Thank you,' he said after a pause.

'I don't think I...realised what it was like when you spoke about it back in England.'

'It would be hard to imagine, I suppose.'

'It's more than that, but…' She let out a soft sigh. 'It doesn't matter now.'

He longed to ask her what she meant, yet some instinct kept him from pressing. This conversation already felt dangerous, flirting with emotions and memories he needed to suppress. As charming as Liza had been tonight, it was very clear that she was still keeping her distance, and Fausto knew he could not presume that anything between them had changed. He certainly had no intention on acting on such a presumption.

Liza's back, slender and tense, was still to him. The shadows lengthened in the room and the silence between them turned hushed, expectant. It would be so easy, so wonderful, to cross the few feet that separated them. So tempting to trail a fingertip down the bare expanse of her back, to hook a finger under the spaghetti strap of her jumpsuit and slip it off her golden, sun-kissed shoulder. Then he would bend his head and brush his lips against that spot, before moving even lower…

Fausto must have made some sound, some indication of his frustrated desire, for Liza turned suddenly, the coffee cup clattering in its saucer.

'I should go.'

'There's no need—'

'It's late, and we have an early start tomorrow.

We're travelling to Lake Como and back all in one day.'

'How long are you staying in the area?'

'Till Wednesday.'

'Then you can come to our garden party this weekend.'

She shook her head as she looked at him miserably. 'Is that really a good idea, Fausto?' she asked quietly.

'Why wouldn't it be?'

'You've already made your point. I don't... I don't need to see any more. Experience any more. I get it.'

'What point is it I'm meant to have made?' Fausto asked, his tone sharpening, but before Liza could reply—not that Fausto was sure she would—Francesca came into the room, followed by Melanie.

'We've seen all the rellies,' Francesca said with a laugh. 'Some of them are so stuffy-looking it's ridiculous.'

'I was just telling Liza that she and her grandmother must come to our garden party this weekend,' Fausto told her sister. Francesca perked right up as he'd known she would, and turned to Liza.

'Oh, yes, do come. It's a tradition we have every year, to say thank you to all the staff and employees. It's so much fun—please say you'll come.'

Liza threw Fausto an accusing look before she

smiled at Francesca and said stiffly, 'Of course, we'd love to. Thank you.'

Fausto could not deny the primal satisfaction that roared through him. He would see Liza again—and who knew what would happen between them then?

CHAPTER FOURTEEN

LIZA COULD HARDLY believe she was back at Villa di Palmerno again, this time for the garden party Fausto had more or less strong-armed her into. Once again reluctance warred with excitement, hope with fear. Seeing him was torture because it reminded her of how attracted she was to him and, more than that, how much she enjoyed his company. How easy it would be to let herself fall in love with him.

Yet she knew just from looking at Fausto that he had no intention of repeating his proposal, or re-establishing their relationship, not that what they'd experienced was even remotely close to that. Still, it had been the most important experience of Liza's life. She was still trying to get over it.

Even if she didn't understand Fausto's motivations for approaching her, she sensed that same reserve within him that had always been there, like a brick wall built against her, and it seemed to go deeper than his understandable concern about her suitability. She recalled his guarded remark back in Norfolk about another woman—was Fausto guarding his heart, the way she had? Too afraid to take a risk again?

In any case, Liza knew she did not have it in her to bring that wall down brick by brick, and he did not seem inclined to do so either. Guarded hearts or proud ones—what did it matter? The result was the same.

As they arrived at Villa di Palmerno the entrance was festooned with bunting and fairy lights and balloons of every colour arched over the villa's magnificent and ancient doorway. Francesca was waiting by the door to greet them, dressed in a plain white shirt and black skirt.

Liza have must looked surprised by her choice of outfit because Francesca laughed. 'Don't look so shocked—I'm dressed as a waitress. Every year when we throw a party for all the staff, all the Dantis do the waiting and serving. There's not enough of us, of course, so we have to bring in people as well—even my mother does her part.'

'And Fausto?' Liza asked sceptically. She could not picture him lowering himself in such a way.

'Oh, yes, he does as well,' Francesca said. 'It was his idea, actually—the tradition only started about five years ago.' She made a face. 'I don't think my father would have considered such a thing, but he was willing for Fausto to make his mark.'

Yet another facet to Fausto that she had not seen before—not been willing to see. 'It sounds fun,' Liza said.

'Go, have a look!' Francesca gestured to the gardens, which were crowded with people. 'There's lots of things to do.'

As Liza wandered around the gardens with her grandmother, she was amazed at every turn at all the festivities that had been arranged—there were carnival games of all kinds and stalls selling everything from plants to toys to delicate wood carvings. On the lawn there was even a small Ferris wheel and clowns on stilts offering balloons to every delighted child. It was utterly magical and she kept turning in a circle, not knowing where to look next, amazed by it all.

Even more amazing, and more humbling, was the vociferous praise she heard from every corner. All the staff attending the party were friendly, and their love for their employer was impossible to deny.

He was a good man, the best man, so kind and generous and fair. There was nothing he wouldn't do for any of them—Liza only half understood the stories several people told her because of the language difference, but the gist was clear enough. Fausto helped them all, he put them before himself, he was wonderful.

Too wonderful, she thought disconsolately, for her. Melanie had become caught up with several women she'd met, and Liza took the chance to slip away. As lovely as the party was, she didn't know how much she could take of all the good humour bubbling up, the joy and wonder and praise...not when she was feeling lower and lower herself.

She slipped through a hedge into a small octagonal rose garden that was blessedly quiet, but still felt too close to all the party mayhem. A little wrought iron gate led to another garden, enclosed by high hedges, a shell-shaped fountain in its centre.

Alone, Liza breathed a sigh of both sorrow and relief. It had been such a happy day, so why did she feel so sad? Not sad, precisely, she told herself, more just...melancholy. And she was afraid to examine its source too closely.

She sat on the edge of the fountain and ran her fingers through the water spraying from the marble shell in a graceful arc. It shouldn't hurt her so much that she'd discovered that Fausto Danti was a good man—proud, yes, but generous, kind and good-hearted. It should be a relief, because of course she'd rather he wasn't horrible. He wasn't the *snobbish, arrogant, rude and unlikeable* person she'd once declared him to be. He was anything but.

Liza let out a choked cry of dismay and bowed her head.

'You look like Venus on the half-shell.'

She stiffened at the sound of his voice, even

though some feminine instinct had known he would come, or at least had hoped.

'Why do you always find me in secret places?' she asked, trying to keep her voice light, but it trembled. She forced herself to look at him; he stood in the entrance to the garden, dressed in a white shirt and black trousers, just like he had been the first time she'd met him. She'd thought the clothes like those of a waiter back then, and today he *was* acting as a waiter, and yet he was anything but. He was so much more.

Standing there, his steely gaze sweeping over her, he looked so handsome he made everything in her ache. The hooded brows…the hard line of his jaw…the lithe beauty and power of his body. She had to look away, afraid her yearning would be evident in her face.

'Why do you always go to secret places?' he asked, his voice a low thrum as he took a few steps towards her.

'I wanted to be alone.'

'Should I leave?'

'No.' Liza knew she didn't want him to. He deserved her apology, at least, as much as it would pain her to give it. 'I wanted to see you. Speak to you.'

'Oh?' Fausto sounded terribly neutral, and she wondered if he was worried she would make some melodramatic declaration. What woman wouldn't, after all she'd seen and heard today?

But no. She wouldn't embarrass them both with such an unwanted sentiment.

'I wanted to thank you for today,' she said, trying not to sound stilted. 'And not just for today. For dinner the other night…and the refreshments and tour from before. You've really been so very kind.'

'It's been no trouble.'

'Yes, but…you really didn't have to.' She forced herself to continue, although her throat had grown painfully tight and every word hurt her. 'Especially…considering how we left things. The last time…in Norfolk.' She risked a glance at him but his face was blank. *Of course.* She had never been able to read him, and she wished she had some inkling as to his feelings—although perhaps she didn't. Perhaps she'd be horrified if she knew what he felt right now, about her. How little he felt.

He inclined his head. 'Whatever passed between us is in the past, Liza. It does not need to affect the present.'

'Yes.' Liza nodded, a bit too much. 'That's very gracious of you.' And even though she suspected—or at least she hoped—that he meant it kindly, those words hurt too. *The past was in the past.* She was just a friend, barely more than an acquaintance. Whatever had happened between them had been all too brief, and probably forgettable as well. *She* was the one who had given it so much importance, who had let it change her whole being, even as she'd fought against it and then thrown it back in his face.

Fausto took another step towards her. 'Why is it, then,' he asked, 'that you look so sad?'

Liza lowered her head so her hair fell forward to hide her face, the chestnut curls resting against her cheek, making Fausto itch to run his hand along her jaw, tuck those wayward curls behind her ear.

'I'm not sad,' she said after a moment, her head still bent.

'Are you sure?'

'I think I know what I'm feeling.' She spoke with humour rather than ire, and Fausto rocked back on his heels, unsure how to handle this moment, or what he wanted from it. The trouble was, he didn't know what *he* was feeling.

Part of him wanted to sweep away all the regrets and memories and simply take Liza in his arms. Forget everything else. Another part of him was wary, not wanting to risk rejection and hurt. And yet another part was trying to be wise, reminding that instinctive impulse that Liza still wasn't suitable, no matter how much she seemed so. Since he'd returned to Italy his mother had put on the pressure for him to find a bride. He had obligations, responsibilities, expectations. Yet that insistent voice was growing quieter and quieter with every moment he spent with this woman.

He strolled over to the other side of the fountain and sat on its edge. In the distance he could hear the sound of the party, laughter and music, a background of joy.

'How have you been these last few months?' he asked. 'Really?'

'Okay,' she said. She ran her fingers through the fountain's water, still not looking at him. 'Ish.'

He hated the thought that he'd been the one to hurt her. He settled more comfortably on his perch. 'How is your family?'

'The same.' She sounded bleak rather than tart. 'It's amazing, what you've done here with the party,' she continued, clearly not wanting to talk about herself. 'Everyone I spoke to sang your praises.'

'They are good people.'

'You're a good person.' She looked at him for the first time, her eyes heartbreakingly wide. 'I want—I need—to say that, especially after all the things I accused you of, back in Norfolk. You aren't any of those things. I'm sorry I said you were.'

Her apology, so plainly stated, touched him deeply, and now he found he was the one who was looking away, to hide the depth of his emotion. 'I'm still proud,' he said, trying for wryness.

'You have a right to be proud, of who you are

and all you've achieved. The people I talked to today told me how you have increased the business, watched out for their welfare, navigated them through difficult times. You are a wonderful employer, by all accounts. A wonderful Conte di Palmerno.' She spoke his title with an attempt at an Italian accent that made Fausto smile even as he ached. He hadn't expected this conversation to be so sweet—or so hard.

'Thank you, Liza.'

'I... I hope there are no hard feelings between us, after everything. Most likely we won't see each other after today, but still. I'd like to part on a good note.' She smiled, her lips trembling as they curved upwards, her glinting hazel eyes searching his face, looking for answers.

He was silent, unable to agree to the assumptions she'd made—that they wouldn't see each other again after today, that they would be saying their final goodbyes.

'Fausto...?' Her voice wavered with uncertainty.

'There are no hard feelings,' he said at last. 'Although I don't like to speak in so final a tone. Today doesn't have to be goodbye.'

'Well...' she shrugged, trying for another smile '...it sort of does, doesn't it? You're back in Italy. I'm in England. And our worlds do not...intersect.' She glanced around the garden, the shadows lengthening on the paving stones as the sky slowly turned to violet. 'I realise that now—how different we are. Our worlds, our…positions. I didn't really understand what you meant. I thought you were just being snobbish, until I came here and saw all this.' She swept one graceful arm to encompass the garden, the villa, the estate, even, he thought, his title. 'I shouldn't have been so scornful about your concerns. In my own way, I was proud too. I see that now.'

Fausto pressed his lips together, fighting an irrational desire to disagree with everything she'd just said. All the things he'd insisted mattered *didn't*, not in the way he'd thought, and not in the way she was now intimating. He didn't care about their *positions*. Heaven help him, how could he have said something so stupid?

'You weren't proud,' he said in a low voice.

'Well…it doesn't matter, does it? Any more.' She made it a statement rather than a question and, unable to argue with her because he had no promises he could make, Fausto stood up.

'Come back to the party. Now that it's getting dark we have a buffet dinner, followed by fireworks. Also, I would like you to meet my mother.'

'Your mother…?' Her expression showed nothing but alarm. 'I don't think…'

'I want you to meet her.' Why, he couldn't say, even in the privacy of his own mind. Viviana Danti, the Dowager Contessa, would be coolly polite to Liza, and no more. Definitely no more.

But perhaps *that* was why. Because he was hardly going to be dictated to by his mother, especially in something like this. *And as for your father...?*

The question reverberated through him hollowly, because he knew his esteemed father would have felt the same as his mother. *Honour is everything. Remember who we are... You have a duty...*

Don't make the same mistake again.

He had promised his father he would marry a suitable woman, after the disaster with Amy. A promise he'd always intended to keep, but now he wondered if it could look different. Liza might not be from the background his parents had wanted, but she certainly had all the qualities he'd look for in a wife. She wasn't Amy, not even close, and he felt far more for her than for a woman he'd convinced himself he was in love with fifteen years ago.

And yet...he'd made promises to his father, promises he'd had instilled in him since he was but a child, and ones he had always, always intended to keep. They'd defined him. But now he felt as if he were spinning in a sudden void, wondering about the bulwarks that had been his foundation.

'Fausto?' Liza regarded him uncertainly. 'I'm not sure it's a good idea to meet your mother.'

'It is,' he said firmly. 'Come with me, back to

the party.' He held out his hand and Liza looked as if it were a foreign object. Then, after an endless few seconds, she put her hand in his. It was small-boned and slender, and he twined his fingers with hers, enjoying the feeling, as intimate as a kiss.

Silently, as if neither of them wanted to break the spell that was being woven over them, they walked from the garden, back to the party.

Dusk was falling softly, a violet cloak dropping over the world. Chinese lanterns were strung through the garden, creating warm pockets of light, and torches had been brought out to the terrace so it was flickering with shadows, an enormous buffet set up by the bank of French windows.

'I'll need to do my job in a moment,' he said, nodding towards the buffet. 'But after everyone is served, I'll introduce you to my mother.'

'Okay,' Liza said, still sounding unconvinced that this was a good plan.

'Come and eat,' Fausto said, and he led her to the buffet and gave her a plate before taking his position behind, as a server. He wished he could have stayed with her, but he knew he would never shirk his position. It was important that all the people who served him so unwaveringly saw him willing to serve them in some small way.

Still, he kept his eye on Liza as she moved down the buffet, a pensive look on her face. She looked so lovely, with her hair wild about her face, her broderie anglaise top matched with a pair of bright blue culottes. Casual yet elegant, a perfect choice for the day, and as he watched her chat to some of the vineyard workers, men with broken English and rough manners, with friendly ease, something warm and sure started in his chest and spread outward. He was glad she was here.

That feeling of gladness, of certainty, only increased as the evening progressed. As Fausto served and chatted, his gaze kept moving to Liza, tracking her around the terrace as she chatted to various people, always friendly and open.

His mother had been holding court in the drawing room for most of the evening, and Fausto decided their introduction could wait. He wanted Liza to himself.

When the buffet had finished he went to join her by the balustrade overlooking the lawn where the fireworks would be set off. 'I'm sorry I couldn't be with you,' he said as he came to stand by her side and she gave him a swift, searching look.

'It's all right.'

'You've been enjoying yourself?'

'Actually, yes.' She let out a little laugh. 'Everyone is so friendly.'

'You are easy to talk to.'

She let out another laugh, this one uncertain.

'Fausto, you're so full of compliments tonight. I don't know what to do with them.'

'Stay,' he said, the word like a pulse, and she gazed out at the darkened lawn, her body so very still. 'Please.'

The first fireworks went off, showering the sky with colour and casting her face in eerie light for a few seconds so he could see how pensive she looked.

'What do you mean exactly?' she asked, her voice unsteady.

'Stay here tonight. With me.'

Another Catherine wheel exploded in the sky, followed by applause and laughter.

'My grandmother...' Liza murmured, and triumph and desire roared through him. If that was her only objection...

'She can stay as well. I will make arrangements for a guest room to be made up. She must be tired. It would be better for her to be here.'

'And me?' Liza asked, turning to look at him, a look of such open vulnerability on her face that Fausto longed to take her in his arms.

'It is better for me,' he said quietly. 'If you stay. I want you to stay. But only if you want to.'

An age seemed to pass as firework after firework burst in the sky and Liza watched them, her expression both thoughtful and hidden. Then, finally, wonderfully, she turned to Fausto.

'Yes,' she said simply.

CHAPTER FIFTEEN

LIZA FOUGHT A sweeping sense of unreality as she and Fausto watched the rest of the fireworks, side by side and unspeaking. She couldn't believe what he'd asked of her, or that she'd agreed. This was the last outcome she'd expected, and yet some part of her acknowledged the rightness of it. She was, amazingly, not surprised.

Neither was she naïve. One night. That was what Fausto was asking of her. One night, and no more. She pushed the thought away as soon as she'd had it; she did not need to remind herself of how fleeting this one night would be. And while it was happening she wanted to savour every precious moment.

The sky darkened as the last sparks fell from it, and people began to trickle towards the front of the villa to go home. In the darkness Fausto gave her a swift searching look.

'I must go and say my goodbyes.'

'Yes. I should find my grandmother...'

'My head of staff, Roberto, will assist you with anything you need.'

Liza didn't reply because she didn't know what assistance she needed, or how she would find Roberto, and part of her just wanted to take cover in the darkness. The *thought* of being with Fausto was far more compelling than the unbearably awkward logistics of making it happen.

He strode off to make his goodbyes, and Liza went in search of Melanie amidst the crowd of happy partygoers. It only took a few minutes to find her; her grandmother had been watching the fireworks on the terrace as well. When Liza explained the arrangements for the night Melanie's eyebrows rose but she acquiesced readily enough.

'I am tired. It will be good not to have to drive all the way back to the *pensione*.' She gave Liza a considering look. 'The Conte is very kind.'

'Yes.'

A man seemed to materialise out of the darkness, smooth and urbane. 'The Conte asked me to show you to your quarters, and make sure you have everything you need.'

'Oh…er…yes.' Liza couldn't help but be flustered. She felt as if her intentions—Fausto's intentions—were emblazoned on her forehead. Roberto, however, was discretion itself and he led Melanie to a sumptuous guestroom upstairs before taking Liza to hers.

'Ring this bell if there is anything you need,'

he said, pointing to a buzzer by the door, and Liza nodded. Her heart had started thumping as soon as she'd entered the room—a spacious bedroom with a huge canopied king-sized bed taking pride of place. *What was she doing?*

The door clicked softly shut as Roberto left her alone. Liza paced the room nervously for a few minutes, before she decided she might as well avail herself of the huge walk-in shower in the en suite bathroom, as well as the thick terrycloth robe hanging on the door.

Twenty minutes later she was showered and swathed in the robe—and still alone. Had Fausto had second thoughts? What if this had all been some sort of a set-up? A payback for the humiliation she'd caused him with her insults and refusal?

But no. After everything she'd learned about him today, everything she knew, she could not believe such a thing of him.

The door opened.

Liza drew her breath in sharply as Fausto stood framed by the doorway, tall and dark and powerful. He regarded her silently for a moment and Liza let out an uncertain laugh, wishing she hadn't decided to don nothing but a robe. She'd been thinking only about not wanting to be hot and sticky, but now she was thinking about being naked.

'I wasn't sure if you would come, after all,' she said.

'Truthfully? I couldn't wait to get away.' His voice was low, and her heart fluttered. She did not reply because she didn't know how to. He took a step into the room. 'You haven't changed your mind?'

'No.' Her voice wavered and she set her chin. 'No,' she said more firmly.

'Good.' Fausto closed the door behind him, and instantly Liza felt as if they'd been cocooned. They were alone, truly alone, at last. Nervously she glanced around the bedroom, conscious again that she wore only a robe.

'This is a very beautiful room, but I imagine every room in this villa is just as beautiful.'

Fausto gazed around the room, his expression indifferent. 'The most beautiful thing in the room is you.'

Liza couldn't keep from giving a sceptical laugh as she shook her head. 'You don't have to soften me with compliments, Fausto. I'm already here.'

He frowned, his dark brows drawing together. 'Is that what you think I am doing?'

'Well…yes.'

'You are beautiful, Liza. I noticed that from the first moment that I saw you.'

'Now I know you're telling lies,' Liza returned lightly, even though it hurt. After all these months, after all that had passed between them, that first little dig still possessed a needle-like pain.

Fausto's frown deepened. 'What do you mean?'

'I heard you, that first night, by the bar. "She looked as plain and boring as the other, if not more so".' She tried for a smile. 'So don't pretend you were blown away by my beauty the first time you clapped eyes on me.'

'I said that?'

'Yes.'

'And you heard?'

'Yes.'

He sighed and shook his head. 'No wonder you took such a dislike to me right away. I did wonder.'

'You *were* rude.'

'Yes, I was. I was tired and I've never liked big social gatherings, but still there is no excuse. I'm sorry.'

Liza laughed and looked away, discomfited by the sincerity of his apology. 'I didn't tell you that to wheedle an apology out of you.'

'I *am* sorry,' Fausto said seriously. 'I never should have said such a thing. If I thought it, it was only because I wanted to dismiss you, and I couldn't, even at the beginning.'

Which brought them to the very prickly nettle neither of them wanted to grasp. Even now, when they were alone together, when Fausto had asked her here, he would still dismiss her at some point. He would still want to. But hopefully not till the morning.

'Never mind about all that,' Liza said as she moved past him to the window, its shutters open to the night air, the gardens swathed in darkness below. 'It's all water under the bridge, anyway.'

'Is it?'

'Yes.'

'Good,' Fausto said after a pause. 'That is how I would like it to be.'

She nodded unsteadily, turning back to look at him, and he glanced towards the bathroom.

'Would you mind if I had a shower first?'

First. Before what? Liza fought an urge to laugh—hysterically. This was all so very much beyond her experience. 'No, of course not.' She gestured to the bathroom, with its marble and gold taps. 'Be my guest,' she quipped. 'Even though I'm yours.'

Fausto gave her a fleeting smile and then disappeared into the bathroom. A few seconds later Liza heard the sound of the shower. Her breath came out in a rush as she sagged with something like relief. This all felt so strange, and yet she *wanted* to be here. Even if only for a night.

Still, she had no idea how things were going to go when Fausto came out of the bathroom. What if he was naked? Where would she *look*? A muffled laugh escaped her and she clapped her hand over her mouth. Assured seductress she was not.

And yet… Fausto still wanted her. Had chosen her, at least for this. And whatever sorrow or heartache tomorrow and the days after might bring, at least she would always have tonight.

Liza hoped it would be a precious, even sacred, memory. She thought it might be. And, she acknowledged as she gazed out at the darkened night, it would have to be enough.

From the bathroom she heard the sound of the shower turning off.

Fausto slowly dried himself as he gazed unseeingly at the steam-fogged mirror. He could hardly believe that he was here…that she was here. When he'd asked her to stay the night it had felt both natural and essential. All he wanted.

And while he wasn't allowing himself to think too much about any possible future, the rightness of this evening, of them being together, burrowed down deep into his soul. It felt, in a way he could not explain even to himself, like their wedding night.

Wrapping the towel around his waist, he opened the bathroom door. Liza whirled around at the sound, her lovely eyes widening at the sight of him.

'Oh…' Her gaze swept up and down the length of his nearly naked body as a rosy blush reddened her cheeks. 'Oh,' she said again, softly this time, and with admiration.

'You seem nervous,' he remarked as he took a step towards her.

'Of course I'm nervous. You do realise the only other time I've done anything like this was on that beach?'

'I wondered if there had been anyone else since.'

'In the last two months?' Liza stared at him incredulously. 'Of course not.'

'You are a lovely woman,' he pointed out with a smile at her outrage. 'You must have admirers.'

'I work all day with an octogenarian,' Liza reminded him. 'And I haven't been going out very much. So no, there haven't been any *admirers*.'

'I'm glad.'

'Are you?' She looked at him seriously. 'You must have had…other women, in the meantime. I wouldn't mind, of course—'

'No.'

'No?' She looked surprised. 'But…'

'I've been working eighteen hours a day, hardly going out at night, and the truth is, I haven't wanted anyone else.' He was amazed at how freeing that admission felt. 'Only you.'

'Fausto…'

'Why don't you believe me?'

'I don't know. Because you're so amazing and I'm so…'

'You're so what?' he asked gently.

She let out an uncertain laugh. 'Plain. Boring. The sister who isn't pretty. The one people skip over, or simply forget.' Each word vibrated with an old, remembered pain and Fausto felt a flash of anger for the idiots who had dismissed her in such a way.

'You are none of those things, Liza. None.'

'I'm not amazing,' she said, clearly trying to sound merely wry.

'You are.' He reached for her hand, because he had to touch her. 'You are utterly amazing.' He brushed his lips against her fingers, and then he gently nibbled her fingertips as he kept his gaze on her, felt his own heat.

'You make me feel amazing,' Liza admitted unsteadily. 'In a way no one else ever has.'

'I'm glad for that too.'

'You're sounding very possessive,' she said with a breathy laugh.

'I'm feeling very possessive,' Fausto answered, and then he tugged on her hand so she came towards him, willing and expectant. Her hips bumped his and heat flared in them both. He felt it in himself as well as in her. She drew a shuddery breath and then, tentatively, placed her hands on his chest, spreading her fingers wide.

'Is that okay?' she asked a little anxiously. 'Can I touch you?'

'Oh, Liza,' Fausto said with a groan. 'You can touch me all you want. Anywhere.'

She laughed as she let her hands slip down his chest, her fingertips flirting with the edge of his towel before skimming up again.

'Go ahead,' Fausto encouraged her in a low, thrumming voice. Already he was more than ready for all she could give him. 'Touch me. Take off the towel.'

'Seriously?' An incredulous smile quirked her mouth.

'Seriously.'

Her hands travelled down again, her breath coming in a gasp as she tugged the towel and it fell away. She glanced down and her eyes widened comically.

'Oh…'

'Nothing to alarm you, I hope,' he said dryly.

'No…it's just I didn't actually *see* you, before.'

'And I didn't see you.' He reached for the sash of her robe and gave it a gentle tug. 'May I?' She nodded. He undid the sash and the robe parted, to reveal the shadowy valleys and curves of a body he ached to touch and treasure.

In one sinuous movement Liza shrugged the garment off and it fell in a heap at her feet. She kicked it away, chin raised, gaze defiant and yet vulnerable.

She was lovely…so lovely, her body pale and perfect, slender and supple. Fausto put his hands on her waist, nearly spanning it as he drew her towards him so their bodies brushed—her breasts against his chest, their hips nudging one another. She let out a shuddery breath and closed her eyes.

He tilted her chin up with one finger. 'All right?' he asked quietly, and she nodded.

'Yes. Very much so.'

'Good.' And then, because he couldn't wait any longer, he kissed her, and it was as sweet as it had been every time before—no, he realised, sweeter. It meant more, because he knew this—what was unspooling between them like a golden thread now—meant more. As he deepened the kiss his mind blurred and he let the thoughts drift away on a tide of sensation.

Liza put her arms around him and as their bodies came in even closer and more exquisite contact another groan escaped him. This was torture—wonderful, wonderful torture.

Stumbling a bit, they made it to the bed. Fausto pulled back the duvet as Liza moved over, her wild curls spread across the ivory pillowcase, her body and heart both open to him. Fausto stretched beside her and hooked one of her curls around his finger.

'Your hair,' he murmured, 'is magnificent.'

She let out another one of her disbelieving laughs. 'It's too curly.'

'Too curly? No. Why do you disparage yourself?'

'I don't know. I've never thought of it that way.' She shrugged slim shoulders. 'I know I've never been as pretty as Jenna, or as spirited as Lindsay, or as clever as Marie.'

'Marie? I haven't met her.'

'No, although you might like her the best. She's quiet and bookish.'

'I like *you* the best,' he said, and then he rolled over and covered her body with his own.

She let out a little gasp of pleasure before he devoured her mouth in a kiss and her arms came around him. She arched up into him, all pliant softness, and it was almost too much.

He kissed his way from her mouth to her breasts…breasts he could feel the ripe fullness of now, could touch and savour in a way he hadn't been able to in their frenzied rush on the beach. Now he would take his time, exploring every hidden curve, every sweet dip. He kissed his way lower.

Beneath him Liza writhed as she let out lovely little mewling sounds of pleasure, her fingers raking through his hair as he kissed her soft thighs.

'Fausto…' she said shakily, half plea, half protest.

'I'm getting to know you,' he murmured, and she let out a breathless laugh as he kissed her at the core of herself and her body convulsed around him.

'Oh, I didn't *think*…'

'Now is not the time for thinking,' he advised. 'Only for feeling.' His mouth moved over her once more, and her body arched sweetly against him.

'*Fausto…*'

He could explore her hidden recesses for ever, but the desperate ache they both felt needed to be sated. They had the whole night in front of them, and he intended to use every single hour of it. But, for now, he reached for a condom.

'Are you ready?' he asked as he rolled on top of her once more, bracing himself on his forearms. Liza nodded, her head buried in his shoulder, her body open to him.

'Yes…*yes.*'

And she was, as he glided smoothly into her, found his way home, and she met him there, thrust for glorious thrust.

It was moments, and yet it was a lifetime shattered and reborn as she enfolded him in her body, clasped him in her arms, and they both broke apart and then came together. *This was where he wanted to be.*

All his concerns about positions or pride, all the armour he'd surrounded himself with to keep himself apart, to keep from gambling on that all-or-nothing risk of loving—it all shattered in this moment.

None of it mattered. None of it mattered in the least.

All he wanted was her. For tonight—and for ever.

He kept his arms around her as he rolled onto his back, their hearts thudding hard against one another in the aftermath of their lovemaking.

'That's just the beginning,' he promised her, and she pressed her forehead against his chest.

'You'll be the death of me.'

And yet, Fausto knew as he kept his arms around her, she was the life of him.

CHAPTER SIXTEEN

LIZA WOKE SLOWLY, blinking in the sunlight, stretching as languorously as the cat that got the cream. And that was how she felt after a night of gorgeous, mind-blowing and body-altering love-making.

She was sore in places she'd never been sore before and her muscles ached in a way that felt delicious. As she lay there in the sunlight, in the dreamy, muted state between sleep and consciousness, a montage of lovely memories danced through her mind. Candlelight on burnished skin. Fausto poised above her. His head bent as he kissed her, her fingers in his dark hair...

And then later, when she'd felt bolder, she'd given him the same sensual treatment. She'd explored every gorgeous inch of his lean, hard body and revelled in her newfound knowledge. They'd fallen asleep in each other's arms some time towards dawn.

Liza turned her head and saw Fausto sleeping next to her, his inky lashes fanned on his cheeks, his chest rising and falling in the steady beat of sleep.

And then, as consciousness crept in, so did reality. It was over. Her one amazing night had ended. And it had been amazing—she had no regrets. Well, not many. The heartache she'd carry with her felt like a heavy yet necessary burden to bear, because she knew now that she loved him. How could she not, after all she'd learned about him? After everything he'd done for her, the kindness, sensitivity and passion he'd shown.

Of course she loved him.

And for a few precious seconds as she watched him sleep she imagined telling him so. She pictured how his face would soften in pleasure and surprise, and then he would take her in his arms and tell her he loved her too.

Of course it was only the stuff of fairy tales. In all the conversations they'd had since she'd come to Italy Fausto had never changed his position on position. On the fact that she was not suitable to be his bride—a fact Liza had felt more and more keenly, the more time she spent at Villa di Palmerno.

She was the Benton sister who had never been anything special, often overlooked or forgotten, one of many rather than a stand-out. She was the woman a man had sneeringly dismissed, had used just to get to her sister. Did she actually think she could be a *Contessa*?

No, of course not.

Slowly, Liza slipped out of bed, not wanting to disturb Fausto. Best if she showered and dressed, made her farewells as quickly as possible. Severed the connection as neatly and cleanly as she could, even if the thought of it hurt more than she could bear.

She'd just taken her clothes into the bathroom when her phone buzzed with an incoming text. Considering it was only seven in the morning, Liza frowned at the sound and swiped her screen. The text was from Jenna.

Are you awake? Need to talk.

Liza pressed 'call' and seconds later she heard Jenna's breathless voice. 'Liza? Sorry to wake you up so early…'

'It's fine, but it's only six in England. What's going on?'

'It's Lindsay,' Jenna said on a jagged note. 'We found out late last night… I didn't want to disturb you…but I couldn't wait any longer. Mum's having fits.'

Liza's stomach plunged icily. 'What's happened?'

'She's been so…oh, I can't even blame her, honestly. She's only just eighteen. Of course her head was bound to be turned.'

'What? Jenna, I have no idea what you're talking about.'

'Lindsay went to London for the weekend,' Jenna explained. 'You remember it's her eighteenth?'

'Yes...' Liza said, although she realised with a stab of guilt that, in light of everything that had been happening here with Fausto, she'd completely forgotten about her sister's birthday.

'Anyway, she told Mum she was seeing me, but she wasn't. She'd met some guy at a club the last time she was here—he invited her to some D-list party this weekend. Honestly, it sounded dire.'

'Oh, no,' Liza said softly. She could picture how thrilled Lindsay would be at such an invitation, how utterly irresponsible she might be at such an event, and also how out of her depth. Poor, foolish Lindsay.

'What happened?' she asked as dread swirled coldly in her stomach.

'I don't know the details, and I'm not sure I want to,' Jenna said with quiet grimness. 'She got involved with some minor celebrity at the party—I haven't heard of him, but Mum had.'

'And?' Liza asked, as everything in her went tenser.

'And there were photos involved. Nude photos.'

'Oh, no, Lindsay...'

'And the guy she was with, this Jack, is threatening to sell them to the tabloids—because this celebrity is apparently big enough for that—if we don't pay out.'

'Jack?' Liza knew even before she asked, 'Jack who?'

'Wick something, I think.'

'Wickley.' She closed her eyes. How could that wretched man be tormenting her family now? If she'd had any doubts about the truth of Fausto's story—and she hadn't—they would certainly have been swept away now.

'You know him?' Jenna asked in surprise.

'No, not really. It doesn't matter. What are we going to do?'

'I don't know. Mum's adamant the photos don't get published. She's worried for Lindsay's wellbeing, of course, but I also think she's afraid of her being expelled from school right in the middle of A-levels. They have a zero tolerance policy about this sort of thing.'

'And if she's expelled, no university,' Liza finished numbly. Despite her sister's seemingly scatty attitude, she had brains and she'd been offered a place studying business in Manchester.

'Her whole life could be derailed,' Jenna concluded miserably. 'Not to mention the humiliation and hurt she would feel. I know Lindsay acts shameless, but she isn't really. She's been reckless and silly, I know that, but she doesn't deserve this. She's trying to act as if she doesn't care, but I think she must.'

'Poor Lindsay.' Liza's mind was racing. 'I'll fly back today.'

'Oh, but your holiday—'

'It will be over in a few days, anyway. And this is more important.' Besides, Liza thought, her holiday already felt as if it were over. Her night with Fausto certainly was. 'I'll text you from the airport,' she promised, and then she disconnected the call.

She dressed quickly, her mind buzzing all the while, and when she emerged from the bathroom Fausto was sitting up in bed with a sleepy smile. Their night together already felt like something consigned to the past.

'Liza…' His smile vanished as he took in her agitation. 'What's happened?'

'Lindsay.' She couldn't keep it from him, as much as she wanted to. As she related the details of the sordid tale, she couldn't help but cringe inside. If there had ever been a measure of how unsuitable she was as his potential bride, now it was taken to the full, but that hardly mattered. She had to think about Lindsay, not herself.

'That bastard,' Fausto said in a low voice. 'He never tires of ruining lives.'

'I don't know what we'll do,' Liza said numbly. 'We can't afford to pay him. We haven't any money, not like that. But I have to go home and help. I need to be there for Lindsay, for Mum…'

Fausto was already getting out of bed and pulling on his trousers. Liza watched him miserably. Could he not get away from her fast enough, now that he knew the full extent of her family's shame?

'I'll arrange for a private flight for you back to England,' he said. 'It will be quicker.'

'Oh, you don't—'

'It's nothing,' he dismissed. 'Of course I will do it.'

'Thank you—'

'I will have it arranged.'

Liza blinked; Fausto's voice sounded so cold. Perhaps he was only offering because he wanted her out of here—out of Italy—as quickly as possible. He didn't even look at her as he buttoned his shirt, and Liza realised his mind was elsewhere; he'd already forgotten her.

Perhaps he was trying to do his own damage control. If Lindsay's photos ended up in the papers and Fausto's association with Liza was discovered she supposed it could reflect badly on the Danti family. She could hardly blame him for wanting to deal with the possible fallout for his own family, and yet the realisation filled her with sadness. Their one amazing night really was well and truly over.

Everything seemed to happen in super speed after that. Fausto left the bedroom without saying goodbye or even looking at her, and when Liza had finished getting ready and gone downstairs he was nowhere to be seen. His mother, Viviana Danti, however, was. Liza recognised her instantly even though they'd never met.

'I trust you had a comfortable night?' she asked in a glacial tone that made Liza freeze where she stood in the entrance hall. She'd just asked Roberto to find her grandmother and she was hoping to make her escape as quickly as possible.

'Yes.' Bravely, a bit recklessly, she stuck out her hand. 'I don't think we've met. I'm Liza Benton.'

'I know who you are,' Viviana Danti said coldly, ignoring Liza's hand. She withdrew it, blushing at the woman's icy hauteur.

'The party yesterday was lovely,' she said after a pause, because the silence was simply too awful. Viviana inclined her head.

'I understand you feel my son has developed some sort of attachment to you,' she said. 'Please don't think it will last.'

Stung, Liza replied, 'I never thought it would, but thank you for making it abundantly clear.'

Viviana smiled, a chilly gesture that held no friendliness. 'I am trying to help you, my dear. A girl such as yourself… It is understandable that you would have hopes.'

Until Viviana Danti had said it aloud, Liza wouldn't have believed she'd had such hopes. She'd reminded herself again and again that she didn't, that she'd walked into last night knowing full well that was all it could be.

And yet.

And yet...

Looking at Viviana's icy elegance, how she looked down her nose at her in the same way Fausto once had... Liza realised painfully that she'd been hoping all along. Hoping so hard, because how could she not, after last night? After how passionate Fausto had been. How tender.

'I have no such hopes,' she stated in as cold a voice as she could manage.

'Are you quite sure?' Viviana asked coolly. 'Because we have been in this situation before, you know. Fausto brought a girl home very much like you. Amy—young, English, poor.' She paused. 'It only took a more tempting offer to make her go away.'

Liza stared at her for a few stunned seconds before she said in a thready voice, 'Are you...are you offering me a bribe?'

'I'm giving you an incentive, along with a warning,' Viviana replied. 'I thought my son had outgrown such foolish fancies, but it appears he hasn't. How much will it take? Fifty thousand? A hundred?' She smiled coolly, and Liza took a stumbling step away. No wonder Fausto worried about gold-diggers. How much had this Amy taken?

'I have absolutely no wish to take a penny from you,' she said coldly. 'And don't worry, because I don't intend to see Fausto again.' The knowledge ripped through her and she drew a shuddering breath. 'Now, if you'll excuse me, I need to find my grandmother.'

The sooner she was able to return home and forget Fausto, she thought miserably, the better.

It had been a long eighteen hours. Long, aggravating, but so very worth it. Fausto glanced at the clock on the dashboard of his car—half past six on a beautiful spring evening. His eyes were gritty and his body ached. Last night he'd barely slept.

He'd checked with his staff to see if Liza had taken advantage of his offer of a private flight, only to learn that she had left with her grandmother in a cab before Roberto had been able to secure it. That knowledge had caused Fausto a ripple of unease, but he'd determinedly dismissed it. Liza had been in a rush to get back to her family. He understood her impatience; now he was in a rush to get back to her.

Unfortunately, finding her was not as simple as he hoped. He didn't have her telephone number, didn't know her address. The only thing he knew was her place of work, but it was evening and she wouldn't be there. He knew he could call Henry and ask for her address, but he was loath to put his godfather, Liza's employer, in such a position.

But he needed to see Liza. He'd left so abruptly in his determination to address the situation, and he feared she might have been besieged by doubts—although could either of them have any doubts after the incredible night they had shared? The aftershocks of emotion and pleasure were *still* rippling through him.

Even so, he needed to see her. Speak to her. *Hold her.* Once he did that, he was sure everything would be all right. It had to be.

He ended up calling Chaz. 'I need Jenna's number,' he stated brusquely.

'*Jenna?*'

'You have it still?'

'Of course I have it.' Something about Chaz's tone made Fausto ask, a little less brusquely, 'Why did you stop seeing her, by the way?'

Chaz was silent for a moment. 'I don't know,' he admitted.

'Was it because of what I said?'

'You told me to think carefully. I did.'

'So what were your concerns?'

Chaz sighed. 'I don't know. That she didn't feel for me as much as I felt for her? It was *frightening*, how much I felt. I backed away from it, I guess.'

Fausto knew all too well how that went. 'But you've been miserable without her,' he stated matter-of-factly. 'You should call her, Chaz.'

'It's been months—'

'So? Apologise. Grovel, if you have to.'

Chaz let out a choked laugh of disbelief. 'Are you, Fausto Danti, asking me to *grovel*?'

'I am.' Because, heaven knew, he might have to grovel too. He had left rather abruptly. 'If she's worth it and, judging from the way you've been these last few months, I think she is.'

'You really want me to call her?'

'Yes, but let me call her first.'

Jenna was as surprised to hear from him as Chaz had been when he'd asked for her number.

'You want Liza's number?'

'Preferably her address. I need to speak to her.'

'She's at home with us, here in Herefordshire.'

'May I have the address, please?'

Jenna hesitated.

'Please,' Fausto said quietly. 'I want to speak to her.' He paused as the words and their truth unfurled and grew inside him. Overwhelmed him. 'I need to tell her I love her.'

Jenna gave him the address.

It was a three-hour drive to the gracious Georgian house smothered with climbing roses in a pretty village overlooking rolling golden fields.

Fausto pulled into the drive and gazed at the house in bemused surprise—yes, the roof clearly needed repairing and it looked a little shabby and worn, but in a lovely, lovable way. The garden was full of bird feeders and ragged bunting, left over from a party perhaps, was strung along the gateposts.

He'd only just got out of the car when the front door was thrown open and Lindsay stood there, hands on her hips, eyes narrowed. Considering the disaster that had been so narrowly averted, she looked none the worse for wear.

'You look familiar,' she said.

'I met you with Chaz Bingham a few months ago,' he said, and she let out a squeal of recognition and delight.

'Oh, yes, you were so grumpy then.'

Faust gave a small smile in spite of himself. 'Indeed I was.'

'What on earth are you here for?' Lindsay demanded.

'Your sister, Liza.'

'Ooh!' The squeal was high-pitched enough to hurt Fausto's ears. '*Li-za!*' she yelled.

Fausto stepped inside the house. It was as lovably shabby on the inside as it was on the outside—all mismatched chintz prints and comfortable sofas, as well as two shaggy golden retrievers who came up to him and immediately sprawled at his feet. Fausto was oddly enchanted by it all, by the homeliness of it, the comfort and care, and most of all the love that radiated from every nook and cranny like a force field. And he'd thought Liza's family would reflect badly on *him*. The realisation, one he'd held in some dark corner of his heart up to even this moment, humbled him all the more.

Then Liza came into the hall—her face was pale, her curls riotous. She wore a loose green sundress and she looked absolutely wonderful.

'Fausto...' Her voice was faint. 'What are you doing here?'

'I needed to see you.'

'Why?'

'Yes, why?' Lindsay asked, clearly having no compunction about being a part of this conversation.

Fausto looked at Liza. 'May we speak in private?'

'Yes...the garden is probably the most private place.' She led him through the house, past her gawking mother, a smiling Jenna and another sister who had to be the bookish Marie. An older man with salt and pepper hair peeped out from a study and then quickly withdrew.

Liza brought him out to a small terrace in the back that overlooked a riotous garden of blowsy roses and bountiful wisteria.

'My father's pride and joy,' Liza said, nodding towards the many roses. 'That and the orchids, but those are in the greenhouse. Nothing like yours, of course. No rare varieties.' She glanced at the kitchen window, where four Benton women were openly staring, and then she nodded towards the lawn that wandered invitingly between trailing wisteria and overgrown rosebushes to a more private space.

'I don't know why you're here,' she said in a rather wooden voice once they were free of the prying eyes and straining ears in the kitchen.

'I told you—to see you.'

'Yes, but why? Has…has something happened?'

Now that he had her here, had her attention, the words bottled up in his chest. He felt overcome with emotion, with certainty, and yet it was so hard to say it. As a boy he'd been taught all about pride and honour, dignity and respect. Not so much about vulnerability or love, yet those were what he felt—and needed—now.

'Fausto…?' The uncertainty in her voice made him ache.

'I love you.' It felt like something that could only be blurted, an admission straight from the gut—and the heart. Liza simply stared, so he decided to say it again. 'I love you. I want to spend the rest of my life with you.' It was like peeling back skin, offering his heart, still beating and raw, on a platter. It *hurt*. Then, to his amazement and horror, she slowly shook her head. This, then, was why he'd kept himself from saying the words for so long. The risk—the pain—were unbearable. 'You don't believe me?' he asked in a ragged voice.

'It's not that I don't believe you,' Liza said. 'Although, to be honest, I'm not sure if I do or not. It's that I'm not sure it matters.'

'What?' Fausto goggled at her, unable to keep himself from it—mouth open, eyes wide. 'What? How can it not? You told me you were holding out for love. That you wanted to marry a man who loved you—you, and only you. Well, I love you, Liza. I love you with my whole heart. My soul. My body. Everything. I've come to realise it—to revel in it!' He couldn't believe he was telling her so much, giving her so much, and yet she still seemed to be rejecting it. *Him*. He'd been so sure…again. How stupid could he be? How arrogant? Once again he'd thought she'd come to him with open arms.

'Yes, that's true,' Liza said after a moment, 'but Fausto, you don't *want* to love me.'

'I fought against it, that's true,' he said steadily. He would not shy away from his past sins. Perhaps now he still needed to atone for them. 'I did, because—'

'Because you didn't think I was *suitable*.' She said the words heavily rather than with scorn.

'No.'

Liza looked at him in surprise, and Fausto continued, this new level of vulnerability hurting him all the more. 'At least that was part of it, but really a small part. The truth was, I was afraid to love you. Afraid to give my heart.' He paused. 'Afraid to be hurt.'

'Like you were before.'

'Yes, although what I felt for her was nothing compared to this. Us.'

Her hazel gaze scanned his face. 'Your mother offered me money to go away.'

Fury streaked through him like a bolt of lightning. 'She's done that before.'

'Yes, she told me. And she told me that... Amy...took the money.'

Fausto's gut tightened at the memory. 'Yes.'

'I'm sorry. That must have been terrible.'

'It was a long time ago.'

'Yet these things still have the power to hurt us.' She paused, her gaze distant and troubled. 'I had a similar experience. I was hurt... Oh, it's a bit ridiculous because it never went anywhere. We only kissed.'

'What happened?' Fausto asked. He already despised whoever the man in question was.

'I met someone at uni. I thought he was interested in me. Well, he acted like he was. He flattered me...spent time with me. But then I discovered he was only interested in getting closer to Jenna.' She sighed, a wavery sound. 'He made that very clear.'

Bastard. 'I'm sorry, Liza.' Now he understood her insecurities, why she didn't believe he could love her. Her, and no other. 'Liza, I do love you,' he said in a low, insistent voice. 'Whatever happens between us, you need to know that. To believe it. I *want* to love you. Yes, I fought against it, and it was foolish of me. But I fought and I won. You won. And it is the sweetest victory, if you'll just…'

A small smile curved her lovely mouth. 'Love you back?'

'*Yes.*'

'I do love you.' Triumph rushed through him, tempered by her next words. 'But does it really change things, Fausto? I fought against loving you, just as you did with me. I can see that now. I was so angry, and that was in part because it felt as if you were making me look at my family differently, critically, and I hated that. I hated who I was becoming.'

'And I hate who I've *been.*'

'But what's changed, Fausto? Really?'

'I've changed,' he insisted. 'I've fallen in love for the very first time. I've seen a woman who is gracious and loving and kind, and I don't care if she was born a princess or a pauper. It doesn't matter.'

'It matters to your mother.'

His stomach tightened again at her despondent tone. 'My mother's concerns are not mine.'

'And yet you made it clear you wanted me gone.' She spoke matter-of-factly, yet he still heard her hurt.

'What?' Fausto stared at her in confusion. This

was not part of the narrative that he understood. 'Why do you think that?'

'You left without even saying goodbye.'

'I was in a hurry—'

'Yes, I know, to do your own damage control. I do understand that.'

'My own...?' Now he could only look at her blankly. 'What is that supposed to mean?'

'Lindsay,' Liza said unhappily. 'I realised that if those photographs were published and our...association...was discovered it would reflect badly on you and your family. I'm sorry for that.'

'But the photos weren't published,' Fausto said slowly.

'No, amazingly they weren't. I don't know what happened. We weren't able to pay the money—'

'I paid the money,' Fausto said quietly, and Liza simply stared.

'You...' Then she nodded slowly. 'Because it would reflect badly on you, like I thought. I am sorry—'

'Liza, do you really think so little of me even now, after everything, that I would see off Jack Wickley simply because of how it affected me?' The pain in his voice was raw and audible, and he couldn't hide it. She'd already told him she loved him and yet she still had these doubts?

'I don't understand...'

'I did it for you, because I love you! And for Lindsay, because she is young and everyone was young and foolish once, including me. And I did it because I could not bear to see Jack Wickley get away with one thing more. I paid him off and I had the photos destroyed, and I have gone to the police with the proof of his embezzling. I didn't do it before because my father wouldn't have wanted the shame on our company and name, which is another kind of damage pride does, but I realised Wickley can't get away with things— it only encourages him to do more, and to hurt more people.' He let out an exasperated, emotional breath. 'I did all that, but I *didn't* do any of it for some sort of *damage control*. I didn't even think about that. I couldn't care less about it now.'

Liza pressed her hands to her cheeks as tears filled her eyes. 'I don't know what you want me to say.'

'Say you love me again and that you'll marry me.'

Tears spilled down her cheeks. 'I'm not...'

'What?'

'Good enough,' she whispered. 'Special enough. Sophisticated enough...'

'You are all that and more, to me. And I will happily spend a lifetime proving it to you.'

'Even though I was so horrible to you?'

'You called me out. I deserved it.'

'You didn't...'

'Liza,' he said with a groan. 'I love you. You've

said you love me. We can argue about the partic-
ulars, but right now I need you to kiss me.'

She laughed and then finally, wonderfully, she
came into his arms and he let out a laugh of both
relief and pure joy. She tilted her face up to his
and he kissed her as he'd been aching to do.

'I do love you,' she said after a long moment.
'So much. I think I fell in love with you ages ago,
and I fought it as much as you did, even though
I didn't realise that was what I was doing at the
time.'

'Then we've both had to surrender.'

'Yes.' She smiled, her face suffused with tenderness and love. 'Sweet, sweet surrender.'

Fausto kissed her again.

EPILOGUE

Seven months later

IT WAS THE wedding of the year. A Christmas wedding and, more than that, a double wedding—two gorgeous brides and two eminently eligible bachelors. The tabloids had a field day. It was on the cover of *You Too!* with an exclusive double page spread in the magazine.

There were four beautiful bridesmaids—Lindsay and Marie, Francesca, and Chaz's sister Kerry, who had thawed when she'd realised Fausto had never even looked at her that way. The ceremony was in the village church in Little Mayton, and the reception was in a luxury hotel nearby. Fausto had rented out the entire place for the occasion.

There would be another party to celebrate his and Liza's marriage in Italy, when they returned to Villa di Palmerno. Liza was going to work remotely for Henry as well as fulfil her duties as Contessa.

It was a fairy tale of epic proportions, and Liza felt as if she had to keep pinching herself. As she took a moment alone at the reception to watch all the gaiety, she did just that. A hard pinch on her upper arm, just to see.

'What are you doing?' Fausto asked, his voice laced with amusement as he came to stand beside her.

'Pinching myself. To make sure this is real.'

'Trust me, it's real.' He nodded towards the twelve-piece band that, on Lindsay's request, was starting a rendition of the Macarena, with Lindsay front and centre leading the dancing.

Liza let out a little muffled laugh. 'You don't mind?'

'Nope.' He slid his arms around her waist. 'Look at them all dancing.'

Liza glanced at her mother, who was giving it as much of her all as Lindsay was, and Jenna and Chaz, who were laughing and dancing, their arms around each other. Her father had even joined in and Henry and, amazingly, Viviana were both nodding along. Her mother-in-law had thawed towards her, if only just, but it was enough for Liza. She understood how hard it was to let go of preconceptions, of pride and prejudice.

'Happy?' Fausto asked as he nuzzled her hair,

and she leaned against him as her thankfulness and joy overflowed.

'Yes,' she said, and turned her head to brush a kiss against his jaw. 'So, so happy.'

* * * * *